Tasmina Perry is the author of the huge *Sunday Times* Top Ten bestsellers *Daddy's Girls*, *Gold Diggers*, *Guilty Pleasures*, *Original Sin*, and, most recently, *Kiss Heaven Goodbye*. She left a career in law to enter the world of women's magazine publishing, going on to win the New Magazine Journalist of the Year award, edit numerous national publications and write on celebrity and style for titles such as *Elle* and *Glamour*. In 2004 she launched her own travel and fashion magazine, *Jaunt*, and was Deputy Editor of *InStyle* magazine when she left the industry to write books full time. Her novels have been published in seventeen countries.

Tasmina lives with her husband and son in Surrey, where she is at work on her next novel and a screenplay. For the latest news, competitions and much more, visit www.tasminaperry.com.

Escape with Tasmina's other novels...

Daddy's Girls
Gold Diggers
Guilty Pleasures
Original Sin

Praise for

Kiss Heaven Goodbye

'For glamour, escapism and a glorious cast, *Kiss Heaven Goodbye* is the perfect beach read' *Daily Express*

'Darker than her previous books but perhaps even more gripping and exciting. We loved every page of it' *Heat*

'Tasmina Perry just gets better and *better...Kiss Heaven Goodbye* is utter *bliss*' *InStyle*

'Pure glittering escapism' *She*

'A sizzling summer read' *Marie Claire*

'All you need for long, hot days spent lazing by the pool' *Sun*

'Expect intrigue and mystery galore' *Star*

'Kiss your social life goodbye ... there's absolutely no escape until the last page is turned' *Daily Record*

Praise for Tasmina's previous bestsellers

'Hold on to your hats – here comes your summer block-buster' *Elle*

'It might blow your luggage allowance but this big, fat, glitzy story will keep you reading all holiday' *Grazia*

'A sexy guilty pleasure you devour like a caramel Magnum' *Glamour*

'Packed with glamour, romance and intrigue, it'll keep you glued from the very first page' *Heat*

'A super-slick, seriously sexy murder mystery. Fantastic' *Company*

'The perfect read to escape the everyday world with enough suspense to keep you hooked' *Sun*

'Intelligent and stylish' *Red*

'Smart, sexy and seriously addictive' *Madison*

'The spirit of *The OC* bottled in a book' *Cosmopolitan*

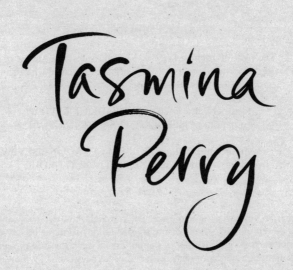

Tasmina Perry

Kiss Heaven
Goodbye

headline
review

First published in 2010 by HEADLINE REVIEW
An imprint of HEADLINE PUBLISHING GROUP

First published in paperback in 2011 by HEADLINE REVIEW
An imprint of HEADLINE PUBLISHING GROUP

1

Cataloguing in Publication Data is available from the British Library

ISBN 978 0 7553 5842 7

Typeset in Sabon by Ellipsis Books Limited, Glasgow

Printed and bound in Great Britain by
Clays Ltd, St Ives plc

Headline's policy is to use papers that are natural, renewable
and recyclable products and made from wood grown in sustainable forests.
The logging and manufacturing processes are expected to conform to
the environmental regulations of the country of origin.

HEADLINE PUBLISHING GROUP
An Hachette UK Company
338 Euston Road
London NW1 3BH

www.headline.co.uk
www.hachette.co.uk

This one's for my sister

Prologue

Summer 2010, Manhattan

He couldn't sleep. How could he? Nobody could rest with such a weight hanging over their head. Miles Ashford turned over and looked at the red digital numbers of his bedside clock: 3.45 a.m. He had taken a Xanax at midnight; it hadn't even made him drowsy. Had it been only twelve hours since his attorney Michael Marshall had called, telling him that a detective inspector from the Royal Bahamas Police Force wanted to question him?

Miles sat up and reached for his cigarettes, hoping it would do something to relieve the anxiety – an emotion he was unused to. A man as successful as Miles Ashford had not got where he was today without being able to handle extreme pressure; he just didn't get rattled. Not when his $500 million residential project had to be shelved in Dubai last year. Not when the banks were breathing down his neck after the collapse of Lehman Brothers. Not even when he had run into a Kosovan gangster when he had tried to buy a series of brothels in London's Soho. All those things were just setbacks, concerns or irritations. This . . . well, this was different.

He swung his legs off the bed and reached for his navy silk robe, pulling it tightly around his body before walking through to his study. It was Miles' favourite room in his Fifth

3

Avenue duplex, with a huge bay window that looked out on to Central Park. After dark, it resembled a black hole in the heart of the city. Whoever coined the expression 'the dead of night' was thinking of 3.45 a.m. in NYC. Even in the city that never sleeps, this sliver of time after the party people had gone to bed and the early risers – the market traders, the workaholic Wall Street tycoons – had not yet started their day was a moment that was eerie and still.

Miles didn't turn on the light, content to just gaze out on to the city, letting the darkness and silence soothe him. He closed his eyes and immediately felt himself transported back to the island. For a second, his memory of that night was so clear he could almost smell the sea air, the pineapple bushes, the mangrove. Growing up, Angel Cay had been his Eden, a private pirate island to explore and to run wild in, rich with imagination and adventures. But not any more, not now.

He turned from the window and sat at his desk. His empire spanned a dozen industries and six continents, yet the glass surface of his work station was remarkably uncluttered. In two hours' time it would be set for breakfast by his butler Stevens and the world's most influential newspapers would be in a neat pile ready for him to read. But now it just contained a stack of contracts, a phone, a copy of *Fortune* magazine and a small desk lamp which finally, reluctantly, he turned on. Blinking in the yellow light, he picked up the sleek black phone and dialled his attorney.

'Miles,' said Michael Marshall. Not a question; the lawyer was used to being woken up at this hour by his employer. Strictly speaking, of course, Michael wasn't just Miles' lawyer. Michael Marshall was his fixer. Miles' father Robert had once had such a man in his employment: Dick Donovan, a super-efficient, can-do sort of fellow, the kind of man you'd trust with your most intimate business. Robert used to ambiguously refer to Dick as 'my man', and when a teenage Miles had once asked Dick what his specific role was in the family company, Dick had simply replied that he was his father's fixer. Miles had liked the phrase; just the right balance of subterfuge and security. Now, of course, Miles Ashford had his own fixer. He also had an army of Harvard- and Cambridge-educated lawyers working for him in his business affairs department who dealt with the complicated mergers and acquisitions and the endless tedious contract work associated with a company of that size. The more sensitive matters were dealt with by Michael. Michael was his personal guard dog.

'This isn't going to go away, is it?' asked Miles. He didn't need to spell it out to Michael; there was only one thing on both their minds that night.

The attorney paused. 'Fifty-fifty,' he replied cautiously. 'I spoke to the assistant commissioner in Nassau when you left the office. He's sympathetic, but they can't turn a blind eye to what's been uncovered.'

Miles nodded. It was as he feared. 'Then set up another meeting with that officer from the Central Detective Unit for me.'

Marshall paused for thought. 'I can stall him, give us a little space to do our own investigations?'

'No,' said Miles. 'We should meet it head on. Tell him I'll go back to Angel Cay.' Despite his anxiety, Miles Ashford was a man of action. Sitting around worrying didn't suit him.

'As you wish. I'll set it up as soon as possible. Anything else?'

Miles hesitated. There were some things he hadn't shared with even his most trusted aide, but now the day had come, he wasn't going to face it alone.

'You need to make arrangements for some others to be present too,' he said. 'Other people are involved, and if I'm going back to the island, they're coming with me.'

He was careful that his voice showed no trace of emotion to his employee. There was a time when Miles knew little about self-discipline and control, when he had always given in to anger and impulse. But time, experience and necessity had changed that.

There was a long pause at the other end of the line.

'Miles, what is this? I can only help you if you tell me everything.'

'There's time for that tomorrow. I'll fill you in on the plane.'

Marshall took a deep breath. It wasn't the first time Miles had made an unusual request, after all. 'OK. What other people?'

'Alex Doyle, Grace Ashford and Sasha Sinclair,' he said in a low, steady voice, knowing that Michael would recognise the names immediately; anyone would. They were three of the most well-known names in the world, names that stood for fame and wealth and influence on an international stage.

'Your sister shouldn't be too much of a problem to get to the island,' began the fixer, 'but the other two . . .'

'Find a way,' said Miles flatly. 'I don't pay you to see problems, I pay you to find solutions. Make it happen.'

He hung up the phone. It had suddenly become warm in the office and he pulled open his robe to let some air on to his skin. Miles tried to picture them, imagine their expressions when Michael called them and gave them the news. He found he could not. All he could see was their faces on the beach that night, the night which had changed all their lives for ever. He turned his chair back towards the window. Now, in the desk lamp's glow, the city had disappeared, replaced only by Miles Ashford's reflection, pale and ghostly. It was time to go back.

Part One

Part One

1

Summer 1990, Angel Cay, the Bahamas

'You're going to dinner dressed like *that*?'

Grace Ashford looked down at her denim Capri pants and French navy T-shirt and frowned at her best friend Sarah Brayfield.

'What's wrong?'

It was what she wore for dinner every night, with flip-flops and a ponytail. How was she supposed to turn up for dinner – in a ball gown and five-inch heels? It wasn't like they were dining at Langan's; they were on holiday, and although *Architectural Digest* had just called her father's Caribbean bolt-hole 'the most idyllic private island in the Bahamas', the reality was it was just low-key and relaxed.

'What's *wrong*?' asked Sarah with a dramatic arch of her eyebrow. 'What's wrong is that we've been on a paradise island for one week now and you have made precisely zero progress with Boy Wonder. We need drastic action. And, more importantly, we need cleavage.'

Grace groaned. Sarah had always been very dramatic. Throughout their entire time at Bristol University her friend had toyed with the idea of being an actress before six job offers on the milk round had made her swap her plans for

9

RADA for law college, declaring cheerfully that she was going to 'sell out'.

Fearing that the night ahead might take an embarrassing turn, Grace realised that it had been a mistake to tell her indiscreet, theatrical flatmate about her secret lust for Alex Doyle, her brother Miles' best friend – especially when they were all holidaying on the Ashfords' private island at the same time: Miles to celebrate the end of A levels and his time at her own alma mater Danehurst School; herself to recover from the late nights and academic rigours of Finals.

Traditionally, Grace had always gone out of her way to avoid spending time with her brother and his friends. Even as a young child, she had always found Miles to be arrogant and underhand, and the people he chose to hang around with were much the same.

That was until he had brought home Alex last summer. Alex Doyle, with his spectacular good looks, sexy northern accent and poet-boy broodiness, was like a cross between the lead in a sixties French movie – Alain Delon perhaps – and John Taylor from Duran Duran, on whom she still nursed a secret crush. She hadn't meant to fall for Alex – after all, he was three years her junior – but ever since he had visited her in Bristol and followed it up with the letter she kept stashed away in her diary, she had felt the attraction was mutual. Or was it? She wasn't sure and she certainly didn't want Sarah tarting her up and making a fool out of her.

'Action? Cleavage?' She grinned at her friend. 'I'm the host this week, remember. It's bad form to go seducing house guests.'

Sarah began touching up her own make-up in the big gilt mirror. 'I'd hardly call your feeble attempts at pulling him seduction. The most you've said to him in the last three days is pass me a pineapple, despite him mooning around you for days.'

Grace felt a jolt of excitement. 'Has he? When?'

'Didn't you see him down on the rocks with his top off? I know I did, but he only had eyes for you, more's the pity.'

Sarah turned to Grace and pouted. 'In the words of Disraeli, action may not bring you happiness. But there is no happiness without action. You have to be bolder. Sit next to him at dinner. I want plans made for the holiday. Arrange to go up to Leeds or wherever it is he's from. Invite him to London. A gig. He's into music, isn't he? Find out from Miles who he likes and get tickets, anything to get him on his own. Seduction is really quite simple you know. Especially when you wear this.'

'Are you sure you should be going to law college? I think Sandhurst might be more appropriate.'

Sarah flung open the wicker wardrobe and pulled out a piece of leopard-print chiffon.

'What's that?'

'Put it on,' she instructed.

'It's see-through!'

Her friend's lip curled upwards in triumph. 'My point exactly.'

Grace hesitated before taking the kaftan from Sarah, wishing she could be more like her friend, the product of unmarried 'resting' children's TV presenters who had brought up their daughter to have a voice, a cause and cast-iron self-belief that she could do anything or be anybody she wanted to be.

Grace's parents on the other hand had given their daughter every material advantage. But the very wealth that had allowed it had drawn Grace into rather than out of her shell. She didn't like attracting attention to herself. She'd spent a lifetime hearing people whispering about her when helicopters dropped her off at school or her father's chauffeured Bentley picked her up from friends' houses. She'd hated it and as a result she liked to blend in.

Get a grip, she told herself, squashing down the

disappointment she had felt all week. You've got a first-class degree; you can get an eighteen-year-old to snog you.

She was surprised as she caught her reflection in the mirror. It wasn't half bad. The kaftan was short and sheer and had a deep V-neck with topaz-coloured beads around it. The colour made her skin look more tanned and her long, thick hair more tawny, and the narrow silhouette added inches to her height. Five feet nine but not in a willowy way, Grace had wide shoulders from sports: lacrosse and netball. *Sturdy* was how her father frequently, painfully, referred to her, as if he was describing an oak tree, but the light chiffon had draped itself over her curves in an elegant and flattering way.

'Very Sharon Stone.' Sarah nodded appreciatively.

'Wilma Flintstone, more like.'

She tried to pull down the kaftan a few inches to hide more of her thighs. 'Heck, it's short. I'm not sure my legs are good enough for something this mini.'

'Nothing a bit of blusher can't sort out,' replied Sarah thoughtfully.

She knelt down and started daubing long streaks of bronzer down the outside of Grace's thigh.

'What are you doing?' shrieked Grace.

'Slimming your legs by optical illusion, of course.'

'Well, well. What's going on down there?'

Grace looked up to see her friends Freya Nicholls and Gabby Devlin at the door. They were both wearing tiny string bikinis, and barely-there sarongs were wrapped around their concave waists.

'Just a little enhancement,' said Sarah, unfazed by the girls' disapproving looks.

Gabby flopped on to the bed, leaving dampness on the coverlet, while Freya pulled a bottle of Moët and another of Kir from her beach bag. Freya had a job lined up at the Lynn Franks PR agency in London as soon as they got back to the UK, and already she had older, more sophisticated tastes than

12

the rest of them. The four girls were unlikely friends – according to Sarah, Freya and Gabby had dispensed with a sense of humour when they discovered that their stunning good looks were all they needed to carry themselves through life. But the two of them had taken Grace under their wing on their first day at Danehurst when she was lost and homesick, and they were sworn best friends for life by the time Grace realised they had almost nothing in common. And when they had followed Grace to Bristol to attend the polytechnic, it had seemed wrong to do anything else but invite them to live with her in the four-bedroom house in Clifton that her father had bought for her time at uni.

'Thought we'd get the party started early,' said Freya as Gabby went to fetch glasses.

'So how was snorkelling?' asked Grace.

'Amazing,' said Gabby, playing with the string of brown beads around her ankle. 'You should have come.'

'And leave *Valley of the Dolls* unfinished?' Grace grinned, holding up a dog-eared paperback. 'After a three-year diet of Chaucer, Milton and Shelley, this is like manna from heaven.'

'Forget the fish, the highlight of the trip was that new boat boy,' said Freya, grabbing Sarah's bottle of red nail polish. 'I'm not sure where he came from but he is cute, cute, cute.'

Gabby took a sip from her tooth glass of champagne and rolled her eyes. 'She's desperate for a holiday shag.'

'What about your boyfriend?' asked Sarah disapprovingly.

'What about him?' Freya smiled. 'What goes on on the island stays on the island.'

Grace took the bottle. 'He must be one of the guys my dad has shipped in from one of the other islands. He's got half a dozen clients coming here tomorrow evening after we've all gone, so they need to put on a show.'

She pressed the button on her cassette player and the sounds of Everything But The Girl floated through the speaker.

Listening to the soulful melody, Grace felt suddenly

depressed and vulnerable. The fact that they were leaving tomorrow meant that all the fun, carefree days of school and university were behind them and the void of her real life was rushing up to meet her. Unlike Sarah, she wasn't sure where her life was going to lead. Since childhood, she had been told that she would go to work in her father's company, but she had no illusions that it would be a glamorous VIP role with a corner office and a place on the board. Her father had always seen Miles as his great successor and gave Grace the impression that her job would be a safe little distraction until she found someone suitable to marry, preferably someone with connections to add to the sheen of the family company, Ash Corp. It certainly didn't make her feel excited; it made her feel trapped and, in a fit of rebellion nine months ago, she had applied for an MA course at Oxford, forging a new fantasy of life as an academic, spending term-time in some dreamy, spired university town and her holidays on Angel writing the new *Gone with the Wind*. Now all she had to do was break the news to her parents.

She poured a generous measure of champagne into her glass, the bubbles fizzing over the top, and drank it down.

'That's the spirit, Grace,' said Freya. 'Let's get in the mood.'

Sarah pursed her lips. 'Grace needs some Dutch courage.'

'What for?' demanded Gabby eagerly, sensing gossip.

'She's going to cop off with Alex tonight.'

'Sarah!' Grace flushed.

'Miles' friend?' asked Gabby, frowning.

'How many other men named Alex are there on Angel Cay?' Sarah replied.

'But he's eighteen, isn't he?' asked Gabby.

'Nineteen in September.'

'You cradle-snatcher!' Freya laughed.

'Actually, that means he's at his sexual peak.' Sarah grinned.

'I can see I'm going to have to get really, really drunk,' said Grace.

Outside, beyond the plantation shuttered windows, the Caribbean sun was setting, flushing the sky the colour of a Bellini. The scent of honeysuckle and jasmine floated on the breeze.

'Where do you think we'll all be in ten years' time?' wondered Grace aloud.

'Back here hopefully,' said Sarah with a smile.

'I want to be married,' said Freya, 'to someone rich, gorgeous and famous.'

They all laughed.

'We'll all be married by then,' said Gabby, as if it was stupid to think anything else.

'Speak for yourself,' said Sarah. 'My mum and dad have got the best relationship I know and they've been happily unmarried for twenty-five years.'

'Your parents are just a pair of old hippies. Any couple not married after ten years do not want to get married.'

'They're hippies all right. But they're right for each other.'

'Screw that,' said Freya, holding up her left hand and waggling her fingers. 'I want a massive rock on here.'

Grace watched them, wondering to what degree their lives were already set. Freya was off to the glittering lights of Soho, Sarah clearly had found her calling as a lawyer – human rights most likely – and Gabby, who had spent her three years at Bristol trawling the students' union for the most eligible Old Etonians, was sure that her research and determination would bear fruit in a good marriage. Grace's parents had decided on her own fate from the moment she was born. But with her MA course tempting her, she knew she could change her destiny. Right here. Tonight, if she could find the courage to tell her dad she didn't want to join the family business.

No pressure then, she said to herself, smiling, feeling a flutter of hope as the champagne bubbles went to her head.

'To sexy men,' said Freya, raising her glass and downing the gently fizzing liquid in one.

'To Angel Cay,' followed Sarah.

Grace felt a rush of hope and expectancy. 'To tonight,' she said, clinking her glass against the others'. 'This is the last few hours of our youth and the start of the rest of our lives. Let's make it a night to remember.'

2

Lying on the deck of *Beautiful Constance*, Robert Ashford's ninety-five-foot motor yacht, Alex Doyle pushed his sunglasses further up his sunburnt nose, still not quite able to believe how a boy from a two-up two-down in Macclesfield was able to live a life like this. As far as the eye could see, turquoise waters stretched out towards the horizon, the blue sea broken only by the outlines of the cays. There were 365 islands in the Exumas – one for every day of the year – and as he lay there, *Beautiful Constance* was heading towards the most beautiful one of all. Angel Cay, the Ashford family's private island, rose like a mirage out of the clear water. Peaks of tropical jungle – mango, palm and coconut trees – were ringed by sugar-white sands. The pale blue Caribbean plantation house stood on the crest of the tallest hill with a wraparound view of sea, sky and tropical vegetation. Squinting, Alex could see specks of bubblegum pink on the beach. 'Flamingos!' he chuckled, pulling out his battered Olympus Trip to take this unlikely snapshot of paradise. Whoever said money didn't make you happy hadn't been to Angel Cay.

Today they had taken the yacht for some snorkelling off the cays, where the fish were as brightly coloured as Christmas baubles, and this afternoon they had cut out towards Harbour Island for some deep-sea fishing. Sitting in the chair struggling with the line, he'd felt like he was living some feverish Hemingway-fuelled fantasy. Over the course of this holiday

Alex had experienced things he'd seen only in James Bond movies – private jets, Jacuzzis, tennis lessons and backgammon, fine wines that cost more than his mother's car, liqueurs you had before *and* after your exotic dinners of lobster and quail. To think he hadn't even wanted to go to Danehurst, the school that had put these opportunities within reach.

The truth was that Alex had been quite happy at Macclesfield's Ryles Park comprehensive until his mother Maureen, a widow, had sat him down after football practice midway through his first year of secondary school.

'I was talking to Mrs Kennedy,' she'd said nonchalantly. 'She had an interesting idea.'

'Oh yes?' he'd asked suspiciously. He knew that his mum had been Mrs Kennedy's cleaner for many years and had become quite close to the rich old lady. He'd been out to her enormous house in the swish village of Prestbury near their home and had been impressed by the size of her cars and the garden; she even had a swimming pool, which to Alex was the height of wealth for anyone.

'I mentioned your talent for music to her,' continued his mother, 'and she thought you could try and get into one of the top boarding schools off the back of it. They offer music scholarships, you know. Mrs Kennedy said it's a brilliant way of getting a first-class education.'

'Boarding school?' he'd replied, appalled. 'I'm not leaving my mates for some posho place down south. No way. Never! *Boarding school.*'

Maureen Doyle, however, was a persuasive woman. She had finally convinced Alex to at least visit one of them. That was all it took; Alex had been seduced by the public school's grandeur and history, the feeling that you were surrounded by the ghosts of people who had done great things and the bodies of people who *would* do great things. So finally, having scored one of their prestigious scholarships, he had agreed to go to Danehurst, a huge gothic pile in West Sussex, which, despite the lacrosse pitches and croquet lawns, felt marginally more normal than the other schools he had visited, plus it was co-ed and in the sixth form you could wear your own clothes. Even better, classes were actually voluntary, although everybody seemed to attend, and in any given year there was likely to be a rock star's daughter or a movie star's son in residence.

People like Miles Ashford, thought Alex, as he peeled off his T-shirt to catch some last rays of sun. Miles was glamorous, rich and connected and had arrived in the sixth form in a silver Bentley and a cloud of rumours, having been expelled from Eton when a master had found a small lump of hashish in his room. He and Alex had not become friends immediately; after all, there were plenty of other privileged neo-aristos for Miles to hang out with at Danehurst. Alex had, unsurprisingly, been considered an outsider, with his northern accent and his strange taste in indie rock, but in the end that seemed to be what Miles was drawn to.

'You're interesting, Alex Doyle,' he had declared, walking into Alex's room one night. 'I'm so bored of all these rich halfwits. You think for yourself, you go your own way.'

Of course, it wasn't long before Alex was going Miles' way, visiting him in the holidays at the family house in the country, or being invited on head-spinning trips like this end-of-term blow-out on the island. But it wasn't all one way; Alex had become Miles Ashford's best friend because, unlike anyone else in his life, Miles knew he could rely on Alex, whatever happened.

Alex reached across to the ice box, pulling out another cold can of Red Stripe, and picked up his Walkman headphones. Ah, the new Pavement EP; he loved the way they were melodic, but spiky and angular at the same time, the way—

'Arrggh! What the . . . !' Alex leapt up howling as he felt

a cold splash of water across his bare stomach. Wrenching off his sunglasses, he saw Oscar and Angus McKay, two of his Danehurst classmates, doubled up with laughter like stupid little schoolboys delighted at their prank.

'What the hell are you doing?' cried Alex, desperately trying to towel off his Walkman and praying it wasn't ruined.

'Just checking you're still alive, Dolly.' The twins knew their nickname for him grated on his nerves, but at least it had never caught on at Danehurst.

'What are you listening to anyway? Brass band music?'

Angus, the smaller of the twins, was still so amused he was clutching his rib cage. Alex fought the urge to punch the little squirt. *Don't screw it up on your last day here*, he thought. *Don't let them get to you.*

Although Danehurst was a liberal, progressive school which tended to attract the children of a rich media crowd, there was still a sprinkling of snooty and arrogant upper-class bores and Oscar and Angus typified the breed. Their father was a Scottish lord, their mother a minor Hollywood actress, and they had inherited both centuries-old snobbery and nouveau riche superiority from their parents. They had invited Miles to spend Easter in Aspen with them and they had all returned to school as thick as thieves, full of private jokes and stories. The twins had jealously tried their best to squeeze Alex out of Miles' affections, and while it hadn't worked, they had spent the final term making his life miserable. Somehow they had found out that his mother was a cleaner and had begun to make snide comments about the dust on the school cups or how their socks needed laundering. And the digs had continued on holiday. To his dismay, Alex had found that two of Grace's friends, Gabby and Freya, had joined in. *It's human nature to want to follow the pack, even if you know you're doing something wrong*, thought Alex.

'Well, make the most of lying about in the sun, Dolly,' said Angus with a cruel smile. 'Tomorrow it's back to processed peas and meat pies. Where are you spending the rest of the summer – stacking shelves in Kwik Save, wasn't it?'

'Yeah, well. Maybe I'll have an island like this one day,' said Alex defiantly. 'When I'm a famous rock star.'

'Yah, right,' said Oscar. 'Dolly wants to be the new Billy Bragg. Up the workers, down the bourgeois. Better not tell the fans about your time moonlighting as a paid-up member of the rich. Then again, interloping hardly counts.'

Alex closed his eyes and pictured himself pushing both of them over the side of the yacht. He would have done it too, if he'd thought that Miles would take his side, but you could never tell with Miles. Besides, after five years at Danehurst, despite his mum drilling her mantra into him that 'these people are no better than you', Alex still didn't feel secure enough in this world to make a stand.

Seeming to lose interest in baiting Alex, Angus pushed past him and grabbed a beer from the cooler.

'Shit, I can't believe we've got this boring dinner with Miles' dad tonight,' he said, pulling the ring off. 'I don't know why we couldn't have gone to Nassau.'

Alex couldn't believe how ungrateful they were. All week they had found something to grumble about, despite the island's incredible hospitality.

'Why did you want to go to Nassau?' he asked, containing himself.

'To go to the casino, of course,' said Oscar witheringly. 'Although I doubt it would have been your scene, Alex.'

'Do you play baccarat, Dolly?' asked Angus.

'Haven't you heard of the Macclesfield Working Men's Domino and Baccarat Club? It's internationally famous,' said Alex, trying to recover some dignity.

'What's going on here?' asked Miles as he walked up from the cabin.

Miles Ashford was an impressive young man by anyone's standards. Not conventionally good-looking, he had a manner

21

and confidence that demanded attention. In shorts and a pale blue shirt, he looked older and more sophisticated than his years. Alex thought he resembled a movie star stepping out for drinks on the terrace.

'Oh, we were just inviting Alex over to Nassau for a flutter on the tables.' Oscar smirked. 'I'm not sure he's keen, though.'

Miles' bright blue eyes darted between the three boys, correctly assessing the mood in an instant. 'Well, I'm not surprised,' he said with an elegant shrug of the shoulders. 'Gambling's a mug's game. Probably why you clowns like it. House always wins – didn't you know that? That's why the smart move is owning a casino like we do.'

Angus curled his lip. 'Business is still gambling, Miles. Stocks, shares. Property.'

Miles smiled. 'In some respects. Then again, there's a difference between calculated risk and pure chance. Incidentally, Angus, the gaming tables in Nassau don't let you in if you're under twenty-one, and I don't think that fake ID you made at Prontoprint is going to get past the casino Gestapo.'

Angus looked embarrassed. 'It might,' he pouted.

'Not when the name you put on it is Ron Jeremy.'

'What's wrong with that?'

'Well, he's a porn star for a start. Incredibly well hung, which is more than can be said for you, if you believe the rumours Emily Reed was spreading round school.'

Angus glowered at Miles but didn't say anything. They were all nervous of upsetting their patron. Miles was the Sun King, with everyone else circling round him like courtiers, and not even the twins, with their brashness and arrogance, dared confront him.

Miles walked over and flung an arm around Alex's shoulder. 'No, the only thing I'll bet my shirt on is talent,' he said, lighting a cigarette and exhaling a smoke ring towards the lavender clouds. 'It's why me and Alex have been friends for so long, isn't it, Al?'

Oscar's face fell.

'Looks like we're about to dock,' said Angus sulkily. 'Think I'll go and find my baseball cap.'

Alex felt a surge of triumph as he watched them go below deck.

'Wankers,' said Miles as he watched them go. 'I don't know why I invited them here. They do nothing but moan.'

'I don't think they like me being here either,' said Alex.

'Ah, they're just jealous of our manly love.' Miles grinned, punching Alex on the arm playfully. 'Listen, Dad's just had some two-man Jet Skis shipped in from Miami. Up for trying them later? Plus I have some charlie back at the house.'

'Jet Skis and coke? Not at the same time, surely?' He said it as a joke, but he suspected Miles was serious. Alex wanted to be a rock star, but if he was totally honest with himself, drugs scared him a bit. Brian Dunne from the Moss estate had started on cannabis in the fourth year at Ryles Park and was a proper junkie now, which was why Alex kept his vices to nicotine and booze.

'Come on, Alex,' said Miles. 'Life on the edge. That's how we like it, isn't it?'

Alex smiled and shrugged. How could he refuse on the last day of the holiday? How could he refuse Miles Ashford anything? Miles had changed his life. He'd do anything for his friend. Anything at all.

3

'Is there anything else you wish me to do, Miss Sasha?'

Sasha Sinclair smiled with satisfaction as she looked at the dinner table shimmering in the light of a dozen hurricane lamps. It wasn't perfect, but it was pretty damn good; better than that mouse Grace Ashford could have done, anyway. Strictly speaking, Sasha was not the mistress of this house and, as a guest, she had no place making the arrangements for the final meal, but if *she* didn't do it, who would? Miles' mother Connie Ashford was at home in London. As for Grace? She was probably off somewhere with her nose stuck in a book. *Poor Grace*, she thought. *No idea of social occasions*.

Sasha walked around the table one last time, rearranging a fork here, a glass there, making sure everything was exactly where it should be. It had been her idea to have the dinner at the long table underneath the tiki hut on the beach; a stroke of genius, even if she did say so herself. The golden glow of the lamps on the sand spilled out glorious, flattering light; not that Sasha Sinclair needed any help looking exquisite. Naturally striking, with glossy honey-blond hair and almond-shaped eyes the colour of parma violets, she had brought three trunks for the week-long trip, but tonight the simplest thing in her wardrobe, an ivory kaftan that set off her deep bronze tan, made her look a million dollars. It had been no surprise to anyone that Sasha had landed a modelling contract with an agency in London; she would be going straight to Chelsea from the island tomorrow.

'Miss Sasha, shall I set the place cards the same as last night?' asked Juan the waiter.

'No,' she snapped, glaring at him. 'Last night was a disaster.'

The previous evening they had dined in the island's main house and Sasha had found herself trapped between Grace and her loud-mouthed friend Sarah. Neither of them had shown any interest in Sasha's funny little story about how she had managed to buy the last Azzedine Alaïa dress from under Patsy Kensit's nose and they had just chattered on about charity and politics and all those left-wing causes Sarah and her crusty parents thought were so important. Tonight Sasha had taken matters into her own hands, positioning Miles to her left, Freya to her right and – most importantly – Mr Ashford directly opposite.

She followed Juan as he placed the cards on each plate, ensuring he didn't make any mistakes. The swarthy odd-job man was a permanent fixture on Angel Cay, but tonight there would be dozens of additional staff – butlers, boat boys, chefs – who had been drafted in to make the stay of Robert Ashford's new guests as comfortable and luxurious as possible, and Sasha couldn't afford anything to go wrong. Tonight was going to be special, she could feel it. Tonight was when Miles' father – *Robert* – would recognise her as his son's future wife and perhaps – though she barely allowed herself to think this – perhaps it would become official with a moonlit proposal. She didn't expect anything too romantic. She knew Miles was not the most demonstrative of boyfriends – sometimes she even wondered whether he was capable of genuine feeling – but Sasha didn't really care about that. What she cared about was *position*. She and Miles were a team, the king and queen of Danehurst, and she had no intention of giving that up now term had ended.

Sasha had set her sights on Miles Ashford the moment she had arrived at Danehurst two years ago after transferring from Wycombe Abbey, an academic school where they had gently suggested that the sixth form might not be the best choice for her. Sasha wasn't fazed; she already had all the qualifications she needed: long legs, full lips and a ruthless focus on what she wanted. Beauty was just as important, *more* important than cleverness, and it had served her well at Danehurst as she had effortlessly seduced Miles. But now she needed to close the deal, make it binding with a ring on her finger before he left for university and she went to London to take up a modelling contract. It was obvious to anyone that Sasha would make the ideal wife for Miles – beautiful, ambitious, a true asset in any society marriage – but she was realistic enough to know that without a permanent claim on him, even she would struggle to keep the relationship together when Miles was at Oxford and she was in London.

'That will be all, Juan,' said Sasha as soon as the table was set to her satisfaction, and he scurried off, leaving her alone on the beach. Sasha looked up towards the main house, where she could see the windows casting out a pumpkin glow. More than anything, she wanted to hold on to all of this. She loved Angel Cay, not only the white beaches and lush scenery but also the house with its dramatic entrance hall and stylish interior, an artfully arranged mixture of expensive pottery, mismatched antique furniture and bright batik drapes. But to keep this in her grasp, she needed Miles.

Sasha smiled at the prospect of marriage. While she found Sarah Brayfield's 'I don't need a man' brand of feminism misguided, she had never expected to want to settle down so soon. But Miles was one of the most eligible young men in the country; even *Tatler* had said so. The timing wasn't ideal, of course; she would much rather have spent her twenties jetting around the globe on glamorous modelling assignments and being wooed by movie stars before she found her perfect man. But sometimes things didn't go entirely to plan and you met a man so spectacular you couldn't let him go; Yasmin Parvaneh hadn't hung around when she'd met Simon Le Bon, or Priscilla Presley and Elvis. Besides. It could be a long engagement.

Steeling her resolve, she thought of her handsome brother Adam, who'd left Durham University five years ago with his 2:1 degree and the world at his feet. On his gap year, waiting for his Civil Service fast-track place to begin, he had met and fallen in love with a Chinese girl, following her to Hong Kong, where he was now a lowly police sergeant with a one-bedroom apartment you couldn't swing a cat in. 'Don't make Adam's mistake,' her mother had said. Sasha did not intend to. Marriage was an alliance, not a romantic ideal.

She turned and stared out to sea, the white caps of the breaking waves just visible in the twilight. There was one fly in the ointment. Alex Doyle. Lately, Miles seemed to spend every waking minute with his best friend from Danehurst. Sasha had no idea what he saw in such an oik or what they found to talk about. Yes, Alex was good-looking, of course, but he was so boring, always going on about politics and miserable indie music. Still, he wouldn't be a problem after tonight; they were off to different universities and everyone knew that childhood friendships soon faded away when you met more interesting and sophisticated people at uni. Sasha felt a rare flutter of anxiety as she realised that the same thing would apply to her unless she managed to have a serious conversation about the future with Miles tonight. She turned and marched back towards the house with determination. She knew what she wanted: she wanted this life, she wanted money, luxury, influence and a five-carat classic-cut sparkler from Tiffany. She wanted commitment from Miles Ashford and she was going to close the deal tonight. And nothing, absolutely nothing, was going to get in her way.

4

On the terrace below the house, two waiters were circulating with trays of canapés. Miles waved them over for a large vodka tonic. Dinner was not being served for another hour, and he didn't think he could get through the night without a decent drink.

He thought of his earlier conversation with Alex – a grand tour of Europe – and wondered why he hadn't thought of it before. Until today he'd had some vague plans about hooking up with a few old Eton friends who were making a killing running illegal raves up and down the country. It sounded fun, but it was still work. After a handful of trust funds had kicked in on his eighteenth birthday, it was not as if Miles needed the money. But with three months of summer stretching out in front of him, he fancied more of an adventure. Already he had thought of a rough itinerary. Marbella for the tarts, the Greek islands for the parties, St Tropez for the little beach clubs, and Rome was always fun, he thought, imagining himself drunk, on a scooter, weaving his way through the streets of the Eternal City.

'Starting a little early, Miles?'

He turned around to see his father looking at him disapprovingly. Even in middle age, Robert Ashford was still an attractive man. Despite a weak chin, he had strong blue eyes and thick brows that framed his face. His pale brown hair veered off uncomfortably into ginger in the sun, but the straw panama he put on to cover it was always worn with stylish rakishness. Miles shared the eyes and the elegant dress sense but had benefited from his mother's better bone structure. They looked like uncle and nephew rather than father and son.

'I'm on holiday,' he replied with truculence.

'Enjoy it while you can,' said Robert wryly.

'What does that mean?' he asked, swigging his vodka defiantly.

'I'd like you to come and see me after dinner. I've prepared a schedule for your time at Ash Corp. Sorry it's taken me a little longer than I thought, but I've been waiting for the right project to come along for you to get your teeth into.'

'Time at Ash Corp.?' Miles looked at his father narrowly, still annoyed at the way Robert had gatecrashed his holiday, elbowing his way into their final-night dinner and then turfing them out a whole three days early because he had clients arriving.

Robert nodded. 'You'll be spending the time until you start at Oxford with me.'

Miles could scarcely believe his ears. 'What?'

'We've discussed this.'

'Me? Work at the company this summer? I thought you were joking.'

'Why would I joke about that?'

'Because I'm knackered. Because I've spent the last six months swotting for my A levels.'

'Not too hard from what I hear. I know Oxford require only two Es, but they do expect you to *aim* a little higher.'

Miles glanced away from his father, knowing the older man had a point. Miles had never been one to distract himself with study when there were pleasures in the world to be indulged in. Miss Lemmon, Danehurst's head teacher, had taken him into her study at the end of the lower sixth and told him he'd be lucky to read theology at a polytechnic if he didn't start applying himself. But beneath the waster front, Miles was fiercely intelligent and had taken Lemmon's words as a challenge. He insisted he be entered for the Oxford entrance examination and after a two-week flurry of cramming had aced his exam and interview and was now due to go to Oriel College to study Modern History.

'Look, it's an interesting project. Surveying potential sites for a premium outlet village. Not a new idea, I know. Basically we're importing the concept from the designer villages like Woodbury Common in New York State. But I think it could really work in this country. The site we want is just outside Coventry. Then there'll be plenty of initial meetings with luxury labels to gauge interest in taking units. This is a huge market for us, a tremendous opportunity, Miles.'

'You want me to spend the summer in *Coventry*?'

'I'm sorry if I've spoilt your fun, Miles,' said Robert Ashford, although his glib tone suggested quite the opposite. 'Remember, it's the business that funds all this. It's not all pleasure.'

'I understand the principles of business,' sniffed his son. 'It's very straightforward, isn't it? I mean, I get why your mates are flying in tomorrow, *for pleasure*. You need financing and generous planning permission to build your skyscrapers, so you fly your contacts out here and ply them with Krug and hookers.'

'Pardon?' hissed his father.

'Prostitutes,' said Miles innocently, prepared to use his trump card. 'I mean, that's why you've sent Dick Donovan into Nassau, isn't it? To sort out the arrival of half a dozen hookers? I have to say, it's not the sort of thing that makes one think more highly of one's parent.'

Robert glared at his son and Miles felt a wave of power surge through him, grateful for the information he'd gleaned earlier that week. He knew his father took mistresses – over the years he'd noticed items of clothing around their London house that were definitely not his mother's, and had heard Robert in his study whispering things that certainly weren't to his business advisers. Then, on Tuesday, he'd heard a couple of staff sniggering about Ashford's 'female entertainers'. Slipping the pool cleaners two hundred dollars to tell him more, Miles had learnt that every year on Robert's corporate Angel Cay weekenders, exotic dancers would perform on the beach, then clients would choose one of the girls for some personal entertainment of their own.

'So Mum knows about the dancers, does she?' challenged Miles. 'Well then, how about we keep it between the two of us and in return you'll let me have one last summer of freedom? It's not that I don't want to work for the company, Dad. I just don't want to work at Ash Corp. quite yet.'

'Don't threaten me, Miles. It doesn't suit you. Now perhaps we should defer this conversation till we both return to London. You've spent enough of your time and my money on ski slopes, exotic beaches and yachts. You are coming to Ash Corp. to work and that is an end to it. So don't even think about trying to get the upper hand with me. Because I will make life so difficult for you it will make your head spin.'

Miles clenched his fingers into tight fists. He would gladly have strangled his father at that moment.

Nothing he had ever done had been good enough for Robert Ashford, from the moment Miles had proudly brought home a prize for excellence from his first school. The teacher had praised his creativity, intelligence and application, saying that through enthusiasm and hard work he was ahead of most of the boys in the year above him.

Robert had taken one look and dropped the certificate in his office waste-paper basket. 'Only *most* of the boys?' he had said. 'Second place is never acceptable, Miles.'

Miles had been five years old.

He had waited in vain for a word of encouragement from his father – for his progress at the Pony Club, on the athletics field or in his exams. Even when Miles had flown through the Common Entrance exam to get into Eton, Robert failed to pass comment. It particularly grated on Miles' nerves that to the outside world, his father was Mr Charming, supporting good causes and working tirelessly for charity. Whispers were that Robert would go into politics; only last month, with Thatcher's power waning, *The Times* had run an opinion poll entitled 'Who would you like to see as PM?'. Robert Ashford had polled over twenty-three per cent: not bad considering he was the only non-politician on the list. 'Isn't he a nice guy?' people would say to Miles. 'He must be so much fun to have as a dad.'

How wrong they were. Miles had never been able to please his father, and so he had rebelled. At fourteen, after a string of misdemeanours, his mother had sent him to see a child psychologist – *a shrink!* – who had suggested that Miles' bad behaviour was the one thing that got his father's attention. And so he partied harder and worked even less, until he was thrown out of Eton for drug use.

Part of Miles didn't even want to go to Oxford, knowing that his looming matriculation there was something that secretly delighted his father. Then again, the elitism of Oxford and the fact that his father hadn't even gone to university, let alone one of the best educational establishments in the world, appealed to him. He wasn't going to turn the opportunity down because of spite.

Without another word, Robert Ashford turned on his heel and sloped off through the sand towards the house.

Miles suddenly felt a pair of warm hands cover his eyes as a damp kiss was planted on the back curve of his neck. He could barely be bothered to turn around and look at her.

'Hey, lover,' purred Sasha, stroking the lapel of his navy

linen suit. 'Why don't you go and change? You look like Gordon Gekko on holiday in that thing.'

'Maybe that's the look I'm going for,' he said flatly. If there was one thing Miles detested it was comments, derogatory ones, made against the sense of style he took very seriously.

'Go and put something more casual on,' pressed Sasha. 'Shorts or something. I've got a few things planned for this evening.'

'Like what? *It's a Knockout?*'

'Don't be silly. Just chilling out. Making out,' she whispered.

Miles felt his eyes close in frustration. Yes, he had enjoyed being top dog at Danehurst, and yes, being a power couple with Sasha had been a large part of that, but it did not make up for the fact that everything she did seemed to annoy him. The way she laughed, the way she flicked her hair, the way she spoke to her friends, it all set his teeth on edge. Even the sex was all a bit try-hard and it didn't really turn him on. He knew it had been a bad idea inviting her to the island but it had been hard not to, especially when she had got wind that his sister and her friends were going to be here too.

She took his reluctant hand and gave it a squeeze. 'So what was that heavy chat with your father about?'

'Me working at the company.'

'Wow! That's a great idea. I mean, really, what's the point in wasting three years at Oxford when you know what you're going to end up doing anyway?'

'I'm going to Oxford,' he replied, irritated. 'He means working for the summer.'

'Still, *amazing*,' she laughed, squeezing his fingers again. 'We can go flat-hunting when we get back to London. A little love nest *à deux*. What about Notting Hill or Chelsea? Yeah, definitely Chelsea. I was looking in the classifieds of *The Times* the other day and there was this great little mews for sale in that square behind Pucci Pizza. Not that I'll be eating pizza once I start modelling, but it was really cheap. The house I mean. Like only nine hundred and fifty thousand pounds or something.'

'I'm not working for my father this summer.'

'Why not?'

'Because I'm going round Europe.'

Sasha looked thoughtful. 'I suppose I could get an agent in Paris.'

'No. I think you should stay in London.'

'But what about Europe? Can we go to St Tropez? *Please?*'

'I'm going with Alex.'

Her face crumpled and he felt a well of disdain.

'What? Alex Doyle? But what about me? Us?'

Miles pulled away from her. Her voice was beginning to sound like the insistent buzzing of a bluebottle. *Us.* The words made him cringe. He wanted to dump her now, finish it for good, but he knew that it would only lead to a scene, and tonight was going to be bad enough with his father as it was. He was sick of women, with their constant chatter and inane obsessions with shoes and gossip. He just couldn't see the point.

'Look, Sasha, we need to talk.'

Suddenly there was an excited yodel from the direction of the tiki hut. Looking over, Miles could see one of the twins – at this distance, he could not tell which one – wrapped around the trunk of the coconut tree, at least twenty feet above the beach.

'What the fuck . . . ?'

There was a loud cry. And then, as if in slow motion, the body descended like a ripe coconut, hitting the sand with an audible bone-crunching thud.

Suddenly the beach was full of the sound of screaming.

Oscar – or was it Angus? – lay on the ground, surrounded by a flurry of waiters and butlers who'd sprung into action and were fussing round the body.

35

'*Nightmare*,' said Sasha, beginning to break into a run. 'I hope the silly sod hasn't hurt himself.'

'So do I,' growled Miles, upping his pace to follow her. 'His mother's American, and if the daft twat *has* hurt himself, I bet she goes and sues us.'

5

Dinner was not a success. Despite the perfection of the menu and the free-flowing, premium-quality alcohol, with Oscar in bed, in pain, everyone had to pretend to be concerned about his welfare and spent most of the meal discussing it, even though they all secretly felt that the night was more enjoyable without him.

Although the formal dining under the tiki hut had been prematurely disbanded, Alex had no intention of letting the evening, *the holiday*, finish there, and when Sasha suggested he get his guitar for a sing-song around the fire, he thought it was an excellent idea.

'Not calling it a night already, are you?'

Alex was coming out of his bedroom, guitar in hand, when he saw Grace coming down the hallway towards him. He felt his mood lift. He had always found his friend's sister approachable and down-to-earth and he suddenly wished he had been sitting next to her at dinner. As it was, he had been stuck at the other end of the table, next to Sarah, opposite Angus and within earshot of Robert Ashford. Feeling intimidated and completely out of his depth, he'd kept quiet until Sarah had seen his red star tattoo poking out from under the edge of his T-shirt, at which point she had asked, in a loud voice that had echoed all the way down the table, whether he was a communist and, with everyone listening, had grilled him with all sorts of tricky questions about nationalisation versus state control. How was he supposed to know the difference between Karl Marx and Stalin? It was just a design he'd picked out of a book in the tattoo parlour in Manchester's Afflecks Palace. The only way Alex had been able to get through the meal had been to keep drinking.

'I was just listening to the football results,' said Grace, pulling a jumper over her shoulders. 'The World Cup. England versus Germany.'

'I can't believe I missed it, but I couldn't find the channel on the radio. Did we win?' he asked hopefully.

'We lost. Gazza cried.'

He swore under his breath and then began to laugh.

'What's so funny? The nation's in mourning.'

'I was just thinking of you following the football.'

'Don't sound so surprised.'

'It's the thighs, isn't it?'

She smiled. It was a nice smile that warmed her entire face. 'Like I get an eyeful of Lineker's legs over the World Service.'

'Touché.' Alex laughed.

'At least Oscar's OK,' she said quickly. 'Nelson, our caretaker, has got his wife to fuss round him. His foot. It's just a sprain. Not a break.'

'So he'll live?' He grinned at her.

'He'll live.'

'More's the pity.'

'Stop it,' she giggled.

'Come on, an arsehole with a sprained ankle is still an arsehole.'

'Point taken. Miles' friends have always been on the exasperating side. Present company excluded, of course.'

He followed Grace through the Great Room and out of the house. Outside, he took a deep breath. The salty air, muddled with smoke from the bonfire and the sweetness of coconut from the sun-tan oil on his skin, was a real taste of the tropics.

'You know, without Oscar on the island, I could stay here for ever,' he said wistfully.

Grace nodded. 'Me too. Except I graduate on Friday so I have to get back, even if my dad wasn't kicking us all off.'

'I thought you *were* a graduate. You've finished uni, haven't you?'

'I've done my finals but not had, you know, the black cape and mortarboard ceremony with the parents clapping proudly thing, thankful that their child achieved something other than cirrhosis of the liver after three years at university.'

'You got a first.' Alex smiled. 'People who get first-class degrees do not drink their way through uni.'

'I do drink,' she said defensively. 'I'm drunk now. Well, drunk-ish. I'm pacing myself because it's my twenty-first on Sunday.'

'Wow, it's going to be one massive long party.'

'Not really. I'm just going out for dinner with a few friends. That's my kind of celebration really.'

'*No party?*'

'What, you think it's better to have a three-ring circus like Miles' eighteenth, with six hundred people too drunk to sing happy birthday?'

Alex laughed; she did have a point. His friend had boasted that it was going to be the party to end all parties and it had been quite a spectacle. Held at the Café de Paris, it was rumoured to have cost Robert Ashford £300,000, which worked out at £60,000 an hour, or £1,000 a minute. Still, at least Miles had enjoyed every single second of it. Unlike Grace, he thrived on being the centre of attention and had swaggered around in a pink suit like Don Johnson's younger brother. The wild rumour was that he'd ended the night in a suite at Brown's Hotel with two high-class hookers, although Alex had never heard Miles himself mention it, which suggested it wasn't true. Miles would never miss an opportunity to boast about something like that.

They were by the pool now, next to the path back down to the ocean. Even from this distance Alex could hear the noise of the ghetto-blaster from the beach, and the braying sounds of Sasha and Grace's friends singing an off-kilter version of 'Nothing Compares 2 U' drifted up to the house. Suddenly he wanted to stay exactly where he was, talking to Grace.

'Do you want to hang around here for a bit?'

'Let's go and sit in the tiki swing.'

As she touched his arm, an unwelcome memory popped into his head and he regretted his invitation. *The letter.* Six months earlier, he and Miles had gone to see The Cure in Bristol, meeting up with Grace and her friends. He'd had a fantastic time and it wasn't just the concert. When Miles had disappeared afterwards they'd all ended up in a dodgy club in St Pauls and he'd gone back to Grace's, where they had stayed up till five in the morning, drinking and laughing. Back at Danehurst Alex hadn't been able to stop thinking about her. He'd spent the evening listening to his Cure album over and over just because it reminded him of her. Seized by the romance of the moment, he'd written her a soppy, over-emotional letter, adding as a postscript the words 'Just Like Heaven', his favourite track, whose lyrics described the way he felt, like some secret message he hoped she'd understand, and had run down to the postbox.

Three days later she'd replied. It was a great letter, smart and funny, inviting him back to Bristol, and she'd signed off with *five* kisses. Alex instantly lost his nerve. Yes, she was smart and funny, a bit too smart if the truth be told. Most importantly she was also off-limits. All it would take was one drunken fumble and his golden ticket into the Ashfords' idyllic inner circle might be immediately revoked. It just wasn't worth it.

So he had defused the situation by leaving it another month to respond, telling Grace quite breezily, as part of his one-page missive, how he'd copped off with Petra Williams, the fox of the lower sixth, and how things with his fledging romance were going 'quite well'. She hadn't written back. It had been for the best.

Grace pulled her legs up on to the swing and tucked them under her as she arranged herself on the cushions. A hummingbird hovered over the swimming pool and the scent from the blue hibiscus bush was so strong it made Alex quite heady.

'You sitting down?'

He shook his head. 'It rocks. The way I'm feeling, I might puke on you.'

'You charmer.'

He sat down on the edge of the pool, a shimmering sheet of turquoise neon in the darkness, and dangled his feet into the water. Still thinking about the letter, and feeling quite intimate in this dark, romantic space, he wondered how long he could leave it before he went back to the beach.

'What are you two doing up here being all antisocial?' asked a self-assured, slightly tipsy voice from the gate down to the shore. 'Come on. We need everyone we can get down on the beach.'

Alex looked up to see Freya standing in front of them, holding an elaborate cocktail.

'We're just hanging out here for a few minutes,' replied Grace, sitting more upright in the tiki swing.

'Is he serenading you?' Freya smiled, nodding her head towards the guitar. She walked over to Alex and picked up the instrument, strumming the strings with her long painted fingernails and making an ugly noise.

Alex winced. 'Careful with that, eh?'

She looked at him and gave a playful half-smile. 'Music's not my strong point. Why don't you show me how to play? Then I can tell everyone the new John Lennon taught me the guitar.'

Feeling flattered, Alex glanced nervously up at Grace, but she just raised her eyebrows.

Sighing, he took the guitar and put his arm round Freya. 'OK, put your first finger here on the G string,' he said.

'Saucy,' she purred.

Alex flushed as he felt his cock go hard. Behind him Grace's sandals clattered on the decking as she stood up.

'I've just got to go somewhere for a minute.'

Alex put the guitar down and frowned. 'Where are you going?'

'Back to the dessert trolley probably,' sniggered Freya under her breath.

He watched Grace disappear through the gate, and by the time he had turned round, Freya had lain down along the side of the pool, her top riding so high up her torso he could see the curve of her tanned breasts. Unable to help himself, he pictured her naked and wondered, not for the first time that holiday, what sex would be like with her. Part of him definitely wouldn't mind finding out.

'Where's home again when we leave Angel?' she asked languidly.

'Cheshire,' said Alex, hoping it sounded posher than Macclesfield.

'Are you ever in London?'

'I will be in September. My college is in Marylebone.'

'My boyfriend has a flat not too far from there.'

'I might bump into you then,' said Alex, wishing he could think of something more funny or interesting to say.

She leant up on one elbow, looking at Alex searchingly. 'He wants me to move in with him.'

'And you don't?' he replied, wondering if they were about to have a deep and meaningful conversation.

Freya sighed. 'I should, he's every girl's dream really. A banker, got a Ferrari and a huge penis,' she whispered conspiratorially. 'But I think I'm too young to be tied down, don't you?'

She sat up, swept her hair off the back of her neck and tied it on top of her head. The long, tanned nape of her neck was beautiful, just like the skin of an apricot.

'I'm going inside,' she said. 'Are you coming?'

Something in the way she was looking at him suggested she wanted to have sex with him, which prompted a sudden, inexplicable flurry of nerves. She looked experienced in bed. Too experienced.

'Shouldn't we go back to the beach? Bit rude to leave everyone for too long.'

Freya touched the top of his thigh. 'I wouldn't bother,' she said. 'Sarah's had a skinful and Grace, I love her, but she's such a bloody bore.'

'I think Grace is a laugh.'

'Are we talking about the same person?'

Her disloyalty surprised him. 'I thought you two had been friends for a million years?'

'Well, yes,' giggled Freya, 'because her daddy's got the best private island in the Caribbean.' She moved towards him and ran her finger down his arm. 'Look, I've got some Es in my room.'

Alex almost laughed. Here he was, on a tropical island with a gorgeous twenty-something girl offering herself – and some expensive drugs – to him, so why was he hesitating? He looked at her. *Yes, she's fit,* he thought. *But she's a bitch.*

'I don't think this is a good idea,' he said.

'Why not?'

'Well, for one thing, you've got a boyfriend back home.'

'A proper rock star wouldn't bother about things like that.'

There was a cough behind them and they both turned.

'Not disturbing anything here, am I?'

Miles' voice was barely audible thanks to the French cigarette that was dangling out of his mouth. He was carrying a slim green bottle and a pitcher of water, which he put on the table by the pool.

'No, no. I was just coming,' said Alex, picking up his guitar.

'Is that so?' Miles smiled, glancing at Freya then back to Alex.

'What's that?' asked Freya, nodding at the bottle.

'Nothing for young ladies,' he said, stubbing his cigarette out on the table.

Freya fixed her mouth into a thin, pinched line and tossed her hair over her shoulder. 'Have it your way, then,' she said, glaring at Alex, then turned and walked into the house.

'So, are you going to fuck her?' asked Miles as she disappeared.

'No,' said Alex quickly.

'Never say never, old boy.' Miles smiled. 'The night's still young, and from what friends in Bristol tell me, she spreads her legs more often than a Russian gymnast.' He looked at Alex with an amused arch to his eyebrow. 'Want a drink then?'

Alex picked up the bottle and looked at it. 'What is it?'

'Absinthe.'

'Really? Isn't this stuff banned?' asked Alex, looking at the label. He'd heard of absinthe – it was supposed to be the drug of choice for artists and poets. He liked the sound of it.

'It's not technically illegal,' said Miles. 'You can get it if you know where to look. This is from Czechoslovakia. I got it back in February when I stayed in Prague.'

Miles produced two small glasses, a spoon and what looked like sugar cubes from his shorts pockets.

'It's eighty per cent proof. Excellent quality,' he said distractedly as he poured a measure of the green liquid into each glass. Placing a sugar cube on the spoon, he dipped it into one of the glasses then balanced the spoon on the rim. Glancing at Alex, he flicked his gold Dunhill lighter and with a 'pop!' the sugar cube lit up.

'Wow,' said Alex, genuinely enthralled by the ritual. It was one thing he had noticed about the rich: they liked their rituals.

Miles tipped the sugar cube into the glass and poured water on top, dousing the flames. He passed the warm glass to Alex, who gingerly lifted it to his lips and took a sip. It didn't taste all that great but he was determined not to show it.

'Baudelaire, Rimbaud, even Aleister Crowley, the wickedest man in the world, loved this stuff,' said Miles as he set his own drink on fire.

'Aren't we supposed to see a green fairy or something?' said Alex, feeling his lips burn.

'Fuck knows,' said Miles, knocking his back. 'Just drink it and see.'

They each had another, then Miles gestured towards the beach.

'Let's walk,' he said. 'And leave the bloody guitar here. I've had enough of Angus' singing tonight.'

'But I've had absinthe,' said Alex with a smile. 'I'm supposed to be at my creative peak. Maybe the world's greatest pop song will come to me as I stare out to sea.'

'I'm prepared to take that risk,' said Miles.

They walked down a path along the side of the house which sloped gently downwards towards the beach at the east of the island. The vegetation thickened and for a few minutes they were walking through dark forest, the only light coming from the moon shining through the trees.

Alex was grateful when they emerged on a small crescent of sand known as Paradise Cove. The moon sent a cone of shimmering silver across the black sea and they walked out to the water's edge.

'Can I ask you a question?'

'Course.'

It was something he had been desperate to ask Miles for a long time. 'Why are we friends?'

It had taken Alex a long time to fit into Danehurst. For

45

the first three years he had taken refuge with the two other music scholarship boys, Kim Yip, a violin prodigy, and Ivan Blade, whose parents had defected from the Soviet Union. They stuck together like glue, bonded by their furious work ethic. Not that Alex needed endless practice because to him, playing music was as natural as breathing. But by the time he joined the sixth form, he considered himself quite cool. He loved bands like the Jesus and Mary Chain and The Fall, read magazines like *The Face* and *ID* and kitted himself out in army surplus clothes. Cool. But not cool enough to be friends with Miles Ashford.

'You've been quite a project in social engineering, son,' said Miles with a slow grin. 'I think I've proved how anyone, even a horrible northerner like you, can acquire social polish just by hanging around with me.'

'Right,' said Alex, fearing all along that that might have been the answer.

'I'm joking,' he said flatly.

Alex felt relief, and then a strong pang of affection for his friend. 'Well in that case, I'm going to miss you.'

'We've got the grand tour of Europe to come yet.'

'I thought you were just showing off to Oscar and Angus.'

'Me? Show off?' Miles smiled.

'Come on, Miles. You know I can't afford a trip like that.'

'If you can pay for your travel, I'll sort out the rest.'

Alex put a friendly arm around Miles' shoulder and took his cigarette off him for a long drag. 'When do you start at Oxford again?'

'October sometime.'

'That's late, isn't it?'

'Short term-time for the elite, my friend,' said Miles as he lit another cigarette. 'Still, you can come down any time of course, although I expect I'll be very busy. The thing about Oxford is that there are more opportunities than there is time to take them up.'

'What do you have in mind? President of the Union? The student paper?'

'God no! The social life.'

'You can come to London, too.'

'And stay in your fleapit student digs?' Miles said mischievously. 'No thank you.'

'I need to sit down. That absinthe is evil.'

'Over here.'

They walked back up the beach to the gentle slope of still-warm sand that ran up to the virgin forest behind them and flopped down. For a few minutes they lay in silence, looking up at the inky star-sprayed sky. Alex wished he had his Walkman with him. A moment like this deserved a sound-track – something bittersweet and melancholic like The Smiths or REM. He closed his eyes, trying to lock the memory into his brain.

'What are you doing?' asked Miles, laughing gently. He had turned on his side and was propping himself up on his elbow, watching his friend with amusement.

'Trying to remember the moment. You know, for when I'm stuck in my fleapit student garret with a view of nothing but dry rot.'

'Alex?'

Before Alex even realised what was happening, Miles had moved towards him, cupping his hand around Alex's chin to pull him closer, his lips descending on to Alex's in a soft kiss. For a moment Alex relaxed into Miles' embrace; it felt strange, but not unpleasant, like biting into some unknown exotic fruit. Miles' tongue gently pushed into his mouth, his breath shuddering with arousal, and they were caught in a moment of desire. But, in a rush, Alex suddenly felt Miles' erection through his thin linen shorts and he sprang away as if he'd been burnt by fire. He scrambled to his feet then froze, paralysed by embarrassment, looking intently away from his friend, not daring even to breathe.

'I thought that's what you wanted,' said Miles quietly. His voice was low, with a hint of menace.

Alex glanced at his friend, who was now lying back on the sand, and suddenly he felt angry. It was typical of Miles to twist this situation and make him feel as if that sudden, unexpected kiss had been his own fault. Alex certainly had affection for Miles, in fact it may even have bordered on hero-worship at times, but this *wasn't* what he wanted, not at all. He felt his stomach clench: had it been what Miles had wanted all along? Was *that* why they had been such unlikely friends? He searched his mind for memories at Danehurst – an unwanted touch perhaps or a lingering look as they showered together after rugby – but there was nothing. He shook his head. Miles wasn't gay; he'd been going out with Sasha for ever.

'Come on, Miles,' said Alex with a nervous laugh. 'We're both just a bit pissed. No need to get all soppy, eh?'

Miles sat up and fixed Alex with a stare as he lit a cigarette. 'You fucking started it.'

Alex suddenly realised they weren't alone. Both boys looked back towards the path. Standing watching them was a young man in Angel Cay's navy-blue staff shorts and polo shirt.

Miles jumped hastily to his feet and gave the boy a confrontational stare. 'What are you looking at?'

The boy took a few steps back. 'Sorry, nothing.'

He had an American accent. Alex could see he was about their age.

'Who the fuck are you anyway?' snapped Miles, his cheeks colouring in the moonlight.

'I'm Bradley. I arrived this morning. Just working on the boats for a few days.'

'Oh yes?' said Miles. 'And what's that?' He pointed to the bottle in the boy's hand.

'Just a beer,' he said defensively. 'I'm just having a drink. It's Independence Day and all.'

'I don't care what day it is,' replied Miles, his voice hard. 'This isn't a holiday for you. You are an employee of my family and you shouldn't be drinking alcohol.'

'I'm sorry. It's just one beer.'

'Don't insult my intelligence,' snapped Miles. 'You're drunk.'

'No, I'm not,' said the boy nervously, backing away. 'Listen, I'd better go.'

Miles flicked his cigarette across the sand. 'If you're not drunk, then walk in a straight line and pick that up.'

For a few seconds the boat boy stood motionless, not knowing what to do.

'Go on,' said Miles, a nasty edge to his voice. 'Pick it up.'

Shrugging, the boy walked slowly over to the cigarette and bent to pick it up. He was still crouched on the sand when Miles took another cigarette from his packet and threw it six feet behind Bradley.

'Now pick that one up.'

Reluctantly, Bradley turned round and stooped to get the cigarette.

'Now that one,' Miles said, flicking another cigarette, 'and that one.'

Cigarettes rained down on the sand. Miles was laughing now as the disorientated boy crawled around, fumbling to pick them all up.

'Come on, get a move on,' he barked. 'It shouldn't be so difficult if you're sober.'

'Miles, stop it,' said Alex. 'This isn't funny.'

'Of course it's not funny,' snapped Miles, pulling his arm away. 'We have a drunk working for the family. I should fire this lying sack of Yankee shit right here and now.'

Finally Bradley had had enough. He stood up and glared at Miles. 'Just because you own this island doesn't mean you can speak to me like that,' he said, his voice trembling.

Miles' mouth remained in a thin, firm line. He took a step

forward until they were just a couple of feet apart and slowly raised the last cigarette to his mouth, lighting it and blowing the smoke into Bradley's face.

'Don't tell me what I can and cannot do, boat boy,' he said coldly. 'This is, as you correctly say, my island and I make the rules here. So I suggest you do exactly what I say: take your lying face and your stolen beer back to the servants' quarters where you belong.'

The boat boy's lips curled into a sneer. 'Asshole,' he whispered.

The next few seconds seemed to happen in slow motion for Alex. He watched Miles' face twist in fury and contempt, his nostrils flaring, his upper lip curling back. He saw Bradley's look of quiet defiance change to fear and disbelief, his mouth slowly gaping. But most of all, he saw Miles lift his cigarette and jab it into Bradley's face. Then, just as suddenly, everything came back into real time: Bradley's stagger, his scream, his hands covering his face. Alex leapt forward, yanking Miles' arm away, but Miles pushed him so hard, he slipped over in the sand.

'Jesus, Miles,' cried Alex. 'What the hell . . .'

The truth was, Alex was afraid of Miles in this mood. He was vicious, cruel, out of control. Alex had seen him reduce people to tears, seen him slap them, but never anything like this.

Miles was standing over the crouched form of the boat boy. 'Go on, fuck off,' he growled, throwing the cigarette butt at his back in a shower of sparks.

With a hurt glance up at both of them, Bradley jumped to his feet and, still holding his cheek, ran up the path towards the house. For a moment it was silent except for the gentle lapping of the waves on the shore.

'What the hell was all that about?' said Alex, but Miles didn't seem to hear him. The look on his face was distant and detached.

'I'm going for a walk,' he said quietly and strode off.

Alex watched his friend disappear away from the house towards the furthest part of the island and felt himself overwhelmed with anger, disgust and confusion. But above all, he felt regret and, to his surprise, loneliness. Because in the space of a few short minutes, he knew that his relationship with his closest friend in the world had changed for ever.

6

Sasha was livid. The dinner on the beach had been her idea. She had arranged it with the staff, decorated the table and spent hours poring over the seating plan – and then what happens? That pompous prat McKay spoils everything by falling out of a coconut tree.

Too busy voicing their phoney concerns for Oscar, not one person had commented on the ambience of the evening or her cleverness for thinking of moving their 'last supper' to the water's edge. To add insult to injury, Miles had practically ignored her for the entire meal and that slut Freya had spent an hour doing some sort of ham-fisted seduction on Robert Ashford. The whole thing had been a disaster from start to finish.

She sat down on the stone wall behind the beach and took a swig from the bottle she was carrying. At least it was Krug; the one positive of Miles' father arriving was that he had brought decent bubbly with him.

Where is Miles? she thought angrily. *What does he think he's playing at?*

Sasha certainly had better things to do than spend the whole night wandering around the island looking for her so-called boyfriend. After dinner, he'd practically sprinted to the beach then spent half an hour goading Angus to drink a bottle of rum and jump over the bonfire. He'd barely looked in her direction. What *was* his problem? She had a good mind to dump him – then he'd come crawling back. Well, maybe. After this evening's performance Sasha wasn't entirely sure of anything. It certainly wasn't going according to plan; she had to admit that it didn't look like a proposal was on the cards tonight.

'Has he abandoned you for the boys again?'

Robert Ashford strolled up to her, cupping his tumbler of peach juice.

'No, just taking a break,' she said, trying to lift her mood. 'Miles' friends can be a little . . .'

'Immature? Stupid? Irritating?' suggested Robert with a smile.

'Yes, exactly.' She giggled.

He took a seat next to her and suddenly she felt very grown-up. Robert Ashford was one of Britain's most successful entrepreneurs. Under the umbrella of Ash Corp., he had a commercial property portfolio that spanned the globe, with interests in everything from hotels to casinos, car parks to out-of-town shopping malls. The smart parts of London that weren't owned by the older, moneyed families like the Grosvenors, Cadogans and Portmans were, by and large, part of the Ashford group. But Robert Ashford was a self-made man and believed in the famous Tory slogan of getting 'on your bike'. He'd started his empire from a run-down guest house in Notting Hill in the 1960s and worked his way up to a billion.

She was glad she had prepared for moments like this. Although her usual reading material consisted of *Tatler* and *Vogue*, in the days before the Bahamas trip she had swotted up on the *Financial Times* to deep-freeze some conversational nuggets.

'So will we be seeing you at Ashford Park over the summer?'

'Well, I start modelling as soon as I get back,' said Sasha confidently. 'But I'm sure I'll be seeing you at some stage.'

He eyed her closely. 'Miles said you had no plans for college.'

'No, but I've been taken on by one of the best agencies in London. It's too good an opportunity to pass up. I'm not convinced about the merits of university to be honest. I sometimes wonder why Miles is bothering with Oxford. Not having a degree didn't stop you from becoming one of the country's most successful businessmen.'

She silently congratulated herself on making this point. She didn't want Miles at Oxford next term, she wanted him in London. And the only thing that could stop it was intervention from his parents. If only Robert could see the good sense in her suggestion.

'I don't know, Sasha. I think college will give Miles the time to mature. Make contacts. You should think about it yourself once you get your A level results. See what you can get through the UCAS clearing system. Modelling isn't easy, you know. Have you thought about how the recession is going to affect the fashion industry?'

She visibly smarted. Was he implying she wasn't beautiful enough to model?

'Well, Linda Evangelista says she doesn't get out of bed for less than ten thousand dollars a day, so I'd say the modelling world is having a boom at the moment.'

'So you're going to be a top model?' he chuckled.

'Of course,' she said matter-of-factly. 'Why wouldn't I be?'

Robert nodded as he smiled. 'I've always liked that about you, Sasha. You're ambitious and you're not afraid to admit it. We're alike, you and I.'

He took a drink and smiled at her. 'Just do me a favour, huh?'

Sasha felt a flutter of anticipation. 'What's that?'

'Never sit around waiting for Miles.'

Her face betrayed her surprise. What was he suggesting?

'I don't intend to, Mr Ashford,' she replied coolly.

'Good,' he said, holding her gaze. 'Because I think you could do better. Much better.'

He looked at his watch and put his empty tumbler on the wall. 'I'm just going to talk to Nelson. A few things to sort out for tomorrow.'

'Of course,' said Sasha. 'And thanks for being an incredible host. I speak for us all when I say we've had an amazing time.'

'You're very welcome, Sasha.'

Sasha watched him go, perplexed and anxious at the same time. Had he just been pointing out the obvious, that his son was a heartless deadbeat? Or had he been coming on to her? If he thought Miles was a deadbeat, at least he had a point. Her boyfriend had certainly been distant and vague all holiday, preferring to spend time with Alex bloody Doyle and ducking the question whenever she wanted to discuss plans for next year. Sasha didn't like to admit to weakness even to herself, but the truth of it was that she had felt lonely, even used.

She shook her head. Maybe she'd just had too many cocktails. She was tired too; last night she and Miles had been up till 5 a.m. screwing. Sasha had used every trick in the book – literally. Unbeknownst to Miles, she had been using a sex manual she'd bought in Soho during the Easter holidays and she was determined to try out every position before the summer was over. She already considered herself sexually experienced, having lost her virginity at fifteen to a thirty-six-year-old Iranian businessman she'd met at the L'Equipe Anglaise nightclub behind Selfridges. She'd told him she was twenty, he'd given her a Rolex. Between him and Miles there had been four others and she had swiftly learnt that there was only one word which would keep a rich man happy and that was S-E-X. It had worked with Miles, after all. Just two months after the start of term in the lower sixth, she had seduced him at the school bonfire party simply by ignoring him. Well, that and not wearing a bra. She had dragged him behind the science block and, their breath puffing in the cold air, panted in his ear that she would do anything he wanted her to. *Anything*. It was a policy she had stuck to ever since to keep their love life on track.

God, this is making me depressed, she thought. *I need a pick-me-up*.

She walked through the house and up to the room she and Miles had been sharing before she had moved into a single room when Robert arrived; Miles had claimed his dad would 'shit a brick' if he suspected they were sleeping together. Sasha rummaged through his leather suitcase. She knew he had some coke in the room somewhere. She walked through to the en suite and checked his wash-bag. 'Ah-ha!' she whispered to herself, finding a little ziplock bag hidden in the side pocket. She fished out the wrap and dug a long fingernail into the white powder, taking a quick hit and slipping the rest into her bra for later.

On her way out, she snatched the cigarette packet sitting on the dressing table and lit one, waving her hand to clear the tarry smell from the air. She knew that Robert Ashford didn't approve of smoking: he was a health nut. Miles had told her – to his great amusement – that his father had recently taken up yoga with 'some fit French bird' and had been on a health kick ever since, as Miles said, so he could keep up with her in bed.

Her jewelled sandals click-clacked down the stairs and out past the pool. In the distance she could make out laughter coming from the bonfire, but she didn't feel like going back there just yet. She turned the other way, taking a path that wound down to a quiet cove. There was a store house for kayaks and a short jetty, and she kicked off her shoes and sat on the edge as she finished her cigarette. There had to be a way of manipulating Miles into a commitment. She just didn't know what it was right now.

A noise behind her made her turn.

'Hey there.'

A boy her age was standing on the path next to the kayak

store. Light from the single bulb over the door shone on his face. He was quite sexy.

'I don't suppose you have a spare one of those on you?' he asked, pointing to the cigarette.

'Sorry, no,' she said, standing up and throwing the stub into the black water. As cute as the boy was, she felt a little vulnerable out here in the dark with a complete stranger.

'Sorry,' said the boy, as if he felt her discomfort. 'I'm Bradley.'

'Ah, you're the new boat boy I heard the girls talking about earlier, aren't you?' said Sasha. 'You were quite a hit.'

The boy shrugged, a little embarrassed.

'Where are you from?'

'West Virginia.'

'I mean recently. I haven't seen you on the island before.'

'I just got here today to work at Robert Ashford's party.'

Sasha began to walk back the way she had come and Bradley fell in step.

'Long way to come, from West Virginia for four days.'

'Ah no, I've been bumming around the islands since I left high school last year, picking up work at the resorts. I heard Mr Ashford wanted some extra crew for some corporate thing he's having this weekend. Money's good and I go to Harvard in the fall, which isn't cheap.'

Sasha looked at him again, her head feeling fuzzy. 'Harvard, eh?' she said. 'Clever boy.'

'We'll see,' said Bradley. 'Anyway, shame it's just until next week. I'd love to work here all summer. Nelson and his family have a real cushy number. I hear the Ashfords are only here a few weeks of the year.'

'Most of the time I come with them actually,' said Sasha with a hint of superiority. 'Miles Ashford is my boyfriend.'

Bradley smiled. 'I know.'

She glanced at him again, smirking. She was flattered despite herself. He obviously had noticed her.

57

'I'm Sasha, anyway. Sasha Sinclair,' she said. 'Although I guess you know that already.'

He shook her hand with a firm grip. 'Bradley Hartford.' He smiled. 'Real pleased to meet you, Sasha.'

A string of hurricane lights hanging from the trees warmed his face. She could see that he was even more good-looking than she had first thought. Nothing striking about his face, but clean-cut all-American good looks that worked well with his plain navy polo shirt and shorts.

'Shouldn't you be down on the beach with the others?' he asked, pointing down the track which led to the beach.

She pulled a face. 'Not much of a party. They're all a bit drunk and acting stupid.'

Bradley nodded back towards the house. 'I've got beers in my room just up there in the staff quarters if you're interested.'

She looked him up and down.

He is cute, she thought, emboldened by most of a bottle of champagne and a snort of coke. *Sod Miles if he can't be bothered to wonder where I am. Why the hell not?*

'You're on, cowboy,' she said, boldly looping her arm through his and walking up the path.

The staff accommodation was all behind the main house. Nelson had an attractive Creole house of his own close to Richmond Cove while Puerto, the head chef, whose job it was to keep Angel stocked with the best food and wine, was in a small annexe. The rest of the cooks, cleaners and groundsmen were housed in a long row of one-storey wooden cabins hidden behind a line of banana trees. Sasha was glad that Bradley's cabin was at the end of the row. For all her rebellion, she didn't really want anyone to see her slumming it, but there were no lights on in the neighbouring cabins.

'I've got my own room. Some of these cabins have got three sous chefs in them at the moment.'

'So how come you got your own space, new boy?' she whispered.

'Charm.' He grinned.

The cabin was basic. Just a narrow single bed and side table, wardrobe and chest of drawers. They both sat on the bed and Bradley twisted the top off a beer and handed it to her.

'So tell me, Sasha Sinclair,' he said with a smile. 'What are you doing all alone by the boathouse when everyone else is having a great time on the beach?'

She shrugged and looked away. She knew it was wrong to be here, but this boy was looking at her as if he desired her.

'Where's your glamorous boyfriend?' he persisted.

'You tell me,' she huffed.

'Uh-oh,' he said. 'Lovers' tiff?'

'More like my boyfriend just doesn't appreciate me.'

'How does that happen with someone as beautiful as you?'

It was cheesy and transparent, but Sasha liked hearing the flattery nonetheless. She could see pure sexual attraction in his eyes, whereas Miles looked at her like she was an embarrassment. A wave of defiance surged up in her. Miles had behaved disgracefully this evening; all holiday in fact. How dare he? Sasha Sinclair was the most popular girl at Danehurst, she had an Elan Models contract, and one day the whole world would know her name. Fuck Miles, fuck them all.

'Hey, what have you done to your cheek?' she asked, lifting a finger to touch the red mark.

'Just a burn. Don't touch it.' He caught hold of her finger, then held it, looking at her for a long exquisite second. Up close, he was even better-looking, with thick lashes, and lips the colour of Scottish raspberries. Looking back later at what little she could remember of the evening, she could never pinpoint why suddenly, as if someone had flicked a switch, she was kissing him; softly at first, getting deeper and harder, so their teeth clinked, tongues tasting lipstick and beer.

Bradley drew away, looking stunned, anxious, elated, then taking her face in his hands he kissed her more softly, as if every taste was like nectar. Sasha felt a shiver of anticipation as a sense of danger rippled through her. Miles had never taken his time in their lovemaking; he always seemed keen to get it over with. Gently, Bradley lowered her down on to the narrow bed. He was firm but unhurried, discovering her kiss by kiss, his urgent breath in her ear, his warm lips on her cheek, her throat. Without thinking, fuelled by anger and desire, she pulled her dress over her head and unclasped her bra. He paused for a moment to take in her naked breasts, ripe and full, cupping them in his hands, then lowered his lips to taste each beige nipple in turn, sucking, savouring them as they grew hard and swollen in his mouth. His need was turning her on and she tugged off his T-shirt, grazing his chest with her long nails. Unlike Miles' slim, effete limbs, Bradley's arms were thick and strong from lugging boats and pulling ropes, his hands rough on her tanned skin. Unbuttoning his shorts, she pulled them off over his thighs. He had a tattoo of the sun on his hip-bone which she stroked with her fingertip.

She reclined on her back. His tongue connected with her belly, heading down towards her navel as her spine rose in an arc. She moaned as his thumbs peeled down her thong, spreading her legs as he pushed two fingers inside her, in, out, in sweet rhythm.

She groaned as his mouth swept down over her damp pubic hair and as his tongue connected with her clitoris, pleasure pulsed around her body with an intensity she had never before experienced.

Miles never did this. Never.

His cock was inside her now, pushing into her with hard strokes, his eyes shut tight, his hands clenching and rucking the sheets. He was fit, keen, hungry. Her arms flung behind her head, she spread her legs wider and felt him slide so far into her, so deep, she felt as if she might tear in two.

As the tense block of pressure in her belly slowly released, she grabbed his hair and screamed out, 'Yes, yes. Yes!' *Oh God, this is what great sex feels like*. And then it was over, his spent body buckling and then collapsing on to hers. Her tawny flesh glistening with sweat, she lay back on the mattress trying to catch her breath, and as the passion subsided, reality rushed back in.

Underneath her thighs a damp patch on the sheet felt ice-cold against her skin. What had she just done?

Miles Ashford was her boyfriend. He was one of the world's most eligible bachelors; had she thrown away a life of luxury for a quick fuck with a boat boy? A quick fuck without a condom. Where the hell was she supposed to get the morning-after pill on a private island?

'I'd better get back,' she said.

'So soon?' His fingers touched her bare back and she flinched. Naked, she felt more than just exposed, she felt vulnerable.

'I'll be missed,' she said, picking up her Dior bra, part of a set that Miles had bought her for Christmas.

Sasha's back was towards Bradley as she hurriedly dressed, but she could feel his eyes on her. Finally she smoothed down her dress and glanced at him. Her head was spinning. 'You're not going to say anything about this, are you?'

He paused for a moment. 'Who to?'

'To Miles, to anyone,' she said, her heart pounding in panic.

Bradley just stared at her.

'Well?' Her tone was brusque and irritable and she immediately regretted it. She was usually so expert at manipulating men, but right now she was spooked, nervous. She knew she had made a mistake that could cost her dear. She wasn't used to being on the back foot.

'What's the matter?' she said, turning towards him. 'Why aren't you saying anything?'

He shrugged. 'Disappointment,' he said, eyes challenging hers. 'What happened just now . . . I thought we had a connection.'

She scoffed inwardly. *A connection.* 'What do you expect happens now, Bradley?' she asked pointedly. 'I'll go out with you? We'll have a nice little holiday romance?'

'Maybe not, but I don't expect you to get up and walk away the second I've come inside you.'

'We're drunk.' She flinched. 'I have a boyfriend. And that's where I am going right now. To find him.'

He paused, then gave a low, shallow laugh. 'I know where your boyfriend is.'

She looked at him sharply. There was an edge to his laugh she didn't like.

'Where?' she asked quietly.

'Making out by Paradise Cove with his boyfriend. You know, the tall good-looking one.'

Her heart was beating hard now. 'What? What the hell are you talking about?'

'I caught them together and that's how I got this,' said Bradley, pointing to the burn on his cheek. 'Your boyfriend stubbed his cigarette out on my face because he didn't like what I had seen.'

Sasha felt cold all over. It was unthinkable, but there was a distant, unpalatable ring of truth in Bradley's words that chilled her to the core.

'You're lying.'

Bradley shook his head slowly. 'Your boyfriend's queer, Sasha.'

'You're lying!' she yelled.

She closed her eyes tight. It couldn't be true.

But it is, isn't it? said a calm, insistent voice in her head.

No, it was just a poisonous lie dreamt up by some low-rent gigolo who wanted to strike back when he found out there would be no repeat performance. It was!

The inner voice mocked her. *You know it's true.*

'My boyfriend is not gay,' she said, fighting to control her voice. 'It's a ridiculous idea.'

'Whatever,' said Bradley sourly, not even looking at her.

She moved towards the door, then turned back. 'You never answered my question.'

'Which one?' he said with a note of insolence.

Right then, she hated him. Her body boiled with fury at this jumped-up nobody who had tricked her into bed. She clenched her hands into fists, using every ounce of willpower to control herself.

'You're not going to say anything to anyone about this.'

He looked up at her with contempt. 'You're all the same, your type,' he spat. 'You use people and then get rid of them at your convenience.'

'I mean it, Bradley,' said Sasha, her voice quivering with anger and frustration. 'Don't even think of breathing a word about what just happened . . .'

'Or what?' asked Bradley.

'Or you'll regret it,' she said, staring at him with cold fury. Then she opened the door and slammed it behind her with such force, the entire cabin shook.

7

Grace wasn't enjoying the party. It was almost 2.30 and she knew she should have gone to bed hours ago. There were over a dozen people on the beach, but the guests were outnumbered by the steel band, chefs and waiters keeping the unending supply of drink and food coming. Only Angus, Sarah, Gabby and herself were sitting by the bonfire and the previous high spirits had long since disappeared. Grace popped a final toasted marshmallow into her mouth – brought to her on a silver tray, naturally – and stood up unsteadily.

'Where are you going?' asked Sarah. 'I thought we were trying to stay up for one last sunrise.'

'I'm just going for a walk. I want to try and sober up a bit or I'll feel terrible for the flight back tomorrow.'

Sarah ran after her as she walked up the sand.

'Are you really feeling ill or are you just trying to torture yourself?'

'What do you mean?'

'Well, you might find Alex and Freya in flagrante behind the sand dunes.'

Grace felt unusually irritable. 'Why are you talking in Latin? You're not a lawyer yet, you know.'

Sarah raised her brows. 'Touchy,' she said and Grace tried to smile.

'I'm not torturing myself,' she replied quickly. 'Freya will want the luxury of soft cotton sheets, not some gritty sand dune. Anyway, I'm not bothered. I'm really not.'

'He's only eighteen, after all,' said Sarah more kindly. 'Probably a bit immature. There're many more fish in the sea.'

Grace nodded as convincingly as she could. 'I just need to walk off the drink. It's a long flight back home.'

Sarah eyed her sceptically. 'You sure?'

Grace nodded. 'I'll be fine.'

Catseye Beach was the longest on the island, a half-mile stretch of sand that shone like a silver ribbon in front of her. It got quieter and darker as she left the bonfire behind and Grace welcomed the isolation. Sarah had been right: the last thing she wanted was to catch Freya and Alex at it in the sand dunes, and she didn't want to go back to the house because Freya's room was next to hers.

What a cow, she thought angrily. Freya was supposed to be her friend! It was bad enough that she had been flirting with Grace's father at dinner but what she had done with Alex was nothing short of a betrayal. *She knew I was interested, we talked about it earlier on,* she thought. Freya had never shown an interest in Alex before. Maybe that was it, maybe Freya just wanted to prove she could pull Alex. For some people friendship didn't matter; everything was just a game. It was all about power, survival of the fittest.

And that was the real reason Grace was angry; she was angry at herself. She'd tried her best by the pool, inviting him on to the tiki swing, letting her kaftan slip off one shoulder ... She cringed. But she was an amateur. Freya was obvious. Subtlety never won prizes – not when it came to sex and eighteen-year-old boys ...

She had reached the end of the beach now and climbed inland through a thicket of red and black mangrove. The dark didn't frighten her; she felt completely at home on the island and loved its remoteness from the world. As a child, she would pretend she was some character in *Lord of the Flies* and spend whole days exploring on her own, looking for sea turtles or exotic flowers.

She was walking up a steep path back towards the headland when she heard a rustle in the long grass next to her. Someone was sitting there, a familiar shape.

'Alex?' she hissed, squinting in the dark. 'Is that you?'

He sat up holding a cigarette and notebook in the strong moonlight.

'Writing some lyrics,' he said, a little embarrassed.

Noting he was alone, Grace laughed, mainly from relief. 'How can you see what you're writing?'

'Can't really,' he said, flicking his lighter so she could see the blank page in his book.

'I see you've found your muse, then,' she said, sitting down beside him.

'Cheeky. These things take time,' he replied defensively. 'Keith Richards used to spend days writing songs without going to bed.'

'Ah, but didn't he have Mick Jagger to help him?' she said, all the time her mind repeating, *Where's Freya? Where's Freya?*

She took a deep breath. *Just bloody ask him.*

'Well, I didn't think I'd see you for the rest of the night, lover boy,' she said as casually as she could. Even in the moonlight, she caught the look of surprise on his face.

'What do you mean?'

'You and Freya.'

He gave a small laugh. 'No, no, nooo . . .' he said. 'Much too scary.'

Grace raised a sceptical eyebrow, but Alex shook his head.

'I mean it. At one point she was going on about some banker boyfriend with a massive cock and a Ferrari. I don't want her talking about *me* like that.'

'Which bit? Your cock or your Ferrari?'

She felt her cheeks flush and was glad of the dark.

Think *obvious*, she chided herself. 'Want to go back to the beach?' she asked and he helped her up, then followed her, stumbling and cursing at hidden tree roots and branches.

'Anyone would think you'd never been to paradise island before,' teased Grace when they were safely back on the sand. They walked along the beach in silence, occasionally looking up at the vast starry sky, the only sound their footsteps and the gentle lap of the waves.

'You glad you came?' she asked softly.

'Obviously I'd rather be in Macclesfield right now.'

She giggled. 'What are you going to do when you get back?' she asked. 'I mean, you don't start music college until September, right?'

'Miles is talking about a trip around Europe but I'd need to get a job first. My mate says there's something going at Piccadilly Records, this really cool record shop in Manchester, but it's a long shot. Anyway, anything's going to be a bit of a comedown after this.'

'Maybe you could have a working holiday.'

He pursed his lips thoughtfully.

'You could go to the Côte d'Azur and be gigolos. Like Richard Gere in that film.'

'Except he got framed for murder, didn't he?' Alex smiled.

'Without the murder.'

'Anyway, I'd be with Miles. Can you see him waiting tables in some Greek taverna?'

'No, I can't.'

'Can I tell you something?' he asked.

'Of course, what is it?'

Alex shrugged. 'I don't want to go to the Royal Academy.'

It was Grace's turn to gape. 'But didn't you get a full scholarship? I thought you were like the most promising musician in the country or something?'

He looked away, embarrassed. 'Yeah, but it's not what I want. I want to get on with playing music, get into a band, start gigging, all that. Studying Gregorian chants or Schubert's Unfinished Symphony just doesn't seem like as much fun. I'd actually rather be going to art school – all the best bands formed at art school: Roxy Music, Talking Heads, Devo . . .'

'I can see you now. Long hair, spray-on leather pants, an electric-blue guitar . . .'

'I'm never going to wear spray-on leather kecks,' said Alex with feeling.

'Oh you say that now, but wait until you start as a gigolo.' She paused and observed his bleak face. 'So why are you going there then?'

'Because it's the Royal Academy of Music,' he said expansively. 'Because it's my mum's dream that I go there.'

Grace laughed. 'Ah, now that sounds familiar.'

'Because it will break her heart if I don't. She's made so many sacrifices for me over the years.'

'She's your mum. She wants the best for you. She wants you to be happy.'

Alex met her gaze. 'So why haven't you told your dad you want to go to Oxford?'

She felt a prickle of shame. 'How do you know about that?'

'You told me in Bristol. Then I heard your dad talking at dinner about you joining the company in August. I asked him about your MA course at Oxford and he looked at me as if he had no idea what I was talking about.'

She felt startled, panicked. 'Oh, no. You didn't mention that, did you? I've not told him. Not yet anyway.'

'Bigmouth strikes again.'

'No, I'm glad,' she said, not entirely convincingly. 'It needs to be said. At least now it might not come as such a big surprise.'

Alex nudged gently into her. 'Wherever we end up, we will stay in touch, won't we?' he said finally.

A beam of excitement pierced through her worry. 'Sure. We could go to, er, a gig or something.'

'You should come up to Manchester,' said Alex. 'We could go to the Haç.'

'The Haç?'

'The Haçienda,' he said, as if it was blindingly obvious. 'You know, the club? One night a week, they even have a swimming pool.'

'Ah, yes,' said Grace, keen not to look completely square. 'Loads of girls on E stripping down to their G-strings lost in love and a wall of sound? I guessed you'd like that.'

'Of course,' he said matter-of-factly. 'Or we could go out in London. I've never been to the Mud Club. Or the Wag.'

'But I might be in Oxford.'

'Then we can go punting.' He laughed.

They kept on walking around the sandy headland. This far away from the house, it was almost pitch black, with just watery moonlight to light their way. Scrambling over a patch of rocks, Alex reached back to take Grace's hand, and even when they reached the flat sand again, he kept hold of it. Grace's heart was pounding, her mouth dry and she didn't dare talk, frightened of breaking the magic.

Just kiss him, you bloody idiot, she willed herself. It's now or never.

'Alex,' she whispered, turning towards him.

'Hey, is that Sasha?' he said suddenly, looking up the path.

Grace felt her heart sink. 'Think so.'

'Should we hide?' He gave her a small embarrassed grin and then dropped her hand. Grace knew the moment was over. She walked on towards the dark figure, feeling as if her heart might break.

8

At the top of Catseye Cove Sasha was feeling sick. Alcohol and a few more hits of cocaine were swirling around in her bloodstream, but the main reason for her nausea was an unfamiliar sense of guilt and – most of all – the horror that she had done something which could not only rock the boat, but could completely capsize it altogether.

What the hell was I thinking? she thought, kicking her toes against the sand. *Why work so hard to hook Miles only to throw it all away on some nobody?*

She breathed deeply, as she had been taught in yoga, and was just beginning to contain her emotions when she saw Miles emerge out of the undergrowth. His shirt was untucked and he looked unsteady on his feet.

'Where the fuck have you been?' she demanded irritably.

Miles shot her a look of disdain. 'Just walking,' he said.

'For the past two hours? I've been everywhere looking for you, worried out of my mind.'

'I've been with Alex if you must know. What are you doing keeping tabs on my every movement anyway?'

Over his shoulder, Sasha saw a figure appear out of the darkness. She recognised the tall, slim silhouette instantly and her eyes narrowed.

'Well there's Alex now with your sister. I thought you said you were with him? Well?'

Miles just waved a weary hand at her, like he was swatting a fly.

'You're such a fucking nag,' he said, looking as if he wanted to strangle her.

Sasha felt her stomach lurch again. Winding Miles up really wasn't helping matters. She had allowed her feelings to run away with her in that tiny cabin; she mustn't do it again – not ever. No, now she needed to get back to what she was good at: twisting men around her little finger. She hung her head and nodded.

'You're right, I'm sorry,' she said. It pained her to say it, but needs must. 'I'm just a bit pissed, you know? And I was worried sick, I thought you'd been bitten by one of those horrid spiders or something.'

She stepped in closer and put her arms around his neck but he just pushed her away.

'Not right now, OK?' he whispered, looking towards the approaching Alex.

Sasha had to struggle to keep her face impassive. What was his problem? Then she had a sudden horrible thought. Surely he didn't know? *It would be just like the Ashfords to have hidden CCTV cameras around the island,* she thought, suddenly resentful of their wealth. *Or do I smell of sex?*

She watched with annoyance as Grace and Alex walked towards them. God, their timing was terrible. Or was it . . . ?

'All right?' asked Alex. He looked subdued and slightly embarrassed. Sensing a scandal, Sasha looked at Grace's face. Yes, she looked a bit upset too. *Hmm, I wonder what those two have been up to,* she thought, making a mental note to do some more digging. You never knew when a little detail like that could come in handy.

'Well, we're glad you're here, aren't we, Miles?' said Sasha with a flash of inspiration. 'It's much more fun with four.'

'What is?' asked Alex.

She crossed her arms and pulled off her dress in one movement. 'Skinny-dipping.'

She was glad to see that Alex's eyes practically popped out on stalks.

Grace laughed nervously. 'I don't think so. It will be freezing.'

'Come on, the sea's lovely,' said Sasha, feeling Alex's eyes on her.

'I'm game,' he said, looking at Grace hopefully.

'Has nobody ever seen *Jaws*?' asked Grace. 'That bit at the beginning where that blonde girl goes running off into the water and the next thing you know she's in pieces on the seashore.'

'Come on, it's our last night,' said Sasha persuasively. 'Let's have some fun!'

She ran off towards the sea. After a moment's hesitation, Alex pulled off his top and followed, turning back to look for Grace.

'Come on!' he shouted.

'There's no way I'm taking all my clothes off in front of my little brother,' she said.

'You don't have to take everything off,' said Alex playfully. 'Not all at once, anyway.'

'Oh ... all right.' She grinned, kicking off her flip-flops and running after the others.

Sasha threw her bra and knickers on to the beach and splashed into the cold salty water. That would get rid of the smell of sex for certain. Turning back to the shore, she smiled to herself as Grace coyly stripped to her bra and black cotton knickers cut low across her pale thighs like PE shorts. No wonder she was pale, thought Sasha. She'd been hiding under a sarong for most of the week.

Alex kept his boxers on as he ran into the water, but Miles stayed on the shore, watching. Sasha turned back towards him, standing waist-deep in the water. She knew she looked good, like some exotic mermaid or Ursula Andress in that Bond film.

'Come on in, the water's lovely,' she said, as he waded reluctantly towards her.

As soon as he was close enough, she pulled him towards her and pressed her naked breasts against his chest, then whispered in his ear, 'We've never had sex in the sea.'

Miles glanced at her, a twisted smirk on his mouth. 'Maybe it's not in your manual.'

'What manual?' She flinched.

Miles laughed. '*The Complete Guide to Sexual Ecstasy*, I believe it's called,' he said, enjoying her discomfort. 'I found it in your case.'

Despite the cool water Sasha felt her cheeks flush. 'What have you been doing rooting around in my case?'

'I could say the same about you,' he said with a flash of anger. 'I came back to the room and all my coke had gone.'

Sasha searched for something to say, but found herself at a loss. She took a deep breath, reminding herself that getting angry would get her nowhere. It wasn't too late to rescue the situation, especially as she was naked.

She pushed her erect nipples against her boyfriend and stroked his chest. 'What's wrong with you tonight?' she asked softly.

'Nothing,' he said flatly.

'There is. I only want to help.'

He turned away from her. 'Don't get all needy on me, Sasha.'

'I'm not needy,' she said petulantly.

'Yes you are, you've been pawing at me all night. All holiday in fact. You're suffocating me.'

Sasha just blinked at him. Her mouth opened, but no words came out.

Miles glanced up at her, then looked away again. 'Look, I think when we get back to England it's best if we spend a bit of time apart,' he said quietly.

What? No! Her mind cried. *This isn't what's supposed to happen.* He couldn't do this to her! She was naked, in the Caribbean Sea, for God's sake! How could he resist her?

'Are you finishing with me?' she said, fighting to keep her voice even.

Miles didn't look at her.

'You shit,' she hissed. 'You *are* finishing with me.'

She felt a tear tremble on her eyelash and blinked it fiercely away.

'Well, fuck you, Miles,' she spat. 'I can do better than you and I will.'

She stormed up the beach, grabbing her underwear, tears running down her cheeks, as she heard Alex and Grace whoop and giggle in the surf.

9

Alex got out of the water shivering. He'd had fun splashing about with Grace, but he wasn't entirely convinced that there were no Great Whites lurking in the water. Just that afternoon in Freetown he'd seen blackboards by the marina advertising 'Shark Dives: Sightings Guaranteed!' More importantly, after what had happened with Miles, it just felt a bit too weird being naked in the water with him and that was why he'd kept his boxer shorts on to go skinny-dipping. Was that also why he had nearly kissed Grace back near the rocks? Certainly, holding hands with her had felt nice, so natural and right. But perhaps it had been more than that, he thought as he dried his damp body with his T-shirt; maybe he had been driven by a desire to get back on the heterosexual straight and narrow after his kiss with Miles.

Did I really kiss my best friend? he thought, unable to grasp it. *What a night.* He watched discreetly as Grace ran out of the sea and disappeared behind a low bush. She returned wearing her dress, her wet underwear rolled up in her hand. Sasha was already out and dressed, sitting hugging her knees up by the path, while Miles stood a little way off smoking a cigarette.

'Do you think anyone will still be down by the bonfire?' asked Grace as she walked over to them.

'Doubt it,' said Sasha gloomily, getting to her feet. Her

earlier buoyant mood seemed to have vanished. She turned and stalked off, her expression stony.

'For fuck's sake,' said Miles under his breath, walking after her. Alex wasn't sure what had been said in the water but it appeared she and Miles were no longer speaking.

They walked for ten minutes in silence, each wrapped up in their own thoughts, an awkward, fractious atmosphere between all of them.

It was almost 5 a.m. Sunrise was not for another hour but thin light was seeping through the blackness, casting the beach in a cool monochrome shadow. The western side of the island was less lush and there were no palm or mango trees along the beach-front, just sand that led up to scrubby dunes. In front of them, about a hundred feet away, Alex could see a long black object on the path at the base of the sandy bank that ran up to the jungle; a piece of driftwood, perhaps? The sea was always coughing up things that littered the beach. Sasha was several paces ahead of him and she stopped suddenly, letting out a little scream.

'Oh my God,' she whispered.

'What is it?' shouted Alex.

The whole world seemed to stand still.

Moving closer, Alex could see it was not driftwood. It was a body, lying completely motionless on the sand. All his nerve endings seemed to vibrate and his skin felt ice cold.

Grace stepped in and raised a hand to her mouth. 'Who is it?' she gasped. 'Are they dead?'

Cautiously, Alex walked right up to the body. It was face down, but it was obviously a man and he was wearing the distinctive polo shirt of the Angel Cay staff.

He looked at Grace, then knelt down slowly and peered at the man's face. All he could see was one closed eye and a gash down the side of his forehead. Blood was congealed around the wound.

'Oh shit . . .' said Alex quietly as he noticed one final terrible detail: there was a small, round burn mark on the man's pale unmoving cheek.

Covering his mouth, Alex turned and fell to his knees, his body ejecting a stomachful of wine and spirits. After retching violently, long strings of spittle hung from his mouth. Wiping them away, he turned back to the body, his hands shaking. He looked around at the faces of his friends.

'It's that boat boy. Bradley.'

Sasha's face was bleached of colour. 'I think he's dead,' she said mournfully.

'Feel his pulse,' said Grace quietly, looking at Alex.

He looked back at her, his face pleading, but someone had to do it. Turning back to the body, he reached out to touch Bradley's wrist.

'Don't be a prick,' hissed Miles suddenly, grabbing his shoulder and pulling him back.

'What's the matter?'

'Don't touch a dead body. You'll leave fingerprints or DNA or something.'

Alex sprang back from the prone figure in alarm. His mum watched police shows all the time and he knew how it worked. The hard-bitten cop would cuff him to the table and say, 'So, Mr Doyle, you were the last one to see the deceased alive. Did you leave him on good terms? Oh, and what can you tell me about these wounds on his face?'

No, Miles was right. Touching a dead body was not a good idea at all.

'We can't just leave him here,' said Grace, taking a small step forward.

'I mean it,' said Miles, blocking her. 'No one should touch it.'

'It?' replied Grace angrily. 'He's one of our staff.'

'He's called Bradley,' said Alex quietly. 'He only got here today.'

'It, he,' said Miles with irritation. 'What does it matter if he's dead?'

Dead. Alex felt glued to the sand. He could feel his heart pumping wildly. *God, how can he be dead?*

How? he asked himself. He looked at Miles and felt a sense of dread well in his stomach, then pushed the dark thought to one side as fiercely as he could.

'We need to go and get help,' he said.

'I think he's past helping,' said Miles in a low, steady voice.

Although he was younger than Alex and Grace, Miles had a natural authority, assisted perhaps by the fact that his father owned the land around them. Sasha seemed happy to toe the line and Alex watched as she slipped her hand into Miles'.

'What should we do, baby?' she asked.

He looked at her, then at Alex and Grace. 'Nothing.'

'Nothing?' asked Grace incredulously.

'Nothing,' repeated Miles. 'We should just stay calm and let someone else find it.'

Alex couldn't believe his ears. 'We have to call a doctor. The police.'

'A doctor?' scoffed Miles. 'He's *dead*. And even if he wasn't, no one will be able to get here for at least half an hour. And the nearest coppers are in George Town.'

Alex pointed to the ground. 'Miles, our footprints are all over this beach. We can't pretend we weren't here.'

'This is our island, Doyle. And let's just say my father has a way of making these things go away.'

'Hang on,' said Sasha quickly, looking up towards the sand-bank above them. 'We're assuming this is some sort of attack or something. Maybe it was an accident. I mean, maybe he fell. It looks like he rolled down this bank.'

Miles shook his head. 'Either way, we should still leave him. Think about it: every one of us is going to look suspicious, running around the island in the dark. None of us can prove where we were every minute of the night, can we? The fact is, he's dead. The police are going to want to point the finger at someone. Who better than the four pissed-up kids who found the body?'

'Come on, Miles. That's a bit paranoid,' said Grace, but her voice lacked confidence.

'Listen, Alex and I had a bit of a pop at him earlier,' said Miles angrily. 'The guy was being a prick, wasn't he, Alex? That's not going to look too good for either of us. I mean, we had nothing to do with this' – he gestured towards the body – 'but who would you believe?'

Alex stared at Miles, his eyes wide. He didn't know when he'd felt more angry and hurt. Was Miles trying to implicate him? He'd always known his friend was arrogant and volatile, but this ... this was *cold*.

'I'm going to get someone,' said Alex, beginning to walk away.

'I'm coming with you,' said Grace.

Miles strode after him and grabbed his arm. 'Stop.'

Alex whirled around, challenging him. 'Why?'

'I can't afford to get mixed up in something I had nothing to do with. Can you?'

'I've got nothing to hide,' said Alex with more bluster than he felt.

'And you want to take a chance on the police believing that?' Miles didn't flinch, holding Alex's gaze, his eyes boring into him.

He turned to Grace. 'You know Father has important clients coming to Angel tomorrow. How is it going to look if there's a police investigation going on? Especially when his son and daughter are right in the middle of it.'

For a few moments no one spoke as the cold chill of Miles' words sank in.

When he spoke again, his voice had an eerie calmness. 'OK, it's five fifteen. Let's get back to the house as quietly as possible. Some of the staff should be getting up any time. Let one of them find the body. They can tell my father and he can sort this out. Agreed?'

He looked at them one by one and slowly, reluctantly, one by one they all nodded.

'Bradley's dead,' said Miles as they began to walk away from the body. 'We can't help him. But we can help ourselves.'

10

It had started to rain as soon as she had got back to her bedroom. Fat, sweet-smelling, tropical rain that lashed against the window and seemed to make the whole house shake. Grace glanced at her watch again; it had been barely an hour since they had been at the beach, but time seemed to be passing horribly slowly.

Down at the beach, Miles' selfish 'let's help ourselves' speech had had a certain perverse logic, but now she'd had time to think, letting someone else find the body seemed wrong on every level. Not that any of them had anything to do with that poor man's death, of course, but to just leave him there . . . It was immoral, heartless, corrupt.

Should I go to see Alex? she wondered. He had been the only one who seemed to have a problem with leaving the body. But his room was next to Miles' and the last thing she wanted to do was alert her brother to what she was thinking of doing. No, Grace knew she had to do this alone. The downpour started to ease. Steeling herself, she slipped on her flip-flops and was just heading for the door when she heard a gentle, almost inaudible knock.

It was Alex, his face grim. 'Can I come in?'

She nodded, glancing up and down the corridor before she closed the door gently behind him.

'We can't just leave that guy on the beach,' he said with quiet urgency. 'I think we should tell your father.'

Grace shook her head. 'I have another idea. Nelson.'

Alex immediately grasped Grace's scheme. Nelson was known as a loyal, efficient man who, while he worked for Robert Ashford, was not afraid to voice an opinion. 'I'll come.'

Outside, the air smelt damp and floral, as if it had been freshly laundered. They walked quickly down the stairs and outside, following the path around the house and past the tennis court, beyond which they could see a weathered but well-kept clapboard house.

'Nelson lived here as caretaker before my father bought the island,' said Grace. 'I've actually always felt it was more his island than ours.'

There was a light on in the top left window, so Grace tapped on the door while Alex hovered nervously behind her. Nelson Ford looked surprised when he answered the door; no wonder, it was just after six. He rubbed his dark, lined forehead as if he were still tired.

'Grace. What can I do for you?'

Grace glanced at Alex, then took a deep breath. 'We thought we saw something down at the beach. I wanted you to come and take a look.'

'What is it?'

Alex hesitated before speaking. 'A body maybe.'

'A body *maybe*?' asked Nelson cautiously.

'We didn't want to get too close,' offered Alex, not meeting Nelson's gaze.

The older man looked at them for a long moment, then turned around and glanced back into the darkness of the house. 'Come on then. Let's go take a look.'

They walked down to the beach in silence, Alex and Grace going at such a brisk pace that even Nelson's long legs struggled to keep up with them.

Getting closer to the beach, Grace felt another stab of uncertainty. *Maybe Miles was right: why should we get mixed up in this when it's nothing to do with us?* The police would be only too happy to pin this on the rich Europeans; there was little love for the flash incomers buying up their own corner of paradise from the native islanders.

At least Nelson was on their side. Or was he? It was hard to get anything straight in her head. Already they had begun lying: *maybe we saw a body*. There was nothing maybe about it.

She stepped on to West Point Beach and immediately sensed something was wrong. In the time between leaving with Miles and Sasha and getting back here with Nelson, the tide had come in, but there was still ten yards of exposed white sand between them and the water's edge. Her eyes scanned up and down the beach and her heart started pounding.

'What are we looking for again, kids?' asked Nelson, slowing his pace to a stop.

The body had gone.

'It was here,' she said, looking around wildly. 'It was.'

Alex had already run further up the shore, looking to see if they had picked the right spot, but Grace was sure of it: this had been the place. She wouldn't forget it in a hurry.

Nelson looked at her cynically. 'Well, there's nothing here now.'

'Tell him, Alex,' said Grace desperately, pointing to the spot on the path. 'There was a dead body right here.'

'It's true, sir,' said Alex, running his hand through his hair. 'We saw him.'

'Him?' asked Nelson. 'Did you see who it was?'

'It was that boy Bradley,' said Alex. 'I think he'd just started as a deckhand or something.'

'Him,' Nelson said disapprovingly. 'I nearly fired him last night. Someone saw him drinking.' His brows knitted. 'Are you sure he wasn't just asleep or passed out? If he was drinking, that seems the most likely thing to have happened here. He woke up and walked off. You did say you didn't get that close?'

Grace shook her head vehemently. 'He wasn't moving. Or breathing, I'm sure of it,' she said, feeling tears well behind her eyes.

Alex examined the shoreline, looking for footsteps, but the rain had smoothed the sand. 'Do you think the tide could have taken the body out?'

Nelson shrugged. 'The sea can be unpredictable, so I guess it's possible,' he said in his thick Bahamian accent. 'But it's not quite high tide. It would have had to be one hell of a freak wave to sweep up and snatch a body.'

He looked at Alex through narrowed eyes. 'Are you sure it wasn't you doing the drinking?'

Alex looked pale in the thin morning light. 'No . . . well, yes, but I know what I saw. He was here!' he said, gesturing at the path. 'We all saw him, didn't we, Grace?'

'You *all* saw him?' said Nelson.

'No, no, I mean, we saw him, me and Grace,' stammered Alex.

'Just you two?' said Nelson.

No more lies, Grace told herself. 'Miles and Sasha too,' she said reluctantly.

'Let's try Bradley's room,' said Nelson finally.

They took the ten-minute walk to the staff cabins and Nelson knocked on the door of the last room. Hearing no movement inside, he pulled a large bunch of keys from his shorts pocket and opened the lock. The cabin was empty, but the bed looked rumpled as if it had been slept in.

'Well, it looks like someone was in here last night,' said Nelson. 'What time did you think you saw him?'

'Around five,' said Grace. 'And we *did* see him.'

'OK,' said Nelson sceptically, locking the door and leading Grace down to the staff mess at the end of the block where they were met by the smell of frying bacon. It made Grace feel sick. Inside, a chef and two maids were having breakfast at a long table.

'Anyone seen Bradley the boat boy this morning?' Nelson asked them.

One of the maids looked from Nelson to Grace and shook her head.

'Maybe he's sleeping in,' said the chef. 'Independence Day yesterday an' all.'

Nelson pulled a face and walked out. 'Well, wherever he's got to, we should tell your dad. Whether he's injured or not, we can't have a missing boat boy on the island when he's bringing over those important clients.'

Grace looked over to the house, feeling as if she wanted to be sick.

'Don't worry,' said Nelson with a sympathetic expression. 'He'll be understanding.'

Grace snorted. *You don't know my father very well*, she thought as they walked back along the path. *No, you don't know him at all.*

11

Alex had run all the way back to the house, ahead of Nelson and Grace, carried by a wave of hope and relief. *Maybe Bradley wasn't dead after all*, he thought as he sprinted up the path. *Maybe we didn't leave a dying man out there.* Back on the beach, when he'd bent over the deckhand, he thought he had seen movement in the boy's face. He wasn't certain, just a flicker at most, but a possible sign of life, certainly. And now the boy was gone – he *must* have been OK.

But you still left him, didn't you? mocked an inner voice. *You still abandoned someone who needed your help.*

It was true. What Miles had said out there had frightened him. He had come so far from a mill town terraced house, living a life of luxury on a private island beyond his wildest dreams, and – he was ashamed to admit it – his first thought when he'd seen the body was that it was all going to be taken away.

Alex stopped by the pool and bent over to catch his breath, then powered on to the house, eager to break the news to Miles. Down on the beach he'd hated Miles for somehow trying to implicate him in that stupid fight he'd had with Bradley. But there was no body. And if Bradley was OK, what was the problem?

He was just feet from his bedroom when the door to the

room next door creaked open. Miles was standing there in a navy dressing gown, his expression flinty.

'Where the fuck have you been?' he spat, looking up and down the corridor warily.

Alex searched for words but could find none.

'I *said* where have you been?' snapped Miles.

He stepped back into his room and Alex followed. Miles closed the door.

'I went to see Nelson,' said Alex finally.

Miles turned around and swept an armful of toiletries off the top of a chest of drawers. 'Fuck,' he growled. He looked away, his top row of teeth biting into his bottom lip.

'Miles, someone needed to know,' said Alex angrily.

'You cretin,' he snapped. 'I thought we had a pact! Let someone else find the body.'

'The more we lie, the more trouble we might get into.'

'What the fuck do you know about troubleshooting?' replied Miles, his eyes dark in the low light. 'Did you say we all saw the body?'

'We didn't mean to.'

'We? You and Grace, I assume. Thanks for fucking nothing,' he sneered.

Alex had seen Miles in this mood before and it frightened him. He held up his hands, trying to calm the situation.

'Look. Just hold on. When we went down to the beach with Nelson, there was no sign of him.'

'No sign of the boat boy?' asked Miles, narrowing his eyes.

'The beach was empty. Bradley was gone. He must have been all right; fallen down and knocked himself out or passed out pissed, but he'd got up and left by the time we got back there.'

Alex saw a look cross Miles' face: confusion? Disbelief perhaps? Or was it guilt? Was Miles feeling the same sense of self-loathing he was?

'He's all right?' said Miles, almost to himself. 'But he was dead, I was sure I . . .'

'We still shouldn't have left him there, mate,' said Alex. 'He's still probably badly hurt.'

'Don't go getting all pious on me now,' sneered Miles. 'You were just as happy as the rest of us to leave him for dead, Alex. You wanted to save your own skin.'

'What? No!' protested Alex.

Miles shook his head with disgust and turned towards the door. 'Well, don't start celebrating just yet,' he said over his shoulder.

There was a soft knock at the door. Alex opened it and saw Nelson standing there, his face expressionless.

'Mr Ashford wants to see you in his study. Have you seen Miss Sasha?'

'We'll be there in a minute.'

They found Sasha sitting on a sunlounger by the pool. Her hair was wet and she was wrapped in a bathrobe, her arms clasped protectively around her knees. She had sunglasses on and seemed to be staring blankly across the water.

Alex hung back and watched the interchange between his friend and his lover.

'My father wants to see us,' said Miles flatly.

'Let me change.' Sasha's voice was vague, despondent.

'Just come.'

She pulled off her shades and looked at them both. A trail of black eye make-up was smeared down her cheek. In the two years he had known her, Alex had never seen Sasha look anything but supremely self-confident and in control. But her open anguish spoke for all of them.

'How does he know about it?' she asked.

'Thank Alex.'

'What are we going to say to him?' she whispered urgently.

'The truth,' replied Alex.

Robert Ashford's study was in a far wing of the house overlooking a sweep of ocean. Daylight had come quickly. Robert was already dressed in a crisp white shirt and dark blue tie when Alex, Miles and Sasha walked in. Grace was sitting sombre-faced in a leather chair facing his desk and Robert motioned to the seats beside her.

'I prefer to stand,' said Miles.

His father shook his head slightly and pulled a sour face. 'As you wish.'

He folded his hands in front of him as if he were about to chair a board meeting.

'Let's get right to it, shall we? Would someone like to explain why Alex and Grace told Nelson there was a body on West Point Beach this morning?'

There was a moment's silence and then they all started speaking at once.

'There *was* a body!' said Grace over the top of the hubbub. 'We thought he was dead!'

Robert made 'quieten down' motions with his hands. 'And who exactly is supposed to be dead?' he asked.

'Bradley someone. He was a boat boy hired to help out with your visitors,' said Grace. 'We were all walking back from Catseye Cove and we found him on the west beach.'

Robert steepled his fingers in front of his mouth. 'Was he breathing? Was there a pulse?'

Everyone looked at Miles.

Alex stared at his friend anxiously.

'I was going to test for a pulse but we decided not to touch the body as the police would want to see it first.'

'He was pretty still,' added Sasha.

'Still?' said Grace. 'He was dead! There was blood all down his face.'

'Were you taking drugs? All of you?' asked Robert finally. Grace was now visibly upset. 'I know what I saw,

89

Dad. And yes, we'd all been drinking, but we weren't hallucinating.'

Robert sat back in his chair with an air of annoyance. 'Well, what I can tell you is that one of the boat boys does appear to have vanished. His bed was slept in, but there's no sign of him on the island.'

'Maybe he was washed out to sea . . .'

Her father held up a hand. 'I haven't finished, Grace,' he said. 'What I was going to say was that Nelson has been down to the boat shed and one of the Boston Whalers is missing.'

'So you think the little shit has done a bunk?' said Miles.

'I wouldn't have put it quite like that,' said Robert. 'But yes, I do.'

'Are you going to call the police?' asked Grace.

'Of course.'

'Today?'

'Immediately.'

Grace looked relieved. 'Are you going to ask them to find out what happened on the beach?'

Her father frowned and shook his head. 'Don't be ridiculous,' he said. 'I'm going to ask them to get my boat back. There are half a dozen islands within a one-mile radius of Angel Cay and I'm going to have each one searched until we find him. Then I'm going to have the little thief clapped in irons.'

'But . . .'

'Until then, I suggest we all keep a tight lid on this. I have very important clients arriving at lunchtime and I don't need the distraction. Let me handle this. You just forget it. Go and finish packing. As you know, the boat will be taking you to Nassau after breakfast.'

Miles gave a small smile of satisfaction.

'But . . .' began Grace again.

'This meeting is over, Grace. The incident is closed.'

Alex lowered his head, his shoulders bowed with regret, fear and shame that, he knew then, would last him a lifetime.

Part Two

12

December 1990

The Knightsbridge offices of the D&D advertising agency were impressive, but Sasha was too cold to notice. The dazzling white marble lobby with ultra-modern glass and chrome fittings and huge abstract artworks hanging on the walls failed to register with Sasha as she pushed through the revolving doors; she was simply glad to be in out of the biting Arctic wind. This winter seemed colder and more miserable than ever, she thought as she unzipped her thin leather jacket and click-clacked across to the lifts in her five-inch heels. But the dark clouds seemed to suit her mood exactly. It had been six months since she had finished at Danehurst and life wasn't turning out how she had imagined it at all. By now she'd thought she'd be the next big thing in modelling, Britain's Christy Turlington or a white Naomi Campbell. She'd had visions of days filled with photo shoots and fashion shows, the evenings spent at glamorous parties with celebrities and millionaires, before returning home to a loft apartment on Chelsea's King's Road with a Saudi prince or an oil baron on her arm.

But no, she sighed, thinking of the indignity of having to arrive at the agency by *bus*. Since summer, life seemed to have been reduced to one round of almost constant rejection, and it wasn't something Sasha was prepared for. Her split from Miles had been traumatic enough, given that she'd had their entire life mapped out in front of them, but the bastard wasn't even taking her phone calls any more. She'd flunked her A levels, and although she hated to admit it, her modelling career had hardly been much more successful – a teen magazine fashion shoot and one day's work handing out leaflets at a fast car show. The worst part, however, had been the castings. Today's go-see was her fourth of the day, the twentieth of the week, and she knew exactly how it would go. The scene at each appointment, whether at an ad agency or a glossy magazine, was depressingly the same. The fashion editor or art director would flick lifelessly through her portfolio as if there was nothing in it of interest whatsoever, look her up and down with a sour expression, then dismiss her with a quick nod of the head. And that was the good ones; sometimes they would actually discuss her shortcomings out loud. *She'll never fit into the Ralph Lauren dress with those arms.*

For someone who had spent her entire life being told she was beautiful, it had been unfathomable. But Sasha was far too proud and stubborn to give in. No, she hadn't spent the last five years doggedly working on improving her social position to give it all up now, Miles or no Miles. Her face would be her fortune or she would die trying. *Let's hope it doesn't come to that*, she thought, tossing her hair back over her shoulders as she exited the lift and strode up to the reception desk.

'In the boardroom, last door on the left,' said a bored brunette, pointing down the corridor.

Sasha took a seat on a chair outside, making sure to straighten her shoulders and back; you never knew who might be watching, although the only people she could see was a huddle of secretaries gathered around a photocopier babbling about the D&D Christmas party that evening.

After a few moments, she was summoned into the room, where the ad executives, a man and an older woman with a chocolate-brown bob, were sitting behind a desk. Unsmiling, the brunette asked for Sasha's portfolio and flicked through it without interest. Sasha tried not to flinch. There were fewer than thirty photos inside it – just test shots, done by up-and-coming photographers to beef it up.

'I'm new,' said Sasha by way of explanation. 'I've been living in the Caribbean,' she added, hoping to sound more glamorous than her body of work suggested.

'How old are you?' asked the brunette.

'Nineteen. Nearly.'

'Have you thought about getting your nose fixed?'

Sasha blinked, trying to keep her face as even as possible. 'Cindy Crawford didn't get her mole done,' she said brightly. 'I think it's sometimes best to leave things as nature intended.'

The male executive smiled and walked over to a video camera mounted on a tripod. 'Shall we?' he asked his colleague, who just shrugged.

The man was young but important-looking, dressed in a black turtleneck and small wire-framed John Lennon glasses; Sasha deduced he was the art director. He waved her over to a chair in front of the camera and she felt an unexpected flurry of nerves. Every rejection she had so far received would be worth it if she scored this one gig. D&D's biggest client was Benson confectionery, and the rumour was that they were currently looking for a girl to front a campaign for a new range of chocolate ice-cream bars. Forget the money – this would mean print ads, billboards and, more importantly, television ads. Whoever landed this would have their face on every street corner and in every front room throughout the summer. It wasn't *Vogue*, but it was big.

'I'd like you to say these words to camera,' said the brunette, making some notes on a yellow pad in front of her. 'Venus ice cream. It's chocolicious.'

Sasha was suddenly glad of the three-week drama summer school she had attended in 1985.

'How do you want me to say "chocolicious"?' she asked. 'Playfully? Sexily? I can put on an American accent if you'd like. I've spent a lot of time in New York and Miami.'

'English will be fine,' replied the brunette thinly.

A red light flicked on and Sasha fixed her gaze into the black depths of the camera lens.

'Try Venus,' she said, pouting. 'It's chocolicious.'

'Can you stick to the script?' said the woman with irritation.

'Of course,' said Sasha, turning back to the camera.

'Venus ice cream,' she breathed, more seductively this time. 'It's chocolicious.'

It better be, thought Sasha, and smiled a dazzling smile.

'So how was the casting? Who was it again? *Vogue*?'

Carole Sinclair was sitting waiting for her daughter at a corner table in Harrods restaurant. In town for last-minute Christmas shopping, she had insisted on meeting Sasha after her casting and 'treating' her to afternoon tea. This annoyed Sasha; as a failed ex-model herself, her mother knew full well that she couldn't actually eat anything.

At forty-eight, Sasha's mother looked ten years younger. She had perfectly blow-dried hair and her skin was lightly tanned from a recent tennis holiday in the Algarve. Around her feet were an assortment of green and gold Harrods carrier bags. Sasha had overheard her father say that they should 'pull our belts in this Christmas' but Carole clearly hadn't been paying attention.

'No,' said Sasha, air-kissing her mother and sitting down. 'It was an ad agency. They're casting for the Venus chocolate girl.'

'So have you got it?' Carole asked with a note of disapproval.

'I don't know yet.'

'Maybe if you didn't wear jeans for your appointments you might be a bit more successful,' she said, looking at Sasha's skin-tight Levis.

Sasha rolled her eyes. 'What do you want me to wear, Mum? Couture?'

Carole picked a piece of imaginary lint from her tailored trousers. 'I just think you might do better if you made yourself look a bit prettier. In my day we got dressed up when we went to see clients.'

'And look what good it did you.'

Carole Sinclair gave her daughter a tart glance. 'I only want the best for you, darling.'

The best for yourself, thought Sasha. At school, Sasha had spent so many years describing her father as the CFO of a multinational company that she had almost come to believe it herself, but the truth was a little less glamorous. Gerald Sinclair was the in-house accountant for a small shipping company and brought home £50,000 a year. A good salary, but not enough to keep Carole in the manner she desired. A townhouse in Belgravia and a chauffeur-driven Roller would have suited her mother's ambitions; instead she had a four-bedroom semi in Esher and a three-year-old BMW.

'Aren't you going to eat that sandwich?'

Sasha shook her head and glared at her mother. Before she'd even had her first casting, the agency had baldly told her that she needed to lose at least a stone, so she had spent the last six months of her life hungry.

'Fair enough. We don't want you putting on too much weight over Christmas, do we?'

Christmas, thought Sasha. Perhaps now would be a good time to bring up the loan. She'd tried asking her father, but every time she mentioned it, he politely changed the conversation. *Well, if you can't ask during the season of giving . . .* she thought.

'Did you and Dad think any more about lending me the deposit for a flat?'

Carole put down her Earl Grey tea. 'I fail to see why you need to move to town when you have a perfectly good bedroom in Esher.'

'Come on, Mum. What about when I go out? It's thirty pounds in a taxi from the King's Road.'

'Why do you need to be going to nightclubs all the time?'

'You *know* I need to go out,' said Sasha, exasperated. 'I need to meet people, make contacts. It was the same in your day.'

Carole shrugged and looked away. 'What about Caroline's house?' she asked.

Sasha cast her eyes to the ceiling. Caroline was a friend from Danehurst who was now working at Pickton House publishers. For the last four months Sasha had had a tacit agreement with her: in return for Sasha getting Caroline and her two housemates into the many clubs and parties which routinely invited models from the agency, Caroline would let Sasha crash in their draughty end-of-terrace in Chelsea's Flood Street. Not that she got a real bed; she was relegated to a camp bed in a corridor where they kept their bikes and coats. She would wake up with a crick in her neck and Caroline banging on about the fabulous night they'd had. She was beginning to think she had got the rough end of the bargain.

'How can I look *pretty* for castings after sleeping on someone's ratty couch?'

'Is this about bringing men home?' said Carole.

Sasha didn't blush. She and her mother had always had a very open relationship when it came to sex; indeed, Carole had instilled in her daughter the importance of using her looks and body to snare a rich man. 'Keep him happy in bed,' she had said, 'and he'll keep your bank account full.'

'No,' she sighed. 'But say I do meet a Hollywood film director in Raffles, I can hardly bring him back to my mum and dad's house, can I?'

Carole sighed. 'Look, we can probably give you the deposit, but how are you going to pay rent every month? You're hardly snowed under with work.'

'I'll sort something out.'

Her mother looked sceptical. 'Sorry, sweetie, I have to fly,' she said, gathering her things. 'I fancy quail tonight and if I don't pop downstairs and buy it now, I'll never make the five fifty train.'

Sasha felt anger rise up in her stomach. It didn't seem so long ago that her mother would have done anything to improve the social lot of her only daughter. Why couldn't she understand? Did she want Sasha to end up stranded in suburbia like her?

'I see,' said Sasha bitterly. 'You can do your weekly shop at Harrods food hall and fill your wardrobe with clothes you hardly wear, but you can't give your daughter a home.'

Carole glared at her. 'Don't speak to me like that.'

'Well, I thought you wanted the best for me.'

'Of course I do, but your father ...'

Sasha frowned. 'What about Dad? Doesn't he want me to have a nice flat?'

With evident reluctance, Carole sat down again, then glanced around to make sure they weren't being overheard.

'If you must know, there's been a change of management at your father's company. They've been talking about redundancies.'

Sasha panicked. 'Daddy's going to lose his job?'

'No, nothing like that. But he might have to go down to three or four days a week. It's this bloody recession.'

Sasha put her hand over her mouth. 'Oh God,' she said. It had been bad enough lying about her background for so long, she couldn't stand to actually be *poor*.

Carole put her hand on Sasha's. 'Don't worry, your dad and I will be fine.'

It's not you I'm worried about, thought Sasha, glancing at her mother's carrier bags with irritation.

'Can I give you some advice, mother to daughter?' added Carole. 'Why don't you give Miles a ring?'

Sasha couldn't believe her ears. Her mother had seen how upset she had been after she had flown back from Angel Cay. And anyway, she had tried to ring him – he didn't seem too keen to pick up the phone.

'What do you suggest, Mother?' she said sarcastically. 'That I should ask him to pay my rent?'

Carole waved the jibe away. 'But darling, he'll be back from Oxford for the holidays. He'll have spent a whole term surrounded by all those plain, swotty bluestockings. Now's the time to strike.'

Sasha stood up and pushed her chair in. 'I can't believe you'd suggest such a thing,' she said, picking up her portfolio. 'You may be happy to whore yourself to a man, but that is something I will never do.'

Registering with satisfaction the look of shock and outrage on her mother's face, she turned on her heel and walked out. *Well, if she won't give me what I want,* she thought, *I'll just have to get it myself.*

And she smiled for the first time in days.

Standing in the warmth of Caroline's bedroom, Sasha pulled the contents of her small overnight bag on to her friend's bed. It was depressingly slim pickings for a night out. One dress, two tops and a pair of white jeans.

'So what's the party tonight?' asked Caroline as she unselfconsciously stripped off.

'Oh, just some drinks company. Are Deborah and Jenny coming out?' Sasha asked. Caroline's two housemates hadn't been in when she arrived.

'No. Deb's got her office party and Jenny's got this new boyfriend.'

'The one she met at Raffles?'

'The one with the Porsche. Anyway, speaking of those two . . .' Caroline took a sip of her Lambrusco. 'Debs was asking when . . . if you're going to start paying some, er, some rent.'

'Rent? For the bike shed?'

'It's part of the house,' said Caroline.

Sasha snorted. 'Barely.'

'Look. Don't shoot the messenger. I don't think they were thinking much. More like a contribution to bills really.'

This was the last thing Sasha needed.

'Frankly, I'm offended,' she said. 'It's fine for me to bunk down when they want tickets to parties and free drinks and boys on tap, but as soon as Jenny gets a boyfriend I'm in the way.'

Caroline looked awkward. 'Listen, between you and me, I think Jenny will be moving out soon anyway, so I'll probably take her room and you could have this one.'

Sasha looked around and sighed. It wasn't the room; it was a lovely room in a great house on one of Chelsea's prettiest back streets. In fact, the prospect of landing a room here was the only reason she put up with sleeping with her face pushed up against a muddy tyre. The only reason, if she was honest, she put up with nights out with Caroline and her giggly friends when she could be socialising with the girls from the agency. But her mother was right: how was she going to pay the rent when she wasn't earning a penny?

'This house is a bargain for Chelsea,' said Caroline.

Sasha caught a flicker of something on her friend's face. Sympathy? God, was it pity? It was fine for Caroline, with her rich parents who had pulled strings to get her a job in publishing. It was a classic holding job for a pretty socialite, something to keep her busy until she inevitably met someone rich enough to marry. That was where she and Caroline differed. Caroline would be happy to settle for a husband called Jonty and the odd long weekend in Klosters. Sasha wanted the world and she wasn't going to settle for anything less. Suddenly she was filled with purpose: she knew what she had to do.

She pulled on a clingy Ozbek tunic that stopped at the top of her thighs. She didn't bother with a skirt; instead she pulled on silver tights and her black patent heels, adding smoky eyes and pale beige lips. The look was bold and striking, like Daryl Hannah in *Bladerunner*.

'Wow! Sexy,' said Caroline.

'That's the idea,' she said. 'Come on, I've got somewhere to take you.'

They walked on to King's Road and flagged a taxi. Sasha leant in to the driver and told him the address.

'I thought the party was in Notting Hill?' said Caroline.

'There's been a change of plan.'

'Ooh, I like surprises,' said Caroline. 'Will there be boys there?'

'That, also, is the idea.' Sasha smiled.

They pulled up outside The Embassy Club, the place Sasha had overheard the secretaries at D&D gossiping about. The queue for the agency's Christmas party was long and boisterous, but Sasha wasn't fazed, striding up to the doorman and giving him the benefit of her widest smile.

'He's got our tickets,' said Sasha, waving towards the queue vaguely. 'But it's cold out here.' She smiled, touching his chest suggestively. He unhooked the velvet rope and waved her through.

'Have we just gatecrashed someone's office party?' whispered Caroline.

'Oh no,' smiled Sasha, taking in the leery gazes of half a dozen men in expensive suits. 'They definitely want us here.'

Sasha had been to dozens of Christmas parties in the past

few weeks and had noticed that gatherings in the festive period had a particular energy, almost as if people had been freed from their usual roles and were allowed, for one night at least, to go wild. The D&D party was no different, with dozens of young women in short dresses and too much make-up eyeing up powerful-looking men with slick haircuts. The atmosphere was buoyed by alcohol, drugs and – particularly – the undercurrent of sex.

'I've got a good feeling about tonight,' said Sasha as Caroline headed off to the bar.

They have to be in here somewhere, she thought, scanning the crowd carefully. She glanced at her watch anxiously; she could imagine that a ball-breaker like the Benson account director would still be in the office, getting ahead of her male counterparts by clocking up overtime.

'Hey, great dress,' said a voice behind her.

Sasha turned to see a woman with sleek blond hair smoking a cigarette.

'Actually it's a top,' she said cautiously.

She looked at the blonde more closely. Now she could see that the woman was stylish and actually quite striking, with almond-shaped eyes and high cheekbones. Handsome rather than beautiful, but still, she had the look of an ex-model.

'Do you work in fashion?' she asked.

'Sort of.' The woman smiled. 'Do you?'

Sasha shrugged. 'Yes, I'm with Elan Models.'

'Well, you really have great personal style. Most people would look like Metal Mickey in that outfit, but you look ... futuristic. Like a sexy robot.'

Sasha narrowed her eyes. Was this woman hitting on her?

The blonde laughed and stubbed out her cigarette. 'Sorry,' she said, holding out a hand. 'Venetia James. I'm a clothes bore, I'm afraid.'

'Sasha Sinclair. What do you do at D&D?'

'I'm freelance. I had a job on one of their commercials yesterday and they invited me to this. I'm a stylist.'

'A stylist?' said Sasha, looking at her with more interest. 'You mean like a fashion editor?'

'Kind of. Except I don't work for a magazine. I used to, though, for *Vogue*.'

'Wow!' said Sasha, letting her pose of bored indifference drop. 'I bet it was amazing!'

Venetia smiled sadly. 'You'd think so, wouldn't you? Bloody hard work and I earned a pittance. Didn't have a trust fund or rich boyfriend like most of them.'

'So what do you now?' Sasha asked, intrigued.

'Catwalk, editorial, record company promos, lots of commercial stuff. Catalogues pay the most, even though I wouldn't dream of telling anyone I work for them. I've got a few personal clients as well. My workload is getting crazy. Actually, you should think about styling, you've obviously got a good eye.'

'Thanks,' said Sasha, 'but I do think I am just one break away from a big modelling career.'

Venetia smiled kindly. 'That's what I said ten years ago.' She grinned and reached into her bag. 'Let me give you my card anyway. You never know when our paths might cross. When I might need an assistant. You really do have a great look.'

Sasha thanked the woman and moved into the crowd. It was always good to make new contacts, but she was still keen to track down the Venus executive. She felt sure she'd screwed up the audition and would do whatever it took to remedy the situation.

'Well, well, well,' said an amused man to her left. 'I didn't know we'd had D&D staff auditioning to be the ice-cream girl.'

At first Sasha didn't recognise him – he wasn't wearing his John Lennon glasses and had swapped the turtleneck for a blue shirt. She breathed a sigh of relief: it was the art director from the casting.

'You,' she said.

He grinned. 'I don't why you're so surprised, I work at D&D, remember?'

'And I'm here with a friend,' said Sasha vaguely.

'Remind me of your name ...'

She felt a pang of disappointment. Surely she must have left some impression?

'Sasha Sinclair. And you are?'

'Martin Newsome.'

'Well, Martin Newsome,' said Sasha as she shook his hand, 'I think my agency are expecting to hear from you about my recall.'

'So you think it went well?' He grinned.

She smiled coquettishly. 'You tell me.'

'Kim and I are talking it over tomorrow. There'll be a recall on Monday.'

'And am I going to be hearing from you?' she pressed. She knew she should be playing it cool, but she couldn't face another night on Caroline's camp bed.

'We'll see. Shall we go somewhere a bit quieter?'

She nodded, and allowed herself to be led towards the back of the club, where topless men wearing sashes of glasses handed out vodka shots.

Martin summoned a waitress. 'Champagne,' he commanded.

Nervously, Sasha threw back her flute in one go.

Laughing, Martin waved the waitress back. 'Better give her another,' he said.

Emboldened by the alcohol – she'd had three glasses of wine at Caroline's and all on a permanently empty stomach – she met his gaze.

'Well, if you want my opinion, I think your script is a bit stupid.'

'Really?' he said with surprise.

'Well, not stupid. Just wrong. I mean, my agent said it was a premium product, which means Benson are going to be charging a lot for it. You want something sexier.'

'Sexier?' said Martin, raising an eyebrow.

'I just think chocolicious sounds a bit cheesy. You should be saying something like "Venus ice cream. My guilty pleasure."'

He gave her a wolfish smile. 'I like the sound of the pleasure part.'

'Please, just call me back,' she said. 'If Kim doesn't like me, let me meet the Benson marketing director.'

She hated the desperation in her voice. This wasn't Sasha Sinclair the confident ass-kicking bitch who ruled the roost at Danehurst. But something had changed in her since she'd arrived in London and she felt she was down to her last roll of the dice. She couldn't go back to that semi in Esher, she just couldn't.

'Listen, Sasha, it needs the marketing director's sign-off, but they are pretty much following our lead.'

'So what are you going to recommend?'

'That we steer away from those stick-insect models. I think we need someone a bit sexier.'

'Like me?'

'Depends if you can do sexy.' He touched her bum and pushed her towards a corridor.

'Where are we going?'

'In here,' he said, holding open the door to the bathroom and leading her towards a cubicle.

Sasha felt her heart lurch. She knew that ad agencies were awash with cocaine, but she didn't take drugs. A lot of the other agency girls did; they said it kept the weight off. Locking the door behind them, Martin tipped some white powder on to the cistern and snorted it through a rolled-up twenty-pound note. Politely she refused his offer of a white line and, shrugging, he took hers too. Then he leant in close, his breath hot on her neck.

'Show me if you can do sexy,' he whispered.

She met him directly in the eyes. 'If I show you, will I get the Venus contract?'

'I think we can safely say we can make this happen.'

She felt a flicker of dread. His fingers played with the zip of his trousers until his cock and sprouts of black hair like spider's legs sprang free. It was not a pretty sight. Then again, they never were.

She hesitated.

'Come on, Sasha. I only need a little bit of persuasion.'

Taking a breath, she dropped to her knees on the cold ceramic floor.

You can do this, she told herself. *You're good at this.*

She held the base of his shaft, then ran her tongue slowly, so slowly, along the sensitive underside of his cock.

'Oh God,' he moaned. 'Yes, yes.'

Closing her eyes, she took him whole in her mouth. He tasted sour. She thought of her small bedroom in Esher, then thought of herself on television. On the cover of *Vogue*. Life was full of choices, and she was making one now.

'Jesus, yes,' he groaned, pulling her head towards him until the tip of his cock hit the back of her throat. She tried not to gag.

'Yesssss . . .'

He slumped against the cubicle wall and Sasha pulled a wad of tissue from the dispenser to wipe a small white stain that had made its way on to her Ozbek top.

'Oh yes,' panted Martin. 'You can definitely do sexy.'

Sasha got up off her knees, looked at him, and then unlocked the door. 'I look forward to hearing from you on Monday,' she said and walked out into the party.

She immediately spotted Caroline draped over a rugby-player type in a badly fitting suit.

'Come on,' she said, peeling her off the protesting beef-cake. 'We're going.'

'What's happened?' asked her friend.

'Mission accomplished,' said Sasha, forcing a smile.

Sasha woke up on the camp bed cold and stiff as usual; but this morning, there was a spring in her step and a new sense of purpose. Caroline and her flatmates had already left for work, so she jumped in the shower, then towelled herself dry as she walked through to the kitchen. She smiled to herself as she opened the fridge and took out a carton of orange juice labelled Jennifer. She was looking forward to living here, and when she did, the fridge would be full of oysters and champagne.

Dressing quickly but carefully, she ran out into the street and – throwing caution to the wind – flagged down a cab, giving the driver the address of her agency in Covent Garden. *What the hell*, she thought happily, *I'll be able to afford it soon.*

She strode into the reception area. 'Hi, Sasha Sinclair to see Hilary.'

'Are you going to come in every day?' Hilary Covington, Sasha's booker, smiled as she walked in. 'You can just call. And you know I'll ring you if anything comes up.'

'I had to come in today. I have news,' said Sasha boldly. 'I saw Martin Newsome for D&D at a party last night. He said I was fantastic and that they were going to send me to see the client, although he seemed pretty confident I was the only one they were interested in.'

Hilary flicked through her call sheet. 'Well I haven't heard from him,' she replied. 'What was the name again?'

'Martin Newsome,' replied Sasha. 'He works with Kim on the Benson account.'

Hilary looked puzzled. 'He works with Kim? Hang on, is he the junior account executive they've just taken on?'

'Junior account executive?'

'In fact I spoke to Kim twenty minutes ago about the Elan girls we sent over. But it looks like they're going with an actress. Someone older.'

Sasha could feel the blood draining away from her face. *Oh God,* she thought, *that can't be true, can it?*

Hilary saw the look of dismay on her face. 'Sasha, you didn't sleep with him, did you?'

'No! Of course not!'

'Good,' said Hilary. 'I know you're too smart for that. But this is modelling and you're going to get asked. Most of the time it's not even worth thinking about.'

'I know,' said Sasha. 'I'm not stupid.'

Hilary fixed her with a long stare. 'Look, Sasha, it's good that you came in, because we need to have a talk.'

Sasha felt her stomach turn over. She had been expecting 'the talk', but not quite so soon.

'We're not really getting anywhere with the jobs, are we?' said Hilary. 'Maybe we need to start considering a few options.'

Sasha didn't reply, her voice choked by anger and fear.

'Maybe we need to turn your hair red,' said Hilary. 'It can limit you, of course, but it might give you a bit of stand-out.'

'But it's just a matter of time before . . .'

Hilary wasn't listening. She gestured towards Sasha's face. 'We definitely need to fix that bump on your nose too,' she said almost conversationally. 'I know a great plastic surgeon who can do it for under two grand. If it's too expensive up front, we can think about taking it out of your fees. It heals much quicker than you'd think.'

Sasha swallowed and forced herself to take a deep breath. Hilary wasn't being nasty, she told herself; in fact she was just trying to be kind. It was a brutal business and you had to be tough to survive.

'Thanks, Hilary,' she said, standing up. 'I'll think about it.'

109

'Just let me know.'

Sasha gave her a weak smile and walked out of the office into the cold street. It looked like it was trying to snow. As she passed a shop window, the mannequins, dressed in glittery red dresses like Santa's little helpers, their arms and legs grotesquely slender, seemed to be mocking her, their featureless faces saying 'Whatever made you think you could do this?'. Arctic wind lashed against her face. She pulled the collar of her jacket further up around her neck.

Maybe they're right, she thought. *Maybe I'm not suited to this business.* She looked again at the window. Or maybe it was just a matter of choosing a different path, doing a little lateral thinking. One thing was sure: Sasha Sinclair was never going to get caught out ever again. Next time she would make the right decision.

13

Maureen Doyle was a magician; it was the only way she could manage. Since the death of her husband Clive ten years before, leaving her nothing but empty gin bottles, she had been forced to become an expert in performing magic tricks with money and time, especially as she had to keep her son Alex in a fancy private school. Plate-spinning was her greatest party piece – simultaneously managing her part-time job in the newsagent's, the cleaning shifts, the envelope-stuffing sideline she did while watching her beloved soaps, while also keeping her own Macclesfield terraced house spotless. But Maureen didn't mind; it was all for her Alex. God only knew why He had seen fit to send her such a talented son, but He had and Maureen was going to do everything in her power to make sure that talent wasn't wasted – everything.

'Going out, love?' she asked, looking up from her Green Shield stamp book.

'Yeah,' mumbled Alex from the doorway of the lounge, pushing a piece of toast into his mouth, spraying crumbs over his Fred Perry T-shirt. 'I'll probably be back late.'

Maureen fought back a surge of disappointment; she had barely seen Alex all week and she had been looking forward to watching the telly with him tonight. Yes, their separate lives were partly to do with Maureen's eleven-hour working days, but there was also something else: Alex seemed to be retreating from the outside world and it worried her. *Is it me?* she asked herself. She had always done her best. The house was always full of Irn Bru and biscuits; she'd bought a second-hand portable telly from the classifieds section of the *Macc Express* and put it in his room. He had his own set of keys and could come home as late as he liked without being asked questions. She had even told him that he could bring any lady friends back if he wanted. But still her son seemed dreadfully, fundamentally unhappy. She stood up to face him, unsure of what to say. Maureen was not a confrontational woman and she was aware that life hadn't always been easy for Alex, but still . . .

'What's the matter?' asked Alex, catching the look on his mother's face.

'Nothing,' she said quickly.

'Don't you want me to go out?'

'No. I'm glad,' she said. Finally she took a deep breath and forced herself to say it. 'I've just been worried about you, love, spending all this time alone.'

Before she'd even finished her sentence she knew how stupid she sounded. She knew that teenagers would rather spend their time listening to records than watching *Coronation Street* with their mothers. But his physical withdrawal upstairs – sleeping all day, locking his bedroom door – echoed a change in his personality that Maureen did not think was simply due to age. Looking back, the change had begun the moment he had come home from that trip to the Caribbean and announced he was going to turn down his place at the Royal Academy. Maureen had been upset, of course – it was exactly why she'd worked so hard all these years, why she hadn't had a new winter coat since the mideighties – but if Alex was going to be unhappy there, then she wouldn't force him. Secretly, she was happy to have him home. She'd missed him desperately when he was away at Danehurst, but he hadn't just withdrawn from her, he had kept away from all his friends too – refusing to take phone calls from Miles Ashford and showing little interest in meeting old friends from Macclesfield. She knew she should have listened to her sister. 'You don't want him going to no posh school,' Rita had warned. 'Won't fit in properly there. Won't fit back.' Maureen was worried she had been right.

'I'm fine,' said Alex defensively.

Maureen nodded sympathetically. 'But you will tell me if you've got problems?'

Alex frowned. 'Problems?'

'Oh, girl trouble ... drugs,' said Maureen, feeling unusually flustered.

'Don't be daft.'

'No, I was cleaning for Dr Gilmore the other day and I was telling him about it and he said that depression is very common in young men. If you're depressed, we can get help.'

'Don't worry about me, Mum,' replied Alex with the hint of a smile. 'I'm not depressed.'

'But I do worry, love. You had everything mapped out. Your place at the Academy, you were going to be a musician. And now what are you going to do?'

'I'm still going to be a musician, Mum. Just a different kind. I'm going to be a rock star, and a degree from the Royal Academy isn't going to help me with that.'

'Well why don't you get a job?'

'I have a job,' said Alex with a hint of petulance.

'Not stacking shelves in Kwik Save; a job that makes use of your music. What about Forsyths, that music shop on Deansgate?'

Alex pulled a face. 'I want to play music, Mum, not sell recorders to ten-year-olds.'

'Then do it!' she cried. 'I love you, Alex, but you have a

113

God-given talent and you're wasting it just sitting in your bedroom. It's breaking my heart.'

They both looked at each other in shock. Maureen didn't know where that had come from; it was almost as if she were watching someone else talking.

'Sorry, love,' she stuttered. 'It's just I've been so worried. I . . . I just want you to be happy.'

Alex cast his eyes to the floor. 'I know, Mum,' he said softly.

And as she closed the front door behind him, Maureen Doyle burst into tears.

Alex slunk out of the house feeling horrible. He knew how hard his mother tried. He knew how much she had sacrificed to send him to Danehurst – his scholarship had helped, but still there were books, instruments, extra tuition, school trips, not to mention all the other things like records and clothes a normal teenager needed when he was away from home. More than that, Alex had always felt the guilt of leaving Maureen to face life alone when she was still getting over the death of his dad. That must have been the hardest part for her. And now he had disappointed her again. She had so wanted her only son to go to the Royal Academy. 'Your father would have been so proud,' she'd told him, her eyes full of tears.

But right now, Alex was where he wanted to be. He almost laughed out loud at that. Macclesfield, the town he had spent his whole life trying to get away from, was the only place he wanted to be in the world. He looked at the grey street ahead of him, the graffiti-dashed walls of a deserted warehouse on one side, the black waters of the River Bollin on the other. To think he'd come straight here from the glistening blue waters of Angel Cay, with its crisp sheets and gentle breeze. But the very thought of the island still made Alex feel sick. He stopped on the little concrete bridge crossing the stream and leant on the railings, gazing down at the sluggish water, wishing he could turn back time. But time wasn't like that; it had an annoying habit of just marching on, leaving you sitting there wondering what happened, just like the rusty shopping trolley stranded, wheels up, under the bridge below him as the river flowed ever on.

No, Macc might not be paradise, but it was where his roots were, like it or not. And anyway, if he was to leave, where would he go? He didn't want to go to the Royal Academy to be surrounded by rich kids with their flute and violin cases – he'd had enough of posh people to last him a lifetime. And he didn't want to live in London, where on any given weekend he might bump into Miles Ashford on a jolly up from Oxford.

He walked on, passing the only curry house in town, passing the Blue Anchor pub, which would be the scene of some ugly scuffles come chucking-out time. Still, the warm glow of the yellow plastic ship's lantern over the door did make him pause. He reckoned his schoolmates Gaz and Dicko would probably be in there, downing pint after pint and making inept passes at Tracey the new barmaid. Maybe that was where he should be. It seemed to be enough for everyone else; why not him? He'd tried that when he'd first got back, tried hanging out with the old crowd. They'd all taken the piss royally, of course, mocking his slightly softened accent and asking him to play them something on his 'fiddle', but there had been affection and familiarity in their ribbing and Alex had loved the way they had completely accepted him back into the fold as if he had never been away. But that was the problem, wasn't it? He *had* been away; he'd had a glimpse of the possibilities of life beyond the pub and the snooker hall and the football ground. He was unwilling to look back to the past, yet too anxious to face the future; that was the bald truth. Squirming, he pulled the collar of his suede jacket a little higher.

At Macclesfield station he hopped on to a train just as it was pulling out. He didn't need to check the destination; every train went to Manchester. Finding an empty carriage, he pulled open his green Millets army bag and took out a can of beer and his copy of *NME*. Cracking open the can with a hiss, he flipped to the 'Musicians Wanted' classified adverts in the back of the paper. 'Wanted: Guitarist for Faces-type band' read the first one. 'DO U WANT 2 B FAMOUS?' He puffed out his cheeks. *Yep, that I do*, he thought. But was 'Ziggy, 21, influences Green On Red, Theatre of Hate and Buzzcocks' the right man to make it happen? Alex had even contacted a couple of the ads over the past few weeks. He'd got on well with a bloke called Matt who had a Stones-influenced band in Birmingham and invited him to audition the following week. Alex had said he would think about it, but knew in his heart that he still didn't want to leave home. Not yet, anyway. One day, yes. But not right now.

It was drizzling when he got into Manchester's Piccadilly station, but he walked with a bounce as he headed into the city centre. There was a buzz in Manchester, an undeniable energy fuelled by acid house, Factory Records and the endless creative melting pot of people who were relying on talent, guts and determination to make it, not connections or money or a family name. It made you feel alive just to be walking on these wet streets.

Threading his way through the grey Victorian alleyways, he passed the Ritz and the Haçienda, ducking under a railway bridge and into The Boardwalk, a small black cave of a club where the ceilings were low and condensation dripped from the rafters. Tonight, as usual, it was full of students. Everyone was in baggy clothes – flared jeans, garish T-shirts, floppy hats; they looked like children wearing adults' clothes. Tonight there was an unsigned band called Verve playing who he'd never heard of. The singer was gaunt and awkward-looking with an angular face, big lips and a long spindly body, like

Mick Jagger stretched on a rack. But when he sang, he held the attention of the audience in the palm of his big hand. They were good, there was no doubt about that, and Alex felt a stab of unbearable envy. *I want to be up there, doing what they are doing*, he thought fiercely. *This is what I've been looking for*. It was the first real strong, visceral emotion he had felt since he had left the island; up to now he had only felt numb or sad.

He turned and pushed his way towards the bar. He really didn't want to think about the island, not when he had been feeling so upbeat, but it kept popping into his head unbidden. It didn't help that Miles kept sending him letters. Alex had never seen Miles as the letter-writing type, but since Angel Cay there had been regular missives, each one sending Alex into a cold sweat, dreading news of a police investigation or some threat to keep quiet. They had been perfectly innocuous and chatty, however, talking about Miles' new life in Oxford, even inviting Alex down during Hilary term, whatever that was, as if nothing had ever happened. He had no intention of taking up that particular offer.

He bought a pint of snakebite and went to stand at the back. He liked it there. He preferred to stay out of the way and watch the competition, noting their instruments and amps, how they played a certain riff or how a song was put together.

'Good, in't he?'

Alex turned his head to see a good-looking boy with dirty blond hair that fell over his ears.

'What? Who?'

'The singer.'

'Yeah, he's good.'

'Great set so far. Lucky fuckers. If there's A and R in the audience tonight, I bet they get snapped up.'

Alex shrugged. Their songs were great, but he thought he could improve them.

In Alex's dream band, everything would be perfect. He'd

117

spent so long planning it in his head, he just knew it would work. And all arrogance aside, he knew the songs he had written were every bit as good as Verve's; in fact, he suspected they were better.

The lad next to him smiled cynically. 'So you're in a band then?'

Alex shook his head. 'Not yet. I'm not even sure I want to. I kinda want to do my own stuff.' He wondered why he was saying all this to a complete stranger, but the truth was he needed to tell someone what he was thinking or he would explode.

'Solo stuff, eh?' said the boy, nodding to the stage. 'It'd be pretty fucking lonely up there.'

'Lonely?' frowned Alex. 'I never really looked at it that way.'

On stage, the band thundered to a halt amid cheers and whistles.

'Listen, d'you fancy going for a pint at the Briton's Protection?' asked the blond boy. 'They've got a decent jukebox and maybe a lock-in if we're lucky.'

Alex hesitated for a moment, then nodded. Why not?

The boy was called Jez and he was in his third year at Manchester Polytechnic studying graphics, although he was originally from Blackpool. Within minutes of settling into a cracked red-vinyl booth in the pub, Jez was boasting that his older brother Graham had been in a 'big' New Romantic band called Bichon Frise who had been slated to support Duran Duran before Graham had got tonsillitis and had to pull out. Alex suppressed a smile; to Jez, his brother's war stories of touring were full of glamour and adventure, but they didn't begin to touch Alex's experiences of paradise islands, ski chalets and private jets. *But then that isn't real life*, he reminded himself. *This is.*

'So what d'ya play?' asked Jez finally.

'Guitar, bass, piano mainly,' said Alex nonchalantly, sipping his drink.

Jez laughed. '*Mainly?* What are you? A fucking musical genius?'

Remembering the all-or-nothing attitude of the singer earlier that night, Alex just shrugged. 'It has been said.'

Jez nodded. 'Fancy a jam with us lot?' He nodded towards the door as two more lads swaggered in, both wearing worn suede jackets like his. 'These pair are in my band, Year Zero. Alex, meet Pete and Gavin. Alex here is a musical genius,' he said with a smirk.

'Excellent,' said Pete, pushing his ginger hair out of his eyes. 'When are you joining us?'

'Am I getting sacked and I don't know about it?' asked Gavin.

'Not you, spastic. Greg. We're hardly going to fire you when you've got a car, are we?'

'Hang on, Greg's leaving the band?'

Jez looked weary and superior. 'I'm going to ask him to reconsider his career choices.' He turned to Alex. 'Greg never shows up for rehearsal. As far as I'm concerned, you're either in or you're out.'

Pete fixed Alex with a stare. 'You interested?'

'Maybe.' He shrugged, but inside he was doing cartwheels. Here was a bunch of cool-looking Manchester-based indie kids who were asking him to join their band. Yes, they could be useless, but they certainly seemed committed, which was half the battle – and they had a car, too!

Alex ordered another snakebite, and as they talked about music, twelve-inches they had bought recently, brilliant gigs they'd been to, swapping secrets about musical discoveries, trying to outdo one another, he felt a little piece of him come back to life. *Yes, this is where I want to be*, he thought. *Right here.*

'Come on,' said Jez, slapping the table. 'Let's have another round.'

Alex looked at his watch with alarm. The last train to

Macclesfield left in ten minutes; if he sprinted, he might just make it.

'I'd better get off,' he said, getting up.

'Lightweight,' jeered Gavin.

'Got to get back to Macc,' said Alex.

'Come back to ours,' said Jez. 'You can always crash on the sofa. We can't let you leave the city before you've sampled Gav's home brew.'

Alex shrugged. What did he have to get back for really?

They continued chatting and arguing about music as they caught the night bus back to the band's student house, a huge orange semi-detached Victorian villa in Fallowfield, a standard student let with swirly carpet and mismatched sagging furniture. He noticed a dark open doorway leading off the living room.

'What's going on there?' he asked. Someone had stuck dozens of cardboard egg boxes on the back of the door.

'Soundproofing, mate,' said Pete. 'The birds in the flat upstairs keep phoning our landlord. One more strike and we're out.'

Gav smiled. 'Which isn't going to happen since Jez banged one of the girls.'

Jez shrugged modestly. 'A man's got to do what a man's got to do.'

He beckoned to Alex and disappeared through the dark doorway. 'Come on, I'll show you the nerve centre.'

Alex followed him down a flight of narrow steps into a damp cellar lit by a single bulb. 'Wow!' he said. There was barely room to stand up, but every available inch of floor space had been crammed with musical gear. They'd obviously gone to quite a bit of trouble with makeshift soundproofing using old mattresses. Unfortunately, they'd become damp and the room smelt of mildew, mixed with the heavier aromas of cigarettes and sweat.

Jez inhaled dramatically. 'Can't you smell it? The scent of

rock.' He picked up a guitar and shoved it into Alex's chest. 'Greg's guitar. He won't mind,' he said.

'Come on then, genius,' said Pete eagerly. 'Let's hear what you've got.'

Alex looked at the ceiling dubiously. 'Shit, Jez,' he said. 'It's twelve thirty. What about those girls upstairs?'

'Don't think they're in. Didn't see a light on, anyway.'

'OK,' said Alex, plugging the guitar in; he'd had too many snakebites to care much anyway. 'Why don't you play me one of your songs and I'll jump in when I can?'

'Let's do "Blood Money",' said Jez.

They launched into a raw rock 'n' roll jam, sort of like 'Diamond Dogs' meets 'Sweet Child O' Mine'. It had an interesting groove, but it wasn't very sophisticated; Alex had no trouble keeping up with the changes, and as his confidence grew, he laid a melody over the rhythm that completely transformed the song. From the grins on the band's faces when they finally ground to a halt, they had been pleased with his performance. Alex wished he could say the same. Gavin was a solid bass player and Pete kept the beat, but from a creative point of view the rhythm section was a desert and Alex could see he would struggle to get much more out of them. Jez was more interesting; his songs were derivative and his voice a bit thin, but he had a huge amount of charisma and Alex thought he'd be an arresting frontman. He was filled with a bubbling excitement. Together, this band had swagger and energy and above all potential. They could be great.

'So what do you think . . .'

The rest of his words were drowned by a loud banging coming from upstairs.

'Oh shit,' muttered Jez, running up the stairs. They all put down their instruments and trooped sheepishly upstairs. Jez was standing at the door talking to a girl, or rather listening as she shouted. She was pretty, with dark red hair that hung messily over her shoulders in a Snoopy nightdress that skimmed the top of her thighs. She stopped her tirade as the other boys peeked around the door and firmly crossed her arms across her chest.

'All right, Emma?' said Gavin with a cheeky smile.

The girl frowned heavily. 'No I am not. It's one o'clock in the bloody morning.'

'Is that the time?' said Jez with a wide grin. Alex could see that his charm was cutting no ice with Emma. Either she wasn't the one he had had sex with, or else she was and he had somehow pissed her off afterwards. Alex thought the latter was most likely.

'First thing in the morning I am calling the landlord,' said Emma to Jez. 'We've warned you a million times, but if you insist on behaving like an ignorant, selfish bastard, I won't lose any sleep if you're chucked out on to the street.'

Alex couldn't help chuckling and Emma rounded on him angrily.

'I'm glad you find it funny. Remind me to ask you how funny it is when you're rehearsing out of a cardboard box in Rusholme.'

'Look, I'm sorry. We all are.' Alex smiled. 'But the muse came and we had to answer the call.'

Emma didn't smile, but even when she frowned, Alex thought she was pretty. Even in that ridiculous nightie.

'Come in for a beer,' he said. 'Come on, Snoopy, you know you want to.'

She pursed her lips but a half-smile pulled at the corners of her mouth. 'Even if you weren't a bunch of shits, I couldn't,' she sighed. 'I've got an essay due in on Monday and I have to do some work in the morning.'

Emboldened by the snakebite, Alex sank to his knees and clasped his hands together. 'Please stay, we'll write a song about you.'

Emma looked down at him. Her face was still serious, but Alex could see she was fighting hard not to laugh.

'Who are you anyway?' she said.

'Alex, Alex Doyle,' he said, getting to his feet.

'Well listen to me, Alex Doyle,' said Emma. 'As soon as I close this door I don't want to hear so much as a single note. Do we understand each other?'

'Absolutely.'

'All right then,' she said and turned away, but Alex saw the grin spreading on her face.

'You sweet-talking son of a bitch.' Jez whistled admiringly.

'It was the snakebite talking,' said Alex.

Jez handed him another can. 'Well let it talk, brother,' he said, as they all flopped down on the sagging sofas.

'Listen, Alex, were you being serious about not wanting to be in a band? From what we saw downstairs, I think that would be a waste.' Pete nodded seriously. 'If you came on board with us, we'd have a right laugh.' Jez popped the ring-pull on his can. 'Together we'll conquer the world!' Pete and Gavin hooted in agreement.

Alex hesitated for a moment, then held up his can. 'Well then, count me in.'

The other three glanced at each other, then leapt at Alex, squashing him into the creaking sofa, yelling and spraying him with beer, until they heard a loud thumping coming from the floor above. Grinning, Alex pushed them off and wiped the beer from his face.

He'd heard that Manchester was the place to be.

He had a feeling that from tonight, life was finally going to get better.

14

May 1991

Grace sprinted for the line. Lunging forward, dipping her shoulders, she shot across, her feet and arms pumping in perfect harmony. Looking up, she saw the time on the scoreboard – a new world record! Her feet thudded to a stop and she leant forward, resting her hands on her knees. As she came to the end of a run, she liked to imagine herself in the final lap of a big race to push herself just that bit harder. Silly, but effective.

Grace's arms were slimmer, her tanned legs more defined and shapely from a month of morning runs along the sand of Four Mile Beach, Port Douglas' longest stretch of sand. Any last hint of puppy fat had been rubbed away by a bout of food poisoning in Thailand, swiftly followed by the healthy living she had taken up in Australia. Although it was the Queensland winter, and not yet eight in the morning, it was already twenty degrees, and drops of sweat were running down her face. *Enough for today,* she thought, flopping down on to the soft sand where the headland rose, curving away to spray-dashed rocks.

She looked out towards the Coral Sea, twinkling silver in the morning light. Over the horizon it blended with the Pacific

Ocean, and beyond that was South America, over six thousand miles away. She allowed herself a smile as she reflected that she was as far away from London as it was possible to be without going to the moon. That, of course, was part of the appeal of Australia. Not the only one, of course: she loved the weather, the 'no-worries' attitude; she even loved the way that while she was greeting a new day with a jog along the beach, in England it was still yesterday. She was separated by time and space – and that was just fine with Grace. She had been out of London nine months and had no plans to return, despite telling her parents that she just wanted a gap year after her degree and before she joined Ash Corp. And, yes, she was sad about not starting her MA at Oxford, but it was worth it.

Brushing the sand off her legs, she returned to the white-washed clapboard cottage she called home.

'God, you weren't out for a run again, were you?' asked Caro, her flatmate, as Grace came down after her shower.

Caro's short platinum hair was sticking up at all angles and she was sitting hunched over a cup of coffee. The previous night they'd both been out to the Cross Arms hotel, the white colonial edifice on the esplanade, but Grace had left her friend surrounded by men and half-empty bottles; no surprise she was feeling rough.

'You should have come with me,' smiled Grace. 'That would have blown the cobwebs away.'

'Some guy with a nose ring did that for me.' Caro smirked. 'Dan? Stan? Dunno, but he just left.'

'So that was the noise in the middle of the night. I thought it was a pack of dingoes.'

Grace had met Caro, a Kiwi from a small town in the South Island, in her first week in Thailand, when they were both staying in a small backpackers' flop-house in Krabi. She was as streetwise as an alley-cat with a knack for seeking out all the coolest places to be. Instantly admiring Caro's carefree attitude, Grace joined her on the boat to Koh Phi Phi, going on to Bali, Australia's Sunshine Coast, finally washing up on the tropical shore of northern Queensland.

Reluctantly, Caro made herself presentable and they both left the house to head into the town. Ten years ago, Port Douglas had been a sleepy fishing village full of locals and the occasional backpacker, but the construction of a large glossy marina a few years before had brought yachts, and with them came upmarket hotel groups, and smart restaurants. The two girls had spent the last four months working on the *Highlander*, a sixty-foot catamaran that transported tourists to the Low Isles, a group of small sandbanks thirty miles to the east where they could snorkel and dive.

'I've got something to tell you,' Caro said as they walked down Macrossan Street, the main thoroughfare sprinkled with cafés and surf-style clothes shops.

'What?'

'I'm thinking of moving on,' she said.

'You're joking.'

'It's getting too touristy around here,' she said, crinkling up her nose. 'And I'm not sure how many more prawn buffets I can serve up on the *Highlander*. I'm supposed to be a vegetarian, fer Chrissakes.'

'Where are you thinking of going?'

'Ah, dunno. India maybe? Fancy coming with me?'

Grace kept quiet. She had built such a happy life for herself here, she wasn't sure if she was ready to leave it.

As they neared the marina, they saw the queue of tourists by the catamaran.

'Check out the guy in the shorts.' Caro whistled as they walked up the gangplank.

'Ssh, don't let the guests hear you,' whispered Grace.

'Fuck the guests,' she said with a casual wave of the hands. 'Actually, yes please,' she added, meeting the dark eyes of the tall, swarthy man.

Grace blushed slightly and began taking the tickets off the passengers. Once everyone was safely boarded, the *Highlander* set sail for the Low Isles and the girls set about preparing meals, serving drinks and making sure the children didn't jump overboard. Grace could see why Caro was getting sick of it; the job was monotonous and in places downright unpleasant, but there were certainly worse ways to earn a living than cruising around the Great Barrier Reef, even if you did have to scrape plates on the way back.

They were just approaching the Low Isles when Neil, the stern Canadian captain, approached.

'You. Come with me,' he said, pointing at Grace.

Raising her eyebrows at Caro, Grace followed Neil forward to the cramped cabin which served as an office and store-room.

'Now then, Grace, I've been watching you over the past few weeks,' he began, 'and I've decided to give you a promotion.'

'Really?' said Grace with surprise.

'No, not really,' said Neil, turning to a locker and flipping it open. 'But I am changing your job description.'

She looked at him wide-eyed; maybe she could move up on deck. She had spent her childhood sailing, and when the sails were at full stretch and the male crew were hauling on the ropes, she longed to join in. Until now she'd stayed below deck, nervous that she might get spotted as Robert Ashford's daughter, which she had mentioned to no one, not even Caro. Luckily in this part of the world, no one seemed to care who you were or where you came from.

Neil pulled out a large black SLR camera and handed it to her. 'You are now the *Highlander*'s official photographer.'

Grace looked at him with her mouth open. 'I've only used Instamatics before.'

'Well now's the time to start learning. It's either you or Caro, and I wouldn't trust her to point it the right way, let

127

alone get a shot in focus. All I'm asking is when we get to the island, take a couple of snaps of the passengers having fun. We get them developed at the marina. We put them in a fancy frame with "I've Been To The Great Barrier Reef" on it and flog 'em back to them for ten dollars a pop.'

Over the tannoy, Neil announced that a small tender boat would be ferrying the guests across and that snorkel gear and anti-jellyfish 'stinger suits' would be handed out when they got to the beach.

Grace rode with them, fiddling with the camera, then headed towards the American family who were struggling to set up camp with a huge amount of beach gear – chairs, ice box, an inflatable dolphin.

'Hello there,' she said, holding up the camera. 'Would you like me to take a picture of you all?'

The father looked at her with hostility. 'Another hidden cost? I've already shelled out for four sodas on your boat.'

'Oh Kevin,' said the mother. 'It will be great.'

She gathered the children around her and the father stood at the back, chin jutting out, clasping a frisbee to his chest as if it were a badge of high office.

Grace squinted through the viewfinder. 'OK, everyone smile . . .' she said, pressing the shutter button.

And nothing happened.

'Sorry,' she said. 'Try again . . .'

Again, nothing. Flustered, Grace looked at the camera, trying to work out what was wrong.

'Bear with me,' she said distractedly.

'Cowboys,' muttered the father as the children began to whine and fidget.

'Here, maybe I can help,' said a voice.

Grace turned to see the handsome passenger she had noticed earlier.

He stepped away from the family, examined the camera then flipped open the back. 'Film's jammed.'

'Bugger. I didn't think I loaded it properly. And now I've left the bag of extra film on the *Highlander*.'

The man dipped his hand in his pocket and pulled out a yellow roll of Kodak. 'Your lucky day.' He smiled.

Bloody hell, he was good-looking, thought Grace, watching him swiftly reload the camera. His skin, the colour of pale coffee, stretched over fine bone structure. His dark, almost black eyes made him look serious, intelligent, even when he smiled.

'Come on,' shouted the father.

'A slight technical hitch,' said Grace, gratefully taking the camera. 'All fixed now. OK, everyone say "Jellyfish"!'

In the end, Neil was right. The holidaymakers all wanted a memento of their trip to the island, so they were only too willing to pose, and now Grace knew which button to press, she felt like David Bailey. She was, however, disappointed that she was busy with her duties throughout the trip back and was unable to thank the man in the Bermudas.

'Thank God that's over,' said Caro as they walked back from the marina. 'So have you thought about coming to India? I reckon a few months there and you'll be the naked one at full moon parties. It will do you a world of good.'

'Thanks, Yoda.' Grace grinned. 'I didn't realise all those pearls of wisdom like "Have another tequila" and "Aw, why don't you just shag him?" were some sort of Zen-like spiritual training.'

'We all have our reasons for coming travelling,' said Caro more seriously. 'We're either trying to find something, or leave something behind. I've never worked out which one it is with you, Grace. What I do know is that you've got to stop living life like you're scared of it.'

They reached the cottage and Caro put the key in the door. 'Shit, we don't have anything in for supper.'

'I'll go,' said Grace, wanting to avoid Caro's latest line of conversation.

She spotted him immediately, standing in front of a seafood restaurant, reading the menu. The handsome, helpful man from the boat had changed out of his shorts into sand-coloured slacks and a white short-sleeved shirt. For a moment, Grace wondered whether to walk past without saying anything, but the man spotted her first.

'Hey, it's Diane Arbus,' he smiled.

'Who?'

'A famous American photographer.'

His accent was American mixed with something else – Spanish she thought from his dark eyes and golden olive skin.

'I thought Americans didn't do sarcasm.'

'Not American, South American.'

'Ah, sorry,' said Grace. 'This place is good, by the way,' she said, 'I can recommend the red snapper.'

'The locals always know the best places.'

'Hardly local,' said Grace. 'I'm on the wrong side of the planet.'

'English, eh?'

Grace nodded.

'The English are known in my country as having excellent taste in all things.'

'I'd better get on,' said Grace, blushing.

The man gestured towards the restaurant. 'Are you hungry?'

She grinned. 'Starving.'

'In that case, I'd be honoured if you would join me here.'

She couldn't believe she was still wearing her *Highlander* uniform, dirty and sweaty from the day's work.

'I don't want to impose . . .'

'Not at all.'

Stop living life like you're scared, she told herself.

'Why not?' She smiled, hoping that Caro could find her supper in the freezer.

He put out his hand. 'Then I believe an introduction is in order. My name is Gabriel.'

130

Grace shook it. 'Grace Ashford.'

The restaurant had a little garden area to the side and they took a table next to a tree covered in fairy lights. The sun had already dipped behind the far hills and the light was dimming to a bluey-grey.

'So. You know what I do,' said Grace. 'What brings you to Port Douglas, Gabriel?'

'I'm a writer.' He shrugged. 'They are making a film out of one of my books in the area, so I'm kind of tagging along on set.'

She looked at him in horror. 'Oh no,' she gasped, her hand covering her embarrassed smile.

'What's wrong?'

'You're not Gabriel Hernandez, are you?'

'I'm afraid so.'

Grace had read about it in the local paper a few weeks before: a big Hollywood studio was filming an adaptation of the massive literary hit *Cast No Shadow*.

'I'm so sorry, I had no idea.'

'You apologise too much.' He smiled.

Grace had actually read *Cast No Shadow* a couple of years ago and had some hazy recollection of him winning a Pulitzer Prize. Or was it a Nobel? Something very impressive, anyway.

'But isn't the book set in the Caribbean?' she said, hoping she had remembered correctly.

Gabriel nodded. 'Apparently the studios will save a lot of money by filming out here. David Robb and Julia Collins only had a ten-week window in their schedules. It's hurricane season in the Caribbean at the moment, so the production was moved out here. It's a good choice: lush, lots of white sand, and those colonial clapboard houses by the harbour could easily be Key West or Bridgetown if you squint slightly.'

The observation unsettled her, but she was distracted by the waiter. They ordered their food – red snapper for both

131

of them – and chatted about diving and sailing and the weather, with just a slight hint of flirtation on both sides. Grace was intrigued and surprised by Gabriel; he wasn't at all the tortured poet she'd expected from reading the book, a story of star-crossed lovers, one driven to suicide by the infidelity of the other. There wasn't anything pompous or gloomy about this man; he was intelligent and witty and warm.

'So where are you going to take me now?' said Gabriel as he waved away the bill, simply handing over his gold Amex.

Grace felt thrilled at his invitation to carry on the evening, quickly followed by horror at the idea of taking him back to the cottage, where no doubt Caro would be lying prostrate on the sofa surrounded by pizza boxes. *Not that it's going to get that far,* she reminded herself.

'Well, it's Tuesday night,' she said. 'That means toad racing.'

'Toads?' he said, raising one eyebrow. 'Toads as in frogs?'

She laughed. 'Cane toads to be precise. They're quite poisonous, actually, but it's kind of the local sport around here if you're a gambling man.'

'Ah, you know us writers.' Gabriel smiled. 'We live close to the edge.'

Grace could tell the races were well under way before they even got close to the Iron Bar near the harbour; men were cursing or bellowing encouragement while shrill female voices shrieked with the excitement of winning a couple of drinks.

'Around here, they say toad racing is better than sex,' shouted Grace over the noise.

'Well I guess that depends on which toad you're backing,' said Gabriel, looking at her meaningfully as Grace felt a shiver of pleasure.

When the race was over, Grace and Gabriel took their drinks to a booth at the back of the dark bar.

After an hour, she felt dizzy from drink and anticipation of where the night might lead.

'Are you from Colombia?' she asked, trying to recall what she'd read on the back of his book.

'I actually live in New York now, but my family are from Parador, just close to Colombia. People call us Colombia's little echo.'

'Meaning?'

'Meaning we have many of the same problems. Coca, from which cocaine is made, is our biggest cash crop, and while we don't produce anywhere near as much coke as Colombia, we still have too much for the needs of Parador.'

'So it all gets exported?'

He nodded. 'The drug cartels are more powerful than the government. Which causes trouble for my family. My brother is leader of CARP, one of the opposition parties in Parador. They pledge to bring down the drug lords. Although how much anyone can really do is questionable.'

'I had no idea,' said Grace, leaning closer. 'So is your dad a politician too?'

Gabriel looked away. 'He's dead.'

'I'm so sorry.'

'He was assassinated over twenty years ago in Palumbo, our capital, just before he was about to be elected president. I was thirteen. Since then, Parador has taken huge strides backwards; we're almost a third-world country now. Two years ago my uncle took over the party and my brother Carlos is the new figurehead, fighting for justice and social initiative, campaigning against our corrupt government who accept money and favours from drug barons.'

'Why not you?'

'I was born second,' he said with a small smile. 'Anyway, Carlos is good; the people believe in him. I'm not sure the same would be true with me.'

'But isn't it terribly dangerous for your brother?' asked Grace, her face so serious, Gabriel laughed.

'All change involves risk,' he said. 'I am proud of him for making a stand.'

'I wish I could say the same about my brother,' replied Grace, instantly wishing she hadn't.

'Really? Do you not get along?'

'Not really.'

'Why not?'

'I'm not sure he's a good person. The frustrating thing is that nobody else sees it. He's been lined up to take over my father's company even though he's arrogant, expectant, underhand . . .'

'Or maybe because of it.'

Grace laughed. 'I suppose so.'

'Anyway, I can understand the pressures of family expectations,' said Gabriel. 'They're proud of my achievements, of course, but Parador is an inward-looking country. To them, anything which happens outside the motherland is irrelevant. Including my writing career.'

'Yeah, my dad's like that with the business. I could be the world's greatest artist or musician, but if you're not doing it for the family, it's not important.'

Gabriel raised his bottle in a toast. 'To being the black sheep of the family. To rebellion!'

Grace was uncomfortable discussing it. Then again, the fact that she had even talked about Miles at all suggested a connection with Gabriel she hadn't felt with anyone else.

'So where next?' she said, not wanting the night to end.

'Actually, I did have one idea,' said Gabriel. They walked back down Macrossan Street until they came to his hotel, and he summoned a valet to get his car.

'Being involved with the movie has one or two advantages,' he confided in a low voice. 'First, they all think I'm some LA hotshot here and treat me like a king. And second . . .' he said, as the valet roared up in a silver convertible Saab, 'I know a few secrets.'

134

They got in the car and drove up into the hills, the head-lights carving their way through the dark. For a second Grace thought how foolish it was being driven off by someone she had known just a few hours. But then she felt the thrill of being in a fast car with a strange man, not entirely sure where she would end up, or how the night would finish. *So this is what adventure feels like*, she thought and giggled.

'What's up?' asked Gabriel, his eyes momentarily flicking across.

She smiled. 'I was just wondering where you're taking me.'

He grinned. 'You'll see . . .'

The car was plunging down some very narrow and steep roads now and Grace could tell from the glorious aroma on the breeze ruffling her hair that they were close to the sea. The ocean at night had a special smell that spoke of mystery, promise and an emptiness waiting to be filled.

Gabriel parked the car and pulled a bag out of the boot. Then he took her hand and led her through the rainforest towards the sea.

'Are you sure you know where you're go— Wow!' gasped Grace. They had walked out of the trees on to the most beautiful sweep of silver moon-washed beach she had ever seen.

'How did you find this place?' she said with wonder. 'I've been here months and I've never heard anything about it.'

Gabriel had dropped to his knees and was leaning over an oil lamp. 'The location manager told me about it.'

'Is this going to be in the movie?'

He struck a match and a dim glow came from the lamp. 'They couldn't use this place as a location because there's no access for the trailers and trucks. But at least we get to see it.'

He spread a blanket on the pale silky sand and they sat down, bathed in soft light. Grace kicked her flip-flops off and stretched her long legs out on to the sand. The intimacy of the situation – their closeness, the complicit silence only punctuated by the gentle roar of the sea – made Grace want to blurt out her innermost thoughts, desires and closely guarded secrets. For the first time since she had left England, she felt light and giddy and *happy*. She felt free, as if she was letting go of her old self, coming up for air in a whole new life where she could be whatever and whoever she wanted.

'What are you smiling about?'

'This.'

'Good.'

He reached over and kissed her, gentle touches at first, growing deeper, his fingers burrowing through her hair. Instinctively she sat up and pulled off her top in one movement as he unbuttoned his own shirt. She pulled the fabric from his arms and stroked the circle of dark chest hair, the hard ripple of muscle, as he unclipped her bra. His hands moved across her body, the curve of her rib cage, the tip of her nipple, which made her gasp.

'You don't know how sexy you are,' he murmured.

For once in her life, she felt it. Not because the shape of her body had changed over the last year, or because she was lit by the flattering glow of the oil lamp. But because of how her skin felt at his melting touch. It had been too long since she had been intimate with anyone, and then it had been student fumbles. Nothing like this. Finally she understood what all the fuss was about.

He unzipped his shorts and slid out of them. His lips brushed her throat, slow butterfly kisses, working down her body as his fingers peeled off her panties. Spreading her legs, he blew lightly on her swollen clitoris, then stroked it with his cock as she groaned in almost unbearable pleasure. Finally he dipped into her, and as they rocked together, feeling his thickness, her stomach knotted in pent-up desire, her back arching as she reached the brink, and then *oh yes, oh yes,* that sweet release, the flood of liquid fire that rippled towards every nerve ending in her body. And then a blissful calm.

Afterwards, they lay on the blanket, damp bodies spooned together, naked in the soft saffron lamplight.

'I've never done that before.'

'Sex?'

'Sex on a beach.'

'Me neither.'

She laughed again and pushed him over on his back.

'What's funny now?'

'Oh, just that I thought a sophisticated literary figure like yourself would be doing this sort of thing all the time.'

'Well, I hope I can keep disappointing you this way.'

'What are you doing tomorrow?' she asked, feeling bold.

'Seeing you, hopefully.'

'For a repeat performance.' She giggled.

'Come back to my hotel with me,' he said, circling his fingertip around her nipple. 'Why wait until tomorrow?'

15

Miles lifted his head from the pillow. What was that? His fuzzy brain, slowed by two bottles of claret at the Bear Inn, struggled to focus. He cursed at being woken up from his slumber. These poky little rooms in Oriel College were too old, too creaky, and with their stone floors and wood-panelled walls, you could hear everything all the way down to St Mary's Quad. Miles grabbed his pillow and pulled it over his head. He did, of course, have one of the better rooms in college, but still it was more than any civilised person could be expected to bear; and what *was* it, anyway?

Growling in annoyance, he pulled the pillow away and lifted his head, cocking an ear. It sounded like singing . . . no, chanting. It was almost haunting, melancholy, like a Gregorian chant, as it echoed down the halls. And then a shout went up: 'We're coming, you wanker!' Finally Miles' sluggish brain made the connection and his heart gave a leap: it was the Carrington Club!

The Carrington was the most elite society at Oxford, nominally a dining club, in reality an excuse for the very top boys from the best families in the university to get together and forge vital links with people who would be the next generation of political leaders and captains of industry. The 'Carrie' was over two hundred years old, and membership was strictly limited: always male, usually second- or third-year undergraduates and almost exclusively confined to those who could

138

afford it – even the uniform, of Oxford-blue tails and amber waistcoat, bought only from Ede and Ravenscroft, cost skywards of a thousand pounds. And of course, you did not ask to be a member of the Carrington Club. You were selected by secret ballot and your invitation to join was delivered by way of a visitation from the club's membership in the dead of night. Traditionally, they would kick in your door, trash your room and force you to undergo a variety of humiliating initiation rituals. A smile crept on to Miles' face. He'd expected his invitation, of course, but not this soon. It was rare for a member to be initiated in his first year, unless they were considered an exceptional candidate. Father won't be able to ignore this, he thought as the noise swelled to a crescendo, bracing himself for the boot on his door.

It never came. The chanting, shouting procession passed on down the corridor, then stopped. There was a sudden terrible silence as Miles strained his ears, frowning. What the hell was going on?

Then there was a crash from next door and a roar of a dozen voices at once, and rising above them all, the shouts of one excited voice calling them all bastards. Miles recognised it immediately: Ewan Donaldson, a boy from the year above him at Eton. He was popular, sporty and clever; more importantly, his father was some influential European ambassador. They had come to initiate Donaldson, not Miles. 'Bastards is right,' hissed Miles, pulling the pillow back over his head. *Bastards!*

Even after the noise had faded, Miles had found it impossible to sleep, tossing and turning, running it over in his head. Donaldson was such a stiff; the only reason anyone talked to him was because he was good at rugger and because they wanted to get to know his father. The Carrington could be so bloody predictable. Finally he admitted defeat when the dawn light began pushing under his curtains, and he got up and dressed, sitting in his window seat, chain-smoking. He tried not to get too worked up but it was a struggle. He was genuinely enjoying Oxford. After the Angel Cay holiday, he'd been desperate to go to university, having spent the rest of the summer staying with various friends to avoid seeing too much of his sister and parents. Oxford had been his sanctuary, his refuge; although at times like this it was traditional and stifling.

At eight thirty there was a knock at the door and Miles glared towards the entrance. He had no desire to speak to anyone this morning, and anyway, who would be bothering him at this hour? Everyone knew that Miles tended to pass on morning lectures as a rule. He stubbed out his cigarette and sighed.

'Enter.'

Jonathon Taylor bounced in. He was an old Etonian friend also reading History at Oriel. He was big-boned, awkward and a little clumsy – Miles had always thought of him as a big floppy Labrador. But like the dog, Jon had hidden teeth, and he always had his ear to the ground regarding gossip.

'Where were you at breakfast?' he said, taking one of Miles' cigarettes without asking and perching on his desk. 'Did you hear about Donaldson and the Carrington?'

'Of course I fucking heard about it,' snapped Miles. 'I could hardly miss it, could I? Bloody racket woke me up and kept me up all night. Don't they realise prelims are around the corner? I've got a good mind to complain to the Dean.'

Jonathon laughed. 'If it's any consolation, they absolutely trashed his room and sprayed fire extinguisher foam all over his Patek Philippe.'

'Boo fucking hoo.'

Jonathon slapped his leg in delight. 'You're jealous!'

'Jealous?' said Miles, snatching his cigarettes back.

'Come on, Ashford. You want to join the Carrie and Donaldson got the nod.'

Miles glared at him. 'What crap. The Carrington's for blue-blooded pricks. Their pranks are idiotic and juvenile. I mean, what's the point in smashing up Dono's stuff? If they'd done that to me, I'd have had the coppers on them so fast it would make their heads swim.'

Jonathon was laughing now. 'So you're telling me you'd have turned them down? Not that they're ever going to ask you, of course.'

Miles narrowed his eyes at his friend. How dare he? At least two members of the Carrington had discreetly indicated they were putting his name forward. But then, Jonathon Taylor was rarely wrong when it came to these things.

'What have you heard?' said Miles.

Jonathon grinned, knowing he'd hit a nerve. 'Come on, Miles, don't act so surprised,' he said. 'You've pissed off so many people over the years, not just here, but at Eton, you can hardly expect there to be a unanimous vote for you.'

Miles was putting a brave face on it, but it was a body blow. He had always assumed that he would be welcomed into all the establishment institutions with open arms – he was Miles Ashford, after all! – but then maybe that was the problem. He may have been a popular figure at Eton and king of the hill at Danehurst, but Jonathon was right: anyone who dared to stick their head above the parapet risked making enemies. And one of those wankers had blackballed him from the Carrington.

'I shouldn't worry too much. It's probably not about you anyway.'

'What do you mean?'

Jonathon shrugged and sauntered towards the door. 'Oh, you know how it is with the Carrie. It's not who you are, it's who your family is.'

'Fucking snobs,' spat Miles after Jonathon had left the room.

Of course he had both suffered and benefited from his

father's status as one of the country's most prominent businessmen over the years. People knew who he was, they knew he was rich, but at Eton, it counted for nothing. At Eton, the seat of kings, it wasn't money that was important, it was *heritage*. Of course money was important to the aristocracy, but a title always trumped a bank balance and the offspring of self-made men were seen as second-class citizens. Miles had risen above it, scrabbling his way to the top by sheer force of personality. Until it had all gone to his head and he had overstepped the mark, stupidly leaving his hash, tobacco and jumbo Rizlas out in an ashtray by his bed for anyone to see. Even he could see that his ego had got the better of him that time, and he had sworn it wouldn't happen again.

Grabbing his cigarettes, he stalked out of the building and into the college grounds. They were unusually empty for such a sunny day. Normally there would be groups of students sitting around on the grass, smoking and chatting, but it was approaching exam time; most people were probably in their rooms studying. Where I should be, thought Miles. If he was honest, his studies at Oxford weren't exactly going to plan. He'd already had a frank discussion with his tutor about his scant attendance and the late arrival of a number of essays, not to mention their somewhat sketchy content.

He marched angrily towards the river. Someone shouted his name, but he ignored them, not wanting to speak to anyone at that moment. He increased his pace and walked on through the water meadows until he came to a white-painted wooden bridge that looked like it would have been more at home in Amsterdam. Stopping in the middle, he leant on the railings and looked down at the placid green waters.

Once he had calmed down a little, Miles tried to trace the source of his anger. In theory, he agreed with everything he had said to Jonathon about the Carrington: it was an old-fashioned manifestation of the British class system, which, while still thriving out here in little pockets of Oxford, was swiftly dying. But still. The truth was, Miles Ashford wanted to be a Carrington man. He wanted the status and position his father would never enjoy; he wanted to be part of an elite only a few were ever asked to join. But it was more than that. Miles wanted to be seen as an individual, someone with his own achievements and persona, not just as the son of 'x', the friend of 'y'. He wanted to be looked up to because he was Miles Ashford. Pure and simple.

And then he had a sudden moment of clarity. *They were threatened by him.* Miles Ashford represented the new guard, a fusion of his father's new money and his mother's old-fashioned British class. He was too good for the Carrington, too good, in fact, for this whole dried-up cap-doffing university. He turned and ran back the way he came, sprinting all the way to his room.

When Jonathon knocked on his door four hours later, he was surprised to find Miles hard at work.

'Rue and Tig and the rest are all going to the White Hart. We wondered if you wanted to . . .' he began, but trailed off, disconcerted by the strange spectacle of Miles Ashford bent over a book, scribbling intently away. 'Are you OK, Miles?' he asked.

Finally Miles looked up. 'Yes, why do you ask?'

Jonathon gestured vaguely at Miles' desk. 'Don't think I've ever seen you hitting the books before. Finally panicking about exams?'

Miles frowned, then shook his head. 'Oh no,' he said, smiling slowly. 'Something much better. I'm starting my own club.'

16

'Are we there yet?' Gavin popped his head around the driver's seat hopefully.

'No,' snapped Jez, turning his head from the steering wheel. 'And if Alex stopped looking at those tits, we might have more of an idea where we were.'

'Actually, I was just reading about that coup going on in Russia,' said Alex, hastily folding up his copy of the *Sun* and picking up the tatty road atlas.

'Russians?' said Gavin. 'They'd better not let the nukes loose. Not before we've had a proper sound check, anyway. That last gig was a disaster.'

'Bollocks to Russia,' said Jez, wrestling with the gear stick. 'I'll just be happy if we make it to Bath in one bloody piece.'

Ah, the glamour of rock and roll, thought Alex to himself.

The last six months had gone by in a blur of exhaust fumes and ringing ears. Jez and Pete had graduated, and Gav had dropped out of his art course. From the night they had first met at The Boardwalk, every spare moment had been spent in the cellar practising until they were ready for their debut gig at the Queen of Hearts pub in Fallowfield. They had gone down a storm with the partisan indie crowd and Alex had felt twelve feet tall. The moment the lads had left college, they each put five hundred quid into the pot so they could buy a transit van. It was twelve years old, almost white and had 'J. & H. Hall Window Cleaners' written down the side in big blue letters. Fortunately it had been a warmish summer and they had been able to sleep in the van between tiny gigs where they would play to six or seven mildly uninterested drinkers then move on to the next place, hoping that this one would cover the cost of the petrol and the service-station pasties. It sounded horrible, but it had been the best few months of their lives. The band, Year Zero, were getting better, tighter with every performance and they all felt they were moving towards something big – whatever that was.

Alex switched on the radio and Bryan Adams' 'Everything I Do, I Do It For You' blared out.

'Is this still number one?' groaned Jez, navigating the traffic. 'Shit, what road are we looking for again?'

'George Street, but the promoter said if we stay on the A4, it will bring us around to the venue.'

'Well where is it then?'

'I don't know!' said Alex, exasperated.

'Come on now, children,' said Pete from the back.

'Piss off!' said Alex and Jez in unison.

It was the same every time they came to a new city. The cameraderie of the road immediately disappeared, to be replaced by annoyance and anxiety; the romance blown away by the reality of rickety stages or playing to empty rooms. No one told you that breaking into the music business was like Dante's Circles of Hell, where you had to suffer for an undetermined period at the first level before scrabbling your way to the next.

Tonight's gig was exciting, because Bath Moles Club was a leap up from the working men's clubs and venues where you were lucky to get fifty quid and a round of drinks to play. When you played Bath Moles, you were on your way up.

Alex hoped so. He had given up his job at Kwik Save and was signing on, and by joining the band he had put all his eggs in one basket; he had to make it work, there was no Plan B. He felt guilty he couldn't give his mum her thirty pounds a week any more, but strangely, she seemed thrilled that he was giving his music a real go.

'Is this it?' asked Pete with disappointment as they finally parked and climbed out of the van. It was evident from their faces that the rest of the band were feeling the same way. The club entrance was a tiny door set into a wall just off the main road: no sign, no posters; it looked like a storage room.

Disconsolately they humped their heavy gear in through the tiny door and set it up on the stage, fitting it into whatever space they could find. The sound engineer, a standard-issue balding guy in a black band T-shirt, ran around plugging cables into sockets and fiddling with the knobs and sliders on an enormous mixing desk at the back of the room.

'All right lads,' he said finally. 'Can you play us something to get the levels?'

'Shall we do "Evermore"?' said Jez. 'I think we should close the set with that tonight.'

Alex frowned. 'What about "Wonderland"?' It was his strongest song and the one they usually ended with.

Jez looked at him dismissively. 'I thought we should mix it up a bit tonight.'

Alex felt unsettled. What Year Zero were desperate for was to get noticed. And as no one really came to see the support band, the best way to do that was to put your good material near the end, where people turning up for the main act would hear it.

'We're ending with "Evermore",' said Jez with finality.

Alex sighed. It was hard to railroad Jez into anything once he had made his mind up. The band was his baby and he was the undisputed leader. He was the one who rang all the venues and charmed the promoters and designed the posters.

Alex accepted that and had no intention of usurping him; he himself just wanted to play music. But Jez had obviously become threatened by Alex ever since he had begun to take over musically. It was the elephant in the room for the band: everyone knew Alex was the better songwriter, and even with their meagre audiences, his songs got by far the loudest cheers. Jez – or Jez's ego – was predictably in denial about it, so Alex always had to tread carefully and had become a master of psychological manipulation.

'How about we open with "Evermore",' said Alex in placating tones. 'Everyone knows you start with your best song and end with the next best. You're right that "Evermore" is the best thing we've got.' He smiled to himself. It was text-book reverse psychology: let the alpha male think it was all his idea.

'All right then,' said Jez, waving a regal arm. 'It's only a support gig anyway, isn't it?'

'Oi!'

They all turned to see the sound engineer standing in the middle of the tiny dance floor, tapping his watch.

'If you ladies are quite finished, I'd like to get this sound check done before the punters get here.'

'Hey, aren't you that big rock star?'

After they had finished the sound check, Alex had headed straight out of the venue, wanting to get as far away from Jez as possible. Jez had agreed to the change in the set list, but as punishment, kept stopping the songs to complain about Alex's playing or to ask him to tune his guitar properly. Head down, mind full of fantasies of strangling the singer, Alex had walked straight past the girl leaning against the railings smoking a cigarette. He looked up in surprise, then beamed. It was Emma.

'What the hell are you doing here?'

'Aw shucks, if I'd known you were going to come over all romantic with me, I'd have been here sooner.'

They both laughed and Alex slipped his arm around her waist to pull her in for a kiss.

'I hadn't expected to see a friendly face in this whole city, let alone you.'

She wrapped herself around him. 'Hitler giving you a hard time again?'

'No more than usual.'

'Well, we thought you might need some support, so we drove down from Manchester this morning.'

'Who's we?'

'Jemma from my course. Her parents live just outside Bath. She says you can all stay tonight.' She sniffed at his shirt. 'If you spend one more night in that van, I think the health and safety people are going to be after you.'

'You mean I smell?'

'Horribly.' She grinned.

'Well I'm glad you've got me a bed for the night, then.'

'If you play your cards right,' said Emma, patting him on the bum playfully. 'And you can start by buying me a drink.'

Alex smiled as they walked hand in hand towards the nearest pub. He was glad she was here. In fact, it wasn't until he'd seen her standing there that he'd realised how much he'd missed her. From that first night in the Snoopy nightie, it had been quite obvious she liked him, so the next day he had gone up and knocked on her door, boldly asking her out for a drink. Six months later, they were still together. Stronger than ever.

They settled into a booth in the corner of a quiet old man's pub.

'Here,' said Emma, licking her thumb and gently wiping

148

it across his cheek. 'Spot of dirt or something,' she said. 'You never know who's going to be watching tonight.'

'There ain't going to be any record company scouts in Bath,' said Alex wearily.

'Well, journalists then. Even if you only get something in the local paper, it all counts, doesn't it?'

Alex looked at her. 'Thanks,' he said.

'What for?'

'For, you know,' he said clumsily. 'For being here.'

'Who would want to miss another performance by the great Alex Doyle?' she teased. 'Anyway, I think Jemma has ulterior motives letting you lot stay tonight.'

Alex raised his eyebrows. 'Not Jez?'

Emma gave a wry smile. 'Who else?'

'Well tell her not to get too attached,' said Alex, taking a sip of his pint.

'Is he that bad?'

'He's not good, put it that way.'

'How many women has he slept with?' said Emma, running a finger around the rim of her glass.

'Dunno. A lot.'

'And how many women have you slept with?'

'This year? One,' said Alex. 'But she wasn't much cop.'

'Hey!' cried Emma, swatting him on the arm.

A sweep of affection for her caught him by surprise. She was easy to talk to and she made him laugh, but she was clever, too. She'd just missed out on getting a first and had ambitions to work in television. Life with Emma had settled into a comfortable routine. She had moved out of the big house in Fallowfield, and when Alex wasn't on the road, they stayed in her bedsit in Withington, venturing out to a gig or to see a foreign film at the Cornerhouse, which – with her fluent French and working Italian – she seemed to enjoy more than he did. And she was always interested in his music, coming to every gig and listening to his demos.

149

'Come on, let's go and be tourists,' he said, taking her hand and leading her out of the pub and down towards the river they'd seen on the way in. Hand in hand they strolled along the banks of the River Avon, the weak sun warming the backs of their necks.

'If you get a record deal, are you going to move to London?' she asked suddenly.

'Maybe. But only if you agreed to come down to the big, bad smoke with me.'

'Really?' she said, unable to hide her delight. 'I didn't think you were the settling-down type.'

'Don't take the piss, this isn't easy for me.'

'I'd jump at the chance,' she said, her mouth closing in a determined line. 'When I said I wanted to work in TV, I didn't think I'd end up as a guide at Granada Studios Tours.'

'Come on. You get to walk up and down Coronation Street every day.'

'We're bigger than all this, Alex. You and me. Why shouldn't we be telly producers or rock stars just 'cos we're not rich or privileged?'

He grabbed her hand in solidarity.

For all his bitching about Jez, Alex was about ten times as happy as he had been before he had joined the band; in fact that black cloud which had been following around in the dark months earlier on in the year seemed to have completely gone. Now happy was a constant state: he was happy writing music, happy going to gigs, happy on stage, although sharing anything with Jez was increasingly hard work. But for the first time in a long time, perhaps ever, Alex realised he was happy just being with another person. He kissed her, hard, sliding his hands inside her T-shirt, stroking her back, slipping his fingers into the waistband of her jeans.

'Steady there, sailor,' she grinned, breaking off. 'Not before the big match.'

'I think you're thinking of boxers there.' Alex smiled.

'Same deal,' said Emma, jumping up and pulling his hand. 'Now come on, stud, let's show all those screaming fans what you can do.'

Three hours later, Alex was ready to kill someone. Red-faced and sweaty, the band clattered off stage, cramming into the tiny backstage changing room. Outside, they could still hear the cheering demands for an encore, but Alex could not enjoy the ecstatic reception they had received.

'You fucking wanker!' he yelled, kicking out at a wooden bench. 'What the hell was that about?'

Jez sauntered down the steps. 'What?' He smiled. 'Can't take the fact that the girls are more interested in me?'

Alex lunged at him, but Gav and Pete caught him first.

'Al, it's not worth it.'

But they looked as angry as Alex felt.

'You really are a prick sometimes, Jez,' said Pete, glaring at him. 'This is a band, you know; we're not your fucking backing group.'

But Jez just laughed at him. 'Well that crowd out there seemed to enjoy themselves. Doesn't matter who they're looking at if they're enjoying the music, does it?'

'But you screwed with the music too, you dick!' yelled Alex. 'You could barely hear the melody over your bellowing!'

'Ah, you're just jealous,' hissed Jez.

'No, Jez, I am *not* jealous,' snapped Alex. 'I don't want the spotlight. You can preen and pose all you like for all I care. What I do care about is when your pathetic ego gets between us and the songs. We *all* make the music, or hadn't you noticed?'

Jez tossed his blond bob back off his face and walked back out of the changing room.

'Wanker,' said the normally mild-mannered Gav.

Alex wasn't sure how long Jez had stayed behind at the

club after he'd left to go for his walk with Emma, but it had been long enough. Clearly he had charmed the engineer into rejigging the sound in his favour. From the start, Jez's vocals had dominated the songs, with Alex and Pete's guitars being turned down at key moments so Jez wouldn't be over-shadowed. He had even fixed it so that the lights were on him for the whole set while everyone else was practically in the dark. Luckily they knew the songs well enough to play without looking at their instruments but it had still affected their performance.

Alex locked himself into the small toilet cubicle and splashed water on to his face.

'Al? Are you in there?' yelled Pete. 'We're going for a drink out front. Wanna come?'

'Be there in a minute, yeah?'

He changed into his least-dirty T-shirt and packed his guitar away. *That's it,* he thought as he fastened the latches on the case. *I've had enough.* Whichever way you looked at it, Jez Harrison was bad news and Alex could feel in his heart that Year Zero's singer was going to get worse not better the more successful they became. He felt relief and anger, but most of all he felt sadness. He had ploughed himself into this band and it was depressing that he would have to start again. *But I will,* he thought defiantly. *My songs are good. I'll form a new band where I don't have to listen to the singer's delusions of grandeur.* It was best to get out now while it still didn't matter.

He pushed through the dressing-room door and out into the busy club. Steeling himself to quit, he stopped when he saw Jez leaning on the bar looking pleased with himself, while Emma was deep in conversation with some old bloke in glasses.

'Hey, Alex, come and meet someone,' said Jez, putting his arm around Alex as if nothing had happened. 'This is Rob Hatton,' he added, catching Alex's eye and giving him a mean-ingful look. 'Rob's from Argent Records.'

The man put out a hand. 'Good to meet you, Alex,' he said. 'Emma here tells me you wrote a couple of the songs. I was impressed.'

'Really?' stuttered Alex. 'I ... well, I'm, uh, glad.'

Jez laughed. 'Alex is more of a musical genius,' he said in a stage whisper. 'Brilliant in the studio, but I think I'll handle the interviews, eh?'

Cocky bastard, thought Alex.

'I drove over from our London office to see the main act tonight,' said Rob.' Good thing I got here a bit early.'

'So did you like it?' asked Alex eagerly.

Rob shrugged. 'Half of what I heard was absolute shit, but there are a couple of pearls in there too. Particularly liked the last song.'

'"Wonderland"? Yeah, that's one I wrote ...'

'We *all* wrote,' corrected Jez.

'So are you interested, Mr Hatton?' asked Emma sweetly.

'I'm definitely interested, love,' he said, looking her up and down hungrily. 'But I want to hear more.'

'Are you saying you'll sign us?' asked Pete hopefully.

Rob started laughing. 'Slow down, kids. I'm saying I want the boss to come and listen to you northern monkeys, see if he hears what I hear.'

'And what do you hear?' asked Alex.

'Cash registers ringing, son: the beautiful sound of money.'

'Come on, Rob,' said Jez, putting a pally hand on the man's shoulder and leading him towards a group of excited-looking girls. 'Let me introduce you to a couple of our biggest fans ...'

'Hey!'

Suddenly Alex was knocked sideways as Emma jumped on him, giving him a crushing hug.

'Isn't it brilliant?' She grinned. 'I *told* you!'

Alex hugged her back and laughed. 'Yes, you did,' he said. Her face was lit up with genuine pleasure at their good fortune, glowing with adoration and expectation for the future. And to think that only five minutes ago, he had decided to leave the band.

Life could change in an instant. He'd learnt that before. Although this time it looked as if things were going to take a turn for the better.

17

'Just five more minutes,' said Grace, pulling the cool white sheet further over her head. It had been a particularly hard shift on the *Highlander* that afternoon. August was the perfect time to visit Port Douglas, so the town was full of honeymooners who all seemed to want to take boat trips to the Low Isles and she had been rushed off her feet.

'No, no more minutes,' said Caro, standing at her bedroom door, munching a huge red apple. 'You have to get ready.'

Grace grunted and waved an arm. 'The taxi's not coming for twenty minutes.'

Caro laughed. 'I can't believe you're going to the biggest, glammest showbiz party this part of Australia has ever seen, and you're still in bed!'

Grace sat up reluctantly. She had been glad that Caro had decided to postpone her trip to India for a few weeks – 'Can't leave you alone with that strange man' had been her exact words – but she could have done without her friend standing over her this evening.

'All right, all right, I'm getting up . . .' she said, swinging her legs on to the floor. She stood up – then immediately sat down again, clutching her head. 'Whoa.'

'You OK, honey?' asked Caro.

Grace forced a smile. 'Yes, I'm fine, just got up too quick. Been feeling a bit off-colour today, that's all.'

'You're not pregnant, are you?' Caro's tone was serious.

The word seemed to drop to the floor and splinter into tiny pieces.

'*Pregnant?*' laughed Grace nervously. 'Don't be daft.'

'I'm not joking,' said Caro. 'You were sick on the *Highlander* again today, weren't you? I heard you in the bathroom.'

Grace waved away the suggestion and stood up, trying to look more vigorous than she felt. 'It was a bad prawn or something.'

'Hey, don't go blaming my seafood buffet.' She kept hold of Grace's hand and pulled her back on to the bed. 'Seriously, Grace. My mum's a midwife and I know the signs: sickness, tiredness – and you never get tired. I've always thought you were battery-powered.'

Grace laughed, but inside she could feel a slow flutter of panic. *Am I pregnant?* she thought. *Would I know if I was?* Even as a teenager, she was never exactly sure when her period would come. She had a long, irregular menstrual cycle which meant she could never pinpoint when it would arrive. Even so, thinking back over the past few weeks, she had definitely missed one, if not two. And Caro was right: for the last couple of days it had been hell on the boat. Grace had tried to put it down to choppy waters, but the truth was it had been calm all week.

Caro was searching her face. 'You've missed your period, haven't you?' she asked softly.

'I'm a bit late, that's all.'

'Late or missed?' pressed Caro. 'Crucial difference.'

Grace forced herself to look at her friend. 'Missed, I guess,' she croaked, her throat dry. 'But I've only been seeing Gabe a few weeks.'

'A few weeks? All it takes is one night.' Caro put her hands on her hips. 'OK, let's find out for sure. We're going to take a test.'

Grace's already sick stomach turned over at the prospect. 'No, Caro, I'm fine,' she said.

156

Caro fixed her with a severe look. 'Take a test. In fact I've got one upstairs. I had a false alarm a few months back with Jago, that backpacker from Stockholm. Anyway, the test came in a two-pack.'

'Caro, I'm just tired . . .'

'Well if that's true, you've got nothing to worry about, have you? Wait here, I'll just be a minute.'

Grace walked through to the bathroom and looked at herself in the round mirror above the sink. All the colour had drained from her face. *Yeah, well things were going too well,* her reflection seemed to be saying.

She wiped a towel slowly over her face. She *couldn't* be pregnant. OK, for the first month of her relationship with Gabe, she hadn't been on the pill – it had felt as if she was tempting fate, as if doing something so planned would put a jinx on the relationship. It had been so effortless, so spontaneous, going to a doctor for contraception seemed far too calculated and unromantic. But it wasn't as if they hadn't taken precautions. For all of Gabe's staunchly Catholic upbringing, they'd used condoms every time they'd had sex. She felt her heart drop. Except that first time on the beach.

Caro ran back in waving a small pink cardboard box. 'I think it's still in its Best Before lifespan.'

Grace took it cautiously, then went into the bathroom. She was a practical girl and she actually found comfort in carefully following the instructions inside the box. It meant she could concentrate on this one task and pretend that the outcome would take care of itself.

Instructions followed, she walked back into the bedroom and handed the stick to Caro. 'You read it,' she said numbly.

'Positive,' said Caro, reaching out for Grace's hand. 'Is that a good thing?'

Grace couldn't speak. This wasn't happening. It *couldn't* be happening. Perhaps she was just ill, delirious. Perhaps she was still asleep in her bed, dreaming this nightmare.

'OK,' said Caro, jumping up and taking Grace's dress from the wardrobe door. 'Here, put it on. The taxi will be here any moment and we haven't done your hair.'

Grace looked at her friend with disbelief. 'And what? Have a laugh and a joke with Gabriel, pretending I'm not having his child?'

Caro shook her head. 'Of course not. You have to tell him.'

'What? No! I can't. He's due to fly back to New York on Friday.'

'Grace, listen to me. You have to go tonight. You have to tell him.'

Exhaling slowly, Grace willed herself to keep calm.

'Put some bright red lippy on,' said Caro. 'Pour yourself into that dress and you'll be ready to face the world, I promise.'

Grace stood up. *Face the world.* That was the last thing she wanted.

Grace gazed out of the taxi window, staring at the dark sea as the car wound around the steep coastline. The party to celebrate the end of filming *Cast No Shadow* was being held at the director's rented Balinese-style house in the lush hills behind Port Douglas. Grace had been more than a little surprised to receive the invitation; after all, she'd only been seeing Gabriel for a few weeks and would hardly have dared consider him her official 'boyfriend'. Since that first night together on the secret beach, they had seen each other at least three times a week, but if Grace was totally honest with herself, there was a good chance this was nothing more than a holiday romance.

Then again, it wasn't as if Gabriel had to be on the set. She had dared to wonder if he had stayed in Port Douglas for her or whether he had just been sucked into the allure of Hollywood. She grimaced. *Whichever. When he hears about this, he's going to be off like a rat up a drainpipe.*

'Grace, there you are! I want you to meet some people,'

said Gabe as soon as she'd seen him through the crowd.

Grace froze. 'Some people' was David Robb, the star of the movie and one of the biggest names in Hollywood. Robb exuded that slick, untouchable confidence that all ultra-successful people seemed to possess. He pumped Grace's hand as they were introduced, holding it for a minute longer than necessary, a trick that her father used to draw people into his confidence and anoint them with his glow, if just for a few precious seconds of his time.

'So, Grace, what do you do out here?'

'I work on a boat.'

'Grace wants to be a writer too,' said Gabriel, sliding his arm around her shoulder in an almost paternal way. 'I'm putting her in front of my agent as soon as we get back to New York.'

Grace looked up at him sharply. New York? 'We'? He hadn't mentioned this to her; in fact he had never spoken about them as a plural or of them having any future together, now she thought about it.

The future. What would that be? A cold sterile room? A nurse with rubber gloves and a tray of steel instruments? How much would it hurt? How late could she leave it? She'd wished she'd paid more attention to those stories in the women's magazines, but back then, she'd thought it would never happen to her.

'Write a role in there for me, won't you?'

'Sorry?'

'A role. For me,' smiled David. 'When you sell the movie rights for your first book, I want to take the leading role. Make him sexy too, OK?'

He was smiling his megawatt smile, but already the star was looking over her shoulder, eager to move on.

'Well, I think you're the first person to ever resist the David Robb charm offensive.' Gabe chuckled.

'Not my type,' she said, forcing a smile.

Gabriel caught the look and frowned slightly. 'Are you OK?' he asked, touching her on the arm.

'Of course,' she said breezily. 'This is my first Hollywood party. I'm a bit overawed.'

'Ah.' He nodded. 'Well I'm a bit out of my depth myself. Writers' parties are nothing like this, let me tell you.'

A waiter passed by with a tray of champagne and Grace automatically reached for one, desperate to calm her nerves, but then instantly recoiled as she remembered her condition.

'I was just telling Gabriel how he should come to LA for six months or so,' said a man in a cap. Gabriel introduced him as Neil Berry, the film's director.

'What do you think, Grace? We need storytellers like him out there and he's sure as shit gonna make more than writing those fruity little books of his. I was on the phone to Joe Eszterhas this morning. The buzz on *Basic Instinct* is good, and if it does great box office, he can charge three million a script.'

Grace nodded and smiled thinly. She was beginning to feel dizzy now. She needed fresh air.

'Sorry, could you excuse me? I'm just going outside.'

'You OK?' asked Gabe.

'Fine.'

She walked into the grounds and sat on the terrace overlooking the party. Sitting in the dark, her hand on her quite flat belly, she felt vulnerable and alone, so far away from home. She was twenty-two; it wasn't too young to have a baby. *But am I ready?*

Through the floor-to-ceiling windows, Grace could see Gabriel inside, effortlessly gliding from person to person – actors, producers, studio heads, all the top people at the party. Writers might be bottom of the totem pole in Hollywood, but not this writer. They all wanted to talk to him, his very presence made them feel more intelligent. Was this man ready

160

to be a father? With her? The reality was she just didn't know, because she barely knew Gabriel. He would certainly be against an abortion. His family were staunchly Catholic, and while Gabriel was more relaxed, his faith was still important to him; his novels were laced with religious symbolism, and every Sunday he went to the local Catholic church for mass. Grace dearly wished she had such strong spiritual principles; at least it would make the decision easier. One thing she was sure of though: she had to be responsible for her own actions. She'd learnt the hard way that you had to make the right decisions, not the easy ones.

Finally Gabriel bounced up the steps towards her holding two flutes of champagne aloft.

'Refreshments.' He smiled, sitting down next to her. 'You know, I've been thinking. Maybe I don't have to go back to New York immediately.'

'Is Hollywood calling?'

'Actually I was thinking of staying here,' he said quietly, taking hold of her fingers. He turned to look at her and she felt a rush of emotion so strong she was glad she was sitting down.

Was this love? she asked herself. Proper grown-up love, complete with responsibilities and difficulties. For a split second she vaguely thought of Alex Doyle, but she could barely recall his face.

'I'm behind on the new novel and there are too many distractions in New York, so I'm postponing my flight home. For a few weeks at least.'

'So I'm not a distraction?' she chided.

'I didn't mean that.' He took a sip of champagne and she watched his lips touch the rim of the glass. 'When are you going back to England?'

'I thought I'd try and stay out here for a while longer.'

'I thought your visa was for a year.'

'I can fly out and come back again.'

161

He looked at her eyes, dark and creamy. 'Like fly to New York.'

'If the offer's open.'

Suddenly he looked awkward. 'You know I can't make any promises about what happens next, but if you do go back to London, it's just a seven-hour flight to JFK.'

'Round the corner, then.'

'It's better than Australia.'

She turn to face him and looked directly in his eyes.

'I think I'm pregnant,' she said, unable to keep it inside her any longer.

The words seemed to hang in the air between them.

'Are you sure?' he said, his voice calm and measured. Grace felt a pang of disappointment and pushed it aside. What had she expected? 'Oh darling, that's wonderful!'?

'I did a test,' she said quietly.

He puffed out his cheeks. 'Fuck.'

Grace gave a little bitter laugh. 'It's not exactly what I had planned either, Gabe.'

He glanced back and touched her leg. 'Sorry, sorry, I'm not thinking straight, I didn't mean how it sounded. It's just it's all a bit of a shock.'

'For me too, Gabe. I wasn't even sure I should tell you, what with you going back to New York, even if you are staying in Port Douglas a bit longer.'

'Have you made a doctor's appointment?'

Grace shook her head. 'I only did the pregnancy test before I came out.'

'So it's not definite?'

'I suppose not.'

He glanced down at her stomach, as if he expected her to have a bump there already. 'I'm surprised you came to the party,' he said.

'Caro forced me. Besides, I couldn't miss out on seeing David Robb's teeth close up, could I?'

He gave a little laugh, but the smile didn't reach his eyes. 'You're right, I should go,' replied Grace.

He took her elbow. 'Don't be stupid. I'm coming with you. We can go to the doctor together in the morning.'

'But it's your wrap party.'

'I've been to enough parties,' he said, taking her hand and leading her out of the house.

When Grace woke, sunlight was streaming through the louvred windows and Gabe's side of the bed was empty. Panicking, she turned over, her fingers finding a note on the pillow.

'Breakfast with the producer. Can we go to the doctor's this afternoon? Gabriel. PS Caro's left for the boat already. She says she'll make your excuses.'

Great, she thought, wondering if he had legged it out of the country.

Determined not to sit in the house moping, she called the doctor's, who could only see her at 5 p.m. anyway. Throwing on a tracksuit, she went to the grocery store on Macrossan Street, filling up her basket with healthy things. At the chemist she bought another pregnancy test, running through the process the second she returned home, chewing her nails on the edge of the bath as she waited for the pink line to appear. 'No question now,' she said as she buried it at the bottom of the trash can.

When Gabriel got back to the cottage at midday, Grace was busy in the kitchen making a chicken salad. He came up behind her and embraced her awkwardly.

'How are you feeling?'

She forced a smile. 'I'm pregnant, not ill, Gabe.'

She brought two plates across to the table and sat down.

'So what did the producer want?' she asked as they began to eat.

His face became animated. 'Apparently the studio want to

green-light *Beachcombers*. They bought the options a couple of years ago but the studio head loves the rushes to *Cast No Shadows* and want to get something else into production.'

Grace put down her fork. 'Oh Gabe, that's fantastic.'

They smiled at each other, both pretending that this strained normality was real, that they were just a couple discussing Gabriel's day at work. Finally Gabriel cracked, pushing his plate away and burying his head in his hands.

'I'm sorry, Grace,' he said, rubbing his palms into his eyes. 'I've been terrible, haven't I? I just don't know how to ... it's all just such a surprise.'

She reached out and touched his hand gently. 'I understand,' she said. 'I'm a twenty-two-year-old Brit on a gap year in Australia. This time yesterday my biggest concern was whether Caro would ever buy a pint of milk for the house. And now I'm having a baby.'

He nodded, looking up at her. 'Do you want to keep it?'

She had expected it of course, but still she didn't want to answer the question. She wanted him to come around the table and hold her, reassure her, tell her it was all OK, whatever happened. She didn't want to make life-changing choices sitting at her kitchen table, looking down at chicken wings.

'Well, what do you think?' she said. She wasn't sure she wanted to hear the answer, but she still needed to ask.

His dark eyes darted away. 'You might not be pregnant. Let's discuss it after the doctor's.'

'I've done two tests, Gabe ...'

'This is the biggest decision we will make in our lives,' he said irritably. 'We can't just discuss it like we're deciding where to go out for dinner.'

'And the one thing we can't do is pretend it's not happening.'

She broke off as the phone began to ring in the next room.

'Are you going to answer that?' he asked flatly.

Glaring at him, she walked through to pick up the receiver, then put her head round the door to call Gabe.

'It's for you,' she said, holding it out to him.

He looked as puzzled as she was. Gabriel lived in a luxurious hotel suite; that was where he did his business and he'd never received a call at Grace's before.

Grace retreated back into the kitchen, but she could hear Gabriel speaking rapidly in his native tongue, too fast to keep up with her schoolgirl Spanish, but she could tell it was serious. For several minutes he was silent, then he marched back into the kitchen and snatched up the keys to his jeep.

'Gabe, what is it?' she asked. 'Where are you going?'

'Out!' he shouted. 'I need to ... I've got to ...'

He paced around the room, his fist gripping the car keys so tightly that his knuckles had gone white. She went across and wrapped her arms around him, but he wriggled from her grip.

'Please, Grace, don't,' he said.

'Gabriel, what's wrong? Can't you tell me?'

Finally he looked at her, and Grace didn't know when she had ever seen anyone look so sad.

'It's my brother. He's dead.'

'Honey,' she whispered, moving towards him, but he just backed up against the door and threw it open. 'Gabriel!' she pleaded. 'Don't go, not in this state.'

'I just need to be alone,' he called over his shoulder. Running out on to the drive behind him, she caught a shower of dust as he gunned the jeep away.

The hours ticked slowly by. Four o'clock. Five o'clock. Her doctor's appointment was missed. She would go there tomorrow. She stayed in the kitchen preparing supper, cleaning, reading, anything to take her mind off where he was. Every ten minutes she put her nose to the window, staring out on to the street, hoping that the silver jeep would come rolling up the drive again. But as the sun set, the streets grew dark and there was still no sign of him. Tiredness engulfed her again, so she crawled on to the sofa and pulled a blanket on top of her.

When she opened her eyes, Gabriel was sitting on the floor next to her, gently stroking her hair, his face wet with tears, his breath stale from alcohol. She pulled him up on to the sofa and they held each other for a while.

'I'm so sorry,' she said quietly. Despite the hours she'd had to rehearse what she should say, everything else seemed to escape her.

'He was shot dead coming out of a restaurant,' said Gabriel, his voice barely a whisper. 'He'd just been meeting friends ...'

For a few seconds there was silence.

'I'm going back to Parador,' he said finally.

She felt a thickness in her throat, but she nodded. 'Of course.'

'Not just for the funeral. I'm going back to stay. My family want me to take over the political party.'

His voice was a monotone; his eyes were just fixed on the wall in front of him.

She sat up to face him. 'Is that what you want?' she said, being careful with her tone.

'I don't want my brother to have died pointlessly. If I can go back and make a difference, then it's the right decision.'

'Then you must go,' she said as evenly as she could. What more could she say? Don't leave me? Stay here to look after me? She couldn't – wouldn't – make him think she was springing a trap. She had already resigned herself that she had to face up to this pregnancy alone and she would do so with dignity, especially given the circumstances. But Gabriel took both her hands in his and stared into her eyes.

'I want you to come with me, Grace,' he said urgently. 'I want us to have this baby.'

For a second she could hardly breathe, and then thick tears of relief and sadness coursed down her cheeks.

He pulled her back into him and began stroking her hair.

'I love you, Gabe,' she whispered.

'I love you, too,' he said into the top of her head.

She had no idea if he meant it, but right then, in his arms, it felt like the only place in the world she wanted to be.

18

December 1991

Annalise Tuttle was the client from hell. Not quite rich enough to afford couture, she was still snobby and spoilt enough to want to look both spectacular and unique in front of her friends on London's flashy society circuit. Sasha groaned as she stood outside the Tuttles' white stucco house in South Kensington, not just in dread at the thought of the evening ahead, but under the weight of the five huge cloth bags that contained a selection of evening dresses for Annalise to try on.

Still, at least she was seeing clients on her own, thought Sasha as she rang the doorbell. She had been working as the assistant to stylist Venetia James, the woman she had met at the D&D party, for almost a year, and in that time she had done little but make coffee, iron clothes and pack suitcases, progressing to doing a little styling of her own. She had always been good at putting outfits together, but she had been delighted to discover she had a real talent for gauging what would look good on a woman. Venetia, however, wasn't so pleased, belittling her selections in front of the clients while secretly using them to her advantage. Sasha had been sorely tempted to try her hand at modelling again, but she stuck with styling because she could see that it was a growing area in every branch of the industry. The biggest names from *Vogue* magazine were being wooed away to lucrative creative jobs at the fashion houses, while others were making their marks styling runway shows for the collections in Paris, Milan and New York. But Sasha had her eye on something else, a niche few other stylists had grasped the potential of. She could see the huge potential in giving individuals their own unique style. Whether you were a celebrity, a politician or a socialite, image was increasingly everything and as most of them couldn't be trusted to come up with that fashion identity themselves, the business of personal styling looked set to explode. Sasha intended to be in the middle of it. *Which is why I need to make this work today*, she thought as she pressed the bell again.

'Where's Venetia?' snapped Annalise, as she opened the door and saw Sasha wrestling with the bags.

'Family emergency,' she lied. The truth was, Venetia was losing her grip on the business, spending more and more time partying with minor celebrities and her coke dealer. She had spent the night with the bassist from a rock band and had rung Sasha at eight that morning, begging her to take this job on her own.

'And who are you?' Annalise sniffed.

'Sasha Sinclair,' she said as brightly as she could, struggling to extend a hand from under the bags. 'I'm Venetia's partner.'

Only a little white lie, thought Sasha as Annalise reluctantly opened the door.

'Well, I hope you've been briefed,' said Annalise briskly, sweeping back into the house and up a long flight of stairs. She led Sasha into the master bedroom, which smelt of roses and had views over Onslow Square. 'The event is my husband's company's Christmas party and naturally I have to look spectacular,' she began, reclining on a vast cream armchair. 'I'm sure Venetia has told you my husband is the chairman.'

'Of course.' Sasha smiled. 'We'll make you look wonderful. Not that you need any help in that department.'

In the beginning, she had pumped clients' egos through gritted teeth, but now the compliments rolled off the tongue like a hot knife sliding through butter. She quickly began opening the cloth bags and laying the dresses carefully on the bed. By the time she got to the third bag, she was already fighting a sinking feeling in her stomach; she could tell that the selection was poor at best. They were all beautiful dresses but completely wrong for the client; the primrose-yellow and cornflower-blue gowns were wrong for Annalise's blond hair and ruddy complexion, while the charcoal theme Venetia had chosen for the rest would age anyone over forty-five. Sasha clenched her teeth together. *Bloody Venetia!* she thought. It was obvious she had just taken the first things off the rack in front of her with no thought for what would work best for the client – and it was Sasha who would have to take the flak.

'Hand me the black strapless,' said Annalise impatiently, standing behind Sasha and holding out her hand.

In full view of the open window she stripped off and slid the long, inky dress over herself before turning to the mirror.

'This is huge!' she said furiously, pulling at the sagging bust-line. 'I told Venetia I've been on the grapefruit and egg diet for the last week and this is just hanging off me.'

'Perhaps we could pin,' said Sasha uncertainly.

'And risk being stabbed all the way through dinner?' She pulled off the dress and flung it on to the bed in disgust. 'I need something else,' she demanded. 'In a size six.'

Sasha scrabbled through the dresses, looking at the labels in rising desperation. She could barely believe it; everything was a size ten.

Annalise looked as if she was about to have a meltdown.

'Seriously, all these gowns are beautiful, but you're right, Venetia hadn't briefed me properly. She told me about your

170

amazing figure and colouring, of course. You really have the most fantastic body of any celebrity I've ever worked with.'

'Hmm,' said Annalise with the hint of a smile.

'No, you need something that will show you off as the most luminous woman in the room.'

'That's exactly what I said to Venetia,' said Annalise. 'If she's not prepared to listen to me, then . . .'

'Between you and me, she's been under a lot of stress recently,' said Sasha in a low voice. 'But don't worry, I know how important this party is and I've got exactly the right piece in mind. Give me until tomorrow afternoon and you'll have the dress of the decade.

Annalise looked at her cynically. 'Well, I'm at John Frieda at midday to have my hair done. Be back here at four and don't even think about bringing me Jasper or Catherine Walker,' she added, taking a sip of iced lemon water. 'Everyone is going to be wearing them. I have to look unique, or believe me, I'm going to tell all my friends how you fouled up on my most important night of the year.'

The next day Sasha was in a fix. 'Shitterty, shit, shit,' she muttered to herself, glancing at her watch in desperation. It was almost two in the afternoon and she had zero options. Yes, over the past year she had built up good relationships with most of the fashion houses and major stores in London, and yes, if she was styling a *Vogue* shoot, she probably wouldn't have a problem pulling in some beautiful pieces. But this wasn't a photo shoot and she'd struggle to convince anyone of the benefits of rushing a dress around to Annalise Tuttle. Even if she lied and said it *was* for an editorial story, most fashion houses did not yet have London press offices and there was simply no time to get something sent over from Milan or Paris.

There was always Harvey Nichols. She had borrowed clothes from the department store on a sale-or-return basis in the past, but of course their stock would be this season's. Annalise was not going to be happy.

How did it come to this? Sasha wondered. In some ways, life was considerably better than it had been a year ago. She was now living in her own studio flat in South Kensington, albeit at the Earls Court end. She had enough money to shop at French Connection and Portobello Market, where she found vintage Ossie Clark dresses and was complimented on her style at least every day. Thanks to her natural fashion sense, she had repeatedly been offered jobs at various magazines, and it was certainly tempting. But she hadn't been able to forget what Robert Ashford had once told her over a family dinner at their Holland Park house: 'Smart people don't work for other people, Sasha,' he had said. 'Smart people don't line other people's pockets. Smart people work for themselves and build their own fortunes.' There were lots of things about that family Sasha had tried to forget, but some things were worth hanging on to.

She knew she *had* to do a great job transforming Annalise from corporate wife to soignée style-setter. Annalise was no great beauty, but she was connected. Her husband was the influential European head of an international media group and she had lots of wealthy friends, women with plenty of money but no sense of style, women Sasha could charge five hundred – no, a thousand pounds a day to look better than their friends. If she could crack this, she could become known for her style, for her power to transform. She could become a brand herself. *But first, I've got to find her something to wear.*

She ran through a mental list of where she could turn next. Grace Ashford's friend Freya worked at Lynn Franks PR and could possibly loan her a dress from one of their fashion clients, but Sasha knew she'd be on one of their 'long lunches'. Then she had a brainwave. She recalled a small piece in *Elle* about a bespoke eveningwear designer working out of south London. She took her mobile phone out of her bag. She wished these things were smaller but she liked her latest gadget. She dialled her friend Louise, a section editor on the magazine.

'Who's that guy with the atelier in Battersea?' she asked. 'Ben someone. You don't happen to have an address for him, do you?'

Scribbling it in her Filofax, she summoned a taxi.

Ben Rivera worked out of a tiny mews house in a Battersea back street. He was about thirty, of slight build and no more than five feet five tall. His bright blue eyes stared at Sasha quizzically as she swept purposefully into the studio.

'Can I help you?' he asked with amusement.

'You're not Spanish,' she said with surprise, as she took in her surroundings. There were rolls of fabric stacked up against every wall, sketches pinned to a huge cork board and mannequins swathed in elaborate folded chiffon and silk. He shook his head.

'My dad's Puerto Rican. Why, what were you expecting?'

'Your name, it sounds Spanish . . . Anyway . . .' She waved her hands in the air as she realised she was wasting time. 'I understand you make couture gowns. I need a dress.'

'OK,' he said, immediately sizing her up and down. 'I'm sure I can do something . . .'

'Not for me,' she said with irritation. 'A client.'

'Ah, you're a stylist?' he said with a little more interest. 'Which magazine?'

'Freelance.'

'Who do you work for?'

Sasha could see there was no point in pretending.

'Look, I've been asked to find a dress for a private client. Annalise Tuttle. Her husband is Richard Tuttle, CEO of News Inc., and she needs a dress for a party tonight.'

'*Tonight?*' Ben folded his arms and viewed her with good-natured cynicism. 'You do know I do bespoke dresses? It

173

takes a minimum of three weeks and four fittings with the client to make one gown.'

'And that's probably why they are so beautiful,' Sasha said, sensing she needed to turn on the charm.

'What about this?' she asked, reaching out towards a mannequin swathed in green silk.

'Don't touch that,' he said, swatting her hand away with a tape measure.

'Don't you have anything ready to wear?'

The designer shrugged. 'What size is she?'

'Thin. A size six. Or do you have a store I can grab some shop stock from?'

He rolled his eyes. 'Shop stock!' he tutted. 'Darling, I repeat, I'm a bespoke operation. This is my atelier and people come to me. I don't have a *shop*.'

Sasha's face dropped. This time she actually thought she might cry for real.

'I'm stuffed,' she said, suddenly feeling dizzy. Annalise would be back from the hair salon any moment, expecting her to turn up with her dress.

'Would it be possible to get a glass of water?' she said, not wanting to go back into the cold quite yet.

Ben pointed towards a tiny kitchen at the back of the studio. As she walked through, she inspected the mannequins and sketches on the walls. *Elle* had been right to feature Ben Rivera, she thought. His designs were sumptuous and innovative, but also flattering to the female form. Approaching the kitchen, she spotted a large French armoire from which billowed pale lilac chiffon, like a cloud at sunset. She stepped closer. The gown was exquisite; such fine needlework and tailoring, it could have been the very finest Parisian couture.

'What's this?' she asked with a rush of excitement.

'It was a costume for the Royal Ballet,' said Ben flatly.

'Has it been used?'

174

'Eventually, no,' he said with disappointment.

'Ballet dancers are skinny, right?' said Sasha, thinking out loud.

He snorted. 'That is *not* a party dress, my dear. It took two hundred hours to make that dress. Five thousand beads sourced from Rajasthan were stitched on by hand.'

'Please?' she said.

'It's not for sale.'

'Please.'

He laughed. 'You march in here, you ask for the earth, you don't even tell me your name.'

'It's Sasha and I'm not asking for the earth. Just this dress.'

'How do I know you are not going to run off with it?'

She smiled. 'You don't.' She met his gaze. 'How many gowns do you sell a month, Ben?'

He looked defensive. 'It's not about quantity . . .'

'Of course, and you can see the quality in every stitch.' She nodded sincerely. 'But the tragedy is I bet you don't do more than twenty dresses a year, do you? A few rich women know your number but that doesn't make you Gianni Versace. Look, this is one of the biggest parties of the year and my client is a very connected woman. *Very* connected. You have an amazing talent, Ben, but you need to market yourself. You can be the best designer in the world, but if no one knows your name, you're going to stay in this room in Battersea for a long time.'

Watching his face, she knew she'd hit home. Unless he was independently wealthy and was doing this for a hobby, there was no way he could afford to turn down selling the dress, and if she could sweeten the deal by offering him the lifeline of ready-made advertising to his key audience, all the better.

'I couldn't let it go for less than eight thousand pounds.'

'Five thousand,' she said quickly. 'Think of the publicity.'

'How will you get me the money?'

'I will take you to her. Bring your pins and your sewing kit. I promise you, Ben, this will change your life.'

'You're late,' said Annalise, opening the door with a stern expression. Her face was fully painted with evening make-up and her hair had been swept up into a dramatic chignon, but she was still wearing a white towelling robe. 'And who is this?'

Sasha walked straight in, taking Annalise's arm and leading her out of Ben's earshot.

'This is Ben Rivera. He's the new Lagerfeld,' she whispered. She didn't want him getting ideas above his station, not before she had the chance to use him to the fullest.

Upstairs, Ben confidently swept the dress out of its linen bag and Annalise's tense facial expression relaxed instantly. The gown floated through the air as if it was made of feathers.

'Is it couture?' whispered Annalise.

Sasha and Ben nodded. Strictly speaking it wasn't couture. Strictly speaking only the handful of designers who showed their collection twice a year in Paris and were members of the Chambre Syndicale de la Haute Couture were considered 'couture'. But the Chambre weren't coming to the party.

'Normally you don't buy dresses like this, Annalise, you *order* them,' said Sasha confidentially. 'But today Ben Rivera himself has come to fit you with his latest creation because I told him about your incredible taste.'

Eagerly Annalise stripped off and allowed herself to be fitted in the gown, Ben weaving his magic with the corset using delicate stitches until it fitted like a second skin. Sasha went into Annalise's dressing room and selected a pair of silver Manolo Blahniks and drop diamond earrings. She looked magnificent. When she moved, the long slits in the fabric, meant for the movement of a dancer, showed off her toned legs in an elegant, sensual way.

'You look beautiful,' cooed Sasha.

'What do I owe you?' asked Annalise, the expression on her face as she looked at herself in the mirror something like love.

'Eight thousand for the gown,' said Sasha, giving Ben just the slightest smile. Without hesitation, Annalise opened a drawer in her dresser and pulled out a chequebook, writing one to Ben, then another for Sasha, which she folded and slipped into her hand whispering, 'You're fabulous.' She pulled a white mink shrug over her shoulders as they all headed down the stairs. 'Wait till my girlfriends hear all about you,' she said. 'They're going to be green with envy.'

Opportunity hung in the air and Sasha reached out for it with both hands.

'How about lunch to discuss a new wardrobe?' she asked.

'Great idea,' said Annalise. 'How about San Lorenzo at one tomorrow?'

'I look forward to it,' said Sasha.

Straight afterwards, Sasha would hand in her notice to Venetia. She didn't need a has-been weighing her down. No, Sasha Sinclair was on her own now, and she was taking Annalise Tuttle and all her high-spending friends with her.

19

The club was called the Youngblood Society and its intentions were clear from the start. Hipper, more meritocratic than the Carrington and Bullingdon, less fey than the Piers Gaveston, more debauched than the Assassins, Miles wanted to create a modern club for a modern Oxford. He did not consider himself a snob, simply superior, and he wanted his club to be full of men like him, brilliant men who would one day be Masters of the Universe and who wanted to play hard along the way.

Wandering around the Youngblood's inaugural Christmas party, he smiled to himself. No wonder some of the Carrington boys were sniffing around, angling for membership. The party was being held at Graveseye House, a four-storey former rectory just outside Oxford. Ideally, Miles would have preferred a grander venue. Then again, as a second home belonging to the parents of Alan Johnson, an eccentric Scot angling for membership, it had cost nothing to hire, which had freed Miles up to spend more money on the actual party. When he'd been researching the history of the gentlemen's club in preparation for creating the Youngbloods, Miles had stumbled across an account of the Great World, a legendary club in 1930s Shanghai, a place that fascinated him for its blend of opulence and debauchery. On the Great World's first floor you could find fortune-tellers and gambling, but by the top floor you would discover opium and sing-song girls, the

Chinese courtesans. That was exactly the ambience Miles had been aiming for, and as he glanced around, he could see that the theatrical set-builders he'd employed to transform the house for the night had got it exactly right. Scarlet silk drapes disguised the Johnsons' flocked wallpaper, gold and velvet oriental furniture had been brought in and the entire space was lit by candles spilling ghoulish shadows around the rooms. It had taken much longer to co-ordinate than he had imagined, but by God, it was worth it.

'Miles!' shouted a dozen voices as he strolled through the ground floor, accepting handshakes and slaps on the back. There were only twenty-five Youngblood members, each dressed in the society uniform of French navy coats with gold frogging and brass buttons, but they were surrounded by models dressed as angels, oriental waitresses and a handful of magicians, contortionists and other performers.

Miles took his place at the head of the dining table.

'I think everyone's expecting a few words, Ashford,' said member Tom Samson.

Miles nodded and stood, straightening his white military tailcoat as he prepared to speak. 'Gentlemen,' he began to hoots and cheers, quickly dying away as he gave them a stern look. 'Gentlemen, you represent the best students at the best university in the world,' he continued, his voice commanding and clear. 'Unlike many elite clubs at Oxford, you've been chosen not because of where you come from, but because of where you're going.'

They all cheered, thumping their hands on the table, rattling the fine china. Miles liked the sound of his own voice but he knew his fledgling hedonists hadn't come here for a lecture.

'Fellow 'bloods, I won't keep you, because there's fun to be had, memories to be created and a bond to be forged. But let this historic phrase ring in your ears: the Youngblood Society is officially in session!'

The members roared their approval as Samson handed

179

Miles a sword and, gesturing for the crowd to stand back, he swung it in a glittering arc towards a jeroboam of champagne standing on the table in front of him. To the amazement and delight of the Youngbloods, it sliced the top of the bottle clean off, the bubbling liquid shooting into the air like a geyser.

Amazing what a little spectacle can do to people, thought Miles as he began to circulate through the throng. On the second floor, two strippers writhed around a brass pole in the centre of a platform specially erected for the evening. Smiling, Miles thought of Alan Johnson's parents – currently in Thailand for Mr Johnson's diplomatic career – and wondered what they would make of this. Their son, who had his head over a long line of cocaine, was clearly not giving it much thought. And what would his own father think of all this? he wondered. Certainly, he knew, Robert would give him hell about his lacklustre academic performance at Oxford, which had been a consequence of all the time the Youngbloods was taking up. Lately his tutors had been on his back for missed essays and poor attendance, but Miles couldn't rouse himself enough to care. Why did it matter whether he got a first- or third-class degree – Ash Corp.'s human resources were hardly going to penalise him for poor exam results, were they?

'Let me fuck the albino,' whispered a second-year PPE student, Ian Thomas.

'I believe her name is Abigail,' said Miles with amusement. 'And she is yours for the right price.'

'Anything, I've got to have her,' Thomas said hungrily.

Miles smiled as he watched him beckon to the girl, who willingly followed him up the stairs. He was pleased with all the women the agency had sent over to act as waitresses and 'companions', each of them beautiful, accommodating and not afraid to multitask. 'High-class escort girls', that was how the agency had described them, but the insinuation was that they were all prepared to do anything for money. That suited Miles perfectly. He had transformed the bedrooms in the eaves of the house into seductive candlelit boudoirs and he would be charging the club members a hefty premium on top of whatever the girls asked. And judging from the constant stream of couples – sometimes threesomes – up the stairs, it looked as if business was going to be brisk.

A tall redhead came and sat beside him. She was older than the others, maybe even thirty. Crossing her legs, long and slim under elegant cream slacks, she leant over to him and stroked the underside of his jaw.

'Is there anything I can do for you?' she breathed.

Miles regarded her coolly. 'Perhaps later.'

She gave a slight shrug but didn't move away.

'I take it from the white uniform that you're the organiser,' she said.

'Founder of the society,' corrected Miles.

'Impressive.' She smiled, running a finger up and down the stem of her champagne flute. 'This is better than some parties I've been to in London and Paris, and believe me, darling, they were organised by some of the best hosts in the business. Movie stars, madams, even an ambassador's wife with a taste, shall we say, for the exotic. You're keeping up with the best of them.'

Miles was enjoying the flattery until she lowered her voice.

'But are you quite sure it's safe?' she whispered.

'Safe?'

'There are some quite high-profile young men here this evening,' she said, nodding towards Juan Carlos Constanta, the son of Mexico's richest industrialist.

'You've done your homework.'

'I find it pays to be informed. An event like this isn't just about the girls and the decor. It's about security.'

'Security from whom?'

She waved a hand. 'Oh, the press, the police. A tabloid

journalist could end careers here before they've even started.'

Miles frowned, privately acknowledging that she had a point. He had gone through life feeling bulletproof; with the exception of his spliff at Eton, he was one of those people who just didn't get caught out. So tonight he hadn't given *security* much thought.

'It's all under control,' he said smoothly.

'I'm glad to hear it,' she purred, putting the palm of her hand across his crotch.

He lifted her hand from his trousers and placed it back on her own thigh. She was annoying, not arousing him.

'If you'll excuse me, this amateur has to go and check out the party,' he said tartly.

He stalked downstairs to the basement, which had been turned into a low-lit opium den.

'Problems, Milo?' asked his friend Jonathon, catching Miles' expression.

'Nothing that won't cure,' he said, reaching for the hubbly-bubbly pipe Jonathon was holding and taking a puff. The smoke filled his lungs and sure enough his earlier irritation began to seem rather distant and unimportant.

'Hey, you heard of the internet?' asked Jonathon in a rather dreamy half-stoned voice.

Miles shook his head slowly as a mellow haze washed over him. 'Should I have done?'

'It's the future, my friend. It's knowledge, power. A guy called Assad, French guy at Magdalen, is looking to start up an internet café in Oxford. He needs investors. You interested?'

'Is he good?' asked Miles.

'Apparently brilliant.'

'Cool. Get me a meeting with him.'

Miles looked through heavy-lidded eyes at the bodies lying around on sofas and plump cushions, some half-naked. He had spent so long looking forward to this event but now he just wanted to lie here and for everyone else to just sod off home.

'Miles! *Miles!*'

He didn't stir, hoping it was a dream. It wasn't until he got a sharp prod in the ribs that he looked up.

Jonathon bent over him and hauled him up by the lapels.

'Get up, *now*!' he said urgently, dragging him up the basement stairs. For a second Miles thought the shouts and screams he could hear were the sounds of carnal pleasure, but one look at the face of the angels and waitresses running towards the front door was enough to sober him up like a slap in the face: they were terrified.

He ran up the stairs to the mezzanine floor, where Tom Samson was standing like a policeman directing traffic, yelling for everyone to get out.

'What the hell's going on, Sam?' yelled Miles, willing his brain to engage.

'Don't you know?' asked Samson incredulously. 'The fucking top bedroom is on fire! One of the candles got knocked over!'

Fire? *Fuck!* The fugginess in his head cleared instantly and Miles turned to Jonathon.

'Get water. In buckets. Now.'

'Where do I get a bucket from?'

'How the fuck should I know? Champagne buckets, anything. Get some others to help.' Spotting a bathroom, Miles ran in and soaked the biggest towels he could find. Sprinting back out, he threw one at Samson. 'Come with me,' he commanded.

Climbing to the second-floor landing, they could see thick acrid smoke pouring down the stairwell and Miles knew instantly that the time had passed for smothering flames with wet blankets. Already he could feel the heat and they were both choking.

'Is anyone else up there?' coughed Samson.

'Fuck knows,' hissed Miles. Sweat was beading from his temples and not just from the heat of the fire. He had no idea who was up there, but he wasn't going to hang around to find out. It was too late to save the party. Too late, probably, to save Alan's house. The least he could do now was save himself.

'Call 999,' he shouted to Samson. 'Make sure everyone's out.'

Samson put the towel over his mouth and began climbing the stairs.

'What the hell are you doing?'

'Someone might be up there. One of the hookers.'

'Fuck the hookers,' spat Miles. 'Let's split.'

But Samson was almost halfway up the stairs. Miles tried to follow him but a shower of flames fell from the roof.

'Samson, get out of there now.'

Samson half ran, half tumbled down the stairs, his jacket glowing with cinders which Miles beat out with his own coat.

'Everyone's out,' he coughed as both boys fled from the building.

The sound of sirens grew louder until their harsh noise seemed to engulf the house. Dozens of partygoers milled around the grounds, some half dressed, some shell-shocked, all looking faintly ridiculous surrounded by the yellow-jacketed firemen running out their hoses with such purpose. Adding to the confusion, a long line of taxis had miraculously started to appear – someone had their head screwed on at least – and Miles saw people fighting to get into them, especially as the blue and red lights of a police car were heading towards them along the drive.

Quickly Miles pulled his mobile phone from the pocket of his soot-smeared tailcoat and stabbed at the keys. His stomach clenched with anger and shame at what he was about to do, but as he saw it, he had no choice. He didn't want to be in any more debt to his father, but he didn't want to go to jail either.

'Come on, come on,' he muttered as he listened to the phone ring at the other end.

He was relieved to hear his father's voice.

'Miles, what is it?' Robert said with irritation.

'I'm in trouble, Dad,' said Miles. There was no point in sugaring the pill. 'I need you to get someone down to Oxford.'

They talked for a few minutes, then Miles calmly put his phone back in his pocket and sat on a wall, watching as a policeman walked over.

'Miles Ashford?' he said. 'I believe you are the organiser of this party?'

Miles glanced at the police officer's uniform. *A sergeant playing by the book,* he thought contemptuously.

'You don't look too clever, son,' said the policeman. 'I should get yourself checked out by the ambulance team. But in the meantime, I'd just like to ask you a few questions . . .'

The college's disciplinary committee were predictable. Judgemental, conservative and holier-than-thou. Miles stood in front of them barely registering what they were saying. *'The importance of pastoral care at the college . . . The necessity to steer other students from drugs . . . The reputation of the university . . .'*

Those wankers. What the hell did they know about life beyond their crumbling flint-knapped walls? Why the hell did he have to stand there and answer to them anyway? It was especially galling as he had almost avoided all of this, almost got off scot-free. To Miles' surprise, his father had done everything he could to contain the story: the vice girls were paid off, the Youngblood membership warned to maintain their silence; even Alan Johnson's parents were persuaded of the wisdom of dropping criminal charges, despite the damage to their home. Yes, Miles had spent a night in the cells at Oxford police station, but Dick Donovan had appeared

185

the next morning and any formal charges had mysteriously melted away. Unfortunately, the Ashford clean-up team hadn't been able to gag everyone: 'an insider' had contacted scandal-hungry tabloid the *Daily Chronicle* and the combination of drugs, prostitutes and an exclusive Oxford society was too irresistible, despite vicious threats from Robert Ashford's lawyers.

The story had prompted an instant investigation by the university. The colleges traditionally turned a blind eye to the raucous behaviour at the elite clubs – clubs like the Carrington had only been suspended a handful of times in their history – but this was in another league entirely. They had no choice but to come down hard on Miles, despite the lack of much real evidence. Miles had been briefed extensively by the Ashford lawyers and knew what to say: the Youngbloods were not a registered university club and the party had not been held on university property; there was nothing to formally link them to the college at all. Moreover, there was nothing beyond hearsay to link Miles to the solicitation of prostitutes or the procurement of drugs – not even the *Chronicle* had been able to find a female party guest willing to admit she had been paid for sex. On paper, Miles had simply organised a party that had got out of control. But that didn't cut any ice with the ancient dons staring down at him.

Miles slowly began to concentrate on what they were saying.

'Aside from the newspaper allegations, Mr Ashford, the quality of your work has been considerably below the required level for this university,' said Professor Stewart, a particularly severe-looking senior tutor. 'Add to that your endless missed tutorials, a sub-standard tutorial report and a woeful history of penal collections. Under the circumstances, I feel we have been particularly lenient when we recommend that you rusticate for a period of one year.'

Miles closed his eyes. Rustication: temporary expulsion from the university. It was one better than being sent down, but still . . .

'Fuck you,' he said.

'I beg your pardon, Mr Ashford,' said the Dean, peering over the top of his half-moon glasses.

'I said "Fuck you",' repeated Miles, enunciating the words as clearly as he could.

The dons exploded: 'What's the meaning of this . . .' 'How dare you? . . .' 'I've a good mind to . . .' *Just as predictable as ever,* thought Miles. Holding his head high, he strolled out of the chambers and into the street, where he leant against the wall, breathing in fresh air, desperate to get the fusty smell of Oxford from his nose.

'Bollocks to rustication,' he muttered to himself as he lit a cigarette, sheltering in a stone archway.

He blew the smoke up towards the grey sky. Since he had been inside, it had started raining. A thin, chilling drizzle that was soaking straight through his Savile Row suit.

A cyclist, his college scarf flying behind him, rode through a big puddle, splashing Miles' trousers, the damp fabric sticking to his legs like cold jelly.

'This place is a shit-hole,' he observed. 'A fucking shit-hole.'

He turned and walked back up the high street. Oxford was over for Miles. It was time to get to where he belonged.

20

May 1992

'Where are the gold lilos?' shouted the photographer. 'And where is that *bloody* unicorn?'

The entire area surrounding the pool at Hartfield Hall was in chaos. The view from the Berkshire country house hotel was obscured by huge lights, a camera on some sort of crane and a fog machine blowing smoke across the water. An army of extras dressed up as fairies were queuing for make-up and in between all of it ran innumerable men and women wearing baseball caps and carrying walkie-talkies.

'It's only a bloody album cover shoot,' said Year Zero's bassist Gavin, staring at the scene from the door of the hotel bar. 'You'd think they were storming the beaches at Normandy.'

For once, the whole band was in a good mood, finally convinced that the record company believed in them, that they were getting somewhere. For the last year they had felt anything but: slogging around the toilet circuit, struggling for any sort of recognition in the music press, releasing a four-track EP that had gone down like a frozen turkey. The biggest blow for Alex was when they had moved down to London. He had always imagined that when he had a record contract, he would be living in a waterside apartment with a Porsche on the drive, but instead, he and Emma shared a mould-ridden Camden Town bedsit where one morning Alex had found a mouse in the toaster. Some days, he had felt like that was a metaphor for his career.

But not any more. Since Year Zero had recorded their debut album *The Long March*, things were changing; suddenly everyone was excited. 'Don't Talk', their first single from the album, had just been released and industry buzz around it suggested that it would go in high when the charts were announced later that day. On top of all that, the record company had employed a team of radio pluggers to get them airplay and the band had even been interviewed on TV. Now they were shooting the album cover with legendary rock photographer Anton Jones. Finally it was all coming together.

'Excuse me, guys?' A girl carrying a clipboard walked into the bar and looked around at the band nervously.

'Can I speak to your manager?' She glanced down at the board. 'Nathan Fox, is it?'

Jez immediately switched into PR mode. 'He's not here, lovely.' He smiled wolfishly. 'Is there anything I can do for you?'

'Oh, well we just need someone to sign off on the car,' she said.

'What car?' said Alex.

'The Rolls-Royce,' said the girl as Jez signed something on her clipboard with a flourish.

'What Rolls-Royce?' said Alex.

'The Roller I'm going to drive straight into that pool!' said Jez happily, taking a swig from a bottle of Bacardi.

'You knew about this?'

'Knew about it? It was my idea! Think of it, all the rock iconography – Keith Moon, Marc Bolan, Bon Scott carking it in a car – it's all there.'

'This shoot is costing a bloody fortune in unicorns as it is.'

Jez threw his arm around Alex's shoulder and breathed rum fumes into his face. 'It's basic common sense: if the label wants to spend a fortune on our album cover, you don't stop them. You want it to look as mental as possible.'

Alex wriggled free and pushed Jez back. 'And who's paying for this, Jez?' he said.

'How the fuck do I know?' said Jez, annoyed.

'We are, you moron! Everything comes out of our advance.'

'Wow, do you two always fight like this?' They both turned to see Liz Gold eyeing them with interest. The *Melody Maker* journalist was at the shoot to get 'some colour' for a four-page story the paper was running on the band. Alex noticed with a sinking feeling that the red light on the journalist's dictaphone machine was on.

'Fight? Nah, we're just hamming it up for the press,' said Jez, squeezing Alex's shoulders. 'Like brothers, aren't we, Al?'

Alex smiled weakly.

Liz nodded, looking from one to the other as if she didn't believe a word. She was right of course. Alex's relationship with Jez had gone from bad to worse lately after Jez had demanded a share of the songwriting credits, threatening to quit unless it happened. The upshot was that Alex had been presented with an impossible decision: agree to Jez's demands, give him equal billing on the songs and let him take credit for all Alex's talent and hard work, not to mention a cut of the publishing royalties, or walk away from a band with a record contract and start again. In the end he had no choice: he caved in, but it did nothing for inter-band morale.

'Listen, I'm just going up to your room where it's quieter,' said Liz, touching Jez flirtatiously on the shoulder. 'Why don't you come up when you're ready and we can do our part of the interview?'

'I'm in there,' said Jez matter-of-factly, when Liz had gone.

'Jez, don't screw up the article by getting frisky with her.'

'What do you care? Anyway, look, your missus is calling

you,' said Jez sarcastically. 'The mini music mogul at work.'

Across the pool Emma was waving at them. Thanks to a tip-off from their manager Nathan, Emma had landed a job as a marketing assistant at EMG, Argent's parent company, which had given her the excuse to attend the album shoot. Her new job meant they hardly saw each other these days, but Alex was genuinely glad she was doing so well in her career; in fact they both shared a dream that one day they would end up in New York ruling the rock industry: she running a major label, him a reclusive musician, occasionally emerging for a huge televised concert at Madison Square Garden or somewhere. And to think this was the girl who used to bang on the floor whenever they turned the music on in the flat downstairs.

'Still looking hot, though,' said Jez, giving Alex a complicit slap on the back. 'Still pretty foxy. You're lucky I gave her to you.'

Alex glared at him. 'You *gave* her to me?'

'Yeah, like after I'd finished with her. Warmed her up for you, didn't I?'

Emma had always denied going near Jez Harrison when they had all lived in the big house in Fallowfield, but Jez was always making sly suggestions that they had slept together.

'Don't worry about it,' whispered Jez. 'Our little secret, eh?'

'Piss off and do your interview, Jez,' said Alex, walking out of the bar. 'And try not to be a total cock this time.'

Emma was waiting for him by the pool. 'I'm off,' she said, kissing him. 'Phone me the second you hear about the chart.' She looked at him and frowned. 'What's up with you?'

Alex groaned. 'Sorry, it's Jez. All this time I've known him and I still can't work out what drives him. Apart from spite, of course.'

'You do know he's jealous of you?' Emma smiled, lighting a cigarette and looking at Alex sideways.

191

'I wouldn't say that,' said Alex.

'All right, he feels threatened, then,' said Emma. 'You're a better singer, musician and songwriter, plus you get more attention from the girls.'

'I do not!' he protested.

'Hey, I didn't say you took them up on it, did I?' She grinned.

'Well, I can't help it, can I?' said Alex. 'Am I supposed to wear a mask?'

'Absolutely not. I'm not having my very gorgeous boyfriend hiding away from anyone.'

He paused for a moment. 'Can I ask you something?'

Emma glanced at her watch. 'I was supposed to be in London an hour ago. But seeing as it's you . . .'

'Did you ever shag him?'

She looked at him with confusion. 'Shag who?'

'Jez, of course,' he said, annoyed.

Her face started to cloud with anger. 'Alex, I've told you a dozen times I didn't.'

'It's just that on the night I first met you, Gavin said he'd slept with one of the girls upstairs . . .'

'I can't believe we're having this conversation, Alex. It was so long ago.'

'So you *did* sleep with him?'

'No, I didn't. I told you.' She shook her head in frustration. 'You're an idiot, d'you know that? It's the biggest bloody day of your career so far and what are you doing? Arguing like children with Jez Harrison. Well, get over it, Alex, because Jez is part of the band. Yes, he's a wanker, but he's a bloody good frontman, and without a frontman there is no Year Zero.'

'I can't believe you're siding with him!' said Alex petulantly.

'I'm not siding with him!' cried Emma, throwing her hands up in the air. 'Are you even listening to the point I'm trying

192

to make here? This isn't about me and Jez, it's about you and your insecurities.'

'You said you were late,' he said sulkily, refusing to meet her gaze. 'Hadn't you better go?'

'Yes, I think I should,' she said, pointedly throwing her cigarette into the pool with a fizz and stalking off to her waiting car.

Despite the nagging guilt over his argument with Emma, Alex had to admit he had actually quite enjoyed the rest of the day's shoot, especially the part where Jez drove them both into the pool. Alex had insisted on riding shotgun in the Rolls, reasoning that he was paying for at least a quarter of it and should get at least half the fun. It had been bloody freezing in the water, though, so he had come up to the band's day room to strip off his wet clothes and have a shower. Opening the bathroom door in a cloud of steam, he padded out into the room with a fluffy white hotel towel wrapped around his waist.

'Oh bugger,' he said. 'Sorry.'

Liz Gold was sitting at the table hunched over a notebook.

'Come to keep me company?' She smiled mischievously.

'Uh, no. Just come to get my jeans,' he said, nodding behind her where they had been drying on the radiator. As he leant over her to get them, she reached out and pulled at his towel, her hand stroking his limp cock.

'What the hell are you doing?' he snapped, recoiling from her.

'Doing what every rock and roll star would want doing in this situation,' said Liz, completely unruffled.

'I have a girlfriend,' he stuttered.

'You and every other musician on the circuit,' she said, laughing. 'But if you're going to get anywhere in this business, you have to learn that you need to keep certain people *onside*.'

Shocked and embarrassed, Alex grabbed the rest of his clothes and stumbled out into the corridor, hastily pulling them on. Jesus, what was all that about?

The truth was, as a teenager he had fantasised about something like that happening when he became a rock star – it was why you got into a band in the first place, wasn't it? *Maybe I need to loosen up a bit,* he told himself. *I have been getting too uptight about everything, letting Jez get to me, taking it out on Emma.* As he reached the door leading to the pool, he could see the band standing by the deep end, all looking up towards the hotel.

'Alex! Get yourself over here!' screamed Gavin.

'What is it?' he called, sprinting across the grass.

Gavin pointed to the hotel, where they could see Nathan Fox through an open window. 'He's got the record company on the blower.'

'The chart position?' said Alex nervously.

Pete nodded, putting a nervous hand on Alex's shoulder.

Through the window, they could see Nathan put the phone down and turn towards them, his face stony.

'You're not going to like this, lads,' he said mournfully, then his face broke out into a Cheshire Cat grin. 'Number fucking nine!' he shouted.

Jez screamed and dragged one of the fairies into the swimming pool with a splash.

'Yessss!' yelled Alex. 'Fucking yessss!'

Nathan came running out of the hotel holding a magnum of champagne then shaking it up and spraying the sticky foam over everyone, Formula One-style.

'Top ten, Alex!' he laughed, pulling him into a bear hug. 'You're on your way now!'

'Oh shit!' said Alex, suddenly thinking of his promise. 'I've got to make a call,' he added, running back to the bar and grabbing the phone at the end of the counter. He dialled the Camden flat and Emma picked up immediately.

'Hello?' she said.

'You're home.'

'Tell me.'

'Number nine!' yelled Alex. 'Number bloody nine!'

'I knew it!' she screamed. 'I just knew it. I never doubted it for a minute.'

'And I never doubted you either,' he replied, wondering how they could possibly have argued earlier.

'Oh, I love you, Alex,' she said.

'I love you too,' he said, suddenly realising it was the first time he had ever said it to her. 'I love you, I love you, I love you.'

Hanging up, he bounced back outside, where he sank on to the grass and smiled. Champagne fizzed in his belly, the sun was warming his face; he felt like he'd just finished a very long race and – to his surprise – had actually won. Across the grass, he watched as Jez climbed out of the water, stripped off his wet clothes and, naked, began to chase the unicorn across the lawn, whooping, 'Number nine, horsey! Number nine!' And for once, all Alex could do was chuckle.

21

October 1992

'How long have you known this friend exactly?' said Isabella Hernandez, her tone dripping with disapproval. Grace turned away from the window to face her formidable mother-in-law. She had been staring out past the Hernandez estate El Esperanza, across miles of velvety rainforest, hoping to catch a glimpse of the car bringing Caro to visit her, but as usual, Gabriel's mother wanted to talk. Or rather, to grill her. Isabella was not yet sixty but looked much older, her face creased with a lifetime of worry for her menfolk, her raven hair streaked at both temples with silver. If Grace had been ten years younger, Isabella Hernandez would have terrified her, but now as an adult, a wife and mother, she accepted her, enduring the daily interrogations and frosty looks, yearning for the day when she could set up a family home of her own. Not that she didn't appreciate living in one of the largest and grandest houses in Parador, but when you had to share that space with an indomitable, interfering mother-in-law, even in the wide hallways and drawing rooms sometimes it felt hard to breathe.

'Oh, we've only been friends a couple of years,' said Grace. 'Caro was there the day I met Gabriel actually. In fact if she hadn't sent me out to buy supper, I don't think I'd be here now.'

Isabella raised an eyebrow that, in one tiny gesture, communicated her general disdain. 'And will this "friend" be gone before the rally in Palumbo?'

Grace knew exactly where this conversation was heading. 'I don't know. Even if she has left, I'm not sure I'll be going.'

'Really? How so?'

'Well, Gabe has turned out to be a natural politician, hasn't he? I'm not sure he needs me hanging around, trying to drum up extra support.'

'Oh, but you must,' said Isabella urgently. 'It's important to understand that you're not just married to the opposition leader, Grace, you're a part of the election. And you are the lady of the house here now.'

Grace was in no mood to be bullied into anything. Motherhood did that to you. Sleepless nights and demanding children toughened you up.

For weeks she'd been pushed by Isabella and Gabe to get more involved in 'the cause', and transform herself into some Latino Jackie Kennedy. But politics, or at least the South American version of it, swinging between the chilling isolation of a bulletproof limousine and the complete emotional overload of a rally – the weeping, the screaming, the thousands of hands reaching out to her in adulation – left her cold. The real truth of it was that she felt a fraud. To accept the adulation felt self-indulgent and, more importantly, hypocritical and wrong. She wasn't a saviour. She was a twenty-three-year-old woman struggling to find her own place in life and she certainly didn't have the answers to Parador's many problems.

Nor could she really blame her mother-in-law for her frosty reception: it was not as if Grace was anybody's idea of a perfect daughter-in-law. Appearing out of the blue the night before Carlos' funeral to announce that they were getting married was never going to be a great start, especially when it became clear that she was a foreigner, albeit a wealthy one. She was still pregnant and, even worse, a Protestant. Of course, Gabriel had gently suggested that Grace could convert to Catholicism, but she had refused point blank, not from any strong spiritual conviction, more that she could picture herself locked in a confessional booth being forced to tell a priest that she had left a young man dying on a beach. In fact, in this recurring nightmare she would have to confess that she suspected her brother of having killed the boy and that she had done nothing about it except flee to the other side of the world.

Outside there was the crunch of car tyres on the drive.

'I think your friend is here,' said Isabella flatly before sweeping out of the room.

Grace clattered down the marble stairs and out into the courtyard as the dusty car drew up. It was hot and humid and the white linen fabric of her skirt stuck to her calves, but as Caro stepped into the sweltering Parador heat, Grace ran forward to hug her.

'Oh honey, you don't know how good it is to see you!' she cried, grinning all over her face.

'Hey, you too. You look amazing. Like a proper lady of the manor. And tell me that's just a shiny green rock on your finger and not a big chunk of emerald.'

'It's an emerald.'

'I can't believe it. And to think I gave Gabriel to you.'

Grace laughed happily. In fourteen months Caro hadn't changed a jot. She was still thin and her clothes still looked as if they could do with a good wash, but most of all she still had that irreverent twinkle in her eye, something Grace had missed more than she had realised.

'Well come and see the manor.' She smiled, moving to take her friend's rucksack.

'No, no, Señora Hernandez, allow me,' said José, Gabriel's driver, stepping forward.

'Ooh, servants now.' Caro giggled.

'It's a long way from Macrossan Street, put it that way,' said Grace.

She gave Caro a guided tour of the house, smiling as her friend gasped at the long formal dining room, the mosaic-adorned indoor pool, their huge bedroom, the voile-draped windows giving an amazing view of the hazy valley below.

'Stone the bloody crows,' breathed Caro as Grace led her out on to the terrace. The infinite green shades of the rainforest looked spectacular from there, especially in the softening light of the late afternoon with the soothing breeze and the soft caw of toucans coming from the treetops. Although it was only ten miles outside the capital city of Palumbo, it felt as if they were in the middle of the throbbing Amazon jungle.

Over excellent mojitos mixed by Isabella's butler, the girls gossiped about old times and new. Caro's life appeared to have changed little – in Goa she had found men, parties and an exotic, bohemian way of life that suited her down to the ground. Excitedly she quizzed Grace about her intimate yet elegant wedding, a candlelit ceremony and reception at El Esperanza. Grace told her how glorious she had felt in her long flowing gown; ripe and luscious like a Botticelli painting, thin folds of chiffon swooping from an empire-line gown disguising her belly from the most conservative and Catholic of guests. It was only in the telling of it that Grace realised just how crazy, exotic and alien her life had become since she had left Port Douglas.

'You're used to it though, aren't you?' said Caro. 'The high life?'

'What do you mean?'

Caro looked away. 'I found a copy of *Hello!* magazine in this hostel in Goa. I flicked through it and there was this story about you getting married to Gabe. Grace, your dad is the twenty-third richest man in the United Kingdom.'

'He'll be disappointed to have slipped out of the top twenty,' said Grace, trying to smile. She shrugged. 'I know I should have told you, but I was . . . well, I was embarrassed. Plus I was trying to get away from all that money and luxury.'

'Doesn't look like you tried very hard.' Caro grinned, looking up at the decorated ceiling of the sitting room. 'I always wondered why you never talked about your family. I mean, what do they make of it all?'

Unwelcome memories flooded back. When Grace had phoned with news of her pregnancy and impending marriage, her father had demanded she come home to 'sort yourself out'. When she had refused, he had flown out to Parador with her mother and a hung-over Miles in tow for the wedding. Somewhere between his irate phone call and arriving at El Esperanza, he had obviously decided it would be good PR to put in an appearance at his daughter's big day, especially as it would make the papers. Thankfully, a takeover bid in London had meant that he could only stay twenty-four hours in Parador and when Miles had made noises to return with him, Grace had actively encouraged the whole party to go and leave her to enjoy what was left of the celebratory weekend.

'So where are the twins?' said Caro eagerly.

Grace glowed with pleasure at the mention of her children. Finding herself married to a world-famous writer was strange enough, especially when you considered he might soon be president of a country she'd barely heard of before. But having children had been even more of a revelation. She'd never really thought about having kids; it was something that would happen much later in life when she'd travelled and had a career and was totally settled. But it hadn't happened like that and she couldn't say she had regretted it for a minute. Oh yes, of course there were times when she was so exhausted she had spent all day in her nightie, and despite the presence of servants and El Esperanza's luxuries – swimming pool,

200

tennis court, hammam – none of it helped with the isolation of raising the twins, especially with Gabriel barely there. But Olivia and Joseph had brought a joy of such depth to her life that sometimes she wondered if she deserved to feel so happy.

She led Caro into the nursery where the twins were sleeping in separate cots.

'These are my babies,' she said, leaning in and scooping up Olivia who yawned, blinking at the room.

'She's so adorable!' cried Caro, taking the infant and sitting her on her knee, making goo-goo noises at her. 'Oh Grace, I can't believe you're a mummy.'

'It's mad, isn't it? You know I found my first grey hair this morning? I'm twenty-three! No one warns you quite how knackering motherhood is.'

'Maybe you should make your nannies work a bit harder.' Caro smiled.

'We don't have one.'

Caro looked at her in disbelief. 'You are kidding me?' she said. 'You have a man to put an umbrella on your cocktail, but you don't have anyone to help with the twins?'

Grace shook her head. 'Gabe is paranoid about the staff. As you've seen, the house is pretty secure but there's still a danger someone might infiltrate the place. One of Parador's top judges was killed at the weekend by his pool cleaner.'

'Fuck what Gabriel thinks,' said Caro with passion. 'He's not the one getting up at five in the morning, is he? If you want a nanny, you get a nanny.'

Caro bounced Olivia up and down on her lap where she gurgled happily. Grace watched her friend. Despite Caro's hard-edged looks – the nose ring, the spiky hair now a rich maple-leaf orange – she was a natural with kids.

'So what are your plans?' asked Grace. She almost hadn't wanted to ask, fearing that Caro would say it was a flying visit.

'D'you mind if I stay a couple of weeks? The flight ticket wiped me out.'

'A couple of weeks?' said Grace with delight. 'That's brilliant! No, I mean, stay as long as you want. The house is big enough. Although you may change your mind when you meet Gabriel's mother.'

'After I get my feet on the ground, I guess I'll head off to Palumbo, see what I can cook up there,' said Caro.

'Parador is a dangerous place, Caro. You don't want to be roaming around Palumbo alone.'

Caro stretched out her toes. 'Could have fooled me. From what I've seen it's like bloody paradise – whoops!' she said, covering Olivia's ears.

'I'm serious, Caro,' said Grace. 'The drug cartels have made it nasty and innocent people get caught in the crossfire.'

'You know me, Gracie,' replied Caro. 'I like to walk on the wild side.'

'This is serious, Caro. I'll only really feel safe if you're here at El Esperanza.'

'Got any jobs then? Need any rancid prawn buffets rustling up?'

Grace looked at her friend for a moment and thought how happy she had been in Port Douglas, how carefree. She loved her husband and her children and she was smitten by the beauty of El Esperanza. At night, it was nothing short of magical, like a fictitious magic box dreamt up by Gabriel for one of his books. But it was also a lonely place.

'Why not work here with me, with the kids?' she said suddenly. She immediately felt stupid, arrogant even, suggesting that Caro might want to work for her. She was her friend, not the hired help.

'What, as a nanny?'

'I guess,' shrugged Grace, a little embarrassed now. 'But I would understand if it was too awkward for you.'

'Are you serious? That would be amazing!' Caro said,

jumping up and hugging Grace. 'But are you sure Gabriel won't mind?'

'Gabe is never here,' Grace said with a note of defiance. Gabe couldn't object to having Caro as their nanny – she was one of her most trusted friends. 'He won't mind,' she said. 'And anyway, this is my house now. What I say goes.'

She hugged her friend again and thought that for the first time since she'd been in Parador, she finally felt at home.

22

Sasha put her foot down and gunned her silver Mazda over the hill, the big houses on either side blurring, the street lights leaving trails behind her. 'Calm down,' she whispered to herself, hitting the brake as she saw the sign for the Hinchley Wood golf club. 'You only have to stay a couple of hours.' She twisted the wheel and practically skidded into the car park; she knew that two hours was going to pass very slowly indeed.

Already people were leaving the party: fifty-something couples in M&S suits and Debenhams taffeta climbing back into their middle-management cars, gleaming Rovers and Ford Mondeos. Strains of disco floated on the night air, and through the plate-glass windows she could see into the Orchid Suite, festooned with paper chains, balloons and metallic banners exclaiming *Happy Silver Wedding Anniversary!*. She could almost smell the warm wine and the sausage rolls without even entering the clubhouse. Sasha hadn't been to a party like this since – well, since her parents' tenth wedding anniversary – and fifteen years later the scene hadn't changed; the people were just a bit more stooped, the dresses a bit more fussy, the cars outside upgraded a notch to the executive model with the walnut dash.

Picking up her present from the passenger seat, she took a deep breath and walked in, immediately spotting old faces: parents of girls she knew from prep school, neighbours from Esher, her father's colleagues, an assortment from her mother's tennis and bridge club circuit. *God, what a nightmare,* she thought. But then she caught sight of one face through the crowd. Instantly she felt guilty at her uncharitable thoughts.

'Hi, Dad,' she said with affection, kissing his papery cheek and wondering at what point over the last five years her father had become old. His hair was fully grey and thinning all over and the once-handsome features had sagged, as if they were giving up.

'Hello, Pumpkin!' said her father, clearly surprised and delighted to see her. 'I'm so glad you could make it. I didn't think you were coming, you've been so busy lately.'

'Oh, I wouldn't miss it for the world,' said Sasha, resisting the urge to add a *darling* at the end of her statement, a word that popped out like a reflex now. 'Where's Mum?'

Her dad waved a hand. 'Off somewhere enjoying the social adoration.'

Sasha thrust the present into his hands. 'For both of you. From Paris. For twenty-five years of marriage.'

He shook the beautifully wrapped box vigorously next to his ear and Sasha flinched.

'No, no. Don't do that. It's from Lalique.'

'Is that one of your fancy fashion labels?' he asked.

'Beautiful glassware actually. Mum will be aware of it.'

'If it's expensive and from Paris I have no doubt she will.' He chuckled. 'By the way, you look absolutely wonderful this evening. Both my girls have done me proud,' he said, gazing across the room at his wife.

Sasha knew she looked good: her dress was a Ben Rivera one-off and she was grateful that her father had noticed she had made an effort. Sasha might be contemptuous of the Surrey commuter belt she had come from, but she had still

205

dressed to impress the parochial crowd she had left behind. The rumour mill in this neck of the woods was more efficient and more vicious than Milan during fashion week. All her old school friends and their parents would have heard about Sasha's relationship with Miles Ashford – he was almost famous, after all – and they would have delighted in the news that it had ended. Hopefully her bespoke dress and her shiny sports car would show those tattle-tale bitches that she didn't need a man to get on. And it was true: Sasha Sinclair was now one of London's most in-demand stylists, not that any of this lot would know what a stylist was. Working on magazines, commercial shoots and private clients, she was making over fifty thousand pounds a year and was still only twenty-one. And to think she could be living here, working in a building society or something. The thought made her shiver.

'You cold, love?' asked her dad.

'No, not at all.' She smiled. The jazz band burst into their rendition of 'Come Fly With Me' and across the room Carole Sinclair, clearly a little tipsy, started motioning urgently at her husband to join her on the dance floor.

'I think you're on,' said Sasha.

Gerald touched her on the arm fondly. 'If your dance card isn't full, would you do your old dad the honour after I've taken your mother for a spin?'

'How could I refuse Esher's answer to Fred Astaire?'

She watched as her father took his wife's hand and proudly led her on to the dance floor. Her mother's dress was coral silk, well-tailored, expensive, probably Escada or even Oscar de la Renta. She guessed that that one dress had hit her father's chequebook harder than the hire cost of the Orchid Suite. Then again, in her mother's mind, she was not in the Hinchley Wood golf club, but in the ballroom of the Dorchester.

Carefully placing the Lalique on the table next to all the other presents, Sasha sauntered over to the buffet table.

'Sasha! How lovely to see you.'

A plump young woman in a tartan dress was smiling at her. For a second, she struggled to place her, until she realised it was Jessica Bird – her father's best friend's daughter. They had been in the same class at prep school, parting ways at eleven when Jessica had scraped into Guildford High while Sasha had gone off to Wycombe Abbey.

'Jessica!' she said with as much enthusiasm as she could muster. 'So what brings you here?'

'Whole family was invited,' she said, stuffing a cocktail sausage into her mouth. 'Of course, I'm just round the corner from my mum and dad now. I finished my teacher training last year and started at St Vincent's Primary in Woking.'

'Wow, that's great,' said Sasha, wondering if the bar had any real champagne. She could see she was going to need it. A tiny diamond ring winked on Jessica's left hand. 'And engaged already?' she asked.

Jessica smiled, glowing from within. 'A bit soon, I know, but I've been with Dan since sixth form, so why waste time?'

Dan from the sixth form, thought Sasha, trying to imagine living in a world of such poor choices, but then she remembered the time she had been desperate for Miles Ashford to propose. *At eighteen! Thank God that didn't happen.* Men were trouble, whether they came from Esher or Angel Cay.

Jessica leant forward, her boozy breath clouding into Sasha's personal space. 'I'm sorry to hear about your dad,' she said, putting a sympathetic hand on her arm.

'What about my dad?' Sasha frowned.

'You know, losing his job.'

Sasha felt suddenly cold. Looking across the dance floor, she could see her father was holding Carole in his arms. He'd lost his job? It was the first Sasha had heard of this, and she was angry they'd let some silly cow in plaid tell her first. Yes, she had been busy, out of the country half the time, but even so.

207

'He told my dad about it on the train to Waterloo a few days after it happened.'

'When was this exactly?'

'It must have been about a month ago now. Of course you know he was still catching the train into the city every day to pretend to your mum that he was still working, which I think was so sweet. He just wants to protect her from the world, doesn't he? I know my Dan is the same. Still, things can't be too bad, can they? They're still having the party and I'm sure your dad has got a lot tucked away.'

'Yes, yes, I'm sure we'll be fine,' said Sasha, making her excuses and heading to the bar, where she got a glass of cava and drank it quickly.

Did he have anything 'tucked away'? Sasha wasn't at all sure, not with the way her mother spent money, using Harrods as her own private boutique. They had not financially supported her for some time, of course, but she was still worried what it meant. *They might have to sell the house*, she thought, suddenly realising how much she was attached to that stupid mock-Tudor semi. She had spent so many years feeling embarrassed by her home and her family, but she still hated the idea of her childhood home not being there to go back to. And would the house be the only casualty? Picking the icing off a thin slice of anniversary cake, she looked at her parents on the dance floor, wondering about the chances of them reaching their thirtieth wedding anniversary. Slim to none, she suspected, when her father could no longer keep Carole in Oscar de la Renta dresses.

'You poor bugger,' she whispered to herself, sitting down at an empty table and filling her glass from a half-empty bottle. Over the years Sasha had experienced many emotions about her father: pity, resentment, frustration at his lack of ambition, talent and sophistication, certainly compared to the Robert Ashfords of this world. But in spite of it all, she loved him and privately acknowledged that she owed him a great deal. Growing up, it had been her mother who had encouraged her to take riding lessons, tap, ballet, flute; *self-improvement is key,* she had always said. But it was her dad who had made it happen. The thought suddenly struck her that he must have been taking time off work to make sure she got to her classes, to ferry her back and forth. No wonder he hadn't progressed in business.

God, I need a drink, she thought, reaching out for the wine. Just as she touched the neck, the bottle was snatched away.

'Hey!' she protested, looking up at a sharp-suited man standing by the table.

'Sorry,' he said, holding up his hand with a half-grin. 'I was just minesweeping.'

'Minesweeping?'

'Leftovers.'

'This isn't the student union, you know,' said Sasha sourly.

'Well, how about we share it?' he said, nodding to the spare chair next to her.

The bottle thief was handsome. Not Alex Doyle handsome, she thought, recalling a magazine feature she had seen about that smug bastard recently. No, this man had that sporty, public boy polish and a gym-toned physique evident beneath his tailored suit. Slightly square, of course, but then this was Hinchley Wood. She held out her glass and shrugged. 'If you must.'

'So who do you know here?' asked the man, topping up his own glass.

'That's my dad,' she said, nodding over in the direction of Gerald Sinclair. 'Poor bastard,' she said despite herself.

'Ah. I heard about his redundancy,' he said.

'Seems like everyone here knows about it,' she said tartly. 'I was just thinking about suing the firm.'

'Which firm?'

'Lewis Bettany, the company where he worked. They gave him redundancy three years short of retirement, presumably to avoid paying his pension. I'm having a friend check out the legality of it all first thing on Monday.'

'Actually I heard they gave him a very generous settlement. Several times their legal obligation, I understand.'

'Which my mother will go through like a plague of locusts.' She sighed, her wine already finished. She held up her glass to him. 'I'm Sasha Sinclair, by the way.'

'I gathered,' he said with a cheeky smile. 'I'm Phil.' He paused. 'Philip Bettany.'

Sasha narrowed her eyes as she examined him. 'Tell me the name's just a horrible coincidence,' she said.

'Sorry,' said Philip. 'My dad is the MD.'

She stared at him incredulously. 'Well you've got a bloody cheek coming here,' she huffed.

'We're invited. My mum, dad, brothers, the whole family.'

'That's so typical of my father,' she said wearily, looking over at Gerald. 'Nice guys come last. I learnt that lesson in kindergarten.'

'Look, Sasha, I don't know the details,' said Philip. 'My dad says it's a decent pay-off and that they held on to him as long as they could. We've all been suffering from the after-effects of the recession.'

'How thoughtful.'

She shot a sideways glance at him. Actually, he was better-looking than she had first thought. Wide, pale grey eyes with thick lashes. If she had seen him at some party in London, she would have thought he was gorgeous.

'So was it you who swung the axe, you arsehole?'

He snorted his wine down his nose. 'Hey, don't hold back.' He laughed. 'Say what you really mean. No, I don't even work for Bettany's. I work at Schroder's, the investment bank.'

Sasha pulled a bored face, but her interest in him rose a notch as her anger softened.

'It's OK, pays the rent,' he said, catching her look. 'But you're right, it's not exactly my childhood dream.'

'Which was what?'

'International-level rugby.' He grinned.

'You're too pretty for rugby. And too thin.'

'Fly-half. I played for Harlequins reserves until I ripped the cartilage in my knee. My career was over before it began really.'

He topped up their glasses. 'So what do you do, Sasha? Model?'

This time she gave him a withering look. 'That's a corny line, even for Hinchley Wood.'

'It's not a line,' he protested. 'I actually heard you were a model.'

'Ex-model. I'm a stylist.'

'Well, that's certainly a great dress,' he said, looking her up and down approvingly.

'I know. I want to buy the company.'

The words came out of her mouth without thinking. She had wanted to tell somebody about her plans to take over Ben Rivera for months, but the world she operated in was so gossipy and tight-knit and she wanted to be absolutely sure she could make it happen. She supposed it was easier to say it out loud to a complete stranger. Ever since that first meeting with the designer in his tiny Battersea workshop, she knew his designs were good enough to become a huge luxury brand – and quickly too. After all, Dolce and Gabbana were the stars of Milan fashion week after less than a decade in business. Giorgio Armani was a global success story, but had only started in the seventies. Society was increasingly design-conscious and label-aware, and Sasha predicted that by the turn of the millennium everyone would be eager for a slice of luxury label validation via designer underwear, scent, T-shirts, even jeans. It was happening already. Calvin Klein had built a billion-dollar empire by expanding into perfume and diffusion lines, making his chic minimalist aesthetic available to the masses *and* the elite.

'Interesting,' said Philip. 'Tell me more.'

She wasn't sure why she wanted to tell him, but she did. Perhaps it was being here, faced with a glimpse of her possible future if she failed to make her mark, that gave her the boldness to share her dreams.

'I work with an incredibly talented designer,' she said. 'He has a clear aesthetic and a loyal client base; he could be huge but he doesn't have the commercial sense to realise his potential. It would be so easy to spin the company out into handbags, scent, shoes . . .' She stopped herself, searching Philip's face. He was smiling, but he didn't laugh at her.

'Interesting sector, luxury fashion,' he said in an even, considered voice. 'But what management experience do you bring to the table? I thought you were a stylist.'

'I might not have been to business school, but I know what women want and I know how to make them beautiful. Plus I've got my own contacts – rich women, celebrities – who I can use as free publicity. I've got a feeling that celebrity is going to be vital to selling fashion in the next few years.'

Philip looked thoughtful. 'And does this designer want to sell?'

She'd had this conversation with Ben recently when she had taken him for cocktails at the Ritz, a celebration for getting one of his dresses on to Whitney Devine, a stunning American Grammy winner who was being photographed for a six-page *Vogue* story. In reality, she'd wanted to sound Ben out before everyone was after a piece of him. He had been disappointingly vague and elusive when she had suggested expanding the business – he didn't seem to have any commercial ambition at all. For him, it was all about the creation of beauty. And there was no money in art. Well, unless you were Andy Warhol.

'Everyone has a price,' she said. 'Besides, it's a tiny operation. He works out of a stable in Battersea. He can't ask much for it, can he?'

Philip shrugged. 'That depends.'

'On what?'

'The starting point is to fix how much the company is worth, which you can do from a series of multiples and calculating from turnover, operating profits, that sort of thing.'

He took a pen out of his pocket and began scribbling some figures on a napkin, his brows knotting in concentration as he explained the principles of a corporate sale.

'There are other factors as well. Does anyone else want to buy the company? How much potential does it have? I'm assuming you can finance the deal.'

He didn't say it unkindly, but there was an implied scepticism that someone like Sasha would have any grasp of the problems of high finance. It only made her more determined.

'Of course I can raise the money. Unless you can tell me a more clever way to do it.' She smiled coquettishly. She hadn't come to her parents' wedding anniversary party to score with a man, but she needed information, and in her experience, dangling sex in front of them often had a loosening effect on their tongues.

'Assuming you're not bringing much capital to the table yourself,' said Philip, 'you're probably looking at private equity rather than a bank, but the fashion sector is still seen as high risk. I mean, the guy specialises in cocktail dresses. If it was jeans or something at the mass-market end it might be more attractive—'

'But if people just see him as the cocktail dress man,' interrupted Sasha, 'then there will be less competition and we have more chance of paying less for the company.'

Philip smiled, clearly pleased at Sasha's quick grasp of the situation. 'I notice you're using the collective term "we".' He laughed.

'If I decide you're the right man for the job,' she said with a little more innuendo than was required.

'Look,' he said more seriously, 'assuming this company is

213

little more than a cottage industry, you could probably buy a controlling interest for tens of thousands, not hundreds. But then what? If the man really is working out of a stable, then it's going to need a major capital injection to move the business forward. We're talking factory production, large-scale distribution, advertising and marketing. Getting the company is just the start.'

Sasha nodded. He was definitely handsome. Didn't rugby players have cauliflower ears and broken noses? He probably had a strong back and legs built for stamina too. She shook off the image; this was business and only business.

'Can't you ask around? You must know lots of money men.'

'I will, but I'm not sure anyone will have the appetite for it.'

'Please. Try.'

Philip grinned and filled her glass again. 'In which case can I take you for dinner to talk about it further?'

'But you're the enemy, Phil Bettany,' she said with a hint of mischief.

'An enemy seeking forgiveness.'

'Well, you might have to work hard for that.'

'I'm willing to beg.'

Sasha laughed. She had no intention of sleeping with him, but he was a banker, a banker with contacts. He could be useful, very useful.

'OK, dinner it is,' she smiled. 'I hope you can stretch to a full bottle of wine.'

'I'll do my best,' he said.

I certainly hope you do, she thought.

23

Sitting in his room in Bangkok's Mandarin Oriental hotel, Miles looked down at the Coutts bank statement in his hand and reread the figure in the 'total' box. It was still there, all six noughts. He looked out of the window, over the Chao Phraya river, a smile spreading across his face. Finally, he was free. Free from his father, free from the golden yoke of being Robert Ashford's son, free to make his own choices, his own mistakes.

Miles had finally turned twenty-one and that meant that his trust funds had finally kicked in. Now he was *really* rich. In the month leading up to his birthday, he had been worried that his father might somehow manage to stop them. Both Connie and Robert had taken a very dim view of his departure from Oriel. He had hoped that when he went home to announce it, his father might have understood; after all, it had all happened in the name of entrepreneurialism. Instead, his mother had burst into tears, while Robert had mumbled that both his children had let him down before retreating silently to his study.

Miles folded the bank statement and put it away. At least that was the last time he'd have to face his parents' small-minded disapproval. He was his own man now – and his first decision as master of his destiny was to go out and celebrate.

He left the hotel and got in a cab to explore Bangkok. He

was in Thailand as part of his own personal 'grand tour' which had begun within days of his dismissal from Oxford. He went to Rio for Carnival, LA for Easter, Greece for summer, then zig-zagged back to New York, then Cape Town and Goa before heading to Thailand. The world was one long party if you knew where to look and Miles' entire address book was a roll-call of socialites, party animals and playboys desperate for the next thrill.

Bangkok was supposed to have been an overnight stop-over en route to Phuket, but the Mandarin Oriental had been so nice he had checked himself in for a week. Miles gazed out of the cab's window at the endless pink and blue neon signs: 'Go-go bar!', '24-hour Sex Show', 'Girls, Girls, Girls!' You didn't need insider knowledge to find the Patpong Road; in fact it would be hard to miss. Although Miles had no great desire to see Thai girls firing ping-pong balls from their vaginas, curiosity about this famous hotbed of wickedness had got the better of him. He left the cab and wandered among the thronging streets, peering at the signs advertising pedi-cures, two-for-one beers and 'full-body massage'. On the pave-ments, petite Thai girls in white vinyl boots beckoned him into their darkened doorways. Miles was having a great time. He hopped from bar to bar, drinking Singha beer and enjoying the alien sensation of being dislocated, surrounded by people who had no idea who he was: giggling couples on a naughty pit-stop to their honeymoon oasis, Western men in denim and football shirts gawking at sights which would stay with them all the way back to Düsseldorf and Tynemouth. It struck Miles that this was the first time he had truly been alone in years. Eton, Danehurst, Oxford, he'd always been surrounded by 'his people', and even when he'd flown the nest, he'd sought out other playboys to join him on his quest for the next high. But here, he was just another *farang*, a foreigner, a fish out of water – and he was loving every minute of it. He could go anywhere, do anything and no one would ever know.

He turned into another street, just as gaudy as the other strips, but here the girls in miniskirts had been replaced by muscular men in vests. In tight groups, their arms casually draped around each other, they watched Miles pass and smiled appreciatively. Miles was mesmerised, frightened, but above all excited. He hesitated on the street, then, taking a deep breath, he pushed his way into a humid basement bar, the throb of the music hitting him in his chest, the condensation dripping down the black lacquered walls – everyone seemed to be sweating, even the club. He elbowed his way to the bar and ordered a Jack Daniel's, knocking it back as he looked around. Men were everywhere, many stripped to the waist, drinking, dancing, even kissing. Miles was aroused by the sheer forbidden nature of the place. *I'm just curious,* he told himself.

'Your first time in Bangkok?'

He looked up. The man was maybe ten years older than him, and there was a trace of a European accent – Dutch? German? He was shorter than Miles but his pumped-up build bulged from the sleeves of a black T-shirt and his dark blond hair was cropped. Part of Miles wanted to run straight out of the club into the fresh air, but his feet felt welded to the spot.

'What makes you say that?' he asked.

The man smiled. 'Just a look.'

'What about you?'

'I come to Thailand twice a year. On business,' he smiled. 'It suits me.'

Miles glanced at the man's rough hands; on his finger was the glint of a wedding ring that both shocked and reassured him.

'You do know what this place is, don't you?'

Miles shrugged. Nonchalant, uncaring, as if he could take it or leave it, but inside his heart was pumping rapidly.

'Should I show you the back?'

'What's there?' asked Miles, finishing his drink. Suddenly his throat seemed very dry.

'What do you think?'

Miles allowed the man to lead him towards a door at the back of the bar where he gave a handful of baht to a bored-looking Thai man on a stool. Inside was a dark corridor smelling of disinfectant, a number of doors leading off to the right. Low sounds echoed behind the walls, moans, murmurs.

Holding one of the doors open, the man indicated that Miles should enter. Nervously, he stepped into a small, dark booth. The heat was oppressive and he felt his body tense. The man was behind him now in the confined space, so close that Miles could feel his breath on the back of his neck.

'Relax. I don't bite,' he said, smiling. 'Not unless you want me to.'

Reaching past Miles, he pushed a token into a rusty slot and a window instantly opened in front of him. Inside, on a vinyl mattress, were three naked men touching, stroking, fucking. For a second, a series of images jumped into Miles' mind, schoolboy fumbles in the dorm at Eton, stolen experimental kisses in the bathroom, the odd encounter on a stairwell in some club in London. But nothing like this. Nothing this – real.

'Do you like this?' asked the man as he unzipped Miles' chinos and reached inside. 'Ah, yes, I think you do.'

Miles closed his eyes, his breath coming in rasps now.

'How's that feel?' asked the man as his trousers fell to the concrete floor.

Miles said nothing, but it felt wonderful. It felt so good to finally release the shameful pent-up desires he'd carried with him for so long, and now, finally, he was ready and willing for the pain and pleasure he was about to receive.

Twenty-four hours later, Miles was in Phuket. The morning after his night out in the depths of Bangkok he checked out of the Oriental, found a stand-by flight and by early evening was weaving up and down the side streets of Patong's Bangla Road with an enormous sense of relief. He felt much more at home here: tanned, slim posh girls on their gap years filled the streets alongside Aussie backpackers on their way to bar jobs. Were it not for the palm trees and the clear blue of the Andaman Sea in the background, it could almost have been a Saturday night along the Fulham Road. At a Thai boxing match he fell in with Tom and Zac, students who had graduated from Edinburgh that summer, and they spent the rest of the evening hopping from bar to bar, enjoying the easy camaraderie of young Brits abroad. Miles felt safe with these boys – they were straight, normal and predictable, exactly what he needed after last night. The thought of it set off a clash of emotions – shame, confusion and, most of all, desire. He pushed the feelings away and herded his new friends into the Disco-a-Go-Go bar behind Soi Seadragon, hitting a wall of neon and sound.

'Welcome, boys,' smiled a petite Thai girl in a tight T-shirt and micro-shorts.

'Hell-oh, mama,' said Zac, gawping at the girl's breasts.

'I hope they're going to be filthy,' said Tom as they ordered beers at the bar and clambered on to bar stools to watch a line of girls sashay out on to a runway. They were mostly Thai, slim and young, wearing an assortment of skimpy clothing – mesh cropped T-shirts, leather shorts, metallic bikinis. The room filled with a sexual charge as the girls danced, hips gyrating, arms circling suggestively. But Miles was only watching one girl. She was different, and not just because she was the only Western girl on the stage. Her long hair was dyed red, swishing back and forth across her curved back. A black crop-top clung to voluptuous breasts and stopped short of a slim, perfectly toned belly. She had spotted Miles watching her and strode over, grinding her taut tummy just in front of his grinning face.

219

'Tuck a fifty in her bra, Miles!' whooped Zac.

'Pounds or baht?' He smiled.

Tom sniggered. Fifty baht was worth less than a pound. Miles gave the girl a hundred-dollar bill, hard US currency. It wasn't like he couldn't afford it, was it?

'Whoa, your round I think, Miles,' said Zac, slapping him on the back.

The dancing girls came off stage to mingle with the crowd, draping themselves over the punters, flirting crudely, cajoling the punters to buy them drinks; small measures, Miles noticed.

'Hey, cowboy.'

Turning, he met the piercing gaze of the redhead.

'Shouldn't you be checking out the dancers, not the bar?' she said with amusement.

'I was just working out how much money this place made a night,' said Miles.

'Fancy the Patong bar game, do you?' She looked at his cream trousers and pink Turnbull and Asser shirt. 'You don't look like the type.'

'Just curious.'

She nodded non-committally. 'So are you going to buy me a drink?'

He smiled. 'A watered-down one, you mean?'

She twirled her finger around her belly chain. 'Oh, I do miss the cynicism of Britain.'

'Where are you from?'

'Hastings,' she said after a minute pause.

'So what brought you here?'

'Same thing as half the other people in Patong. Money, adventure, excitement.'

She gave him a suggestive half-smile. To his surprise, he found he was enjoying her attention.

'And did you find it?'

'Business is good.' She smiled slowly. 'I probably make a great deal more money than most people my age, even posh

Home Counties ones with fancy educations like you.'

He smiled at her naïve suggestion that she somehow had more money than him. But she had a 'screw you' attitude that appealed to him. She wasn't going to sweet-talk him just to get the commission for a few overpriced drinks. Still, he couldn't help goading her.

'So how exactly do you make that money?'

She visibly bristled. 'This is a decent place. The dancers here aren't hookers.'

She waited, hands on hips, for a smart remark, but Miles just met her gaze.

'I make money because I'm pretty,' she continued with irritation. 'Because I'm European. Because I don't want to get married to the first guy who shows interest. And the Asian guys love me. I don't fuck. I just dance, and I make a lot of cash doing it. Speaking of which, are you going to buy me a drink? My bosses are watching.'

'I don't pay to talk to girls.'

'Yes, you have that look about you,' she said, turning on her heel.

Miles pulled her back. This girl was affecting him. Not in an obvious sexual way, but there was something about her that made him want to keep talking to her.

'Why don't we meet later?' he said. 'Not for money. Because you want to.'

She was about to laugh it off, but then saw Miles was serious. She hesitated.

'I'm at the Marriott in Karon Bay,' he said quickly. 'Come by for a drink at the bar later.'

She shook her head slightly. 'When I'm off duty, I'm off duty.'

Miles smiled. 'Come on. I thought you came to Phuket for adventure.'

She raised that sculpted eyebrow again. 'You could be anyone.'

'Do I look like Jack the Ripper?'

'Just because you're wearing Ralph Lauren doesn't mean you don't want a freebie fuck with a go-go girl.'

Miles smiled slightly. 'Thanks for making me sound so cheap,' he said. 'Not many people can do that, believe me.'

She laughed. Suddenly she seemed to make a decision. 'I finish at one a.m.,' she said. 'There's a little bar in Karon Bay called The Red Parrot. One drink. And I'm buying.'

And with that, she walked off into the crowd. Miles grinned at her back, feeling strangely buoyant.

'Strike out with the redhead?' said Zac sympathetically. He had a Thai girl with waist-length hair sitting on his knee, simpering.

'Can't win 'em all, can you?' said Miles, signalling to the barman and wondering how long he could leave it before he got rid of Tom and Zac.

24

She was twenty minutes late. Miles had considered leaving, but when she walked through the door in white jeans and a tight red T-shirt, he was glad he had swallowed his pride and stayed. She looked fantastic and Miles was particularly pleased that she looked even better in this relaxed setting. Karon Bay was just two miles down the Suwang Road but a million miles away from the fluoro pink lights and sex tourists of Patong. Chrissy Devine ('The name on my birth certificate,' she smiled. 'I was born to be a go-go dancer, wasn't I?') had been in Thailand for almost eighteen months, lured to the exotic East when an ex-boyfriend had told her about the money to be made on the strip. She ordered Miles a cocktail – not bothering to ask if he wanted one – and pulled him over to the pool table where she expertly potted four balls in quick succession.

'So that's me,' she smiled, lining up her next shot, breasts almost spilling out of the low scoop of her T-shirt. 'What about you? On a round-the-world ticket with Daddy's money until he finds you something at the family firm?'

Miles laughed. He loved the fact that she didn't mind pissing him off. Girls usually tiptoed around him, twirling their fingers in their hair, careful not to say the wrong thing, careful not to upset the highly eligible Miles Ashford. Chrissy was different, crackling with sexual energy and attitude. Miles could feel himself getting aroused as much as the night before.

'You're right about the round-the-world trip. But wrong about Daddy's money.'

'So you work?'

'No. Inheritance.'

'Lucky you,' she replied with a small throaty laugh. 'The only thing I got from my family was a rejection complex.'

'Really? What happened?'

Chrissy waved a hand in the air. 'Oh, just the usual story. My dad pissed off when I was nine, Mum got a new boyfriend, and they started breeding like rabbits to get a bigger house off the council. Once the new kids came along, me and my brother were pushed to the side. My brother didn't handle it very well. You can see him hanging around Hastings harbour now trying to score heroin.'

'Christ,' said Miles, trying not to look as shocked as he felt. He had never met the benefit scroungers he'd read about in the tabloids, and he'd certainly never met a junkie. 'Sorry.'

'Don't be sorry,' said Chrissy. 'My brother was always a loser. I got out as soon as I could. I went to Amsterdam when I was seventeen, then Tokyo, working in bars for a couple of years until I'd saved up the cash to come here.'

He did the arithmetic. 'So you're twenty-one?' He was surprised. She didn't look the same age as him. He was suddenly more impressed with her worldliness. 'How long are you going to keep doing this?'

'I've already been sounded out by Sundown on Soi Bangla to be a mamasan in the New Year.'

'What's that?'

'A manager.' She smiled. 'It's a promotion.'

'Really?'

'As mamasan I'll get a cut of everything my dancers make. It's good pay; it's dirt cheap to live out here. I reckon to make a hundred grand before I'm thirty.'

Miles whistled. 'Shit, you have it all worked out.'

Chrissy potted the black with a decisive thunk.

'Then again,' said Miles slowly, 'a hundred grand? That's not particularly ambitious.'

'Sorry if it doesn't sound much to you,' she snapped. 'But I'll have earned it, not just pulled it out of my trust fund.'

'I didn't mean to sound patronising. And it doesn't matter where you come from, Chrissy; if you want it enough, you can be as big, as rich as they come.'

She eyed him up slowly. 'I thought you'd be a snob.'

He laughed. 'Not me. At school, my best mate was the scholarship boy.'

'How fucking generous of you.' She laughed, taking a long drag of cigarette. She wasn't as beautiful as Sasha, thought Miles, but she had something more raw, more animal. Even so, put her in jeans and cowboy boots and behind the wheel of a BMW on the King's Road, she'd fit right in.

'Want to come back for a smoke?'

Chrissy's flat consisted of one large room with a bathroom, but it was tidy and surprisingly feminine: purple velvet cushions and rose petals by the bath. Miles sat on a small sofa pouring vodka into two old china cups, while Chrissy sat cross-legged on the floor, expertly rolling a double-size joint.

'I thought the Thais were zero tolerance on drugs,' said Miles as she passed it over. 'The papers are full of stories about the Bangkok Hilton.'

Chrissy let the fragrant smoke out with a sigh. 'You don't want to get caught dealing,' she said. 'They still enforce the death penalty for trafficking. But the police are always open to a bribe for anything recreational.'

Miles moved to sit next to her on the floor.

'I'm a bit drunk,' she said with a laugh. 'I think you're a bad influence.'

'It's not the first time that's been said,' drawled Miles.

He felt his cock stiffen. Carefully he pushed back the scoop

225

neck of her T-shirt and kissed her shoulder, tasting her skin, soft and moist like chocolate butter.

'You know I don't usually do this,' she murmured.

'Neither do I,' he replied truthfully.

The ceiling fan revolved lazily above them as his hand slid up to her breasts, and as he rubbed his palm over her nipples, she tipped her head back and groaned. Turning, she kissed him hard on the mouth, pulling urgently at his belt, pushing down his jeans. Her fingers found his cock, and as her hand moved up and down the shaft he grew, to his enormous relief, harder and harder in her grip. Her mouth sank down over his cock, taking him whole.

He moaned, pulling out with a soft 'pop'. He scrambled to shed the rest of his clothes, then tore at hers, falling on to the rug, his greedy mouth on hers.

She slipped a condom on him, and they fucked on the floor, urgent, hungry, her back arching as he kissed her ear lobes, her throat, his hands sweeping over her slicked skin, pulling her hips to him, and she came quickly, shuddering as he gave one last feral thrust into her, collapsing on to her breasts, their bodies pressed together. And Miles grinned to himself as he turned his head away, listening to the hard beating of her heart.

Harsh white sunlight breaking through the thin curtains woke him. Blinking, for one moment he wondered where he was, then he smiled as he saw Chrissy making breakfast in the small kitchen area, naked except for a blue lace thong and a white shirt she had left undone. He lit a cigarette and scratched his balls with satisfaction.

'What's on room service?' he asked.

'Lipton's tea,' she said, padding back through and thrusting the mug into his hand. 'The best I can do, I'm afraid.'

She perched on the edge of the bed and, smiling, slipped her hand under the covers to rub his cock.

'Oh, I think you can do better than that,' he said, putting his tea down.

'Hey, I thought I was going to show you the island,' she protested.

'The island's not going anywhere,' he smiled.

Two hours later, Miles found himself standing on a pier, watching with fascination as Chrissy jabbered away to an old fisherman in Thai. Whatever was said, it ended with Chrissy handing over a fistful of notes and the little man leading them to a small fishing boat that took them out into the Andaman Sea.

It was a perfect day for a trip across to the outlying islands. The boat scudded across the bright emerald waters, past shanty towns clustered along the shore, washing hanging to dry and herds of longboats crowding the docks. Chrissy pointed out sea gypsy communities and glittering temples seemingly placed at random. As they got further out to sea, the landscape grew more dramatic, with huge karst rising from the water like giant limestone fingers. Miles closed his eyes as the warm wind whipped through his hair. He was used to travelling in luxury, private jets, de luxe hotels, but the raw natural beauty caught him by surprise.

Finally the boat's engine chugged to a stop. The captain pulled a battered kayak from beneath a tarpaulin and Chrissy helped him to lift it over the side.

Miles sat at the back of the kayak and followed Chrissy's lead, raking the green foam first with one paddle, then the other. They ploughed through the water towards the sheer cliffs until he saw a gaping hole in the side of the rock, barely big enough to squeeze through.

'Open Sesame,' said Chrissy, turning around to smile at him.

'We're going into a cave?' said Miles incredulously.

'Come on, rich boy, live a little.'

227

In seconds they were in an eerie blue-grey darkness, cold and strange after the baking sun of the open sea.

Miles shivered, unnerved by the strange twilight of the cavern, nothing below them but lapping blackened water. Suddenly they slid around a corner and the narrow walls opened out into a cave mouth, cliffs rearing behind them, a cornflower-blue sky above.

'Holy shit,' said Miles, truly incredulous. They had passed straight through the wall of the island and into a hidden lagoon. Directly in front of them was a curve of blinding white beach.

At twenty-one, Miles considered himself a man of the world. He had dived off the cliffs in Mexico, skied down treacherous off-piste runs in Whistler, but this was unlike anything he had ever experienced.

'Pretty cool, huh?' said Chrissy as they dragged the kayak up the beach. She peeled off her denim shorts and lay on the sand in her black bikini, her legs looking even longer and browner than before.

Laughing, Miles threw himself down next to her and kissed her. 'Thanks, Chrissy,' he said.

She looked surprised. 'What for?'

'For being different.'

'Ah, now different I can do,' she said, reaching for his zip.

It was hot on the beach and the two litre bottles of water they had brought were quickly drunk. Trying to cool off, they swam across the lagoon and tried to climb the rock face, finally giving up in a tangle of screams and laughter. And then they sat on the rocks and fucked again, slowly this time, touching, tasting, enjoying each other's deepest and most sensitive places. It was one of the best days of Miles Ashford's life.

When they got back to Patong, Chrissy had gone to work and it had seemed the most natural thing for Miles to hang around her flat, just drinking tea, watching badly dubbed movies on cable and reading Chrissy's collection of hard-boiled detective fiction. He had dozed off when he heard the click of the door and Chrissy climbed naked into bed beside him, curling herself into the hollow of his body like a cat.

They spent the next day together and the day after that, and the day after that. After a week, Miles stopped paying for the room at the Marriott and moved his bags into Chrissy's studio and their days fell into an easy routine. By day they would swim, explore the island on scooters and make love in lonely coves off the beaten track; by night, he would smoke dope in her little studio and wait for her to return from work. But slowly, the nightly absences began to get to Miles. He was missing London, his old life and the certainties of his position in the world.

One night it was getting him particularly down. By the time she got home at 4 a.m., he was spoiling for a fight.

'You still up, baby?' she said, coming over to kiss his neck. He pushed her away impatiently.

'Where have you been?' he snapped.

'Where do you think?' she said. 'At work.'

'Oh yeah?' he said petulantly.

'Miles, what's going on?'

'I think you should leave the bar,' he said flatly.

'I am leaving the bar,' she said, walking through to the kitchen and filling the kettle. 'You know I'm starting at Hooters in January.'

He looked at her, his face like thunder. 'You're not listening. I don't want you working at Sundown either.'

She slammed the kettle down. 'Piss off, Miles.'

'Chrissy, you're better than this.'

'Better than what?' There was ice in her voice.

'Better than tarting around clubs in tiny skirts, jiggling your tits at Japs. Better than this shit-hole.'

'Fuck you, Miles,' she shouted. 'This is my shit-hole, paid

for with my shitty money. I work bloody hard for what I've got, but that's not something you'd know about, is it?'

He stood up unsteadily. 'I know what you're really doing to earn that money,' he began, but she silenced him with a stinging slap across the face.

'Get out,' she growled.

Miles stared after her, touching his stinging skin. 'Come to London,' he said.

She didn't speak, just shook her head.

'You think your life is better than mine, don't you?' she said eventually. She looked so defiant, so angry, so sure of her place in the world that Miles almost laughed.

'Come back with me,' he repeated.

'I'm happy here.'

He threw his hands up. 'Well I'm not.'

The anger in her face melted into sadness. 'I'm sorry,' she said. 'I didn't know.'

He strode across to her and took her hands in his. 'It's not you, Chris, don't think that. It's just this place, it's closing in on me, and we've got the whole world to explore together.'

Miles knew he didn't want to stay in Thailand for ever. Sure, it was fun and cheap, like a teenager mainlining on Thunderbird, but the novelty of slumming it was wearing off, and he was missing the familiar luxuries of his London life. But he didn't want to lose Chrissy. It had been a long time since he had felt he had a partner in crime – not since he'd buggered it all up with Alex, in fact – and he loved how she made him feel: clever and adventurous and brave. How shallow and sapping his relationship with Sasha had been, how pointless the interchangeable society blondes he'd toyed with at Oxford. Chrissy was real, an equal, a genuine soulmate.

'Look, Miles,' she said softly, 'it's fine if you have to move on ...'

No! he thought, his heart lurching. The more she pulled away from him, the more he wanted her.

'I have money to buy a flat. Something smart in Chelsea, South Ken. We could live there,' he began.

'And do what? Play happy fucking families?' She laughed harshly.

He hesitated. 'You and I are so alike, Chrissy. We're good together. We can have a better life in London.'

She stepped forward and put her arms around his neck. 'Look, Miles, I really, really like you. But I know how these things work. I move to London and you get back with some posh ex-girlfriend your daddy approves of and I have to start all over again. Besides, I like it here.'

An idea popped into his head so remote, so stupid, so wrong, it seemed right. He pulled her closer.

'I want you, Chrissy Devine.'

'I'm not a fucking sports car, Miles.'

He paused, his mouth suddenly going dry. *Oh fuck it,* he thought.

'Marry me.'

Chrissy blinked at him, a flicker of a smile crossing her face. 'Marry you?' she repeated.

Miles started chuckling. The last six weeks had been incredible fun. He felt armour-plated when he was with her. He dropped down to one knee, still holding her hand.

'You're not kidding, are you?' she giggled.

Miles shook his head. 'I've never been more serious about anything.'

Carefully, she knelt down to face him, looking into his eyes and threading her arms around his neck.

'OK,' she said.

'What?' said Miles, a smile spreading across his face.

'I said yes.' She laughed.

'Really?'

'Yep,' she said. 'I mean, why the fuck not?'

231

Cackling with laughter, he grabbed her face and kissed her again and again.

They flew back to London via Vegas, and after a twelve-minute ceremony at the Little White Chapel of the West, Miles Ashford and Chrissy Devine became man and wife. They spent their first night in a suite at the MGM Grand, drinking champagne and taking coke. Lying back on the huge circular water bed as Chrissy stroked his cock, Miles couldn't remember when he had experienced feeling this high, unfettered and free, the fact that he had not yet told his parents only heightening the delicious feeling of rebellion and power. In his quieter moments he preferred not to dwell on the fact of whether he really did love Chrissy – he supposed he cared for her as much as any married couple did these days. Whatever, he was looking forward to playing Professor Higgins to his own Eliza Doolittle. The first thing he proposed to do when they got back to London was to take her shopping and change his dirty little sex kitten into a Chelsea Blonde. He chuckled to himself. Whoever would have thought he'd be married at twenty-one? Well, he did pride himself on being a little unconventional. He drifted off to sleep, knowing that his night in that filthy booth in Bangkok seven weeks ago was well and truly erased.

25

December 1992

Miles had been to many parties at Ashford Park, his parents' thousand-acre Oxfordshire estate. He could remember summer parties for the company being held on the large lawns that led down to the lake, where there would be pony rides for the children, a huge marquee serving Pimm's and an open-air dance floor by the water. Robert Ashford had built a reputation for his hospitality, but as he drove his rented Mercedes up the driveway towards the main house, Miles could tell that the boat had really been pushed out for his mother's fiftieth birthday party. The dove-grey Bath stone façade of the forty-roomed manor house was bathed in klieg lights and an army of valets were parking a fleet of expensive vehicles – Bentleys, Ferraris, Porsches – in a fan shape to one side of the house. It was like a festival for motor enthusiasts.

'Nice pad,' drawled Chrissy in the seat beside him.

He glanced across at her and laughed. The way she said it, so casually, as if she saw places like this every week.

'Most people seem to agree with you,' he said. 'It was on the cover of *Architectural Digest* three years ago and we only gave access to four rooms and the gardens.'

'Fancy,' she said, checking herself in the mirror, pulling the shoulders down on her chic Armani cocktail dress to reveal more flesh.

'Do I look white?' she asked, touching up her make-up. 'I can't believe my tan is fading.'

He glanced across and winced at the long, square fingernails that gripped her scarlet lipstick. Miles' Professor Higgins project had been a success – forgetting the nails, she looked every inch the well-dressed Sloane – but still he was nervous about tonight. Would she embarrass him? They had been back from Phuket for four days now and had been staying at the Capital Hotel in Knightsbridge. Miles had been keen to show off his home town to Chrissy and told her he wanted to spoil his new wife, taking her into London's finest shops in preparation for their first meeting with his parents. At Harvey Nichols she had wanted a sexy Dolce and Gabbana dress, but Miles had steered her towards the more conservative Armani concession. Before her hair appointment at Michaeljohn, he'd had a quiet word with the stylist, asking him to tone down Chrissy's vivid red hair into a softer shade of chestnut. And tonight, as they had dressed in their sumptuous hotel suite, Chrissy had spent half an hour looking for the ankle bracelet which Miles had thrown in the bin the day they had arrived. Miles had married Chrissy because he loved her overt sexuality and her fiercely independent streak, but at the same time he didn't want the attributes he found so attractive to rock the boat tonight.

'Look, about meeting my parents,' he began as they pulled up a little way from the house. 'They are going to ask a lot of questions. So maybe be a bit vague about Disco-A-Go-Go.'

'Why, are you ashamed of me?'

'No, baby. But my father can be quite conservative.'

'I thought you didn't care what your father thought.'

Miles rolled his eyes. 'At some point I'm going to have to start working at Ash Corp. and my father's an awkward bastard when he feels slighted. I want my pick of the company departments – I don't want him dumping me in Finance or somewhere, because he can.'

'And you think I'm going to get you sent to Siberia?'

Miles smiled. 'Maybe. He's going to be pissed off enough that we got married without asking his permission. I don't need to make it any worse.'

'I promise I'll be a good girl,' said Chrissy in a mocking tone. 'Now, have you got the coke?'

Miles laughed and racked a couple of fat lines out on a road atlas, rubbing the residue into their gums.

'OK, husband,' purred Chrissy, her eyes suddenly more bright. 'Let's do it!'

'Well, well. What a surprise,' said Robert Ashford. 'The prodigal son returns.'

Stiffly, Miles and his father shook hands at the door of Ashford Park. All around them was the rich smell of cinnamon and pine cones, and the happy sound of four hundred party guests enjoying themselves at someone else's expense. The huge entrance hall was dominated by a twenty-foot Christmas tree festooned with Austrian crystal baubles and banners hanging from the ceiling declared 'Seasons Greetings!' and 'Goodwill to all Men!' And yet despite not having seen one another in almost twelve months, the atmosphere between father and son was sub-zero.

'Not pleased to see me?' said Miles.

'On the contrary, Miles,' said Robert, 'I was beginning to think I would have to go to the expense and inconvenience of sending a search party. Your turning up out of the blue is something of a boon in that department.'

Miles' instinct was to turn around and leave straight away, but with Chrissy there he couldn't, not without losing face.

'Yes, I know I said I was coming back in February,' he said in a more even tone. 'But, well, there was a change of plan.'

'Did the full-moon party scene finally lose its appeal?' said Robert. He turned to Chrissy, holding out a hand. 'I don't believe we've met,' he smiled.

'Christine Devine,' she said with a deferential nod. 'Call me Chrissy. Pleased to meet you.'

Miles watched his father quickly size up his wife.

'Judging from the tan,' said Robert, 'I'd say you two met abroad.'

'Thailand,' replied Chrissy.

'Wonderful,' he replied with little enthusiasm. 'And were you travelling too?'

'Working.'

'Really? Whereabouts?'

'In Phuket. I worked in a hotel.'

Miles smiled inwardly, grateful for the lie.

'Oh, which one?' asked Robert. 'I was in Patong last summer looking at resort sites.'

Chrissy answered without hesitation. 'The Coral Cay, lovely place . . .'

'Miles! I don't believe it!' said an excited voice, breaking the interrogation. It was Connie Ashford, and Miles gratefully embraced his mother. Always a beautiful woman, she looked especially chic in a long midnight-blue silk gown which fell to the floor. Her blond hair was swept off her face in a chignon, her delicate features enhanced by soft sweeps of colour to her cheeks and eyelids. Her extreme beauty often made people think she was haughty, but when she smiled, which was often, her Grace Kelly froideur softened, giving her a warmth that her husband lacked.

'Happy birthday, Mum,' said Miles, kissing her cheek.

'I couldn't have asked for a better present.' She smiled.

'Mum, this is Chrissy,' he said, quickly manoeuvring her away from his father.

'Lovely to meet you,' said Connie, shaking her hand.

'Well, I'm glad we have both of you here,' said Miles

quickly; he wanted to get this over with. 'We have some news.'

'Tell me you're staying for New Year?' said Connie, looking from Miles to Chrissy expectantly.

Miles shook his head.

'We're married.'

There was a stunned pause as both parents blinked at him, not quite sure if they had heard him correctly.

'Married?' said Connie, nervously tucking a curl of hair behind her ear. 'My word . . . that certainly is news.' Regaining her characteristic poise, she stepped forward and embraced her son and his new bride. 'Congratulations to both of you,' she said, her eyes glazing with tears. 'I'm bowled over. But it's wonderful. Isn't it, Robert?'

'You never stop surprising us, Miles,' said Robert, his smile thin and tight. 'I'll give you that much.'

'You know I like to keep things interesting, Dad,' said Miles. 'Wouldn't want to disappoint, would I?'

Connie saw the challenge in Miles' jutting chin and stepped in between the two men before it could escalate.

'Well, I think we all need to celebrate, don't you?' she said, leading Miles and Chrissy into the crowded hall, chattering to cover the silence. 'I think Robert is planning to make a little speech later, so we can announce it then.'

'Tonight is your birthday celebration, Connie,' said Robert haughtily. 'I'm not sure we should be muddying the waters.'

'No, I think Mr Ashford's right,' said Chrissy, glancing at Miles and looking very awkward. 'We don't want to steal your thunder.'

Connie was just beginning to object when Miles' father interrupted.

'Darling, John and Norma Major have just arrived, I think we should say hello. We can all talk about this later.'

Connie nodded, then took her son's hand. 'I'll get Consuela to prepare your room. Tomorrow we can go to Le Manoir for dinner and make plans. Chrissy, we'll have to do something girlie.'

'Constance. Please,' said Robert sharply, beckoning her over.

Miles watched them go, feeling angry but not entirely surprised. He had actually expected more of an explosion from his father, but then he had been caught on the back foot. Miles felt sure Robert would have more to say on this later.

'They're not happy, are they?' said Chrissy, a note of sadness in her voice.

'Don't take it personally. They were never going to do cartwheels at the news. Secretly, I think my mother is delighted, although I'm sure she feels a bit cheated. She lives for planning: birthday parties, charity events, company outings; she loves to work out every detail. And considering my sister Grace went off and had a shotgun wedding in the South American sticks, she's missed out on both of the big ones.'

Chrissy didn't look convinced. She folded her arms in front of her chest. 'Your dad hates me.'

'No he doesn't. He disapproves of my lifestyle choices. It's not you, it's me.'

'Right then,' she said, deliberately ignoring him. 'Just because your dad's a grumpy old bugger, let's not let it ruin the night. Come on, let's get pissed and have sex in the hayloft.'

'We don't have a hayloft,' said Miles, slightly affronted. 'This is a Robert Adam manor house, one of England's finest, actually, not some farm.'

Chrissy leant in close to Miles and gently bit his ear lobe. 'Well maybe you'd better show me,' she laughed in her sexy, smoky way. 'Architecture turns me on.'

They took two bottles of champagne from the bar and Miles took Chrissy on an impromptu tour of the house: the library stuffed with rare first editions and eighteenth-century tapestries, the big kitchen with the giant bread oven, his old

238

bedroom in the west wing, still decorated with sports cups and Airfix model aeroplanes. Her open amazement at the place charmed him. There was a quiet competitiveness between the rich which meant anyone of their level would not be able to bring themselves to compliment someone else's house beyond asking who their decorator might be. Only Alex Doyle had been as wide-eyed at the grandeur of the Ashford family home as Chrissy.

'Miles, this place is like a fairy-tale castle, only more beautiful. Is it as nice outside? Do you have one of those big maze things?'

Her eyes were slightly glassy from the champagne, but she was genuinely excited by Miles' lifestyle; not in a 'I've just hooked an eligible bachelor' way; more that she was actually pleased to be here, as if she couldn't believe her luck.

'Do you really want to go outside?' he asked. 'It'll be freezing out there.'

She giggled. 'I'll warm you up, don't you worry.'

They returned to Miles' bedroom, where they had sex and rolled a joint and sat giggling, semi-naked, on his old single bed.

An hour later there was a sharp rap on the door. Robert Ashford entered the room and Miles waved his hand in the air to diffuse the sweet smell of dope.

His dad's eyes blazed. 'So here's where you are. It's your mother's birthday and she's seen you for literally two minutes.'

'Sorry,' Miles said smirking.

Robert sniffed the air. 'Are you high, Miles?' he demanded, his voice quivering.

'No,' he lied. Chrissy giggled.

Robert glared at her. 'I'd like a moment with my son if you don't mind.'

She looked at Miles, who nodded.

The two men watched in silence as she put on her dress and carefully closed the door behind her. When she was gone,

Robert drew himself up to his full height and clasped his hands behind his back.

'How many times are we going to be in this situation, Miles?' he asked.

'I'm twenty-one, Father,' he replied defiantly as he pulled on his jeans. 'I don't need you telling me how to live my life.'

'Evidently you do.'

'Dad, it's just a joint . . .'

'I mean about you marrying this tart on some beach in Thailand. Did you think for one minute how it would affect the family?'

Miles narrowed his eyes. 'She is not a tart,' he hissed. 'She is my wife!'

Robert chuckled, a cruel smile on his face. 'I was being polite. Whore might be nearer the mark.'

'Don't you *dare* speak about her like that!' yelled Miles. 'You don't know anything about her.'

'I know she didn't work at the Coral Cay hotel,' said Robert in a superior tone. 'I phoned them an hour ago and they had no record of her. Where did you meet her, Miles? A go-go bar? A sex show?'

Miles could feel every muscle in his body tense, a thudding headache building in his temples. He'd been here before, right on the edge of control, and he knew that if he let himself, he could walk across the room and tear his father apart. *Not now, not this way*, he said to himself. There were other ways to hurt a man like Robert Ashford, ways which would wound him far deeper than a punch ever could. *You've just made yourself a dangerous enemy, Father*, he thought. He took a long ragged breath, clearing his vision.

'She was a dancer,' he said finally.

Robert was looking at him as if he was some unpleasant worm he'd found crawling across his path.

'Is she pregnant?' he asked.

'No,' sighed Miles, suddenly weary of the whole charade.

'Was this ceremony legal?'

'Do you mean were we married by a witch doctor who blew smoke rings into the air when we said "I do"?'

'Well was it?'

'Yes, it was legal. We were married in Vegas.'

'Damn,' muttered Robert.

Miles barked out a harsh laugh. 'You are a horrible snob,' he said, shaking his head.

Robert laughed with an air of self-righteousness. 'Speaks the boy who walked around Oxford for twelve months in a gown . . .' He trailed off as Connie Ashford walked into the room.

'What's going on?' she said irritably. 'I've just found poor Chrissy crying on the stairs.'

Robert waved an angry hand through the air. 'Poor Chrissy?' he mocked. 'She's a gold-digger, an opportunist. She is a destructive influence and Lord knows Miles doesn't need any help in that department.'

He glanced at his watch, as if this was all taking up too much of his precious time.

'On Monday morning I am speaking to Peter Murray, family law expert at Farrar's. Preferably this so-called marriage can be annulled rather than go through divorce proceedings. The last thing I want is to give her any money, but if that's what it takes for her to clear off, I suppose we can arrange something.'

Miles looked at his father with cold hate. Chrissy made him feel like a man in bed and out of it; there was no way he was giving her up.

'I am not divorcing Chrissy,' he said evenly.

'I'm not asking, Miles.'

'And I'm not one of your business pawns you can manipulate and bully. I am a man now and you will treat me like one.'

Ignoring him, Robert ploughed on. 'You bum around the

world on hand-outs, then you come crawling back with a hooker for a wife and an STD no doubt.'

'Robert, please,' pleaded Connie.

'Unless you get rid of that girl and sort yourself out, there is no future for you at Ash Corp.,' said Robert. 'And there will be no further money from our coffers. I mean it, Miles.'

The two men's eyes locked.

'Good,' said Miles, his voice shaking. 'I don't need your pathetic little company.'

'It's my pathetic little company that has given you this house, your education—'

'I don't want *any* of it!' screamed Miles. 'Don't you understand that? I don't want anything you can give me, Father – *nothing*!'

Robert Ashford was already by the door. 'You have until New Year to think about it,' he said, and walked out of the room without turning back.

'Miles, wait—'

Connie could see that her son was in a rage, out of control. There was no telling what he would do if he caught up with his father, so she stepped out, blocking the door.

'Mum, don't,' Miles growled, his cheeks flushed, but Connie shook her head firmly.

Robert had never understood Miles or the anger, the violence he kept inside him, but Connie had known about it from the moment he was born, when he took one look at the world and let out a terrible scream. Miles had an energy, a dark urge she hadn't felt with Grace – or anyone else for that matter. He had huge untapped talents, hidden depths that were capable of great things, she was sure of it, but neither of his parents and none of his teachers had been able to do anything about it. Connie realised that a line had been crossed tonight – and she also knew this might be her last chance to reach her son.

'Miles, sit down,' she said, closing the door.

'I've got to go to Chrissy,' insisted Miles.

'Chrissy is fine, darling.'

'But you heard what Dad said.'

'Yes. And I think your father is wrong.'

Although Connie Ashford came from money – considerably more money than her husband if truth be told – she was not a snob. She did not judge Chrissy just because of her accent, the way she looked or how she made a living. She remembered only too well the way her own family had looked down their noses when she had first introduced them to Robert Ashford. Poor Robert had come from nothing and had clawed his way up – but not very far. He was destined for great things, but by then all he had was a five-bedroom guesthouse in Notting Hill and an estuary accent that hinted at his working-class roots. Over the course of their year-long courtship, Connie's father, Sir Reginald King, had refused to acknowledge Robert, even when he was in the same room.

'I've never told you this, but I had the same thing with my father.'

Miles frowned. 'What do you mean?'

'When I told him we wanted to get married, he threatened to cut me off from my inheritance. He called your father all sorts of names and said he was after my money. Your dad is only doing what he thinks is best. The problem with him is that he's spent so long trying to be something he never was, he forgets where he came from. He doesn't mean to do it, but he's been acting in a role for so long, he doesn't know how to stop.'

Connie examined her son carefully and wondered what it was about Chrissy that had bewitched him. It was true she wasn't the sort of woman they had expected him to choose – in fact, they had rather expected that nice girl Sasha to tie him down – but then love wasn't logical or easy to understand. *The heart wants what it wants*, that was the phrase, wasn't it?

'I do what Dad says now, I'm going to carry on doing what he wants for the rest of my life,' said Miles more quietly.

Connie looked at him. Her baby was so grown up. It only seemed like two minutes since she was pushing him around Holland Park in his stroller. Her birthday today had only served to remind her how quickly time was passing.

'Do you love her?' she asked.

'Chrissy? She's my wife.'

'I know that. I asked if you loved her.'

'Yes, I do,' said Miles softly. 'But this isn't about her, it's about me. You know that.'

His mother nodded slowly. 'So what are you going to do?'

'My own thing.'

She smiled. That had always been his way. Miles was her complicated child. Charming, manipulative and in many ways brilliant, he had the raw tools to succeed at whatever he wanted to be. But he could be lazy, expectant, the polar opposite of Grace, who saw her family's personal wealth as a reason to prove herself, not an excuse for coasting through life. Connie felt a stab of guilt. Had she failed as a mother? Why were they both so distant from her? Physically and emotionally, they had both ended up on the opposite side of the world. Now was the time to narrow the gap. She walked across to Miles and cupped his face.

'You're my son, Miles. You're clever enough to succeed at anything. You can do whatever you want to do in life. But most of all I want you to be happy, so you take your girl and you go off and do whatever it is that makes you feel whole. I'll always be there for you. No matter what.'

There were tears in Miles' eyes when he looked up at her. 'Thanks, Mum,' he said simply. Then he hugged her and stood up. 'Now I think I'd better go and find Chrissy. We've got to look after each other now.'

I hope it works out for you, my darling, Connie thought as she watched him go. *It didn't for me.*

26

It was the biggest Christmas tree Grace had ever seen. Standing outside Palumbo Cathedral, the huge bushy ombu tree glistened and glittered in the warm night air, its branches and leaves tied with thousands of silver ribbons and streamers. For Grace, walking towards the cathedral for midnight mass carrying a lit candle, this Parador Christmas scene was strange and familiar at the same time. The small differences she noticed, such as the way people put nativity scenes on their front step, or how all the children wore white to symbolise 'El Niño Dios', the Child of God, made Christmas in Parador special, but also served to remind her how far from home she was.

Gabriel linked his arm through Grace's and pulled her close. Glancing over her shoulder, she saw Caro carrying Olivia, with Gabe's uncle Hugo just behind, Joseph sleeping on his shoulder. Grace smiled softly and for once she felt at peace.

The following morning, there was a rowdy, good-natured breakfast and as everyone unwrapped their presents, the whole house was full of life and noise. Feeling full after an excellent late lunch, Grace retired to the conservatory, her favourite room in the house, with a glass of brandy. Gabriel had gone into Palumbo for a short visit to a mission and for once, Olivia and Joseph were asleep at the same time.

She sat in a wicker chair and watched as the view beyond the window slowly changed. Light was falling from the sky, and the jungle started to blacken against the ribbons of pink and lavender clouds. She sipped the brandy and thought about the phone call she had just had with her mother. Miles was *married*! She still couldn't take it in. She supposed the shock might have been less had his new wife been Sasha Sinclair. She remembered how withdrawn the younger girl had been on that flight back from Nassau after their holiday in Angel Cay, how devastated she had seemed. Grace had almost been moved by her plight. Then again, she recognised Sasha as an operator, so she had often wondered whether she would reunite with Miles – after all, she certainly had leverage because of that night. That secret. But no, Miles had met someone travelling and had fallen in love, just as Grace had done in Australia. Had her brother changed? she wondered. Had he softened? She smiled at the thought. *Not Miles*.

'Knock, knock.'

Grace turned to see Caro standing at the door of the conservatory. 'I come bearing gifts,' she said, producing a shiny red parcel from behind her back.

'Ooh!' said Grace excitedly, tearing off the paper to find a fancy-looking camera inside.

Both women burst out laughing.

'I couldn't let your photographic skills die once we left the *Highlander*, could I?'

Grace gave Caro a reproachful glance.

'Tell me this is point and shoot.'

'Nope. It's got loads of expensive twiddly bits. You can be David Bailey with this piece of kit. You can take pictures of the kids, a photo diary of the election maybe, I don't know.'

'Wow. It's fantastic. Thank you,' she said, pointing it towards the horizon. It felt good in her hands. It felt like she had a purpose.

'So where's Gabe?' asked Caro, sitting in the chair opposite her friend.

'In Palumbo, at the mission.'

'He never stops, does he? You have to hand it to him, campaigning on Christmas Day.'

'It's just a goodwill visit.'

'It's Christmas! He should be with you.'

Grace smiled to disguise her frustration. Caro had a point. These days she felt completely sidelined in Gabriel's pursuit of votes. The election was still over a year away and yet he was away from El Esperanza six nights out of seven. Not once had she ever suspected him of unfaithfulness, but what she felt was worse: she felt abandoned. At least with another woman, she would have something tangible to fight against. But how did you compete with a whole country?

'Join me for a drink?' she asked, waving her glass in the air.

Caro shook her head. 'Better not. I'm supposed to call my folks.'

'In that case, I'm going to start snapping,' said Grace excitedly. 'I think Gabe's got a box of film in a drawer in his study.'

'Watch out for the porn.' Caro laughed as she went.

Grace knew Caro was being ironic; it was a running joke of hers that Gabriel – at least, Gabriel the politician – was the most strait-laced man she had ever met. He'd certainly lost a lot of his breezy charm over the past two years. It was understandable, of course: with the pressure to win, the seriousness of Parador's situation and the constant reminders of the living conditions many of the population were forced to endure, anyone would find it hard to smile. But it didn't stop Grace from wanting the old Gabriel, the charming, happy, spontaneous man she had met on a street in Australia, to come back.

At the top of the stairs, she paused. Even now, she hesitated before entering Gabriel's study. It wasn't officially out of bounds, of course, but her husband liked to see it as his man-cave, his own private space. It's my house too, after all, she told herself, pushing the door open. She walked across the room and sat at his desk, smiling as she looked at the photograph of them both in front of her.

Putting her camera on the desktop, she opened the bottom drawer. Reaching inside, something familiar caught her eye, hidden between sheafs of paper: Gabriel's old notebook.

Glancing around, she pulled it out, running her fingers over the leather cover. Gabriel had carried this battered old book around with him all the time in Australia. *Just ideas,* he'd told her at the time. *Maybe something will turn into a novel, who knows?* She flicked through the pages and her heart leapt: it was clearly more than 'just ideas'; it looked like at least a dozen chapters, written in longhand. Moving across to the sofa, she curled her feet under a cushion and began reading. It was a love story set in wartime Australia, and from the first sentence, she was transfixed. It was good, very, very good, one of those raw books that touched your life and made you want to share it with people you cared about.

'What are you doing?'

She hadn't even noticed the study door open. Gabriel walked slowly into the room and sat in the chair opposite her. She held up the notebook.

'I found this when I was looking for film,' she said.

He frowned and shook his head. 'Put it away. Please.'

She sat up, clutching the notebook to her chest as if it might be snatched away, as if she did not want to let go of the life they could have had together.

'But Gabe, this is incredible. Has your agent or editor seen it?'

She knew Gabriel had barely been in contact with his New York-based publisher since he had arrived back in Parador, and despite repeated phone calls from his agent, he seemed content to let that part of his life melt into the past. He waved a dismissive hand.

'Grace, I haven't got time for writing.'

'But it's such a waste!'

'It's not a waste,' he snapped. 'I'm trying to achieve something bigger, better here than mere words.'

Frustration boiled inside her. 'What's happened to you, Gabriel?' she said.

'What do you mean, what's happened to me? Nothing has happened to me.'

She had avoided this conversation before now because she knew how important politics had become to him, but lately she had been wondering if it was all worth it. They had arrived in Parador with a romantic ideal: Gabriel was going to avenge his brother's death; he was going to save his country. But over the last year, she had begun to wonder if it was actually possible to save Parador. Corruption seemed to be eating the country from the inside. Gabriel and his mother seemed blind to it – they were too close to the issues – but Grace was able to see the situation from a different angle. Corruption in Parador had become so entrenched, so much a part of everyday life, she doubted that any new government would be able to wash it clean again. And the sad truth was that Gabriel's CARP party was so stridently anti-corruption, so against playing Parador's unique little games, it actually stood little chance of success in the 1994 election. The reality was that politics was a dirty game and anyone who tried to play it whiter than white was going to get crushed. Grace had seen it happen in her father's empire; she'd heard the conversations behind closed doors. Success always came at a price. Deals had to be done, people paid off, the powerful made promises. It was the way the game was played, and if Gabriel wasn't prepared to get his hands dirty, he was doomed to fail.

'Do you think you can win, Gabe?' she asked simply.

'Yes. If only we can reach more people, work harder, do more.'

'How much more?' said Grace, balling her hands into fists. 'You're missing your children grow up. We don't have a life together. You've even abandoned your talent, your one-in-a-million gift for writing.'

'I think it's worth it.'

'Nothing is worth this!' she cried.

He came off his chair and knelt down in front of her, taking the notebook from her hands.

'Help me, Grace. Help me win. We need one big push, and you can make a difference. You need to get on the campaign trail, be there by my side. Twelve months of your time. That's all I'm asking.'

She pushed his arms off. 'Have you been listening to a word of what I have been saying?' she said. 'I can't stand it any more. I don't want this political life.'

'But I promise you, once we are in power, then we can have more time together.'

He wrapped his arms around her and for a second she pulled away. He didn't even smell familiar these days.

'Listen to me, I can do the presidency for two terms. That's just ten years, Grace. It's nothing; you'll be thirty-three, I'll be in my mid-forties and then we'll have the rest of our lives to write, talk, just be together. But life will be better, sweeter, because of the difference we've made.'

He looked at her intently. 'Have you ever done anything bad, Grace?'

The question startled her and she flinched. *Anything bad?* Her heart was thumping and she could hear the ticking of the study clock getting louder and louder. She had never told him about that night. She had always meant to. He was her husband. They shared everything: a bed, a family, a life, secrets.

'Yes,' she said quietly and a look of complicity darted between them.

'We all have,' he nodded, taking her hands. 'I left my family, I moved to New York. I was selfish and pursued my own

251

dreams and ambitions and didn't once think of the bigger picture. Everybody has regrets, things they wish they could change. But it's never too late to put things right.'

She looked at him, and a surge of hope filled her. Was that the answer? Since Angel Cay, she had felt as if she had been running, constantly on the move, never once daring to stop and look back. She was weighed down by the guilt of what she had done – what she had failed to do – that night. She had never believed that the boy on the beach had got up and walked away, much less stolen a boat and run off to a nearby island. It was all too convenient. No, that whole terrible mess had her father's filthy fingerprints all over it; it was a glittering illustration of the corruption Gabriel was fighting against, a horrible example of all the deals done to make things go away and to keep things the same. Perhaps Gabriel was right, perhaps this was a way to atone for that one mistake. Maybe it would lift the weight that was pushing her down, bending her double. She looked into his eyes and nodded.

'OK, I'll help you,' she said finally. 'I'll do whatever you want me to do.'

'Thank you,' he said, kissing her forehead. 'Thank you, my love.'

She held up one finger. 'But on one condition.'

'Name it,' he said.

'Promise me that when we're done and all this is over, you'll get that sexy ass back on that chair and finish your novel.'

He threw his head back and laughed, and as he did so, he looked younger, more like the man she had seen that balmy night on Macrossan Street.

'You've got a deal,' he said. 'Now come on downstairs and let's grab some champagne.'

27

'Should I wear this, or this?' asked Chrissy, holding up a slinky black dress in one hand and a tiny scarlet one in the other. Lying across the bed of their Capital Hotel suite, Miles barely looked up from the copy of *The Times* he had been reading. Neither dress was from their Harvey Nichols shopping trip before Christmas and both of them looked tarty. Then again, he was a long way past caring.

'The black one,' he said, his eyes not straying from the article he had become engrossed in: a review of a gig Year Zero had done the night before at the Brixton Academy. Rereading the text and examining the photo of the 'hot Manchester four-piece', Miles found himself becoming very irritable. Alex bloody Doyle, making the papers before him – and *The Times* at that! He pushed himself up and stalked to the minibar, unscrewing two bottles of Jack Daniel's and pouring them into a glass simultaneously. It was the second time this week he'd felt a stab of envy: a Christmas card from Grace he'd seen propped up on the mantelpiece at Ashford Park had had the same effect. It was an expensive embossed affair featuring a black and white photograph of Grace, Gabriel and the children. Who did she think she was, Princess Diana? It didn't seem two minutes ago that Alex was living with his mother in some horrid northern town and Grace was working as a deckhand in Australia, but that had all changed, hadn't it? The grandeur of the Christmas card and the size of the review in *The Times* spelt out one thing in big capital letters: SUCCESS. His sister and his former best friend had found it, Miles hadn't. Things weren't supposed to have played out like this. He was Miles Ashford. A leader, an achiever. But honestly, what had he ever done? Burnt down a house in Oxfordshire?

Chrissy emerged from the bathroom in the red dress, tottering on a pair of very high black heels.

'Come on, we're late,' she said, prodding Miles in the side with her cheap clutch bag.

'No we're not. It's New Year's Eve. Nothing is going to get going until ten at the earliest.'

'By which point we won't be able to find a taxi and the tubes will be packed.'

'I'm not getting the *tube*,' said Miles with disdain.

'I forgot,' said Chrissy sarcastically. 'It's beneath you.'

'No, I just have standards,' he said, pulling on his coat.

She touched his cheek, but he flinched away. 'What is it, honey?' she asked. 'Are you still pissed off about your dad?'

'No, I'm not.'

'Well, you've been in a bad mood since the party,' she said. 'You're not still thinking about it, are you? He was just angry about the wedding. He'll come round.'

Miles was trying to put a brave face on it, but the truth was he hadn't been able to stop thinking about the party. Nor had he told Chrissy about his father's ultimatum. *Annul the marriage or you're out of Ash Corp. You have until New Year to think about it.* He still didn't know what to do. He didn't want to annul the marriage, and he felt sure that a grovelling apology and a promise to send his new wife to finishing school would be an acceptable compromise. But did he want a life at Ash Corp. working as his father's lapdog? For all his bluster in front of his mother, right now, he had no other better alternatives.

'Let's not talk about this now,' he said, avoiding Chrissy's searching gaze and heading for the door. 'You're right, we'd better go or we'll be forced to get on the bloody tube.'

Piers Jackson was an old friend from Danehurst now working at Saatchi's and living in a huge loft apartment in Covent Garden. The loft was full and thumping with dance music by the time Miles and Chrissy arrived, the guest list a mix of young adland, the old boys' public school network and a smattering of assorted interesting others, models, DJs, and West End hipsters.

'Milo!' cried Piers as he walked out on to the roof terrace. 'And who is this lovely young thing?' he added, drinking in Chrissy and her tiny red dress.

'This, Piers, is my wife.'

Piers did a double-take, then roared with laughter. 'Good God, Milo, you had me going there for a moment.'

Chrissy smiled sweetly and stepped forward, offering her hand. 'I'm afraid it's true,' she said in her best plummy accent. 'I'm Christine Ashford, delighted to meet you.'

Piers took her hand and, not taking his eyes from hers, kissed it. 'Well I have to say, the pleasure's all mine, Mrs Ashford,' he said lasciviously. 'Miles always did have cracking taste in women. Whatever happened to that Sasha you were shagging at school?'

Miles shrugged, trying not to catch Chrissy's eye. 'I hear she's modelling.'

'Men only, I hope.'

'So how's the ad game?' asked Miles quickly, trying to steer him well away from past conquests.

'Fantastic, even if I do say so myself,' said Piers. 'Lot of bollocks, of course, but the money's OK and it's a laugh. Why don't I have a word with the recruitment director at Saatchi? You're exactly the sort of person we want,' he said, pouring them both a glass of red wine. 'Could probably get you in at the junior account level.'

His cheeks flaring, Miles shook his head. *That shit.* 'What was it Raymond Chandler said?' he asked as casually as he could. 'I think it was: "Chess is as elaborate a waste of human intelligence as you can find outside an advertising agency." I won't waste my time with either pursuit, Piers.'

Piers shrugged. 'Fair enough, offer's there. Fancy a line?' He passed Chrissy a CD case which had four lines of cocaine already chopped out. 'Ladies first,' he smiled, handing her a rolled twenty-pound note. When it was his turn, Miles was only slightly surprised to see that the CD was Year Zero's debut album. It didn't stop him hoovering up the powder.

'So what are you up to now, Milo?' said Piers, pouring them both more wine. 'Working for the old man?'

'No,' said Miles quickly.

'Yes, sorry, Milo,' said Piers with a sickly smile. 'I did hear your dad had given you the old heave-ho, some bust-up at Chrimbo, wasn't it?'

The rich man's grapevine works fast, thought Miles with a sick feeling in his stomach.

'Miles is working on his own project,' said Chrissy confidently. 'Property. It's very exciting.'

'Oh really?' said Piers, putting his arm around Miles' shoulders. 'Listen, I've got a line on this myself. Me and a few chums have a bit of spare cash, trust funds and whatnot, we're going to cash in on the Docklands Light Railway expanding out east – build some sexy little shag pads for the bankers. Wondered if you'd like to chuck a few shekels into the pot?'

'Hmm, possibly,' said Miles. 'How much are we talking?'

'Oh, eight or nine each, I thought.'

'Thousand?'

'Million?' replied Piers casually.

Miles looked incredulous.

'Well, not to worry if you can't lay your hands on it,' said

256

Piers, sniffing. 'Thought you had a few readies, but I s'pose they were all Daddy's, eh?'

Miles almost laughed out loud. Piers' father was one of the richest landowners in the country; this flat hadn't been bought with his salary as an advertising executive, that was for sure. Clearly, however, his friend's trust fund had been slightly more generous than his own.

'I'll think about it, OK?' he said, trying to save face.

Piers nodded sceptically, his attention wandering towards a pneumatic blonde across the room. 'Catch you later, eh, Milo?' he said with a sly smile. 'Give me a bell if it doesn't work out, yeah?'

His humiliating conversation with Piers had done nothing to help Miles climb out from under his black cloud. *Another* of his contemporaries doing well, investing in the future, making cash, while Miles stayed where he was, unable to jump one way or the other. He looked at his watch; it was a quarter to twelve. Usually he felt fantastic on New Year's Eve – invariably out of it, but always excited about the possibilities of the year ahead. Not tonight. Tonight he felt unsettled, edgy. A door at the far end of the loft led to an iron staircase and then the flat roof of the building. Walking out into the cold fresh air, he leaned against an old stacked chimney pot and lit a cigarette, looking out over the rooftops of London. The music from the party sounded woolly in the background, until it was cut through by the striking chimes of the illuminated church clock far off over the skyline. Muffled cheers rang out from the party and the streets far below. The door to the loft clattered open and Chrissy staggered outside, unsteady on her high heels, a bottle of champagne in one hand.

'Happy New Year, honey!' she grinned, flinging her arms around his neck.

Miles glanced at the church clock. *Time's up*, he thought,

imagining the Ash Corp. corner office with his name on the door. It wasn't what he wanted, but he didn't know anything else. He was frightened to be left outside looking in.

'Nineteen ninety-three is going to be our year. I've got a feeling,' said Chrissy, taking the cigarette from him and blowing a smoke ring. She examined his face. 'You're looking moody. Does that mean you've decided to go to work for your father?'

'No,' he said resentfully. He thought about telling her of his father's threats, getting rid of her, wondering how she would take it. Then he closed his eyes and shook his head. It would be so easy to blame all this on Chrissy, but the truth was, none of it was about her. He wasn't rejecting his father's ultimatum in some grand gesture of love; he was doing it for himself, because it was the only way to finally find his own place in the world. He just wished he had a clue where to start looking.

'So what are you going to do?'

'I don't know,' he said crossly. 'I'll think of something.'

Chrissy nodded and dropped the cigarette on to the roof, carefully grinding it out.

'The first thing to think about is what are you good at.'

'Enjoying myself,' he said with a distracted laugh.

'Fun. There's money in that. It's a talent, you know, helping people have a great time.'

'I've tried that, remember? The Youngblood Society.'

'Don't think of it as a disaster,' said Chrissy. 'Think of it as a trial run.'

He looked at her with interest. 'You think I should open a club?'

She nodded. 'Look around you, Miles. It's New Year's Eve. See it. Feel it.' She was drunk, but her words were spoken with passion. 'If you could bottle this feeling and serve it up every night of the year, you'd make a million.'

'A billion,' said Miles, feeling the confidence beginning to creep back into him.

It wasn't a half-bad idea and plenty of people had done it before. There was Annabel's and Tramp, old-school hang-outs for old-school money and their faster new-moneyed friends. The Groucho Club had opened in the eighties, an elite drinking den for London's media and liberal intelligentsia. But there was definitely room for something else, something with more energy and style. It could be the most elite private members' club in London and then he could roll it out to other cities, maybe even extending the brand into hotels, restaurants and one-off events. His mind buzzed with the possibilities. It was so simple; it was playing to his strengths, doing something he knew about, and if he did it right, it could be a little gold mine.

'Chrissy, you're a fucking genius!' he said, grabbing her and planting a big kiss on her mouth. Suddenly he saw it all clearly: he wasn't going to join his father, he was going to take him on. He had a five-million-pound trust fund. He had the idea, and for the first time in his life, he had the absolute drive and determination to see it through.

'Hand me that bottle,' he said. 'It's time to get the party started.'

By the end of January, Miles and Chrissy had viewed a dozen places all over London. To Miles' surprise there had been a paucity of real contenders as a site for their new club. Most buildings had the size but not the location, or they had the location but were way out of his price range. Finally they got lucky with a double-fronted townhouse in Covent Garden being sold, as part of a divorce settlement, at a knock-down price. Glorious red brick, five storeys high, with a roof terrace, Miles knew it was right the moment they set foot inside. Immediately he was picturing power lunches, launch parties, even perhaps a jacuzzi on the roof for those decadent late-night trysts. It was in budget, and more exciting, the surveyors they employed were certain that the adjoining house was going to come on the market in the next two years, should further expansion be necessary. They spent a frantic five months acquiring planning permission, then a further manic three transforming the interior. Chrissy was there every day in her hard hat, yelling orders at the terrified builders, while Miles worked the phones and the lunch circuit, building a members' list, creating a buzz, getting press. By the end of the summer, everyone in London's hippest circles was talking about Miles Ashford, wanting to get close to this dynamic and ambitious new face. Nobody mentioned his father. And on the first of October 1993, when the Globe Club opened for business, the *Evening Standard* ran a picture of Miles on the front page, with the caption 'King of the World'. Miles couldn't have put it better himself.

28

November 1993

Alex had never been inside the Dorchester Hotel in his life, but he guessed that on a normal night, it didn't look like this. The double-height marble lobby had been transformed into a circus tent, with brightly coloured canvas draped from the ceiling, acrobats performing in front of the reception desk and in the centre of the room, in a polished steel cage, a slightly bored-looking tiger.

'Roll up! Roll up!' bellowed a man dressed in the red coat and top hat of a ringmaster. 'Come and see the greatest show on earth!'

'Check this out,' Alex whispered to Emma, as they pushed through the buzzing, excited crowd. 'They've taken over the whole hotel. It must be costing them a fortune.'

Music industry legend had it that EMG Records always spent a tenth of their year's profit on their lavish annual party. This year had obviously been a good one, partly due to the resurgence of home-grown talent like Year Zero, but mainly because the company had released their entire back catalogue on CD: they'd managed a minor miracle of selling their assets twice over, often to the same consumers.

They moved towards the ballroom, but every five paces someone would stop Alex to air-kiss him, flatter him about the new album or offer a raucous anecdote. There was a great buzz about the room, boozy and self-congratulatory – the best he'd experienced since the Brits earlier in the year, when Year Zero had been nominated but lost out to some dance act. Finally they got to the clown-staffed bar and ordered two of the garish 'Big Top' cocktails, clinking their glasses together.

'Next tour, I reckon we'll do something like this,' said Alex. 'Theme up the venues like Atlantis or something.'

Emma dug him in the ribs. 'Alex, you're not U2 yet, you know.'

'Next year, babe. Next year.'

'Maybe,' said Emma seriously. 'But it's tough out there. There are some really great bands coming out of nowhere. I saw this band Oasis at the Powerhaus the other day. They were fantastic, almost what you're trying to do but better.'

'Cheers, Em,' said Alex sourly. 'I thought you were supposed to be on my side.'

'I am. I'm just worried you're going to get left behind. You're not writing enough songs . . .'

'Give me a fucking chance! I've been on tour for half the year, recording the other half, not to mention doing stupid Norwegian TV shows hosted by puppets! I barely have time to sit down and write you a postcard, let alone a hit record.'

'OK, OK,' said Emma. 'Don't get all worked up. If I can't say what I think, Alex, who's going to? Jez? Your management? They're far too tight for my liking anyway.'

'And what do you mean by that?'

'I just think Jez and Nathan have a different agenda to you. For Jez, well, it's all about Jez, isn't it? But for Nathan, it's all about making money and obviously that means pushing Jez to the front – Jez is always going to mean bums on seats.'

'So where does that leave me?' said Alex sulkily.

She shrugged. 'Year Zero isn't being sold on the music any

more, is it? You're like these cheeky-chappie Britpoppers who look good and give a catchy quote. Whoever talks about the songs any more?'

Alex gestured angrily towards the rest of the party. 'All these people!' he snapped. 'Didn't you hear them as we came in? They were all saying how much they loved the album—'

'Don't be so bloody naïve, Alex,' she interrupted. 'The bloodsuckers in this room would slap you on the back and call you a genius if you'd written "The Birdie Song" and it had made them money. What matters to them is that you're keeping them in Ferraris and coke.'

'When did you get so cynical?' said Alex. He knew she was right, of course. For all their front covers and chart positions – four top-ten singles in a row – Year Zero weren't exactly rolling in it, and if he was honest, he was increasingly uncomfortable with the way Jez had become the face of the band, constantly making the tabloids for some outrageous quote or being pictured rolling out of Browns nightclub in the company of models or soap actors. Worst of all, she was right about the music. The creativity of their first couple of years seemed to have disappeared.

Alex swallowed the rest of his cocktail and gestured towards a clown. 'Can you get me a Jack Daniel's?' he asked. 'Make it a double.'

Emma put her hand on his. 'I'm sorry,' she said gently. 'You're right. Let's just enjoy the party. Seems like Jez has already made a start.'

'He's here, is he?' said Alex, knocking back his whiskey.

'There he is. With that supermodel. Sophia whatsherface.'

'You're kidding,' he said, spinning around quickly.

He watched the beautiful brunette wrap her arms around Year Zero's frontman and almost coughed up his drink.

'I can't pissing believe it.'

Emma chuckled. 'Don't get so wound up about it. Word

is she's a right music groupie. She'll be moving on to the next *NME* cover star tomorrow.'

She drew a finger to his cheek. 'Look at you, all pink. Admit it, Doyle, you wish you were going out with a multi-millonaire supermodel rather than a lowly marketing exec. Although I do think I have better tits.'

She was making a joke of it, but Alex knew she was pressing home a point.

'My lovely marketing executive does have better tits. In fact she has better everything. But that's not the point. I just can't understand how he does it,' he said, his voice beginning to wobble.

'Look. There's Clive from the New York office. Are you going to come over and say hello?'

'No.'

'Alex. He's the big cheese over there. Schmooze. Network.'

'I need another drink.'

'Fine. Calm yourself down,' she said, rolling her eyes and disappearing into the crowd.

Alex couldn't help his gaze wandering back in the direction of Jez, preening himself in front of his audience, loving every minute of his reflected glory. His irritation wasn't exactly new; everything Jez did these days seemed to annoy him. His stupid political slogan T-shirts, the artfully done floppy hair, the way in interviews he always referred to the band's songs as 'my songs', as if no one else had lifted a finger. And yet here he was with one of the world's sexiest women on his arm. And then it clicked and in an instant Alex realised just what it was about Jez which so wound him up. Somewhere, somehow, in setting off to find a new life away from Danehurst, Alex had found another Miles. Another charmer, another self-interested manipulator who snaked his way through life with his hand out, expecting to be given everything. *Jesus Christ*, he thought, laughing to himself. *Why didn't I spot this before?*

He ordered another drink and threw it back, grimacing. By rights, he should have been incredibly drunk. He'd started drinking at lunchtime – just a few beers at the Engineer in Primrose Hill – and hadn't stopped. But these days he never got the sort of happy highs he used to with alcohol. Now it was just a matter of trying to feel normal.

Emma was laughing with Clive Benson now. She was doing so well at the company and he had no doubt that within ten years she'd be running the show, but his pride in her was bittersweet; she was always working, always coming up with some new scheme. They never seemed to relax these days, enjoy one another's company, enjoy what they had. *I can talk*, he thought, putting his glass down on the bar. Emma had reminded him recently that he should be happy with what he had achieved; stop and enjoy the moment. After all, he had the life he'd always wanted: he was a successful musician, he lived with a fantastic woman: people would kill for his life. So why did he feel so miserable all the time?

'Penny for your thoughts?'

Alex turned to see two sapphire cat-like eyes looking at him: Sophia Brand.

'Uh, sorry?' he mumbled with complete surprise.

'Just you looked like you were struggling with some deep thoughts there,' she said in her syrupy Deep South accent.

'No, just the usual. Sex and football.'

Sophia laughed and the blue eyes began to sparkle.

Fuck, she's beautiful, thought Alex. Up close she wasn't as physically perfect as the magazine covers suggested – she was only late twenties, but fine lines were already collecting round her eyes and mouth and her pale olive skin wasn't completely smooth. But those tiny flaws almost made her more striking, more real. He searched his mind for something witty or interesting to say.

'Drink?' he asked.

'Jack and Coke, thanks. I've got a room here in the hotel so I don't have to stagger very far.'

'Don't you live in London?'

'In New York mainly. After ten years of modelling I think I'm addicted to hotels. I just prefer them to home. They make life feel more exciting.'

'I didn't think you had any problems in that department.' Alex smiled. Sophia Brand had a reputation as a rock chick, a full-on party girl. For five years she'd dated Danny Gregg the movie star, which kept the papers fuelled with decadent stories of orgies in his Jacuzzi, but they had split recently in a flurry of juicy accusations of abuse on both sides. As far as Alex knew, Jez was her first new suitor.

'So you're in a band?'

'Year Zero.'

'Jez's band,' she squealed. 'You're kidding me.'

Alex smarted. Jez's band?

'You must be Alex.'

He grunted. 'So you're with Jez now, then?' he asked as he handed her the drink.

'I like the word *with*,' she said, holding his gaze as she sipped. 'It's suitably vague.'

She glanced over at Jez, who was now schmoozing the same record executive Emma had gone to speak to. 'How come you're not ass-licking your paymasters too?' she asked with a sour expression.

'I leave all that to Jez.' Alex smiled. 'He's better at it than me. And also because I think, what's the point? Is having a laugh and a joke with Clive Benson going to get us a US recording deal or a *Billboard* chart position?'

Sophia suppressed a smile. 'Is that being idealistic or just idle?'

He laughed.

'Can I ask you a question?' said Sophia, stirring the ice cubes around in her drink.

'Of course.'

'Have you ever thought about modelling?'

'Are you trying to pick me up?' He chuckled. 'I'm sure half of those slimy marketing guys over there will be asking the circus girls exactly the same question tonight.'

'I'm serious,' she said.

'No, I haven't. Why?'

'Because you look great in jeans,' she said playfully.

Alex could feel himself blushing again, but Sophia carried on.

'Look, I have a contract with the fashion label Ellis Cole. I front all their advertisements – jeans, scent, underwear – and we're just about to do a new campaign. Ellis wants to use a male model with me in this one and he kind of wants rock vibe for it. I think a great-looking musician is going to be better than a great-looking model. I saw you across the room. When you told me you played in Jez's band, I couldn't believe it.'

Alex couldn't help laughing. 'I'm flattered,' he said. 'But why not Jez if you want the rock thing?'

Sophia pouted. 'He's not as pretty as you.'

Alex felt a rush of triumph and then immediately looked around for Emma.

'I tell you what, let's phone Ellis,' said Sophia decisively, pulling a mobile phone out of her bag.

'What for?' said Alex lamely.

'I want to tell him that I've found the perfect guy for the campaign.'

'You're not joking, are you?'

'No,' she said, looking at him with those deep blue eyes that had peered from a thousand billboards. 'I'm not.'

Just then there was a sudden blast of music as James Cook, one of EMG's most successful solo acts, came on stage.

Sophia grabbed Alex's hand and shouted in his ear over the music: 'Let's find somewhere quieter.'

On the other side of the room he could see Emma laughing with a TV presenter. *Ah sod it,* he thought. It wasn't like he was doing anything wrong. Emma had said it herself: you had to flirt with these people, make them think you were their friend. And an ad campaign with Ellis Cole – that had to be a six-figure deal if Nathan negotiated it properly. For weeks now, Emma had been making noises about a place in the country. Somewhere she could ride and he could write and they could have dogs and go for walks. Besides, he thought with a smile, it would really piss Jez off.

They went out into the foyer, where dozens of people were still milling around, pointing at the bored tiger, but even out here the music was deafening.

'Why don't we go upstairs to my room?' said Sophia, leading him towards the lift. 'We can call him from there.'

Sophia's suite was on one of the high floors. It had an impressive view across Hyde Park and was decked out with expensive antiques and silk furnishings. She went into the bedroom and opened the minibar, her tight white dress riding up her thighs as she crouched to pull out a chilled bottle of vodka, splashing it into two glasses. Then she took a little paper wrap, opened it and tipped the white powder inside on to a small mirror.

'Will I need to send over a press photo or something?' asked Alex.

'What?' she said distractedly as she arranged the powder into lines.

'Do I need to send a photo to Ellis?'

As she shrugged, her dress fell off one shoulder.

'Ellis tends to listen to my opinions,' she said, offering him a straw. 'So you're coming round to the idea, then?'

He snorted a line of coke. It was only now, with the offer of a major modelling gig on the table, that he realised how much he had hated Jez taking on so much of the publicity and promotion for the band. He hated it that people thought

Year Zero were simply Jez's backing band. Lately he'd been getting the distinct feel that Jez's increased profile was all part of a plan cooked up by Nathan and the record company to pave the way for a glittering solo career for Jez Harrison and Jez Harrison alone.

'Where did you and Jez meet?' Suddenly it seemed very important. Just how *did* a berk like Jez hook up with a super-model?

'At a mutual friend's dinner in New York last month.'

'Who's that?'

'Clive Benson,' said Sophia, hoovering up a line.

Fuck. He hadn't even known Jez was in New York two weeks ago. He knocked back his vodka and took another line.

His coke habit had crept up on him slowly. He had resisted at first – he didn't want to become a rock cliché – but it was insidious: coke was everywhere. To celebrate in the studio after you'd laid down a track; before a party to get you 'in the mood'. People you'd just met would invite you to the loos for a line; it was like a music industry handshake. It never made him feel bad; actually coke made him feel great most of the time. And he often congratulated himself on not progressing to any of the harder stuff that was rife on the circuit. Smack to come down. Crack to go back up. Coke was subtle and had a sheen of sophistication, how could it be that bad?

'You don't do things by halves, do you?' said Sophia, coming up behind him, running her hands over his shoulders. 'Now, before I call Ellis,' she whispered in his ear, 'I'd better check there's no pasty body hiding under there.'

She slipped her hands under his T-shirt and pulled it over his head.

'Mmm . . . very nice,' she said, stepping away and admiring his six-pack. 'Why don't you hold that thought for me,' she purred, turning to go into the bathroom.

Alex knew he should leave the room, but his feet felt welded to the floor. He looked up and Sophia was standing in the doorway to the bathroom, naked except for her black heels. Alex could only stand there, staring. Her breasts stood round and firm, her pert nipples begged for a mouth to suck them whole. A lick of pubic hair between her thighs, not like Emma's slightly untidy bush, looked soft and inviting. She slowly walked over to the bed and knelt down in front of him, brushing herself against his chest. He groaned as her lips swept the side of his neck.

He forced himself to pull away.

'Look, Sophia. Jez . . .'

'Do you know what I love doing?' she said, her warm mouth nuzzling into his ear.

His throat was too dry to speak.

'Fucking on coke,' she whispered, pushing him back on to the bed and straddling him.

Hell, I'm only human, he thought as her hand sank to the waistband of his jeans, unbuckling them and pulling them down. His cock was erect and almost painful with need, pushing at the material of his boxer shorts. Looking deep into his eyes, she took his index finger and lifted it to her mouth, sucking it, swirling her tongue around it, then slowly, slowly, pulled it out, saliva glinting in the soft light. She stretched over to retrieve the mirror and dipped his fingertip into the small mound of cocaine. Putting the mirror down, she slid off him and knelt on the bed, lifting her perfect arse towards him, licking her own fingers and stroking the dark crease, opening her tight rosebud, and leaving him in no doubt about where she wanted the cocaine administered. Alex got up and went behind her.

'Oh God, yes, there,' she panted as Alex ran his free hand down her spine, towards her peachy buttocks.

He was mesmerised by this woman, drunk with desire. *Fuck you, Jez*, he thought as he pushed his finger into her.

He didn't even hear the click as the bedroom door opened,

270

but he heard the gasp. He whirled around to find Emma standing there, her hand over her mouth.

'Oh shit, Em, I . . .' he stuttered, but she turned away and ran. By the time he made it to the corridor, she was gone.

He ran through the fire escape and took the stairs down, guessing she would have taken the lift. He clattered down the concrete steps four at a time, crashing into walls, finally bursting into the hotel lobby and startling the tiger, which finally lifted its head and gave a half-hearted growl.

'Emma, stop!' he shouted as he saw her push through the revolving doors. He rushed out on to the street just as she sprinted across Park Lane, barely looking at the speeding traffic.

'Wait! Please!' he called, as a bus came from nowhere, causing him to stumble backwards on to the pavement. It had started to rain, but he could see her on the other side of the road, her red dress as vivid as a poppy. There was a break in the traffic and he ran across the road.

Where had she gone? Then he saw a flash of red a hundred yards ahead of him; she'd run into the park.

'Emma! Come back, please!'

He pounded after her, so full of adrenalin he didn't feel the cold drizzle soaking his thin T-shirt. And then finally he saw her, slumped on the steps of the bandstand, her shoulders heaving. She was sobbing, her face buried in her arms.

'Em, I'm so sorry,' he began, reaching out to touch her shoulder, but she jerked violently away, scrambling backwards.

'Sorry?' she screamed, bending at the waist from the effort.

Yellow light from the old-style streetlamps illuminating the park pathways fell on to her face, and Alex could see she was ghostly white, except for sickly pink spots in the middle of her cheeks.

She closed her eyes and he could see a cloud of breath escape from her lips.

'You are so *predictable*,' she spat, her entire body shivering.

'Nothing happened,' he said lamely.

'Nothing?' she said with a harsh laugh. 'You were naked, putting coke up her arse, like some sad fucking rock cliché.'

'We ... we went upstairs to phone Ellis Cole,' he said, knowing how pathetic it sounded.

'Of course!' said Emma, flapping her arms at her sides. 'That's what you go *upstairs* to a hotel room for. Well it's a good job I saw you go off with that tart, isn't it?' she said sarcastically. 'A good job I followed you, a good job the house-keeper let me in, because otherwise *something* might have happened.'

'She said I could be in this campaign,' he pleaded. 'She pulled my T-shirt off to see if my body ...' He trailed off.

A guttural part sob, part laugh pierced the night air. 'Don't stop,' she said. 'I'm dying to hear the part about how Ellis answered the phone and told you to take all her clothes off and stick coke up her backside.'

'We didn't have sex,' he said, looking at the wet ground.

'Yes, you did,' she said quietly, then turned and walked away.

He followed her slowly, at a distance, not knowing what to do or say. She looked so small and vulnerable, all he wanted to do was hug her and tell her how sorry he was and how he would make it up to her. Finally they came to the Serpentine lake, long, black and still save for where the rain pitted the dark surface. Alex reached out to touch her.

'Don't, Alex. Just don't.'

'I'd had too much to drink,' he said sheepishly. 'It was *Sophia Brand*. I was impressed. She was with Jez ...' But as soon as the words came out of his mouth he could tell that honesty was not the best policy. He fell into silence, listening to the hiss of rain on the water, the distant growl of the traffic.

'Do you think it's easy for me?' she said softly. 'I don't have a beautiful face or a fantastic figure, I'm not famous or clever. Don't you think I hear the whispers every time we walk into a room? "What's he doing with her? Surely he could do better?" And I try not to listen, but I'm not stupid, Alex. I love a man that half the women in the country want to sleep with, because you're beautiful and because you write songs that touch them. Women are always going to want you. But you don't have to take up those offers. You're better than that. *We're* better than that. Or I thought we were.'

His mouth was stale from alcohol, dry from remorse.

'Just go,' she whispered.

But he couldn't go. He needed her and the thought of leaving her here was making his heart ache.

'I love you, Emma. Please, please forgive me.'

She looked at him with such a probing gaze that he was frightened of what she could see, that she could see right inside him, see his faults and weaknesses. See his secrets.

'I love you too, Alex. But things have got to change.'

Hope sparked in his heart. 'What? Anything! Just tell me.'

'No more other women. Groupies, models, whatever. And the drink, the drugs, they've got to stop.'

'You've never mentioned that before,' he said defensively.

'Alex, I *have*. How many times have I told you to go easy at the bar or backstage or in your hotel room? How many times have I asked you to come to bed and you've stayed up caning it on your own? I know you're a rock star, but it's getting out of control and I think you know that. The bottom line is that I won't share you with other women and I won't share you with an addiction either.'

'I'm not addicted to anything!'

She looked at him fiercely. 'Then prove it to me.'

'Em, I don't know if I can,' he said, looking down at his hands. 'I feel lost, I feel empty, I . . .'

She took his hands and held them tight, painfully tight.

'Do you love me?' she asked.

The thought of her walking out of the park, out of his life, made him feel as if every organ was about to be ripped out of his body.

'Yes, God yes. You mean everything to me, Emma.'

'Then don't hurt me again,' she said. 'Because if you do, you really will be on your own.'

29

Grace jumped out of the limo with a spring in her step, smoothing down the red light woollen suit and smiling for the photographers waiting on the pavement outside the Palumbo Hilton. Inside the foyer, she drew an elegant hand across her forehead. It was a particularly muggy day and she would have liked nothing more than to be by the pool with her children, but with the elections only twelve weeks away, every minute of her day was filled up helping Gabe on the campaign trail, in keeping with the promise she had made to her husband at Christmas. That morning she had shown a journalist from London's *Sunday Times* around a Palumbo orphanage and then been interviewed for a six-page feature on Parador for that publication. And now she was on her way to support Gabe at a press lunch. On the way to the hotel, her assistant Manuela had read out the latest election polls from the local paper. Since Grace's involvement with Gabriel's campaign and the launch of her orphanages charity, CARP's popularity had increased by two per cent. It wasn't a huge amount, and anyway, she doubted the reliability of these polls – this was Parador after all – but it still made her feel good.

Nor could she ignore that her relationship with Gabriel had vastly improved since she had joined the campaign trail. For a start, they were together much more often, which not only gave them more to talk about, but meant that they often shared the same bed at night. Their sex life, which had dwindled away to almost nothing over the past year, had reignited; it was like they were discovering each other all over again. It made her remember how much she missed it. But the truth was, while she wholeheartedly believed in the aims of the CARP party, Grace wouldn't weep if they lost the election. Win or lose, though, it had to be better than the tense limbo they were now in. She loved Gabriel and wanted him to succeed, but most of all she just wanted it over.

She was ushered through the hotel by her bodyguard and up to a large conference room. The huge suite on the mezzanine floor was full of journalists all looking towards a dais where Gabriel was standing in a navy suit deftly answering questions with wit and authority, although even from the back of the room, she could see the tension on his face. He was under fire and he desperately needed the support of the press. A month earlier, CARP had unveiled a plan to hand over a parcel of land to the paramilitaries terrorising the rural south in return for a ceasefire. It was brave and forward-thinking, but it was also political dynamite.

'What makes you think the rebels will be satisfied with this deal?' asked one journalist. 'If you reward terrorism, surely that will just encourage them to burn more crops, rape more women and butcher more innocents so you will give them more land?'

Gabriel shook his head. 'This is a one-off deal, a final settlement. I am not just expecting a ceasefire, I am expecting a timetable of decommissioning arms.'

'And if they don't do what you ask?'

Gabriel smiled slightly. 'Then we will talk to them again. Only this time, we won't take no for an answer.'

A ripple of laughter ran around the room. Grace caught her husband's eye and he winked at her. He was still able to send little shivers up her spine. She tapped Manuela on the shoulder.

'I'm just going to wish my husband good luck.'

She walked around the back of the dais, climbing up on the platform behind Gabriel. One of the journalists she knew – Juan Moreno from the *Parador Internacional* – spotted her and waved his notebook at her.

'Mrs Hernandez!' he called. 'Can you give us your take on your husband's new policy?'

Gabriel put up his hand as if to veto the question, but Grace stepped forward.

'This is Parador, Mr Moreno,' she said with a sweet smile. 'On this platform, whatever my husband thinks is exactly right. However, when I get him home, whatever I say goes.'

The room cracked up with laughter and Gabriel dipped his head to the microphones. 'And I think that's a perfect place to leave it, thank you, gentlemen.'

More black-suited security men led Grace and Gabriel towards a back entrance. As they waited for their cars to come around, Gabriel turned to her and grinned.

'Brilliant as ever, Mrs Hernandez,' he said, leaning over to kiss her on the neck.

'You weren't so bad yourself.' Grace grinned.

Gabriel pulled a face. 'You missed the tricky parts. Not all of them agree with what we stand for.'

'I shouldn't worry, Gabe,' she said. 'All journalists in Parador have a closet liberal streak; they all secretly want change, otherwise why would they stick around here? Not for the twenty-thousand-dollar salary.'

Gabriel laughed. 'I didn't know when I married you that I'd gain a wise counsel as well as a wife.'

'You just remember that when you come to buy my next birthday present.'

Just then, Gabriel's car drew up, ready to take him to his next hand-shaking engagement. He was about to climb inside when Grace grabbed his hand and squeezed it.

'You deserve this, honey,' she whispered. 'If I forget to say it later, I'm proud of you.'

She watched his car roar off, sending up the inevitable cloud of dust.

'Excuse me, Mrs Hernandez?'

She turned to face a young woman perhaps a year or two older than herself. She was wearing a press photo pass.

'My name is Maria Santos,' she said. 'I am a reporter with *Parador Scrivener*.'

Grace smiled politely. 'Pleased to meet you.'

'I wondered if I just ask you a couple of questions before you leave?'

Grace glanced nervously over at one of the security men, but then reminded herself that she could make her own rules now.

'Of course,' she said.

The woman produced a dictaphone, the red light already on. 'Can I ask what you think of the allegation that your husband has been taking political contributions from the Andres family?'

Instantly Grace felt the colour drain from her face. She was used to difficult questions coming from left field on the campaign trail, but this was different. The Andres brothers headed one of Parador's most powerful drug cartels; the suggestion that her husband was taking money from the most hated bandits in the country was preposterous, it was against everything he stood for.

'I think it is absolute nonsense,' she replied as steadily as she could.

'We have some very reliable sources who say it is not nonsense, Mrs Hernandez.'

'I am sure you are aware that my husband is running his campaign on a "no corruption" ticket, Ms Santos,' said Grace steadily. 'I would suggest you are very sure of your sources before you start making such wild accusations about a respected and popular man.'

'Oh, we are sure, Mrs Hernandez.'

'This is ridiculous,' said Grace, noting with relief that her car was just turning into the hotel's forecourt.

'Your husband isn't the first to take a pay-off and he won't be the last,' said the reporter, looking at her evenly. 'Politics is full of people who start out wanting to make a difference,' she continued. 'But they quickly discover you can't make a difference without power, and to obtain power, you need the support of influential people. Your husband has clearly decided that the price of that power is worth paying. How do you feel about that?'

The car pulled up and Grace jumped in, glad to be inside the armoured cocoon, behind tinted glass.

How do I feel about that? she asked herself. *I feel sick, that's how I feel.*

'Where to, Mrs Hernandez?' asked the driver.

'Take me home,' she said.

30

No one could deny that the Globe Club was an exceptional place. The design was worthy of any coffee-table book about stylish interiors. They had the most beautiful staff – all resting actresses and models, hand-picked by Chrissy – and the first-floor haute cuisine restaurant was outstanding, overseen by Pierre Girard, a Michelin-starred chef Miles had poached from Paris. The rooftop spa had surpassed all his expectations: it was the last word in sybaritic luxury, with therapists flown in from Bali and Phuket and the best gym equipment that money could buy. No, there was only one problem with the Globe Club. It was empty.

Sipping an extra-strong espresso and trying to stave off another hangover, Miles was in a particularly filthy mood as he did his morning inspection of the club. He just couldn't comprehend what had gone wrong. Chrissy had tried to tell him that they needed more time to build up their profile and that by this time next year the Globe would be the hottest place in town. But time was one thing Miles did not have. He had ploughed every penny he had into the club, even cashing in the chunk of Ash Corp. stock he had received on his twenty-first birthday, but the wages bills, rates and running costs would put him out of business within the year if they didn't start generating some profit soon. As a sideline, he and Chrissy had been operating a discreet service of high-class escort girls to keep their heads above financial waters, but Miles didn't want to be a male Heidi Fleiss. He wanted to be Ian Schrager, running a successful design-led hotel group. Worst of all, he knew that people – his father in particular – were watching the Globe very closely. Failure was simply not an option.

Outside the spa reception, Chrissy was supervising their florist as she placed an elaborate arrangement of lilies on a mirrored table.

'Fancy lunch in about ten minutes?' smiled Chrissy as she saw Miles walk over.

He ignored her and turned to the florist. 'You're fired,' he said flatly.

'Pardon?' said the florist, looking flustered. 'Are you not happy with the flowers?'

He pulled at a soft petal and glowered. 'I'm not having my club looking like a bloody funeral parlour. Go on, clear off,' he said, stalking out of the spa and down the walnut staircase to the restaurant. He took his favourite table by the window which had been set with starched white napkins and water and wine glasses.

'An omelette and some water,' he said without looking up at the pretty waitress. He stared out on to the street, feeling angry and frustrated. Out of the corner of his eye he saw Chrissy enter the dining room.

She stood at the table for a few seconds, then, realising that Miles was not even going to look up at her, took a seat opposite him anyway.

'What's wrong?'

'Nothing.'

Chrissy put her hand on top of his. 'It's going to be all right, babe.'

'Of course it's going to be all right,' he snapped. 'We've got the best fucking flower arrangements in London.'

'We *did*. Until you just fired her. By the way, that was

281

totally out of order, no matter how worried you are about the finances.'

'I'm not worried,' he said tartly, aware that Chrissy would see through the lie; she probably knew him better than anybody in the world. 'We've got to make this work,' he said softly.

'I know. And we will, but not by running around throwing tantrums.'

She was right; she usually was. He had to admit he had been blown away by Chrissy during the setting up of the club. Hard work combined with great ideas and a dogged determination made her a perfect business partner. She was a natural with the guests and with the staff she was firm but fair – at her core was an iciness, a hardness that meant no one dared take advantage.

'Do you think the membership fee is too high?' he asked her. Before he had met her, Miles Ashford had never asked anyone's advice, but he knew could rely on Chrissy to give him a frank response. She shook her head.

'The problem isn't the fee. It's not even the number of people we've got coming to the club – it's the *kind* of people. We need the cream, Miles, the biggest names in London. Every A-list star that comes to town has got to want to come here.'

'Thanks for the recap on my original idea,' he said sulkily.

'But that was only half the idea, wasn't it?' she said. 'The big idea was in the mix.'

Again she was correct. 'The mix' was one of the things they had identified as being crucial to making an outstanding club. You could have the most stylish interior and the world's greatest chef, but if you didn't have the right blend of people, you were never going to stand out. Studio 54 had it: artists rubbed shoulders with musicians, princes with whores. Truman Capote's Black and White Tie Ball had it: the greatest fusion of actors, writers and socialites ever seen. But the Globe most certainly did not have it.

Somewhere between the spa therapists and the attention to the wine cellar, 'the mix' had been forgotten.

'We need to sprinkle this place with stardust, Miles,' said Chrissy, passion sparkling in her eyes. 'At the moment it's just Piers Jackson and his advertising cronies hanging out with your posh mates from Danehurst and a few rich kids from west London. That might make a decent New Year's Eve party, but it's never going to make people queue around the block. We want celebs worth their salt knocking at our door whenever they are in London.'

She paused.

'Why don't you call Alex Doyle?'

Miles couldn't even pass a weak smile at that suggestion. He'd thought of that already, of course, but hell would freeze over before he begged Alex Doyle to bring his music crowd down.

'That loser isn't a big enough star,' said Miles. 'I seriously doubt he's got Bono and Madonna's numbers.'

Chrissy grabbed his hand and squeezed it. 'Come on, let's think. Who's in town right now?'

Miles looked out the window. 'Euan O'Neil is in rehearsals for a play at that theatre around the corner,' he said. 'He's been in a couple of times for lunch.' The handsome Irish actor had been one of the top names in Hollywood for a decade and was making headlines by daring to tread the boards in an edgy West End version of *Hamlet*.

'Perhaps we can host a party here for the cast and crew?' said Chrissy.

Miles shook his head. 'One night's hardly going to kick-start a revival of our fortunes.'

'Well, we have to start somewhere,' she said, waving the waitress over and ordering two large glasses of wine. 'What do we know about him?'

Miles sighed. 'He married that girl from that sitcom, what's it called?'

'*After You.*'

'That's the one – Jeanie Peters, standard blue-eyed blonde bimbo.'

'Yeah, but I read in the *Enquirer* he was screwing loads of dark-haired, dark-skinned cocktail waitresses until Jeanie threatened him with divorce.'

Miles looked at her. 'But how does that help us?'

'I'm thinking, I'm thinking,' she said as she clinked her glass against his.

In the corner of the bar, Euan O'Neil sipped his fourth Jack Daniel's and Coke and wondered if he should call his wife. He glanced at his watch. It was gone midnight London time, which made it – what? – mid-afternoon in LA. She'd be on Rodeo Drive or getting a colonic or some shit, but he still better call. America might see Jeanie Peters as their favourite girl next door, but America had never been on the receiving end of one of her screaming tantrums. She hadn't been happy about Euan coming to London in the first place – with good reason, he guessed – so he knew he ought to try and keep her sweet. Goddamn bitch had him by the balls. He pulled out his cell phone and dialled the number, but when it went straight to the answering machine he sighed with relief.

Euan had known eighteen months earlier that their marriage was over, but the truth was that he and Jeanie both realised that they were a more valuable Hollywood commodity together than apart. For now, anyway. That, in fact, was the main reason Euan had decided to take the risk of coming here to do the play. At thirty-seven years old he was still a big Hollywood star. But when his last two films turned out to be turkeys, he had decided it was time to regroup and refocus. He'd fired his agent and manager and agreed to a serious theatre role – six weeks in London, then a two-month run on Broadway. People thought he was insane, but it had been a savvy move: it was the biggest event in theatreland for decades, and if the press buzz was anything to go by, his acting credentials had been firmly re-established. Now he'd be offered Oscar-worthy roles, he'd be offered more money, and more importantly, thought Euan, as he let the amber liquid slip down his throat, he might finally be able to get rid of Jeanie.

He went out on to the roof terrace for a quick cigarette in the cold night air; the booze was making him sluggish. *It's a pretty cool place,* he thought looking back into the club. Quiet. Discreet. He was glad to get a gold Globe Club member's card delivered to him by courier this afternoon, especially as all the barmaids were so hot.

'Could I have a light?'

He turned to face a stunningly beautiful woman with long raven hair and a black dress so tight it was like shrink-wrap around her body. He felt his cock stir. He hadn't had sex in a month and it was getting to him – his wife might be a regular on *People* magazine's 'Most Beautiful' list, but Halley's Comet came around more often than she put out.

He held the flame of his Dunhill lighter up to the cigarette dangling from her glossy red lips.

'You know, if I was auditioning for a film noir femme fatale, I'd cast you in a minute.'

She smiled. 'Good job I'm not an actress then,' she replied. 'So what do you do?'

'Spend my husband's money,' she laughed, blowing a smoke ring.

'At least you're honest.'

'Oh, it's not as if I don't deserve it,' she said, narrowing her chocolate eyes. 'I go to parties, talk to people; I'm his eyes and ears around London. Last year I identified five investment opportunities for his company that have already doubled in profit. I'm recommending he looks into investing in this place, actually.'

'I was just thinking LA could do with somewhere like this.'

'Oh really?' said the woman. 'Do you live out there?'

He nodded.

'What do you do there?'

He smirked. It was actually rather refreshing; it had been years since he'd spoken to anyone who didn't know who he was.

'I work in the movies,' he said modestly.

She looked at him more closely. 'Have you seen the screening room?'

He shook his head.

'Come on, I'll show you,' she said, taking his arm.

He watched her round arse twitching as she led him down a dimly lit corridor, his heart beating with a mixture of anticipation and apprehension. Yes, this woman was the perfect combination of classy and sexy, but still, he didn't want to get spotted going into a darkened room with her. Jeanie had spies everywhere.

'This way.' She smiled, opening a heavy soundproofed door and pulling him in. It was a snug little room with three rows of red velvet tip-up seats and a screen at one end. 'I think you can even lock it,' she whispered, flipping a switch.

'Hey, I don't know . . .' he began, but never finished the sentence, as she took his hand and put it on her breast.

'How's that feel?' she growled. 'Does it feel good?'

'Yes,' he said, surprised. This was quick work, even for him. 'Yes, it does.'

'How about this?' She slid her hand inside his trousers and held his erect cock.

'Pretty good,' he gasped. She pushed him back into one of the screening chairs, and as she unzipped his flies, he pulled her Lycra dress down to free her bra-less breasts, fantastic natural orbs that yielded to the touch.

'Naughty,' she purred, rolling her dress up her thighs to show him she hadn't bothered with panties either. She straddled him, and using the fingers of one hand to part herself, guided his throbbing cock into her wetness. Vaguely an alarm bell was ringing in his brain. A producer friend in LA had warned him about London – the kiss-and-tell culture of the tabloids, the girls who would do anything for their fifteen minutes of fame and a cheque in the bank. But he was Euan O'Neil; he couldn't be expected to abstain from women completely. He just had to choose carefully. Surely a lonely, lovely socialite with a rich, powerful husband wasn't going to run to the tabloids or whisper to her friends? No, a memory of a night with Euan O'Neil would be kept hidden in the box marked 'special memories', along with her vibrator.

'You are sure you locked the door?' he moaned as she gripped her thighs around him, swivelling her hips to control the pace and rhythm. He could feel her clench around him, hot and tight. Holding on to the back of the chair, she slowly lifted herself off him so the very tip of his cock was tickling her neatly trimmed pubes, then she plunged back down, grinding herself on to him. He groaned, but the sound was lost as she leant forward and pulled his bottom lip into a sultry kiss.

'I'm going to come,' he growled as her nipple brushed his lips.

'Not yet,' she whispered, pumping harder. She was doing all the work, fucking him, pleasuring him, totally in control. Completely calling the shots. He loved it.

He groaned again, finding the energy to push her off him as he came, shooting over the red velvet like an over-eager eighteen-year-old. He pulled out his handkerchief to wipe it up, vaguely embarrassed, but it was better than having a love child floating around London.

'Wow,' breathed the woman, tossing her long hair back and rolling the Lycra tube back down her body. He realised he didn't even know her name.

'Let's keep this between us, hey?' he said hopefully.

She leant down and kissed him on the cheek. 'I wouldn't

want it any other way,' she said, then opened the door and walked out.

He slumped back down in the chair, panting. 'Shit, why didn't I come to London years ago?'

Miles glanced casually at his watch as he made his way towards the stage door. It was five o'clock, twenty minutes after the *Hamlet* matinée had finished, which meant Euan O'Neil would be back in his dressing room. A male crew member with a walkie-talkie was having a smoke on the street.

'I need to speak to Mr O'Neil,' said Miles coolly.

The boy shook his head apologetically. 'Sorry, can't let you in. Mr O'Neil usually has a massage after the performance.'

Miles took out a wodge of money from his breast pocket and handed it over. 'This is important,' he said, knowing the money was more than a theatre hand would make in a week.

'Follow me,' said the boy.

They wound down through the back corridors of the theatre. *What a shit-hole*, thought Miles, looking at the peeling paint and concrete floors. Finally the lad pointed at a door and stuffed the money in his pocket.

'He's in there.'

Miles knocked and entered without being asked. Euan O'Neil was sitting in front of a long illuminated mirror where a young girl was carefully taking off his make-up. *Get yourself a new agent*, thought Miles, looking around at the shabby dressing room. It was small, simple, dotted with a couple of vases of wilting flowers, and a portable TV and video on the counter. Ah, that was good, thought Miles.

'Can I help you?' said Euan, turning to look at him.

Miles extended a hand. 'Miles Ashford. From the Globe Club.'

O'Neil glanced at the make-up girl, then waved her away.

'Of course, Miles,' he said, shaking Miles' hand, back in

full PR mode. 'Thanks for the membership, it's a great little club.'

'Did you have a good time the other night?' Miles said.

Euan's Hollywood smile faded. 'How can I help you, Mr Ashford?' he asked. 'I'm very busy.'

Miles placed a padded envelope on the counter in front of the mirror.

'At the Globe Club we value discretion, privacy, but also security. As you probably know, our membership is wealthy and private, and we make every effort to ensure it stays that way.'

In the reflection, Miles watched Euan's handsome face frown, the panstick making the lines on his face look darker, thicker and troubled. He reached into the envelope and pulled out a black, unmarked video cassette.

'What's this?'

'Footage from the club.'

He stepped over to the TV and slotted the tape into the machine, waiting as a grainy black-and-white image of Euan and the brunette crackled on screen. The accompanying soundtrack was a series of moans and urgent panting. Impatiently, Euan reached over and clicked it off.

'OK, enough. I get the fucking message. Who's seen this?'

'No one besides myself and the Globe's head of security.'

Euan looked relieved and then irritated. 'I'm assuming you're here to give me this back?'

'Of course.'

His face softened. 'Thanks.'

'As I say, the privacy of our members is paramount. You can imagine if that tape got into the wrong hands it would be worth millions.'

Euan's face changed instantly. 'Are you trying to screw me?' he said angrily. 'Because I warn you, Ashford, my lawyers will have you in court before you can blink.'

Miles smiled to himself. He hadn't expected the actor to

be a complete pushover. He'd met enough celebrities in his time to know that you didn't get well known without being tough and ruthless.

He shook his head slowly. 'I don't want your money, Mr O'Neil. Ask around, I've got enough of my own.'

'So what do you want?'

'Nothing. I just wanted you to know that this will go no further.'

Miles had been sceptical, but Chrissy had been right once again. They couldn't blackmail Euan O'Neil, especially when he'd already been caught with his pants down. Instead, they needed him on side, spreading the word to his Hollywood friends about this hot new club where the women were sexy and discretion was guaranteed. And where the A list came, so would lesser mortals. They wouldn't be joining some club owned by London rich kid Miles Ashford; they would be joining a secret cabal made up of the industry's hottest movers and shakers.

'This is yours,' said Miles, ejecting the tape and handing it to the actor. 'There are no copies. This will just be between us.'

'Oh,' said Euan, looking down at the tape. 'I'm sorry if I was a little hasty there. This is very good of you.'

Miles nodded sympathetically. 'My pleasure,' he said and began to turn towards the door.

'Hey, listen,' said Euan. 'At least let me buy you a drink? I've got a few hours to kill before the next performance. I'd like to say thanks.'

Miles glanced at his watch. 'Sure, maybe just the one.'

Chrissy was waiting in the office.

'So?' she asked, pouring two fingers of ice-cold vodka and handing him the glass.

'He'll be on the membership committee and he's getting Tom, Brad and Harvey to join him. He'll have the VIP party for his next London premiere at the club, and he's coming for dinner with his wife when she's back in London in a fortnight. Make sure the paps are outside. We can't have the Ivy hogging all the Covent Garden action.'

Chrissy grinned and took a drink. The cameras had been hastily put into the screening room the day before Euan's first visit, but maybe it was a good idea to install CCTV everywhere in the club. You never knew when this sort of thing might happen again, with or without a little helping hand. She picked up her phone and dialled a number.

'Lauren? Chrissy. I have to say, congratulations are in order.'

Lauren was the raven-haired woman with the chocolate-brown eyes. Chrissy knew her from the Tokyo hostess circuit, but she was now one of London's most elite call girls. Chrissy and Miles had put quite a bit of work her way in the past few months.

'I aim to please,' replied Lauren.

'I'm transferring the five thousand now. By the way, what was it like fucking the sexiest man in Hollywood?'

Lauren giggled. 'Messy.'

Chrissy hung up and turned to her husband, leaning across the desk to clink their tumblers together. The Globe Club was suddenly in business.

31

February 1994

Sasha pushed the glass door and stepped out into the bright sunlight of Lombard Street. It didn't happen very often, but at this moment, she felt like crying. She scrabbled around in her bag looking for a tissue, but could only find a cocktail napkin from the Atlantic Bar, seizing it to dab at her eyes.

Philip Bettany put a reassuring arm across her shoulder. 'Hey, don't worry, Sash,' he said. 'We'll find another bank. It will all work out in the end, I promise.'

'It's not that, I've just got something in my eye,' she muttered, turning away. The truth was, the endless stress of trying to take over the Ben Rivera label was finally getting to her: she wanted it so much, but the harder she pushed, the further away it seemed to be. She had spent the last twelve months walking a dangerous tightrope, on the one hand trying to interest Ben in selling his company and raise the finance to buy him out, while simultaneously trying not to alert any other investors to the potential of the brand.

It was an impossible task, especially as part of her job was to tell everyone how amazing Ben Rivera's designs were – and of course they *were* amazing, but she didn't want anyone else to twig that Rivera might be a future gold mine with the right strategic investment. The last thing she wanted was for him to be poached by one of the big fashion giants like Dior or Versace for a well-paid in-house design position.

The thing that was giving her the most sleepless nights was the difficulty in finding the money. It wasn't as if she didn't know plenty of wealthy people. The problem was, Sasha was a twenty-two-year-old ex-model with zero commercial experience. They'd take her for dinner, sure. But hand over upwards of a million pounds for turning Ben Rivera into a ready-to-wear label with a London boutique outlet? Not a chance. The one genuine lead she had, a wealthy Iranian called Razzi Akbari, had put her off seeking private investment overnight. Sasha had been brilliant at their meeting, presenting her business plan with passion and gusto, answering all his concerns, even indulging in a little light flirting. But when she'd overheard Razzi's wife at a party boasting that her husband was about to buy her 'a little fashion company to play with', Sasha had immediately shut down all communication. Ben Rivera was *her* find. She wasn't going to be elbowed out of the way by anybody.

Which was why she was standing in the City, fighting back the tears. This was the sixth bank to turn her down flat. Philip's generous attendance at the meeting had definitely helped things along – having an analyst from Schroder's in the room meant she hadn't had to face the 'but what financial experience do you have?' question this time. But his presence hadn't been enough to make it happen.

'It's bloody over, isn't it,' said Sasha, her voice cracking. 'There's no one else to go to.'

'Chin up, Sash,' said Philip bullishly. 'Look around you. We're in one of the greatest financial capitals of the world. Somewhere nearby is someone with money to invest in the company; it's just a matter of finding them.'

She forced a smile. He was being kind; he was always kind. After their flirtatious beginning at her parents' anniversary party, Sasha had discouraged any romantic interest, but to her surprise, Philip had stuck around. It had been strange at first – Sasha had never had a platonic male friend before; in fact, working in fashion, she didn't have many real friends at all beyond the kissy-kissy, 'see you at the next party' variety. But Philip had been a rock, happy to give up his weekends to help her draft a comprehensive business plan, celebrating the completion or refinement of every draft with suppers at Pucci Pizza, drinks at the Hollywood Arms or just a video and popcorn in his small Chelsea Harbour apartment. It was actually nice to have a friend without any of the sexual complications; Sasha wondered why she hadn't done this years ago.

Philip stuck his arm out, flagging down a cab.

'Listen, I'll bet you're starving,' he said. 'Come back to mine, we'll get a takeaway and work out how to crack this.'

'I'm way behind on work for the label,' she said, shaking her head. 'I really should get back.'

'Oh no,' said Philip firmly. 'You can't wriggle out of it that easily. I'm not having you moping all night when I bet the answer is staring us in the face.'

It was true, she was hungry. She hadn't eaten all day, partly through nerves, partly because she had been so busy preparing for the meeting.

They ordered Chinese from the cab using Philip's mobile, and it was there by the time they arrived. Philip arranged the cartons on the rug in the living room and laid the business plan out next to it.

'So let's look at this logically,' he said thoughtfully. 'The banks are a no-go without a big injection of your own cash. What other avenues can we try?'

'Are you sure your dad isn't interested?' said Sasha, reaching for the noodles. She'd never met Leo Bettany, but she still hadn't forgiven him for making her father redundant. His selfish attitude to his kids hadn't helped; although Philip had all the polish of a successful Young Turk, not a penny had come from his father. Leo Bettany believed in leaving his children to their own devices and had vowed to bequeath all his wealth to charity.

'Tried him,' said Philip sheepishly. 'He says he only invests in areas he understands – that doesn't include cocktail dresses apparently. Besides, you're a friend of mine, which definitely counts against you.'

He sat up, pursing his lips. 'Look, we need at least a million pounds' investment and the banks have refused us,' he said. 'There's the venture capitalist firms, but they usually like dealing with bigger investments.'

'So let's ask for more money.'

'And give up seventy per cent of the business?' He shook his head. 'I don't think that's the way to go. I still think we need to chase down private investors, despite what happened with Razzi. Investment is about people, and you are definitely the right person to turn Ben Rivera into everything it can be.'

'Sweet of you to say,' she said. 'But no one seems to agree with you.'

Philip paused for a moment.

'Look, I have about two hundred thousand pounds of my own funds we could put in,' he said. 'Private investors might be more willing to look at you if we put in some capital of our own.'

Sasha stopped and gaped at him, a spring roll halfway to her mouth.

'You'd really do that?'

'Well, when you first told me about your idea, I was sceptical. But that was before I knew you, before I knew how determined you are, what a taste-maker you are, how special you are.'

'You're a sweetheart, you know that,' said Sasha with sincerity. 'Everything you've done over the past few months, everything you've helped me with ... I don't know how to thank you.'

She felt the atmosphere in the room change. Dusk was settling across London, and while Philip's apartment was small, it had floor-to-ceiling windows with a view right across Chelsea Harbour. Suddenly Sasha was very aware of the soft glow of the setting sun filling his living room.

'You know how you can thank me,' he said quietly.

It was true. She'd steered their relationship towards friendship not because she didn't find Philip attractive, but because she couldn't handle the distraction. She'd learnt the hard way that men were bad news, that love was a false promise. Even sex came with a price. She didn't need it. She didn't need any of it.

'You're a nice guy, Philip, but ...'

'What's wrong with the nice guy?' he said, stretching over, his fingers touching hers.

God, why does he have to be so bloody handsome? she thought, feeling her guard slip. He brought his hand to her face, cupping it gently, then slowly, very slowly, lowered his soft lips for the most tender of kisses.

She shivered; both anticipation and fear. She'd had sex only once since her episode with the D&D advertising executive three years earlier. It had been on a work trip to Italy and he'd been a macho Milanese fashion executive; the experience had been stiff, painful and awkward to the point where she faked an orgasm after just a few minutes to get the whole thing over with. But this wasn't like that, not at all. As Philip slowly unbuttoned her shirt and unclipped her bra, she groaned, pushing her firm breasts towards him. She wanted him, wanted his touch, wanted it hard and fast. But Philip was in no hurry. For someone who had so obviously wanted her for so long, he was maddeningly slow, taking each moment leisurely to kiss, taste and savour every inch of her body, his tongue discovering secret pleasure spots she had never even known existed. The tip of his finger circled her nipple, delicately at first as it hardened to his touch, then when it was ripe he lowered his mouth, sucking and gently biting. He repeated it on the other side, then kissed down her belly, swirling his tongue around the insides of her thighs. Waves of white-hot desire rippled from her belly before he had even entered her. But then he was inside and she was crying out in pleasure, her hands gripping the rug, her feet kicking the takeaway cartons across the floor. The orgasm that was building from her throbbing, molten core was so deep, so electrifying, so blissfully, blindingly exquisite, she pleaded with him to stop. When it was over, she relaxed into the curve of his body, enjoying his musky, manly scent of sex and sweat, and the feeling of sweet, satisfying release.

'That was every bit as good as I hoped it was going to be,' he said, his face silhouetted in the low light.

She nodded, realising that the deep knot of tension and anger inside her was no longer there.

Her eyes stared at the ceiling.

'I know who I can get the money off,' she said slowly. She hadn't wanted to ask him, although from the start he was the obvious person. But having sex with Philip, creating a new bond with someone who made her feel safe, galvanised her to do it.

'Well that's fantastic,' Philip breathed into her ear, reaching around and cupping her breast, his finger and thumb getting to work on her hardening nipple. 'But it'll wait until morning, won't it?'

Sasha gave another gasp of pleasure and turned back to him.

Yes, she guessed it would.

32

'Where's Gabriel?' snapped Isabella, sweeping imperiously into the hall. Grace had already searched the whole of the ground floor of El Esperanza. His cousin's wedding was due to start in forty-five minutes and the church was at least half an hour's drive away. It was one thing waiting for the groom to be kept waiting by the bride, but not by random members of the family.

'I'll look upstairs,' said Grace, hitching up her long silk dress to climb the steps.

'When you find him,' called Isabella after her, 'please tell him that I am leaving for the church in exactly five minutes, whether he's coming or not.'

Grace ran into his study, her heels clattering on the stone floor. Gabriel was sitting in front of his computer, wearing jeans and an unbuttoned white shirt, furiously making notes on a yellow legal notebook.

'You're not even changed?' she gasped.

Gabriel glanced up, then went back to his notes. 'I don't know if I can come,' he said distractedly.

'You're kidding.'

'CBS want to interview me tomorrow,' he said. 'I'm just waiting for the producer to call and confirm.'

'Gabriel, it's your cousin's wedding in less than an hour! The interview can wait.'

'The interview *can't* wait, Grace,' he snapped. 'It's the election in three weeks' time.'

'Yes, and CBS is an *American* cable channel.'

'A very influential American cable channel.'

Grace squeezed her eyes shut, trying not to explode.

'Go without me,' he said finally.

'Fine,' she sighed, walking to the door. 'Do you want to give me the present, then? I can take it to the wedding along with your apologies.'

Several months ago, Grace had found out that Gabriel's cousin Amelia had first met her fiancé at an exhibition of Luis Marquis, one of Parador's most prominent sculptors. She and Gabe had commissioned him to make a small piece as a wedding gift for the happy couple.

'What do you mean, do I want to give you the present?' He frowned.

'You said you'd pick it up from the Marquis studio yesterday after your meeting at the CARP office.'

'Oh shit,' he whispered. 'I completely forgot.'

'It's fine,' she said tersely, turning away.

'Grace, it doesn't matter.'

In the scheme of things, it probably didn't matter – they could have it sent over after the wedding – but it was just one more thing which reminded her that life outside politics just didn't exist for Gabriel any longer.

She ran back downstairs, willing herself not to cry. Caro was waiting for her at the bottom.

'What's wrong?' asked her friend, kneeling down to tie pink ribbons around Olivia's pigtails.

'Oh, Gabe forgot to pick up the wedding present when he was in Palumbo yesterday.'

'Don't worry, I can go. I wasn't really invited to the church service anyway. I'm only in it for the party.' Caro grinned.

'Do you mind? Take Gabe's car. We were going to take it, but there's been a rethink. I'm going with Isabella. We'll see you at the reception.'

Caro ushered the twins towards their mother and gave

them a stern look. 'Now you be good for cousin Amelia, OK? No shouting out in church.'

'Yes, Caro,' they chorused solemnly.

Grace suppressed a smile. Who'd have thought her wild Kiwi roommate would have become such a great mother hen?

Caro ran outside while Isabella pulled on her cream taffeta coat.

'Let's go,' hissed the older woman. 'If Gabe's not coming—'

She never finished her sentence. There was a split second when all the air in the room seemed to expand, then a white flash followed by a deep sickening boom that Grace felt in her chest. She was thrown into the steps, her arms still around the twins. She was dimly aware that she was covered in tiny pieces of wood and glass and that Olivia was lying on top of her screaming, but the noise seemed to retreat around her as if she was underwater. She pulled Joseph to her; he was bleeding from his forehead and shaking violently. Then, in a rush, the noise came back and everywhere was shouting and running footsteps and the crackle of flames.

'Grace! Are you all right?' For a moment, Grace didn't recognise Gabriel and drew the children closer to her. 'It's OK, baby, it's me, it's me,' he said soothingly, pulling her up and sitting her on the marble steps.

Unable to reply, she looked down and was horrified to see that her arms and legs had been lacerated by glass from the shattered windows. The huge double front doors had been blown clean off their hinges; beyond that, all she could see was thick billowing smoke that had engulfed El Esperanza's courtyard.

'Oh my God, Caro . . .' She staggered to her feet and ran to the door.

'Grace, don't go out there!' shouted Gabriel, his arms tight around the children. She ignored him and ran out into the bright courtyard. A hundred feet in front of her, Gabriel's car was now a ball of twisted metal and flame. She shielded her face from the intense heat.

'Caro!' she screamed. 'CARO!' Then she sank to her knees, sobbing, knowing that there was nothing she could do to save her friend.

Gabriel grabbed her and pulled her back from the burning car. 'Don't look, don't look,' he whispered.

Grace couldn't breathe, couldn't take it in. *She* should have been in that car. They *all* should: her, Gabriel, the twins. They should be dead, not her friend, not Caro.

'Oh God,' she said, turning her bloody, tear-marked face towards Gabriel. 'What have we done? What have we done?'

33

According to the police, it had only been a matter of time before a car bomb took out a senior member of CARP. It was a popular method of murder in Parador. During the troubles in the seventies, not a week had gone by without a judge or politician being eliminated in this way, and twenty years later it was the chosen assassination method of the drug cartels. The fact that it had happened within the grounds of El Esperanza, where they spent hundreds of thousands of US dollars on security, had shaken the entire family to the core – not just for the questions it raised about their own safety but for the future of democracy in Parador. If their enemies could reach right into the heart of their organisation, they could get to anyone, anyone at all.

In the days that followed Caro's murder, Grace had walked around like a ghost. With security breached and El Esperanza badly damaged, she had taken the children to their house high in the hills, where they had been under twenty-four-hour armed guard. She played with the twins, she dressed her wounds and she tried her best not to fall apart. Despite Gabe's appeal that she carry on and help him provide a united front in the run-up to the elections, she could barely bring herself to get out of bed in the morning. Racked with guilt, she played endless games of 'if only': if only Caro hadn't come to Parador, if only Grace hadn't asked her to work at

302

El Esperanza, if only she hadn't asked her to pick up that sculpture. *If only*. You could drive yourself mad with that game.

There was no body to take back to New Zealand, but Caro's family were holding a memorial service in their home town. Grace had been surprised when Gabe had insisted they all go and take the family jet, although no opportunity was wasted: a CNN film crew was at the airport to see them off.

Caro's family lived in a small town forty miles from Christchurch airport, where the rich green rolling countryside reminded Grace of rural Oxfordshire on a particularly lush hot summer's day. It was a beautiful part of the world and Grace wondered why Caro had spent half her life running away from it; then again, Grace knew about the desire to run away from a life that, on the face of it, seemed perfect.

They drove straight to the church, a white clapboard jewel on the outskirts of the village, for the small and discreet service, followed by a wake at Caro's parents' farmhouse. Isabella's PA had checked them into a luxury lodge a short drive away from the church, where they were to stay the night before returning to Parador. Gabriel immediately went out on to the balcony with the telephone and began talking intensely, so Grace unpacked their few belongings and put the twins to sleep in the two travel cots. There were still a couple of daylight hours left, and in the distance she could see a river glistening silver, so she knocked on the adjoining suite and asked if Isabella could sit with the twins while she got some fresh air.

Although it was February, it was New Zealand's summer. The air smelt crisp and full of promise and new life. Grace grimaced at the irony of it. She walked away from the lodge across an emerald meadow and sat on a bench on the river's edge. She had eaten very little all day, but still she felt nauseous. In the church, she had not been able to shake off a terrible sense of shame; it was like some physical weight pressing down on her. *If only*.

Hearing footsteps behind her, she turned. Gabriel had changed out of his sombre funeral suit into jeans and a blue shirt that made his skin look more olive and golden.

'We have dinner reservations at seven thirty,' he said. 'Apparently the restaurant at the lodge is excellent. We need to be refreshed for the flight home, anyway.'

'I'm not hungry,' said Grace, looking away.

'Why not?'

'Why not?' she snapped. 'We've just been to my best friend's funeral, that's why not. The funeral of a friend who was murdered at our house – with a car bomb meant for us. Is that enough?'

'She was unlucky,' said Gabriel quietly.

'Unlucky?' Grace hissed. 'Gabriel, she's dead. *Dead*. She died and we lived, don't you feel bad about that?'

He looked at the ground but didn't speak.

'I have to ask you something, Gabe,' she said suddenly. 'Have you been dealing with the cartels?'

He shrugged, his eyes still on the floor. 'You know I've met them.'

'Yes, but what I'm asking is did you accept money from them?'

His cheeks flushed. 'What? Of course not!'

'Don't lie to me, Gabe,' she said, her voice wavering. 'They didn't plant a bomb in our car for no reason.'

'Don't be ridiculous!' cried Gabriel. 'They put it there to destabilise our campaign. The bomb was meant for *me*.'

Should she believe him? His cheeks were pink and his eyes wide, but all powerful men lied, they *had* to. She had heard enough of the glib half-truths coming from her father's tongue to know that much.

'A journalist at the Palumbo press conference told me you'd

304

been accepting contributions to your campaign from the Andres brothers.'

'That's a complete lie,' he spat. 'Did you believe him? Did you really think I would stoop so low?'

'I didn't believe her, Gabe. Not once did I doubt you, which is why I never brought it up. But now . . . now Caro is dead.'

Tears were rolling down her cheeks now. The shame and guilt of Caro's death when the car bomb had been meant for them was almost too much to bear. Could she have acted when the journalist had told her about Gabe's corruption? Could she have saved Caro?

'You asked me once if I'd ever done anything bad,' she said, struggling to get her words out. 'I found a body on my father's island, the body of one of his staff. And I did nothing, I turned a blind eye and there was never any justice for the person who had killed him. I'm not going to let that happen again.'

'So what do you intend to do?' said Gabriel angrily. 'Expose your husband as a corrupt politician, tell the world I took bribes from the drug lords? Do you really think that will bring Caro back?'

'Did you take money, Gabe?' she insisted. 'Answer me!'

'No,' he said, looking away from her, across the river.

'Oh my God,' she gasped, her eyes wide. 'You did, you took a kickback.'

'Yes!' he yelled. 'If you really must know, I did take money, but not from those animals the Andres brothers, or from any of the cartels.'

'So who did you take it from?'

Gabriel glanced at her. 'The Americans,' he said simply. 'When I went to Washington at New Year, it was to discuss a military counter-narcotics programme.'

'So why didn't you tell me?'

'Because I was ashamed!'

'But you did it for the right reasons,' said Grace.

305

'Yes, Grace, but there's always a price to pay, isn't there?'

'Caro, you mean?'

'Not Caro,' he said dismissively. 'The debt we will owe the Americans. Don't you understand, Grace? I have sold my country to a superpower. Yes, they want to stop the spread of drugs, but they're far more interested in having countries like us in their debt, jumping to their tune.'

It was only at that moment that Grace could see how far her husband had got away from her, how little there was left of the man she had married. He had started with ideals, a passion and a duty, but now he couldn't even see that someone dying in his place was tragic. He couldn't see that his plan to free Parador had almost got him and his children killed.

'Do you really want to win this election so much?'

'Of course I do,' he replied incredulously.

'I'm not sure I do, Gabe. I want to help people, and I've come to love the people of your country. But do I want to change the world? In Parador at least, that price feels too high. I'm twenty-four years old, Gabe. We have a family. I just want us to be happy. Safe.'

He shook his head. 'We've come too far to turn back now,' he said.

'No, Gabe,' she said, clutching his arm. 'We haven't, we can always change. If you don't win this election, you can return to your books. You can still lobby the West to help your country, but sometimes you can be more effective outside politics than inside.'

'If I don't win, Grace,' he said firmly, 'then I'm going to try again. The next elections are only in four years' time. And there'll be risks again. You know that.'

'But look how big the risk is, Gabe! Caro is *dead*! What good will it do if you die too? Or me? Or the twins? You can't help people if you're dead.'

She felt a deep, unsettling selfishness saying it, but it was the truth, and it was also a relief to say out loud what she had been feeling for months, perhaps years.

'Are you sure this is what you want? Do you want to live like this, always looking over your shoulder?'

'I want to be *president*, Grace,' he said, his eyes blazing. 'It's my destiny.'

She took a long, hard look at Gabriel's face. She didn't see sadness, guilt or anger at what had just happened. All she saw was desire. Somewhere along the line, the quest for change had become the need for power. And power, she knew, was a drug too hard to kick. Deep down, she knew her marriage was over.

'Grace!' cried Gabriel as he watched her walk away. 'Come back, goddamn it!'

But she kept walking. She closed her eyes and let the summer breeze wash over her, knowing exactly what she needed to do.

Gabriel ran up and caught her arm. 'Where are you going?' he said irritably.

'I'm leaving Parador.'

'That's ... that's insane!' stuttered Gabriel. 'How is that going to look to the electorate, my wife abandoning me?'

'I don't care how it looks, Gabe,' she cried. 'I want our kids to be safe.'

'They *are* safe!'

'Clearly not.'

'I thought you wanted to make a difference, Grace,' he mocked.

She shrugged. 'What is more important to you, Gabe? Your family or your ambitions?'

'I want to save my country,' he said, puffing his chest out.

'No, Gabriel, you want to be *president*. There is a huge difference.'

She stormed up the path back to the lodge. Still shaking with anger, she dried her face and took a few moments to compose herself before she went back into the suite. Isabella was in a chair by the open window reading a book, the twins still asleep. Grace wondered how much her mother-in-law had seen or heard.

'So, my dear,' said Isabella, putting a bookmark between the pages. 'I suppose you'll be leaving us.'

Grace looked across at her sharply. 'Did you hear?'

'No,' she said softly. 'But I know what I'd be thinking, as a wife and a mother. If I were you, Grace, I would leave Parador.'

Grace gaped at her and Isabella chuckled softly. 'Don't look so shocked. I've made many sacrifices for my country. I've lost a husband and a son. You think you can fix things with good ideas and principles and passion, but sadly, I've come to realise that that just isn't the case.'

'I do want him to win, Isabella, I do, but I can't live like this.'

The older woman nodded. 'Go,' she said simply. 'I don't want to lose anyone else. Nothing is worth that, believe me.'

Grace felt the tears come again. This was the last person she had expected kindness from.

Isabella walked over and gently lifted her chin. 'Look after my grandchildren for me.'

'But I thought . . .'

'You thought I would hate you? No, Grace, I am proud of you. Proud of what you have achieved in Parador, proud of the woman you have grown into. And now I am proud that you are doing the right thing. I only wish that I had had your strength when I was your age.'

Grace could barely move her mouth to speak. Isabella nodded towards the door, where Grace could see her suitcase standing.

'I've packed all your things,' she said. 'Now gather your children; your car is waiting downstairs. There's a jet at Christchurch airport which will take you wherever you want to go.'

Grace pulled Isabella into a smothering hug. It was only then that she realised this was the first time she had ever embraced her mother-in-law. 'Thank you, Isabella,' she said simply.

'You're very welcome, my dear,' said Isabella, straightening herself back up to her usual elegant posture.

Quickly Grace scooped the unstirring twins up and walked to the door as Isabella gave them a final goodbye kiss.

'You will look after Gabe, won't you?' she asked, tears in her eyes.

'Of course, he will be fine.' Isabella opened the door and Grace stepped through. 'And Grace?' she said. 'You'll be fine too.'

I only hope you're right, thought Grace, biting on her lip to stop herself from sobbing. *I only hope you're right.*

34

March 1994

Sasha had never spent more time preparing for a meeting; she would hardly have taken more care over her appearance if it had been Oscar night. She had tried on everything in her wardrobe, rejected the lot, then trawled Bond Street before deciding that her favourite Ben Rivera day dress was by far the most flattering and, of course, appropriate. As she was shown up to the office, she felt pretty good. She was tall and slender thanks to four-inch heels and a week on a drastic Ryvita diet and her blond hair was long and glossy thanks to a three-hundred-pound cut and colour at Neville. Of course, she would have preferred to be coming here with a successful career to boast about – at the very least, an eight-carat engagement ring. But then this wasn't a social call. She had only come because she had to.

'Hello, Miles,' she said, walking into the Globe Club office, swaying her hips. The years had been kind to Miles Ashford, she thought, taking a seat opposite him. In a sharply tailored navy suit, accessorised by just a tan, her ex-boyfriend had transformed from an attractive yet gangly youth into a handsome twenty-three-year-old man oozing confidence and polish.

I'd be oozing confidence if I owned the Globe, thought

Sasha begrudgingly. The Covent Garden club was unquestionably the hippest, most elite place in town. On the way up to Miles' top-floor office, she'd seen two actors, a rock band and a group of writers in intense discussion over cappuccinos. London was gathering a buzz as the place to be – not since the sixties, when Mary Quant, Shrimpton, Bailey and the Stones had helped make it a global mecca for all things cool had the capital had such a feeling of possibility and excitement. And right now, the Globe Club was at the epicentre of it all; the place to be seen.

'Tea?' asked Miles, reclining in his Eames chair and buzzing his secretary. Sasha bristled at being treated like any other corporate guest, but then again, any hopes of a private, intimate tête-à-tête had been dashed when he had suggested meeting at his office.

'Only tea?' She smiled. 'In the old days it would have been a cheeky lunchtime martini.'

'I don't drink on duty, Sasha. In fact, I rarely drink at all these days.'

'Things have changed,' she said, genuinely surprised.

A beautiful girl dressed in tight black cigarette pants came in and placed a tray of tea on the leather-topped table. Miles barely took his eyes off the girl while she was in the room, a gesture Sasha felt sure was for her benefit.

'So how are you?'

'Fine.' She smiled. 'Congratulations on your wedding, by the way. What does your wife do again?'

Miles' mouth tightened into a line. 'Chrissy is a partner in the business with me.'

'Yes, I heard she was a hostess. That must be useful with a place like the Globe Club.'

They looked at each other, two fighting dogs circling, neither willing to back down.

Miles put a dainty cup in front of Sasha, rattling it in the saucer.

'What do you want, Sash?'

'I have a very exciting business opportunity for you.'

Miles gave a small laugh. 'You mean you want to borrow some money.'

Sasha had always known this wasn't going to be easy, but she was determined not to wither under his mocking gaze.

'You're twenty-three years old, Sasha. What do you know about business?'

'I could say the same about you.' She smiled sweetly. 'But here you are, on top of the world.'

'I found my calling,' said Miles grandly.

'Well it's the same with me,' she replied. 'The aim of my business is to help make women look fabulous. And I was always top-notch at looking good, wasn't I?'

Miles just shrugged non-committally and suddenly Sasha hated him. Miles Ashford with his family money and Oxbridge attitude. Without his trust funds he'd be nothing, and yet here he was, lording it over her like some ancient king. If she and his other friends hadn't kept quiet . . . She took a breath. She was here for a reason, not to dredge up the past.

'I am working with a couturier called Ben Rivera,' she said, trying to maintain a businesslike tone. 'It's a small operation making red-carpet gowns; he's as good as Lagerfeld or Lacroix, better even. The trouble is his outfit has little commercial backing, and as yet, it's not geared up for any mainstream production or distribution.'

Miles curled a lip. 'And I am interested in Ben Rivera because . . . ?'

She had to be honest with him. This office was the Last Chance Saloon. She had spent the last eighteen months walking a commercial tightrope; she needed wealthy investors, but she knew that looking for money on her rich social circuit might alert people to Ben's potential. Already word was getting round the industry that he was a name to watch out for, especially since he had made a gown for Princess Diana. So Sasha

312

had encouraged him to stay small, working on spectacular bespoke pieces while she tried to find someone to give her the money to steal the business out from under him.

'You should be interested because everyone is interested in fashion now; everyone wants to buy into a slice of designer living. Image is everything, Miles. You've bought into that yourself with the Globe. But in the next ten years the top fashion houses will become billion-dollar brands with infinite brand extension opportunities. Here's the business plan,' she said, putting a slim folder in front of him. 'That will show you how I'm going to do it.'

Miles sighed, flipping through the folder without interest. 'And how much are you looking for?'

'A million pounds,' said Sasha calmly. 'Three hundred thousand to buy Ben out, the rest for capital investment: a store in a chic street in London and the nuts and bolts of creating a ready-to-wear operation. Fabric, a manufacturer in Italy, distribution and so on.'

Miles folded his hands in front of him on the desk. 'So let me get this right,' he said with a superior smile. 'Three hundred thousand buys you a controlling interest in Ben Rivera. Let's say a sixty per cent stake. But you want to keep hold of a majority shareholding, which is fifty-one per cent. The designer also retains a share. So where does that leave the investor? You can't honestly expect anyone to invest a million pounds for a ten per cent stake in a back-street fashion designer, can you?' He gave a little laugh she recognised well, the laugh he reserved for people he pitied or felt were beneath him.

'Ben Rivera is not a back-street designer,' she said firmly. 'His will be the next big name in fashion.'

Miles looked bored. 'And who's the management team?'

'There's me, of course.'

Miles laughed. 'Spending money was always your strong point, Sasha, not making it.'

Sasha tried not to flinch. The management team was the

weak part of her plan. She was completely convinced of her own abilities and the potential of the Rivera brand, but she was well aware that investors saw 'creative' types as a liability. They wanted to see that other people like them – steady, analytical people with a track record in business – were prepared to get involved in the project.

'I have Philip Bettany, an analyst at Schroder's, as my financial director.'

She hadn't officially asked Phil if she could use his name, of course, and she had zero expectation that he would give up a glittering career in the financial sector to help his sort-of-girlfriend out with her silly dresses, but she wasn't going to let Miles know that.

Miles nodded, looking much more impressed. 'Well, he should know what he's talking about at least,' he said, tossing the business plan on his desk. 'Trouble is, I haven't got a million quid to give you.'

Sasha swallowed. She had expected resistance, even out-and-out refusal, but not this.

'Bullshit, Miles,' she said. 'What about your trust funds?'

He held his hands open. 'They're bankrolling this place.'

'I thought that was your father's job?'

Miles shook his head. 'You have the wrong information.'

She felt panic rising. She couldn't leave this room without the money; what would she do? She'd tried every other avenue and it was only a matter of time before someone else spotted Ben's potential.

'You owe me, Miles,' she said quietly.

'And how exactly do I owe you?'

'You know what I'm talking about. That night on Angel Cay, the body of the boat boy.'

'What body?' he said. 'There was no body.'

'Really? Well perhaps we should get the Bahamas police to interview Grace and Alex. That should jog everyone's memory.'

He held up a hand. 'Look, OK, so we all saw this guy on the beach. We all agreed to ignore it. *All* of us. But then it turns out the fucker wasn't so dead after all. He nicked a boat and buggered off. So don't pretend you have something over me. All we had was a thief, not a body.'

Sasha shook her head slowly. 'You almost battered someone to death, Miles. How's that going to go down with your little showbiz chums? I can't see them flocking around when the story gets out.'

'I did not batter anyone,' he growled, gripping the front of his desk.

'You know it, I know it, Grace and Alex know it. Why else do we all avoid each other like the plague?'

'You don't know anything,' he spat. 'Why the hell would I even care about that stupid deckhand?'

She paused, picking at an imaginary thread on her skirt.

'I fucked the boat boy, Miles,' she said casually. 'On the last night, in his cabin. I think he came to find you and I think you attacked him. And I know you were coming from West Point Cove just before we found him.'

His face was like stone. 'I did not do it,' he said quietly, his voice betraying just the slightest crack.

'But you had motive, didn't you? And opportunity. And it would be just like you to attack someone from behind.'

Their eyes locked.

'What's that supposed to mean?' he hissed.

'Whatever you want it to mean, Miles.'

Suddenly he jumped up, leaning on the desk. 'This hangs over you too, Sasha,' he said. 'You're planning this hotshot fashion career. You have just as much to lose.'

Sasha laughed. 'Miles, right now, I have nothing to lose.'

Cursing, he turned away and walked to the window.

'We all agreed to keep quiet,' he said, looking down at the street. 'And now you come here threatening me.'

'This isn't a threat, it's a business opportunity. I'm not

asking for cash to keep quiet, I'm offering you a slice of a global fashion brand with the potential to make us all rich. I just needed to get your attention.'

'Well you've certainly done that, Sasha,' he said, not turning to look at her.

Sasha wondered if she'd pushed him too far. She knew what he was capable of and she certainly didn't want Miles Ashford as an enemy, but what she had said was true: she really didn't have anything to lose.

'For old times' sake,' he sighed, 'and because I actually agree with you about the potential of the fashion sector, I could offer five hundred thousand for a fifty per cent stake.'

Sasha's heart gave a lurch. She had him, but she couldn't let go yet.

'You don't appear to be listening to me, Miles,' she said coolly. 'Half a million isn't enough.'

'It's all I can afford.'

He had to be bluffing: half a million was pocket change to someone like Miles Ashford. Besides, it was academic: she needed more.

'Twenty-five per cent of the company for seven hundred and fifty thousand, and that money is in the form of a loan. After four years, if I can pay you back, then your share-holding reverts to me.'

'I want interest at ten per cent.'

She snorted. 'You get interest at five per cent and think yourself lucky,' she said.

It was Miles' turn to laugh. He put out a hand and they shook. 'Maybe I was wrong about you having no head for business,' he said.

'A head for business, a body for sin, isn't that the phrase?' said Sasha, her heart speeding up as she felt Miles run his eyes over her body. Then, abruptly, his face changed, softened.

'I didn't kill him, Sasha,' he said, looking into her eyes.

'It's all in the past.' She shrugged. 'Like you said, there was no body.'

For a long moment it was like the years had fallen away: they were both eighteen, walking hand in hand on the beach, a life of possibility ahead of them. Then that moment was gone and he dropped her hand.

'Now,' said Sasha, smoothing down her dress, 'when can I expect the cheque?'

She walked out of Miles' office and down the walnut-panelled stairs, into the ladies' cloakroom. Sunlight flooded in through a window, dappling the floor with colour. She went over to the sink and looked into the mirror, taking deep breaths. Then she turned away, stumbled into a toilet cubicle and vomited.

35

April 1995

Alex took another belt from his bottle of Fukucho sake and lurched out into the late-night Tokyo traffic. The Hondas and Nissans swerved, tyres screeching, horns blaring, but Alex just roared back at them, holding up his clawed hands like bear paws. 'Hello, Tokyo!' he bellowed, their headlights blurring into the endless neon. Reaching the far pavement, he tipped his head back and spun around, gazing up at the towering skyscrapers above him and reflecting that he couldn't remember having more fun. It was as if someone had created Tokyo as a personal neon-lit playground just for Alex Doyle. Everything about the place was quirky, unreal or upside down. Stumbling over a sign advertising 'Octopus Balls', he bumped into a suited businessman who bowed rapidly and scurried away. He had been warned that the Japanese thought all Westerners were insane, so he guessed a six-foot-two long-haired Westerner in biker boots was going to be terrifying.

'*Gomennasai!*' he shouted after the retreating figure. '*Gomennas*-fucking-*ai!*'

Alex had certainly had plenty of need for both of the two Japanese phrases he'd learnt on Year Zero's short tour of the country: '*Gomennasai*' for 'sorry' and '*arigatou*' for 'thank you'. The thank yous had begun the moment Year Zero had stepped off the plane and been mobbed by obsessive – but polite – fans, many of whom had brought gifts: teddy bears embroidered with the band's logo, sweets in hand-made boxes, even T-shirts and shoes. Gift-bearing, camera-waving fans seemed to be everywhere: at the hotel, at the club, in the restaurants, often waiting for them in lifts or toilets. Luckily Jez was only too pleased to bathe in adulation wherever he found it, often inviting five or six girls back to his room for what he called a 'tea party'. They often saw tearful girls fleeing down the corridors; presumably he wasn't serving cup cakes.

Alex was much more interested in visiting temples and markets, soaking up the weird atmosphere of the Far East he'd read about as a teenager, but it quickly became apparent that playing the tourist just wasn't possible. Six months ago, the band had shot a TV commercial for Fiju beer which had meant he was recognised everywhere he went. Besides which, the band had a punishing schedule: six shows in six different cities over six nights, squeezing in appearances on TV, radio interviews and in-store acoustic gigs. Year Zero were genuinely Big in Japan: a number-one album and single plus sold-out arena shows. It was the same in Sweden, France and Germany, but in the UK, the band had, in record industry parlance, 'failed to break out'. Yes, the *Long March* album had been a hit, but then Blur and Oasis had come along with *Park Life* and *Definitely Maybe* and completely stolen their thunder. In fact, Pulp, Supergrass, Elastica, even the Boo Radleys were on *Top of the Pops* more than Year Zero. It was the most exciting period for British music in decades – Britpop, they were calling it – and Year Zero were sitting in the second divison, facing relegation.

Alex finished the last of the sake and dropped the empty bottle into a rubbish bin with a clang. Nothing was going to dampen his mood tonight. Ducking into a doorway, he pulled out his bag of coke and, using the corner of his hotel room key, scooped up a generous pile and snorted it.

As he left his hidey-hole, he spotted a flashing sign reading 'Rock Club' just down the street. Outside, there was a queue of teenagers wearing black leather and studded belts. Pushing his way to the front of the queue, he slapped a five-thousand-yen note on the counter. A huge bouncer in a black vest stepped out in front of him, but a girl jumped up and began jabbering in Japanese. The only words Alex could make out were 'Alex san', and 'Fiju beer'. The man reluctantly moved aside and Alex plunged inside.

'*Gomennasai,*' he said, elbowing his way to the bar. He pulled out another note and waved it in the air like a distress flare. 'Oi, mate!' he called to the barman. 'Sake over here, mate.'

''Scuse, Alex san.'

Alex turned to see the girl from the front of the club standing next to him. She was pretty, with big almond-shaped eyes thickly lined in black and a Cleopatra-style bob. She also had a studded dog collar around her neck. 'May I help?'

'Just trying to get served, darling.' Alex smiled, continuing to wave his money.

'With respect, Alex san, he will not serve you,' said the girl.

'Oh really?' he said, looking at her with interest. 'Why not?'

'Because in Japan, waving money is very rude. Also, the word "mate" in Japanese means "wait!" or "stop!". It is very confusing for him.'

'Oh, bugger. Can you do it for me? Get yourself a drink too. And say sorry to him for me, will you?'

She bowed and went to speak to the barman, returning with a bottle of sake and two beers.

320

'I am Maiko,' she said, bowing. 'I study English at college and I love Year Zero very much.'

'Well, you're a lifesaver, Maiko,' he said, slumping into a booth and sinking half the beer in one.

'Why you drink so much, Alex san?'

'Because I should be in Osaka.'

He thought back to that morning when he'd woken up feeling unwell after a bender the night before. He'd started the day with a line of cocaine anyway, which had made his nose start to bleed. Worse than his poor health was the realisation that he had long passed the point where he could survive without either a wrap or a bottle. Three hours later, he'd had to leave Tokyo for Osaka with the rest of the band. On the train he'd found himself paranoid, shaking and insular. He just didn't want to be around his band mates any longer, so when they had arrived at Osaka Arena, he had hung back, then got a taxi to the station and the bullet train back to Tokyo.

'I should be on stage right now,' he said sadly, the bravado replaced by guilt. 'I've fucked up, Maiko. I've let them all down.'

'It is sad if you fail others, Alex san,' said Maiko seriously. 'But it is tragedy if you fail yourself.'

He blinked at her. She had hit the nail on the head. The drink and drugs were just masking his unhappiness. Deep down he hated what he was doing. He had set out wanting to make music, not just to be a rock star. He wanted to write songs as singular and affecting as all those bands he had listened to in his room at Danehurst, but instead he had cobbled together something he thought would appeal to everyone when it hadn't even appealed to him.

'I think that calls for a drink,' he said, splashing sake into two cups, then knocking both of them back.

'Hey, Alex san!' said Maiko, cocking her head. 'It is your song!'

Alex grabbed her hand. 'Come on,' he replied. 'Let's have a dance.'

He woke up to the smell of noodles. Turning his head painfully, he saw a black plastic bowl sitting on a low table beside the bed. He didn't recognise the bowl, or the bed for that matter. In fact, he didn't recognise any of it. For a moment he felt scared, flustered, searching the room and his memories for a clue. Except he couldn't remember anything about the night before.

'Hello, Alex san.'

The door opened and a pretty girl came into the room. He immediately wondered if he had slept with her and felt both aroused and ashamed.

'You feel better?' she said, pouring Alex some tea.

'Er. Where am I?' He tried to sit up, but his head hurt and he lay back down. 'How do we know each other again?'

'I am Maiko. We meet in club, Alex san.'

'Last night?'

Maiko giggled. 'The night before. You drink very much. You sleep on the street.' She smiled, which made him feel a little more reassured.

'But why am I here?'

'I did not know where you stay,' said the girl. 'So you stay here. Yesterday, you sleep.'

Now Alex did sit up, clutching his head. 'You mean I've been here *two days*?'

She nodded.

'Oh Jesus,' he breathed. That meant he had not only missed the Osaka show – he remembered that much – but a shit-load of promotion.

He tried to work out the time, but evidently somewhere in the last thirty-six hours he'd lost his watch. He was just about to ask Maiko if she knew where it had gone when he heard a knock on the door and a loud English voice in the hallway. The bedroom door swung open and Alex was startled to see Jez standing there.

'Do you know how long it's taken me to find you?' he yelled. 'You selfish wanker!'

Jez launched into a tirade. Alan their tour manager was currently at the police station. An acoustic gig at one of Tokyo's biggest record stores, scheduled for the night before, had had to be cancelled. Writs were being issued and their visas were in jeopardy.

'The record company is going apeshit,' said Jez, taking a sip of the green tea and then spitting it back into the cup. 'Who knows how much fucking money the insurance is going to have to pay up because we were a no-show in Osaka.'

'Well that's what insurance is for,' said Alex, annoyed by Jez's self-righteousness. 'It's not the end of the bloody world, is it? Anyway, I don't know why you didn't do it without me. You know all the guitar parts.'

'Of course I could do it without you,' said Jez haughtily. 'But that's not the point, is it? Those punters paid to see fucking Alex san from the beer ad, didn't they?'

'There are four of us in the band, Jez.'

'Yeah, right, like anyone turns up to see Pete.'

Alex shook his head. Jez was such an egotistical prick.

'So how did you find me?' said Alex, standing up to pull on his jeans.

'God, you are fucked up, aren't you, Doyle?' snorted Jez. 'I suppose you don't remember phoning me at about four in the morning, crying your eyes out, telling me you loved me,' he mocked. 'Then you told me you were going to marry this Maiko chick and that I was invited to the wedding.'

'So why did it take you so long?'

'*So long?*' shouted Jez. 'Do you realise how many Maiko Takahashis there are in the Tokyo phone book? You're lucky we managed to track the little slut down at all, otherwise you'd have been stuck here in Nipland for ever.'

'Don't talk about her like that,' spat Alex angrily. 'She's my friend.'

Jez bent down over him so close Alex could see the red veins on his eyeballs, and his lip curled upwards in a sneer. 'She's your friend? You're a fucking loser, Doyle,' he said, jabbing a finger. 'I hope you're happy that you've screwed up my whole tour.'

'*Your* tour?'

'Yes, *my* tour!' shouted Jez, spittle flying in Alex's face. 'Who else do they put on the front pages? It ain't Gav and it's not you since you went all moody and fat. You're a fucking waste of space, Doyle.'

With a contemptuous look, he stood up and stalked into the next room. Alex followed, turning to Maiko.

'Listen, Maiko,' he said, 'thanks for all you did for me—'

'Oh shut up, Doyle,' said Jez, throwing a five-thousand-yen note on to the table and pulling Alex towards the door.

'*Gomennasai*,' said Alex over his shoulder. 'I really am.'

Outside in the corridor, Alex contemptuously shook Jez's hand off. 'You've just offended that girl,' he said.

'Oh boo-hoo,' sneered Jez. 'I bet she's on the phone to the newspapers right now.' He pointed at Alex again. 'If this gets in the Japanese press I will personally kill you. You know the Nip market is important to us.'

'Nip market?' said Alex, incredulous at Jez's racism.

'Don't pretend you care about your slanty-eyed friends,' spat Jez. 'You're over here for the same thing as the rest of us – some quick bucks and a shitload of yellow pussy.'

Alex flung out his fist, catching Jez in the mouth, splitting his lip and knocking him on his backside.

'You're out of the band, Doyle!' shrieked Jez, spitting blood on to the floor. 'Out, do you hear me? I hope it was worth it, your little fucking Oriental bunk-up.'

'I didn't have sex with her,' said Alex to himself as he walked away. 'She's my friend.'

Year Zero flew home from Tokyo that night. At check-in, Alex arranged to exchange his business-class seat for an economy one. The student who moved up front in his place was ecstatic. Alex knew the drinks trolley wouldn't be quite so free-flowing back in cattle class, but it was worth it not to sit with the rest of the band.

He wasn't sure if Jez was serious about kicking him out, but neither was he sure if he wanted to fight too hard to stay. If he left Year Zero, what the hell was he going to do? It was a little late to take up his place at the Royal Academy and he wasn't really qualified for working in a bank. He resolved to spend the whole flight thrashing it out, drawing up 'pros' and 'cons' lists, but instead he drank three Bloody Marys and woke up as they were descending into Heathrow. Emma would know what to do, he thought as the taxi pulled up in front of their Notting Hill apartment. They had moved here six months ago and he was still excited to think that the proud white stucco townhouse was theirs. *Home, sweet home*, he thought with a smile. Although how he was going to pay the mortgage if he got booted out of the band was another thing.

Alex knew something was wrong the moment his key turned in the lock. His footsteps sounded hollow on the floor and there were boxes in the hall. Emma was sitting on the bedroom floor sorting through a pile of CDs, an overflowing ashtray in front of her. Two large suitcases were open on the bed and the wardrobe was empty on one side.

'What are you doing?' he said.

Emma continued to flip through the CDs without looking up. 'What does it look like, Alex?'

'You're leaving? But why? I don't get it.'

Finally she looked up, her face cold. 'I know all about it,

Alex,' she said. 'I know you went missing for three days high on who knows what. I know you were found in some Japanese model's bed. I know everything.'

'It was two days, and she wasn't a model. A nice student took me to her flat because I collapsed in a nightclub.'

She snorted. 'Do you think I was born yesterday?'

Alex's confusion gave way to anger. 'Who told you all this? Jez?'

'Yes, if you must know. He was worried about you.'

'Worried?' Alex laughed. 'That lying bastard never worried about anyone but himself. It's lies, Emma! Bullshit!'

'Well, the tabloids don't seem to think so,' said Emma, flinging a paper at him.

He picked it up: the headline read 'Big Trouble In Little Tokyo' and featured a shot of Alex dancing cheek to cheek with an 'unidentified' Japanese girl he immediately recognised as Maiko. According to the story, he had been ejected from the club after trying to snort cocaine from another girl's breasts.

'Oh shit,' said Alex. 'The PR guy said it wasn't a big story.'

'Well your mother read it,' said Emma. 'I've had her on the phone in tears.'

'I didn't sleep with her, Em,' he pleaded. 'She looked after me.'

She gave a caustic laugh. 'Is that what they call it now?'

He tried to touch her, but she lashed out at him. 'Don't come near me!' she screamed, backing up against the bed. 'I can't do this any more, Alex,' she said, and the misery in her voice made his heart crack.

'Listen, Em, I got drunk and I missed a gig, that's all it is.'

She looked at him, her eyes puffy red crescents. 'No, that's not all it is,' she said sadly. 'You're on self-destruct, Alex; something's eating away at you like maggots and I can't stand by and watch you destroy yourself any more.'

Hazy morning light was pouring through the windows.

Six months in the flat and they had never got round to putting curtains up; they hadn't been there enough for it to matter. Sunlight sparkled off her deep red hair and he could see her eyes were glistening. In a strange way she had never looked more beautiful.

'Emma, please, I know this isn't what you want.'

She shook her head. 'No. It isn't what I want. But it's what I need.'

'Marry me,' he said, sinking to his knees and grabbing her hands.

She pulled away from him. 'Ah, the big romantic gesture that makes it all go away.' She laughed sarcastically. 'It's too late, Alex, much too late.'

'It's not just a gesture!' cried Alex. 'I'm asking you to be my wife! Please, all I want is to be with you. Just tell me what's wrong, and I can change.'

She shook her head. 'You're not going to change, Alex,' she said regretfully. 'Not until you work out what's wrong.'

He looked at her sadly, wishing he could talk to her about the one thing in his life that was screwing him up. He had never told her about the island. He had wondered many times if it was why it sometimes felt lonely in the relationship. Secrets isolated people. Secrets made you dishonest. And how good could a relationship be if it was dishonest?

He clenched his fists together, dismissing the thought. This relationship *was* a good one. *Emma* was a good one.

She stood up and picked up her denim jacket and her handbag. 'I'll get someone to pick the boxes up later in the week.'

He felt in free-fall. 'Emma, please! You can't go!' he shouted, his voice choking.

But she was already at the front door. And then she was gone.

36

Sasha was broke. So broke, in fact, she wasn't sure she could afford the taxi fare. She looked out of the window as London slipped by and wondered how she had managed to spend three quarters of a million pounds so quickly. First of all, buying a majority stake from Ben had cost her more than she'd thought once he'd got a lawyer involved, then there was the scandalous cost of a leasehold on a small retail premises on Belgravia's Ebury Street, not to mention the crippling costs of turning the bespoke operation into a ready-to-wear label: fabric, pattern cutters, shop staff, plus regular visits to the Milanese factory manufacturing the designs. Some days it just felt like they were shovelling cash into a big furnace and watching it burn.

And now she was the boss, Sasha had to deal with everything from electricity bills to managing Ben's ego. It had taken every ounce of her charm and patience to persuade Ben that while his gowns were the last word in luxury, they were not going to build a fashion empire with red-carpet dresses – they needed clothes women could wear every day. So, after weeks of cajoling, he had finally agreed to expand his designs from eveningwear into daywear – and what designs they were. Cashmere sweaters beaded with seed pearls, light wool pencil skirts, jackets with nipped-in waists and crystal buttons, shirts with tulle appliqué detail. It was a confection of timeless, low-key luxury; it was perfect.

But the clothes, of course, were only the beginning. Next they had to persuade the fashion press that Rivera – Sasha had insisted the 'Ben' be removed to avoid it being too aligned to its founder – was a label worth talking about. Which was exactly why Sasha and Philip were in a taxi pulling up in front of BAFTA's headquarters on Piccadilly.

'Hang on,' said Philip, as he saw the party decorations. 'I thought we were here to see a film?'

'No, this is work,' said Sasha. 'It's always work, remember?'

Philip rolled his eyes. It was a standing joke between the two of them that Sasha had become a serious workaholic. She was working fifteen hours a day shuttling between the studio, the shop and after-hours parties to network and spread the word. She was CEO, creative director and head of public relations all in one.

'This is a cast and crew preview for *By Midnight*,' she explained, linking her arm through his. 'The premiere is in two weeks and the word is it's going to be the biggest British movie of the year. I've had to pull every string just to get us in here.'

'But what's this got to do with the label?' he frowned.

'Kate Williams is the star of the movie and I want her in a Rivera dress for the premiere.'

Philip gave her a cynical look. Even he knew it was a long shot, but long shots were all they had left. They had spent the last month brainstorming marketing plans, but everything they came up with, even the wildest ideas, cost money. Philip had been pushing to run a print campaign for the Autumn/Winter collection in *Vogue* but Sasha knew it was hopeless. Financially, magazine advertising was way out of their reach: a photographer to shoot the thing, models, locations, film, processing, on top of the cost of actually placing the ad. They were talking a hundred grand before they even blinked.

'Come on, we can do this,' said Sasha, smiling up at him as they entered the BAFTA offices. She certainly looked the part of ass-kicking fashionista: in skin-tight black cigarette pants with a cashmere Rivera twinset, she looked like a sexy cross between a Mitford sister and Marianne Faithfull.

Philip reached over and squeezed her hand, but she let go of it immediately. 'Business, remember,' she said and walked inside.

Shit, Kate Williams isn't here, she thought with sinking disappointment as she scanned the bar area.

Lately she couldn't help but think she was swimming against the tide. The company needed a break and they needed it quickly. Without a much higher profile, Rivera was doomed. She looked around the crowd, hoping for the late arrival of the leading lady. As she did so, Jason Abbot, one of the supporting actors in the movie, gave her a lazy, mischievous smile. It was a look Sasha was used to: interest, desire. She smiled back and wondered if she should cross the room and follow it up. A famous boyfriend would certainly be beneficial when it came to the business. But then she glanced over at Philip laughing with the film's director and she felt a flush of guilt. She wasn't in love with Phil Bettany – she had no time for any such complications – but she was certainly fond of him. More importantly, she needed him. Not only did he have a six per cent shareholding – a condition Miles had stipulated for his investment – he had also given up his job at Schroder's to become Rivera's chief operating officer and was proving invaluable on the commercial side of the business, negotiating with the factories, structuring credit facilities with the fabric suppliers: keeping the ship steady. She glanced at the actor again: he was still looking. *No*, she thought firmly, *I mustn't. I really mustn't.*

'Hey, great sweater.'

A blonde woman with feline eyes stepped over to Sasha and touched the beading on her top.

'Thanks,' she said. 'It's my own label, actually.'

'Really?' asked the blonde appreciatively. 'Where do you stock?'

'Rivera, the store is in Ebury Street,' said Sasha, handing her a business card.

'Well I'll definitely pop by,' said the blonde, passing Sasha her own card. *Lucinda Clarke. Director Image PR*, it read.

'You do publicity?' said Sasha.

'Talent publicity, yes.'

'Who's your client tonight?'

Lucinda smiled. 'Kate, although she's not here of course; she's filming in Croatia of all places.'

Sasha immediately saw an opening. 'I'm actually looking for a publicist for Rivera,' she said as casually as she could, 'although I don't suppose you do corporate work?'

'Honey, it's my company.' Lucinda laughed, touching Sasha's arm. 'We'll take the work I say we take.'

'Interesting,' said Sasha, leading the woman towards the screening room. 'In which case, I have a proposal for you.'

'I can't believe you've taken on another publicist,' said Philip, storming his way into the small office above the Ebury Street store. Two weeks on from the *By Midnight* preview, the company's financial woes had not improved. 'Do I need to remind you we're already paying for a very expensive publicist and that we have six months of their contract to run?'

'Different sort of publicist,' said Sasha, sitting down at her desk and spinning her Rolodex. 'Not only is Lucinda going to get her clients into our clothes, she's going to represent me.'

'What on earth do *you* need a publicist for?'

Sasha just smiled inscrutably. She actually couldn't believe she hadn't thought of it before. While having every star in

Hollywood wearing Rivera creations would be invaluable publicity, no one was a better ambassador for the brand than Sasha Sinclair herself.

'You're sure this PR bird can get Kate into the dress for tomorrow's premiere?' said Philip sceptically.

Sasha unzipped the clothes bag hanging on a rail and pulled out the dress Ben had created specifically for the star. It was a beautiful red silk sheath that wrinkled and shone in the light.

'Yes, I'm sure,' she said. 'It was one of the conditions of Image PR getting our business, so stop worrying.' She blew him a kiss, then picked up the phone and dialled Lucinda Clarke.

'Darling, it's Sasha at Rivera,' she said briskly. 'I was just wondering whether to bike Kate's dress over to your office or to her hotel?'

There was a long, ominous pause down the receiver.

'About that . . .' said Lucinda slowly. 'Kate's LA manager wanted to know who the designer of her premiere dress was going to be. When I said Rivera, he had a typical LA hissy fit.'

Sasha felt her pulse quicken. 'I don't understand what the problem is,' she said.

'This is LA, Sasha. He wants his client in a named designer. Armani or Gaultier, something like that. Yes, I know it's narrow-minded and snobbish, but in Hollywood, management calls the shots.'

You double-crossing bitch, thought Sasha, but this was no time to let emotion get in the way.

'Lucinda,' she said coolly, 'I thought we had an agreement.'

'Darling, I've tried,' protested the publicist.

Sasha took a tiny sip of her iced water. She was livid, but she knew she had to tread carefully. This was still her best chance of saving the label and Lucinda was one enemy she could not afford to make – even if she had just stitched her up.

'So what are you going to do about it? We have' – she glanced at her watch – 'approximately twenty-two hours to salvage something from this.'

'I've been thinking about it,' said Lucinda. 'Maybe I could get Greg Nicholls' girlfriend to wear one of your dresses?'

Sasha put a hand over her eyes. *A girlfriend?*

'Who is this girlfriend?' she sighed.

'Giselle Makin.'

'Never heard of her.'

'She's an actress and model, absolutely beautiful. And Greg *is* the movie's leading man. She'll be very visible on the red carpet.'

As if the tabloids would be interested in a nobody like her, thought Sasha. She looked across at Philip who was desperately making 'What the hell's up?' gestures. But then she noticed something behind Phil. Propped up in the corner of the office was a roll of blush-pink silk georgette. And Sasha had a sudden flash of inspiration.

'Visible on the red carpet, you say?' she said, smiling.

Sasha and Ben worked around the clock. At 3 a.m., when Ben started making irritable noises about needing to leave, Sasha took the only key they had to the studio door and flushed it down the toilet.

'We're not getting out of here until Philip lets us out at eight o'clock tomorrow morning,' she told him sternly. Sasha could sympathise, of course. It was impossible to make a bespoke dress to Ben's exacting standards in eighteen hours – usually it took weeks – so they were adapting an existing sample instead. Carefully Sasha unpicked a long satin-faced organza skirt from the old dress while Ben got to work constructing the bodice. It was Ben's design but Sasha's vision; she knew exactly what she wanted the dress to achieve.

By the time the birds starting singing in the street outside, the gown was taking shape, and at nine thirty, black rings under her eyes, Sasha took the dress directly to Giselle Makin's Notting Hill apartment where she met Lucinda. Sasha wasn't entirely surprised by Giselle's reaction the first time she tried the dress on; clinging to every generous curve of the actress' body, it left very little to the imagination.

'Oh God,' she said as she looked in the mirror, her eyes wide. 'Greg is going to kill me.'

'Greg won't be able to keep his eyes off you,' said Lucinda reassuringly as Sasha made some adjustments with her stylist's pin box and sewing kit. Giselle did indeed look sensational. Her deep strawberry-blond hair looked like the most precious amber against the natural pink blush of the gown. Sasha just knew the media were going to go mad for her – hell, she was even going to have Hollywood knocking on her door after this red-carpet appearance. Lucinda was obviously thinking the same thing.

'She looks incredible,' she gushed. 'How can I thank you?'

'You can start by sorting out a couple of VIP tickets for the premiere,' she said. 'I need them biking around to Holland Park immediately.'

Lucinda looked puzzled. 'You and Phil have tickets, don't you?'

'Oh, they're not for us.' Sasha smiled. 'They're for another *very* important guest.' The second stage of her plan was about to begin.

The two most sensational women on the red carpet at the *By Midnight* premiere were wearing Rivera. One of them was the fashion company's CEO. Striding out confidently in her silver minidress, Sasha bathed in the blinding light of the paparazzi's flashbulbs, knowing this was the start of the media's serious interest in her. But it was Giselle who made the press erupt into a feeding frenzy. As she followed Greg out of their limousine, she kept a respectful two paces behind him, but not for long. The silk georgette corset of her dress, which in the car had looked merely a soft pink, appeared to turn completely transparent in the glare of the flashbulbs. The roar of the crowd in Leicester Square was deafening. 'Giselle! Giselle! Over here!' they yelled, ignoring all the other stars walking up to the theatre. She played her part brilliantly, a half-smile on her face as she moved slowly along the red carpet, the wide graceful skirt of the dress billowing like a cloud of apple blossom, her semi-translucent corset revealing her dark brown nipples. It was an incredibly flattering dress, one that made Giselle look part saint, part sinner, a beautiful fallen angel caught between heaven and hell.

'I think we can call that a job well done,' whispered Philip, planting a warm kiss on the back of Sasha's neck.

'Not quite yet,' said Sasha, looking back down the carpet, her eyes searching for new arrivals. Then finally she spotted them: Robert and Connie Ashford hurrying past the photographers.

'What have you got up your pretty little sleeve this time, Sinclair?' Philip chuckled as he watched a satisfied smile spread across Sasha's face.

'We're going to expand into America,' she said simply, ignoring his confused expression.

'I know,' said Philip. 'We have meetings with Neiman Marcus and Saks in a week's time.'

'No, I mean *really* take America. I want our own Rivera store on Fifth Avenue, Phil,' she said, turning into the cinema.

'But we can't afford—'

She cut him off. 'And I want it by this time next year.'

The next morning, Giselle Makin was on the front of every major publication, although her erect nipples had been discreetly airbrushed into respectability. And from the *Sun*'s women's pages to the *Telegraph*'s fashion column, they were all asking if the designer of Giselle's dress, Rivera, was the New Dior. Not since Gianni Versace had sent the four supermodels down his 1990 Autumn/Winter runway had a designer made such a splash. It was better than Sasha had dared hope. Lucinda Clarke was calling her every five minutes with another request for an interview or a quote from the new fashion sensation, but Sasha had something else to do first. For a moment she let her hand rest on top of her battered old 1990 Filofax. Miles had given her Robert Ashford's direct line just before their holiday to Angel Cay that summer. *It's strictly for emergencies, Sash*. Well, five years later, Sasha felt it was time to make the call. Not an emegency per se, but important enough.

'Robert. It's Sasha Sinclair.'

'Sasha, what a surprise,' he said, sounding genuinely pleased to hear from her. 'I believe we have you to thank for yesterday's impromptu night out.'

'I know you and Connie have always been so supportive of my career. I've never forgotten your words of wisdom and encouragement.'

'I believe I told you to go to university. Shows what I know.' He laughed.

She took a breath, then ploughed on. 'Listen, Robert, I have a proposal for you. It concerns my fashion company Rivera. If you've seen this morning's papers, you'll be aware of it.'

'Continue,' he said, his bonhomie immediately replaced by a businesslike tone.

'It's a win-win situation if you like,' she said, purring into the telephone. 'I want to expand the company into America, you always want to make more money and get a foothold in a new market. And Robert, here's how we're going to do it . . .'

37

Alex shifted his hired Jeep into second gear as he turned into a tight hairpin bend. *Ibiza is hot*, he thought tapping the air-con. *I wish I had a drink*. The last seven days had been the first time in years he had been completely sober. Ironic really, considering this was one place where anything you wanted was freely available. He wound down the window and breathed in the air – a wooded blend of pine trees, salt and dusty soil that seemed unique to the northern tip of the island. *Two weeks ago, I wouldn't have noticed any of that*, he thought. It hadn't been any fun staying straight, that was for sure, but there were a few up sides, he supposed. Besides, he knew it was his only chance of survival. It had been ten days since Emma had left him and he had immediately gone on a huge bender; he could barely remember any of it, but he did know he had been found slumped in a cubicle in the toilets at the Groucho, blood and vomit caked on his torn shirt. His girlfriend's departure had left a huge gap inside him and it was far too tempting to keep pouring booze into that deep, deep hole. So he had caught a taxi straight to Heathrow and taken the first flight he could get – it just happened to be going to Ibiza.

He ducked his head to squint at the expensive villas on his right. There it was – Villa des Fleurs. He felt a shiver despite the heat. It was hard to believe that pure chance alone had brought him to this island. It couldn't just be

337

random, could it? He turned into the driveway, then leant over to press the intercom buzzer next to the high steel gates. He felt a terrible flurry of nerves as the gates swung open and he caught sight of the rambling whitewashed villa and the pink bougainvillea climbing up to the teak shutters.

For a moment, he thought about throwing the Jeep into reverse and getting the hell out of there. *But someone or something wants me here,* he reasoned. *No point in fighting it, is there?* He parked the car and clambered out just as the villa's front door opened.

'Hi, Grace.' He smiled. Her thick, dark-honey-coloured hair hung loose down her back, her fringe framing her deep blue eyes. She wore brown leather sandals, jeans and a white shirt in some flimsy fabric that looked a little see-through in the sun. He'd seen pictures of her in the broadsheets looking grown-up and intimidating in smart dresses and dark sunglasses, just like the politician's wife she was. But this style suited her better; she looked like the old Grace.

'So are you going to invite me in or let me burn to a crisp out here?' he asked.

'I forgot.' She smiled. 'Musicians never see daylight, do they?'

Walking into the villa, he looked around the cool rustic space while she poured him a glass of fresh lemonade.

'I can't believe you're here,' she said, shaking her head. Neither could he. When he'd arrived in Ibiza, he'd deliberately taken the most isolated hotel he could find, needing to sleep, detox and just hide away from the world, but by the third day he was feeling stir-crazy – and, if he was honest, desperate for a drink. He'd headed into Ibiza town, gone into the first bar and ordered a frozen marguerita. While it was being mixed, he picked up a local magazine on the bar and read about a photography exhibition featuring the work of one 'Grace Hernandez', the politician's wife, who now lived on Ibiza's north coast. He left a thousand-peseta note on the counter and walked out of the bar without looking back.

Grace took the jug of lemonade outside into a shady courtyard where two children were riding around on bikes.

'Wow! Little Grace clones!' he laughed, looking at their thick blond hair and tanned skin. 'They're gorgeous, Grace. But then they would be.'

Grace led him to a shaded terrace where they sat down with their drinks.

'So, come on, Mr Rock Star, what brings you to Ibiza?' she asked. 'Some big gig at one of the clubs?'

Alex shook his head and looked away. 'Just getting a bit of space,' he said with a shrug.

'Ah, the life of a celebrity,' said Grace. 'I tasted a bit of it in Parador. I didn't like it much, I have to say.'

'But what about you?' said Alex. 'What's the new Evita doing in Ibiza?'

'Three afternoons a week I teach at the local school, which I'm loving. And then there's the photography which you know about.'

'No. I meant what brought you here.'

'Well, that's a bit more complicated. An assassination attempt, a failed marriage. Discomfort at being the "new Evita" as you put it. Take your pick.'

'And I always thought it was Miles who was surrounded by drama.'

As they sipped their lemonade, Grace filled him in on the last few years. Her trip to Australia, meeting Gabriel, the wedding, the twins and her life in a gilded cage in Parador. Then the car bomb, Caro's death and Gabriel's subsequent election defeat. Listening to her problems, Alex felt the weight of his own lift a little. Yes, they had both been trapped and both been hurt, but at least no one was trying to kill him. Looking more closely, he could see the tired rings under

Grace's eyes, the fact that she'd lost a lot of weight since the last photos he'd seen.

'I was in England when the old government was re-elected in Parador,' she was saying. 'We flew out here straight after the election.'

'Why Ibiza?'

Grace shrugged. 'I wanted somewhere quiet, safe and Spanish-speaking for the kids.'

'So you're really divorced?'

'Officially the marriage was annulled; the family have Catholic friends in high places. I like to think the Pope gave me a get-out-of-jail-free card,' she said, trying to smile, but Alex could see the sadness in her face. It was obviously hurting her more than she wanted to let on.

'Anyway, what about you?'

'You came to Ibiza to start a new life, I came here to escape my old one.'

'Women trouble?' Grace smiled.

'Everything trouble.'

Grace stood up. 'Ah, well that sounds like a long story,' she said. 'Shall I make some food? The kids haven't had a sleep today so they'll be in bed in an hour.'

'Cool. You whip us up something hot and Spanish and I'll play with Joe and Liv.'

'Hot and Spanish you say? You're not on tour now, you know.'

'Hey, I'm a good boy, you know,' said Alex. 'You ask your friend the Pope.'

And he ran off down the garden making monster noises to the delighted squeals of the children.

What am I doing? thought Grace as she leant into the mirror to reapply her lipstick. *He's just an old friend, remember?*

Before his unexpected phone call that morning, it had been a long time since she had thought about Alex Doyle.

340

Not in a conscious way, at least. He'd appear as a faceless character in a bad dream or part of a vague sense of dread that she sometimes woke up with in the middle of the night. But she certainly hadn't been longing for him. No, for the first time in a long time, she was happy again. She loved the villa, she loved working at the San Josef Primaria, a small rural school just a few miles away from her hamlet, she loved running the photography club, buying camera equipment with her own money, which brought enormous pleasure to both herself and the pupils of the heavily under-resourced school. And she was happy alone, just her and the kids. There was no room for anything or anyone else in her life.

So why are you putting lipstick on? she asked herself. *Why didn't you make an excuse when he rang?*

She went back into the kitchen. Outside she could see Alex chasing the shrieking kids with a leaky garden hose. Quickly she snatched up her camera and shot off a roll of film of photographs, smiling as she thought what a natural Alex was with the kids. As the sun dipped in the sky, and the crickets came out with their brittle nighttime chorus, she put the children to bed with no trouble – Uncle Alex had exhausted them.

While Grace put the finishing touches to the food, Alex opened a bottle of wine and walked around the dining room looking at the black and white prints on the wall. 'These photos are fantastic, Grace,' he called. 'You should do it professionally.'

'Oh, it's just a hobby,' said Grace, poking her head around the door. 'The exhibition's going to be fun, but I don't think David Bailey is going to be quaking in his boots.'

Alex helped her carry the food outside on to an old wrought-iron table on the terrace and they lit some oil lamps; the sky had turned purple behind a line of olive trees. Grace served up a chorizo stew with garlic polenta and a big bowl of salad brimming with ripe red tomatoes. As they ate, Alex slowly filled her in on his own life.

'So are you going back to Emma?' she said.

'I'm not sure she'll have me,' said Alex. 'She says I drink too much.'

'Then stop.'

'I'm going to try,' he said with a half-smile.

'No, you have to be serious, Alex,' she said. 'Join AA, go on a retreat, show her that you mean business. And we'll start by taking this away,' she said, reaching over and moving the second bottle of Rioja out of his reach.

'Grace, please.'

'No, Alex, I think Emma's right. You're a talented musician; you keep this up, you'll throw it all away.'

He pulled a face. 'Might be a bit too late for that. The songs have dried up and now Jez wants me out of the band.'

'So leave.'

'And do what?'

'Start a new band. Or go solo. What is so difficult?'

'I'm in a pretty successful band, Grace,' he said. 'I like playing at Glastonbury. Being Big in Japan. '

'Ah, so the best reason you can think of not to do it is because you're comfortable?'

'I don't know if I *can* do it,' he said quietly. Grace's heart jumped as she realised there were tears in his eyes. She had been sitting here being a cheerleader, saying 'Come on Alex, you can do it!' without realising how defeated and broken he really was.

'You are too brilliant to hide all that talent,' she said. 'And you are too bloody gorgeous not to be out there centre stage.' She blushed as she said it, but she had to do something to help him crawl out of the hole he had fallen into. That was what friends did, wasn't it?

'I know it's hard,' she said softly, 'but you have to try. Because I think that what you're doing, making music that

342

touches people, makes them happy and sad, I think that's more important than any of your problems with Jez or Emma.'

Alex looked touched. 'I will,' he said.

Their eyes met and Grace felt a crackle of electricity between them, like the old spark, leaping across the space between them.

'Listen, I should get back,' said Alex suddenly, standing up.

'Alex Doyle,' she scolded, 'don't even think about it. You've had way too much to drink and I'm not going to let you kill yourself. There's plenty of room here.'

'Grace . . .'

'Alex, please. I'll make up the spare room. Stay in bed as long as you like, but I warn you, the kids get up at the crack of dawn.'

She showed him the way and gave him towels and blankets and a spare toothbrush. He reached over and touched her cheek.

'Thanks, Grace,' he said softly. 'You know I've missed you.'

Her heart jumped.

'You were always so sensible,' he continued. 'You always make things make sense.'

She nodded, fighting down the feeling of disappointment. Creamy moonlight streamed through the window and for a split second they were both back there on West Point Beach. She flinched and then knew he'd felt it too.

'That's what friends are for, Alex.' She smiled. *And friends is all we'll ever be*, she thought sadly.

38

June 1996

Alex stepped off stage at LA's House of Blues, propped his guitar against the wall and sank down to his haunches. He was exhausted. He couldn't remember when he'd worked as hard. And where had twelve months of soul-searching, discipline and back-breaking graft got him? A measly acoustic gig on a dead Tuesday evening. OK, so it was one of LA's top rock venues, right on the Sunset Strip, and yes, he'd got a pretty good reaction considering, but he was playing as the first warm-up act to some local hair metal band. Headlining at the Hollywood Bowl it wasn't.

Hauling himself to his feet, he stripped off his T-shirt and used it to wipe the sweat from his face, smiling at the thought that when he was in Year Zero, their live contracts had stipulated that each band member '*must* be supplied with four brand-new forest-green towels'. He had always wondered why they had to be forest green. One of Jez's demands, no doubt. At least he hadn't had to listen to that cock for the last year, he thought with a grim smile.

Alex had quit the band the moment he got back from Ibiza; he had been more than a little annoyed that no one had begged him to stay and that the label had issued a statement saying that while his departure was 'regrettable', it would be 'business as usual' for Year Zero. In the usual scheme of things, this would have been the perfect excuse for Alex to drink himself into a coma, but that was the old Alex. The new Alex went back to the Notting Hill flat, packed a backpack, grabbed his guitar and flew straight to Ireland. He rented a tumbledown crofter's cottage on a tuft of windswept headland in Connemara, grew a beard and slept in his clothes. He'd wake with the dawn, go for brisk walks and drink nothing but strong Irish tea. It was the ultimate in cold turkey, but he was also writing tunes that felt better than anything he'd ever written. On long hikes over the purple heather, the lyrics had come too. Verses of love and loss, romance and regret. Even memories, emotions he hadn't allowed himself to think about were revisited and rechannelled into the music. He knew it sounded wanky, but in that little cottage he felt reborn.

And then he'd come out here, to LA. From the sublime to the vacuous, the home of the silicone breast and the coke spoon, the last place he wanted to be but the one place he needed to be if he was going to crack America. *Some bloody hope*, he thought, pulling on his one clean T-shirt. He snapped his guitar case closed and headed out on to the Strip. He had wanted to see the main act – he had a secret affection for spandex and drum solos – but it would have meant hanging around the bar. After almost one year sober, he couldn't take that sort of risk.

'Alex, Alex! Wait!'

He turned to see two pretty teenage girls, one blonde, one brunette, running towards him.

'Can we have your autograph?' said the blonde, handing him a black marker pen.

'You sure?' he said, bemused.

'Hell, yeah,' said the brunette, opening her denim jacket and thrusting her breasts towards him. 'Can you sign my T-shirt?'

'You were *amazing*,' said the blonde.

'Was I?' he said.

'Hell, yes. Those songs, they were so personal, so sensitive. I melted, man – I fucking *melted*.'

'Hey, d'you wanna come to a party tonight?' said the blonde, biting her lip playfully.

Alex laughed. It was certainly tempting, but he'd promised himself no more one-night stands, no cheap thrills in the club toilets. In fact there had been no one in the year since Emma had left him, but the attention was flattering nonetheless.

'Ladies, it's fantastic to meet you.' He smiled. 'But I've really got to go.'

'Go where?'

'My hotel. I leave for Santa Barbara tomorrow.'

'When are you coming back?'

'Soon. I promise.'

He kissed each girl on the cheek and started walking back up Sunset, whistling. In LA, everyone went everywhere by car, but it wasn't far to the hotel and it was a nice night to walk. A sweet, balmy breeze fluttered through the palm trees and Alex swung his guitar case happily; he felt relaxed, free and hopeful. *People came out to see me!* He was more excited about that than he would have been if a record executive had turned up. Because this time, Alex was making the music he wanted to make, not the music he hoped would get him a record deal.

His hotel rose like a gothic fairy-tale castle from the garish wonderland of Sunset Boulevard. The Chateau Marmont was Alex's favourite hotel in the world, a place where you could not help but feel like a rock-and-roll star even if you were a carpet salesman from Wisconsin. He'd blown a huge chunk of his savings staying here, but Harry Cohn the hotel's founder had summed up its magic when he said that at the Chateau Marmont you could be whoever you wanted to be.

Right now, that seemed like a potent idea to hold on to.

Walking through the doors, he was confronted by the bar, fizzing with people and sound. It looked so inviting, so welcoming. It was one of the things he had really missed about giving up the booze: the warmth and social mix of pubs and bars. *Fuck it,* he thought. *I can do this.* He settled into a booth, put his guitar under the table and ordered a Virgin Bloody Mary.

To distract himself, he began doodling on a napkin, writing up his itinerary for the next fortnight: Santa Barbara, Palo Alto, San Fran, Portland, Seattle. Most of the gigs were in small bars on student campuses, plus a few interviews with college radio. Not much, but it was a start. Then he heard laughter and looked up – and froze. Miles Ashford was standing in the lobby, joking with the hotel concierge. Alex's heart began to pound as he watched the sharp-suited figure cut through the crowd towards him. Miles did a double-take, then walked straight up and stuck out his hand.

'Alex Doyle,' he said, shaking his head and grinning. 'I don't believe it.'

For a second Alex didn't know how to respond. He had known that their paths would cross one day, of course, and he had rehearsed what he would say a thousand times over. But now, with Miles standing right in front of him, no words would come.

'Miles,' he said simply, shaking his hand.

'May I?' asked Miles, indicating the space next to him.

'Sure,' said Alex, wishing he had the strength to say no.

'This is incredible. This calls for champagne,' Miles said, signalling to a waitress.

Alex shook his head. 'Not for me.'

'Ah yes, I heard you were off the sauce,' said Miles.

'Really?' said Alex, slightly unsettled. He hadn't spoken to anyone about his self-ministered withdrawal in Ireland. 'Been keeping tabs on me?'

'Not really,' said Miles, giving the waitress his order. 'But it's amazing what gossip you pick up working in the club industry. I'm seriously thinking of starting my own scandal rag.'

'So are you staying here?'

Miles nodded. 'Scouting sites for a West Coast Globe Club. The whole thing has gone crazy, I've got a three-year waiting list from half of London wanting to become members. Difficult thing is marrying expansion with exclusivity.'

It was typical Miles, thought Alex, always boasting about his latest wheeze, telling you how well-connected and clever he was, but now the old brash arrogance had been replaced by a smooth self-assurance. Alex had kept tabs on Miles too via the papers and the occasional snippet of gossip, and he knew that the tailored suit and the Rolex had come from the success of the Globe clubs rather than his father's generous allowance.

'So how're things with you? Still singing and dancing?'

Alex ignored the jibe. 'Yes, I've just done a gig at the House of Blues.'

'Well done,' said Miles without enthusiasm. 'So you left that band, eh? Brave decision. I hear the music scene is really taking off in London, all that Britpop shite. Hey, I think Jez Harrison is a Globe Club member, do you want me to get him blackballed?'

Alex pulled a face. 'I wouldn't bother.'

'That's the spirit,' said Miles, clapping him on the shoulder. 'Don't get mad, get even and all that. Good plan coming out to the States actually; all the serious money is here. Jez would shit a brick if you made it out here.'

The thought had crossed Alex's mind, but if he was honest, it wasn't looking too rosy. Three knock-backs from record labels and a handful of college gigs – he was hardly Michael Jackson.

'I haven't actually got a recording contract yet.'

'Oh really?' Miles with a sideways glance. 'Bad luck.' He lit a cigarette and blew a smoke ring into the air. It was a simple gesture, but it was so familiar to Alex that suddenly he needed a drink. He reached out and grabbed the champagne flute, knocking it back in one.

'Hey, I thought you were clean and serene,' said Miles.

'Just the one,' said Alex, grimacing as the alcohol burnt its way down. Clearly his feelings for Miles were as raw as ever and it made him uncomfortable just being in the same room.

'So how long are you in town?'

'Just until tomorrow. I've got a few college gigs up the West Coast.'

'College gigs! Balls to that,' said Miles with disdain. 'You know who you have to meet? Falk.'

'*David* Falk?' said Alex, almost choking. 'You know him?'

David Falk was a legend in the music industry. He ran one of the biggest media companies in the world. Equally known for his amazing ear for hits and for his appetite for debauchery, he had not only made the careers of dozens of global stars, he had supposedly seduced a good few of them too. Alex was astonished that Miles was now mixing with the highest inner circle of the entertainment industry.

Miles shrugged casually. 'Yeah, Dave's having a party tomorrow night. Amazing house in the Hollywood Hills, even I was impressed. You should come, I think he'll like you.'

'Miles, I can't. I have to be in Santa Barbara tomorrow. I have a gig.'

Miles suddenly looked serious. 'You don't get it, do you?' he said, locking eyes with Alex. 'Why do you think people like Jez Harrison are successful despite having no talent, while you're out here with no record deal? Networking, Alex. It's putting yourself out there and showing people how good you are. Jez would be there in a flash; any musician who was serious about succeeding would. It's a music *busi-*

ness, Alex, a record *deal*. You need to start sweet-talking the money men.'

He threw a fifty-dollar bill and his business card on the table.

'Nice seeing you, Alex,' he said, standing up. 'Give me a call if you make the right decision.'

Then he walked away without looking back.

Alex hated it, but Miles was right. After a fretful night's sleep, punctuated by vivid, brutal dreams, he got up early and called the number on the card. He could keep slogging away on the American version of the toilet circuit and hope that some record company scout happened to walk by, or he could cut out all the pain and uncertainty and go straight to the top. And anyway, it was just a party. He wasn't there to talk to Miles, or renew their friendship. It was just business.

Alex remained silent and tense for most of the twisting climb up into the Hills as Miles chattered about his many successes. The Falk mansion didn't look particularly impressive as they turned off Mulholland Drive high above the city, just a black gate and a lot of shrubbery. But as they climbed out of the car and Miles handed the keys to a valet, Alex had to stop in his tracks. The house was astounding, like a glistening silver spaceship hovering over the twinkling carpet of Los Angeles. A series of pools encircled the whole house, connected by waterfalls and bridges, and the entire ground floor opened out on to a huge entertaining deck which tonight was packed with hundreds of household names mingling and laughing with a supporting cast of beautiful scenesters.

'Impressive, huh?' Miles grinned. 'Told you it was worth coming.'

Alex had been to loads of showbiz parties in his time, but this one was in another league. London might be swinging, but this place was red hot. In a huge hot tub, talking box office receipts, were two of the most powerful men in

Hollywood, while in another corner, Rosalind the supermodel was semi-naked and fellating her billionaire boyfriend in front of a small, encouraging crowd.

'She's an exhibitionist,' said Miles unnecessarily.

They moved through the party, Miles shaking hands and slapping backs, until they reached the bar, staffed by topless male waiters. 'Don't be so nervous,' hissed Miles. 'It's just a party; let's have a good laugh. Like old times, eh?'

Alex ordered a Pepsi and watched Miles effortlessly flit from group to group, chuckling, swapping anecdotes, confident, garrulous, in control. Alex had tortured himself over the years with the question of whether his friend could actually have killed that boat boy, but watching him tonight, he did not look like a man with a burden. He looked completely at ease with himself and his environment. Did that mean anything? Probably not. Alex was sure there were people in this room whose pasts weren't whiter than white.

'Like those, do you?' asked a short man with salt and pepper hair. Alex had been admiring a display of electric guitars hung along a wall like works of art.

'What a collection,' said Alex, gazing up.

'The one at the end used to be John Lennon's,' the man said, pointing to the black and white Rickenbacker. 'Everyone thinks Yoko's got it, but we came to an arrangement,' he added with a wink as Alex realised with a blush that the man was the party's host, David Falk.

'Alex is a musician too,' said Miles, walking over. 'He's really good. Used to be in Year Zero, that British band? '

'I know Year Zero,' said David to Alex. 'A bit hit and miss, but you had potential. You were at the House of Blues the other night, weren't you?'

Alex nodded slowly but his heart was racing.

'I had a scout there. I hear good things. '

'Which is why I thought you two should meet,' said Miles. 'A lot of people have been showing interest, haven't they, Al?

351

But I told him not to sign anything until he spoke to you or at least gave you his demo.'

Miles nudged Alex, who reluctantly pulled out a cassette of some of the songs he'd written in Ireland.

Falk gave a lukewarm smile and put it in his pocket.

'So you'll listen to it?' pressed Miles.

'Boys, this is my fucking birthday party, not open mike night,' said Falk. 'So come on, let's enjoy ourselves, huh?'

A slim Oriental boy, naked except for a black thong, had appeared at Falk's side. 'David, are you coming?' he asked.

Falk chuckled and began to move away. 'Going to hit the Jacuzzi. You're welcome to join us, Alex,' he said, looking him up and down and smiling.

Alex smiled weakly. 'Maybe later.'

When Falk had gone, Alex let out a long breath and turned angrily to Miles. 'That went well,' he said sarcastically. He felt like he'd had a golden opportunity slip away.

'Well maybe you should have gone to the Jacuzzi,' shot back Miles.

Their eyes locked for a moment, then Alex looked away.

'Listen, I should go,' he said.

'Oh come on, stop sulking,' said Miles. 'It wasn't that bad. I thought he liked you.'

'He'd like me to jump naked into his Jacuzzi, that's what he'd like. What about the music?'

'Alex, stop acting like a big girl,' said Miles with irritation. 'You just gave your demo to David Falk. People would literally kill for that opportunity. If he likes it, he'll call you. Now don't ever say I owe you one.'

Suddenly Alex wanted to get away from this place. He shouldn't have come here, he knew that now. He felt soiled and shameful just being close to Miles Ashford. Miles corrupted everything he touched.

'I have to get back to the hotel,' said Alex.

'Call yourself rock and roll?' said Miles with a mocking laugh. 'And how do you intend getting back to the Chateau?'

'I'll find a taxi.'

'You'll be lucky.'

'Goodbye, Miles.'

Miles was right. Again. It took Alex thirty minutes of walking through the dark before he could flag a taxi, and when he got back to the hotel he ordered a triple Jack Daniel's which sent him into a deep, medicinal sleep until ten o'clock the next morning. The phone woke him, a shrill ring that clattered round his fragile head. He clawed for the phone and pulled the receiver under the covers.

'Ungh? Whoizit?' he mumbled.

'OK, here's what I think,' said an unfamiliar voice down the line. 'One minute you're trying to be Jeff Buckley, the next minute you're trying to show off what a brilliant experimental musician you are, and if that's what you want you should be trying to join Philip Glass' orchestra, not touting yourself to me.'

Alex immediately sat up in bed, stars popping in front of his eyes. 'Mr Falk? Is that you?' he asked incredulously.

The mogul wasn't listening. 'But there're moments of fucking genius on this tape, baby. Total genius. And it doesn't hurt you look so hot either.'

'Wow,' stuttered Alex. 'Thanks ... So you're interested, then?'

'I'm only going to say this once, Alex. Sign with Falk Records and I'll sell you two hundred million records.'

'Whoo-hoo!' screamed Alex, trying to punch the air, but getting tangled in the sheets and landing with a crash on the floor. 'Mr Falk? You still there?' he said, grappling with the phone.

'There're lots of things we need to talk about. Management. I'm thinking about putting a band around you too, like

Springsteen and the E Street Band. I know you're talking to other labels so I want to move quickly to get you in our studio. We have a movie coming out next summer. It's going to be hot with the sixteen to twenty-four crowd. We've been looking for a title track and that song on your tape, "Angel Falls"? It's good, really good. It's about a woman, right?'

'Actually, a place,' said Alex more quietly.

'Place, woman, we can fix that,' said Falk. 'I'll see you in my office, three this afternoon.' And he clicked off.

Alex stared at the receiver in disbelief. Then he let out a whoop of delight and ran around the room doing a victory dance, finishing with a screaming dive back on to the bed. He stared at the ceiling, a big grin on his face. This afternoon he was supposed to be in Santa Barbara playing to students; instead he was going to sign a record deal with *the* biggest star-maker in the business. He thought of Miles. He thought of Angel Cay. And then he thought of nothing, as he got up, had a shower and prepared himself for the first day of his new life.

39

March 1997

Philip paced up and down the deep-pile carpet checking his watch. The suite at the Peninsula was costing the Rivera company three thousand dollars a night and that was before Sasha had transformed it into her romantic vision of a Parisian fitting room. A dozen vases of ivory lilies gave the whole room an exotic perfume, while light refreshments came in the form of iced Cristal and chocolate-dipped strawberries. In the bedroom of the suite were rails of Ben's most exquisite gowns in a rainbow of colours together with neatly paired heels and Judith Leiber handbags to complete the look.

'Are you sure anyone is going to come?' he said.

'Relax,' said Sasha as she made last-minute adjustments to the room. 'It's going to be fine.'

Philip was such a worrier, thought Sasha irritably; always focusing on their cashflow, he never took the time to see the big picture. The fact was that the Beverly Hills store was due to open in April and without this afternoon of dressing-up and canapés there was a very real chance the whole company could collapse. In two days' time, LA would be locked down for the biggest event in the city's year, the Oscars ceremony, and they desperately needed to get the actresses and wives walking along that red carpet in Rivera gowns. They had launched the company on the red carpet three years ago with Giselle's daring, dazzling dress and it had been a massive success, making Rivera a household name and ensuring the London store had to employ a queuing system in order to deal with the demand. But getting a dress into the Oscars would mean global exposure; the coverage was watched by thirty million people in the US alone. With the cost of hotels, flights, catering, not to mention the gowns, this afternoon was a huge risk for them, but Sasha firmly believed it was worth it.

'This afternoon is going to put us on the map, sweetie,' she said, allowing herself the tiniest sip of champagne. 'Two years ago everyone thought Prada was just a handbag line. They get Uma Thurman in that lilac dress at the Oscars and bam, they're the hottest fashion label in Milan. This isn't Giselle Makin making waves in London. This is the big time, Philip.'

Philip didn't look convinced. 'What time is the first appointment?'

'One thirty. Why?'

'First of all, I'm worried we're going to have a bottleneck of starlets arguing over the same bloody dress. And two, where is our bloody publicist?'

Marina Schwartz had been the biggest expense of this afternoon's showcase, but she was essential to the operation. One of LA's top celebrity publicists, she had – for a very large fee – agreed to spend the day bringing her roster of clients over to the suite to try on the gowns one by one. She had also got Sasha on the guest lists for the most important Oscar-night parties.

'She'll be here,' said Sasha. 'You look very handsome today, you know,' she said, adjusting his collar. He was being a pain in the backside, but Sasha needed him to stay on side. If he had wanted to, he could easily have derailed the whole scheme. 'I hope you're not going to distract these greedy little starlets too much from the dresses,' she purred.

Finally he smiled and pulled her towards him. God, men were so easy to manipulate.

'When we've got rid of them all, why don't we make the most of the suite?' she whispered.

Philip pulled a face. 'Remember we've got dinner with Doug Petersen tonight. I've got us reservations at Spago.'

Sasha shook her head. 'Not tonight. Marina is taking me to some pre-Oscars party in the Hills. I need to be out there being seen to be glamorous, especially just before the Rodeo Drive opening; we need the face of the company in all the pap shots.'

He clicked his tongue in annoyance. 'But this is Doug Petersen, Sash,' he said. 'You know he's Robert Ashford's top guy in America. We've got to keep Ash Corp. sweet.'

He was right, of course. Expansion on to America's West Coast had only been made possible with strategic investment from Robert Ashford, who had rented the label one of the units Ash Corp. owned on Rodeo Drive in return for a small stake in the US arm of the business. Impressed by their business plan, Robert had also been swayed by his wife's enthusiasm for Ben Rivera's designs – 'as good as Lagerfeld' she had remarked after a visit to their Ebury Street store. Sasha also suspected that part of Robert's interest in Rivera was due to the fact that Miles was also a shareholder. He might no longer hold financial sway over his son, but at least with access to the books, he could legitimately keep tabs on him.

'Don't worry about Ash Corp.,' smiled Sasha. 'You know I go a long way back with the family.'

Philip picked up a strawberry and bit into it. 'Aren't these starlets going to want to meet the great designer himself?'

'I am the face of the label, Philip,' said Sasha with irritation. 'Anyway, Ben didn't come for a reason. He's been getting bloody snarky lately, always wanting to know why he isn't doing any interviews in *Vogue* or the fashion pages of *The Times*. I can't tell you the amount of times I've had to stop myself from reminding him that no one wants to see a camp little midget as the frontman of the company.'

Philip winced. 'Oof, more than a little harsh there, baby. He's just finding it hard to let go.'

'No, he's clinging on for dear life,' said Sasha. 'He knows we don't need him any more. I swear it's like pulling teeth these days; when I mentioned a diffusion collection, he threw another hissy fit.'

'But we do need him, Sash,' said Philip gently.

'No, Phil, we don't,' she said angrily. It was the one thing that drove her mad about the business. Sasha Sinclair was seen as a well-dressed arse-kicking businesswoman, while Ben took all the credit for the designs. But the collections were all her vision, her *look*. With each season, she had more input in the design process, adapting the label's classic shapes and seasonal staples with inspired changes, or choosing a template of colours that would flatter any woman. And now that the clothes were being made in ready-to-wear factories in Italy, Ben's skills as a tailor and couturier had become superfluous. They were not just selling dresses, they were selling a lifestyle. *Sasha's* lifestyle. She was about to say more when the door of the suite buzzed. In swept Marina Schwartz in a cloud of expensive scent.

'Showtime, darlings!' she purred, air-kissing them both. 'You know Nicole, of course?'

A petite girl with waist-length copper-coloured hair came into the suite carrying a tiny dog.

This was a promising start, thought Sasha to herself. Nicole Barton was the star of the hottest new ABC drama and a fixture in the US celebrity style magazines. She had been nominated for Best Supporting Actress for her first big screen role as a downtrodden servant girl in a lavish adaptation of a Henry James novel.

'Am I the first?' she said, running over to the rail of dresses with a little squeal of pleasure.

'Of course you are, Nicky,' said Sasha, pouring on the fashion charm. 'We wanted you to have first pick. We have so many wonderful gowns, but I thought this one would look amazing on you . . .'

By three o'clock there had been a steady stream of celebrities and superwives – the partners of Hollywood producers and directors – passing through the suite. Nicole had been so delighted with her amber scooped-back column dress, she had phoned all her young Hollywood friends and told them to get over to the Peninsula immediately. They had quickly adopted an efficient system: Philip and Marina would entertain the incoming actresses, stylists and assorted hangers-on in the living room while Sasha took the next in line into the bedroom for a consultation.

With a break in the traffic, Sasha flopped down on the bed and helped herself to one of the exquisite hors d'oeuvres standing on a crystal tray: perfect choux pastry wrapped around Ligurian truffles. They had remained completely untouched throughout the day: no one ate so close to the ceremony. Peeking around the door to make sure no starlets were still inside, Philip came in to join her.

'This is getting out of control,' he moaned, taking off his suit jacket and fanning himself with a room-service menu. 'Marina is telling all of them that if they wear the gown on the red carpet they can keep it!'

'I told her to say that,' said Sasha calmly. 'I'm absolutely sure Armani is saying the same thing.'

'But what about the dresses that get taken and not worn?' said Philip, exasperated. 'How many of those do you realistically think we are going to see again?'

Sasha sighed. She was getting tired of his penny-pinching. 'Does it matter?'

'Of course it matters!' cried Philip. 'Forty dresses have gone out so far and their wholesale price is three thousand bucks apiece. Assuming we never see thirty of them again, that's almost a hundred thousand dollars we're going to have to write off.'

'Which is a bargain if we even get *five* celebrities to wear a Rivera dress down the Oscars red carpet,' said Sasha patiently. 'That's what we're doing this for, remember?'

Marina popped her head around the bedroom door. 'Important client alert,' she whispered. 'Ginger Wilson.'

Sasha and Philip looked at each other.

Ginger wasn't strictly speaking a celebrity herself, but as the wife of Steven Goldberg, one of Hollywood's biggest producers, she was one of the most powerful women in LA. The fifty-something walked in wearing fitted jeans and a cashmere T-shirt with a crocodile Hermès Birkin hanging from the crook of her arm. Pulling off her sunglasses, she went straight over to the clothes rail.

'Oh my God, I just love this,' she said, removing a long sequinned sheath dress and holding it aloft so it shimmered in the light. 'I've just got to try it on.'

'A perfect choice,' smiled Sasha, shooing Philip out of the room as Ginger grabbed a pair of silver shoes to go with it. Sasha had noticed that in Hollywood, the richer the woman, the more she wanted a freebie. Sasha didn't mind, as long as she could get something in return.

'This looks amazing,' said Ginger, admiring herself in the mirror.

'Well there's more where that came from,' said Sasha. 'It's the opening of the Rodeo Rivera store next month. Maybe we could talk later about you hosting a little launch there.'

'*Absolutely*,' gushed Ginger. 'I just know all my girlfriends are gonna go green when they see me in this.'

The doorbell rang again and Sasha was dumbstruck when Ben Rivera flounced into the room.

'*Ben?*' said Sasha and Philip in unison.

'In the flesh,' he said. 'I just couldn't stay away.'

360

'So you're the design genius I've been hearing about,' said Ginger, extending her hand. 'One of my girlfriends came here this lunchtime and said your stuff was to die for. I had to come and check it out, and you know what? She was right.'

'Umm, that colour is so good on your skin,' said Ben, one camp finger to his lips. 'Although I think I might be able to add something here . . .' he said, pinching the material at the waist.

'Could you?' she gushed. 'My husband's mistress is going to be there on Sunday. I want something that's going to knock them both dead.'

'I will make you even more stunning than you already are.' He smiled.

'Actually, I'm having a little pre-Oscars drinks party tonight,' said Ginger. 'Perhaps you could come over and we can talk about it? My girlfriends will love meeting the man who's going to make them look so *pretty* tomorrow night.'

'Of course,' said Ben. 'That is what I am here for!'

Sasha coughed discreetly. 'Ben?' she said. 'Can I just have a word with you for one moment?'

She led him out on to the terrace, her cheeks burning with fury.

'What the hell are you doing here?' she said as soon as the doors were closed. 'I thought you were holding the fort in London.'

'How could I stay there and miss all this?' he said with a note of petulance. 'This is my company too. I don't want to be left in a dark room with a tape measure round my neck.'

That's where I'd like it to be, thought Sasha. *Tied really tight.*

'We have roles, Ben,' she said angrily. ' *I* am the ambassador. *You* are the designer.'

'Exactly, which is why people want to meet me today. You heard Ginger.' He smirked. 'I am the man who makes women beautiful.'

361

'No, you are the little queen who bitches about everything.'

Ben gasped. 'How dare you speak to me like that?'

Sasha knew she should back off, save this for a better time, but this fight had been coming for months and she was incensed at Ben's game-playing. He knew this would embarrass her and undermine her hard-won position in LA, yet he'd come anyway. Well, she wasn't going to have anyone steal her thunder, not now.

'I want you out of here,' she said, her voice rising.

'Who the hell do you think you are, Sasha?'

'The woman who has turned this company into the hottest new label in town,' she spat. 'Who do *you* think you are?'

Philip put his head around the door. 'Ginger is leaving,' he said with a warning glance. 'You might want to have this conversation later, in *private*.'

Sasha tried to compose herself. She knew it was unprofessional to leave such a big client, but the whole afternoon was beginning to wind her up. Philip's disapproving looks every time someone opened a bottle of champagne, Marina's constant backhanded compliments about how such a small company was doing so well, and the endless grabbing expectancy of the actresses when they knew how important exposure at the Oscars was to a label.

Squeezing her eyes shut and taking a deep breath, she walked back into the suite, where Ginger kissed Ben on the cheeks. 'Make me look hot, hot, hot and I'll get you into the *Vanity Fair* party at Morton's tomorrow night,' she said with a wink as she left. 'We're going to make you into the new Dior.'

As the door clicked shut, Sasha glared at Ben, but he just smiled smugly. 'The *Vanity Fair* party,' he beamed. 'I knew it was worth coming.'

Sasha grabbed her clutch bag and stalked out of the suite. Philip followed her into the hallway.

'Sasha, come on,' he called. 'Don't blow it up out of proportion. It's not the end of the world.'

Sasha glared at him. 'It better not be.'

She walked quickly down to the elevator, but instead of pressing the 'L' for 'Lobby' button, she went up to the top floor where the roof garden restaurant had a lavish rest room. Leaning into the mirror, she put some blusher on her cheeks, thickened her lashes with mascara and drew a slick of gloss across her lips. Smiling to herself, she hitched up her skirt and removed the cream lace La Perla thong she was wearing, hiding it in her clutch. Walking purposefully back out, she turned away from the lift bank and took the stairs down two floors, the thrill of danger surging through her body as she strode along the soft carpet of the corridor. She took a deep breath, then knocked on the door of the corner suite. It swung open and he was standing there, casual in suit trousers and a blue shirt open at the neck.

'Hello, Robert,' she said as she stepped into the suite.

Robert Ashford smiled at her. 'How's it going up there?'

'Ben bloody Rivera has just turned up,' she said. 'He is getting to be very troublesome. Philip too; always complaining, never able to see the big picture. I'm sick of both of them. They just don't share our vision.'

'Well, we should think about getting rid of them.'

'How?'

Robert smiled. 'It shouldn't be too difficult,' he said, walking over. He wrapped his hands around her waist, unzipping her skirt and letting the thin fabric fall to the floor. Sasha followed him into the bedroom, thinking that sometimes, business did come before pleasure.

40

February 1998

Nothing that Sasha Sinclair ever did was accidental. Every move was thought through, considered, the options examined and carefully weighed up. And in truth, that was how her affair with Robert Ashford had begun. She had wanted to expand into America and Robert could make that happen, so she had invited him to the premiere. It was a business arrangement, something they both could profit from. But then there had been the long meetings to discuss strategy over lunch, the innocent flirtation, the touching of fingers as they both reached for the wine. Their occasional lunch meetings became suppers; soon she didn't want to go home when they'd finished discussing net gearing ratios or whatever the subject had been.

The sex, when it had finally happened, almost eighteen months after they had first renewed contact, had been on a weekend trip to view a shop Robert had in mind for Rivera. It had seemed like the perfectly logical conclusion not just to their months of professional liaison but to a decade of interest. Looking back, there had been a flirtation, a connection, at Angel Cay. What had Robert said on that final night on the island? 'You can do better than Miles.' It turned out he was right.

364

In the penthouse suite of the Ashford Canary Wharf hotel, Sasha sat on the bed in her white towelling robe, reading through a contract Robert had handed her. Connie Ashford thought her husband was in Texas for a meeting with the underperforming Ashford Houston hotel, while Sasha had left the Rivera office early telling Philip she had a Pilates lesson and massage. He'd had no reason to question her.

'Are you sure LVMH won't buy us?' she said, looking up. After all, why shouldn't someone like the Louis Vuitton group be interested in them? Rivera was one of the hottest fashion labels in the industry; with seven stores, presence in all the prestigious department stores and a forty-million-pound turnover, it had become one of the favoured labels of the rich and famous.

Reclining at the end of the bed, Robert Ashford watched her, an amused smile on his lips.

'Don't run before you can walk,' he said. 'Rivera is barely out of the starting blocks. Right now you're too small.'

She swivelled off the bed in anger. 'Why too small? LVMH bought Marc Jacobs when he was tiny.'

'Marc Jacobs had been established twelve years when LVMH acquired a stake in his label,' replied Robert smoothly. Not for the first time, he surprised her with his detailed industry knowledge.

'But I want to sell to someone prestigious,' said Sasha petulantly.

Robert laughed. 'What you want to do is to get rid of Ben, Philip and Miles,' he said. 'What you want to do is to dilute your own shareholding to raise capital and liquidise some of your assets. What you want is a supportive strategic partner who will let you stay creative director and invest money into the brand so we can finally branch out into accessories, scent, even more stores.'

'And who's that strategic partner? You?'

Robert shook his head. 'A private equity outfit.'

She walked over to the window, pursing her lips in thought. In front of her, the regenerated Docklands twinkled in the darkness – the lights from offices and expensive flats like citrines sprinkled over a pad of black velvet. Although they were both stubborn and self-righteous, she respected Robert's opinion completely. He knew so much about everything. Dynamism oozed from every pore of his skin. He was the only man that had ever made her feel both valued and ... what was the word? *Protected,* that was it. She felt that nothing could go wrong when she was with him. He came up behind her, sliding his hands around her waist, untying her robe.

'You can conquer the world, you know that,' he said, stroking her breasts. 'I always thought that about you. You're strong and clever.' He kissed her neck. 'And you're not afraid to take risks.'

She moaned as his lips tickled her ear. 'Hey, I've got to read the contract,' she said.

'Later,' he said, slipping off her gown.

She looked at her naked reflection in the glass. She wondered if anyone could see them and the thought thrilled her. Sasha Sinclair and Robert Ashford atop Canary Wharf. Lovers, equals, like the king and queen of the world.

Still standing behind her, he slipped his hand between her thighs and curled his fingers into her warm, damp pussy. 'Come back to bed,' he said and she went willingly, already aroused. If she had first thought that sex with an older man, a much older man, would be staid and routine, she had been mistaken. At fifty, Robert's body was in impeccable shape, but it wasn't his stamina or his experience that made it such a thrilling, erotic experience. Their lovemaking had an emotional connection and sensuality that she had never reached with Philip or anyone else.

'I've got you something,' he said as he lay back on the pillow afterwards. He reached over to his jacket and pulled out a slip of folded paper.

'What's that?' she asked.

'A cheque.'

'What for? Services rendered?' she said with a note of irritation.

'Open it.'

The cheque was for three quarters of a million pounds. She looked at him, her eyes wide.

'I believe that is what you need to exercise your option to purchase a certain shareholding in Ben Rivera.'

A certain shareholding, meaning Miles'. Although Miles was his son and an investor in Ben Rivera, Robert always avoided mentioning his name. In a few weeks' time, it would be four years since Miles had given her his initial investment in Rivera. Under their original agreement, she could buy back his stake – and Sasha wanted to do it desperately.

'Is this a loan?' she asked, waggling the cheque at him.

'We'll see,' said Robert. 'The important thing is to simplify the company's shareholding structure as much as possible pre-sale. If you can get rid of him, it will make Rivera more appealing to buyers.'

She crawled over and kissed him on the lips. 'Thank you, Robert,' she said simply.

'My pleasure. I like you very much, Sasha Sinclair.'

Shit, that's progress, she smiled to herself. She had never pushed Robert about commitment, never fished for compliments – what was the point? She knew there was unlikely to be any traditional permanent future between them. He was bound to Connie with golden handcuffs. And men like Robert rarely appreciated threats or demands.

'I like you too.'

He stretched over and touched her cheek. 'Listen, I've been thinking. Why don't we go and spend a week at Angel Cay?'

Sasha froze. She hadn't allowed herself to think about that place since her affair with Robert had first begun. She didn't want to think what his role had been in that whole mess.

'No. I don't think that would be a good idea,' she said, looking away.

'Why not?' he said, stroking her neck. 'We can swim, eat, or my personal favourite, just stay in bed.'

It did sound tempting, of course. After all, it was all so long ago, and what had they done wrong really? That boy Bradley had stolen a boat and got away, hadn't he? But still, she didn't want to go back there. What she had with Robert was starting to feel so precious, she didn't want to let anything break the spell. What if he had covered it up? What if he had been involved?

'Not Angel Cay. It's Connie's island,' she said quietly. 'We can go to any other private island in the world, but not Angel.'

'Since when have you been one to take the moral high ground? Besides, Connie won't ever know. I can say I'm in Sydney on business.'

She looked into his strong, intense gaze. There was nothing she'd like more than to spend a week on a sun-drenched private island with him right now. But she couldn't go back there. She couldn't.

'I just don't think it's a good idea, Robert. We're trying to sell the company. That's going to take up every second of my time. I can't be flying off to Angel Cay. I can't. Just leave it, OK?'

He looked at her, but she simply shook her head. As far as she was concerned, the matter was closed: she would never go back to Angel Cay. Never.

Six weeks later, Sasha was feeling just as uncomfortable, but for very different reasons. She walked into Philip's living room to find the dining table set for two with a starched linen tablecloth, scented candles and a gleaming set of white bone china that Sasha had never seen before. Her heart sank. He'd obviously pushed the boat out and she could guess why. Philip had been bugging her to move in for six months, but so far she just had a small drawer of underwear, a few cosmetics and a toothbrush on the bathroom shelf.

'You said you didn't want to go out for supper,' said Philip. 'So I thought we could do something special at the flat.'

Sasha smiled thinly. She was too tired for Philip's unsubtle seduction techniques. The amount of sneaking around she'd been doing – the snatched meetings with Robert, the secret planning, the under-the-radar strategising – it had all been exhausting. Besides, she'd come here for a reason and it was obvious it didn't fit in with Philip's plans.

'I said I didn't want to go for dinner because we have to talk business,' she said briskly.

'Will you relax, Sash?' he said, walking over to rub her shoulders.

She wanted to pull away, but she knew she mustn't. This wasn't Philip's fault; he was a nice guy. Sasha was fond of him and he had worked very hard for the company. But business was business. She went to sit down at the table to get away from him, propping her document folder next to her chair.

'You look all wound up,' said Philip, sitting opposite. 'Do you want to tell me about it?'

'I'm fine,' she said, avoiding his gaze.

'In which case, do you want wine or champagne?' he asked, turning to the ice bucket beside him.

'Are we celebrating?'

'We'll see,' said Philip, pulling a bottle of Krug out of the ice. Actually, he was looking particularly handsome tonight, she thought. Freshly shaved, hair well cut, a crisp white shirt that set off his olive skin and pale grey eyes. Why did he have to be so considerate, so good-looking? For so many women he would be the perfect man. She cursed silently, wishing this had been done at her place. Still, it could wait until after dinner, she told herself. *What's another half an hour?*

In the end, Sasha could barely eat a thing. Philip had obviously spent ages on the food, but she could do nothing more than push her sea bass around the plate.

'More wine?' he asked when he had cleared her untouched dessert away.

'No, I'm driving,' she said. 'I want to get back to the apartment tonight.'

He looked offended. 'Why?'

'I've got things to do.'

'Well at least stay for coffee,' he said, going into the kitchen and coming back with a tray bearing a silver coffee pot and a box of Ladurée macaroons.

'Gosh, where did you get these from?' The macaroons were her absolute favourites but the famous patisserie was in Paris. He just tapped the side of his nose mysteriously.

'Open the box,' he said, looking serious.

She pulled open the pale green lid. Surrounded by pale pink and sherbet-lemon macaroons was a small black velvet box.

Oh no, she thought, suddenly understanding what all this effort had been for.

'Take it out,' he urged.

'Phil . . .' she said gently.

He came round the table and knelt down next to her, his face filled with hope.

'I love you, Sasha,' he said softly. 'I know you've been nervous about moving in with me, but commitment can be scary. The thing is, though, there's nothing to be frightened of. We're a team. We belong together.'

'Phil, I—'

'Sasha Sinclair,' he said, grasping her hands, 'will you marry me?'

She knew what she was supposed to do. She was supposed

to shriek with delight and fall into his arms. She was supposed to say 'Yes, yes, yes!' She was supposed to feel like the happiest woman on earth. But Sasha rarely did what she was supposed to do. She bent down and picked up her leather document folder. Without saying a word, she unzipped it and pulled out a set of contracts.

'What's this?' he said, frowning.

'An offer has been made for the company,' she said coolly. 'A fifty-five-million-pound offer.'

Philip looked incredulous. 'Sasha, I am asking you to marry me and all you can talk about is the bloody business!'

'Hear me out, Phil. This is important.'

'And so is this!' he snapped. He stood up quickly, his face a scowl. 'Fine. You want to talk business? Then my first question is why is this the first I have heard about an offer for the company?'

'Because the approach came to me.'

'Oh yes,' he said sarcastically. 'As ambassador for the brand?'

'Listen to me, Phil,' she said. 'Absolute Capital are one of the most exciting investment vehicles in London and they are interested in Rivera. This could be good for all of us.'

'*All* of us?' he said cynically.

She paused for a moment. 'Well, yes, they would want to bring in their own management team,' she said carefully.

'The COO would be Lucian Grey, a co-investor in the fund. He has considerable experience in the luxury sector. I've known him for years; he's a good man.'

'I'm sorry?' said Philip. 'You're saying he would replace *me*?'

'Philip, you fell into this business. It was never what you really wanted.'

'I gave up my career for you, Sasha,' he said, banging his hand on the table. 'I gave up everything to help you build your dream and now you're selling me down the bloody river.'

'Philip, you have a six per cent shareholding,' she said tersely. 'This sale will make you a rich man.'

'It was never about the money,' he said. 'Don't you understand that? It was always about you.'

'Well I want this to happen,' replied Sasha.

Philip walked over to the window, looking out into the darkness, then turned back suddenly. 'You need a majority shareholder vote for a sale,' he said. 'You only have forty-five per cent. You need me to make this happen, don't you? Just like always. You've always needed me to push decisions through.'

She pitied the note of desperation in his voice.

'I'm speaking to Ben tomorrow,' she said.

'Ben's never going to allow the company to be taken from under him,' said Philip dismissively. 'You still need me.'

It was harsh, especially after what had just happened, but she had to say it.

'No, Philip, I don't. I will have more than fifty per cent anyway.'

She reached into the folder and pulled out a Coutts banker's draft, putting it down on the table. It was made out to Miles Ashford for £800,000.

'That's everything I owe Miles, with interest,' she said simply. 'Tomorrow I'm going to exercise my option to buy back his shareholding.'

He looked at the cheque, then back at her, his eyes narrowing. 'Where did you get the money from?'

She looked away. 'It doesn't matter.'

'Really?' he said bitterly. 'I suspect it matters a great deal.'

Of course Philip would find out eventually. She knew that and she knew that he would hate her.

'I'm sorry, Phil,' she said, picking up the papers and putting them back into the folder. 'I didn't want it to end like this.'

He didn't say anything, just looked at her and shook his head. Then he walked back to the table and snapped the black velvet box shut.

'There's more to life than just money, Sasha,' he said closing his hand over the box. 'One day you'll learn that.'

'Maybe if we can just talk about this ...' began Sasha.

But Philip wasn't listening. 'I think you'd better go.'

She picked up her coat and slowly walked past him. 'Phil, I wish you'd—'

'Just go,' he said, walking into the bedroom and closing the door.

41

September 2001

Alex's life had undergone a transformation. For a start, he wasn't Alex Doyle any more. He was Al Doyle now, multi-Grammy-award-winning British songwriting superstar. In the last two years alone he had sold twenty million records, filled stadiums across the globe and his videos were on MTV and VH-1 almost on a loop.

He sat on the steps of his trailer looking out on to the shady Manhattan side street just off Times Square. They had been shooting the video for his latest single 'Moving On' through the night and they still weren't done. A runner brought him a tea and a bacon sandwich with ketchup running all over the paper plate. Alex was happy enough sitting around on a warm New York fall morning. He loved the Big Apple, especially now, with his star in the ascendant. He was invited to every party, he could get a table at any restaurant and everyone was so ambitious, so caught up in their own world, they were too busy to pay any attention to him. LA was the direct opposite. It was an industry town, a hotbed of 'look at me' self-indulgence; everyone wanted to be noticed, from the stars down to the waiters. Even though Alex had a house in Laurel Canyon, he hated it there.

A black Town Car stopped in front of the blue barricade blocking off the section of street they were shooting in. Alex recognised the small figure of David Falk stepping out of the car, accompanied by a blonde woman. He was always pleased to see Falk. It still felt like yesterday he'd had that first meeting with him at his LA headquarters. From the second he had walked into Falk's corner office, Alex had known that this man was going to change his life – and he had. He had used Alex's debut solo single 'Angel Falls' as the title track to one of the movie hits of the nineties, and instantly Al Doyle was a household name. Hit followed hit, and his transition from nobody to megastar had been so seamless, Alex wondered if the years of struggle with Year Zero had just been a bad dream.

'Hey, Al. How's it going?' said Falk, walking over, his hand out.

'Still standing.' He grinned, holding up his tea. 'Caffeine helps.'

His eyes were drawn to the blonde woman standing just behind David. He recognised her immediately: Melissa Jackson, one of the hottest new actresses in Hollywood; in fact he had heard that Falk's company was producing her next vehicle.

'Have you met Melissa?'

'No, no, hello . . .' said Alex, wiping his hand on his jeans, then shaking hers. 'Sorry,' he said. 'Ketchup all over it.'

She smiled. 'Happens to me all the time.'

'Say, you going to Julia's party tonight?' said Falk.

Alex nodded. 'If this shoot ever finishes.'

'You got a date?' Falk's direct manner was legendary. He hadn't got anywhere in his business without getting straight to the point.

Alex laughed and looked at Melissa. 'Why do I feel I'm being set up?'

'Obviously neither of you kids needs to work too hard for

375

company, but Melissa's new movie is about a failed pop singer, and . . .'

'And you thought, "Hey, which losers do I know?"'

'Sorry, Alex,' said Melissa. 'I did try to tell him how crass he was being, but you know Dave . . .'

Alex laughed.

'Hey, talk about me as if I'm not here, why dontcha?' said Falk.

'It would be great to pick your brains about touring and playing small dives and so on,' she continued with a shy smile. 'And you don't have to think of it as a date.'

'Ah, don't ruin it,' smiled Alex. 'This is the best offer I've had in months.'

Actually, he was only half joking. He was on tour six months out of twelve and spent most of his time with the burly men who moved the stage around; even a big star needed a little help in the romance department. Sometimes all he wanted was someone to talk to who understood his life now – he felt quite sure both Emma and Grace would have ribbed him mercilessly about his entourage today: an assistant, a make-up girl, a stylist, a record company PR and a driver – but he guessed Melissa would understand how mad and unreal it all felt. And it didn't hurt that she was gorgeous.

Martin, the director, waved at him. 'Al, we're ready to go again in a minute,' he called.

Alex stood up and stretched. 'Sorry, guys, no rest for the wicked.' He smiled. 'I'll see you tonight at—' He was cut short as he was almost knocked flying by the runner who had brought him his bacon sandwich. The boy was red-faced and out of breath. 'Whoa, slow down there, mate,' said Alex. 'What's the rush?'

'Haven't you heard?' said the runner. His eyes were wide and frightened. 'A plane has just hit the World Trade Center.'

'What? You're joking?' said Falk, shooting a look at Alex. 'How do you know?'

'I've just read the tickertape in Times Square. Everyone's yelling about it down there, it's chaos.'

A burly man in sunglasses and an earpiece approached them swiftly from David's Town Car. Alex had met him before; he was an ex-Navy Seal who served as Falk's bodyguard and security adviser. He took Falk's arm and led him to one side, speaking urgently out of earshot. Alex watched David's expression become more grave.

'OK, you two,' said David, taking both Alex and Melissa by the arm and steering them towards the car. 'You're coming with me.'

'Where are we going?' asked Alex.

'Out of Manhattan.'

'Why?' Alex looked behind him. Everyone was crowding around the location van watching a small television.

'Come *on*, Alex,' growled Falk, tugging his arm.

'We can't just leave,' said Alex, looking to Melissa for support.

'He's right, David,' said the actress. 'What about all the others?'

'Just get in the freaking car,' said Falk sternly. 'They think it could be a terrorist attack. There're rumours of other planes being hijacked. The city might be under siege.'

'Oh shit.'

Alex felt his heart thumping. The tall buildings appeared to be crowding in around him, each one suddenly seeming to have the capability to explode on top of them at any moment. Falk pushed Alex and Melissa into the car and they sped off across Broadway towards Eighth Avenue. David leant forward to switch the car's TV screen on, flicking to a news channel. They watched in silence as the unbelievable footage was shown: shaky amateur film of a jet liner crashing into a gleaming skyscraper. The news cut to a reporter standing close to the tower, holding a microphone. Behind him, they could see the chaos: people in suits running away, people in uniform running towards it. There was a weird dislocation: they were watching this on the television, but it was happening right outside. Just as they crossed Eleventh Avenue, heading for the West Side parkway, the driver had to swerve to avoid two fire trucks, their lights and sirens screaming. Alex turned to look out of the window and could see a thick column of smoke rising from the south of the island.

'Jesus, this is really happening,' he said, glancing at Melissa. She looked scared and instinctively he reached out to squeeze her hand.

'Look!' said Falk suddenly, causing Alex to spin back around. He frowned, not sure what was happening on the screen.

'Is that another one?'

The on-screen camera pulled out rapidly and they could see that a second plane had flown into the other tower.

'Fuck,' whispered Alex. He wasn't sure if he knew anyone who would be so far downtown at nine o'clock in the morning. Then again, the horrors unfolding on the television were so shocking and surreal, it was impossible to think clearly about anything.

The driver pressed his fingers to his earpiece. 'Sir, I have a contact who says fighters have been scrambled,' he said, glancing into his rear-view mirror. 'There's a plane heading for Washington, maybe a couple more.'

The car was hurtling towards the George Washington Bridge at over fifty miles an hour, but they were forced to slow as they reached the on-ramp. A crush of traffic was causing a bottleneck and police vans were pulling up, officers unloading barriers.

'Get us through,' ordered Falk.

'Hold on, ladies and gents,' said the driver. They felt a bump as the car mounted a kerb, then swerved around a barrier. There was frantic beeping and a policeman jumped out waving his arms, but the driver ignored him, squeezing the big car between a truck and a minivan, losing a wing-mirror in the process. Alex could see that they had just made it on to the bridge; the barriers were right across the four lanes behind them.

'God help anyone still on there,' said David as they watched the island metropolis disappear.

Alex thought of friends living in SoHo, and Tribeca. Mike, Josh, Marty, all the crew in the van in midtown.

He was running away again. It was what he did best.

The car took them upstate to the sumptuous country home of David's friend, the fashion designer Todd Barabosa. Within a few hours it had become a refugee camp for the super-rich and influential: all of the celebrities, powerbrokers and foreign dignitaries with the influence and connections to get them out of Manhattan had come here, spirited into the gated estate by armed drivers. Todd's staff made food and kept the coffee flowing but no one was in the mood to eat or drink. People stood in small huddles close to the huge plasma televisions, watching the terrible events unfold, some crying, others stunned into a muted disbelieving silence. Everyone in the room knew they were going nowhere; the airports were in lock-down, the bridges and tunnels in and out of Manhattan closed, and until they knew what was really happening, they were in the safest place.

Alex didn't feel safe. He felt vulnerable and isolated. Everyone seemed to have someone to call – loved ones, families, connected people with information. Alex had called his mum, who burst into tears of relief when she heard his voice, but he didn't really have anyone else. He smiled at the irony. Thousands, no, millions of girls would chop off an arm to get close to him, yet there was no one out there frantically calling him, checking he was OK. Feeling hemmed in, he walked outside into the garden, a gush of balmy late-afternoon breeze ruffling his long hair.

'Alex, wait!' He turned to see Melissa running after him. 'I don't really know anyone in there. Do you mind if I tag along?'

'Not at all.'

They wandered through the luscious grounds, not talking – there didn't seem to be anything to say. They took a dusty path through the mowed lawns studded with beds of foxgloves and roses, up towards a shady copse that overlooked the whole estate. From there, Alex could see the colonial house, a glinting lake and a paddock of horses grazing peacefully. No one would know that anything was wrong with the world from this distance. They sat down on the hillside and he stole a sideways glance at Melissa. She really was an incredibly sexual creature: pillowy lips, high cheekbones and pale blond hair that she pulled back from her long neck. Most of all, though, he liked the way she seemed human; genuinely devastated by the events.

'You didn't know anyone in the towers?'

He shook his head.

'You live in LA, don't you?' It wasn't really a question. It was one of the strange things about being famous; people knew things about you. He was also amazed at the way other celebrities would instantly bond with you, a complicit understanding that you were part of their club. They talked vaguely about the people they knew in common, sharing silly stories and amusing anecdotes, talking of a life far beyond the tragic scenes of lower Manhattan. As the sun began to slip from the sky, Alex realised they had been there over an hour and that it was turning cold.

'I think I'm going to get back to the house,' he said.

'Stay with me just a little while longer,' she said, still staring out over the fields.

He shrugged. 'OK, cool.'

And when she rested her head on his shoulder and he pulled her close, it seemed like the most natural thing in the world. On a day like this, everybody needed someone to make them feel just a little bit less vulnerable and afraid. Because for all their money and fame and acquaintances, neither of them had anyone to hold them. They were both alone.

42

January 2002

'This is so spooky,' said Olivia, grabbing her mother's hand so tightly she could feel the wedding ring dig into her flesh. Not for the first time, Grace wondered why she still wore it, even if she had switched it to her right hand.

'Actually, darling, I think it's rather beautiful,' whispered Grace. 'Like somewhere a fairy princess might get married. It's very romantic.'

On any other day, the loch-side chapel would have looked bleak and severe against the deep violet Scottish sky, the highland hills pressing in on all sides. But this evening, it looked otherworldly, illuminated by torchlight that flickered long shadows against the stone.

'Do you think Bonnie Prince Charlie came here?' asked Joseph as they clambered out of the Land Rover which had brought them from their B&B. 'We did him at school. He had a claymore sword. Can I have a sword, Mum?'

'No, darling, you can't,' said Grace, pulling the collar of her cashmere coat up around her ears and leading the children past a lone piper in full clan tartan and into the church.

'Bride or groom?' asked a handsome usher in a midnight-blue kilt.

'Bride,' she said, accepting her order of service printed on thick vellum. As they sat down, Grace discreetly leant forward to look at the groom. She had never met him, but had occasionally read about him in the society pages, thanks to his status as the eldest son of one of Scotland's richest land-owning lords.

With the triumphant flourish of Handel's 'Arrival of the Queen of Sheba', the two hundred guests all stood and turned to watch the bride make her way up the aisle, resplendent in ivory bridal couture.

It was no surprise to Grace that her old friend from Danehurst Freya Nicholls was marrying well: in a few minutes Freya would become the Countess of Kalcraig. The surprise – to Grace at least – was that she had accepted the invitation. In the twelve years since they had shared a house together in Bristol, Freya had barely been in touch – sporadic postcards and emails and one random visit two years ago when Freya was in Ibiza to spend the weekend on a friend's yacht. But when a 'Save the Date' announcement had arrived at her Ibizan farmhouse four months earlier, Grace had felt compelled to reply. She still wasn't sure she'd made the right decision; it certainly hadn't been any fun making the seven-hour journey with two whining ten-year-olds. They had perked up since they had seen the castle, though.

'Wow, look at this place,' said Olivia as they followed the procession back from the church to the Kalcraigs' family home, where the wedding breakfast was to be held.

'It's like a real palace. Is this where Countess Freya is going to live?'

'One day, I think,' said Grace. She suspected that Freya would almost certainly stay in the double-fronted townhouse in Notting Hill the couple also owned; she had never visited, but it had appeared in countless interiors magazines.

'She's beautiful, isn't she? Countess Freya, I mean,' said Olivia. 'I bet all the boys used to like her at college.'

'They did,' replied Grace. 'Including some of the boys I used to like.'

'So why are we at her wedding if she used to do that?' said Joseph, bristling.

'I was *joking*, darling.' Grace smiled. She loved how Joseph was so protective of her, but she worried that the divorce had affected the kids more than they let on. Gabriel didn't visit very often and was formal and distant when he did. He had aged visibly since they had left Parador: the party's fortunes hadn't improved much and the strain of keeping the movement alive was taking its toll. The children rarely mentioned their father when he wasn't there and had taken diametrically opposed positions on marriage: Joseph was staunchly against any sort of relationship, saying it was 'stupid' while Olivia had romanticised it to the extent that she believed in Disney-style happy endings. So Joe would snarl at any man who came near his mother, while Liv would scare them even more by immediately grilling them on their preference for summer or winter weddings. Not that Grace had the time or inclination for a relationship; she was still licking her wounds from the last one.

'Can we meet the Countess, Mummy?' said Olivia, tugging at Grace's hand as they moved into the huge vaulted hall of Kalcraig Castle.

'Of course, Livvy, it's traditional to greet the bride and groom when you arrive at the reception.'

They joined the line crowding to give their congratulations to the happy couple. Ahead of her, Grace recognised a BAFTA-winning actor, several famous authors and a *Vogue* cover girl, but no friends or acquaintances of her own. She supposed the real reason she had accepted Freya's invitation was because she had been hoping to meet up with old friends from Danehurst and Bristol, almost all of whom had dropped off her radar. Lately she had found herself becoming quite nostalgic; she certainly regretted cutting herself off so ruthlessly after that 1990 summer. Time and maturity made it easier for her to admit that she had been both rash and dramatic, and she had spent many hours on the internet lately, particularly on a site called Friends Reunited, looking up people from the past.

'Gracie!' squealed Freya as they shuffled up, clasping her to her breast, smothering her in silk. 'It's so amazing to see you.'

'Congratulations, you look stunning,' said Grace, suddenly feeling frumpy and old next to her friend.

'I ought to, I've been working towards today for five months. I swear I haven't eaten anything solid since New Year.' She lowered her head towards Grace's ear. 'I think you're going to love the table plan. Guess who you're sitting next to?'

Grace held her breath, half expecting her to say Alex Doyle. She wouldn't have put it past Freya to reacquaint herself with Alex especially now that he was a Grammy-winning musician.

'Sasha Sinclair.' She giggled.

Grace tried not to show her dismay. 'I didn't know you were in touch with Sasha,' she said.

'We weren't, but then I met her at a party a few months ago. You know she runs Rivera? Absolutely divine. I told her I was getting married and how US *Vogue* wanted to do something on the wedding, so she offered to do my gown at cost. And isn't it *fabulous*?'

'Beautiful,' said Grace distractedly, glancing around for the face she had seen so many times in style magazines; and there she was, already seated at table nine. *Calm down, Grace,* she thought to herself. *It's only Sasha Sinclair, not Freddy Krueger.* After all, she had seen Alex in Ibiza and there had only been a flicker of discomfort. And she saw Miles too, perhaps once a year, and they managed to be civil to each other at least.

385

'Hello, Grace,' said Sasha stiffly, standing to give Grace a brittle embrace. 'I wondered if you might be here.'

'Freya's been talking about marrying a rich, powerful man for nearly twenty years; I couldn't miss it now it's happened,' said Grace.

'Are we sitting together?' asked Sasha, looking down at the place cards.

'You are now,' said Joseph, moving around the table to put Grace and Sasha's cards together.

'Joe, I don't think you should . . .'

'No, he's right, Mum,' said Olivia, moving another card around. 'And I'll sit on the other side of Sasha. I've seen you in *Vogue*,' she said eagerly, climbing into her new seat. 'I want to be a fashion designer too.'

'Do you now?' said Sasha with an imperious smile. 'Well I'll have to see what you know, won't I?' adding in mock-confession, 'Although strictly speaking I'm not a fashion designer.'

Grace smiled. She was not surprised that the self-confident eighteen-year-old had grown up into the slightly intimidating, successful beauty in front of her. They were joined at the table by the groom's unmarried cousin, his former nanny and her septuagenarian brother, plus a braying friend from Cambridge who monopolised the first half of the meal regaling them with highly inappropriate stories of the groom's sexual adventures at university.

'I think we can safely say we got the duff table,' whispered Sasha as the dessert was brought around. 'And to think I practically *gave* her wedding dress to her.'

'Don't let my father know you're giving dresses away at cost.'

Grace detected something in Sasha's expression. *Discomfort?* For a moment she entertained the idea that Sasha had spent the last decade being plagued by memories of the island too, then dismissed the thought. *Stupid*, she scolded herself. If that was the case she would hardly have taken Robert Ashford's investment in her company, would she?

'You should come into the Bond Street store yourself while you're in the UK,' said Sasha quickly. 'Our silk jersey wrap dresses will look incredible on you. You have an amazing figure now.'

Now? Is that a backhanded compliment I hear? thought Grace.

'Well, I'd recommend a divorce and an assassination attempt to anyone as a diet plan,' she said.

'Oh, I'm so sorry,' said Sasha, touching her hand. 'I had heard; I didn't think . . .'

'Don't be silly, I'm kidding. I'd love to come and try a few things on, but my mum's convinced me to stay with her in Oxfordshire for the week.'

'Then you must come to my thirtieth,' said Sasha with enthusiasm. 'It's at my friend Iftaka's house in Berkshire and I think your mum and dad are coming anyway.'

'It's lovely of you to offer, but . . .'

'Alex Doyle will be there,' said Sasha with a sly smile.

'You mean *Al* Doyle,' said Grace. She actually hadn't seen Alex since his visit to Ibiza. It didn't surprise her, given the way his career had taken off. Every now and then she would get a postcard sent to the farmhouse, postmarked Las Vegas, Sydney or Tokyo, with some sweet or cryptic message. Olivia was always very impressed.

'I didn't know you and Alex were friends,' said Grace.

'Darling, in my business I have to touch base with everyone. This party is an excuse to see everyone important in one fell swoop.'

'Mummy, Mummy! Come and dance!' said Olivia and Joseph in unison, bouncing up and down and pulling at her hand as the ceilidh band began to play.

'I'd better go and strut my stuff,' she said, excusing herself.

'And then I'd better get these two to bed before they have any more sugar.'

Sasha nodded and touched her on the arm. 'You know, we should have spoken earlier,' she said softly.

'Yes, I know,' replied Grace.

'And you will come to the party?'

Part of her desperately wanted to say yes. Twelve years of being haunted by the memory of what happened on Angel Cay was far too long; she wanted to move on. But she still wasn't sure if she could handle all four of them being in the same place at one time.

'Is Miles going to be there?'

Sasha shook her head. 'I don't see him. And I don't think he'd want to come, to be honest.'

There was a look of understanding between them. A secret nod of support from woman to woman.

'Sure, I'd love to come,' said Grace. 'Thirty, eh?' she added as she was hauled towards the dance floor. 'We're almost grown-ups now.'

And it was time to start acting like one.

43

February 2002

Alex wasn't entirely sure where he had heard the phrase, but in the world of celebrity, it was certainly true that one and one made eleven. Before his relationship with Melissa had finally leaked in a three-page *National Enquirer* story called 'Beauty and the Beat', the tabloid press had only a passing interest in him. Yes, he was a platinum-selling artist, but he was a serious musician, not a red-carpet regular. Interesting to music geeks and teenage girls, but not the sort of star who could shift millions of newspapers. Melissa was a bigger celebrity, of course, but she was not in the same league as Catherine, Julia or Jennifer. Together, however, Alex and Melissa created a strange alchemy that had sent the paparazzi crazy and turned their world upside down. Wherever they went, photographers were there. Leaving the house, at the airport, visiting a restaurant; they were mobbed going in and coming out and the paps would crowd around the windows trying to take pictures of them – shock! – eating noodles or – hold the front-page! – popping to the loo. Not a week went by without front-page splashes about their relationship – in love, splitting up, sometimes both in the same paper – or speculation about an imminent elopement or secret love-child.

Alex was still struggling to make the adjustment, both to

his new relationship and to his new mega-stardom. Some days were good, some days horrible, but today had been one of the good ones – one of the best, in fact. Alex lay back on the four-poster bed in his favourite London hotel, Blakes, feeling happy and relaxed. For once, he and Melissa had managed to spend the entire day together, doing exactly what they wanted; no interviews, no phone calls, just them. Melissa was in London waiting to start filming at Pinewood Studios. Alex had just finished recording at Abbey Road. At his suggestion, they'd spent the day doing all the touristy things Alex never did when he lived there. Suitably disguised in sunglasses and baseball caps, they had strolled around London Zoo, gone boating in Regent's Park, then taken a black cab out to Hampton Court, where they'd gone for a long walk down the Thames towpath all the way to Richmond. Alex didn't know when he'd felt happier.

'You know what's great?' he said, watching Melissa strip out of her jeans and sweater. In the low light, with the cream voile drapes fluttering behind her, she looked like an angel.

'I don't know, tell me,' she smiled, crawling up the bed towards him. As she leant over to kiss him, he could smell her; a delicate blend of raspberries and vanilla he had always loved.

'Feeling together,' said Alex. 'Feeling settled.'

Melissa laughed. 'You say it like it's this strange and crazy thing.'

In a way, it was. Even when he was with Emma, there was always something that made him feel displaced or anxious: his insecurities about Jez Harrison or the worry of failure. But with Melissa, he felt safe and confident. All the pressure seemed to lift when she was around.

'Well, how do you feel about being Mrs Alex Doyle?' he asked.

Her hand covered her mouth, her blue eyes wide. She looked shocked.

'What?' he asked.

'Al, you're not proposing to me, are you?'

It was his turn to look surprised. Actually he had simply been asking if she was feeling as contented and fuzzy as he was; did she like being seen as 'Mrs Alex Doyle', his *missus*. But still . . . It wasn't such a mad idea, was it? In idle moments, he'd been toying with the notion of growing old together, having a tribe of beautiful mini-Melissas and retiring to a ranch in Wyoming or somewhere. And God, she was beautiful, he thought, gazing into her perfect, beaming face, breathless with anticipation. *What the fuck are you waiting for?* he asked himself.

'Yes, I am,' he said.

'In that case yes, yes, yes,' she squealed, straddling him and covering his face with kisses. Laughing, he rolled over on top of her, but she was squirming so much that they slipped off the bed with a thump. There was a moment's delay, then they both burst out laughing. Scrambling to his feet, Alex grabbed the bedside phone. 'OK, this calls for a celebration,' he said, dialling room service. 'I'll get them to send up their biggest bottle of champagne. One of those Necubanezzers or whatever they're called.'

'No, don't,' she said, taking the receiver from him. 'Let's go out to celebrate.'

'Out where?'

'I promised a friend of mine we'd go to her party.'

Alex pulled a face. 'Can't we just stay in bed and pour Dom Perignon all over each other?'

She put her hands on her hips and pouted. 'The sexiest man in the world has just proposed to me. I want to tell the world!' she said.

'Well, if you put it that way . . .' He smiled. 'So where is it?'

'It's at this amazing house in Berkshire. Belongs to some Middle Eastern gazillionaire. Plus it's my friend's thirtieth birthday.'

'OK,' said Alex. 'But only if I can help you dress,' he added, sliding his hand inside her lacy panties.

'Please!' Melissa giggled. 'I'm an engaged woman, what would my fiancé say?'

'I think he'd say I was a very lucky man,' he growled, pushing her back on the bed.

It took over an hour to get to the party, but pulling through the gates of Chambrey Park estate, a huge, wildly romantic Jacobean manor house set in extensive grounds, Alex knew it was going to be a lavish affair: the perfect place to celebrate.

'You've not even told me who your friend is,' said Alex. He had spent the entire journey happily listening to Melissa debate whether the Santa Ynez ranch or the Post Ranch Inn would be the perfect place to have the ceremony.

'Oh, she owns a fashion company, I wear a lot their stuff on the red carpet. Rivera, they're just amazing.'

'You don't mean Sasha *Sinclair*?' he said incredulously. Alex didn't know much about women's fashion, but it would be hard to live in LA and not be aware of Sasha's incredible rise as a style icon.

'Do you know her? I guess she's British too, so you would, right?'

'We went to school together actually,' he said, feeling suddenly nervy. 'On holiday too.'

'You didn't sleep with her, did you?' Melissa said, narrowing her eyes.

'Of course not,' he said defensively. 'She went out with my best friend. I haven't seen her in over ten years.'

'Well in that case,' said Melissa, brightening, 'you can have a little reunion, can't you? It'll be a double celebration.'

'Yeah,' said Alex. 'Smashing.'

Flashbulbs popped as they went into the party. 'Oi, Melissa, one of you on your own, eh love?' shouted a photographer and Alex stepped to the side as she posed alone. It had happened before, of course – for some reason Alex's music hadn't taken off in the UK in the same way as it had in the States – but tonight it annoyed him more than usual. *We're supposed to be together, tonight of all nights*, he thought. Finally, they went inside and Alex immediately approached a waiter holding a tray of drinks.

'Champagne, please,' he said.

'Oh no, can you fix us two Virgin Bellinis?' interrupted Melissa.

'But we're celebrating, aren't we?' frowned Alex.

'Al, we don't need to get wasted to celebrate, you know.'

He was just about to argue when a face across the room caught his attention. *Grace was here!* He looked up and waved.

'Who's that?' said Melissa.

'Who?' he said distractedly.

'The fat one in the blue dress.'

He turned on her. 'Hey, that's an old friend of mine.'

Melissa pouted. 'Someone else you've slept with, then.'

'No! I haven't slept with her, she's just an old friend. And a lovely person.'

Melissa's face softened. 'Sorry, honey,' she said, slipping a hand around his waist. 'It's just I don't want you getting away from me now I've snared you.'

Snared me? thought Alex. 'I'm not going anywhere, you know that.'

'Well, great, let's go and tell your friend the news.'

'What news?'

'The "we're getting married" news, stupid.'

He felt his cheeks flush. 'Of course. Well, maybe later,' he said, suddenly feeling tongue-tied and embarrassed. 'Don't you want to tell your friends first?'

But Melissa had already gone, trotting over to another super-groomed blonde woman. 'Darling,' she said, 'you'll never guess, but I've got some fabulous news ...'

And when Alex looked around for Grace, she had gone.

Sasha loved the venue for her party; she only wished it hadn't come with strings attached. Chambrey Park was not quite the biggest private residence in the Home Counties but it was, quite possibly, the prettiest. The cut-glass chandeliers sparkled diamonds of light around the restored ballroom which was lined with beautiful modernist art: Warhol, Basquiat, Matisse. Its owner, Abu Dhabi billionaire Iftaka Khani, had been extremely generous in offering Sasha his house for her thirtieth birthday party. Generous, but not altogether altruistic. He had taken a great shine to the beautiful entrepreneur, lavishing her with gifts, dinners and invites to his many homes around the globe, and as Sasha was officially single, and he was one of the most eligible bachelors in London, he clearly thought it was only a matter of time before they would become an item. He certainly had made an effort. The catering had been done by the Fat Duck restaurant, just a stone's throw away in Bray, and the music was courtesy of Fatboy Slim. That alone must have cost a fortune. *Still not enough*, thought Sasha with a shiver, thinking of Iftaka's fifty-inch waist and hairy hands.

She walked through the party exchanging air-kisses and compliments, then stopped on the mezzanine balcony. Behind her through long windows she could just see the River Thames glinting in the moonlight, while in front of her the party was crackling with laughter and energy, the guest list a glamorous mix of old money, new money, fashion legends and Hoxton hipsters. She smiled as she remembered the times she'd had to sweet-talk bouncers to get into the sought-after London parties. But fashion had been kind to her, sweeping her up on the crest of a wave and giving her a place in society, not to mention a flourishing business. What was it that *Vogue* had said about the Rivera label recently? That its fans were buying into the fantasy of Sasha Sinclair's lifestyle: chic, successful new millennium glamour. Well it was a fantasy she had created all by herself, she thought. This party was full of so-called 'self-made people' who'd actually been backed by family money or wealthy spouses. Yes, Sasha had needed investment too, but she had used every ounce of ingenuity, every contact, every business advantage; she'd worked ruthlessly to make it happen.

Ruthless. That was what Ben Rivera had called her when she'd finally pushed him out kicking and screaming, although she'd noticed that he didn't refuse the five-million-pound pay-off. 'Rivera will never succeed without me!' he had declared. Well he was wrong. She'd swiftly hired a talented young French designer, and with Sasha firmly steering the design, she had taken the company to even greater heights – it had recently been valued at a hundred million dollars. No, it was an amazing place to be at thirty, but still Sasha felt a pang of sadness. There was one person missing from this party: her father. Twelve months ago Gerald Sinclair had had a stroke which left him paralysed down one side. Although some speech and mobility had returned slowly, he was still a shadow of himself and she hadn't been surprised when her mother had turned up at the party without him. She smiled to herself. If Ben Rivera thinks I'm ruthless, he's never met my mother.

Her mobile phone was buzzing. Irritated, she snapped it open and then smiled at the message. 'First bedroom on the second floor,' it read.

Robert was waiting for her, silhouetted against the window. She locked the door and went over to him, running her hands over his shoulders.

'Where's Connie?' she whispered.

'Talking to Iftaka Khani.'

'Ironic,' said Sasha.

He looked at her seriously. 'There's nothing going on there,

395

is there? You and Iftaka. I mean, it's good of him to do this
. . .'

'I've never made him promises.'

'Good.'

His smile pleased her. Recently they'd celebrated the fifth
anniversary of their relationship. It was longer than most
marriages in their world. Yes, Sasha sporadically dated other
men, but whenever Robert called, she would come running.
He was her north point, the only other passion that co-existed
with her business in her universe. She didn't like being
possessed, even if it was her choice, but she still wanted to
feel desired.

'I'm a single girl, Robert,' she said. 'I can do what I please.'

'Don't go playing hard to get,' he said, turning her around
and kissing the back of her neck. 'Not when I've got something special planned for us both tomorrow.'

He slid his hand into her dress and cupped her breast,
rubbing the nipple with his palm. She tipped her head back
and moaned. She wanted him inside her now, and from the
hardness of his cock, she could tell he wanted her too.

'The door's locked,' he mumbled into her hair.

Suddenly she took a step away from him and turned
around. 'Well you'd better go and unlock it,' she said. 'I've
got to get back to the party.'

He looked at her, puzzled. 'Sasha, we've got a private minute
here. Let's make the most of it.'

God, she wanted him, but she knew it was time to play a
different game. It was time to start calling the shots. The truth
was, she'd hated seeing him arrive with Connie, hated the polite,
remote way he'd spoken to her when they had been standing
with mutual friends. She knew it was the price of their secret
romance, but it was a price she was no longer going to pay.

'Sasha. I can't go back out there. I've got a hard-on the
size of Africa.'

She looked him up and down witheringly. 'Hmm. Looks

like you're going to have to stay here for a little while then,' she replied flatly, handing him an interiors magazine from the bedside table as she headed for the door. 'But don't worry, we can pick up where we left off tomorrow.'

'Remind me why I'm here?' said Sarah Brayfield as she watched Sasha Sinclair glide down the stairs.

'She's not that bad,' smiled Grace, glad that her former flatmate had come to the party with her. Sarah's no-nonsense approach hadn't changed over the years – Grace suspected it was essential in her job as a media litigation lawyer – and it was refreshing to go to a society party with someone who didn't think everything was 'fabulous'.

'She *is* that bad, Grace!' said Sarah. 'You might have forgotten what a pain in the arse she was that holiday in Angel Cay, but I haven't. She's poisonous and she always will be.'

'Ah, the tolerance, the generosity of spirit; Sarah Brayfield, how I've missed you.' Grace giggled.

The two women clinked their cocktail glasses together. As part of her plan to build bridges she had burnt over the years, Grace had contacted Sarah straight after Freya's wedding and was delighted when she had agreed to be her 'date' for the party. It was hard to believe that she hadn't seen her since she had left for Thailand all those years ago. That, Grace now realised, was the real tragedy of Angel Cay. It had robbed her of her friends.

'When are you coming back to London, Gracie?' asked Sarah. 'I've still not forgiven you for buggering off to Australia and marrying Che Guevara.'

'You mean the father of my children,' she said, raising one eyebrow.

'Yes, him. And then you go off and lead the bloody good life in Ibiza. You know I never saw you as the Spanish Felicity Kendal. Come on, you've got to admit you miss London?'

Grace pulled a face.

'Well all right then, you must miss me at least? I promise I've cleaned up my act. I don't even drink snakebite and black any more on a night out. It's all elegant cocktails and good behaviour now.'

'I should think so. I'd hate to think of you staggering around the High Court reeking of booze.'

They laughed.

'Seriously, though, we do have to get out on the pull,' said Sarah. She had never married – another of the things she had inherited from her hippy parents was a distrust of the institution – and had only recently split up from her barrister boyfriend of three years. 'I mean, when was the last time you had sex, Grace? If you tell me it's last century I'm going have to batter you with this cocktail umbrella.'

'It's hard being a single mum.'

'Excuses, excuses.'

'I'm serious,' protested Grace. 'I was at Glasgow airport the other day and this Ewan McGregor lookalike smiled at me at the baggage carousel. You should have seen his face when the kids came to help me with the luggage.'

'Well I saw Julian Adler clocking you earlier.'

'The artist?' said Grace. 'Don't be silly. He was probably just looking for the loos or something.'

'Well I think he's pretty sexy in a "going to seed but knows it" kind of way. I bet he'd be filthy in bed too – sensitive fingers.'

Grace laughed, but she couldn't help scanning the crowd to see if she could spot the famous painter.

'Have you seen Alex yet?' she asked. 'I thought I saw him through the crowd but then he disappeared.'

Sarah looked at her wide-eyed. 'Alex *Doyle* is here? So that's why you've dragged me out to bloody Berkshire.'

'Don't be daft.'

'Well I hope not, because you do know he's got a superstar girlfriend, don't you? I suspect even you can't compete with her.'

Grace shook her head, surprised at how disappointed she felt at the news. 'What superstar girlfriend?' she asked.

'Whatshername, Melissa Jackson. Hollywood sex-pot.'

Grace almost snorted her drink down her nose. '*What?* He goes out with *her?*'

Sarah tutted. 'Don't you ever read *Heat?*'

'Not in rural Ibiza, no.'

'Well, they're LA's hottest power couple; they're practically joined at the hip.'

Suddenly Grace felt the music getting louder, the crowd pressing in.

'Listen, I'm going to the bar,' she said. 'Do you want anything?'

'Don't worry about me,' said Sarah. 'I've just spotted that guy Iftaka, the one who owns this place. I'll put in a good word for you!'

'Oh God, don't . . .' But Sarah was already tapping the stocky Arab on the shoulder.

Blushing, Grace headed in the opposite direction, suddenly remembering why she preferred her quiet farmhouse in Ibiza.

Alex had managed to give Melissa the slip. Not that he wanted to get rid of his fiancée exactly, but he wanted to tell Grace about their engagement privately, without Melissa making a big deal of it. He had no reason to break it to her gently, of course, but he felt she would appreciate hearing it from him, rather than reading about it in the papers.

He found Grace in the orangery, sitting on a marble bench sipping a glass of champagne. 'Guess who?' he said, coming up behind her and covering her eyes with the palms of his hands.

'Al Doyle. Rock and roll superstar,' said Grace with her throaty chuckle. 'I thought I saw you coming in.'

'It's still Alex to you, by the way,' he said, sitting down next to her. 'I haven't turned into a complete knob quite yet.'

'I wasn't suggesting you had.' She smiled.

'Here, give us a swig of your bubbly,' he said. 'I've got a throat like a badger.'

She covered the glass with her hand. 'Are you allowed?'

Alex rolled his eyes. 'Not you too. The person I came with is on a zero tolerance alcohol drive at the moment. Some health kick in time for the Oscars. It's all mung beans and green algae drinks.'

'The person you came with?' She smiled. 'Would that be your Hollywood girlfriend?'

He nodded. 'Yeah. Melissa's cool.'

'She was terrific in that film about the lost puppy.'

'Are you being sarcastic?'

'No! I'm the mother of two ten-year-olds,' said Grace. 'It kept them quiet for two hours on a flight to Parador.'

There was a moment's awkward silence.

'It's good to see you, Grace,' he said, nudging her. 'Haven't seen you in ages.'

'Two years.' She smiled slowly. 'But in Hollywood years that's probably about two minutes, right?'

'I'm surprised you're here,' said Alex. 'You know, because of the . . . Well, I never thought you and Sasha were particularly close.'

Grace shrugged. 'I could say the same thing about you.'

'Ah, well Melissa didn't actually tell me whose party it was until I got here.'

'I came willingly,' she said with a sheepish grin. 'Actually, Sasha told me you were coming and I thought that unless I went to Wembley or somewhere, it was my best chance of seeing you.'

'Hey!' protested Alex. 'I've been busy.'

'I know, I know,' teased Grace. 'Rock stars aren't allowed to use the phone.'

She looked around the orangery. 'So do you have body-guards lurking in the shrubbery?'

'Not tonight.' He smiled, a little sadly. 'In England, people still think of me as that bloke from Year Zero.'

'Come on, even I know you've had three number-one albums.'

Alex laughed. 'Hey, listen. This was all your idea. If you hadn't told me to go solo in Ibiza, I'd be living in some bedsit in Catford by now remembering the days when about five people knew I was the guitarist in some band no one can remember the name of any more.'

'Whatever happened to Year Zero anyway?'

'Drugs, cabaret, fatherhood, in that order,' said Alex. 'Jez, the singer, is still out there searching for his big break, although he's been dropped by his record company and I hear he's got badly into drugs, not that I'm one to talk. Gav is playing in a show band on the cruise ships and having the time of his life by all accounts. And Pete has gone into teaching and become the proud father to a baby girl called Isabelle. He's asked me to be godfather at her christening, would you believe?'

'Heavens,' laughed Grace. 'I guess Cool Britannia really is well and truly over.'

Alex shifted on the cold bench slightly. He knew he should tell her about the engagement, but it didn't seem like the right moment.

'So what about you?' he asked, playing for time. 'You still in Ibiza? I must come out and see you again, if the offer's open of course. I loved it out there.'

'I've been thinking of coming home, actually,' she said, looking at her hands. 'Not full time, just term-time, if I can get Joe and Liv into good schools over here. I want them to have the best of both worlds, and it would be good if they could spend more time with my mum, too.'

'You should come back,' said Alex. 'I think England agrees

with you; you seem back to your old self. Not that there was anything wrong with you in Ibiza,' he added quickly.

'Well it will give me the chance to give my photography a proper crack. There isn't much call for it in Ibiza beyond shooting another line of olive trees for *Condé Nast Traveller*.'

'Hey, why don't you take my picture?'

'What, now?'

'No, I mean do my album sleeve.'

She started laughing.

'I mean it,' said Alex. 'Those portraits at your house were amazing and my label have been talking about doing something black and white, gritty. They want me to be taken a bit more seriously.'

'As opposed to being a teenybopper adored by millions of teenage girls? Besides, you're too pretty to look gritty.'

'Well, the girls might not be so interested in me when I'm married.'

He watched as Grace's smile slipped temporarily.

'Married?' she said quietly.

Alex felt his neck flush with embarrassment. 'I proposed to Melissa tonight.'

'Congratulations,' she said warmly, clasping his hand. 'That's fantastic news.'

Alex surprised himself by feeling disappointment at her reaction. *What did you expect?* he thought angrily. *That she would break down and weep?*

'I mean we've only been going out five months; in fact it all kind of happened by accident,' he said nervously.

'You proposed by *accident*?'

'Don't ask. But it feels like the right thing to do, you know? She's good for me. Even the booze ban, and the mung beans and shit. It's good for me. Everyone needs someone who's good for them.'

She sighed. 'Tell me about it.'

'No men on the horizon for you, then?'

402

He'd already looked at her left hand, but her wedding ring was still on her right hand as it had been in Ibiza and there were no new rings there. With a sinking feeling, Alex realised he hadn't even thought of getting a ring for Melissa. *Must get down to De Beers tomorrow first thing*, he reminded himself.

'Well, I met Julian Adler at the bar,' said Grace. 'He invited me to an exhibition at the White Cube. Does that count as going to see his etchings?'

'Are you going to go?'

She shrugged.

'Well if you do, wear that dress,' he said, nodding at her inky-blue cocktail dress. 'You look lovely in it.'

'Maybe,' she said, glancing at her watch.

'Sorry, I didn't mean . . .' said Alex quickly, hoping he hadn't said anything stupid or egotistical.

'No, no, it's just I've got to get back to London. The kids are with a friend and I said I'd be back by midnight.'

Alex stood up and offered his hand. 'Come on then, Cinderella,' he said, leading her back towards the party. 'Let me give you my cell number. And let's stay in touch this time, shall we?'

'Of course. I don't want to miss out on a big Hollywood wedding.'

'It's going to be the party of the century!' he cried and she giggled.

'No mung beans, though.'

'No, no mung beans. Maybe that's what I'll call the album.'

He gave her his best smile, but when she turned to walk away, he could feel it slowly slipping from his face. And he stood there, not wanting to go back to the party, wondering why he felt so sad.

44

When she woke up the next morning, Sasha was disappointed to find she didn't feel any different, even if it was her thirtieth birthday. For many people she supposed three-zero was a big milestone, the end of youth or something equally traumatic, but she had felt grown up for a long time. She had her own multi-million-pound company and her picture was in glossy magazines all around the world. People knew who Sasha Sinclair was; in fact they wanted to *be* her. Still, she felt disappointed. Unfulfilled. But why? She had everything she could ever want. Lazily stretching her arms out, she realised what it was: there was no one next to her. She was alone.

Her bedside phone rang and she snatched it up.

'Happy birthday,' said a voice.

'Good morning, Robert,' she replied, smiling as she swung her legs out of bed and scrunched her toes in the deep cream carpet. 'Where are you?'

'I'm on Sloane Street, heading your way.'

Her heart gave a little jump; he was almost there. 'Just give me five minutes,' she said. 'I'll see you downstairs.'

She leapt in the shower, taking care not to wet her blow-dried hair, then pulled on the outfit she had carefully selected the previous afternoon before leaving for the party. Grabbing her leather overnight bag, she blew the apartment a kiss and ran out of the door. She knew she shouldn't be running down the steps, giddy with excitement that a man was coming to take her on a romantic day out. She was Sasha Sinclair, ball-breaking businesswoman and style icon. She didn't chase after men. And yet here she was, skipping across the road, swinging her bag, her day brightened by the man sitting in a silver 1960s Aston Martin. *Remember*, she thought. *You're calling the shots now*.

'Nice car, mister,' she said, climbing inside.

'Only forty of these ever made,' said Robert proudly. 'I like to take her out on special occasions.'

She touched his leg gently; he took his left hand off the steering wheel and squeezed her fingers.

God, what am I doing, falling head over heels with a married man? she thought to herself. She was thirty, after all. She didn't want to wake up alone every morning. *Not now*, she scolded herself. *Just enjoy your birthday*.

'So where are we going?' she asked.

He flashed her a smile. 'The coast.'

'I thought you were strictly a Côte d'Azur man.'

Robert shook his head. 'Today it's all about long pebbly beaches, ice cream and crabbing.'

'Crabbing?' She laughed. 'What do you know about crabbing?'

'I wasn't always an international playboy, you know,' he said. 'I went on horrible family seaside outings like everyone else.'

'You'll be taking me on a donkey ride next.' She grinned.

'Oh, I've got plans for that too,' he said with a wolfish smile.

On the open roads of Hampshire, Sasha wound the window down and let the breeze bring in the aromas of grass, flowers and wood smoke. It was a bright winter's day and the sky was the soft blue of a robin's egg. She wanted every weekend to be like this, not stolen afternoons in hotels. She wanted to wake up with him and kiss him in the street and sit on the sofa listening to music while he massaged her feet. But for now, on this lovely afternoon, all she wanted was what she had: Robert and her together, an adventure in front of them.

'You know what?' she said. 'I'm really . . .'

She never got to finish her sentence. At that moment, time seemed to slow and she could feel herself moving but could do nothing about it, as if she was floating above, tied to the windscreen like a child's balloon. She watched helplessly as the front of the car turned abruptly, swerving off the road, Robert desperately wrestling with the wheel. She could see the tension in his arms, the tendons standing out, the sudden left and right movements of his hands as they mounted an embankment. She saw the line of trees looming in front of them. And then she saw nothing.

When her eyes opened, blinking at the harsh fluorescent light, she was looking up at chipped polystyrene ceiling tiles. She felt a flutter of fear as she immediately realised she was in a hospital bed. She tried to move her arms, to sit up, but she felt pain in her chest and her head and her legs – everywhere.

'Don't try and move, darling.' She turned her head slightly to see her mother leaning over her, stroking her head. Her first thought was how she hated Carole seeing her like this.

'What happened?' asked Sasha weakly. 'The car . . .'

'Yes, you were in a car crash,' said Carole. 'But the doctors say you'll be fine. Just concussion, a couple of cracked ribs, a broken wrist and lots of bruising. You might have to be kept in overnight, but only for observation.'

'Where's Robert?'

Carole didn't say anything for a moment.

'I didn't know that you and he . . .'

'Where is he?' Sasha repeated.

Carole's eyes dipped to the floor and Sasha felt a flutter of dread.

'Robert has some very serious injuries,' she said. 'They don't think he was wearing his seat belt.'

Fragments of the morning came back into focus. Getting into the car, putting her belt on. Robert getting out of the car at a petrol station. Did he put his seat belt on? She couldn't remember. *Why can't I remember?* she thought angrily. Then: *I've got to go to him, be with him.*

She pulled her weak, bruised body up. 'Where is he?'

'Sasha, I'm not sure that's a good idea,' said Carole, putting a hand on her arm. 'His wife is here.'

She stopped and looked at her mother sharply.

'I guess you messed up again, Sasha.'

'What?' She felt like she had been slapped. 'I *messed up*?' she repeated.

'Well, it didn't work out with Miles, did it?' said Carole with a smug expression. 'And now you've been caught out with his father. You never could close the deal, could you?'

'Deals?' she hissed. 'Relationships are not deals, Mother.'

Carole laughed cynically. 'Well, perhaps you take after me more than I thought.'

At this moment, the idea of inheriting anything from her mother was a revolting thought. 'How on earth can you think we share anything?' she spat.

'Three years ago I was going to leave your father,' said Carole, a wistful look in her eyes. 'I met someone at the tennis club. Eddie owns Kingly Haulage and he has a beautiful house on the St George's Hill estate. He kept asking me to leave your father, but I put it off. First it was his birthday, then it was Christmas. And then he had the stroke. And of course I can't leave him now.'

Sasha snorted. 'I wouldn't put anything past you.'

She shuffled around the bed, heading towards the door.

'I only hope he's provided for you,' said Carole.

Sasha stopped. 'What do you mean "provided"?'

'In his will, of course.'

Sasha shook her head in disbelief. 'Just go, Mother.'

She walked down the corridor, feeling the aching in her chest and her legs. There was a livid green bruise on the back of her right hand and her wrist was in plaster. She desperately tried to remember what had happened, but all she could see was an image of a line of trees coming towards her. She turned a corner and at once she knew that Robert was in the room in front of her. A man in a grey suit was sitting in a chair outside reading a magazine. She had no idea who he was. An exec from Ash Corp. waiting for a meeting? Connie Ashford's driver? Her heart beat faster – was she still in there? The man stood up and walked towards her, his hands held up to stop her.

'I'm sorry, Ms Sinclair, you can't go in there.'

Sasha tried to dodge around him, but she was in no shape to get very far. 'I *have* to see him,' she said desperately, craning her neck to see in the window, but the blinds were down. 'Please, you don't understand,' she said. 'I was with him in the car. I have to see him.'

The man looked sympathetic, but he still shook his head and turned her around. 'His family don't want anyone near him. Especially you.'

'I'll be back,' she said defiantly, but allowed herself to be taken back to her bed. She lay down, feeling weak and shaky, squeezing her eyes shut to prevent the tears coming out. *I won't cry,* she thought to herself. She couldn't let them get to her, they couldn't keep her away from him for ever.

When she opened her eyes, she gasped. Miles was standing at her door.

'Don't you think you've done enough?' he said, his eyes cold.

Shame and fear rushed over her and she shivered. 'I love him,' she said quietly, only now daring to say the words she had never admitted to herself or Robert.

'Like you loved me?' he sneered. 'You were only interested in the money. You're just a cheap social-climbing whore.'

'I care for him!' she said, sticking her chin out. 'And he looked after me!'

'Oh, I'll bet he did,' said Miles, his tone mocking. 'But don't pretend you cared for him, you little slut. You have only ever cared about yourself.' He moved towards her, his hands curled into fists.

Terrified, Sasha leant over and grabbed the emergency alert button, yanking it out of the wall. An alarm began to sound.

'Help!' she shouted. 'Nurse!'

Miles smiled, his face full of cruel fury. 'Don't think this is over,' he said as he backed towards the door. 'You can kiss that precious little business of yours goodbye.'

'Get out!' screamed Sasha. 'Get out before I have you thrown out!'

Two male nurses came running in, but Miles had already gone.

'Are you OK?' asked one of them.

'Fine,' said Sasha, the tears finally rolling down her face. 'I'm just fine.'

Grace arrived at the hospital late. She had been in the air, flying back to Ibiza, when her mother had called her, leaving a message about the accident. She picked it up in the arrivals hall and headed straight for the booking desks to get a flight back to Heathrow.

'This is stupid, Mum!' whined Joseph. 'We just got off the plane!'

'Grandad Ashford isn't well, honey,' said Grace firmly, hastily writing fresh luggage labels for them all. 'We have to go back.'

Joe remained irritated rather than alarmed the whole flight back and Grace felt a stab of guilt at how remote from her parents the twins had become. She knew that it was a choice she had made for them and suddenly it felt very wrong.

It was eleven o'clock by the time Grace had dropped the children with friends and raced to the hospital. The corridors were eerily quiet as her heels clacked along them. Her father was lying motionless in his room, ghostly and wan in the weak light of the single lamp above his bed. It was only then that Grace could see how serious it was. All the way over she had been telling herself that he'd come away with cuts and bruises, maybe a fracture or two, but now ... now she could see her father was critical.

His mouth was covered by a plastic mask attached to a machine by a long rubber tube. A series of drips hung from a rack beside the bed. His arms, lying both sides of his body on the blue acrylic blanket, looked pale and old. Connie Ashford was sitting on a plastic chair by the bed. She looked tiny in the semi-darkness, her face in half-shadow. She stood up and gave Grace a sad embrace.

'He's going to be OK,' said Grace. 'He's going to be fine.'

But Connie's silence suggested otherwise.

'Do we know any more about what happened?'

Her mother told her what they had managed to piece together: Robert's Aston Martin had swerved off the road and ploughed into a tree. The crash alerted a farmer who called the ambulance and fire brigade, who had to cut both the passengers from the wreckage. Robert's injuries were extensive: a punctured lung and ruptured spleen plus spinal damage, the severity of which was unknown; various specialists were being flown in to treat him.

'Who was the passenger?' asked Grace, sitting down.

'That woman ...' said Connie, her voice cracking as she spoke. 'It was Sasha Sinclair.'

'Sasha?' Grace whispered incredulously.

Connie could barely manage a nod. 'I can't believe he took me to her party last night,' she said, her brow creased in confusion. 'I knew he was having an affair, of course. I always did. But I never thought for one moment it would be with *her*. She was Miles' girlfriend, for God's sake!'

Grace was amazed. She had always known Sasha was an operator and had therefore been surprised when she had let Miles slip through her fingers, but maybe that was because she had her eye on the bigger prize. Could she have been seeing Robert for that long?

'Is she here?'

'Not any more. She was admitted for a few hours but she's been discharged.' Connie let out another sob.

'Are you sure?' asked Grace gently. 'I mean are you sure that they were together? Dad had invested in her business, maybe they were going to a meeting . . . ?'

Connie shook her head sadly. 'There was a diamond bracelet for her in his jacket pocket. A birthday present.'

Grace squeezed her mother's hand sympathetically. 'Well, none of that matters now. All that matters is that he gets better.'

Connie nodded slowly, looking at her husband with red-ringed eyes. 'I need a walk,' she said, standing. 'I doubt the canteen is open but I'm sure there's a vending machine some-where.'

She closed the door behind her and Grace listened as her mother's heels retreated down the corridor. She turned back to her father, so still and small. Robert had always been an imposing man, someone to look up to, someone to fear. She couldn't actually remember ever doing normal father–daughter things with him like outings to the park or playing hide and seek. It was just accepted that Daddy had important work to do, that he was too busy to play and that birthdays and school prize days were difficult to schedule. In her early years at boarding school, Grace had kept a scrapbook of cuttings she had collected from the business and society pages of the news-papers: Daddy shaking hands with another man, Daddy going to a party, Daddy opening a new hotel. It was her version of a family photo album; Robert Ashford was never home long enough to have any photos with his children. In fact, now Grace thought about it, the only other time she could remember being alone with her father like this was when he had summoned her to his study to discuss her school report when it was anything other than a string of A's.

'I want the twins to know you, Dad,' said Grace. 'I don't want them to be strangers to you, like I was.'

She brushed at her face and was surprised to find a tear running down her cheek.

'It's never too late to start making amends, that's something I've only just learnt,' she said. 'If you can just stick around for a while longer, we can make a little time to be together, can't we? Nothing's more important than that.'

She reached out to touch his hand, lying there on top of the covers. It was so warm, so alive, but his face was so still and deathly.

'Did you hide the body?' she whispered, searching his face for a trace of movement, the slightest sign. 'I've always wanted to believe what you said about the boy leaving the island. But I never did.'

Grace had always clung to the idea that Robert had moved the body, hidden it, covered the whole thing up. She had never bought the story of the missing boy and the stolen boat. That boat boy had been dead. Her father was a powerful man – why wouldn't he make it all go away if he could? So for all these years she had directed her anger towards him, hiding her own shame at leaving the body by focusing on her father's corruption and arrogance. But sitting here, next to his frail body, she finally realised why he had done it: because he had been protecting his son. Miles had killed that boy and Robert had helped him. And Grace couldn't honestly say she wouldn't have done the same thing had it been Joseph or Olivia.

'Come back to us, Daddy,' she said through the tears. 'I understand now. I don't want you to be the bogeyman any more.'

She heard movement behind her and turned. Connie Ashford was standing there with two cups of coffee. Grace swallowed; how long had she been there? What had she heard? She quickly rubbed her face, embarrassed at her tears.

'Don't, darling,' said her mother. 'Don't be ashamed of loving your father.'

She put the coffee down and sat next to Grace, holding her hand. 'God knows, there are times when he didn't deserve it. I'll admit there are times when I hated him. Sasha is not the first by any means, even if she thinks she is.'

'Mum, I . . .'

Connie put a finger to her lips. 'You're a grown woman, Grace, and I'm so proud of how you've made a life for yourself. I don't know what we did to make you need to leave, but things are different now – *you're* different. I know it's a selfish thing to ask, but I want you to come home.'

Grace had been thinking about it, weighing up the options, knowing it would be good for the kids, maybe even good for her. But still she hesitated.

'I . . . I'm not sure, Mum,' she said. 'I'm not sure I'm ready.'

Connie looked into her eyes. 'If we waited until we were ready for everything, we would never leave the nest. Nothing's perfect in this life, Grace,' she said, looking at her husband's prone figure. 'But you have to take a chance and hope you're doing the right thing.'

Grace nodded, knowing she was right.

'Come back to us, Grace,' said her mother, holding her hand tight. 'We need you.'

413

45

Robert Ashford's funeral was held in the church in Sweeton village, just a couple of miles from the family estate. Mourners were ferried in by helicopter or blacked-out limousines and the pews were filled with celebrities, captains of industry, even members of the Cabinet. A military-trained security company had to be employed to keep the press and rubber-neckers from invading the area. At the request of the family, the service was kept short and solemn.

Connie quietly wept on Grace's shoulder in the church, but dried her eyes and held her head aloft as they walked out into the quiet graveyard. She was dignifed and elegant as she accepted the hushed words of condolence at the wake in the red drawing room of Ashford Park. Grace was impressed by how well she held herself together, considering the bottom had fallen out of her world. Grief was hard enough to deal with on its own – Grace knew that well enough – but her mother had an extra burden to shoulder: the pain and humiliation of the way in which Robert had died.

'Can I get you anything, Mum?' she asked, as the last of the mourners left. Connie looked tired and drawn, her eyes ringed with dark circles no make-up could hide.

'No thank you, darling,' her mother said, patting her hand. 'Everyone has been so kind. The trouble is everyone thinks they should talk to me, but no one knows what to say.'

Grace smiled. 'Well you let me know. I'm just going to speak to Miles.'

Her brother and his wife were standing by the long French windows leading to the terrace, each with a glass of white wine. Grace immediately sensed an atmosphere, as if they'd just been arguing.

'How's it going, sis?' said Miles, raising his glass.

'I've had better days, Miles,' said Grace.

Miles nodded and looked away. 'Mum seems to be bearing up pretty well, considering.'

'At least Sasha Sinclair had the decency to stay away,' said Chrissy. She was wearing a demure Chanel shift dress with a Hermès scarf round her neck. No one would have suspected that this woman had ever been out of the Home Counties, let alone spent years as an exotic dancer. Money and success had rubbed away her history like footprints on the beach.

'I don't think even Sasha would want that sort of publicity,' said Grace. Miles looked as if he was about to say something, then took a long drink of his wine instead.

'I see Alex Doyle sent flowers,' said Chrissy, trying to fill the awkward silence.

'That was kind of him,' said Grace.

'Mum says you're moving back to Britain?' said Miles abruptly.

'Yes, for the winter anyway. I'll see how it goes after that. How long are you staying?'

Miles scowled. 'I'm getting out of here as soon as humanly possible,' he said. 'Coming back here . . .' He trailed off and stared out of the window.

'The family lawyer is going to read the will after the wake, I hear,' said Chrissy with a little too much enthusiasm.

'Really?' said Grace. 'I hadn't heard.'

She caught Miles flashing her a warning look.

'Sod this,' he said, draining his glass. 'I'm going for a ride.'

'Ooh, that sounds good,' said Chrissy.

415

'On my own,' he said pointedly and stalked out of the room.

Miles rode the mare hard, her hooves sending clods of earth flying behind them. He followed the line of the river, jumping fences and fallen logs, then pushed her up the hill to the wood right on the edge of the estate, glorious in the bleak colour palette of winter. Having been based in New York for the last two years to oversee the American Globe clubs, he was glad to be back in England.

'Good girl,' he said, patting the horse's neck as he dismounted, tying her to a tree and letting her graze while he lit a cigarette and gazed out on to the vastness of the estate, a carpet of green, grey and heather. *All mine*, he thought with a twisted smile. *Well, maybe if I'd played it differently.*

Miles had thought about this day many times, the day his father would pass on. He had imagined he would feel triumphant and elated that he had just succeeded his father to the throne. Even though Robert had disinherited Miles, his father's death still made him head of the Ashford dynasty. The money would go to Connie, he supposed, but for Miles, Robert's death meant one thing: freedom. No one ever looked down on a reigning monarch and scoffed, 'Oh, well his father *gave* him that title.' Now the king was dead, Miles could finally escape his long shadow.

But Miles felt no note of victory, just an aching sadness that he had seen so little of his father over the last decade, that Robert had never acknowledged his success, never patted him on the head and said 'Well done'. Because Miles had never hated Robert Ashford, he had just wanted his recognition. All of his drive, all of his achievements had come from a desire to please his father. In fact now Miles could see that without his father's ultimatum over Chrissy that Christmas, he would probably have frittered his trust funds away like

Piers Jackson and all his other friends in London, earning a low-six-figure salary and living in a semi-detached house in Putney or Fulham.

He threw his cigarette away and snorted at the irony. Of all the things his father had done for him, his rejection had been his greatest gift.

'Thanks, Pops,' he said quietly.

He narrowed his gaze and saw another horse approaching from the house. He shook his head. It was just like Chrissy to go against his express wishes. But as the animal drew nearer, he could see that the rider was an expert: Connie Ashford.

'Mum?' he said, taking her horse's reins as she dismounted. 'What are you doing out?'

She pulled off her helmet and swept her ash-blond hair back from her face. She looked strangely calm and controlled.

'The other option is to stay wallowing in the house. I thought blasting the cobwebs out might help.'

'Are you OK?' he asked as he tied her horse up.

'Why shouldn't I be?'

Miles smiled. 'No reason,' he said.

Connie sat down on a fallen log and Miles joined her.

'So why are you out here?' she said after a while. 'Not another argument with Chrissy?'

Miles looked away. He hated how his mother seemed to be able to tap straight into his moods and thoughts. Some sort of maternal voodoo, he supposed.

'Do you know how much I hate Sasha Sinclair?' he whispered.

'Miles, let it go. It's not worth it.'

He closed his eyes, then opened them again, sweeping his gaze across the stunning rural vista. 'Do you think Dad ever came up here and looked at everything he had?' he said finally.

'Your father was very proud of you, you know,' said Connie.

Miles looked at his mother cynically. 'I think he made it

perfectly clear how he felt about me at your birthday party, Mum.'

'That was a long time ago, darling. A lot of things have changed since then.'

'You're not telling me he mellowed in his old age?'

'Not him, Miles. *You.* He watched you grow up and become a man. He would read about you in the papers and talk about how you should talk to this person about planning, or that bank about funding. He always knew where you were and what you were doing.'

Miles felt his heart lurch. Could it be true? Had his father really cared about his business? Had he really watched him make his way in the world? Miles felt a gnawing in his stomach and he looked away from Connie, turning his face to the sky. There was a pink cast to the clouds and it would be dark in less than an hour.

'You know our lawyer is coming to the house this evening?' said Connie.

'Ah yes, the will.'

'It's a big responsibility, Miles,' she said, looking at him sideways. 'The assets are considerable.'

'What's that got to do with me?'

'A great deal. I already know the contents of the will and I wanted to speak to you first.'

Miles laughed. 'Wanted to soften the blow, eh? Not even left me a pair of cufflinks?'

'No, Miles, he left you the business.'

Miles jerked backwards, almost losing his balance on the log. 'You . . . you're serious?' he stuttered. 'But we haven't spoken in over nine years.'

'That didn't mean he didn't love you, Miles. You were always his son. Ever since that first club, he's believed you were the best person to move the company on. He was just too proud to pick up the phone.'

Miles could barely take it in. It was an enormous undertaking. Ash Corp. was owned by a complex series of limited companies and trusts, but Robert Ashford had ultimately had control of all of them. The assets would run into billions.

He rubbed his chin nervously. 'I'm not sure I . . .' he began, but trailed off. 'It's so big a job,' was the best he could manage.

'Well, your father's shareholding has gone to you, but it doesn't mean you have to be CEO,' said Connie. 'Pete Stone could step up.'

Miles gave a short laugh. 'After the way he handled the PecOil merger last spring? I wouldn't trust his judgement.'

Connie smiled, obviously pleased that Miles had also been following Robert's fortunes in the business pages.

'I can't tell you what to do, Miles,' she said. 'I'm so proud of you, what you have done and if the Globe and your own business interests in America are your life now, then so be it. But I'd like you to come back to Ash Corp. Forget New York. I'd like you to come back to England.'

He raised an eyebrow. 'Both me and Grace, eh?'

'I'm not trying to use your father's death to emotionally blackmail you both, if that's what you're implying,' she said tartly.

'I didn't mean that,' he said, putting a hand out to touch her knee. 'I just . . . oh, I don't know what I meant. But I can't make a decision now, Mum.'

'I don't expect you to,' she said carefully. 'But this is what your father wanted, Miles. Come back and fulfil your promise.'

46

March 2002

The weeks after Robert's death passed by in a daze. The ferocity of her emotions had taken Sasha by surprise, her grief made worse by the fact that she had to face it alone. She could count on one hand the number of people who knew about her relationship with Robert, so most people assumed that her complete withdrawal from the business and the social circuit were due to the injuries she had sustained from the accident. There were whispers, of course. The death of one of England's most prominent businessmen had been a big story, but the Ashford PR machine had done a good job in containing the story. Only gossip linked her to Robert now, a thought that gave Sasha no comfort whatsoever.

'You have a visitor,' said Sally, her housekeeper, coming into the room and plumping the cushions. 'Lucian Grey.'

Sasha looked up from the copy of the *Financial Times* she had been reading on her table by the window.

'Thank you,' she said, fastening her silk robe tighter and limping through her apartment into the living room. She still had to use a stick to walk even short distances, but she could feel she was getting stronger every day. Somehow, that just added to her anger; it seemed like a betrayal of Robert that she could recover when he never would.

'Sasha, how are you feeling?' Lucian rose from the red velvet sofa to gently embrace her. An elegant sixty-year-old with four decades of experience in the fashion industry, he was fair and wise, with an instinctive fashion sense which was rare in a money man. Sasha had recommended him to the private equity house as a replacement for Philip when they had bought the company. He was one of the few people she trusted entirely.

'I'm getting there,' she said. 'You know I'm coming back in to work on Monday?'

'Are you sure?' he said with concern. 'I thought you'd been signed off for six weeks.'

'It's my company, Lucian,' she said firmly.

He didn't press the point and Sasha was grateful. It wasn't her body that needed to recover, but her heart, her mind. Sitting around in her apartment with only Sally and occasional visits from the physiotherapist, she had nothing to do but dwell on might-have-beens and she feared that if it went on any longer, she might not crawl out from under her black cloud. The truth was the company was the one thing in her life she could control. Yes, there were other forces at work – competitors, the economy – but it stood or fell by her own efforts, her own decisions. That was what she loved about it.

Sally brought in a tray of coffee and Lucian helped Sasha to the Venetian glass table, sitting opposite her.

'You know the press office have been swamped with interview requests for you,' he said. 'No one's saying it out loud, of course, but they all want the story on the crash. Everyone has heard the rumours.'

She groaned. 'That's the last thing I need.'

'You should do it,' said Lucian, reaching for the silver pot. 'A bit of notoriety never hurt anyone.'

'I don't want this to be painted as some of sort of Ted Kennedy at Chappaquiddick.'

'Don't underestimate the power of your lifestyle, Sasha,' said Lucian. 'I might be old, but I haven't lost my nose for this. I can't remember when there has been so much excitement for a growing business. You are our greatest asset; people look up to you. Handled in the right way, this can help us. This is tragedy, not notoriety.'

'I don't want to make money from Robert's death,' said Sasha bitterly.

Lucian shook his head.

'You're not; you're making money from your life, Sasha.' He took a sip of coffee and gave a small smile. 'And I think making money is something Robert would have approved of.'

She stared out of the window. 'You should know that Robert left me his shareholding in the US business in his will,' she said quietly.

'When will probate clear?'

'I don't know yet,' she said. 'As you can imagine, I haven't exactly got a hotline to the Ashford family any more.'

Lucian didn't smile. 'Well we need to get that moving as soon as we can,' he said urgently. 'Because Absolute Capital are looking to sell.'

Sasha looked up with alarm. 'Because of the accident?'

'No, because they've had their investment with us for four years and because they think it's the right time to exit.'

'Do you?'

She respected Lucian's opinion. He was tougher than Philip, although she missed the sense of a shared journey she'd had with Phil, that they'd built it up together. But Lucian knew business better and he didn't spare her feelings.

'Yes. It's absolutely the right time to sell. Share prices of luxury companies are rocketing. Plus celebrity is the new currency and you have it by the bucketload.'

Sasha thought of Robert and that evening in Canary Wharf when he'd first suggested getting private equity investment, how he'd told her he loved the way she took risks. It had been a risk ditching Ben, it had been a risk expanding into America. And it had been a risk loving Robert. But she had done it all and she was glad she had, even with all the pain it had caused.

'Let's do it,' she said, feeling some of her fire return. 'As soon as the shareholding comes through, let's sell.'

Lucian smiled. 'That's my girl,' he said.

Nine months later Rivera Holdings were taken over by another private equity company. The big fashion conglomerates of LVMH, Richemont and PPR had again refused to bite, but the one hundred and ten million sale price paid by Duo Capital more than made up for it. The agreement banked Sasha more than thirty million pounds, while also allowing her to keep hold of a small stake in the company and retain her position as president and creative director.

Steven Ellis, the new CEO installed by the owner of Duo Capital, was a sombre fifty-something Scot with sharp suits and even sharper business instincts, who had turned around a failing Swiss watch company and made it the horological must-buy for the new Russian money. He had a degree from Yale and an MBA from Insead, the French business school, and Sasha could tell from the minute she met him that he could do great things with her company. Six months later, after a few well-placed interviews and dozens of sessions of therapy, it was business as usual, the hole in her heart mended, a pile of party invitations on her desk. Sasha Sinclair was ready to face the world again. And this time, she thought, the world could take her as she was.

47

September 2003

Miles was enjoying being back in London. He walked to the window and peered out into the garden of his Notting Hill townhouse. The long sloping lawn was slightly unkempt and the rose beds were scattered with unraked leaves, but the very thought of having a garden made him smile. In New York you were lucky if you had a window box, but here you could smell flowers, hear birds, watch the changing seasons; he had forgotten how much he missed it. Since the growth of the Globe empire in the States, he had spent less and less time in England. He had a management team to deal with the Covent Garden club and gym while the concierge service was raking in hundreds of thousands with virtually no investment, but the real money had been in the States, where the Globe Country Club franchise was going stratospheric, with seven locations along with golf courses and spas. But that was nothing compared to the global reach of Ash Corp.

Sitting down at his heavy wooden desk – an antique the dealer had assured him had come from one of the Duke of Wellington's residences – Miles flipped through a file showing all the businesses Robert Ashford had owned or had a significant interest in. There were literally hundreds, based in hundreds of cities around the world. Miles shook his head with dismay as he ran his eyes down the list. Alongside the manufacturing and commercial property wings, Ash Corp. owned a dry-cleaning chain, a business card supplier and a haulage firm which specialised in frozen goods. Frankly, it was a sprawling mess. Robert Ashford had been a shrewd investor, no question of that – and individually, Miles felt sure that most of these businesses would turn a good profit – but such a wide spread of interests had made Ash Corp. flabby and unfocused. Somewhere along the line, Robert Ashford had taken his eye off the ball.

Possibly around the time he started screwing my ex-girlfriend, Miles thought bitterly. But then again, the evidence in front of him suggested the old man's brains had been going soft long before that affair began.

The problem was that Ash Corp. hadn't moved with the times. In the sixties and seventies, Robert Ashford had built an empire by taking a series of calculated risks coupled with some audacious yet well-timed takeovers. He quickly gained a reputation as someone who could sniff out trends and capitalise on them. In the early eighties he had seen the need for out-of-town supermarkets; the experts had derided it as fool-hardy, but he had been right.

So what went wrong? wondered Miles, reaching over for a decanter of Scotch and pouring himself a generous measure. Clearly his father had been resting on his laurels for the best part of a decade. Yes, Ash Corp. had a number of other prof-itable divisions, but they were stodgy, meat and potatoes oper-ations; nothing creative, nothing exciting. Miles turned to the section dealing with the hotel division. Ash Corp. owned a number of hotel chains and resorts in all the best locations – the Bahamas, Hawaii, the French Alps – but they were old-fashioned and fusty, appealing to an ageing clientele, while the young money was going to the new rash of funky boutique hotels. People wanted stylish, they wanted modern, they wanted to feel that they were part of a select elite. They didn't want a snooty manager in pin-stripe trousers looking down his nose at them because they didn't have a title. The Ash Corp. hotels – and indeed the rest of the company – desperately needed to be stripped right back and rebuilt from the ground up. And that was why Miles felt that London was the perfect place to begin restructuring. Since he had opened the first Globe Club ten years ago, London had transformed from a moderately important if bustling city into the most exciting city in the world. You could feel the energy in the boardrooms, the nightclubs, even the arrivals lounge at Heathrow. Cool Britannia was over, but it had left behind a vapour trail of talent and wealth. Rag-trade billionaires, restaurateurs, a melting pot of Italians, South Africans, Swiss, Indians and Americans. It was the most exciting time to be in London in decades, and Miles was right at the centre of it all, in charge of one of the biggest international corporations in the capital.

He tossed the file on to the desk and walked towards the marble staircase. He and Chrissy had moved into the five-storey white stucco townhouse just off Portobello Road in May. It had an outside hot tub, basement gym and six bedrooms; to be honest, it felt too large for them except when they entertained. He climbed up to the master bedroom on the third floor, looking at his watch. He and Chrissy were due to catch the Eurostar to Paris that night for a meeting with a hotelier interested in running the Globe concierge service as a franchise.

'Chris?' he called. 'You up here?'

The bedroom had deep cream carpets and a huge oval bed covered in olive-green silk, but the room was dominated by a Marlene Dumas painting of a naked woman on all fours. He walked past it and through to the en suite bathroom, a white-tiled wet room with twin showers and a huge white marble bath. Chrissy was lying in it, swathed in bubbles, her face almost obscured by the rising steam.

'Hi, lover,' she smiled, lifting a hand and blowing a cloud of froth towards Miles.

'We need to talk,' he said, sitting on the edge of the bath and trailing a hand in the water.

'Too right we do,' said Chrissy. 'We have a problem with Martin.'

Miles smiled to himself. While he got to grips with the spidery Ash Corp. structure, he had handed the running of the Globe business over to Chrissy and she was ruthlessly pruning the dead wood from the London club.

'What's he done?'

'It's what he's not done,' said Chrissy before rattling off a long list of complaints.

'So fire him.'

'I already did. I poached the deputy manager from the Lanesborough – young, ambitious, efficient, plus he's taking a pay cut to come across to the Globe. It's a win-win.'

Miles nodded grudgingly. Lately his relationship with Chrissy had been going downhill fast. Everything she did seemed to annoy him – the way she said 'sat' instead of 'sitting', her fixation with soap operas – in fact, some days he could barely stand to be in the same room as her. But when it came to the business, she was indispensable. She was tough, clever and one of the few people Miles could trust to give it to him straight.

'I've been going through the Ash Corp. structure,' said Miles. 'Can you believe my dad bought a dry-cleaning chain?'

'Well, I do need someone to do my cashmere,' she smiled.

Chrissy had come a long way since her skin-tight minidresses and stilettos when they were first married. She now had accounts at most of the shops between Sloane Square and Knightsbridge and an entire bedroom off the main suite as a giant walk-in wardrobe.

'The whole thing needs slashing back,' said Miles. 'It's like the old man wasn't living in the modern world.'

'Well let's start with what you can fix: off-load the best stuff, shut down the rest. Then you need to look at the worst areas and fire everyone not pulling their weight.'

'You can't fire everyone,' he said, rolling his eyes.

'Well where are the weak spots?' asked Chrissy, reaching out a suds-covered arm for a sponge.

'The hotels division is a mess.' Miles sighed.

Chrissy snorted. 'The problem is no one wants to go there,' she said. 'Remember Cannon Bay?'

'How could I forget?'

Cannon Bay was a five-star hotel resort on the French side of St Martin in the Caribbean. They had gone to St Martin to inspect a golf course complex when they were planning to extend the Globe Country Club franchise earlier that year. As Cannon Bay was the most exclusive resort on the island and an Ash Corp. hotel, they had booked a suite from curiosity. It had been awful. The staff were unfriendly, the food was bland and the paint was peeling. When Chrissy politely complained to the manager, he told her she was 'lucky to stay here'. Chrissy had replied, in her sweetest, poshest voice, that he was lucky to keep his teeth. He was the first Ash Corp. employee they had fired.

'Our spies are telling us that it's the same in all the hotels. Old-fashioned, stuck-up and wasteful.'

'Made in the image of their owner, darling,' said Chrissy.

He frowned. Chrissy had good reason to hate his father, that was true, but he felt uncomfortable when she criticised Robert.

'The good thing is that the hotels are all in great locations,' said Chrissy, oblivious to Miles' annoyance. 'It's much easier to revamp an interior than to build from scratch.'

'Hmm . . .' said Miles. 'But how to revamp them? We don't want to lose the old clientele.'

'Bollocks to the old clientele,' snapped Chrissy. 'What have you always told me? You have to be bold. We should be

428

offering luxury right across the whole division for every different taste.'

She was exactly right, of course. There was no reason why they couldn't vary what was offered: some small and exclusive, some catering for the business travel and conference market, but all adhering to one trusted brand manifesto: 'spend your money here and you'll get the very best'.

Chrissy pulled the plug with her toes and stood up, pulling a towel from a heated rail behind her. Miles felt his heart give a little thump as he watched her dry herself. She still had the power to arouse him, not that he had acted upon it for a long time. Too much energy required elsewhere.

'I've actually been thinking about this,' said Chrissy, wrapping herself in a robe. 'Ashford Hotels needs a flagship, the one place that embodies everything we stand for – unattainable luxury you can attain.'

Miles chuckled. 'Snappy tag-line. Do you mean like a super-hotel?'

'Not a hotel, a resort,' she said, her excitement visible on her face. 'What says total luxury better than your own private island, like Branson does with Necker or David Copperfield has with Musha. White sands, palm trees, blissful isolation.'

The smile on Miles' face faded. He knew her well enough to realise where she was going with this.

'Angel Cay still belongs to my mother, Chris.'

'But can't we buy it from her? We could create the world's most luxurious island resort.'

'Let's just leave Angel Cay out of this, shall we?'

'What's the matter, Miles?' she said, allowing her irritation to show. 'Why do you hate talking about the island? Why do you change the subject whenever I mention we go?'

He looked at her sharply. 'Because I don't want to go and waste two weeks on a bloody desert island. That's not how empires are built, Chrissy, and you know it.'

She shook her head. 'I think we need to go, Miles.'

'Why?'

'Because all we seem to do these days is row. I for one wouldn't mind two weeks on a desert island. Just me and you. It could be our second honeymoon.'

He glanced at his watch. 'I've got to go. I've got a conference call in ten minutes. Sorry, Chrissy. We'll take this up another time.'

Miles stared out of the taxi window as the cab drove through the Paris streets towards the Seine. It was almost 6 p.m., but he and Chrissy had only just left their lunch meeting at Chez le Anges. It had gone well; François Bernard, the French billionaire who owned some of the finest hotels in Europe and spoke his own version of Franglais, had loudly proclaimed Miles a 'fucking genius', causing every head to turn their way. In fact, the Globe pitch had been Chrissy's idea, not that he was going to tell François that. She had suggested that the Globe concierge service could be used as a sort of super-butler for François' high-rolling clients, being put at their disposal before and after their visit to arrange transport, prepare the room, ensure the best seats at the opera and the best tables in restaurants, then make sure their onward journey went just as smoothly, checking that their luggage, shopping and business documents were waiting for them when they arrived at their next destination. It would be like having your own Jeeves-style manservant – albeit for a limited period. It was exactly the sort of thing they planned for the Ashford hotels, only this deal was infinitely more profitable, as Miles had negotiated that François would sub-contract the service, allowing them to take a percentage of every outlandish request, plus he would pay a licensing fee to use the Globe name, giving the brand increased visibility and cachet.

Miles looked across at his wife, looking chic and relaxed in Chanel. He had been nervous about handing the Globe over to her, but he had to admit he had underestimated her once again. Not even Miles could run both Ash Corp. and Globe simultaneously, so it made sense to delegate the smaller operation, but he had an emotional attachment to his 'baby'. *Even babies have to go out into the world sometime*, he thought.

'Are you pleased with me?' Chrissy asked.

'Yes, I'm pleased with you,' he said, kissing her.

'Good, because you're going to love how I plan to celebrate.'

'Where are you taking me, exactly?' he asked, peering out of the window as they passed Le Garnier Opera.

Chrissy smiled and tapped the side of her nose. 'You'll see. And stop looking at your watch. We need a night off, Miles; since you took over Ash Corp., you've been working practically non-stop.'

'I said I'd call Bill Loxley,' said Miles impatiently, name checking the general manager of the London Globe. 'And we need to discuss your plans for expanding the clubs into Europe.'

'See?' said Chrissy. 'You can't stop for a minute, can you? And I'm sure Bill would rather go home and watch *Eldorado* than speak to you.'

Finally the taxi stopped outside a hotel in the Fifth. Miles peered out of the window, frowning. It was a pretty but slightly run-down area with narrow streets and old-fashioned streetlamps. There were a few bars and brasseries with awnings and neon signs which reflected down into the streets, shiny and treacle black from the earlier rain.

'What is this?' said Miles, looking up at the hotel dubiously. It was shabby chic personified; a crumbling beau monde frontage with double-glass doors. 'Are you proposing to buy this too?'

'No, silly,' smiled Chrissy, hooking her arm though his and leading him inside. 'This is the surprise.'

Miles watched his wife speak to the manager in fluent French and the old man handed her a key.

'Is this a joke?' he hissed as they stepped inside the old-fashioned wrought-iron cage of the lift. 'Give me thirty seconds and I can call the Crillon and see if the penthouse is available.'

'It's not a joke,' said Chrissy, pulling open the concertina lift gate and leading him towards a pair of dark wood doors. Inside, it was like a miniature version of the king's chamber at Versailles. A huge four-poster bed with turned gold-leaf uprights and red, dusty velvet drapes. Gold plaster cherubs surrounding a large oval mirror and a cracked crystal chandelier. Chrissy stripped off her coat and dropped it on a chair.

'What are you doing?' said Miles.

'What do you think?' she said, a sexy smile on her face. 'We have dinner booked at a little brasserie just around the corner at eight. But first ...' She slid her hand inside his jacket and began to unbutton his shirt, planting a kiss on his neck.

'In this shit-hole?'

She moved behind him and slid off his cashmere overcoat. 'It's romantic,' she whispered into his neck.

'It's revolting,' said Miles, looking at the bed and feeling his skin begin to itch. She pulled down the shoulders of her dress and let it slide down her lithe body. Underneath she was wearing a black push-up bra and stockings and suspenders – no panties. She was slim, boyish, with breasts he could cover with the palm of his hand. Holding his gaze as she moved, she slid down his body and unbuckled his trousers, reaching inside for his cock.

'We are a team, honey,' she whispered. 'In life, in business, in bed.'

She took him into her mouth and he gasped. It had been so long since they had done anything sexual, but then it had

432

been so long since he had felt a hint of the sexual chemistry he remembered from those heady days in Thailand.

She gently pushed him towards the bed and straddled him, pushing herself down on him, hot and wet.

'Oh God,' he moaned, falling back on to the bedcover.

'Relax, honey, just relax,' she whispered, undoing her bra and letting her hard nipples skate over his chest. 'Imagine we're back in Patong,' she breathed into his ear. 'We're in my little flat. We didn't get out of bed for days. We *fucked* and *fucked*.'

Miles tried to remember; he tried to send himself back to that hot, cramped apartment, to that time when they had been so happy, so together. She was grinding herself down on him now.

'Come on,' she gasped. 'Fuck me.'

But he couldn't. Suddenly he knew it was all wrong, and his erection ebbed away and slipped out of her.

'I'm sorry, Chris,' he said, pushing her off and quickly pulling his trousers back up. 'I'm tired, tense. There's too much stress at the moment.'

He looked back at her, sprawled on the bed, hugging her arms around herself protectively, her eyes hurt and pleading. It was the first time he could remember seeing her look vulnerable.

'I'm going out,' he said quietly.

'Fine,' she snapped, putting her clothes back on.

'Don't be like that, Chris. I just need some space.'

He got dressed and went out on to the street, where a taxi took him into the Marais. He was angry, frustrated and couldn't even put his finger on why. Wandering the back streets, he found himself at a club which, from the clientele hanging around outside, he guessed would suit his needs. He turned and stepped inside, looking forward to an anonymous Frenchman finishing off the job that Chrissy had started in bed thirty minutes earlier.

48

September 2003

'Do you think this is too daggy for school?' asked Olivia, looking at herself in the mirror. She was wearing tight jeans, a candy-striped T-shirt and hot-pink baseball boots.

'I know you don't have to wear uniform, Liv,' said Grace, 'but it's still school, not a fashion show.'

'I've got to look good on my first day, haven't I?' said her daughter. 'I bet you were the same.'

Grace frowned; now she thought about it, she couldn't actually remember. She had blocked out so much of her early years; some parts had been completely erased from her memory. Maybe it was just the strain of the day, she thought as she looked at her watch for the third time in as many minutes.

Where is Julian? she thought, walking to the window. *Calm down, Grace,* she told herself. *It's not the end of the world.* But it felt like it. Ever since she had left Parador, Liv and Joe had been her world, the reason she got up every morning. And now they were leaving for Danehurst, she felt as if she was waiting for a hospital operation. She'd have much preferred them to go to a local day school near their new home, a farmhouse on her mother's Oxfordshire estate. But the twins had been adamant that they wanted to go to Danehurst.

'It looks amazing, Mum!' Olivia had said when they had got the school prospectus. 'I can't believe you and Uncle Miles both went there.' Grace suspected her daughter was secretly rather more impressed that Sasha Sinclair had gone to Danehurst. Since their meeting at Freya's wedding, Olivia had taken out a subscription to *Vogue* and had declared her intention of becoming an 'international brand' like Sasha. Of course the children had not been told of Sasha's involvement in their grandfather's death, but Grace still found it galling that Olivia should regard her as such a role model.

She looked over at Joseph, dark-eyed and moody, the perfect image of his father. He was leaning over his trunk – the same one Miles had taken to Eton almost twenty years ago – rummaging inside with one hand while holding his neatly written checklist in the other. Joe was the one she worried about. He was much quieter than Liv, more serious and deep, but with a dry sense of humour. Olivia on the other hand, currently letting Connie take her bags to the car while she read a magazine, was very much her father's daughter. Beautiful, charming, flamboyant, a little egocentric. She would do fine.

Outside the farmhouse a horn pipped.

'That must be Julian,' Grace said, jumping up. 'Now are you sure you don't mind if he takes us all to the school?'

'Don't be silly, Mum,' said Olivia, still flicking through her magazine. 'We like Julian and we're glad you've finally found someone who can put up with you.'

'I know, darling,' said Grace, stroking her daughter's hair. 'But it's your first day at school and it should be your dad taking you ...'

'Mum, we're *eleven*!' said Olivia. 'We understand what's happened. Loads of parents get divorced, it's no big deal.'

435

She got up and hugged Grace. 'Julian's nice and Dad lives on the other side of the world. What more do you need?'

Grace laughed. Getting relationship advice from her eleven-year-old daughter now!

'Anyone want to go to school?' shouted Julian from downstairs.

Grace and the children came downstairs into the farmhouse's chalky pink living room.

'I found a load of boxes outside, so I put them into the car,' smiled Julian, ruffling Joe's hair affectionately. 'I hope they're yours?'

'Hey, not the hair!' said Joe, dodging him and sloping outside.

'Sorry, I forgot. You need to look gorgeous for all the girls. Talking of which . . .' He grabbed Grace and drew her close, kissing her on the lips.

'Eww,' said Olivia, pushing past. 'Get a room!'

Grace's relationship with Julian Adler had started slowly in the weeks after Robert's death. He had sent her a large bouquet of lilies with his condolences and a note reading: 'The one time people leave you completely alone is when you're standing in front of paintings. If you ever need peace and quiet, just call.'

The first time she called, he had given her a very personal tour of his exhibition. He had been funny and engaging, but he had also given her space. So she had called again, just for a coffee, which had led to dinner, which had led to . . . Well, eighteen months later, she found she couldn't imagine a time when he hadn't been there. He was part of her motivation for moving back to England full-time and his energy and *joie de vivre* were exactly what she needed to pull her out of her grief. She had lived with a creative man before, of course, but life with Julian was the direct opposite to the cloying, monitored, cosseted existence of Parador. Together they travelled to New York, Rome, Moscow, even the northern reaches

436

of Finland, where they had swum in lakes under the midnight sun and camped in a teepee made of reindeer skin. He was a media darling – invited to everything – and he took her to showbiz parties: premieres, gallery openings and wild soirées in boho lofts belonging to artists. Having lived a very gentle existence in Ibiza for eight years, he made her feel bolder, stronger, which was precisely why she needed him at her side today.

They squeezed everything into Julian's Jeep and Connie came to wave them off. Looking out of the back window, Joe nudged Grace.

'I guess this is it, huh, Mum?' He smiled.

'I guess this is it,' said Grace. It was time to go back to her past.

The drive from Oxfordshire to West Sussex took less than two hours. As their car pulled through Danehurst's stone gates, two decades seemed to melt away. In many ways the pupils and parents gathered around the front doors counting suitcases and kissing goodbye didn't look that much different from when she had first started at the school back in 1980. The clothes were a little different, but there was the same polish and confidence in both generations, although there were more obvious signs of money now: the black helicopter by the tennis courts and the stacks of matching Louis Vuitton luggage. There was even a gold Hummer belonging to an LA rapper who was sending his son for an English education. It had always been a creative, media school, smiled Grace, watching Joe's awed expression as he saw the car.

Grace crunched across the gravel drive to embrace an old woman wearing a stiff tweed suit. 'Still here, I see, Miss Lemmon.' She smiled.

'Just about,' said the head teacher. 'I'm finally retiring next year.'

The formidable Miss Lemmon had been a source of considerable fear for the pupils of Danehurst, but holding her shoulders now, Grace couldn't believe how small and fragile she was.

'Is that Julian Adler?' she whispered, looking behind Grace.

'My boyfriend, I'm afraid,' said Grace, a little embarrassed.

'How exciting! Get him to doodle on a school programme before he leaves. We've got a charity auction coming up in a few weeks' time; might raise enough for a new roof for the library.'

'Oh, I'm sure we can do better than a few doodles,' said Grace, suddenly remembering the hours she had spent in that self-same library looking at books on Greek sculpture and laughing at the willies.

'You're in the creative arts yourself, I believe?' said Miss Lemmon. 'I always thought you'd become a writer, but I saw your portraits of that Peruvian tribe in the *Sunday Times* the other week and thought they were quite wonderful.'

'Yes, it's all starting to work out,' Grace replied modestly.

'You're a photographer with two wonderful children, turning up with one of the world's greatest living artists. I'd say that was a little better than working out, Grace Ashford. And how's your brother these days? He seems to be doing well if the papers are anything to go by. I believe you also knew Alex Doyle and Sasha Sinclair? The pupils get very excited when they hear those two are ex-Danehurst.'

Grace gave a thin smile. 'Well, I think I'd better sneak off while the twins aren't looking,' she said. Across the driveway, they were both talking excitedly with other children. 'But do keep a watchful eye on Olivia. She can be a handful.'

'They always are, Grace.' The headmistress smiled. 'Give me the girl of eleven and I'll give you the woman.'

'That's what I'm afraid of,' said Grace.

Julian drove back, sitting in silence as Grace wept, waiting for the storm to pass.

'Sorry, darling,' said Grace finally as she wiped her face and blew her nose. 'It's been quite a day all in all.'

He squeezed her knee. 'Don't worry, I've got something to take your mind off it.'

'What is it?' asked Grace.

'You'll see.'

He took a detour around some smaller B roads, cutting across country back towards Oxford, driving through pretty chocolate-box villages and leafy glades. They pulled off the road and proceeded down a long winding drive, flanked with lime trees, which seemed to go on for ever. Grace could see no clues as to what this place might be. Not a farm – too well kept; not a big hotel – no golf buggies or helpful signs 'to the Spa'.

'It's massive,' she said when she finally saw the stately home in front of her. A huge high-gothic mansion complete with castellations and stained-glass windows. 'Very Brideshead,' she added appreciatively.

'At the risk of sounding like a geek, Brideshead was actually filmed at Castle Howard in Yorkshire,' said Julian, pulling up a little way from the front. 'But Stockbridge Hall was designed by the same architect. It's Grade I listed, naturally. Thirty-five thousand square feet of space.'

'Well, I think it's a work of art.'

Julian grinned. 'I'm glad you said that,' he said.

'Why?'

'Because I've bought it.'

She laughed with surprise. 'What?'

'Why not?' he said, shrugging.

'Well for one thing, look at it.' She giggled. 'It's like the Taj Mahal. It isn't just a house, it's a national monument. It's not the sort of thing you buy on impulse, like a pair of shoes.'

'I did give it some thought,' he said, reaching into the glove compartment for some papers.

'I can see you've got a plan.' She laughed.

They got out of the car and took in the lazy September sun spilling across the honey-stone façade.

'I thought this could be a project. Our project,' he said putting his arm around her shoulder.

'Our project?' she said.

'We should renovate it together,' he said, unfolding the paper he was carrying and spreading it over the Jeep's bonnet. It was a set of blueprints for the revamp. 'I thought that whole east wing would be perfect as a gallery for my work and for other artists,' he said, pointing to the plans. 'We could make it as important as Tate Modern. I thought you could look after the living quarters. Add those girlie little touches you're so good at.'

'Hey!' she said, punching him on the arm. 'But this will take years, won't it?'

'Not that long. Besides, as it's closer to the kids' school, you could see them at weekends.'

She threw her arms around his neck and kissed him.

He lifted her up on to the bonnet of the car, standing between her legs.

'So what are you suggesting?' she asked playfully.

'That we move in here together when it's completed. What do you say?'

He slid his hand up the back of her T-shirt and pulled her closer, rubbing his crotch against hers.

'Not here, Julian,' she whispered, glancing around.

'Why not here?' He smiled, now pushing his hand up her skirt. 'No one's looking. Listen – silence.'

He was right. No sight of anyone, anything around them, except the looming shape of the house. And no sound, particularly no lively children's chatter from the back seat. It was strange, but at the same time oddly liberating.

'Grace, relax,' he murmured into her ear. 'Remember you're not just a mother. You're a woman too.'

And as he slipped his fingers inside her panties, feeling her wetness, dipping inside her, she groaned in pleasure. And she knew she had finally come home.

49

March 2005

From the twenty-fifth floor, Las Vegas lost some of its glamour. Standing at the window of the Ash Corp. Vegas office, Miles could see the whole of the Strip and much of it looked like a building site. At night, when the neon and the funfair fantasies of the castles and the pirate ships were all lit up, Las Vegas still looked like a Day-Glo rollercoaster of fun and sin, but in the harsh desert sunshine, you could see behind the façades and hotel fronts and it just looked dusty and a little forlorn.

'So where are we up to with buying the Aladdin?'

He turned back to face Michael Marshall, the American attorney he had appointed to oversee Ash Corp.'s commercial property interests, including the acquisition of a Las Vegas casino. The lawyer was a serious-looking man in his thirties with a straight nose and dark eyes.

'I'll be frank, Miles. I don't think it's going to happen,' he said.

Miles frowned. Since he had taken over his father's company, he had become used to the marketing speak and double-talk of the business world. Everything was 'in the pipeline' or being 'run up the flagpole'. They hid behind bland clichés either because they didn't know what they were doing, or because they didn't want to tell the boss that they couldn't give him what he wanted.

'That's not what I want to hear, Michael,' said Miles.

'I appreciate that,' said Marshall. 'But the facts are clear. Las Vegas is essentially a closed shop of Nevada-based investors creating a front for a number of well-connected syndicates and individuals, the biggest of which being the Mormons, who own most of the land out here. In short, the people who own Vegas don't want you here – and you can sympathise.'

'Sympathise?' said Miles. 'Whose side are you on, Marshall?'

The young lawyer gave a slight smile. 'It's nothing personal, Miles. It's pure economics. Why allow an international player of Ash Corp.'s size and financial muscle on to the Strip? You're only going to take money away from them, especially given your own personal reputation for reinventing the wheel.'

Miles nodded. It was true: he was becoming a victim of his own success. His overhaul of the Ash Corp. hotel group had been a triumph. He had sold off the dead wood, then broken the remaining hotels down into groups – prestige, business and affordable – rebranded them and given all a complete refit from the bathroom tiles to the entertainment systems. It had cost the company hundreds of millions, but it had been a shrewd investment. Now people knew what they were getting from an Ash Corp. hotel: quality and value for money, even if they were staying in the James hotel chain at the budget end of the scale. At the top end of the market, the hotels were winning awards for unparalleled service and the interiors were being featured in design magazines. In the space of a year, Miles had doubled capacity and trebled the turnover. No wonder the Las Vegas establishment were reluctant to allow him free rein in their own personal playground.

'OK, so what's the big stumbling block?' he asked, sitting down at his desk.

'Two things: construction and licensing. The gaming commission are raising questions about Ash Corp.'s experience in this sector.'

'We have gaming experience,' said Miles. 'Don't they know we own The Laing?' He knew it was a weak argument. The Laing was an old-school gentlemen's casino in Mayfair catering to high-rolling Middle Eastern sheikhs and the Euroaristo circuit. It was chic and discreet and it made huge profits, but it was a world away from the large-scale walk-in casinos of Las Vegas.

'With respect, The Laing is a very different animal to say Caesars Palace, or the MGM. It's rather like comparing Le Gavroche to Pizza Hut.'

'So we buy in experience,' said Miles. 'We poach someone from Caesars or Steve Wynn's outfit.'

Marshall nodded. 'Already done. We have the general manager from Mandalay Bay to head up the team when we're ready to move and he's agreed to come on board as a consultant when we go in front of the gaming commission.'

'Good. I don't want to let this one slip through the net.'

The US was in the middle of a huge economic boom, but history told Miles that where there was a boom, bust wouldn't be too far behind. But a Las Vegas casino was as close as you could get to a recession-proof business: when times got hard, people wanted to gamble.

'How important is this to you, Miles?' said Marshall. 'Because it's going to take some, uh, shall we say, fancy footwork.'

Miles liked this man. He had only met Marshall twice before: once to sign off on his appointment, once to thrash out the initial approach to the gaming commission, but it was clear he was exactly the kind of man Miles needed in his organisation. Someone entirely focused on getting the job

444

done, overcoming the obstacles by whatever means necessary. He also liked him on another level: Marshall was good-looking and energetic. Miles briefly allowed himself to imagine a scenario, then pushed it away. *Back to business,* he smiled to himself as the lawyer brought out a file.

'What do you have there?'

'A proposal for the casino project. I've done some initial projections, and to cut to the chase, getting blackballed in Vegas might be a blessing in disguise. Nothing is cheap in Vegas at the best of times and construction costs here are insane. I'm projecting one point five billion US – and that's conservative.'

'Jesus,' said Miles. Even for a company of the size of Ash Corp., that was an enormous investment, more so when you considered they were putting all their eggs in one basket. But Miles hated being told 'no' and he hated being blackballed even more. He looked at Marshall. 'Tell me about this fancy footwork of yours.'

Marshall paused for a moment. 'My gut feeling is we're banging our heads against a brick wall with the commission. Plus, none of the existing casinos are going to approve of us building a rival right next door to them, especially with the Wynn just opening.'

'Agreed. So what do we do?'

'It's a little left field, but I think it can work. We already have a hotel in Vegas – we remodel that.'

The Las Vegas James hotel was part of an old low-end Ash Corp. hotel chain, more of a motel-cum-flophouse jammed between the Stardust and the Frontier, two of the more run-down casinos at the north end of the Vegas Strip, away from all the glitz and glamour of the newer casinos such as the Bellagio and the Luxor to the south. Miles pulled a face.

'The James hotel is a stinker, Michael. It's in the wrong part of town. We can't even get the fifty-dollar-a-night slot machine crowd in there.'

'That's where the left-field idea comes in,' said the lawyer. 'We forget the casino and concentrate on the hotel. Do what you do best, high-end luxury. Make it exclusive and hard to get in.'

'But we're missing the point of the exercise,' said Miles. 'The money is in the gamblers. The casino can make a million dollars on one spin of the wheel.'

'And you can lose it too,' said Marshall. 'OK, so a hotel isn't going to make that sort of money, but we have the space for a six-hundred room all-suite hotel, and if we establish it as *the* place to stay on the Strip . . .'

'But why would the high-rollers stay so far from the action?'

'That's your job, Miles. No one is better at persuading people that your establishment is the only place to be.'

Miles nodded. 'OK, but even so, it's still a wasteland up there.'

Marshall smiled. 'The big guns are moving north, they have to. Trump is looking in the north end and Wynn's already there. If those guys are there, it's on the money. Plus there's even talk of a huge retail park.'

'How do you know?'

Marshall shrugged modestly. 'I've seen some development plans, heard a few rumours. It's my job, Miles. It's one of the things you pay me for.'

He pushed forward another document. It was a set of drawings of how the remodelled hotel could look. It looked great – chic, tasteful, relaxed, everything Vegas was not. Miles raised an eyebrow at the name above the door.

'Vegas Laing?' he said.

'The brand is already established,' said Marshall. 'It says European, exclusive, stylish, all the things you stand for, Miles. It says quiet money.'

Miles laughed. 'Quiet money. Two words to sum up Vegas.'

Marshall nodded. 'People like to flash their wealth in

Vegas, that's true, but that will change if the economy takes a downturn. And the real high-rollers prefer staying under the radar.'

Miles turned the pages of the document and found more drawings of a much bigger development. 'And what's this?'

'This is the future,' said Marshall, walking around the desk. He pointed to a sketch of a high-rise building. 'This is phase two. Once we're established on the Strip, we stand a much better chance of getting past the gaming commission to build a proper casino resort. Even if we don't get permission to build a casino at the Laing, we could build off the Strip where the land is cheaper.'

Miles traced a finger over the plans, enjoying having Michael standing so close to him. 'Is there room?'

'It's a deceptively big plot,' said Marshall, 'but the rumour I hear is that the Stardust and Frontier are leaking money. One or both could go under in the next six months. If that's the case, we could either demolish them or absorb them into the Laing.'

Miles looked up. 'My word, Mr Marshall,' he smiled, 'you are full of surprises today.'

'As I say, that's what you pay me for,' said Marshall, gathering up his files. As he walked back around the desk, Miles took in his lean physique.

'Well perhaps we'd better think about giving you a raise,' he said.

50

Sasha had wanted to open a Moscow branch of Rivera ever since the ultra-rich, high-spending tide of Russians began sweeping into London. She'd spent eighteen months doing her homework on the former Soviet capital, working out what the high net worth women of the city would want. If there was one thing Sasha had learnt from her time in the global fashion industry, it was that while all women loved shopping, their spending habits varied from country to country. The French bought fewer, more classic items, but they were prepared to pay for quality, while the Brits were more into trend-led impulse purchases. So when her research revealed that rich Russians liked their fashion to be an overt statement of their new-found wealth, she set out to make the launch of the Rivera Moscow a lavish, no-expenses-spared event, hiring the most prestigious firm of party planners to make it happen.

As the Rivera store was only small – she couldn't believe the price of premium retail space in Moscow – they had decided to host the trunk show and party at one of the city's prestigious venues. There had been an embarrassment of options: from the State Museum, whose address of One Red Square had almost swung it, to the Park Hyatt hotel which served cocktails at forty dollars a pop. In the end she had plumped for the library dining room of the Café Pushkin, which had practically become the local canteen for oligarchs, Russian politicos and supermodels.

They arrived in force. Men fattened with the proceeds of the newly capitalistic state. Wives dripping in sable mink and pink diamonds. Girlfriends and mistresses with angular faces and beautiful bodies. Sasha wasn't intimidated; she knew she could compete with any of them. She had upped her personal Pilates classes from three to five times a week which had made her body even leaner than usual, and the quarter-head of Botox had smoothed her skin and given her a glow. Her favourite dress from the Spring/Summer collection had been customised especially for the Russian market, with crystal embellishment and a lower scooped neckline, accessorised by high metallic Rivera heels and a butter-soft Rivera clutch. Not only was she working hard to make Rivera a global brand, she knew she had to position it as a luxury goods company and not simply a fashion house.

'Do you speak English?' asked a male voice behind her.

She turned round to see a slim man in his late twenties with incredible blue eyes.

'Of course I do,' she replied. 'I own the company.'

'Phew!' said the man, miming wiping his brow. 'I thought I was going to have to walk around saying *da* and *niet* all night, hoping I got lucky.'

'Well, I can teach you the Russian for "The Rivera store opens on Saturday" if you like.'

They laughed complicitly.

'Have we met before?' she asked and he smiled.

'I get that a lot; I'm covered in a helmet half the time.' He held out his hand. 'Josh Steel. I'm a racing driver.'

'Sasha Sinclair.'

'I know,' he said with a flirtatious smile.

'What are you doing in Moscow? I didn't know there was a race here.'

449

'There isn't,' said Josh. 'The season hasn't started. But our team are looking for sponsors. I'm kind of here to schmooze.'

And so am I, thought Sasha, feeling cross with herself for wasting time on someone who wasn't going to buy her clothes.

'Well, good luck with the language barrier,' she said, spotting the wife of a high-ranking politician across the room. 'I've got to mingle.'

Two hours later, the show was over and Sasha was glowing with a social and business triumph. Rivera's Russian PR Karla had already warned her that they might have to reorder stock before the Rivera store had even opened – already a handful of women had proclaimed that they wanted 'everything', and neither Sasha nor Karla thought they were joking. Slipping on her russet-red fox fur, Sasha headed out into the chilly Moscow night air. She was the last to leave Café Pushkin and she was left alone on Pushkin Square.

Where's my bloody car? she thought anxiously. The last thing she wanted was to get stuck in the middle of nowhere, not even knowing the word for 'hotel'. The white boxy shape of a Muscovite taxi turned the corner. Cold, tired and desperate to get back to her hotel, she put her hand out to stop it.

'Hey, missus,' called an amused voice. 'You don't want to be getting into taxis all alone at night.' Josh Steel was leaning out of the window of a black Mercedes, his blue eyes twinkling.

'I'm screwed then, aren't I?' she said.

'Too early to tell.' He grinned, popping the passenger door open.

She walked across and got in.

'What hotel are you at?'

'Park Hyatt.'

'Splendid, so am I,' he said, gunning the engine.

450

'I hope you're going to stick to the speed limit, Mr Steel,' she said in mock alarm.

He smiled. 'I'm fast but I'm safe.'

'I bet you say that to all the girls.'

Back at the hotel, Sasha pretended to hesitate when he asked her for a drink. They took the elevator up to the tenth floor bar, overlooking the city, packed with businessmen and blondes wearing jewels as big as ice cubes.

'Bloody hell, the drinks are expensive,' said Josh, flipping through the menu.

'I didn't realise you were looking for a cheap date,' said Sasha.

'Just social observation. Down the street you can get vodka for fifty roubles.'

'The Russian way. Everything is either very cheap or very expensive. They're still caught between communism and capitalism.'

They slipped into easy conversation, swapping stories about their lives and people they knew in common. Josh was easygoing and fun, 'the only way you can deal with such a stressful job', he reasoned. It felt like a long time since Sasha had really laughed, and not talked about business, just fun throwaway things like people, parties and gossip. She loved that they were in such an exotic, alien environment and yet she could feel so familiar and relaxed with this stranger.

'How do you think it went tonight?' said Josh, swirling the vodka around the bottom of his glass.

'Very well,' said Sasha. 'Which is a relief, as Rivera's investors were divided over whether we should even have the party. They were worried we might devalue the brand if we were too aligned with new Russian money. It's preposterous! I mean, where does that logic lead? We don't sell to the Chinese because of their human rights track record?'

He held his hands up and laughed. 'OK, OK, I'm on your side. Maybe we shouldn't talk about business.'

'Sorry.' Sasha winced. 'Was I ranting?'

He held up his thumb and forefinger. 'Just a little.'

They sipped their drinks and fell into an amiable silence.

'Hey, you know I have seen you before,' he said after a pause. 'At that party at Somerset House recently. I was going to come to speak to you but someone told me not to bother.'

'Really? Why?'

'They told me you batted for the other team.'

'No!' she gasped, truly amazed.

'They said you never have a boyfriend.'

She drew herself up in the chair. 'What a ridiculous thing to say, just because I don't flaunt my love life all over the papers. Actually I dated my finance director for four years. Then there was someone else . . .' She hesitated. 'Someone I shouldn't have been seeing.'

'What happened? Wife find out?'

'He died,' she said, knocking back her vodka.

'I'm sorry.' He put his hand over hers and she felt her anger simmer down. She glanced up and he was looking at her with his Paul Newman eyes.

'I'll walk you back to your room,' he said, signing the bill. 'You never know who might be lurking behind the plants.'

They rode the lift down in silence and stopped outside her room. As she reached into her clutch for her key-card, he took her face in his hands and kissed her. He tasted sweet and sour, the vodka and his lips, and suddenly she wanted him. She popped the door open and, without turning on the light, he pushed her up against the wall, his mouth hot on hers, desire running from her navel to her groin. Then, just as suddenly, she pulled away from him.

'What's the matter?' he whispered.

'It's . . . it's just been a while, that's all,' she said honestly. 'Bit nervous.'

'You're kidding me?' he said, chuckling.

It was true. There had been nobody since Robert, and she

felt so closed off, so resistant to the desire that was searing round her body, she felt a physical ache as he touched her.

'We'll take it slowly,' he whispered, sliding his hand behind her, unzipping her dress. 'You just relax. I'm going to remind you exactly what you've been missing.'

51

'Will you stop looking at me like that?' said Melissa as Alex drove their 4x4 up Highway One towards Pacific Palisades.

'Like what?' asked Alex, glancing towards the passenger seat.

'You're looking at me weirdly,' she said with a disapproving pout. 'Like I'm a stranger or something.'

Alex chuckled and squeezed her knee. 'Maybe it's because you do look like a stranger. My wife left for the hairdresser's at nine o'clock this morning and she hasn't come back.'

Even members of Melissa's fan club would be hard pressed to spot her tonight. Her face was nearly make-up-free, her usually red lips muted with a pale beige stain. A four-hour session at Guido, Beverly Hills' most sought-after hairdresser, had turned her glossy blond mane chocolate brown, while her knee-length navy tea-dress hadn't quite extinguished her sex appeal but had made her less available, more serious.

'I want this part, Alex. Tonight I'm going to show him I *am* Danielle.'

Alex chuckled to himself. They were on their way to dinner with Christopher Hayes, the maverick director and screenwriter whose latest project was adapting *Next Door But One*, a Pulitzer-prize-winning book about sexual tension in 1950s suburbia. Melissa had already been offered the role of Nancy, the young temptress who seduces a Madison Avenue advertising executive away from his wife. But she didn't want to be Nancy; she wanted the smaller but more pivotal role of Danielle, the wife.

'Nancy gets you the front cover of *GQ*,' she'd told Alex while reading the script in bed. 'But Danielle wins you an Oscar.'

Most of the time Alex tried to avoid Hollywood's power-broking party circuit, but he'd agreed to come along tonight because he was a huge fan of Christopher Hayes. The director had spent the eighties and early nineties making deeply intelligent and often quite weird films – studies of small-town paranoia, many of which Alex had seen with Emma at the Cornerhouse, the little art-house cinema in Manchester. Every actor in Hollywood wanted to work for him, and judging by the huge Spanish-style mansion overlooking the ocean, his off-the-wall movies were big business.

A maid in grey uniform answered the door and led them through to an open living area facing the Pacific, which was fading from view as the sun sank behind dusky clouds. Alex couldn't help but grin inanely when Christopher came over and shook their hands and introduced them to the other dinner guests.

'Al, Melissa, you both know Justin Coe?' he said.

'We've met,' simpered Melissa. 'And of course I'm a huge fan.'

'Oh, I can't think why,' said Justin, flashing his perfect white teeth.

Justin Coe was one of Hollywood's biggest and most bankable stars. He had signed up to play the role of Ray, the advertising executive in the movie.

'So what do you do, Al?' he asked.

'Oh, Al's just a singer,' said Melissa.

'Really?' said Justin, his smile dimming slightly. 'You done anything I might have heard?'

'Nothing much yet,' said Alex. 'Made a few demos, hoping to get a few gigs in the valley.'

'Yeah, good luck with that,' said Justin, steering Melissa away. 'You really have to meet Daniel over here ...'

At dinner, Melissa was seated between Christopher and Justin, while Alex was relegated to the other end, next to Christopher's wife Jennifer, an impressive and rather intimidating woman wearing a camel-coloured trouser suit. Alex sat quietly, just absorbing the Hollywood shop talk – who was making what, who was screwing who, who had a terrible coke problem, who was in rehab – swinging between boredom and awkwardness. By the time the dessert was brought out, he had taken to playing a game with himself, counting the times the word 'awesome' was used in conversation. He watched as Melissa and Justin stood up, heading out towards the swimming pool 'for a smoke'. He was just about to follow when Jennifer touched his arm.

'You really shouldn't have fucked with him, you know,' she whispered.

Alex looked at her, startled. 'Who?'

'Justin. Or Teeth as I like to call him,' said Jennifer. 'It's not the done thing to make the star look stupid, even if he doesn't realise.'

'Sorry, he was being a knob.'

Jennifer laughed, a full-throated, fruity chuckle. 'Knob,' she repeated with relish. 'I love the way you speak – and that wasn't supposed to sound patronising. You wouldn't believe how much bland shit I have to listen to at these things. It's nice to meet someone who says what he thinks.'

Alex smiled politely, trying to remember everything Melissa had told him about Jennifer in the car. She was a former columnist for the *New York Times* turned scriptwriter and novelist. That might explain her forthright approach.

'So with that in mind, why don't you tell me what you thought of *Firefly*?'

456

Firefly was Christopher Hayes' last movie, a twisted tale of unrequited love set in a remote town in the Midwest.

'I thought it was brilliant,' said Alex. 'I loved the homage to French New Wave in the scene at the gas station.'

Jennifer glanced over towards her husband, who was locked in earnest conversation. 'Crock of pretentious shit if you ask me,' she muttered, and Alex had to cover his mouth to stop himself from coughing his blueberry tart across the table.

'I'll be honest, Jennifer.' He laughed. 'I wasn't expecting you to say that.'

'I know. The soignée Hollywood wife. Come on. I used to be a journalist. I'm a New Yorker. If I think *Firefly* was just an exercise in artistic masturbation, then I'm going to say so.'

'You'd love it in my home town,' said Alex. 'Everyone says exactly what they mean up there. That's why there are so many fights outside the chippy.'

'That's what drives me nuts about the West Coast, Al,' said Jennifer, pouring him more wine as the dessert was cleared away. 'You never say what you think out here, you say what you think you should say. It's one of the reasons I prefer writing books to screenplays. I call the shots. Writing a movie, you've got fifteen different people telling you what to do, all trying to outmanoeuvre the other guy. You're a pawn, not an author.'

She saw Alex glancing towards the door Melissa had left through.

'You know, LA is full of very smart people who think they have to play stupid,' she said quietly.

'Oh, Melissa's not stupid.'

'I gathered that the second I saw her. I take it she's after the part of Danielle and not Nancy?'

'Is it that obvious?'

'I've seen every trick in the book. People will do anything to get the part.'

'Well, if you'll excuse me, I think I'd better check where she's got to,' he said, pushing his chair back.

He walked out towards the pool, and for a moment he couldn't see Melissa anywhere. Then he spotted her, hidden away in a corner, sitting on a teak sunlounger, cosied right up next to Justin. Her tea-dress, that had looked so decorous when they had left the house, had risen several inches up her thigh, which was now covered with Justin Coe's hand.

As they drove back towards Mulholland, snaking their way up through the hills, Melissa was beaming, her cheeks flushed.

'Great that you were talking to Jennifer back there,' she said. 'Good strategy to get in with the wife.'

'She was actually the only human in the room,' he said.

'What's got into you?' She frowned.

Alex glanced at her, then looked back towards the road, fuming.

'What?' she said.

'I don't know why you bothered with this prom-virgin charade tonight if all along you planned on behaving like a ... like you did back there.'

'What are you talking about?' she said defensively.

'What am I talking about? From the minute we got there to the minute we left, you were flirting with Justin like a bitch on heat.'

'We were talking about the movie,' she said.

'Oh yes? And did he need to put his hand up your skirt while you chatted?'

'I wasn't flirting,' protested Melissa. 'I was demonstrating chemistry.'

'Of course,' he said, shaking his head. 'How naïve of me.'

'Look, Christopher is one of the most powerful directors in the world, but Justin will still have the final say-so on his co-star.'

'And that makes it OK, does it?' snapped Alex. 'Think

about how it feels for me, Melissa. Married to "the sexiest woman in the world". I know you have to network and connect with future co-stars, but you're married and there's a line you don't cross.'

'And do you think it's easy for me? You out on tour, surrounded by screaming girls, never home?'

Suddenly Alex had déjà vu so powerful he shivered. He was almost transported back to the Year Zero days and having almost exactly the same conversations with Emma.

'Have you ever seen any evidence of that? Don't you think those groupies would sell their stories to the tabloids in a heartbeat? Have you ever seen a pap shot of me out with another woman? Have you ever caught me feeling up Courtney Love?'

Melissa looked out of the dark window, slowly shaking her head. 'Justin is gay,' she said quietly.

'What?' he said, glancing at her. Was she kidding? He'd heard the gay rumours before, of course – and not just about Justin Coe. If you listened to the gossip, half of Hollywood's leading men swung the other way. And some of the gossip was true. The 'commitment-phobe' heart-throb who was never without a model, starlet or waitress at his side but who actually had a long-term boyfriend he was deeply in love with. Or the happily married action star who had a secret life cruising Sunset Boulevard and taking discreet male lovers. But Justin ... He just couldn't believe it.

'Justin Coe isn't gay. Isn't he supposed to be secretly engaged to that bird off that sitcom?'

'It's the best-kept secret in Hollywood, but yes, Justin is gay.'

He frowned at her, wanting to believe her, but not sure.

'How do you know?'

'Because he told me!' she cried, exasperated.

'Oh,' said Alex, feeling his cheeks flare. 'Really? I have to say I'm surprised.'

He thought for a moment. 'So why did he have his hand ...'

'We were acting, Alex! We're actors! It's what we do!'

'All right, all right, I get the message,' said Alex. 'I'm sorry, I just thought ...'

'I know what you thought, baby,' she said, scratching him behind his ear. 'But I think it's about time you started trusting me. Justin thinks I'll be perfect as Danielle, and frankly so do I. I need to be creatively stretched, Alex. I need to reach my potential. I don't want to be the sexy blonde for the rest of my career. I want to win awards, I want to be Meryl Streep ...'

He put his foot down on the gas pedal, gunning the engine. He didn't want to hear the rest.

52

August 2006

After the huge publicity from shooting two of Alex Doyle's platinum-selling album sleeves, Grace's photographic career took off like a rocket. She was constantly in demand to shoot magazine covers and for editorial spreads and private commissions. Above all, she loved doing portraiture, not the volumes of celebrity stuff that was regularly sent her way, but what she called 'real-life people': farmers in the fields, single mothers on sink estates, scientists at work in their laboratories. She loved capturing the lines on their faces, the expressions in their eyes, hoping her camera could reveal their inner secrets.

Today she was doing a portfolio for *Rive* magazine called 'Bright Young Things', subtitled 'A snapshot of the new millennium's gilded youth'. She was about to turn the job down – the Stockbridge Hall renovations desperately needed her full attention – when she got a call from Olivia saying that she had been chosen to appear in the very same photo story. Although she wasn't too pleased with her daughter being described as 'gilded youth', Grace had thought it wise to oversee her modelling debut, so had agreed to the commission.

461

'Let me look. Let me look!'

Olivia came running across the grass of Davidson House, a bucolic Georgian manor on the outskirts of London. In skin-tight jeans, huge wedge platforms and floaty white Chloe top, it was no surprise she had been chosen for the shoot. With her long dark hair and huge green eyes, she was growing into a very beautiful young woman, thought Grace with a sense of pride. She handed Olivia the Polaroid of the shot she had just taken; six Bright Young Things, the twin daughters of a rock star, a handsome eighteen-year-old lord who starred in the latest Abercrombie and Fitch campaign, two pretty actresses and Olivia playing croquet with gold balls on the front lawns.

'Wow, I look amazing!' said Olivia. 'Can you make my boobs a bit bigger when you make up the prints?' she said hopefully.

'No I will not,' said Grace.

'Please, Mum. I've already been in touch with a modelling agency, and they want me to send some photographs in. They're going to freak when they know I've already done a *Rive* editorial. The work will just pile in.'

Grace took a deep breath. It was clear from Olivia's school reports that she was not going to be an academic, not through a lack of intelligence but from an absence of interest in anything beyond make-up and fashion magazines.

'Olivia, we've talked about modelling before,' she said. 'You're fourteen years old and I think you should be concentrating on your GCSEs and all the stuff you love at school. What about the tennis team and the film club?'

Olivia rolled her eyes. 'I haven't done those things for ages, Mum. They're so boring.'

'Well, I think you're too young to model.'

'Julian says loads of models are my age.'

It was just like Olivia to start getting ammunition from Grace's partner.

'I don't care what Julian says. He is not your mother.'

Olivia glanced critically at her. 'It's only because you needed a chaperone at my age.'

Grace gasped. 'Do not talk to me like—' she began, but she was interrupted by her assistant, Tim.

'Sorry, Grace,' he said. 'Catrina wants you. She wants to know which shot you're planning on doing next so she can style the models.'

'I'll come inside.' She sighed, watching Olivia run back to the croquet lawn where she slipped her hand around Lord Freddie's waist, whispering something in his ear. Not for the first time, she wished that her daughter wasn't away at boarding school. If she had lost touch with Olivia's interests, she certainly had no idea of her social life. Was she dating Freddie? Grace was realistic enough to know that if her daughter wanted to horse around with boys, or smoke – or even do drugs, she thought with a grimace – nothing could stop her, but she wished she had a better relationship with Olivia, wished her daughter wanted to confide in her.

Perhaps it's my fault, she thought as she walked towards the house. Three months ago, Gabriel had announced that he was remarrying, which had upset Joseph but hadn't seemed to bother Olivia. Maybe this rebellion was her way of showing her hurt. Or maybe it was more than that. Olivia was beautiful, charming and bright, but she also had a lazy, expectant streak and a nose for trouble. The real truth was that she was starting to remind Grace of Miles.

The manor's library had been turned into a makeshift dressing room. Catrina, the magazine's fashion editor, was fighting her way through a long rail of designer clothes. Grace was going through the next set-up with her, which was to be the rock twins running through the orchard in long sundresses, when they heard an insistent beeping coming from a pile of coats and bags flung on a chaise longue.

'Where *is* that bloody noise coming from?' said Catrina.

463

'It's been beeping for the last ten minutes and it's driving me crazy.'

Tim rummaged through the pile and lifted up a brown Mulberry satchel that Grace immediately recognised as Olivia's.

'That's my daughter's,' said Grace. 'I'll take it to her.'

The satchel was heavy, weighed down with shoes, magazines and make-up.

No need to take the whole bag out, she thought, stopping in the hallway and rummaging through it looking for the phone. Then her fingers touched something and she stopped, holding her breath. It was a thin metallic strip of tablets. It was the pill. Looking up, she could hear footsteps.

'I need a drink,' said Olivia, running into the house.

Grace stood up. 'Olivia, can I talk to you for one moment?'

'Later, Mum,' she said, trying to dodge around her. 'Me and Freddie want a Pepsi.'

'Now,' said Grace, taking her by the arm and leading her into an empty study. It was a formal space with a walnut writing desk and a captain chair that made Grace feel like a Victorian father.

'I found these in your bag,' she said simply, handing her daughter the strip of pills.

Olivia's green eyes blazed at her. 'What the hell were you doing going through my bag?'

'That's beside the point. I asked *you* what you're doing on the pill, Olivia.'

'I've only just got them,' she said sulkily.

'How? Why?' Grace asked, shaking with anger. 'You're fourteen years old, you're still a child.'

Olivia did not look like a child, standing six feet tall in her wedges, her hands on her hips.

'I'm not a child!' she spat. 'It's about time you realised that, Mother. Freddie and I are having sex and you can't stop us,' she added with a note of malice.

Grace quivered with anger, but she knew she wouldn't get anywhere with Olivia by shouting. God knows she'd tried often enough.

'I just think you're too young, darling,' she said in a softer tone.

'Too young for modelling, too young for sex,' said Olivia sarcastically.

'You need to be responsible . . .'

'Ha!' said Olivia. 'Take a look in the mirror, Mum. Maybe you should have been a bit more responsible yourself.'

Grace gasped at her daughter's insolence. 'What do you mean by that?'

'I'm not stupid, Mum. I can do the maths. You got pregnant almost as soon as you met Dad. That's why you went to live in Parador and got married. No wonder it didn't all work out with him; you shouldn't have got married in the first place.'

'How dare you!' whispered Grace. 'I loved your father . . .'

'Love?' said Olivia cruelly. 'Don't make me laugh.'

With a flick of her hair, she stalked out of the room. Grace could only stand there staring at the spot where her daughter had been. Slowly she turned and walked to the window, where she could see Olivia running up to her boyfriend like an eager puppy. How had this happened? In the blink of an eye, her sweet little girl had become a woman, a woman she barely recognised.

Olivia was right, of course: she did still think of her daughter as a child – a baby, even – and she knew she couldn't hold on for ever. She curled her hand into a fist. She should never have confronted Olivia in that way; she shouldn't have trotted out the old clichés about waiting and responsibility. No wonder Olivia didn't want to confide in her. She had certainly played this particular episode badly. But was Olivia also right when she said she had played it *all* badly? For fourteen years, Grace had tried to do the right thing for her children, putting them first, pushing her own needs to one side to make sure they had the best start they could have. Had she been a bad mother? She could certainly have done things differently, that was true. But should she have done?

'Grace?' called Catrina from the doorway. 'Do you want to look at the outfits for the next shot?'

Grace quickly brushed a tear away. 'Sure, I'll be there in a minute,' she said.

Out in the garden, Olivia was sitting next to Lord Freddie, her head resting affectionately on his shoulder.

Just don't make the mistakes I did, darling, thought Grace, picking up her camera and turning away. It was the best she could hope for.

53

Alex Doyle felt without a care in the world. Fregate Island, a private Seychelles atoll thirty miles east of Mahe, was beautiful, remote and the last word in barefoot luxury. A riot of coconut palms, cashew and almond trees perfumed the whole island like a bottle of Melissa's bespoke scent. For five days that week the lush secluded oasis was especially exclusive as Alex and Melissa had hired out the entire island for a holiday of paparazzi- and people-free luxury. Melissa was just about to go on a twelve-country promo tour for the Christopher Hayes film *Next Door But One* and Alex had finished a twenty-one-date tour of South American football stadiums; they felt they deserved it.

'I'm nervous about the movie,' said Melissa, turning towards her husband. They were lying on wooden sunloungers positioned right at the water's edge of Anse Parc Beach, a small table between them holding cocktails, their ice slowly melting. Fregate wasn't entirely deserted, of course. This was a luxury resort for the super-rich and there was an army of waiters, chefs and gofers to make sure their two guests never went without.

'What are you nervous about, honey?' said Alex, putting down the book he was reading – a biography of hair metal band Motley Crue – and peering at her over his sunglasses. 'The early buzz on the film is great. Hayes said he'd work with you again in a heartbeat and you got a six-million-dollar pay packet. Sounds OK to me.'

She frowned, shielding her eyes from the sun. 'None of that matters, Alex. All that matters is box office and the Academy.'

'I'm not an expert,' said Alex, 'but the two things don't necessarily go hand in hand. I mean, look at *Die Hard*. Brilliant movie, big box office, but where was Bruce Willis' Oscar? You can't necessarily have both.'

'*Next Door* is not an *action* movie, Alex,' she said sourly. 'All I'm saying is that I want people to enjoy the movie, of course, but I also want recognition from my peers about my craft.'

Alex rolled his eyes at the mention of the *craft*. Melissa was taking herself very seriously these days. Having acting lessons with a teacher at Lee Strasberg and searching for scripts that involved a physical transformation – her logic being that Nicole Kidman, Charlize Theron and Halle Berry had all won Oscars in roles where they'd had to put on weight, don a prosthetic nose or wear little make-up.

'Christopher thinks I should stay a brunette.'

'I've been telling you for months you should stay as a brunette.' In fact, Alex wasn't entirely sure what Melissa's natural hair colour was: she had her roots done every two weeks and her pubic hair had been waxed, dyed and buffed with the same regularity as the hair on her head. 'Brunette definitely suits you, baby,' he said, but Melissa had already closed her eyes, concentrating on her tan. He started reading his book again, but quickly put it down – all those stories of shooting up and orgies with groupies made him feel uncomfortable. He rolled over and grabbed the stack of tabloid magazines that Melissa had picked up at the airport. She professed to loathe the things and had taken out lawsuits against a number of them, but they were a guilty pleasure for her as much as the next person.

He flicked through the first one casually, enjoying the tittle-tattle, the dress disasters, the celebrity meltdowns. He closed his eyes, relishing the cool breeze coming off the Indian Ocean, like a lake of shimmering jade in front of him. He had to admit, it had taken some persuading to get him to a private island. For many years he had been uncomfortable being by the sea at all. The year before, he and Melissa had had huge rows when she wanted to move to Malibu, because Alex was not sure if he wanted to wake up every morning to the sound of lapping waves. He hadn't told Melissa the real reason about his preference to stay in their Hollywood Hills home.

Reaching across, he got his cocktail and sipped it slowly as he leafed through the magazine. He couldn't pinpoint the precise moment he'd started drinking again, but it was usually only a couple of Budweisers every day and Melissa had been either on set or too self-absorbed to notice. Suddenly he stopped on the centre-spread story in *US Weekly*, his eyes wide. *Too Hot To Handle!* screamed the headline. There were two blown-up pictures on facing pages – one of Melissa and Justin in bed together, the curve of her breast and his bronzed, rippled torso totally visible. The other was a grainy long-lens shot of the two of them in deep discussion. That one made him feel like puking. In it, they were completely clothed, but Justin's hand was held up to Melissa's face, stroking the under-side of her jaw. It was such an intimate gesture, it was like a punch to the stomach for Alex. Maybe Melissa could explain the bed shot away – although he had no idea how – but this one, this was unmistakably a photograph of two people who were in love.

He wanted to throw the magazine away, but he couldn't take his eyes from the page, vainly hoping it would change. The chatter about an on-set affair between Melissa and Justin

469

had been fairly continuous throughout the filming of *Next Door But One*, but Melissa had kept reminding him about Justin's sexual preference. He only had her word for it, and even she couldn't dispute the intimacy in these pictures.

'Melissa,' he said.

She opened one eye lazily. 'What?'

He held up the magazine.

Melissa groaned. 'Not this again?' she said, snatching it from him. 'When are you going to get over being so damn insecure?'

'A picture of you and Justin naked together isn't really helping things, Melissa,' he snapped.

'Oh get real, Alex,' she said wearily. 'This shot is from the movie – the *movie*! It was leaked by Brett – it's all part of the publicity.'

'So now your publicist is whipping up trouble about our marriage in the tabloids?'

'He released one on-set photo taken months ago.'

'Of you having sex, which by the way I thought was supposed to be a closed set. Just you, Justin and the director.'

'What is your problem?' she said fiercely. 'I'm getting sick of this jealousy, Alex. I'm an actress; sometimes I have to play parts that involve intimacy, and when I do, I do it well. And I'm not going to apologise for the way the studio does its publicity – that's just ridiculous.'

Emotion welled up in his throat. Everything had gone so well over the past few years: his music career, his marriage to one of the world's most beautiful women. He knew it was more than he deserved and in his darker moments, usually alone on tour, awake in the middle of night, he expected it all to come crashing down.

'I just want us to be happy,' he said sadly.

Her expression softened. She swung her legs around his body to straddle him, pressing her bare breasts against his back as she kissed the nape of his neck.

470

'It's just publicity, honey. I love you, Alex. I love you so much.'

He relaxed into her, feeling reassurance in her words and her warm skin brushing against his.

'I want to try for a baby,' she whispered.

He turned round to face her. 'You do?'

The only time children had been mentioned before was on their honeymoon in Ireland. Sailing across Lough Neagh, a gorgeous blood-red sunset had settled over the water and, overcome with its beauty, Alex had turned round to his new wife and told her he wanted to have at least six children. Melissa had just giggled and said, 'We'll see'. Alex had never pushed it because he knew her career came first. *Always* came first. But he had always wanted children, desperately wanted them. Perhaps it was some desire to make up for the failings of his own family, or a need to create something whose love would be unconditional, whose love he would never have to question.

'Are you sure this is what you want?' he asked. 'You start shooting another movie in a month, and I've got the European tour.'

He knew he was pushing her, testing her. A baby was exactly what he wanted – but he wanted her to want it just as much.

'After this film and after the tour, then we'll start trying,' she said, nibbling at his ear lobe. 'But in the meantime, why don't we start practising?'

She squealed with laughter as Alex scooped her up and rolled on to the floury-white sand. Lying half naked on the shore, a wave of surf washed over them.

'From here to eternity.' She giggled.

God, I hope so, thought Alex, pulling at her bikini briefs. *I really do*.

54

March 2008

Sitting outside a café on the Left Bank, Alex had an old Frank Sinatra tune in his head. What was it? Something about loving Paris in the springtime? And it was true: Paris seemed idyllic whether it was covered in blossom or frost, but Alex particularly loved it for the simple reason that he couldn't do this in any other city in the world. In London, New York or Berlin, he would have been mobbed by fans and star-struck tourists, but the French were too cool to bother you over lunch. A leisurely *moules frites* was sacrosanct in Paris. Alex offered a chip to his manager, who politely declined. Ted Sullivan was a straight-talking Brit – something of an anomaly in an industry which seemed to produce foul-mouthed ball-breakers on a production line – but he had been with Alex ever since he had become Al Doyle and Alex trusted him implicitly.

'So how's Melissa?' asked Ted.

'Great.' Alex shrugged. 'Well, as far as I know, anyway.'

Alex was coming to the end of his European tour and Melissa was currently shooting her latest movie on location in Vancouver, so it was hard to find time when they could talk on the phone, let alone see each other. Melissa had managed to fly out to see him in Rome a few weeks earlier, but they had been living separate lives for months. Ted looked at him awkwardly.

'Look, I didn't want to bring this up, and part of me thinks it's none of my business, but as your manager and your friend, I think you should know.'

'Know what?'

'The rumours about Melissa and Justin Coe having an affair.'

Alex smiled and took a sip of his beer. 'I appreciate your concern, Ted, but Melissa and Justin are not having an affair.'

'How do you know? Those red-carpet pictures of them together on the *Next Door* promo tour looked pretty cosy.'

'I just know.'

'How?'

Alex sighed. 'Because he's *gay*.' He hadn't wanted to say it; if it was Hollywood's best-kept secret, then he respected that. But when he was starting to get grief from his manager, who was a discreet, no-nonsense man, it was time to put the record straight.

'Are you sure?'

Alex rolled his eyes. 'No, I don't have CCTV link-up into the man's bedroom. But I trust my wife, Ted.'

Ted went back to his burger. He took a bite, then put it down again, distracted. Alex looked at him.

'What is it? Come on, Ted, tell me.'

'Are you sure she's up in Vancouver filming the new movie?'

'She's got a couple more days' shooting,' said Alex, feeling a flurry of anxiety. 'Why do you ask?'

'Because a friend of mine saw her in New York last week.'

'Oh, big deal,' said Alex with irritation. 'So she had a couple of days off and went shopping. You know what women are like.'

'New York *State*, Alex, not Manhattan. Some fancy hotel in the middle of nowhere.'

It was hard keeping tabs on his wife's movements when

473

he was on the road, but he was sure Melissa hadn't mentioned being in New York at any point over the last month.

'Well maybe she . . .' stuttered Alex. 'Maybe she just needed a break,' he finished lamely.

Ted took out his wallet, pulled out a business card and put in on the bistro table. 'As I said, it's probably none of my business, but if you're concerned, give this guy a ring. Mike Stone's his name. Tommy, the drummer from Kool-Aid, was having concerns about his wife last year. They had a pre-nup, with a no-cheating clause. Anyway, he got this PI to check out Suzie's movements. Turns out she had some guy tucked away in Vegas and was about to file for divorce.'

Alex was incredulous. 'Are you suggesting I put a private detective on Melissa?'

'At the risk of sounding like your mother, Alex, I just don't want you to get hurt. Emotionally or financially.'

Back at the hotel, Alex called the Vancouver house Melissa was renting during filming. The housekeeper answered and said that Miss Melissa had not been at home for the last two days. Fetching himself a large Jack Daniel's, he picked up the business card that Ted had given him and made the call.

If Alex had been expecting evidence of Melissa's infidelity, he was disappointed. According to the investigator's meticulously logged reports, over the next two weeks Melissa went to the gym, to her hairdresser or out to the Ivy for lunch with Christopher Hayes. The PI managed to get close: they were talking about a new script Hayes had in mind for Melissa. In the end, the matter was settled by an unexpected source.

The night before he was due to fly back to LA, Alex was in the make-up room at the BBC, having powder applied to his nose by a camp young man named Will. He was due to appear on a late-night chat show and was enjoying the make-up artist's endless string of gossip.

474

'You know, I can't wait to see that new film your wife just did with Justin Coe,' Will said.

'Me too.' Alex smiled, not wanting to reveal too much. He was aware that some celebrity make-up artists and hairdressers supplemented their income by tipping off the tabloids.

'You know my boyfriend used to date Justin,' said Will boastfully.

The news made Alex sit up. 'I didn't know Justin was, er, gay.'

'Not good for business, is it?' Will laughed. 'Dan, that's my boyfriend, was a hairdresser in LA for a while. When they split he had to sign a confidentiality contract thicker than his dick. Nice pay-off. Used it as a deposit for his house in Santa Monica.'

Alex put in an awful performance on the chat show. Usually he was a natural on screen, affable, funny and open with his rock-industry anecdotes. But that night he was distracted and anxious. Part of him felt flooded with relief, while the other part felt wretched about his suspicious and irrational behaviour. Setting a private investigator on his wife! What was he thinking?

Back at his hotel, he called Mike Stone, the private investigator.

'Hi, Mike, it's Alex. Listen, I've been thinking about the investigation, and I think it's time to stop ...'

'You got my photos, then?' said Stone.

'No, what photos?'

'You near a computer? I sent them to your email.'

Quickly Alex opened his laptop and clicked on his inbox – immediately he was confronted with a grainy shot of Melissa coming out of an anonymous office block. In the background, he could just see part of the sign; it read 'Clinic'.

'What's this?' Alex frowned. 'A cosmetic surgeon's?' It wouldn't have surprised him. With the advent of High

475

Definition, every actress in Hollywood over twenty-five was freaking out over every visible line and open pore.

'Uh-uh,' said Stone. 'Try ob-gyn.'

'An obstetrician?' Alex said with delight in his voice. 'That's the best fucking photograph I think I've ever seen.'

Alex took the first flight back to LA. His driver collected him from Santa Monica airport and he went straight to Neil Lane, Melissa's favourite jeweller's, picking out a twelve-carat eternity ring that sparkled like the ocean in summertime. Back at their Hollywood Hills home, he rolled his sleeves up and got to work preparing his wife's favourite meal of cold poached salmon, and gave Ana, their housekeeper, the rest of the day off. By the time he saw Melissa's Prius turn into the drive, he had already laid a table with starched linen, crystal goblets and candles out by the pool. He had hidden the ring clumsily under a napkin, but the velvet box was peeking out.

'Hey, stranger.' She smiled, coming through the door and kissing him on the cheek. 'What's going on?' she asked as he led her out to the table.

'A surprise welcome home.'

'Oh now you've made me feel guilty,' she said coquettishly. 'Sorry I couldn't have been back earlier, but you know these meetings run on and on. Oh look, Ana's made my favourite poached salmon salad.'

'My own handiwork, actually.' He smiled.

'My, my. You should go away more often.'

'So how's it been without me?' he asked as they sat down.

'Wretched, of course,' she said in a faux British thespian accent. Her next movie was a period piece and she had just started working with a dialogue coach.

'Oh shit,' said Alex suddenly. 'Can you eat salmon?'

'What? Why not?' she said.

'You're not supposed to eat fish, are you?' he babbled. 'Bad for the baby, I think. Or is it just raw fish?'

'Babies?' she said with a weak smile.

He leant over and grasped her hand. 'Sorry, honey, I heard you were at the ob-gyn yesterday,' he said, hoping she wouldn't think to ask how he knew what she was doing yesterday. 'I just put two and two together . . .' He trailed off, seeing the downturn of her mouth, the way she avoided his gaze.

'You're not pregnant, are you?' he said slowly, trying not to let his disappointment show.

'Yes, I am,' she said simply.

'You are? That's fantastic!' he cried, picking her up and spinning her around. 'Was it that night in Rome? That's so romantic! Maybe we should call him Gino if it's a boy, what do you think? Too Dexy's Midnight Runners?'

Too late, Alex realised Melissa wasn't smiling.

'Rome was ten weeks ago, Alex,' she said quietly. 'I'm five weeks pregnant.'

He felt all the joy fall out of him. 'Five weeks?' he said. He didn't even need to do the arithmetic. 'Are you sure?' he asked, feeling his heart beating too fast.

'It's not your baby, Alex.'

He could barely breathe. So it was true about Melissa and Justin.

'But Justin's gay,' he said.

'The baby is Chris'.'

'Chris? Christopher *Hayes*?' he said incredulously.

'It's been going on for a while. We didn't want you to find out like this. We all want to avoid bad publicity . . .'

'*Bad publicity?* Is that all you care about?'

'Of course not,' she said, taking a step towards him. 'I'm so sorry, Alex.'

'But why?' he whispered. 'Why?'

'He's good for me,' she said.

'Good for your career, you mean. Good for getting you a bloody Oscar.'

'It's not like that, Alex,' she said defiantly. 'Christopher and I are equals.'

Alex knew what she meant by that. Hayes would give Melissa the sheen of respectability she craved. He could take her where she wanted to go – acceptance as a serious actress, not just a pretty face. She had her own money. Fame. Alex could offer her nothing but himself – and that wasn't good enough.

'What about us?'

'There is no us!' shouted Melissa. 'Can't you get that through your head? It's over, Alex! Chris is going to end it with Jennifer. It's serious between us. Especially now.'

'Serious?' he yelled, pulling the ring out and thrusting it in her face. 'This is an eternity ring, Melissa. That's how serious I am about you. I wanted to grow old with you, I wanted us to be together for ever!'

He strode to the edge of the terrace and, pulling his arm back, flung the ring out towards the lights of Hollywood. It twinkled briefly, then it was gone.

55

As the low outline of the Pennines came into view, Alex leant over and switched off the radio. He didn't want any distractions as he drove into Macclesfield. It had been eight years since he had last visited his home town and he wanted to absorb everything. Peering through the drizzle spotting the windscreen, he took in the cramped grey terraces with their narrow ginnels, the tiny shops selling lacy ladies' things and unfashionable lamps, the chippy, the church, the endless pubs with their welcoming orange glow. Suddenly all these things he had once loathed and rejected seemed more solid and important than anywhere else. This was where his roots were and, like it or not, where his heart was.

He drew the black Mercedes into the kerb, noting that a caravan was still parked outside number thirty opposite as it always had been, except this model looked whiter and shinier. Alex had not seen his mum in over three months, when he had flown her out to Athens for one of his live shows. She had always wanted to see the Parthenon and was giddy with excitement as they walked around it. Since he'd come into money, Alex liked giving gifts – over the years he'd spent a fortune on art, jewellery and clothes for Melissa and bought two sports cars for Ted – but the look on his mum's face that afternoon had been worth every last bit of the struggle it had taken to get there.

'Alex, love!' Maureen Doyle's face lit up as she saw her son.

'All right, Mum.' He gave his mother a hug, shocked how much older, thinner, smaller she'd become, even in that short period of time. He'd made countless offers over the years to relocate her to LA, but she had insisted she was happier in Macclesfield, in her home, surrounded by people she had known for decades.

'Not brought the reporters with you, then?' she said, peering around the front door.

'I'm not sure anyone at the *Macc Express* knows who I am, Mum.'

'And where's Melissa?'

'Oh, filming,' he said vaguely.

It had only been three days since she had told him about the baby. Melissa had not offered to move out – Christopher had yet to tell his wife that their relationship was over and Melissa didn't want to 'rock the boat' until that point. Unable to stay under the same roof as her, Alex had gone to stay with Ted for a couple of nights. It was Ted and his wife who had finally persuaded him to get as far away from LA as he could. Alex had decided not to tell his mum anything about their split. He told himself it was because he didn't want to burden her, but in reality he was hoping Melissa would change her mind.

'Well it's lovely to see you anyway,' said Maureen. 'I'll put the kettle on, shall I?'

'Cool. I'll just go and put my bag upstairs.'

She popped her head around the kitchen door. 'You're staying here tonight?' she said, surprised.

'Not many five-star hotels in Macc, are there?' He smiled.

He walked up the narrow stairwell past the bathroom. The avocado suite had gone and had been replaced by something white and slightly more modern-looking, apparently installed by nice Mr Singh from down the road. His bedroom hadn't changed at all except for one platinum record that hung on the far wall. Maureen was much too discreet to have it on show anywhere else, but it looked just right there next to the shelf full of music trophies from Danehurst, the dusty stack of *Melody Makers* and the little ceramic pot full of plectrums.

Dropping his bag on the bed, he walked to the window. Outside, he could see a man strapping his kids into the back of a slightly battered Fiat Punto. With a lurch, he realised it was 'Mad' Dave Kinsella, a lad he had gone to school with. They'd played in the school football team together and Dave had earned his nickname for creeping into the girls' showers for a dare. For a moment, Alex thought about going down there, saying hello – but then what would he say? 'All right, Dave, how are the kids getting on? Going swimming are you? To the park?'

Here he was, one of the biggest rock stars in the world, a platinum disc on the wall of his bedroom, and yet 'nice Mr Singh' was the one looking out for his mum and Mad Dave was the one with the happy family life and a shiny new caravan. Here in the real world, your dreams might be smaller, but they were still dreams and they could still come true. With a wrenching gut, Alex realised that the part of his life he'd treated as an afterthought – marriage, children, stability – was the thing he had always wanted the most.

Turning away from the window, he spotted something he hadn't seen in years – cassette tapes, neatly lined up along the top of his chest of drawers.

'Wow,' he said, rifling through the carefully hand-written labels. The Pixies, the Breeders, Nick Drake. 'Damn, I had good taste back then,' he muttered. He opened a drawer and found other things, things that suddenly seemed important to him. A handful of scout badges, a paperback book that Grace Ashford had given him on that trip to Bristol, a harmonica that had belonged to his dad, a ticket stub for

481

that fateful Verve concert where he had met Jez, Gav and Pete.

'Hey, Mum!' he shouted, putting his head over the banisters. 'Have you got a box I can use to put some stuff in?'

'There's a shoebox on the sideboard,' shouted back Maureen. 'Just got letters in it. You can leave them on the side.'

Alex bounced down the stairs in three jumps and went to the sideboard, emptying out the box. As he put the letters down, a few slid to the floor and he bent to pick them up.

'Christie's?' he said to himself, seeing the logo on one letter. He felt his heart begin to pound.

'I've only got fig rolls . . .' said Maureen, walking through holding up a packet. She stopped abruptly when she saw her son holding the letter.

'What is this, Mum?' Alex said.

'Just a check-up at the hospital.' She tried to smile, but her eyes were full of pain.

Alex had been past Christie's Hospital dozens of times on the bus. It specialised in cancer treatment. 'This isn't a check-up, Mum,' he said, looking at the letter. 'This is asking you to report to admissions.'

'I just need some chemotherapy.'

'*Just* some chemotherapy?' said Alex.

Maureen had walked back into the kitchen and began opening the biscuits with jerky movements. 'Stupid things . . .' she muttered.

'Mum. Just stop for a moment,' Alex said, putting his hand on hers. She dropped the packet and began shaking. He put an arm around her and gently led her to the kitchen table.

'Tell me, Mum,' he said, sitting down opposite her.

'The doctors want to try the chemo first before they do the surgery. I think they want to try and shrink the tumour.'

Tumour. His mother had a tumour.

'Why didn't you tell me?'

'I didn't want to worry you. Not before I knew if it was serious. Everything is going so well for you and Melissa and I didn't want to burden you. Jean and Brian were going to come with me to the hospital.'

'Jean and Brian are your next-door neighbours,' he said angrily. 'I'm your son.' He clutched her hand. 'Listen, you're coming back to America with me. We're going to get you the best treatment available.'

'Alex, Christie's is one of the best cancer hospitals in the country. I'm lucky, really.'

'Don't be such a fucking martyr!' he shouted, banging his fist on the kitchen side.

He saw her alarm and took a deep breath. 'I'm sorry, Mum,' he said, his voice pleading. 'I just want to make you better.'

'I'll be fine, love,' she said softly. 'It's going to be all right.'

He rested his head on her shoulder and began to sob, feeling ashamed and alone as she stroked his hair and held him tight. 'Don't you worry about a thing,' she whispered. 'We'll get through this together.'

We have to, thought Alex. *Because she's all I've got left.*

56

April 2008

The flight from Dubai arrived earlier than expected. Miles' dinner with the sheikh had been cancelled due to 'pressing state business', so he was on the ground at City airport before 9 p.m. As his Bentley left the terminal, it was tempting to go straight to Soho. He felt he had been neglecting the Globe over the past few months. Yes, Chrissy seemed to be doing a good job, but it never did any harm to keep an eye on things, keep the staff on their toes. He imagined the look of surprise and fear on their faces as he walked in, as the barman fumbled to get his drink on the bar, as the buzz went around the club. And then he imagined all the people who would want to talk to him. 'Miles! How are you? Now about that investment opportunity ...' 'Long time no see, any chance you could help me out with the planners?' 'Miles, you said you'd call ...' And that was before the manager and the sommelier and the receptionist would want to talk to him about budgets and restocking and membership queries.

Screw 'em, thought Miles, leaning forward to his driver. 'Take me home,' he said.

Their house in Notting Hill was sumptous. Three rooms on the ground floor had been linked to create a sunken living-cum-entertaining space with a huge kitchen diner overlooking the garden, accessed by French doors which folded right back for summer parties. The garden, too, had been landscaped to make it a series of enclosed areas where guests could sit and drink or smoke. There was even a sunken hot tub which cast a blue-green glow up the side of the house, adding to the atmosphere.

Miles let himself in and threw his keys on to the hall table. The house was quiet, only a few lights on – probably just on the timers. Chrissy would be at the club until midnight at the earliest and Miles felt a little rush of excitement at being home alone. He chuckled to himself as he walked into his study: *simple things*. The problem with success was that you were never alone. Everyone wanted a moment of your time, to make decisions on a current project or to talk about plans for the next one. Then there was the endless schmoozing of politicians or socialising with useful contacts. In Dubai, where refusing hospitality of any kind was considered a terrible snub, that claustrophobia had been tripled. Not that it had been a chore. Miles could feel that the opening of the Laing resort in Dubai was going to be a triumph, and he had plans to use the same formula for super-luxe getaways in Mexico, Cape Town and Rio.

He poured himself a brandy, then flopped down in his favourite squashy leather armchair. He kicked off his shoes and scrunched his toes in the carpet. *Bliss*. He'd had this study built as the ultimate man-cave, with a walk-in humidor and every kind of sports, movie and porn channel piped into the entertainment system, but he'd rarely had time to take advantage. He grabbed the remote control for his plasma-screen TV. His thumb hovered over the 'on' button as he heard voices. He cocked his head. No, not just voices, distant laughter. *God, I hope the neighbours aren't going to have some sort of bloody party tonight*, he thought.

He got up and walked in his stockinged feet out of his

study and down to the kitchen. He didn't turn on the lights – didn't want to alert them before he could see what was going on. But he could tell straight away that it wasn't the neighbours. The laughter was coming from his own garden – there was someone in the hot tub. The pool lights had not been switched on, but he could see the dim turquoise glow of the water and the steam coming off the surface. Making sure he was hidden in the shadows, Miles crept closer, until he could see. It was Chrissy, her hair wet and slicked back; her shoulders were under the water, but he could see she was topless. And her arms were around Bill Loxley, the general manager of the London Globe.

Miles' fists clenched. Only a few years earlier, he would have exploded, but he was bringing his vicious temper under control. A road-rage incident two years ago plus innumerable verbal attacks on staff members had made him seek help from a celebrity shrink who taught him 'coping techniques'. He closed his eyed and inhaled through his nose.

Had he known? He and Chrissy had spent days, sometimes weeks apart, and when they were together, they were often at each other's throats. But that was just the way married couples were, wasn't it? Similarly, their sexual relationship, so passionate in the beginning, had dwindled to nothing; surely that too was a common thing in marriage, especially after fifteen years? But the honest answer was no, Miles hadn't known. In fact, the thought of Chrissy wanting, needing another man had never entered his head. But of all the people to choose: Bill Loxley! He was an *employee*. What he made in a year wouldn't even cover Chrissy's clothing allowance.

Opening his eyes, he watched Bill's hand snake round the back of his wife's neck, stroking her shoulder, looking into her eyes. Miles felt sick, genuinely nauseous. He'd much rather he'd caught them in flagrante; the easy and intimate way they laughed together in the blue shimmering water was harder to take. They looked like a couple in love.

He stepped backwards, padding away into the darkness, quickly grabbing his shoes and coat and turning off the lights. As he was heading for the door, he stopped and went back into the study, emptying his brandy glass and wiping it clear. He didn't want anyone to know he'd ever been there. Out on the street, he quickly walked around the corner and pulled out his mobile phone, his breath puffing in the cold air.

First he called for his driver, then he scrolled down to Michael Marshall.

'Michael,' he said, surprised at how calm he sounded. 'Sorry to disturb you so late, but I was wondering if I could just pop round? I wanted to test your knowledge of UK divorce law.'

Four weeks later, Miles was standing on his private terrace in the penthouse of the Dubai Laing, gazing out at the Arabian Sea shimmering like a sheet of black onyx in the moonlight. It had been a good day. A very good day. A 737 had shipped in the crème de la crème of London and New York to the launch of the latest Laing Resort. People of taste, influence or simply celebrity, they had each been given one of the 'restricted suites' with huge open-plan living space and personal spa complete with full-time masseur and private thirty-metre pool with direct sea views. Pampering, first-rate service and a gorgeous room, followed by a decadent no-holds-barred party on the beach: that was the way to spread the word about the unrivalled luxury of the Laing. A hotel was only as good as its reputation, and after today's launch, *everyone* was going to want to check into the Laing.

He heard footsteps and turned as Michael Marshall approached him carrying a glass of champagne.

'Are we celebrating?'

Michael nodded. The Dubai sun had bronzed his face, bringing out the colour of his eyes. In a blue shirt and cream trousers he looked liked Cary Grant. To his surprise, Miles felt himself becoming aroused, or maybe that was the thought of what was about to come.

'They disappeared to the Bridge Suite about an hour ago and have just returned downstairs,' said Michael, handing Miles a disc.

'Good,' said Miles, sipping the wine. 'Give me twenty minutes and then send Chrissy up to see me.'

Miles finished the champagne watching the party scene below him. It was still in full swing, but for him, at least, it was over. He showered and changed into his silk pyjamas and monogrammed slippers. He heard the door open just as he was walking back through – perfect timing.

'Hey,' said Chrissy. 'Michael said you wanted me. Are you OK?'

'Fine,' said Miles, handing her a glass of champagne. 'Great party, by the way. You did very well.'

Chrissy had made such a success of the Globe clubs, Miles had felt no qualms about bringing her on board for the development and launch of the Laing ventures. She had been invaluable in softening and feminising his design vision for the Las Vegas hotel, and in sole charge of the opening night, she had struck the perfect balance between glitz and discreet luxury. Here in Dubai, she had once again shown her talent, making full use of the resort's amazing pool and beach area, keeping the dress code casual – 'no shoes' – and handing out Slush Puppies and hot dogs. Yes, the Laing is sumptuous and elite, she was saying, but it's also somewhere you can have fun. Chrissy had really turned into an asset. She was worth having around, but only if he could keep her under control.

'So why did you want me?' she asked.

'I wanted to talk to you about something. I want to renew our vows.'

Chrissy's face gave nothing away, she merely raised her eyebrows. 'Why would we want to do that, Miles?'

He smiled thinly. 'Not exactly the reaction I was hoping

488

for. "Darling, what a wonderful idea", perhaps, or "I can't wait to tell everyone". Not "Why?"'

Chrissy took a sip of her champagne. 'Well, things haven't exactly been brilliant between us recently, you have to admit that.'

'Then what better way to get through this rough patch?' said Miles. 'We can have a fresh start; it will be just like the old days.'

Chrissy laughed wearily. 'The old days are long gone, Miles, long gone.'

Miles shook his head and looked at her for a moment, then raised his glass in salute.

'Have it your way,' he said. 'You can't say I didn't try.'

'What do you mean?'

He picked up a remote control and clicked a button. The wide-screen television flickered into life, showing a single shot of two people making love. Chrissy's face flushed with embarrassment and anger.

'You and Bill seem to have had a particularly good time at the party,' he said, turning down the volume as the orgasmic groans grew particularly loud. His wife looked shell-shocked.

'I'm in love with him,' said Chrissy finally.

'How touching,' sneered Miles, clicking off the picture. 'Shame it can't go on.'

'Don't blame Bill,' she snapped. 'This is your fault. If you'd shown the slightest interest in me over the last few years, maybe I wouldn't have had to go to another man. And Bill *is* a man, Miles.'

The colour drained from his face. 'What's that supposed to mean?'

She shook her head. 'Don't you think I know, Miles? You're gay.'

He looked at her scornfully. 'You're being ridiculous.'

'How many dicks have you had in your mouth? Is that

489

how you like it? Or do you prefer to give? Pretend that you're still a man that way?'

He smiled callously. 'I really don't think you should be throwing stones in this particular glass house, Chrissy. You've built yourself a very comfortable life here, but it doesn't take much to destroy someone's reputation. The Hastings past, the junkie brother, the sordid little lesbian shows in Phuket. I could go on.'

She looked pale. 'I've told you before, I was just a dancer . . .'

'Don't be so bloody naïve!' he snapped. 'Do you think any of those girls you worked with – who you *performed* with – would keep quiet for you? All it took was a few baht.'

'It's lies!' she cried. 'I never did anything like that.'

'I know everything, Chrissy,' he said fiercely. 'You fuck people for money. That's what you've been doing since the second I laid eyes on you.'

She stuck her chin out defiantly. 'I want a divorce.'

Miles laughed in her face. 'Divorce is out of the question. I can't have that sort of distraction when we're at such a delicate stage of our expansion. It wouldn't go down well here. Dubai is a very moral country.'

She snorted. 'What would you know about morals?'

His expression softened and he raised his hand to touch her face. He'd known she wouldn't take this lying down.

'I do love you, Chrissy,' he said. 'We're good together. Look what we've built.'

She glared at him. 'You really expect me to go along with this? Play happy families with you?'

'Think of it as playing a role, pretending to be something you're not. You've always been good at that.'

'You really are a bastard, aren't you?'

Miles gave a small smile. 'It has been said. Oh, and one other thing, Chrissy.' He walked over to the desk and picked up a document.

'What's this?'

'A post-nuptial agreement.' He put the paper on the table next to her and twisted his Montblanc fountain pen open. 'You see, my father was right about protecting the family interests, and, well, it was the exuberance of youth getting married without doing that.'

Chrissy picked the document up, scanning it, her eyes growing wider as she read.

'Take my word, it's a fair agreement,' said Miles. 'In the unlikely event of a divorce, you will receive a ten per cent share in Globe Holdings with a ten million ceiling. Don't let anyone ever say I haven't appreciated all your input into the business.'

'You are kidding me?' she gasped. 'Ash Corp. is worth billions!'

'Yes, it is, but I think ten million pounds is a fortune for a hooker from Hastings, don't you?'

'You can't do this.'

'Oh, I can,' said Miles. 'You see, if you don't sign this now, I am calling the police.'

'The *police*?'

'You'll be aware that infidelity is a criminal offence in Dubai. Punishable by twelve months' imprisonment, I believe. It's rarely upheld for foreigners unless a strong complaint is made to the authorities, but, as you know, I am very well regarded in the United Arab Emirates. And once the Dubai authorities see this DVD, I'm sure they'll want this sort of behaviour held to account.'

Chrissy ran at him screaming, her fingers clawing at his face, but Miles caught her wrists and flung her into a chair.

'I won't do it!' she hissed, her eyes blazing. 'This is black-mail! I'll fight it every inch of the way.'

'You'll be fighting it from a jail cell, and I hear the condi-tions in prisons over here are pretty grim. Mind you, I'm sure they'll be interested in your lesbo show.'

'Fuck you, Miles!' she shouted.

'No, fuck you,' he spat, grabbing the contract and the pen and shoving them into her hands. 'Did you really think you could screw me over, flaunt your affair with some underling in my face? No, you've fucked up, Chrissy, and there's a price to be paid. Now *sign*.'

She looked up at him, her face a mask of hate. Then her shoulders slumped and her head hung down. She took the pen and signed the contract. Miles picked it up and slipped it into a leather document folder, then locked it in the safe. When he turned back, Chrissy was looking at him like a wolf with its leg caught in a trap. *Which I suppose she is*, he thought.

'Please understand, this is just protection, Chrissy,' he said in a soothing tone. 'It's going to be far better if we work with each other rather than against one another.'

'You can't stop me seeing Bill,' she said insolently.

He smiled cruelly. 'I think you'll find I can. I'm offering him the job as general manager of the Globe Sydney. That should be far enough to keep his filthy paws off you.'

'He won't take it.'

'Oh he will. If he doesn't, by the time I've finished muddying his reputation he won't be able to get a job shovelling shit from the pavements in Soho.'

He stretched across to the small mahogany table and picked up the phone. 'Room service?' he said. 'Mr Ashford here in the penthouse. I'd like you to prepare something special, perhaps that thing you do with quail? And retrieve a bottle of forty-seven Petrus from the cellar. My wife and I have something to celebrate.'

57

December 2008

When the Stockbridge Hall renovations were finally completed, after almost four years of work and five million pounds on structural and cosmetic alterations, Julian decided to throw a weekend house party to celebrate. To Grace's disappointment, he invited art dealers, collectors and gallery owners, a very staid and serious crowd, and she was beginning to wish she'd laid on hors d'oeuvres on the terrace instead of a hog roast.

'Never let it be said that your boyfriend doesn't like the sound of his own voice,' whispered Sarah Brayfield, loitering at the back of the west wing gallery, sipping a much-needed glass of red wine. Grace giggled behind her hand, feeling like a naughty schoolgirl bunking off a field trip. They were forty-five minutes into a guided tour and had yet to leave the gallery, where Julian was standing in front of his paintings and talking expansively about his early abstract period.

'He's just proud of what he's done.' Grace smiled.

'Well I'm not sure about the paintings, but you can't fault what he's done with this place,' said Sarah. 'I'm just hoping you're going to adopt me and I can move into the bedroom in that Rapunzel turret.'

Her friend was right. Stockbridge Hall was absolutely spectacular. The house itself was a labyrinth of rooms, secret turrets and huge bedrooms, while the grounds had miles of woods, lush meadows and lanes flanked by lavender and cow parsley where Grace would spend hours riding her bike in the sun.

'Well that's enough about my daubings,' said Julian. 'Now I've got something a little special to show you. Follow me, everyone. To the screening room.'

Grace smiled at the guests, showing them towards Julian's specially constructed darkroom. He was keen to show off his new project, 'Newspeak', a wall of sixty-four television screens which would randomly flick between TV stations around the world. He had installed a giant satellite screen on the roof for the purpose.

'I think I've seen enough for one day,' whispered Sarah as they sloped off to hide in the kitchen, toasty from the Aga filling the room with heat. 'Feels like we're back in the Bristol house,' she said, settling at the farmhouse table. 'Remember how the boiler was always on the blink? Either tropical conditions or icicles on the cold tap.'

Grace nodded and filled up their glasses. 'That seems a lifetime ago.'

'For you maybe,' said Sarah. 'I'm still single, childless, careless . . . only difference is its five-hundred-quid Frette sheets keeping me warm at night.'

'You were adamant last month you like being single.'

'I said I'm not afraid of being single. Thing is, I don't want just *anyone*. I want the right one. Speaking of which, did you read about Alex and Melissa's divorce? Sounds messy.'

'I spoke to him a few weeks ago,' said Grace. 'I invited him down tonight actually, but he couldn't make it because his mum isn't well.'

'Still carrying a torch for little Alex?' Sarah teased. 'Can't imagine what you'd see in a gorgeous millionaire rock star like that.'

'Sarah, I'm a happily unmarried woman,' said Grace, feeling herself blush.

494

'I know that, but we can still talk about our "What if" men, can't we?'

If Grace was honest, she had been dwelling on that very thought lately. She had begun to wonder how she had managed to end up rattling around another big, beautiful mansion with an absent partner and just a handful of staff for company. Julian was away four nights out of seven working on his 'urban study', an extension of his Newspeak project which involved installing a series of TV screens in and around east London. For that end, he was using a rented studio in Shoreditch rather than the five-thousand-square-foot space he'd just had built in the grounds of Stockbridge Hall. It felt like history was repeating itself.

'So how's life in the castle?' asked Sarah.

'Julian is giving up smoking, so he's snapping like a little dog,' said Grace, dodging the question. 'I'm actually glad he's up in London half the week.'

'I think you're bored,' mused Sarah. 'You know what you should do?' she smiled mischievously.

'What?'

'A film – a documentary. You've got a fantastic visual eye.'

'Come on. Julian's the one playing around with videos. I'm a photographer, not a director.'

Sarah took another sip of wine. 'I'm not talking about you being the next Spielberg, but I think you could do an incredible documentary. Michael Moore has won Oscars from getting on his soap box with a camcorder.'

Grace loved how Sarah believed in her, thought she was capable of anything. She had none of her friend's confidence in her own abilities and for a moment she wondered if the years living with bullish, driven men like Gabriel and Julian had sapped her self-belief.

'I can help with investment.' Sarah worked in one of the country's biggest media law practices, with contacts across the business.

'You know I don't need it.'

'Film finance isn't just about money. I know a couple of guys who could exec-produce it for you.'

For the first time in a long time, Grace felt a flurry of excitement.

'The big four zero is out there, Grace. When it comes, we want to be forty, fulfilled and fabulous.'

'I'll drink to that,' said Grace.

Julian hated the idea. Grace wasn't entirely surprised; he hadn't been all that supportive of her photography, deriding it as 'populist' and 'commercial', two things he found completely unacceptable in any artistic venture. Grace also suspected that he disliked the idea of her stepping on his toes. He was the visual artist in their relationship and he didn't want her stealing any of his thunder. Grace had spread a series of black and white prints of photographs she had taken in Parador on the big table in the conservatory, a sort of makeshift mood board for a possible documentary. Julian gave them a cursory glance.

'Say something,' said Grace with gathering frustration.

'OK,' he said. 'I just don't understand why, of the million subjects in the world, your documentary has to be about Parador.'

'Because there's a great untold story there.'

'And your desire to go back there has nothing to do with your ex-husband?'

'Don't be so childish, Julian,' said Grace. 'You know Gabe has a new wife.'

'I just think it's strange, that's all I'm saying.'

He walked back into the house and she followed him. She was angry that he could be so dismissive of her interests and ambitions, yet he expected her to drop everything and muck in when he got excited about a project.

'Don't walk away from me, Julian,' she said. 'This is important to me.'

Julian stopped and crossed his arms. 'Is this about you reasserting some ludicrous sense of independence?'

'No! Why would you even think that? And what's so wrong about having my own career anyway?'

He snorted. 'Be honest, Grace,' he said. 'This whole thing is just about you showing me and your precious Gabriel how clever and creative you are.'

'I can't believe you're behaving like this.'

'Fine,' he said, flapping a dismissive hand. 'Do whatever you want. Fly off to Parador. But don't expect me to go running after your kids if they want to come home from school for the weekend. Or go dashing off to your mother's if the poor dear has a fall.'

She stared after him, wondering if she had ever really known this man at all.

'Have you lost your mind?' cried Gabriel, pacing up and down the lawns at El Esperanza. 'You left Parador, left our *marriage*, because you were terrified about safety, and now you want to go running around some of the most dangerous barrios in the world to make a *movie*?'

Grace was furious. This was the first time she had been back to Parador since she had left Ibiza years before, and she hadn't exactly expected to be welcomed with open arms. But she had expected a little more support, considering that the reason for her visit, if it came off, would help Gabriel's precious cause.

'Gabe, don't you start. Julian didn't speak to me for three days when I told him I wanted to do this.'

'Well for once I agree with Julian,' said Gabriel. 'I told you on the phone I can't be responsible for what happens to you, and if you choose to blatantly disregard what I say ... It's *dangerous* out there, Grace.'

At forty-five, Gabriel was still a handsome man. The flecks of grey in his hair gave him the elegance and dignity of a forties matinee idol. But the fire she had seen in his eyes when they had first come back to Parador had dimmed. His words were laced with bitterness and anxiety. After three attempts at winning the presidency, he had resigned himself to life as a senator in the Parador assembly, and that all-consuming drive for change and justice had gone. He seemed smaller somehow, his shoulders less straight.

He still travelled in a bulletproof car, but the truth was the CARP party was toothless, far too weak to be a threat to anyone. Even so, Grace had hoped Gabriel of all people would understand her desire to bring the problems of his country to a wider audience.

'You wanted to make a difference, Gabe. It's the reason you ran for office, it's the reason our marriage failed.'

'Don't blame the party for—' he began, but she cut him off.

'Our marriage failed because Parador was the most important thing to you. I just want to go out into the barrios and show the world what's happening.'

Gabriel stopped and looked at her. 'This is about Angel Cay, isn't it?' he said.

'What? What, I . . .' she stuttered, remembering the time she had told her husband about the island. He'd once asked her if she had ever done anything bad and after Caro's death she'd admitted what had gone on that hot summer night.

'Just because you once found a body and did nothing about it doesn't mean you have to spend the rest of your life being a saint, Grace. The charity work, the photographs, the documentaries. It's all atonement for one stupid mistake.'

'It's not,' she said vigorously.

'Are you papering over the cracks, Grace, or is this really making you happy?' he asked her, his blue eyes boring into her. 'Because I want you to be happy, I really do.'

'Gabe, I . . .' she began, but just then Gabriel's wife Martina appeared at the French windows of the house and came across the lawns with a tray bearing three cold drinks for them. She was in navy slacks and a cream silk shirt; elegant, decorous, the politician's wife Grace had never been able to be. Grace watched Gabriel's face as Martina approached and she didn't miss the little smile, the softening of the eyes. He loved her, there was no doubt of that. She wished she could feel happier about it.

'Will you be staying for lunch, Grace?' Martina asked, hooking her arm through her husband's.

'No, no. My car should be here in twenty minutes to take me into Palumbo.'

'But you'll be back for dinner?'

'*Si dios quiere*,' said Gabriel, shaking his head.

If God wills it.

She spent eight hours in 'El Tumba', Parador's worst slum, which clung forlornly to the hillside overlooking Palumbo. She interviewed orphans and farmers who had lost everything after the paramilitary sequestered their land. She spoke to them of hunger and suffering, she spoke to them of disease and squalor, but most of all, she spoke to them of hope and their amazing, inspiring belief that God would provide, that one day they would come down off the hill and make a new life for themselves.

Back at El Esperanza, she stripped off her clothes and stepped into the shower, tipping her head back as the hot water washed away the stench. Wrapping herself in a clean white terry robe, she sat at the desk by the window watching the sun set across the jungle, a sight at once so familiar and yet so alien to her now.

Gabe peeked around the door. 'Can I come in?' he asked.

'I'm decent,' she said, thinking, *Nothing you haven't seen before*.

'How was it?'

She shook her head slowly. 'A quarter of a million people

in one slum,' she said. 'It beggars belief. Did you know one child dies a violent death there every eight hours?'

'Do you think you got enough for your film?'

'I wish,' she said ruefully. 'There were so many stories to be told: happy, sad, some even terrifying. But I'm still missing the angle. At the moment it's just a lot of very poor people in appalling circumstances. I need a narrative to pull it all together.'

Gabriel took a piece of paper from his pocket and held it out to her.

'What's this?'

'Phone numbers,' he said. 'The first one is for Father Diaz. He looks after six hundred orphans in twelve sites around Parador. His brother was Pablos Cavalas, one of the most notorious drug-dealers in the late eighties. The second number will help you arrange an interview with the president.' He smiled. 'Although I doubt you'll get much there, I'd be interested how he justifies El Tumba to you.'

'And the last one?'

'The third number is for Felix Philipe, coach for the Parador national football team. Five years ago he opened a soccer academy for the children of the slums. Half of his squad are men who've grown up in the barrios.' Gabriel shrugged. 'I think you should find your angle in there somewhere.'

Grace stood up and hugged him. 'Thank you, Gabriel,' she said simply, resting her chin on his shoulder. They stood like that for a long moment, then Gabriel turned back to the door.

'I'm proud of you, Grace,' he said, his eyes flicking to hers and holding them for a second. 'I really am.'

And for the first time in a long time, Grace felt the same way.

58

Alex came to, jerking awake.

'What the hell?' he mumbled, before wincing at the pain in his neck.

I fell asleep on the sofa again, he thought numbly. In the corner of the room, the TV was still playing with the sound off. *Breakfast TV. Bloody hell, I haven't seen that in years*.

Squinting, shading his eyes from the bright morning light, he pushed himself on to one elbow, shook a bent cigarette from the pack and lit it, coughing the smoke straight out again. He sat forward, trying to ignore the thumping in his head, and picked up the various cans and bottles crowding the coffee table. Empty . . . empty . . . a-ha! An inch of whisky sloshing around in the bottom of the bottle. He tipped it up, feeling the chink of the glass on his teeth, and gagged it down in three swallows. And that was when it hit him, as it did every morning: the sinking, churning feeling in his stomach – the feeling that he was still alive and had another day to face. He ran to the toilet and vomited.

Walking back into the lounge, wiping his mouth, he could see that every available surface was covered in crushed cans, open tins and pizza boxes. *What a shit-hole*, he thought. He had barely left his west London home since he'd returned

501

from his mum's funeral six months earlier. He had an arrangement with the man in the off-licence to bring him a box of booze and snacks every day, taking the empties away when he left, although Alex had to admit he'd been getting a little lax on tidying up over the past week.

Maureen had died in her sleep, but that brought him little comfort. He had watched her suffer for weeks, months, the pain creasing into her face. She'd been brave, of course, hadn't wanted Alex to see how much she was suffering, but the cancer swept through her so quickly, the doctors had struggled to keep up with the morphine. During the last days, they had let her come home, and Alex had even allowed himself to think she was getting better. She was sitting up in bed, her eyes bright and clear, talking about the old days, when she and Alex's father had bought their first car, a Hillman Imp, and had taken it for a run out to Southport. Now, Alex thought it had all been for his benefit, to make him feel better, not her.

'It's going to be OK, love,' she would say whenever he cried. 'You'll be strong for me, won't you?'

Back in London, Alex closed his front door and quietly fell to pieces. He felt utterly lost, adrift in the world with nothing solid to cling to. All he could do was blot it out, drinking anything that came to hand: sherry, gin, the ouzo he had brought back from his trip to Greece with his mum. Drugs were all around him in his part of London, and he tried them all, plus a long list of prescription drugs. He just wanted the pain to stop.

He walked over to the TV and snapped it off, then slowly climbed the stairs, running a tepid bath. When he was ready, he took a cab into Soho. No one bothered him in the West End's busy, grimy streets. Two weeks' beard growth and unwashed hair helped, as did the bottle in his hand. No one wanted to bother the crazy drunk guy with the red-rimmed eyes. Besides, since his split with Melissa, Al Doyle was no longer a 'celeb'. He was back to being an everyday, common or garden musician. He barely rated a mention on Perez Hilton any more.

He dropped in at the Coach and Horses, still quiet before the lunch rush. He ordered a double brandy and a pint and retreated to a corner to read his book, an account of the 'Enfield Poltergeist', a malevolent spirit that had apparently possessed a teenage girl in the 1970s. He had always been interested in the unexplained, but since his mum's death he had begun to think about it a lot more. Maybe good spirits could come back and watch over you, he thought. Or maybe bad ones, angry ones, could come back and screw you up. *Maybe we're all ghosts*, thought Alex. *Maybe this whole thing is all an illusion.*

By seven o'clock, Alex had been in eight pubs, an off-licence and a sushi restaurant, where he drank the sake and left his teriyaki untouched. By nine o'clock he was in Soho House, slurring his words as he said, 'Dom Perignon, barman,' banging his hand on the counter. 'And make it snappy.'

That was the last thing that Alex would remember clearly, the point where his anchor gave way. Time seemed to be telescoping and contracting. He felt shaken up and disorientated, like he was on a rollercoaster he couldn't see. He was blacking out, then tuning in again, with no idea what had happened in between. First the waitress was bringing the champagne over to the table, then the bottle was empty, upside down in the ice bucket. Next he looked up and there were two girls sitting next to him, then he glanced away and they were gone. *Drink through it*, said a voice in his head. *Keep drinking and it will all go away.* He ordered some tequila, then some brandy, then some exotic beer that tasted of leaves. Then he found himself sitting on his own. Had he been asleep? Suddenly all these jump-cuts were starting to scare him. He wanted to get home. But where was home exactly?

'Here you are, mate,' said the driver. 'Camden High Street.'

'What? Why are we here?' Alex couldn't remember getting into the cab, let alone telling him to go to north London.

The cabbie gave a world-weary shrug. 'You tell me, pal.'

Alex looked around as the cab pulled away. At least now he knew where he was. He was standing at the door to the flat where the rest of Year Zero had lived all those years ago. The buzzers were the same; only the labels had changed. The top flat bell, which the lead singer had labelled as 'Jez and the Others', now read 'Taya B.' In fact, now he looked, a lot of things had changed. The kebab shop opposite the station was now a florist's and the corner shop that sold cheap bread was now a bistro. It had been cleaned up a lot. Alex didn't feel at home here either. He stumbled along the street, the headlights of the passing cars blurring into streams and trails, the people walking past giving him a wide berth. *Another drink*, the voice whispered, *just to steady your nerves*. Haltingly, he approached a pub – wasn't it a bank? – but a penguin-suited bouncer stepped out, one hand up. 'Not tonight,' he said not even recognising him. Alex began to protest, then saw the look in the man's eyes and kept walking, turning into a convenience store with a neon sign in the window: '24/7'. *That's me all right*, thought Alex, giggling to himself. He pinballed down the narrow aisles, bouncing off shelves either side, colliding with a carousel display of cheap plastic children's toys and sending some crashing to the floor. 'Sorry! Sorry!' he said, gathering them back up. 'My mistake, no harm done.' Glancing towards the counter, he grabbed a water pistol and stuck it into his pocket. *That'll teach the buggers to rip me off*, he thought crazily.

Suddenly the shopkeeper, a small Korean man with half-moon glasses, was standing in front of him.

'What you want?' he asked. It was only then that Alex noticed the man was clutching a broom.

'Drink,' he said. 'Just want a drink. Tequila.'

'No tequila!' shouted the man, waving his broom angrily. 'You go!'

'What about gin?'

'No drink!' barked the man, prodding Alex with the end of his broom. 'I call police.'

'Just a half-bottle,' said Alex, almost pleading now. It looked as though the old man had taken against him for some reason and he really wanted that gin. 'Look, I have money ...' He reached into his pocket for his wallet and instead pulled out the water pistol.

The shopkeeper jumped backwards as if electrified. 'Police!' he yelled, running towards the door. 'Call police!'

Alex looked down at his hand, the misunderstanding slowly dawning on him. 'Oh no, this is just a toy ...' he said, tripping over a pile of newspapers and crashing into a shelf of baked beans.

'There he is!' shouted the shopkeeper. 'He smash up store!'

Next to the old man was another figure, wearing all black, talking into a radio.

'Stay calm, sir,' said the policeman, walking forward. But Alex wasn't waiting. He ran towards the back of the shop, crashing through a door. All he could think was that he had to get away. It was some sort of storeroom: stacks of cardboard boxes, pallets of tins covered in clear plastic. He ran towards a door at the rear. It was locked. He looked around. There were no windows.

'Let me out, you fuckers!' he shouted.

Outside he could hear the wail of police sirens.

'Oh shit, oh shit,' he said, running back and slamming the storeroom door, bolting it closed. He'd read about people getting shot by armed police. He leant against the door and pulled his mobile out of his pocket. Who to call? Who could help? His heart was hammering, and sweat was rolling down his face, despite the coldness of the storeroom. Outside he could hear shouts and heavy footsteps.

He picked up the phone and scrolled to a number he hadn't used for years.

'Miles. You have to help me.' Alex spoke quickly, his voice trembling.

'Go on,' said Miles. Calm, unflappable. The police were banging on the door now.

Alex quickly explained. 'What should I do?'

'OK, I'm in New York,' said Miles. 'But I'll call my lawyer, he's in London. His name in Michael Marshall. He will find you and I promise you he will fix this.'

'Thanks, Miles, thank you, thank you.'

'A friend in need and all that,' said Miles.

The door lurched inwards. 'Miles, they're kicking the door in, what should I do now? *Miles, help me.*'

'Stay calm, Alex. Don't do anything stupid. Michael will come and find you. Leave it to me. Oh, and Alex?'

'What?'

'I'd get away from that door.'

Just as Alex moved out of the way, the wood splintered and flew inwards, rapidly followed by three policemen. Alex started sobbing. He drew the water pistol and pushed it against his temple.

'Stop there or I'll shoot,' he cried as a policeman wrestled him to the ground and cuffed his hands behind him.

'I only wanted a drink,' he whimpered. And then he blacked out.

59

May 2009

Approached along the long crunchy drive, Second Chances looked like a particularly elegant country house hotel, the sort where guests took high tea and debated which spa treatment to try next. But the eighteenth-century Bath-stone manor house was a very different type of residential property. The front door could only be opened with a master key, the rooms had narrow beds with foam mattresses and the food tended to come from large catering tins, warmed in a vat. You didn't come to Second Chances for a holiday; you came here because you had no other choice. Its literature described it as a 'rehabilitation facility', but this was no overgrown health farm for stressed-out celebrities who'd overindulged on the party circuit. Second Chances was a real hospital, for people with real problems. And for the last three weeks, it had been Alex Doyle's home.

He could only remember fragments from the first few days of his arrival. He had been isolated and sedated, a nurse monitoring him around the clock. He'd vacillate between shivering, begging for more blankets, then rolling sweats and diarrhoea as the drugs and alcohol left his system. It was a little-known fact – to Alex at least – that withdrawal from alcohol was infinitely more drastic and life-threatening than from drugs such as heroin. Booze could take days, even weeks of physical pain, hallucinations and genuine sickness. Alex ran the gamut. But slowly, very slowly, he had come up for air.

After isolation, he was assigned to share a room with a young man named William – everyone was paired up with a buddy; no one was allowed to sit and mope alone. Their illness, they were repeatedly told, could be mastered, but only through constant vigilance. The addiction wanted you to be weak, it wanted you to feel sorry for yourself, it wanted you to go and get wasted. So all day and late into the evening, in group sessions and individual one-to-ones, they were told to confront their shortcomings, confess to their transgressions. Alex found he had plenty to say.

'Don't rush it,' said Dr Wilson, the morning of Alex's fourth week. 'If you'd broken your leg, you wouldn't expect to be able to run the hundred metres so soon, would you?'

'But I do feel better,' said Alex. 'I'm not shaking or nauseous and I'm sleeping better than I have in years.'

'That's good. But remember, addiction is both physical and mental. Your body may be free of the toxins, but your brain needs time to heal too.'

The trouble was, Alex had never been much good at patience. He had always been anxious to get on to the next thing. He had mastered the piano, so he learnt the violin, then the rest of the orchestra. Then, when he outgrew the music department at Danehurst and was due to go to the Royal Academy, he wanted to jump forward again, so he had joined a band. There was always another peak to climb. The therapists pointed out how 'enabling' his choice of lifestyle had been for someone prone to addictive behaviour. Yes, drugs were available in the music industry, sure, but what was damaging was the emptiness of Alex's life. As soon as he had a nice guitar, he wanted a bigger amp. As soon as he had an Aston Martin, he wanted a helicopter. He had a nice girlfriend, but he wanted a movie star. He was constantly chasing the next high.

Finally, in group therapy one morning, another patient had

asked the question he had been avoiding: 'What are you running from, Alex?' And suddenly, without warning, Alex began crying, his shoulders heaving with the sobs.

Glancing out of the window of the day room, a glass-fronted conservatory where the patients would sit between sessions, Alex could tell visiting hours had begun. Visitors were strictly vetted – they didn't want your dealer turning up – and were limited to a two-hour visit twice a week. For someone who had hundreds of so-called friends all around the world, Alex had only managed one short visit from Ted Sullivan, who had filled him in on everything being done to contain the news of his 'little break'.

Today, however, it was different. Today, Alex had a real visitor and he was as nervous as a teenager going on his first date. Unable to sit still, he walked towards the front door – and almost bumped right into her.

'Hello, stranger,' said Grace, hugging him warmly. 'I love the new look.'

Alex laughed, relief flooding through him. When Grace had written to request a visit, he hadn't known how he would react, but now she was here, he felt relaxed and comfortable.

'I thought it was time for a change,' he said, rubbing his hand over his straggly beard. 'But you look fantastic.' She was wearing a cream sweater and a grey pencil skirt – sexy but elegant, Grace Ashford's signature look, he smiled.

He led her out into the grounds, where the sunshine warmed his face, and they began to walk slowly down towards the water.

'Well it's nice to see you looking so good,' said Grace.

Alex chuckled. There were no mirrors in Second Chances – they were broken too often – but he caught his reflection in the windows at night. His eyes were sunken and his jeans hung loosely around his shrinking waist. 'It's kind of you, but I look like shit,' he said. 'Is that what they told you to say?' He nodded towards a nurse who was subtly keeping tabs on the patients.

Grace frowned. 'No one told me to say anything.'

'Sorry, it's not paranoia,' said Alex. 'It's just they have this policy at Chances – no negativity. There's a guy who was drinking lighter fuel before he came in here. His skin looks like tissue paper and his eyeballs are pink, but everyone keeps telling him how amazing he's looking.'

Grace smiled and put her arm through his. As they walked, he filled her in on his situation. The blackouts in Soho House, the raid on the off-licence and his frantic call to Miles. From his talk with Ted, he told her how Miles' lawyer had paid off the Korean and persuaded the police and the hospital he had been taken to not to section him – as long as he came straight to Second Chances.

'Well he's done a good job of keeping it quiet,' said Grace. 'I haven't read anything in the newspapers about it.'

'Apparently David Falk – the guy who owns my record label – was toying with the idea of leaking it to the press. Said the idea of me being sectioned might give me a more edgy image. But Ted and Miles talked him round and they've kept a tight lid on it. I don't want to be seen as a bloody freak show.'

'Has anyone recognised you here?'

He nodded. 'It's kind of hard to avoid – we do nothing but talk about ourselves in group therapy. But people are pretty cool about it and everyone wants to help each other get well. Of course there are plenty of people round here more famous than me.'

'Really?' said Grace, wide-eyed.

He pointed. 'That guy over there told me he was Jimi Hendrix yesterday.'

She punched him on the arm.

'Honestly, though, they ponce this place up with words like recovery and rehabilitation, but really it's a psychiatric unit. A nut-house.'

'It's a hospital, Alex, and they're just here to make you well.'

He laughed. 'You sound like the doctors.'

'Well, maybe that's because they know what they're talking about.'

They walked a little way further.

'So if I haven't made the papers, how did you know I was here?'

She pulled a face. 'Miles told me.'

'Ah. Discretion was never his strong point, was it? Has he sent you to baby-sit?'

'I wanted to come.' She turned towards him. 'You know, I wish you'd told me about what was going on. You needed someone, Alex, and I feel horrible that I wasn't there for you.'

Alex waved a hand. 'Grace, I didn't want anyone to be there for me. Besides, I'm learning all sorts of things about myself in this place, and one of the blinding revelations is that no one could have stopped me being an arse. I had to hit bottom before I even knew I was in a hole. So don't feel bad. Not even *I* knew I needed a friend.'

'I wish I'd been able to try.'

'Tell you what, why don't you take me out when I leave this place?'

'Where do you want to go?'

'Anywhere with food. The grub's so awful here, I've started to make mental lists of all the things I'm going to eat when I get out, like prawn cocktail crisps and spaghetti carbonara and Marmite sandwiches – God, I miss Marmite!'

She giggled as they sat on a bench by the lake.

'So what are you going to do when you get out of here, Alex?' she said more seriously. 'You know you're welcome to come and stay with me and Julian at Stockbridge, that's if you're not heading back to LA.'

'I don't think I'll be heading anywhere within a one-thousand-mile radius of Melissa.'

'Have you heard from her?'

He shook his head. 'And don't get all sad about it,' he said.

511

'It's funny, in the middle of all this madness I can actually see things more clearly now. Me and Melissa should never have got together. I mean, we met on the morning of 9/11, did you know that? The thing that brings people together isn't always love. It's timing, convenience, sadness, guilt.'

'Like us?'

He gave a slow smile.

'Do you ever think about him?' Grace said finally. 'The boy from that night?'

'At first I couldn't stop thinking about him,' said Alex. 'But then slowly it got less and less – it's tragic, but you move on with your life. At least it seemed that way, but deep down I think I've always carried it with me.'

He paused, looking down at the bench, running a fingernail along the grain of the wood.

'It's funny, you take drugs to make yourself feel good, but since Angel I've never felt truly good, never really liked myself. But being here, I've realised that it's not all down to one night. There's plenty of other stuff to pick from: my dad dying, the guilt of not being able to look after my mum, the loneliness of going to Danehurst because it was what I thought she wanted. In actual fact, we'd both have been happier if I'd stayed at home.' He laughed. 'Sorry for sounding like a self-pitying bastard, but it's what we do here.'

Grace put her head on his shoulder. For a split second Alex felt they had been transported out of Second Chances hospital and whizzed through the air. Now they were two lovers, two ordinary people, sitting by the boating lake in Regent's Park, enjoying a happy, comfortable silence. It was wonderful, a perfect moment that made his heart want to burst. And then it hit him. He was happy because he was here, right now, with Grace. It was Grace who made him happy. *I love her*, he thought with overpowering clarity. Emotion welled inside him. All he wanted to do was just kiss her.

'Alex?'

He turned round to see the white uniform of one of the nurses.

'You have to come inside for your medication in a few minutes, Alex.'

He nodded, feeling a terrible sense of loss and disappointment as Grace let go of his hand and stood up.

This isn't how it works, he thought angrily. *This isn't how it happens in the movies.* He was supposed to take her in his arms and kiss her as a fiery sun set over the lake. But this wasn't *An Affair to Remember*. It wasn't the top of the Empire State Building. It was a psychiatric unit. No one wanted a madman to declare undying love, even if he was Cary Grant.

He tried to compose himself. 'OK, so before you go, tell me some news from the outside world,' he said as they strolled back towards the house.

'Well, believe it or not,' said Grace, 'I'm making a film.'

'Wow.'

'Actually, it's more of a documentary, and I tell you, I feel as if I'm making it up as I go along.'

'No negativity, remember?' said Alex. 'I bet it's brilliant. Hey, who's doing the score?'

'We're quite a way off from that yet. Why? Know anyone?' she said with a smile.

'Ah, so that's why you came here today,' he teased.

She looked mortally offended. He nudged her arm.

'I'd do it in a heartbeat, Grace,' he said. 'But something tells me I'd be a liability to any project at the moment.'

'Well when you get out, we can talk about it over Marmite sandwiches, OK?'

They stopped at the front door.

'I'd like that, Grace,' he said, hugging her.

'You know you're going to get well, don't you, Alex?' she said, squeezing his hand one last time.

'I know,' he said. 'I know I am.'

513

60

December 2009

'God, I hate Christmas,' said Josh. 'The parties have all been shit this year.'

Sasha raised an eyebrow, looking around the palatial Chester Row townhouse belonging to Euro-millionaire Flavio Torres.

'I do believe they're calling it the credit crunch, darling. A lot of people have lost a lot of money the last few months. That's why everyone is serving cava – it sends the right message.'

'For God's sake, it's like swapping your Ferrari for one of those horrible Prius things.'

Sasha didn't say so, but it was actually an appropriate metaphor for Josh's career. For years he'd cashed in on his glamour-boy image on the Formula One circuit. There were always better drivers out there, but the media had conveniently overlooked the lack of podium places when he was twenty-five and as handsome as a movie star. But now he was pushing thirty-five, he simply couldn't compete with the likes of Jenson Button, who had good looks *and* a Formula One World Championship. The rumour was that Josh's contract with Alliot Bown, his team, wasn't going to be renewed; and then what? She stole a sideways glance at him.

For a second she couldn't believe how long they'd been dating. What had started out as a quick fling had become a four-year on-off relationship. She supposed he was good-looking, but he'd become very snappy recently, resenting her work trips and the increasing attention as the business grew. But he was pretty good between the sheets.

'OK, if you're not feeling festive,' she said, putting her flute on the white marble mantelpiece, 'let's get going.'

'Come on, Sash. It's Christmas.'

'I thought you just said the party was terrible.'

'What's the option? Going home?'

'I'm sorry if that sounds like such an unappealing prospect.'

'Let's at least have a mingle.'

'Ten minutes.' She sighed. 'And if Elton's not here, I'm going home.'

They walked around the ground floor of the house. It was a beautiful place with high ceilings, wonderfully decorated with long gilt mirrors and old oils. Sasha knew Flavio a little and she was sure it was the work of an interior designer; Flavio's taste was slightly more *exotic*. The house was crowded. Josh was right that the crunch had led to some rather anaemic Christmas parties, so when someone like Flavio did it properly, the beautiful people came in droves.

'I've just seen Steve Darling,' said Josh into her ear.

'That awful sports agent?'

'He's not that bad,' he replied. 'Anyway, he said the party's really happening upstairs. Come on.'

Reluctantly, Sasha followed him up the marble staircase. The disadvantage of dating a sportsman – if you could call driving a car a *sport* – was that they tended to flock together: the drivers, the footballers, the boxers. Some were very nice, of course, but many were just plain chavvy. All that gold jewellery and tattoos: she shivered. No, she really needed to start rethinking her relationship with Josh, especially as he'd been badgering her about his idea for a men's clothing line. Like *that* would ever work.

'There he is,' said Josh eagerly, taking Sasha's hand and leading her into a darkened bedroom. There were half a dozen people lounging around watching two girls dancing to banging dance music. Steve Darling came over wearing a brown silk shirt and a fixed glassy smile. Sasha instantly stiffened.

'Hey-hey!' cried Steve, throwing his arms open wide. 'The glamour couple are here, now the party can really get started.' He held up a rolled note and gestured towards a bedside table where lines of cocaine were already chopped out. 'Fancy a nose-up? It's Christmas after all.'

Sasha saw the look of interest on Josh's face, but after a glance at her, he shook his head. Sasha never took drugs and he knew she didn't approve. 'Maybe later, eh, mate?'

'Well have a drink then,' said Steve, turning to a blonde girl in a red minidress who was gyrating her hips against a tall man Sasha recognised as Premiership footballer Gary Shute. 'Here, Louise, get Josh and his lady friend a drink, will you?'

The girl flashed Sasha a narrow look as she reached for a bottle chilling in an ice bucket. Sasha almost laughed out loud. *Like I'd ever be interested in some footballer, sweetie*, she thought.

'Not for me,' she said. 'In fact, we've got to be going, haven't we, Josh?'

'Come on, not yet,' said Steve, stroking the shoulder of the blonde. 'Louise here is a dancer and she was just going to put on a show for us.'

Not waiting to hear any more, Sasha turned and walked straight down the stairs. Josh came clattering after her.

'Sash!' he called. 'Hey, where are you going?'

She stopped on the landing and turned to face him. 'I'm getting as far away from your sordid little friends as I can.'

516

'They're all right,' said Josh defensively. 'Train hard, play hard – they're just a bit pissed, that's all.'

'If you say so. Either way I'm going home. Are you coming?'

'No, I think I'm going to hang out here for a while.'

'Fine,' said Sasha. And as she stalked towards the front door, she found she was actually very relieved to be leaving Josh behind.

Sasha was woken by an insistent ringing.

For a few moments, she tried to ignore it, pulling the warm duvet tighter around her, but it was no use. Moaning, she switched on her bedside light and groped for her watch: 5 a.m.

'What the hell?' she whispered. It was still pitch black outside, and as the doorbell kept on ringing, her annoyance quickly turned to fear. She adored her four-storey Chelsea townhouse, but for several months now she had been thinking about moving into an apartment with CCTV and twenty-four-hour concierge, or at least getting her study turned into a panic room. You couldn't pick up a newspaper these days without hearing horror stories leaking out of the smartest enclaves of London. There was Karin Cavendish, the swimwear designer, who had a stalker. Then there was that violent robbery in Chelsea. No, you couldn't be too careful these days. Especially when you were beautiful. Or had money. Or both.

She grabbed her mobile, tapping in 999 ... they could be here in minutes ... but before she could press 'call', the phone began vibrating in her hand. 'Josh' read the LCD display. 'Bastard,' she muttered.

'It's me,' said Josh as soon as she picked up.

'I know,' she hissed. 'And you've just fucking scared the life out of me.'

'I'm outside. You have to let me in.'

'Strangely enough, I'm not in the mood for a booty call.'

'Please, Sasha. This is important.'

She heard a waver of panic in his voice.

'What's the matter?'

Maha, Sasha's burly Hungarian housekeeper, poked her head round the door. She was carrying a solid-looking torch.

'Is everything OK, Miss Sasha? Shall we call the police?'

'Go back to bed. It's fine.'

Usually she would have let Maha answer the door, but she was curious to know what was making Josh so agitated. Wrapping herself in her silk robe, she padded downstairs and let him in.

'This better be good,' she said, retreating into the kitchen. She opened the fridge and poured herself a glass of Maha's freshly squeezed orange juice. She didn't offer Josh any. 'Well? What's so bloody important?'

Josh looked terrible. Two grey crescents hung under his eyes. There was a stain on the front of the blue shirt that was brand new the night before. He looked like a tramp. *If your sponsors could see you now*, thought Sasha, taking a sip of her juice.

'I'm in deep shit, Sash,' he said. 'There was a situation at the party. The police want me to go to the station.'

'What sort of situation?'

'I think the *News of the World* is going to call it a roasting.'

'Roasting?' said Sasha. 'You mean a rape?'

'No,' he said firmly. 'She was up for it.'

Sasha put her glass down on the distressed oak table and walked back to the door. She put her hand on the lock.

'Out,' she said.

'Sasha, please . . .' he began.

'Get out of my house!' she shouted.

Josh came over to her. 'Hear me out, Sasha, *please*. It wasn't like that. I wasn't involved.'

She saw the desperation in his eyes. He really was scared. It couldn't hurt to hear what he had to say; she could always call Maha down with her torch.

'All right, start talking,' she said, sitting down at the table and crossing her arms.

'After you'd gone, I stayed in that room,' he said, his voice trembling. 'Steve went off, but there were those footballers ...'

'And those sluts,' said Sasha.

Josh looked down and nodded. 'We had some champagne, a bit of coke. We were all out of it.'

'Then ...'

His face looked pale in the dark of the kitchen. 'Then it all started getting a bit playful. That girl you saw, Louise? She stripped off and Martin started having sex with her on the bed. When he finished, his friend Wayne took over. Then Gary joined in ...'

'And was the girl still *up for it*?' she said with sarcasm.

He looked away once more and fell silent.

'And what were you doing at this point?' she said.

'I left.'

'You left,' she repeated, letting it hang in the air. 'So why do you look as if you're stepping up to the executioner's block if you're so completely innocent?'

He was looking increasingly uncomfortable under Sasha's direct gaze.

'When she took her top off, I felt her tits. I mean, she asked me to! She wanted to prove they were real. I just jiggled them for a second. We were just having a laugh.'

'Hilarious, yes,' said Sasha.

'Listen, I'm in trouble, Sash,' he said, his eyes pleading. 'It was dark in that room and the girl was out of her head. She didn't know who fucked her and who didn't. But I swear to you, I didn't do anything.'

He put his head in his hands.

'Gary called me. She's saying she was raped, and the police have pulled Martin and Kevin. They're all denying it of course, and who knows if she actually said no.'

'Do you really think that would have mattered?' shouted Sasha, thinking of her first few months in London. Men with power, influence, or just the illusion of it, exploiting girls for disposable pleasure.

'So if you're all such great mates, how do the police know you were there?'

'The girl went to the police station with her friend, the other one who was in there. She identified all of us.'

Sasha thought for a moment.

'Would Gary or Martin say you left the room?'

'No chance – you know how the papers work. It suits them for me to be dragged into this. They're all Premiership foot-ballers, but they're not Beckham or Rooney, not household names. But if I'm involved, the media will home in on me, won't they? Formula One Ace in Roasting Scandal and all that? No one will be interested in them.'

Sasha knew he was right. Not that Josh was entirely an innocent party here. After all, he'd fondled a drunken girl and then watched the other men have sex with her.

'Go to the police,' she said. 'Tell them what you've just told me.'

'What I say isn't going to matter!' he cried. 'That girl will say I was in the room, she might even say I had sex with her. And that bastard Gary said he would take me down with them unless I kept my mouth shut.'

He looked at her hopefully. 'There's only one way I can see out of this . . .'

'What?'

'Come with me to the station, Sash. Say I left the party with you at two o'clock. I'll admit to having a drink with them but then say I left the room.'

'You want me to *lie*?'

'Why not?' he said. 'You're a respected businesswoman. I admit I was wrong being there, but I'm not taking the heat for something I didn't do.'

He stretched his hands over the table and grabbed hers. 'Sasha, you have to help me.'

Snapshots of the past jumped into her head as she looked at his pleading eyes. The advertising party and the feel of the cold tiles in that toilet stall. Then the island, and Miles Ashford's face on the beach. Power and lies, lies and power. She couldn't do it again.

'I can't,' she said, pulling away. She knew the media would tear Josh apart unless she backed up his story, but he had brought it on himself. And the truth was he wasn't the only victim here. Sasha had her own reputation to think about. She'd built up one of the most successful fashion houses in Europe from the ground up; she wasn't going to let some sordid little coke orgy screw that up.

'Why not?' he said. 'Why can't you help me? We're partners, friends. That's what friends do for each other. They help each other, protect each other.'

'That's over, Josh,' she said simply. 'I don't want to be in this relationship any more.'

'I can't believe you're saying this, Sasha. Not when I need you.'

'What you need, what we all need is just to tell the truth. It's simpler that way.'

He stood up and walked to the door. 'Well I didn't think I'd hear you of all people say that.'

As he closed the door behind him, she felt a thick sob swell in her throat.

No, neither did I.

61

January 2010

Miles paced up and down the Ash Corp. offices high above the Las Vegas Strip. He was in a particularly foul mood this morning. Not even the blow job he'd received from Hans, the Canadian sous chef in the executive kitchen, had done much to cheer him up.

'What are we going to do?' he demanded. 'The whole project is going tits up and you're all just sitting there with pokers up your arses. Give me solutions, people!'

The Ash Corp. management team exchanged glances, but none of them spoke.

'Come on!' shouted Miles, banging his desk. 'I pay you good money to fix these things. I need ideas.'

Miles knew he needed more than ideas; he needed a miracle. After the runaway success of the Laing hotel and its rapid extension into luxury apartments on the Strip, the Las Vegas gaming commission had had a sudden sea change in its attitude towards Ash Corp. As long as certain conditions were met, they said – Miles suspected that 'certain conditions' meant 'heavy investment' – they were open to an approach vis-à-vis building a casino. Work began on Ashford Towers almost immediately: a vast upwardly mobile hotel, casino and condo project. It had been started in late 2006 when the whole of America was riding on the crest of an economic wave. Sin City was recession-proof, everyone said so. In its entire history it had only suffered one downturn, immediately after 9/11. But then no one could have predicted the scale and impact of the 2008 financial crisis. Sub-prime greed, arrogant hedge-funders plus the hubris of the US banks meant that the world economy not only wobbled, it toppled to the ground, taking Lehman Brothers and a whole house of cards with it. To Miles' fury, Ash Corp. was left badly exposed. If he had stuck with his father's policy of diversification, they might have been able to roll with the punches, but he had restructured to focus on leisure, travel and construction – three of the most vulnerable sectors in a recession. Now Ashford Towers seemed to stand as a shining monument to his folly, its rooms empty, the gamblers shifting to Hold 'em Poker, the only game in Vegas where the house failed to win.

'Well, we could refinance,' said Greg Barbera, the Ash Corp. COO, cautiously. 'It's a risk of course, given the current climate, but it might help us ride it out.'

'No, that's just throwing good money after bad,' said Miles. 'Besides, we haven't got the time. Every hour it's open, the casino is sucking up more electricity than the whole of New England. We need to make money, not borrow it.'

'Perhaps if we look at the projections?' said Jonathon Cohen, finance director. 'I've run a few figures, and if we experience a bounce effect, we may gain some breathing space.'

Miles jabbed his finger at the spreadsheet in front of him. 'Screw your projections, Jon,' he said. 'Look at the figures from last month. Hotel booking down thirty per cent on your worst-case scenario. What kind of confidence do you think that instils in me? We need to face facts: it's far worse than anyone dared guess.'

'It's not just us. Have you seen where MGM Mirage stock

prices are? Steve Wynn has just had to cut employees' salaries by ten per cent.'

'I don't care what other people are doing,' said Miles. 'I only care what we're doing.'

He looked around at each of the team. 'Right. No more double-talk and marketing-speak bollocks. I want each of you to go away and come back with real-life workable solutions for rescuing Ashford Towers – and Ash Corp.'

He clapped his hands. 'Go on, piss off.'

Silently they all gathered their notes and filed towards the door.

'Not you, Michael,' said Miles, gesturing to Michael Marshall to close the door. He walked over to his drinks bar and poured himself a malt whisky. 'Snifter?' he asked, but Marshall shook his head. 'OK, Mike, tell me you've got an idea.'

The lawyer had started out in the company by getting Ash Corp. a foothold out here in the desert; now Miles needed him to perform another of his sleight-of-hand tricks. Marshall had risen up the ranks by doing Ash Corp.'s dirty work, but now he was Miles' *consigliere*, the one man he trusted to dig them out of this hole, because the alternative was grim: the whole company could go down.

'I do have one idea to get hotel occupancy up, but I'm not sure you're going to like it.'

'If it works, I'll like it, Michael,' said Miles, sipping the amber liquid. 'We've run out of elegant solutions. Ugly is all we got.'

'All right,' said Marshall. 'Hotel occupancy is down, gambling is down, people have fallen out of love with Vegas – no one gets excited about blackjack when they're struggling to keep a roof over their heads.'

'My heart bleeds,' said Miles. 'But continue.'

'There's one other thing Vegas does that people will always want – showbiz. This place does over-the-top razzle-dazzle like nowhere else on earth, and people will come for that, because in hard times, everyone loves escapism – plus they feel they're getting value for money. Now Cirque du Soleil continues to pack 'em in, and Celine Dion's residency at Caesars has taken over fifty-five million dollars in ticket revenues over the first twelve months.'

Miles nodded. 'It's an interesting angle, but let's say forty mill of that is profit – forty large isn't going to fill our hole.'

'Exactly, but fifty-five million ticket sales equals at least a couple of hundred thousand customers passing our way. They all need food, lodging and gas. And if they're happy, in a great mood having seen a great gig, it will get them into the casino.'

'But who's big enough in the States to pull in that number? Madonna?'

'Too expensive.'

'Well who else sells tens of million of albums?'

Michael looked at him and nodded. 'Time to call in a favour, Miles.'

Alex didn't say yes or no; he just laughed. The speakers in the conference call system crackled as his laugh boomed out.

'Tell me you're joking, Miles?' he said down the line. 'You have to be kidding, right?'

Miles struggled to keep his voice calm. He had been reluctant to call Alex at his home in London, but Michael had persuaded him that it was the only way to bring in enough bodies to get the casino working again.

'I'm completely serious. We both have a lot to gain.'

'You have a lot to gain, you mean,' said Alex.

'Think about it, Alex. It's a golden opportunity to really reach your core audience. You tour all over the world, but you sell far more albums here in the States. They love you here. And it's good for you, too. You've been quiet for the last eighteen months. AWOL from the industry, from your fans. And this way, you can stay in one place throughout the residency, instead of flying from country to country.'

There was a pause.

'OK, I'll admit that appeals to me,' Alex said. 'Touring is one of the things I hate the most about this job.'

'Exactly,' said Miles. 'And you could build whatever kind of set you liked, be really creative with the way it's presented. You won't get that when you're playing in football stadiums.'

'What, are you thinking like a theatre in the round or something?'

Miles looked at Michael, who just shrugged.

'Anything, the sky's the limit on that score,' said Miles enthusiastically, leaning over his desk.

'I don't know, Miles,' said Alex. 'I've just got out of rehab, I'm feeling good about myself. I'm not sure I'm ready to go out there yet.'

'But you must have new songs you want to showcase, a new direction perhaps?'

'Maybe,' said Alex. 'How long were you thinking?'

'Seventy-five nights. Maybe more.'

'Whaaaat!'

'We'll give you two hundred thousand a show.'

Alex was laughing again. 'I don't need money, Miles. Right now I need my sanity.'

'You owe me, Alex.'

'I'll always be grateful for your help. But a seventy-five-night residency! I've been ill, Miles, you know that.'

'Not ill enough not to work for my sister.'

'That's a film score. I can do it from home.'

'Don't let me down, Alex,' said Miles, his tone turning angry. 'You're saying no to me? After everything I've done for you?'

'You know what?' said Alex. 'For once in my life I am saying no to you, Miles Ashford.' There was a soft click through the speakers.

'Alex?' said Miles. '*Alex?*' He looked at Michael. 'Get him back, Marshall!' he shouted. 'Get the fucker back on the line!'

'He's gone, Miles. He said no.'

No one said no to Miles Ashford, no one. He looked out of the window at the silver tower twinkling in the sun. And roaring with frustration, he swept his arm across his desk, smashing the phone to the floor.

62

Alex pressed 'save' on his hard drive, feeling a familiar rush of excitement. It was the same feeling he remembered getting when he pressed 'stop' on his battered old tape recorder, having just committed a song to cassette. Only this time, he wasn't sitting in that mouse-ridden house in Fallowfield; he was in his recording studio in the basement of a Georgian mews house in a quiet pocket of Highgate. And this wasn't a song; it was his first film score – two whole hours of sweeping, soaring music that had pushed him to the limit of his abilities as a composer. The last few months he had spent working on Grace's film had been some of the hardest he'd had to go through, constantly questioning himself, constantly pushing himself harder until he'd created something he just knew was better than anything he'd done before. More than anything else, he felt proud of himself. Six months ago, he had been shivering and puking on the floor of his room in Second Chances; now he was sober, hopeful and content to just be here, doing what he loved. With a new song, he could connect with people, he could make someone cry, he could make his fortune. But here, he felt he had turned a corner in his life. Here he had opened a new door.

He sat back in his Aeron chair. Usually at this point he would have celebrated by going to the pub and not coming back for days. He smiled. That was one reason why he liked living in Highgate: it was only a couple of miles from fashionable, happening London, but it was just far enough out. It was quieter, older, more serene. Not like the 'Twin Hills of Temptation', Primrose Hill and Notting Hill, where there was always someone asking him down the pub or to a party, which was where his troubles usually began.

He reached for his coat, locked his studio and headed out towards Waterlow Park; it was a lovely afternoon for a walk – cold but crisp. He thought about Grace Ashford and smiled. The documentary score had given him a renewed sense of purpose and a reason for getting out of bed in the morning. A reason to think about the future and not dwell on the past. But it was their renewed friendship which had really saved him from sliding backwards. After he left Second Chances, he'd declined Grace's offer to stay at Stockbridge – there was something about Julian that aggravated him – but he had seen her at least one a week: trips to the movies, a walk around the Heath, or for brunch to discuss the documentary. He'd put any romantic thoughts to one side – jumping into another messy relationship was the last thing he needed right now – but their platonic mini-dates had really brought him back to life and he would always be in her debt for that.

He walked past the tennis courts, breathing in the air and enjoying the squeals of a group of children trying to climb a tree. At Second Chances they'd called this 'the Technicolor Rush', the pure pleasure of seeing the world again through clear eyes, enjoying simple things like birds and flowers for what they were. Alex knew he wasn't completely free from that little devil on his shoulder whispering about how nice a pint would be right now, but he was learning to ignore it. It was easier when you were surrounded by grass and trees and ... *God, I'm turning into a hippy*, he smiled to himself.

He paid his three pounds and walked into Highgate Cemetery. This was one of his favourite places in London; he loved the poetic bleakness of the place. Around the edges, the graveyard was pretty and well-kept – fresh flowers in front of polished headstones, tourists posing in front of the Karl Marx memorial – but if you ventured into the middle, where the tottering headstones were overgrown and choked with ivy, it was somehow more beautiful and serene. A place for the dead, it was one of the few places Alex felt at peace. He sat on a weatherworn bench and smiled as a young mother pushed a toddler by in his buggy. He waved at the little boy, who giggled, hiding behind his stuffed rabbit. For a second Alex thought of Melissa and their plans to start a family. He'd heard from Ted that Christopher Hayes had gone back to Jennifer, but that part of his life seemed so distant and strange, as if his marriage had been part of a bio-pic movie about someone else.

It was starting to get dark, so Alex put on his iPod head-phones and began to walk back up towards the gates. He had come so far in such a short space of time and he wondered where he would be if he hadn't gone on that bender in Soho, if he hadn't gone to Second Chances. *Would I still be lying on the sofa at my old house?* He would never have had the strength to say no to Miles' offer of the residency at his Vegas hotel, that was for sure. Part of him still felt bad about letting Miles down, but he did not want to be bound to him any longer. He'd paid that debt.

He pushed his hands into his pockets, lost in the music he was listening to – the funk-groove soundtrack to an obscure blaxploitation movie. He didn't hear the running footsteps behind him, didn't know anything of the attack until he felt the blow on the back of the head. The ground swung up to meet him, the gravel digging into his ear. He tried to cover his head, to roll into a ball as he was repeatedly kicked in the face, back, legs, only vaguely aware that his headphones and wallet were being torn from him. And then all he could hear was a baby crying: 'Mama! Mama!'

63

February 2010

Stockbridge Hall had never looked more magnificent. In the decades before Julian had bought the mansion, it had changed hands a number of times – one wing had been used as a conference centre, then briefly turned into an old people's home – but it had been neglected and allowed to peel and crack. Now it had been fully restored, it made perfect sense to reintroduce Stockbridge to polite society with a modern version of a debutante ball. Hurricane lights twinkled like fireflies, hanging from the long row of lime trees that flanked the drive; a marquee on the rear lawn seated three hundred for dinner around a koi carp pool, while the ceiling of the ballroom was covered in black velvet pierced by thousands of fairy lights to give the impression of dancing under the stars. It had taken all Grace's powers of persuasion to convince Julian to throw an eighteenth birthday party for the twins. Unsurprisingly, he wasn't keen to have hundreds of drunken teenagers marauding through his lovingly rejuvenated stately home, especially considering the priceless art in the gallery wing. But once Grace had pointed out that Joe and Liv's friends were the sons and daughters of the super-rich, people they could subsequently invite to parties, screenings and gallery openings, he decided it was to be a no-expenses-spared event. A funk band, a DJ from Pascha and musical fireworks were arranged, with accommodation laid on for all the guests in a series of local hotels and B&Bs. It was going to be a night to remember.

'Come on, Livvy,' called Grace. 'Looks like your guests are starting to arrive.' Sitting on the window seat of her daughter's bedroom, she peered out of the long windows and could just make out the headlights of a coach bringing the first lot of arrivals. The door to the en suite bathroom opened and Olivia stepped out.

'How do I look?' she asked, doing a dainty pirouette.

In five-inch heels and an ivory minidress, her hair tied up in a top-knot, she looked both sexy and elegant and far more mature than her years.

'You look like a goddess,' said Grace with maternal pride. Mother and daughter had gone through some difficult times after Grace had found the contraceptive pills in Olivia's bag. They had rowed constantly over boys, drinking, clothes and money. Olivia had defied Grace, sworn at her, stayed out all night. In the end, however, they had got over the worst. Olivia was less truculent and rebellious, Grace less protective and controlling. It had been a long journey for both of them, and Grace realised she had needed to grow up a little too. Six months ago she had celebrated her fortieth birthday, and yet she still wasn't ready to accept that she had a daughter who was beautiful enough to grace the cover of any fashion magazine in the world.

'Wait. How about something in your hair?' she said, picking up a black velvet box she had left on the side.

'What is it?' said Olivia.

'Just something your grandmother gave to me when I moved to Parador.'

Olivia opened the box and took out a beautiful silver and diamond hairclip. 'Gosh, Mum, it's lovely.'

'It's been in the Hernandez family for three generations – now you make it four.'

Isabella had given it to her that second Christmas, as a belated 'welcome to the family' gesture. Grace had been touched nevertheless, and as she clipped it into Olivia's hair, she felt a warm sense of having completed a circle.

The party filled up quickly as two coaches ferried in guests from Danehurst, the local tennis club Joseph belonged to, as well as private homes in London and Oxfordshire. After much debate, an alcohol bar had been provided along with catering by the Admirable Crichton, who had been responsible for the Posh and Becks nuptials.

'Are you sure this is an eighteenth party?' said Sarah as the guests filed in. 'It looks like a particularly decadent night at Studio 54.' The presence of Sarah, Grace and Connie as unofficial chaperones was the one concession the twins had been forced to agree to for their party, although Grace was not looking forward to an evening acting like some prison guard, separating horny teenagers. Besides which, Sarah was right, none of the guests looked like teenagers. The girls, especially, seemed impossibly glamorous and sophisticated.

'Now you're not going to get in the way, are you, Mum?' said Olivia. 'You must remember what it was like to be eighteen.'

'She doesn't, but I do,' said Sarah. 'So no funny business, OK?'

Connie walked in holding a silver envelope and handed it to Olivia. 'Special message for Mr Joseph and Ms Olivia Hernandez,' she said.

'Joe!' shouted Olivia. Her brother ran over as she tore open the envelope. He was wearing a midnight-blue dinner suit and had his father's dark eyes and thick, floppy hair. Sometimes Grace would look up and catch sight of him and think she was back in Australia.

'What's it say?' said Joe eagerly, peering over his sister's shoulder.

'"Sorry I can't be there, but hopefully these might make up for it. Uncle Miles."'

Olivia looked at her mother, but Grace shrugged. She had no idea what this was about. Her daughter turned to Connie.

'What is it? What's Uncle Miles got us?'

Raising her eyebrows, Connie pointed towards the front door. Squealing, Olivia ran outside, closely followed by Joe and the rest of the party. Two gleaming silver sports cars were parked outside.

'Ohmygod! Ohmygod!' said Olivia, dancing on the spot. Joseph had already opened the door of the first one and all his friends were crowding around, clapping him on the back.

Grace went over to Julian. He was smiling, but she saw that he looked put out. He didn't like to be upstaged.

'They can't even drive,' he said, walking back inside.

Olivia was squealing again. 'Look, there's platinum Globe Club membership in the glove compartment!'

Frantic discussions began between her and her friends about when they could first head off to London, before someone had the more extravagant plan of flying out to New York to sample the Globe Club there.

Olivia ran over to show her mother. 'Why don't we see more of Uncle Miles, Mum? He's so cool.'

Grace flashed her mother a look, and Connie gave her a small smile. 'He's a very busy man, Liv. He's out of the country most of the time.'

'Can I go to New York in the summer?' Olivia said. 'It'd be so brilliant.'

Grace was about to say 'no, you're too young to travel alone' when she remembered her own disappearing act when she was not much older than her daughter.

'We'll see, honey,' she said. To her surprise, Olivia grabbed her, giving her a hug.

'You're so cool sometimes, Mum,' she said.

534

The next two hours passed by in a blur for Grace. As the guests got progressively more drunk and frisky – one couple were found completely naked in the gun room – the adults discreetly patrolled the party making sure behaviour wasn't getting too out of hand, and that the security in the roped-off parts of the manor, such as the indoor pool and the gallery, hadn't been breached. For all his pre-party worrying, Julian didn't seem all that concerned with what was going on; in fact he seemed to be enjoying himself holding court in the kitchen, surrounded by adoring girls bombarding him with questions about art and the celebrities he knew. By ten thirty Grace felt fit to drop and went to the bar for a fortifying glass of red wine.

'With two hundred teenagers to watch over, I thought I might find you at the booze supply,' said an amused voice behind her.

'Alex!' she cried, turning to hug him. 'You're here!'

'I've been here a while actually,' said Alex. 'Sarah had me collared in the conservatory.'

For once, Grace didn't feel jealous, possibly because she and Alex had spent so much time together over the past six months while he'd worked on the score for her documentary. After he left the clinic, he had declined her offer to stay at Stockbridge, but he had seen her at least once a week: trips to the West End, walks around the village, or brunch to discuss the documentary. She'd come to look forward to their time together, all the 'coupley' things she should have been doing with Julian, who never seemed to have the time. And it had been wonderful to see Alex slowly come back to life. Despite the recent mugging, Alex still seemed remarkably upbeat; the old twinkle was returning to his eyes, especially when he'd played her the music. It was amazing: dramatic, romantic, moving. Everything she had hoped for – for both of them.

She got Alex a tonic water from the bar, then led him to the library, where she could rest her aching feet and they could hear themselves above the thumping bass of the funk band.

'You know Joseph asked me to do an acoustic session in the stables later on?' Alex said.

'You're not going to, are you?'

'I said I'd have a jam with a few of the lads if they were interested. But get up on stage? Not a chance. They're going to want to see Lady Gaga or JLS. A bunch of eighteen-year-olds aren't going to be interested in some old fella with a guitar.'

'Even one who's sold a hundred million records?'

'*Especially* one who's sold a hundred million records. I think I'm officially Mum and Dad's music now.'

They stared into the library fire, listening to the muffled sound of the DJ.

'So what did Sarah collar you about, then?'

'Oh, the state of the music industry, how the old songs are better than all this new-fangled rubbish. Your average party conversation.'

Part of Grace felt that Alex and Sarah were the answer to each other's problems. He needed someone strong and dependable, while Sarah was looking for a decent DNA donor before her biological clock ran out of steam, but she felt an out-of-character flush of relief that he did not seem remotely interested in Sarah.

She cupped her hands around her wine glass. 'I can't believe my kids are eighteen. They'll be off to university this year.'

'Does this make you officially an empty-nester?'

'It makes me old.'

'Nonsense,' said Alex. 'Plenty of women are just having their first child at your age. Maybe it's time you settled down.'

'Well, Julian does propose to me sporadically. I might have to take him up on his next offer just so I don't feel like some crabby old spinster.'

'You should,' he said, staring into the fire. 'It's good to

536

have someone to look out for you. What's been stopping you all these years?'

Grace shrugged. 'I've done it once before, remember?'

'Still holding a torch for El Presidente?'

She shook her head. 'No, I saw a lot of Gabe making the movie in Palumbo. He's moved on, he's happy. He's got a wife who's good for him.'

'I thought that about Melissa, and look where that got me.' He took a sip of his tonic water. 'I see Miles sent elaborate gifts.'

She grunted. 'Like two eighteen-year-olds need sports cars and club membership.'

'Miles always was good at buying his way into people's affections. It's when you've got to pay him back that it becomes a problem.'

Out in the courtyard, Olivia was enjoying a Gauloise cigarette. She liked the French brands; they made her look cool. Not that she needed any help in that department. Over Christmas she'd been shopping in Topshop and was spotted by scouts from both Storm and Models One. Olivia knew what she wanted to do when school was finally over. Her brother might have a place at Cambridge, but what guarantee was that of getting on in the world? Good looks and contacts, that was what mattered, and she was determined to work her advantages to the max.

She looked up as she heard the door open: Julian, wearing a dinner suit with a white T-shirt underneath and box-fresh plimsolls. She didn't bother to hide the cigarette; she was eighteen now and he wasn't her father, was he?

'Enjoying your birthday, Liv?' he asked.

'Yeah, it's been cool,' she said nonchalantly. 'The car is fantastic but I don't think Mum approves. Then again, she doesn't approve of anything these days, does she?'

Olivia was pleased that Julian didn't stick up for Grace.

Although she had disliked him as a child, as the years had passed she had come to view him as an ally. Years ago, after her mum had found her pills, she had heard her and Julian arguing about it. 'Treat her like a grown-up, Grace!' he'd said. 'If she wants to have sex, she'll have it whether she's on the pill or not.' Well, he was right there.

'Have you seen your mother anywhere?'

'Talking to Alex Doyle last time I saw her. As always,' she said mischievously.

Julian smiled. Olivia had noticed he had a dirty, sexy smile, as if he was always thinking about something naughty.

'I mean, don't you get embarrassed how they're always off whispering in corners? People wondering, you know, if there's something going on?'

Julian laughed softly. 'I don't think your mother is the type to have an affair,' he said.

Olivia blew a smoke ring. 'A lot of people think that about their spouses. Until they get presented with an opportunity.' She was pleased to see a cloud of concern pass over his face.

'Can I have a pull on that thing?' he asked. He took the cigarette from her fingers and drew it to his mouth.

Through the smoke she looked at his face, lined and worn from experience, fun, life, excitement, success. Julian was not a particularly good-looking man but there was something about it that made him incredibly attractive. Certainly her friends from London were terribly excited to meet him. Art was the new rock and roll these days, or so she'd read in some glossy magazine. She had no idea what he saw in such a square and earnest woman as her mother.

'I got a car from Uncle Miles, the trust fund from the family, the watch from Mum,' said Olivia. 'What am I getting from you?'

'What do you want?'

'A picture.'

He smiled. 'That shouldn't be too difficult to sort out.'

538

'No, I want a picture of me. Come on, draw me.'

'What, now?'

'Of course. Every girl wants to be an artist's muse.'

She could see desire spark into his eyes and she knew he wanted her – but then she'd known that for a while now. Last summer, when she'd been sunbathing alone by the stream running through the grounds, he'd come down and asked her if she fancied a swim, his eyes lingering over her tiny Eres bikini.

It felt good being desired by a man like Julian. Anyone could get a red-blooded, constantly horny eighteen-year-old interested in them. Boys were easy prey. Real men, now they were more of a challenge.

She walked up close to him.

'Come to my room in five minutes,' she whispered, stamping her cigarette out under her heel and disappearing back into the house.

Ten minutes later there was a polite knock at her bedroom door.

'Lock it,' she said. He did as she instructed and she knew he was putty in her hands.

'So what does a muse do now?' she said, tipping her head to one side.

He stood a foot away from her and folded his arms across his chest.

'Let me look at you,' he said, a quiver in his voice.

'OK,' she said, unzipping her dress and letting it fall to the floor. She'd removed her panties before he'd got there and stood naked in front of him except for her red-soled Louboutins.

'Come closer,' she said, enjoying the sense of power she had over him. She hadn't felt this aroused, this in control, since she had fucked Mr Browning, her English teacher, twelve months ago. He'd been a terrible shag, but at least he had let her coast through his A level class ever since.

'You're beautiful,' he whispered.

'I know.'

'I want you.'

'I know.'

He put his hand out, tracing around her dark beige aureole with the tip of his finger. His skin felt grooved and rough like an emery board, and as he moved his fingers down her long, lithe body she groaned, desperate to feel him inside her.

'Touch me,' she said, parting her legs, feeling his hand moving between her thighs. She gasped as he dipped two fingers into her warmth, then circled her hips, clenching around him.

'Happy birthday,' he whispered, pulling out of her to unfasten his trousers.

She felt a glow of pleasure and accomplishment. 'Make sure you make it one to remember.'

Connie Ashford was a careful woman. Over the years, she'd had to learn to be. She did not like to think ill of the dead, but life had certainly not been easy with Robert Ashford. She'd known that her husband had been having affairs since soon after their children had been born, and she knew it went with the turf when you were married to a rich and successful man. But having made the decision to stay married to him, she had spent over two decades on red alert, safeguarding her position, ensuring none of his mistresses got too serious, and with the exception of Sasha Sinclair, she had been expert at detecting when women were closing in for the kill on her husband.

So when she'd seen her granddaughter and Julian talking, flirting in the courtyard, sharing a cigarette, she had been suspicious. She had never liked Julian, whom she considered too cocky and self-important by half, and Olivia had always been so precocious, rebellious and selfish. It was not surprising that she might be flattered by her mother's glamorous boyfriend, but she couldn't know what he had in mind, what foul idea was growing in his head. Age might have dulled Connie's senses, but life experience had sharpened her instincts. So she watched and waited.

The whole of the south wing had been closed off to the party and the corridors were dark. Approaching Olivia's bedroom, she could see that the door was closed, but she could hear noises coming from inside. Horrible, horrible noises. The guttural groans of frantic, passionate sex.

How could he? She was just a child! It was tantamount to incest. Connie's anger rose: she couldn't have this, she wouldn't allow it. Through Robert's selfishness she had been robbed of seeing her own children grow up, and she was fiercely protective of her granddaughter.

'Stop this!' she shouted, banging her hand on the door. 'Stop it at once!'

She listened: frantic whispers, then footsteps. The door flew open and Julian was standing there naked, his face flushed, his penis still erect. Behind him she could see Olivia sitting on the bed, her knees pulled up, clutching her dress to herself, her expression shocked and guilt-stricken.

'Connie!' gasped Julian. 'I can explain; it's not what you think . . .'

She slapped him hard and he stumbled backwards.

'I'm going to tell your mother,' she hissed at Olivia. 'I'm going to tell her right this second.'

She turned and hurried back down the corridor, heels tapping the granite floor, eyes glazing over with tears.

It was dark. Connie was unfamiliar with the house and did not know where the light switch was. She was confused. Anxious. Maybe she should tell Alex or Sarah Brayfield first. This would just destroy her daughter.

She reached the top of a small flight of stairs that led back to the main wing of the house.

She began to descend the steps, but her shoe slipped on

541

the polished stone, turning her ankle over. Her thin hand grabbed the banister, but she was moving too fast: the momentum carried her forward, pitching her over, crashing down, down, hitting her head against the stone. Seeing flashing light, momentary pain. And then she felt nothing.

64

From the comfort of her business-class seat on a BA flight from Salzburg to London, Sasha read the news item in that morning's paper with wide eyes. She couldn't believe Connie Ashford was dead. The brief story on page nine reported that the sixty-five-year-old wife of the late billionaire businessman Robert Ashford had been killed in a tragic fall at the eighteenth birthday party of her grand-children Olivia and Joseph Hernandez. For years Sasha had resented her former lover's wife, but reading about Connie's demise was sad and uncomfortable, bringing to the surface all the guilt she had long tried to ignore.

Don't dwell on it, she told herself. There were more important things to think about. The launch of Rivera Chinawear range at Selfridges on Tuesday. An interview with the *Evening Standard*, then three days in New York to meet executives at Saks, Henri Bendels and Bloomingdales about expanding their floor space in the city's most prestigious department stores. Oh, and there was a board meeting at eleven o'clock this morning and it was already gone ten thirty. Sasha felt a vague sense of guilt, as Steven Ellis, the Rivera CEO, had been making a big fuss about her being there. It wasn't as if they could start without her, she smiled to herself. She was the president of Rivera, in charge, in control. Everyone made time for Sasha Sinclair.

Take the past weekend, for example. She had been staying

at a fabulous schloss just outside the Austrian capital to attend the wedding of Princess Marie Louise of Hamburg. Marie Louise had not married in Rivera – not through lack of trying on Sasha's part – but Sasha had still accepted the bride's invitation to the nuptials, knowing the event would be bristling with the high-profile Euro-rich. And everyone had wanted to talk to her: oligarchs, billionaires, princes, wives of princes. Most exciting of all had been George Liu, the Hong Kong retail magnate, who had sounded her out about a consultant's position with his company. She had stayed up late into the night discussing the proposition with him, missing her lift back to London on a friend's private jet. Which was why – she glanced at her watch – she was going to be a few hours late for that bloody board meeting. They would wait for her. They always did.

'Where is everyone?' snapped Sasha, running into Rivera's Chelsea headquarters.

Harriet, Steven's PA, looked apologetic. 'In the board meeting.'

'They've started without me?' she said incredulously. 'Why did no one contact me?'

'We knew you were flying. Steven said not to bother you.'

'Did he now?' she said, striding up the stairs to the second-floor boardroom. If Steven thought he could do anything without consulting her first, he had another think coming, she fumed as her heels click-clacked up the steps. She stopped suddenly at the top. The boardroom door was open and they were all filing out. Sasha walked straight up to Steven.

'You've finished?' she said, fist on hip.

'We waited until eleven thirty, Sasha,' said Steven, glancing about nervously. 'Randall couldn't wait. He has to be in Geneva this afternoon.'

'Randall was here? Why didn't you tell me?'

Sasha was even more furious she had missed Randall Kane,

chairman of Duo Capital, who owned the majority share-holding of the company. And she was sure Steven would have given her absence his own particular twist.

'Can we just have a quick chat back in the boardroom, Sasha?' he said, pointing behind him.

She smarted at the tone of his voice. How dare he make her feel as if she was a teenager caught smoking behind the bike sheds? His beady eyes and weak chin added to the image of an ineffectual head teacher. She followed him in, crossing her arms.

'What?' she said.

'AF Holdings have gone into administration,' he said simply.

AF Holdings were an Italian licensing and production company that manufactured the Rivera diffusion line.

Sasha shrugged. 'Well, we find someone else.'

'This is serious, Sasha,' he said. 'We'll have to cancel the show.' The Rivera Sport fashion show was due to be staged in Paris in ten days' time.

'How ridiculous. We show the collection and then get someone else to manufacture the line. It's inconvenient, yes, but hardly a disaster. To be frank, Steven, this is exactly the problem with the Rivera management at the moment: too much flapping, not enough doing.'

Sasha watched with satisfaction as Steven jerked back in his chair. That one had hit home, she thought.

'Well if that's how you feel, perhaps you could have made your feelings known at the meeting instead of gallivanting around Europe.'

'*Gallivanting?* I was up until four o'clock this morning being the face of this company at one of the most high-profile society events of the year. As I do almost every night of the week. My networking is worth millions of pounds of marketing to this company.'

'So you keep telling me,' said Steven, a sour look on his face. 'But forgive me for questioning what this company has to sacrifice in order for you to do it. You're barely in the office these days. There's always a lunch or interview or party. Perhaps you'd like to come in and tell us how to magically sort out the company's problems.'

'I am the president of this company, Steven!' she said. 'I should not have to be sorting out problems for you. The Rivera staff are handsomely paid to handle any blip like this.'

Steven stared at her. She could tell he was just as angry as she was, but his bland expression gave nothing away. They had rarely seen eye to eye over the running of the company, but Sasha could do little about it. Steven had been appointed by Duo Capital, the private equity house that currently owned the majority share in Rivera, so she would be unable to manoeuvre him out.

'I'm glad you brought up the subject of money,' he said. 'Your so-called marketing initiative of going to parties does have a monetary cost. Last year, five hundred thousand pounds went on your clothing allowance and fifty thousand on your driver alone. That's without adding in the cost of international travel and hotels, et cetera.'

'Do you expect me to catch the bus to go and meet the editor of *Vogue*? Besides, those were the terms of my contract at the last buy-out.'

Sasha closed her eyes tight. She refused to let Steven's jealousy get to her. She had worked ferociously for Rivera for well over a decade, built it up into a prestigious luxury brand, extending their range from clothing to accessories to scent and homeware, with thirty stores worldwide and a flourishing wholesale business, supplying to all the major stores in the world. She wasn't going to let some stick-in-the-mud jobsworth dictate to her.

'What's the real problem, Steven?' she said. She thought she knew exactly what it was. In the New Year's Honours list she had been granted an MBE for services to fashion, and Steven had almost blown his top at the news. 'It's my gong, isn't it?' she said triumphantly. 'People know my name, not yours, and you hate it.'

His expression soured. 'This is business, Sasha, not a popularity contest.'

'We are in the business of popularity, Steven,' she snapped. 'That's why I work so hard getting the right people into our clothes, getting them seen in the right places. Rivera is a fashion brand. The moment we cease to be fashionable, we are dead.'

She looked at her watch. Damn, it was half past one already. She had a lunch to get to.

'And this is exactly why I can't stand here arguing with you,' she said, moving towards the door. 'I'm just off to meet Princess Jali Hassan. And before you ask, it's work. Not pleasure. I have an interesting commercial opportunity for us.'

'What is it?' he said sceptically.

She didn't have time for this, but she was aware she needed his support. She sighed and turned back.

'As you know, the princess' family owns half of Abu Dhabi. They've seen what's happened in Dubai and are looking to be the new tourist force in the Middle East.'

'What has that to do with Rivera?'

'They want to stage a major polo tournament out there and are looking for an international luxury brand to be the headline sponsor.'

She frowned at the silence, watching Steven's round face crinkle, the glasses pushing up his nose. He was so conservative.

'I'm not sure how relevant hospitality marketing is any more in this climate.'

'Hospitality marketing is *completely* relevant, Steven,' she said, her irritation mingling with a slight sense of panic. She'd already told Princess Jali that of course Rivera would be the headline sponsor. The lunch today was to get the ball rolling, and Sasha was especially looking forward to fleshing out the details – preferably at Jali's family palace on the Gulf Sea.

'Times are tough, Sasha, even for luxury brands, and we need to look really hard at where we put the marketing spend.'

God, he's so small-minded, she thought.

'But this isn't just about marketing, Steven. One of our company priorities is global expansion. The Gulf is a hugely important market for us and Abu Dhabi is eclipsing Dubai as the new Middle East playground and honey-pot for investment. Look at Formula One. The newest race on the circuit is there.'

'You're right, Sasha,' he said, pausing just long enough to make her think she had won, then continued. '*One* of our company priorities is global expansion. But in an economic downturn, we still have to tighten our belts, and I won't sanction wasting hundreds of thousands of marketing money on sponsoring a polo match.'

Sasha ground her teeth. She could tell when Steven was about to dig his heels in, and as chief executive he had the final say-so on sign-offs unless it was a matter that needed board approval. How was she supposed to explain *that* to Princess Jali over Dover sole?

The answer it turned out was simple: she postponed the lunch, citing a migraine, and made a call. If there was one person more powerful than Steven in the company, it was the chairman of Duo Capital, Randall Kane, who in essence was their owner. Randall had a hands-off approach to the business which Sasha usually appreciated; she didn't like anyone micro-managing any part of her life. And anyway, why would Randall care how Rivera was run, as long as it was making him money? The label was just one of his many investments, spread out over the globe, and so he was constantly in the air, taking meetings in New York, Houston or Shanghai.

She booked the best table at Scott's restaurant and was

wearing her most flattering figure-hugging cashmere dress as she slowly walked to the table, swinging her hips.

'Randall,' she smiled, leaning across to give him a kiss and a brief flash of cleavage. 'So sorry to miss you at the board meeting the other day. You know how it is with these royal weddings.'

'No I don't,' he laughed. 'But I hope you're going to tell me.'

Randall was a fifty-something East Coast WASP who had made a fortune in hedge funds over the last decade. Sasha was sure this was why he was investing in Rivera – lunches with one of the most desirable women in fashion, plus the social ammunition of Sasha's juicy insider gossip which he could then use at his next dinner party.

'Funny you should ask about that.' She smiled. 'I actually have an exciting business proposal for you involving a princess.'

'A princess? She single?'

Sasha laughed. She knew she had him. Steven wasn't going to like her going over his head, but he had forced her hand. It was dog eat dog out there.

'Well, you know Abu Dhabi is the most exciting Gulf state right now,' she began, touching Randall's hand conspiratori-ally. 'Oil-rich, progressive. Well, an interesting commercial opportunity has just presented itself . . .'

65

April 2010

Miles sat on the deck of the super-yacht *Simba*, listening to the gentle breeze ruffling the sails and the chink of the ice in his vodka. He had his own tub of course – the 125-foot *Conifer* he'd inherited from his mother – but the *Simba*, belonging to the Indian steel magnate Anil Chawla, was magnificent. Two hundred and forty feet of sleek engineering genius, it could glide along with wind power like an America's Cup winner, or cruise effortlessly across the Pacific in a gale using the Rolls-Royce engines. Plus it had its own swimming pool. Luxury yachts were the boardrooms of the twenty-first century, where global deals were hatched in secret, and it was infinitely preferable to talk business here, moored off the coast of Corfu, than it was in some bland air-conditioned office block in London or Manhattan. Miles was not prone to envy, but he certainly admired this boat – and the man who owned it.

'I'm sorry about your mother, Miles,' said Anil. He was sixty years old and looked twenty years younger, his latte-coloured skin remarkably free of lines, his wiry body yoga-toned. He was worth a conservative estimate of twenty billion dollars, but the whisper was that there was far more hidden away.

'Thank you,' said Miles, looking away and sipping his drink. His grief was still raw. He had never been particularly close to Connie, in fact had only seen her two or three times a year in the past decade, but her loss had hit him harder than he had imagined. He had felt quite choked speaking at the funeral in front of four hundred people; his grief being worse because he simply hadn't expected it. Despite her slight frame, Connie had always been the Ashford family's power-house, and he just couldn't believe she was dead. The precise events surrounding her death were still unclear, but apparently it was as simple and tragic as that she'd had a few too many drinks celebrating her grandchildren's birthday and had got disorientated wandering around Julian's monstrous mansion. One fall in the dark and that was it – she was gone.

They talked for a while about the people they knew in common. It felt good to be treated as an equal by someone of Anil's stature.

'I hear that the Chelsea Museum is about to come on the market,' said Anil.

Miles had heard that rumour too. Every heavy-hitting developer was going to be after the site. It was without question the most exclusive pocket of London.

'Are you going to bid?'

Miles shook his head. 'Unlikely. I think I have enough property in London at the moment.' The truth was that he wasn't sure he could afford to take on the project. The last two years had been tough; they'd only just managed to scrabble out of the Las Vegas debacle by the skin of their teeth and he'd lost millions in the project in Dubai when the Middle Eastern bubble burst. The money was still coming in, but Ash Corp.'s reputation had been dented and Miles badly needed to spread out into new markets. And for that he needed allies.

'Yes, I have seen your developments there – and in New York,' said Anil. 'In fact I bought my son one of your Hyde Park penthouses.'

Miles was of course aware of that. In 2007, at the height of the market, Anil had bought it for forty-five million as a wedding gift for his son.

'Well if London is overplayed for you, perhaps you will be more interested in this,' said Anil. 'I have just purchased a parcel of land in Mumbai. I have money to invest but not developing expertise. I think we could work well in partnership.'

Miles did not betray his feelings, but he was immediately excited. Ash Corp. had suffered in the downturn, but it was not a global depression. There were pockets – vast pockets – of prosperity. Wealth was shifting from the West to the East, the emerging nations riding a wave of conspicuous consumption, and India was a future super-power. Miles knew that his strategy of courting the super-rich, building them apartments beyond their own lurid dreams, would work perfectly there. But first he needed to establish a foothold.

'What sort of figures are we talking about?' he asked casually.

Anil shrugged and named a figure. A huge figure. A figure that represented a big risk for Ash Corp. If it succeeded, of course, Miles could buy his own version of the *Simba*. Something even bigger, sleeker. But if it failed – and foreign developments were fraught with endless hidden pitfalls, as he had found to his cost in Dubai – then the company would be dangerously exposed. Miles pursed his lips thoughtfully, his face a diplomatic mask. His poker face. Should he bet or fold? Push all his chips in the middle or stick with the safe option?

He smiled to himself. Safe wasn't in Miles' vocabulary. He had been adamant he would keep investing through the recession. Like a shark, if you stopped swimming, stopped moving forward, you just died. But the banks had tightened up their lending facilities even for clients as wealthy and prestigious as Ash Corp. They were unlikely to extend more credit to him unless he liquidated some assets first. He would need to free at least fifty million dollars in liquid cash just to get started. How could he get hold of that money so quickly without going to the banks?

A butler dressed in an all-white uniform handed him a glass of ice-cold lassi. It felt thick and creamy on his tongue. Corfu glistened in the distance and the answer became instantly clear to him. *The island*.

Not a year went by without someone making a serious offer for Angel Cay. American oil men, the wealthiest Hollywood celebrities, de luxe hotel groups. Lately it had appealed to Russian oligarchs and the new Chinese super-rich. But Robert Ashford, and then Connie, had always refused to sell. It was their sanctuary. Miles had no such love for the island, and after his parents' death, it was his to do with as he liked. In fact, he would be glad to be free of it.

He put out his hand to Anil. 'I think you've got yourself a partner.' He smiled.

66

June 2010

Although it was a ninety-minute journey from London to Miles Ashford's Oxfordshire estate, everyone who had an invitation to his summer party came. It was a tradition his father had started – gather the top players in every field together, ply them with the finest wines and make them feel as if they were at one of the best parties of their lives. Miles had to hand it to the old man, it was a clever move. The party cost almost half a million pounds but it paid dividends in goodwill, great contacts and information.

As Miles looked down on to the lawns from the terrace, he knew he had scored another hit. It was the perfect sort of hot Sunday afternoon, the kind of hazy English summer day which made Ashford Park look particularly spectacular, and his party planners had done a splendid job converting the gardens into a vision of an Edwardian English park. There were pedaloes on the lake, a brass band playing a medley of Beatles hits in a striped bandstand, while the peacocks strutting around the lawns were no match for the guests – Mayfair hedge-fund kings, Hollywood stars, national treasures, sporting legends, Euro-royalty and dot-com billionaires. This wasn't just a party. Miles' summer party was now one of the key social events of the year.

He smiled as his friend Arnaud Dauphin the financier approached with two other guests.

'Excellent party, Miles, as always,' said Arnaud. 'Do you know Randall Kane and Steven Ellis?'

Miles smiled broadly, shaking the men's hands. He was aware of both men's involvement with Rivera.

'I've heard of both of you by reputation of course. Randall, I believe we met when I was out in New York?'

'I do believe I dropped by the Globe Club more than once.'

'You and the best of Manhattan.' Miles smiled. 'So how is the lovely Sasha?'

'She's fine,' said Randall. 'You two go back a long way if I remember correctly?'

'We do. And of course I was the backer in the early days of Rivera. Is she still earning her keep?'

Miles did not miss Steven Ellis' tight, fake smile: it told him more about the state of the company than anything a market analyst could cook up.

'Sasha is Sasha.' Steven shrugged, his smile never slipping.

After a few minutes of polite chit-chat, Randall and Steven disappeared across the lawns to check out the vintage car collection that had been parked beyond the bandstand. Miles and Arnaud exchanged raised eyebrows.

'So what's happening there?' asked Miles. 'Steven looked like he was sucking on a lemon at the mention of Sasha.'

'No love lost between him and Ms Sinclair.' Arnaud smiled.

Arnaud and his Argentinian wife Letizia were legendary social entertainers and were always to be found at the epicentre of London's elevated social scene. Consequently, he could usually be relied upon to know the latest gossip.

'Letizia was at lunch with Steven's wife at Harry's Bar on Friday,' he said. 'Apparently Steven and Sasha are barely speaking to one another these days.'

'Why not?'

'Steven is furious that despite all the hard work he puts into the company, Sasha takes all the reward. You heard she's got an MBE for services to fashion?'

Miles shrugged. 'To be fair, she did build the company up from nothing before the private equity boys got involved.'

'Maybe,' said Arnaud. 'But she has never really been hands-on with the business side. That was always left to Steven and Lucian, the previous CEO. The company has only become an international force since they had a chief installed who knew what they were doing.'

Miles chuckled. 'I don't see what the problem is. After all, Sasha has always been a brilliant self-publicist. And now she's just a glorified figurehead for Rivera, it gives her the opportunity to do what she does best: flouncing around the world in sexy little dresses talking about herself.'

'Well, either way, Steven is pissed off. He's tired of the entire business community thinking that Sasha is Donald Trump in stilettos, when really all she's doing these days is confusing marketing with partying. She should be careful anyway. It can't be good for business when the CEO and the president of Rivera can't stand being the same room.'

Miles nodded, his neutral expression never betraying how he was absorbing every detail and formulating a plan. He had been watching Rivera more closely for a while now. Just before Christmas he'd had one of his team prepare a report on the company which told him that the label hadn't been too affected by the recession thanks to clever diversification and a flourishing accessories and scent line. However, the fact that Steven and Sasha were at each other's throats was good news; in fact, it was excellent news. Looking back, Miles had been naïve to get rid of his holding. At the time he had been happy with a hefty return on his original investment, but now, quite suddenly, he wanted Rivera back. After the death of Robert Ashford, he had promised his mother that he would not interfere with the company out of spite or revenge, but now she was gone, and anyway, circumstances had changed. He would never forgive Sasha for what she had done; plus this was business. Miles could do with a company like Rivera; a luxury goods firm would sit nicely next to the Globe and the Laing brands. It wouldn't do his own image any harm either – he could be seen as a style leader, and that could open up all sorts of opportunites for Ash Corp.: cars, travel, jewellery, media, any area where design and trend-setting were key.

He stared out into the party as he began to think. Certainly the timing was bad. If he made a bid for the company now, it wouldn't come cheap. He had an injection of cash coming in this summer – the Fairmont hotel group had made an excellent offer to buy Angel Cay – but that was all earmarked for the residential Mumbai project with Anil. And then there was Sasha to consider. Although she was only a minority shareholder and couldn't officially block a sale, she could still make things very, very difficult. No, what he needed was an interim buyer, someone who wanted to get in and out quickly with a tidy return – but not too tidy. A name popped instantly into his head. Simon Assad. He was the French guy he remembered from Oxford, the one who had made his first million with a string of internet cafés in the big university towns and had gone on to be one of the sharpest financiers in town. Assad had a fund that was comprised partly from his own wealth but with the financial muscle of other major investors. And he loved short-term investments that would turn over a quick profit.

Miles took a long drink of his wine as he felt a surge of excitement: he was sure that Simon was the man for the job, but how to play it? He couldn't tip Assad off directly that Rivera was ripe for an approach. No, he would have to share this information with a trusted source, who could then advise Assad to make the move himself. And then Miles would be perfectly poised to take the company over.

Seeing that Peter Mandelson had just arrived, he walked down the steps to greet him with a renewed spring in his step. *Thanks, Daddy*, he thought to himself. *This party really is quite a splendid idea.*

67

At thirty-seven, Simon Assad was a man in a hurry. He had graduated from Oxford at twenty, finished his MBA at Stanford three years later and quickly made his name with Denton Barnes, one of London's top investment brokers. Now he was out on his own, he worked eighteen-hour days, six days a week and for the past five years had taken no holiday longer than a three-day break. The plan was to retire at forty, and as that milestone was hovering in the distance, he had just three years to make another hundred million dollars. Rivera would help him some way towards that goal.

On paper Rivera had been one of the most exciting investment opportunities in some time. A strong, glamorous brand, it had enormous potential to expand quickly and successfully into the Chinese and Indian markets which would make for a fast and profitable return – exactly what Assad was after. The tip-off had come to him from Nat Churchill, a friend from Oxford who was now one of the most respected bankers in the City. An initial bid had already been made to Randall Kane, which had allowed Assad to start due diligence: the process of assessing a business' true worth before a sale.

Sipping a glass of mint tea, Simon looked at the documents in front of him. They were transcripts of interviews he had commissioned with the staff, getting their opinions on the company's strengths and weaknesses. Staff members were often reluctant to take part, seeing this sort of thing as disloyal or even dangerous – after all, who knew if the sale would go ahead and they might be left having slagged off the MD? But in this case, the company staff had been particularly open, either singling out Steven Ellis or Sasha Sinclair for praise. Everyone in the company was agreed that Steven was an excellent CEO but Sasha's contribution, while more nebulous, was just as, if not more, crucial. She was a powerhouse networker and marketeer. More importantly she was the face of the brand, the person thousands of women wanted to be. For Simon it was a dilemma, as it was just as clear that Rivera couldn't continue with them both. If he was going to buy the company he had to choose which one to keep as part of an ongoing management team. Which was why he had arranged supper at Mark's Club with Nat Churchill, having asked his old friend to invite along Miles Ashford. Miles had been an early backer of Rivera, plus Nat had told him that he'd dated Sasha at school. Hopefully Miles would be able to give him some insight.

Ashford was late of course, breezing into the club with a silver-tipped umbrella and talking to half a dozen diners before he even got to the table.

'Simon. You remember Miles Ashford from Oxford?' said Nat as Miles finally sat down opposite him.

'Of course,' said Simon. Everyone knew Miles Ashford at Oxford. Assad had never actually met him – but he had seen him in the pubs along the river or smoking outside the Bodleian in his gold-piped military coat, like Napoleon on his lunch break. Usually Assad hated the gilded elite with their flash cars and braying girlfriends, but in a strange way he had admired Miles. The short-lived Youngblood Society was the stuff of Oxford legend, and Miles had gone on to make a huge success of the Globe brand without any support from his wealthy father, something which certainly demanded

560

respect. Simon had expected him to spend supper boasting about his successes and name-dropping his celebrity connections, but in actual fact he was quiet and polite, laughing along at Nat's overblown account of his recent expedition to Antarctica.

'Just going for a slash, then I'm off,' said Nat, glancing at his watch.

Both men watched him go.

'Do you have to go too?' asked Miles.

Simon shook his head. 'Not really, why?'

'I've got some excellent Scotch back at mine. Vintage single malt from a tiny distillery on Jute. We didn't really get to chat tonight and I assume that's what you wanted?'

Simon smiled. He should have known Miles Ashford would have seen through his 'old mates together' ruse.

'Sure, that sounds good.'

Six months earlier, Miles had finally separated from Chrissy. Although he had no intention of divorcing her quite yet, she had stayed in their Notting Hill home whilst he had moved to a huge penthouse overlooking Hyde Park.

Back home he opened a drinks cabinet hidden behind a series of mirrored panels and poured two generous measures of the Scotch.

'May I smoke?' asked Simon.

'Let's go on to the terrace,' said Miles.

They went out into the mild night air. The terrace was illuminated by soft light and a black granite water feature provided a soft gurgling soundtrack.

Assad leant against the balcony, and as he watched Miles take a seat on a mahogany recliner he felt an erotic stir. He wasn't sure whether it was because his family were staunchly conservative French Catholics or because the macho culture of the City forced people to stay in the closet, but he had only recently admitted his true sexual orientation to himself. But he couldn't allow himself to be distracted from the job in hand.

'So I hear you've offered for Rivera,' said Miles, swirling the amber liquid around the bottom of his glass.

'Did Nat tell you?'

'No, just a rumour,' he replied. 'But I'm assuming it's true, otherwise why else are you here? Not just for my excellent Scotch.'

They exchanged a flirtatious glance. Assad had heard the whispers about Ashford's sexuality, that he liked men *and* women. It wouldn't surprise him. Men like Ashford wanted everything.

'What do you make of Sasha Sinclair?' he asked.

Miles put his hands behind his head and looked thoughtful. 'I think she's ambitious and a talented marketeer,' he replied. 'But I don't agree with the style magazines who say she's the most brilliant fashion and business brain of her generation.' His laugh did not convey unkindness, rather affection, and Simon was intrigued. He'd done his homework of course; Miles had known Sinclair for two decades and had directly invested in her company. The chances were he knew her better than anyone.

'I suppose what I'm asking is whether you think Rivera can thrive without her?' said Simon.

Miles downed his Scotch. 'Look, I'll be frank. In the early days Sasha's vision and drive was crucial. But now? Things move on, Simon. Gucci didn't exactly go to the wall when Tom Ford left the business. Besides which, Sasha was never even the designer, just the stylist. Yes, she's an ambitious woman with good taste and a fat contacts book. But since Rivera has become big business, she's only really been, well, just a very pretty figurehead.'

Simon nodded. He'd almost been convinced by the arguments of the Rivera staff and respected observers of the fashion industry that Sasha Sinclair was *the* key component of the label. But from a purely commercial viewpoint, that made no sense at all. Steven Ellis was a strong leader backed up by a talented design team. What role did Sasha Sinclair play beyond being a photogenic and well-connected brand ambassador? Then there was her million-dollar clothing allowance and her seven-figure remuneration package: outrageous for the amount of time she appeared to be in the office. No. What Miles Ashford was saying made perfect sense: Sasha Sinclair was well past her sell-by date.

He glanced at Miles, his legs slightly apart on the lounger, two buttons open on his shirt, and allowed himself a moment to imagine in what other capacity he might well be useful, but then pushed the thought away.

'Well, thanks for the Scotch, Miles, it was excellent,' he said, standing up.

'Leaving so soon?'

'Perhaps we can talk again if this bid comes off.'

Miles held his gaze. 'I'd like that.'

Simon walked towards the door. Temptation wasn't what he needed right now. In the world of Simon Assad, everything was strictly business.

In the back of her car on the way to Claridge's, Sasha flicked through her diary, both pleased and concerned that every single weekend was booked up until September. Hen nights, house-warmings, polo matches, fortieths in Ibiza and weddings in the Loire – if any more invitations came through, she was going to need a bigger mantelpiece. The weeks in between were no less hectic: parties, openings, premieres; it was getting hard to squeeze the business meetings in between. But when Simon Assad had called her the day before to invite her for dinner, she made a space in her diary immediately.

As a director and shareholder in Rivera, she had been aware that Assad had made an initial bid to Randall. She wasn't necessarily against another sale, of course. After all, diluting her shareholding would net her several more millions and finally propel her on to the *Sunday Times* Rich List, but she was also well aware that Simon would not want both Steven and her attached to the new management. She'd already had quiet words with key members of staff, enticing them with bonusess and promotion assurances if they would tell Assad that Sasha was an irreplaceable visionary. Hell would freeze over before she allowed Steven Ellis to push her out of her own company, she thought as she left her driver idling by the kerb and walked into Claridge's.

Despite her resolution not to sleep with him – Sasha had met few men for dinner who did not want to finish the evening in bed – she had made a special effort for their meeting, even getting her blond hair cut into a severe bob which made her feel more in control and powerful. Assad was already waiting for her in the elegant dining room at a quiet table by the window.

He got up from his seat and kissed her on the cheek, but she was disappointed when he didn't even show a flicker of appreciation for how she was looking. In fact his manner was brusque, efficient, purposeful. If she'd been expecting lingering aperitifs, flirtatious small talk and footsie, she was very much mistaken – she knew immediately that this was strictly business. And serious business.

'Sorry for getting you here at such short notice,' said Simon. 'But this shouldn't take long. You'll be aware I have made a preliminary offer for Rivera.'

'Of course.'

'Then you also probably know that this company cannot continue with you and Steven steering the ship. The atmosphere is toxic, Sasha, and it's starting to affect staff morale. More importantly, the industry is getting wind of it, which is going to affect business.'

'I agree that something's got to give, Simon,' she said, trying to keep her tone light and non-confrontational. 'If you ask around, I'm sure they'll tell you that Steven's "steering" has lacked the vision a creative company like Rivera requires.'

564

Sasha knew that someone with a purely commercial mind like Assad might favour Steven's contribution to the business and she had to stay focused on what she wanted out of the Assad deal. She wanted Steven out, yes, but she also wanted a financial windfall from selling part of her shareholding and a greatly improved remuneration package. The only way to do that was to make Simon see that while bean-counter CEOs were ten a penny, an international player, a creative visionary, like her was indispensable to the business. Then again, she didn't want to seem callous.

'I don't think you should be too hard on Steven. As you'll see from the figures, we're on course for a fifteen per cent sales uplift this year, so while Steven Ellis isn't my favourite person in the world, his presence is not actually harming the company. Perhaps if we could find some other role . . .'

'No,' said Simon firmly. 'One of you has to exit the company and sell your stake. It's the only way forward.'

'Well then your choice is made.' Sasha smiled. 'I am the founder of Rivera. It needs me.'

'I'm not sure that's the case any more,' said Assad.

'I beg your pardon?'

'Rivera needs to expand globally and I want someone to lead this label who has the international experience to do that. Steven has worked in Hong Kong, Paris, New York.'

Sasha tried to speak, but found the words failed her. She had never considered that Simon would push her out. She was Sasha Sinclair, for God's sake, a style icon!

'So you've made your decision?' she stuttered. 'You want Steven and not me? Steven is just a number-cruncher.'

'We both know that's not true.'

'I can't believe you don't understand the principal allure of Rivera,' she said. 'People are buying into my lifestyle, Simon. The fantasy I have created.'

'Sasha, please. Do people buy Chanel because they want to look like Karl Lagerfeld?'

'No, but Stella McCartney gave her label rock and roll chic. Tamara Mellon gave Jimmy Choo its glamour . . .'

'Sasha, I've made my decision.'

A waiter hovered, holding menus, but Sasha knew she wouldn't be needing one. She could feel her hands trembling. It was inconceivable to think that Simon would choose an accountant over Rivera's founder, the beating heart of the company.

'This is insane. I won't stand for it,' she said.

'I don't need your approval to make this deal happen, Sasha,' said Simon.

He was so casual, so off-hand, as if this was just another day at the office. But this was her life, a company she had created with her own hands, a company she had imagined into being. It was part of her.

'Fuck you, Simon,' she said in a low, hard voice. Then she stood up and walked out on to Brook Street, her head held high.

Getting into the car, she sat silently for a few moments trying to collect her thoughts. Had that really happened? Had she really just been fired from her own company? Was she really unemployed?

'Where to, Miss Sinclair?' asked Matthew, her driver.

She held up a finger to indicate 'one minute'.

Think, Sasha. Think.

She took out her mobile and dialled Randall Kane.

'Randall, where are you?'

'London,' replied her chairman cautiously. 'Why?'

'I need to see to you urgently.'

'I can switch a few things around tomorrow so we could do breakfast.'

'Too late,' she said, feeling her heart beating hard. 'I need to see you now.'

'Sasha, I can't tonight. I have dinner guests.'

'Ten minutes of your time, that's all I need.'

He paused for a moment. 'At least tell me what it is.'

She was not going to give him the chance to make excuses. 'I can't discuss it now,' she replied with a sense of urgency.

He sighed heavily. 'If you must. You know the address. And it's ten minutes, Sasha.'

Long minutes later her car drew up next to one of west London's most prestigious addresses. Randall owned a huge white stucco house at the Notting Hill end of Kensington Park Gardens. *What an incredible place to live*, she thought, looking up at the double-fronted building. As she climbed from the car, she wondered how much it would cost her to buy a place like this. Too much, she decided. London might be in a recession, but super-prime properties like these were still selling for sixty, seventy million, fuelled by foreign money and the huge bonuses still awarded to the biggest City players. Light jazz drifted on to the street, and from the shadows of dozens of people at the windows, Randall was having more than a quiet dinner party. As a uniformed maid let her in, Sasha craned her neck to see inside the reception room which was crammed with at least fifty people. Any other time she would have been piqued not to have received an invitation, but for once, she had no desire to socialise.

Randall appeared at the door holding a tumbler of cognac. 'Sasha, why don't we go outside,' he said, leading her on to a terrace at the back of the house. There would have been a time when she would have found this intoxicating; alone with a handsome, successful man in one of the finest homes in London, but now all she felt was anxious and out of control. She took a deep breath.

'Assad wants me out,' she said simply.

'I know.'

'*You know?*'

'He told me yesterday.'

'Has this always been the plan? To push me out?'

'No, Sasha. There was never a plan. But there are

management issues, even you must admit that. We're lucky that Assad is even interested in buying the company with a president and CEO wanting to kill each other.'

'I am not stepping to one side, Randall,' she said, her voice fierce.

He looked at her for a moment. 'Why?' he asked.

'*Why?*' she said with a laugh. 'Why would I?'

'Because you've been working full throttle since you were twenty-one years old,' said Randall. 'Because you've made yourself a very rich woman; because you have the respect of the entire industry and should be confident enough to take a break, look at other options, have a baby . . .'

'A *baby*?'

Randall pressed on. 'How old are you, Sasha? Thirty-eight, thirty-nine? You are one of the most beautiful women in London, yet you are alone.'

'Don't patronise me, Randall.'

'I'm talking as a friend, Sasha. Why not cash in now, why not make a fortune? Then you'll have time for a relationship, family.' His grey brows knitted together with fatherly concern.

'What I want is this company,' she growled, feeling her eyes prick with emotion.

She blinked angrily. Now was not the time for a show of weakness. The worst thing was that there was a whiff of truth in what he said. Recently she'd seen a picture of Grace Ashford and her children at the Cannes film festival; the smiling photograph of a successful woman with her two teenage children and glamorous artist partner had filled her with a crushing sense of loneliness that had lasted for days. But she couldn't let sentiment like that overcome her. She was Sasha Sinclair, one of the country's top businesswomen. She lived for the cut and thrust of business.

'I'll fight it, Randall,' she said, a note of desperation creeping into her voice.

568

'Don't make trouble, Sasha,' he said. 'I know how much you love the business and I know how hard it must be to let go, but do the right thing and step aside.'

She left without another word and walked down Kensington Park Gardens towards the High Street. To her left, smoky lilac dusk was setting across the park. Fleetingly she considered speaking to Randall again, but she couldn't bear the humiliation; she knew they had made up their minds. To them it was just another deal, just another line of numbers on a spreadsheet. They had no idea what she had sacrificed to get to where she was; they had no idea what she had put into that company. And now they were yanking it out from underneath her. Slowly she walked back to the car.

'Just take me home,' she said.

Matthew was just about to move away when an Aston Martin coming from the other direction pulled up at the kerb. Two men jumped out, crossed the street and began climbing the steps towards Randall's front door. At first, in the dark, she wasn't sure it was him, but then she recognised the pale camel jacket he had been wearing at Claridge's: Simon Assad. But it was his shorter, slimmer companion that made her catch her breath. It was Miles Ashford.

Miles slapped Simon on the shoulder as the door opened and they stepped inside. Matey, familiar, celebrating their good fortune. And finally the last piece of the puzzle clicked into place. What had changed Simon's mind so suddenly? Why had he chosen to replace her instead of an interchangeable number-cruncher like Steven? The answer was right there in front of her: Miles Ashford. Coming along to destroy all her hard work on a whim, just as he had done twenty years ago. For a moment back there on the terrace, Sasha had felt defeated; she had even begun to think that perhaps Randall was right, it was time she took her foot off the gas, settled down and started a family. But not now. Now she was going to fight. And if that was what it took, she was going to fight dirty.

68

Back in the comfort of his Manhattan office, Miles Ashford held his copy of *Forbes* magazine aloft and allowed himself a smile as he read the words on the cover: 'Going The Extra Miles: How Ashford Conquered New York' read the headline over a very flattering David Bailey portrait of himself.

Although the Big Apple was no longer his home, Miles still felt a great attachment to the city and was glad of this visible and prestigious recognition of his achievements. Not that he had any plans to rest on his laurels. The New York Globe was still incredibly popular, but Andre Balzas' Penthouse bar at the top of the Standard was generating the sort of excitement the Globe had drawn at the start of the decade, and if there was one thing Miles hated it was other people stealing his thunder. There were residential opportunities to exploit too: two landmark buildings were coming up for sale downtown and Miles was determined to have them for his own.

Tipping his chair back, he looked around his office at the trappings of success: the Francis Bacon that hung above the leather sofa; the collage of photographs of Miles with assorted luminaries – Obama, Clinton, Mandela. He wasn't about to give any of this up. Yes, the recession had shaken him badly, but things had to be on the upturn, especially since he'd gone in with Anil on the Mumbai deal – on a personal level as well as professionally. Randall Kane's get-together the other night was the sort of macho back-slapping party he usually found boring, but Simon Assad had made it much more interesting. Firstly because he had told Miles that he was forcing Sasha out of the company – exactly the sort of thing to perk him up – but mainly because of Assad himself. He intrigued Miles, excited him. That night in his penthouse when Miles had cracked open his best whisky, he'd wanted to carry on the evening and show Assad *exactly* why all work and no play made Simon a very dull boy. He smiled to himself. There would be plenty of time for that. He swivelled his leather chair so he could see the New York skyline in front of him. First he had a city to conquer.

There was a knock at the door. Irritated, he turned back towards the office. 'Enter.'

Michael Marshall came in and took a seat under the Bacon, and immediately Miles noticed the troubled expression on the lawyer's face.

'Trouble?' he asked.

Marshall nodded. 'It's about Angel Cay.'

The warmth seemed to disappear from the room. Miles' skin felt cold and his mouth dry.

'Angel?' he repeated as steadily as he could.

The Fairmont hotel group who were buying the island were keen for a quick sale – as far as Miles was concerned, he couldn't get rid of the place quick enough. But any sale was dependent on a detailed survey to see whether it was suitable for the required level of construction for the proposed two-hundred-room resort.

Michael put his hands up. 'I don't think it's anything to worry about just yet, but I have just got off the phone with the Royal Bahamian Police.'

'What on earth about?'

Michael pushed his lips out as if he were pondering a difficult problem. It was a gesture that always unsettled and yet excited Miles – no one was better at finding solutions to problems than Michael. Over the years, Miles had come to rely on him to find ways out of tight spots. Michael was by far his most trusted and valuable member of staff – the one most like him. But if Michael Marshall was troubled, Miles knew it was serious.

'I've been speaking to our contact at Fairmont. Apparently surveyors have been on the island for about a week. They've been taking soil samples from around the island. Suitability for building work and so on – I understand they were planning on building the spa at a place called West Point Beach on the far side of the island?'

Miles realised he was gripping the edge of his desk and deliberately relaxed his fingers.

'Miles, they found a body.'

His heart was thumping. 'A human body?'

Michael nodded. 'Well, decomposed remains anyway. Of course, the first thing the surveyors did was call the police in George Town. Second thing they did was call Fairmont, and they called me.'

'So the police are on to it?' He could feel sweat collecting at the back of his neck, dampening the collar of his shirt that felt suddenly too tight around his throat. He'd dreamt about this moment before – in distant nightmares of his youth – but had never actually prepared for it, never really believed that it could actually happen.

'Two officers from the Royal Bahamian Police force are on their way to Angel Cay now,' said Michael.

'Have you spoken to them?'

'Not the investigating officers. I've left three messages.'

Miles tried to compose himself and think more rationally. 'Do we know how long the body's been there?'

'No idea. I'm sure forensics in Nassau will be able to date it.'

Michael sat forward slightly, and Miles could feel him searching his face.

572

'Miles, you don't know anything about this, do you?'

'What the fuck are you suggesting?' snapped Miles.

Michael shrugged. 'As your lawyer and adviser, I have to ask the question.'

Miles knew he had to be convincing. 'Look, I'm as surprised and horrified by this as you are,' he said. 'My family has owned that island for thirty years and I can assure you I know nothing about any body. Anyway, we have no idea how old these remains are, do we? It could be the bones of bloody Blackbeard for all we know.'

Michael nodded, his eyes still searching Miles' face. Did he see something there? wondered Miles.

'Have they interviewed Nelson?' he asked, if only to deflect Michael's scrutiny. As soon as the deal with Fairmont had been announced, he had made sure Michael dealt with Nelson's severance from his job. He didn't want to run the risk of the long-term caretaker being viewed as a sitting tenant. A temporary handyman had been installed in Nelson's place.

'No.'

'Well make sure Nelson is out of the way; pack him off to Timbuktu if you have to. And make sure this new handyman keeps quiet too. I want us to deal with this directly.'

Michael's expression was still serious. 'You do know they are going to want to talk to you?'

'I can understand that,' said Miles. 'But we really have to nip this in the bud before there's talk. You need to get out to Nassau – today. In the meantime, we need to contain the story.'

'Miles, I think you should come with me,' said Michael.

'What? For some old pirate bones?' he snapped. 'Don't be ridiculous.'

Michael shook his head. 'Even so, you need to go. The police are going to get suspicious if you don't cooperate fully and it's going to look strange if this does leak and you're sitting in an office in New York. If the press twist this the wrong way, it could be a major scandal. Now's not the time, Miles.'

Sighing, Miles nodded. Michael was right. There was no point hiding from this; they needed to get it sorted as soon as possible. Everything could be solved or hushed up when you had power and money.

'Very well. Arrange for the jet to take us to Nassau.'

Grace was in the kitchen of their Spitalfields house, reading a trashy novel at the huge farmhouse table, when Julian poked his head into the room.

'Can you fix us a snack?' he said. 'We're getting a bit peckish. Some sandwiches with that nice cheese maybe.'

He had been locked in a meeting with his business manager Lars Johnstone for a couple of hours now. Grace fought her irritation. He was spending more and more time with Lars and his trendy east London artist crowd and only seemed to notice her when he needed something. Yesterday he'd walked in and said, 'You do know we're out of bog roll,' like she was a maid who wasn't doing her job. Perhaps she wasn't. Julian didn't seem to be satisfied with anything about her at the moment.

'Sure,' she said, shutting her book. 'What are you doing down there anyway?'

'Just talking tactics.'

'Oh yes? For what?'

He sighed. 'We're thinking about having a big one-off auction of my latest work. Lars thinks *Zenras at Moonlight* might go for twenty million.'

Grace frowned. 'I thought you were planning to show that collection at the Singleton Gallery?'

'Nah. Thought we'd cut Neil out of this one.'

Neil Singleton was Julian's long-term dealer, the man who had plucked him straight out of Goldsmiths and navigated his career into the stratosphere. Admittedly, the forty per cent commission he took from all his sales was more than adequate compensation, but Grace was a little unsettled by Julian's casual dismissal of someone who had been so pivotal in his development.

'Isn't Neil going to be a bit pissed off about being bypassed?'

'I make the rules now, Grace,' Julian said. 'If we make what Lars thinks we can make at auction, I'm thinking of buying something really special. An island. A massive yacht.'

She laughed nervously. 'Julian, we don't need a yacht.'

His eyes narrowed and his voice took on a petulant edge. 'Strictly speaking we don't need anything, do we?' he said. 'This book. That pan. That clock on the wall. None of it's really necessary, is it? But you want it all, don't you?'

She could tell he was spoiling for a fight again. It was happening more and more these days. Julian would sneer and snipe at her until it blew up into a row, then he would have the excuse to storm off and spend the night 'at Lars''.

'OK, OK,' she said, standing up and walking over to the big steel fridge. 'I'll just make those sandwiches, shall I?'

It had all started to go downhill at that horrible party when Connie had been found dead in the south wing at Stockbridge. Olivia had been inconsolable and Julian had become sullen and withdrawn. She was surprised how hard it had hit them both. Julian had refused to talk about it with her and became angry when she pressed him about it. By contrast, Olivia had cried on her shoulder for a week and as a consequence they had become much closer, spending more quality time together. Grace supposed that Liv had been brought face to face with mortality and didn't want to lose her mum in the same way. Whatever it was, Grace was glad to have her daughter back. In fact she had spent the weekend helping Olivia move into her new Chelsea flat, which had been bought with an inheritance from her grandmother. Two days of painting, cleaning, lifting boxes, unpacking had left her with a vague fluey feeling. *Onset of middle age*, she thought to herself.

Piling a stack of sandwiches on a plate, she took the narrow staircase to Julian's basement den. Grace was not a big fan of this part of London. It was too trendy, intimidating and gritty. But she loved Julian's Georgian terraced house, tucked away just past the market; it was light and roomy and it had the whiff of Dickens about it. As she approached the study door, she could hear Julian and Lars talking.

'Do you honestly think we can get fifteen million for the Zoltar?'

'Not normally, no,' said Lars in his crisp public school voice. 'But if we get Chris Abrams and Hugh Benton bidding against each other then we'll make it.'

Julian did not sound convinced. 'But we're barely out of recession. I know the Russians and the Chinese are still swimming in cash, but are Chris and Hugh prepared to pay eight figures in this climate?'

Lars laughed. 'The purpose of this auction is *for* them to pay over the odds for your work. To bid against each other until one of them pays an inflated price.'

'Why?'

'Because both of them own at least a dozen of your works, Julian. Estimated value may be one hundred million dollars. This auction will set a new benchmark price for your work and the value of their collection increases twenty, maybe thirty per cent overnight. That's better than any stock pick, I tell you.'

Grace left the sandwiches by the door and tiptoed back up the stairs.

Julian came into the bedroom an hour later. Grace had been trying to get to sleep but she couldn't; too much was going around in her head. Julian took his shirt off and threw it on the armchair. His belly was round and slack, hanging over the edge of his waistband.

'I heard you talking about the auction.'

'Really? Learn anything?' he said without looking at her, his voice bored.

'Actually I did. You're rigging it.'

He didn't even deny it. 'Get off your fucking high horse, will you,' he said. 'Since when have you been all *art is for the people*? You seem pretty happy to live off the proceeds.'

She gaped at him, stung. 'What's that supposed to mean?'

'You know exactly what I mean,' he said. 'I know you like pissing about taking your little black and white photos of slum kids, but two hundred and fifty quid a day jobs don't buy houses like Stockbridge.'

'Well I'm sorry that it's not all about the money for me, Julian,' she replied. 'I'd rather people wanted to look at my little black and white photos because they were interesting, not just because some self-interested collector decided they were valuable.'

'I didn't see much of this gritty integrity when you were swanning about hob-nobbing at Cannes.'

Cannes again. Every time they argued he brought up Cannes. She had taken her documentary to the film festival and it had been a roaring success. There was even talk of a possible Oscar nomination for *El Tumba* in the factual film category. And yet Julian had used this success against her like a weapon and his mood had been on a hair trigger ever since. She couldn't swallow it any longer.

'Why don't you just admit you're jealous of my success, Julian?' she said. 'You're happy when I'm buttering sandwiches and making small talk with your collectors, but as soon as I step out of your shadow, you become a child.'

'Jealous?' he sneered.

'Yes, jealous.'

He snorted and started to pull his shirt back on.

'Where are you going?'

'Out,' he said.

'Julian, it's nearly midnight.'

'So?'

'Well where are you going?'

'Dunno,' he said, shrugging his shoulders defiantly. 'Anywhere where I don't have to listen to this sanctimonious shit.'

And as the door slammed shut and she heard his footsteps fade away on the cobbles outside, Grace wondered how a person like her – a person who had so much love in her heart – had ended up with a man she was beginning to despise. And then she began to cry.

69

It was only the third time in twenty years that Miles had been to the Bahamas. Despite the huge potential of resorts on the islands, particularly due to their proximity to the States, he had always avoided the area, even declining any invitations to nearby islands. It just wasn't somewhere he wanted to be. If that was true in the normal run of things, it was doubly so right now, as he walked down the narrow steps of the corporate Gulfstream on to the hot tarmac at Nassau airport. He felt sick just being this close to Angel Cay.

A car met Miles and Michael and took them to the Ashford Nassau, where the penthouse suite had been lavishly prepared for the chief executive's arrival. Miles took a shower and, wrapping himself in a white robe, walked out on to the roof terrace.

'I hope you're not going to make me go to the bloody police station,' he grumbled, looking out over the city, a carpet of pale low-rise buildings fanning out to stripes of white sand and vivid green ocean. 'Those places make you feel like a criminal as soon as you've stepped foot inside.'

Michael looked up from his laptop and shook his head. 'I've arranged all that. A detective from Nassau's Central Detective Unit is meeting you here at four.'

'Detective? From Nassau?' said Miles. 'I thought the George Town lot were dealing with this.'

'Miles, don't worry,' said Michael soothingly. 'It's best we talk to the top men in the area and get this over with as soon as possible. We don't want you repeating yourself to a bunch of local flatfoots.'

Miles didn't want to be talking to the police at all, especially not here where the afternoon sun was so oppressively hot. He retreated into the bedroom, drew down the blinds and stayed there fretfully until he heard Michael's knock on the door. He'd had a couple of shots of bourbon an hour earlier to steady his nerves, but now realised that the police would smell the sour oaky liquor on his breath: not a good start. Running into the bathroom, he scrabbled around for his toothbrush, then gave up and swilled some toothpaste around his mouth until he was ready to answer the door.

'Miles Ashford, this is Detective Inspector Carlton,' said Michael.

Carlton was fiftyish, short greying hair contrasting with his cocoa skin. Miles showed him into the suite and they sat on facing sofas. Miles wished he had taken the meeting on the terrace where sunglasses could have hidden his eyes. *Calm down*, he said to himself, *you have nothing to be afraid of. No evidence, a twenty-year gap, there's nothing left to find.* He smiled at the detective.

'So how can I help?' he asked.

'I assume Mr Marshall has filled you in?' asked Carlton.

Miles shrugged. 'As much as he could. Neither of us knows a great deal, but we'd be grateful for anything you could tell us. As I'm sure you're aware, I have a fifty-million-dollar business deal at stake here. Fairmont – the company buying Angel Cay – won't exchange contracts until they get a satisfactory survey, and I'm sure you can appreciate that finding a dead body where they'd like an infinity pool to be hasn't exactly gone down well with their board of directors.'

Carlton simply nodded. 'So you know nothing about the body other than the details we have told Mr Marshall?' he asked.

'Of course not. My family have owned the island for nearly thirty years and we've had no reason to ever think that something like that was buried on the west coast beach. Can I ask how old you think the remains are?'

Carlton held out his hands. 'Forensics isn't an exact science, I'm afraid, particularly when the body is so decomposed. But the initial report from the lab dated the time of death between twenty and thirty years ago.'

Miles felt his heart jump. 'Which suggests the previous owner of Angel Cay might know something about it?' he offered helpfully.

Carlton flipped over a few pages in his notebook. 'A gentleman named Ron Casey. Lives in Las Vegas now. It's not making our lives easy, all you people being so far-flung.'

'I can only apologise,' said Miles with a sympathetic laugh.

For the next twenty minutes, Carlton continued questioning Miles. What could he remember about the guests they had had on the island? Did he ever remember anyone unconnected to the family docking on Angel Cay? Did his father only invite business associates or did he rent the island out to friends? Miles was able to honestly answer that he had little recollection. He had only visited the island as a young man on family holidays. How his father used it in between was a mystery to him.

'And you can't remember anyone ever going missing?'

Despite the air-conditioning, Miles knew that his hands were clammy. He felt dehydrated and dizzy, but he had to maintain a cool exterior. He'd been under worse pressure than this, many times.

'Missing?' he said.

'A guest, a member of staff . . .' suggested Carlton.

Miles shook his head. 'No, although I'm sure we've had staff do a moonlight flit on us.'

'*Moonlight flit?*' said Carlton. 'I'm sorry, I'm not familiar with that term.'

581

'My apologies. It means they left the island without notice. I do remember someone made off with my mother's pearl earrings once.' He smiled. 'But missing, no, I don't recall anything like that.'

Carlton nodded slowly, his eyes never leaving Miles'.

'I assume I'm allowed to go to Angel Cay?' asked Miles. 'I wasn't expecting to make this trip, but now I'm here, it'd be nice to have one last look around the family home before the developers move in.'

'We can't ask you to stay in Nassau, Mr Ashford. Not yet,' said Carlton, rising and shaking Miles' hand. 'But I trust you'll be available to speak to us at any time?'

Not yet? Miles thought with unease.

'Our forensic team will be there another day or so,' said the policeman. 'Although it's big enough for us to section off the appropriate area.'

'Just the west beach?'

'More or less.'

'Have you spoken to Nelson Ford?' asked Michael, leading Carlton to the door. 'I gave you the up-to-date contact details we have for him.'

'Not yet. He's not at any of the numbers you gave us. Anyone would think he had gone underground.'

Miles laughed. 'Not Nelson. He's a sixty-five-year-old man, not a master criminal.'

'Let's hope not, Mr Ashford,' said Carlton. 'I hate to have mysteries like this hanging around. Here in the islands we find that secrets don't stay that way for long.'

70

When Grace woke up the next morning, Julian's side of the bed was empty. It had happened before; after eight years together, Grace was used to his hot temper and mood swings. In happier times, his mercurial disposition had manifested itself in spontaneity: leaping into the car to drive to the Cornish coast or the Scottish highlands simply because the muse had taken hold of him. Back then, Julian had been romantic and exciting. Now he was childish and petulant, using arguments – picking fights – as an excuse to go out to parties and bohemian dive bars. For a while Grace had put up with it; Julian was an artist after all and given to sensitivity. He certainly hadn't taken Connie's death well – it couldn't have been pleasant to be the one to find her lying at the bottom of those stairs, thought Grace with a shiver. But lately, his behaviour had simply left her angry and dismayed. The pointless argument of the previous night had made her wonder if she really knew him at all.

She showered, dressed and had a breakfast of grapefruit and black coffee, but she still felt edgy. She thought about calling Joe who was at tennis camp in Marbella but it was too early. Usually when she needed to clear her head, she would go for a run: all those long jogs along Port Douglas' Four Mile Beach or the muddy bridle paths around Stockbridge. But you never saw people jogging around this part of east London. Slouching, yes; scowling with studied indifference, that too. But jogging? No.

So I'll clean! She smiled to herself, grabbing the keys to her scooter. Weaving through the streets of London, her hair streaming in a long ribbon from under her helmet, she immediately felt better. Grace's friends had laughed at her for getting a scooter at forty, but it was her little shot at rebellion. She'd spent her entire life being sensible, doing what she thought was right, so why not have a little fun? At the time when she should have been falling out of nightclubs, sleeping with unsuitable men and feeling carefree and unfettered, she'd been bringing up two children in the stifling atmosphere of El Esperanza with a dark secret that would barely let her sleep at night. Come to think of it, she should get a real motorbike, she thought as she parked the scooter. That would really raise a few eyebrows.

Olivia's apartment was in a red-brick mansion block behind Cheyne Walk. It had been a probate sale, still full of an old lady's things, curtains from the fifties and knick-knacks not removed by the family, so Olivia had made Grace promise to come back to help 'sort it'. Grace opened the front door with her spare key and went up the stairs. The apartment was still in the same mess she had left it yesterday: overflowing boxes, designer clothes hanging off every surface, thick layers of dust on the windowsills.

There was no sign of Olivia, but then it was still only nine o'clock and she had probably been out clubbing till all hours. Putting the kettle on, Grace went down the corridor to rouse her daughter from bed.

'C'mon, sleepyhead, rise and . . .' she began, the words dying in her throat. Olivia was lying on top of the well-upholstered body of a man, his face buried between her tanned, slender thighs. She was completely naked, her skin sheened in sweat, and her long hair could not disguise the fact that her mouth was on his cock. As Grace stood there, Olivia looked up, her hair dishevelled, her cheeks flushed, her moist lips glinting in the hazy morning light.

'Mum. Shit.'

She scrambled off the naked man and knelt up on the duvet, her face suddenly blanched of colour.

The man sat up, and Grace thought she was going to die on the spot.

'Julian,' she croaked. Her whole body felt like lead, unable to move, revulsion and fury rising in her chest like boiling magma until it reached her throat. Finally she took a breath and let out a scream.

'You little whore!' she spat.

'Mum, I'm so sorry,' said Olivia, jumping off the bed, knocking over a bottle of wine that leaked on to the carpet.

'Get out!' Grace bellowed at Julian, picking up his jeans, shirt and shoes and throwing them out of the door.

'Grace, please,' he said meekly.

'Don't you *dare* say another word,' growled Grace. 'I said *get out*!'

She watched him leave, his plump body scampering into the corridor. In the other corner of the room her daughter covered her naked body with a small pink robe with a teddy bear motif on the front pocket.

Olivia was frantic. 'I know how this looks.'

'You know how this *looks*? It looks like you're a cheap, cheap *slut*, that's how it looks.'

Olivia's face immediately became defiant. 'I love him, Mum.'

'Love?' She tried to roar but it came out as a pathetic little squeak. 'The only person you love, Olivia, is yourself.'

'It's been over between you and Julian for months.'

It was a slap in the face and Grace willed herself not to crumble. 'Who told you that? Him? Because last time I looked, we'd been living together for five years.'

Olivia wrapped her robe tightly around herself and squared

up to her mother. Grace could smell the musky scent of sex on her teenage daughter's face and stepped away, repulsed by the thought of where it came from.

'Do you know why I care about him?' said Olivia.

'Because he's a world-famous artist?' said Grace, tears streaming down her cheeks. 'Because you're spoilt and vicious and you want the one person you know you can't have, like some sick, sad power trip?' She didn't recognise herself in the hard, harsh words coming out of her mouth.

'Because he cares about me,' said Olivia, her voice level. 'Because he gives me attention. Which is more than you've ever given me. You've always been flying off around the world helping orphans, empowering poor people, running photography clubs for fucking peasants. What about us, Mum? What about your children? And I don't mean lecturing us on our moral well-being. *Be careful. Don't have sex. Take the pill,*' she mocked. 'You've been so busy being a do-gooder, trying to save the world, when really you should be looking at how to save your *own* life. Look at you. You've got a boyfriend that doesn't love you. Children you hardly know . . .'

'Is that what you think?' She could barely see now through the glaze of tears. It was like a knife through her heart. Forget Julian, he barely seemed to matter any more. But after everything she had done for her kids, her daughter's words were shattering.

'Yes,' said Olivia simply. 'That's what I think.'

'Then you'd better just go,' said Grace, too weak to fight any longer.

'No,' said Olivia quietly, lifting her chin. 'This is *my* flat. You go.'

Looking at her daughter, the pit of Grace's stomach welled up with love, sorrow, disappointment. She stumbled back into the corridor, out of the door, taking the flight of steps down two by two and out on to the street, gasping for air as she sank down onto the cold concrete pavement. Desperately she tipped her handbag out on the ground, scrabbling for her mobile phone, her fingers shaking as they stabbed the numbers.

'Be there,' she whispered to herself as she held the phone to her ear. 'Please, please be there ... Alex, is that you?'

'Grace?' came the familiar voice. 'What's wrong? Tell me.'

'I need you, Alex,' she sobbed. 'Come quickly. Please, just come and get me.'

71

Few people liked going to parties by themselves, but it was something that had never particularly bothered Sasha Sinclair. She was attractive, funny and a master networker; after nearly twenty years on the party circuit, she usually knew at least half a dozen people at any gathering. Today, however, that was a distinct disadvantage. Normally a party like Amelia Hambro's fortieth, held in the gardens of Inner Temple Inns of Court along London's Embankment, would have been an ideal opportunity for Sasha to flirt, make contacts and exchange gossip. The trouble was, today the gossip was about her. Word was out about the Assad bid for Rivera and everyone was whispering about Sasha: was she leaving the company – and if so, was she jumping or was she being pushed? For the first time, Sasha had no desire to talk to anyone. She felt adrift, dislocated. Everywhere she looked, happy couples were laughing, talking about their holiday plans for Tuscany or Provence, their children at expensive prep schools: normal everyday life. The truth was Randall had been right when he said she had been consumed by her ambition. If she lost her place in the fashion world, she genuinely wouldn't know how to behave. Of course there were thousands of things she could do with fifty million pounds in the bank and two decades' worth of experience in the fashion industry. But right now she couldn't think of any of them –

she didn't *want* any of them. What Sasha Sinclair wanted was her life back.

'I thought it was you.'

She had been sheltering from the furtive glances and the whispered gossip under a lime tree a little way from the party. She spun round and opened her eyes wide.

'Philip Bettany!' she exclaimed. 'What on earth are you doing here?'

She leant in to kiss him, wincing inwardly. She had always regretted treating Philip so badly. He was a good man and a good friend, but she had pushed him aside in favour of her ambition and her feelings for an unsuitable married man. He was still looking good. His hair was peppered with grey at the temples, and his skin looked sun-worn, but at forty-seven he was still the most handsome man at the party.

'I didn't even know you were in the country,' said Sasha. 'The last I heard you were in Hong Kong.'

'I was in Sydney for eight years. I moved back two months ago, escaping the Aussie winter.'

He smiled. It was a warm, genuine smile although there was no reason for him to be so happy to see her. Sasha remembered the final days of their relationship: Philip's marriage proposal, her plan to oust him from the company, his quiet, dignified exit. How could she have been so selfish, so brutal? Looking at him now, she wondered what it was that hadn't worked. Certainly, she could have shown more grace.

'So who are you here with?' asked Philip.

'Just me. I was only popping my head in,' she said. 'I try not to dwell too much on fortieths, with mine being just around the corner.'

'Forty? Try having fifty out there.' He laughed. 'You're lucky I didn't bring my walking stick today.'

'I think you're looking great, Phil,' she said, blushing slightly and rushing on to cover her embarrassment. 'So tell me everything. What were you doing in Sydney?'

589

'CFO of a car manufacturing company. Not as sexy as evening dresses.'

'But you always loved cars, didn't you?' She glanced down at his left hand. 'Married? Kids?'

'Both.'

'Great.' She smiled too brightly.

'Well, the marriage is past tense, actually. It didn't quite work out as I'd hoped. Ended rather badly in fact.'

Sasha raised her eyebrows. 'A horror story you wish to share?'

Philip pulled a face. 'I wish it was something original,' he said, 'but it was just plain common-or-garden infidelity. Natalie, my wife, is English. We moved out to Sydney together, had Lily, our little girl. And then Natalie had an affair. End of story, really.'

Sasha touched his arm. 'I'm sorry to hear that.'

He shrugged. 'The day she told me she was leaving me and taking Lily, it was such a blow, I wrote a cheque for half of what we had in the bank and told her to get out.'

'Very dramatic of you,' said Sasha. 'Like an eighties mini-series.'

Philip laughed. 'Turns out it was a big mistake. In Australia, you can't begin divorce proceedings until you've been separated for twelve months, by which time she'd spent all the money I gave her and came after me for another half. I got screwed twice.'

'Gosh, Phil, that's so not like you,' said Sasha. 'At Rivera you watched every pound, shilling and pence.'

'Love makes people do the strangest things.'

She nodded, hating the thought of Philip being hurt so badly again. He deserved better.

'And what about you?' he asked. 'I've watched from afar, of course. I'm proud of what you've done with the company, Sash, but then again, I always knew you'd fly high.'

She snorted. 'Well right now, I'm about to crash and burn.'

'Really?'

Sasha quickly filled him in about Assad's takeover and being forced to leave the company.

'I thought something was wrong. You look worn out.'

If anyone else had said it, Sasha would have felt insulted, but from Philip it had the quiet intimacy of someone who knew her well. She reflected that he probably knew her better than anyone else. *That's a tragedy on its own*, she thought.

She looked out beyond the gardens, towards the darkness of the Thames and the twinkling South Bank and the soaring, majestic London Eye on the other side of the river. It was a romantic, inspiring vista.

'Listen, I'll understand if you say no,' said Sasha, 'but could we go out and talk about it?'

He chuckled. 'You want *my* advice?'

She touched his arm again. 'I can't let my company go without a fight, Phil. Besides, I always valued your advice. I just didn't show you how much I appreciated it.'

He looked at her for a moment, then smiled. 'What are you doing tomorrow?'

'Wallowing.' She grinned.

'I have a house in Tetbury. Nothing fancy. But it's quiet. There're horses, fields, long walks. It's the perfect place to convene a council of war.'

'So you'll help me?'

'Sasha, I've never stopped wanting to help you.'

She wanted to hug him, feel his reassuring warmth against her, but instead she just said, 'Thanks.'

He chinked his champagne glass against hers. 'I'll pick you up at five o'clock. And be ready for once, OK?'

'Oh I'll be ready,' smiled Sasha.

72

Miles couldn't concentrate. In the Pool Room at New York's Four Seasons restaurant, he should have been in his element, charming the group of Japanese bankers opposite him, cutting deals, laying the groundwork for his next attack on another territory ripe for exploitation. But with yesterday's trip to Nassau still weighing heavily on his mind, he could barely order coffee successfully, let alone impress new financial backers. He'd been like this all day – so distracted and wound up he'd had to leave the Ash Corp. offices and go to the driving range to work off some of his anger and frustration. How had he allowed this to happen? Why had he sold the island? If he had kept it in the family, no one would have gone anywhere near that bloody beach.

His phone was vibrating in his pocket, but he let it ring out: the Japanese were always sticklers for politeness. Its angry insistence made him feel under siege. Finally, the Japanese group began to leave, citing early flights back to Tokyo. Smiling and bowing, he waved them off, then let out a long breath and headed straight to the bar by the Grill Room and ordered a large gin and tonic, then took a seat in a quiet corner to make a call.

'Michael, you called?' he said.

'Yes, it's probably nothing, but Detective Carlton has been in touch.'

Miles closed his eyes and let his gin slip down his throat.

'Apparently they've spoken to an ex-Angel Cay employee,' continued Michael. 'A chef who worked there in the late eighties, early nineties. He remembered one of the casual staff disappearing – 1990, 1991, he thought.'

Miles was determined not to let his anxiety show. 'Hmm, yes. I vaguely remember that too. It was 1990, because I'd just finished at Danehurst. It was some boat boy and he hardly disappeared. He was drinking on the job and bunked off nicking one of our boats before he got fired. Damn inconvenient it was too. My father had a very important corporate event going on and didn't need the hassle of disappearing staff.'

Miles was surprised at his own calm manner as he spoke. He certainly would have found this more difficult to say if he had been with his lawyer face to face. That probing look Michael had, like he could see straight through whatever you were saying.

'Well, either way, you're going to have to go back to Nassau,' said Michael.

'But I was only bloody there yesterday!' cried Miles.

'We have to give them something, Miles. They want to know if you have any contact details for this boat boy at least.'

'Of course I don't,' snapped Miles. 'I was eighteen years old.'

'Carlton wants to know if there are any records of staff on the island or at the company offices.'

Miles felt his anger flare into red spots of heat on his cheeks. 'Michael, don't bother me with this shit. Sort it out. Pay someone off.'

'Look, Miles, I am trying to get them off our backs,' said Michael with irritation. 'Forgive me if I don't have as many police contacts in Nassau as I do in London or New York.'

The tone of Michael's voice made Miles shiver. Michael Marshall was a top-notch fixer, always happy to roll up his sleeves and get dirty; he never baulked at anything Miles asked, dealing with it with implacable calm and efficiency. In all the years they had worked together, he had never been tart or sarcastic. The fact that he sounded harassed and anxious made Miles think that the situation was more severe than Michael was letting on. But this was no time for rolling into a ball and giving up.

'Michael, I don't expect you to know every spook on the planet. But I do expect you to get on top of the situation. If you don't have the contacts, get them. Everyone, especially policemen, has their price. Try fucking harder.'

He slammed twenty dollars on the bar and stormed downstairs, out of the restaurant on the warm midtown night. His driver was waiting for him and took him uptown to his Fifth Avenue home, the lights of Manhattan slipping past in a blur of colour. Back at the apartment, he took a hot shower and a Xanax. He needed something to help him sleep. He needed something to make him forget.

73

It was almost eight o'clock by the time Philip's Range Rover pulled up outside a detached grey stone farmhouse with a low-slung gable roof, in an idyllic spot behind Westonbirt Arboretum. The journey from London hadn't been nearly as awkward or uncomfortable as Sasha had been expecting, not once she'd employed the tactic of just letting Philip talk about his daughter. There didn't seem to be any limit to Philip's pride and affection for Lily. It was bittersweet for Sasha to listen to him; she was happy to see his face light up, but sad that she had no one she could speak of with such warmth or love.

Dusk was still an hour off but light had already fallen from the sky, smudging it with a peachy glow like a wash from a watercolour brush. *This is a summit meeting, not a bloody mini-break*, she told herself as she took her overnight bag from the boot and made her way into the house.

'The blue room at the front of the house is the nicest guest room,' said Philip. 'Put your bag upstairs and I'll start dinner.'

Sasha had been in many country house guest rooms before – confections of four-poster beds, de Gournay wallpaper, Jo Malone candles and well-chosen antiques. But an interior decorator hadn't been near this place, she thought, looking at the uneven floor, chintzy curtains and rickety white wooden furniture.

Unzipping her holdall and removing the slim skirts, three

pairs of high heels, Hermès riding boots, jodhpurs and assortment of silk and cashmere items, she felt immediately ill-equipped for the weekend ahead. This was a chunky jumper and Hunter wellies sort of place, not a dress-for-dinner one. She also felt ill-equipped for spending so much time with Philip. Emotionally, she was raw anyway, but it was somehow worse seeing Philip so well and so ... sorted. She'd always assumed that he'd have spent his days pining away for her, but he'd moved on, healed whatever wounds he had.

A cast-iron claw-foot bath sat in front of the huge bay window that looked over fields and hills, just smudges of olive and charcoal in the twilight. She turned the stiff brass taps on, and the bath quickly filled.

There was a knock at the door. 'You decent?'

Smiling at the propriety of it all, she saw Philip's arm appear around the door holding a glass of wine which she took gratefully.

'Thanks, Phil,' she said.

'Don't mention it,' he mumbled as she heard him thudding back down the rickety stairs. Taking off her clothes, she stepped into the bath and slid down until her shoulders dipped under the soapy water. All was silent, except for the evening song of a cluster of blackbirds outside and the gentle popping of bubbles against her skin, and she relaxed, feeling the tension ebb away. Maybe it wasn't such a bad idea coming here after all.

Finally she came downstairs in the most casual clothes she'd brought: a pair of cashmere jogging pants and a sheer knit that just took the edge off the cool summer evening air. Philip was standing at the Aga with his shirt sleeves rolled up, grinding pepper into a bubbling pot.

'Just in time,' he said as he served up two plates of calorific-looking stew. They went through to the large living room, where a fire had been lit and stacks of papers set up on the table.

'What's that?' she said, pointing to the paperwork.

'Business school case studies of fashion company buy-outs, everything I could find on Simon Assad, profiles of other investment houses, company accounts . . . loads of other more boring stuff.'

She smiled, unable to hide how impressed she was. 'You've certainly done your homework.'

'Anything for a friend.' He smiled, then looked away. 'Anyway, what I don't understand is why Assad can't see the value you bring to the company.'

'I think he did, but he's been persuaded otherwise.'

'By who? Randall Kane?'

Sasha shook her head. 'On Thursday I saw Miles and Simon go in to Randall's party together. I think Miles Ashford has poisoned Assad against me.'

'*Miles?*' said Philip, almost choking on a mouthful of stew.

'It's female intuition, Phil. I know it.'

'But why would he do that? It's just petulant.'

'Miles always has been angry, peevish and destructive. Plus I think he's struggling a bit – did you hear how his Dubai project went under? – and he's pissed off because he cashed in his Rivera investment before he made any real money.'

She paused, taking a sip of wine.

'And he'll still be bitter about my relationship with his father.'

'That was a long time ago, Sasha,' he said.

She could tell he didn't want to talk about it, but it was the elephant in the room and she needed to broach it, however painful it was.

'You do know I was with Robert in the car accident that killed him?' she said quietly.

'I heard a rumour,' said Philip, not meeting her eye.

She reached across to touch his hand. 'I didn't mean to hurt you, Phil, I really didn't, but . . . I suppose I was swept off my feet, or something along those lines anyway. I certainly wish I hadn't been such a bitch to you.'

'As I said, it was all a long time ago.'

'Not for Miles,' said Sasha more fiercely. 'Miles hates me and I hate him right back.'

'Hate is a pretty destructive emotion, Sash,' said Philip. 'Nothing good ever comes of it. Have you confronted him about it?'

'As you might expect, Miles and I no longer talk.'

Phil sat in silence for a while, drinking his wine slowly, the cogs turning in his head.

'Look, there is a way out of this,' he said finally. 'You've tried appealing to Randall and to Simon but it hasn't worked and they seem happy to make this deal happen without your consent. You could threaten them, tell them how much negative publicity you could generate for Rivera, but you don't want to be seen as bitter and unprofessional. So let's find another buyer. A buyer who will make a more attractive offer than Assad.'

Sasha looked dubious. 'We haven't got much time. Simon's exclusivity on the deal lasts until Monday but he's going to be ready to formalise it any day.'

Philip shook his head. 'That doesn't matter. He's only made his first offer. It will take months, believe me.'

'I'm not so sure,' said Sasha. 'Randall gave me the impression it was a done deal. I don't want to take any chances on this, Phil.'

She sat back in her chair, rubbing her temples with her fingertips. She felt better off-loading her problems to Phil, just talking to him made things simpler, but it was all too much for her at the moment; her nerves were too raw.

'Can we do this tomorrow?' she asked, surprising herself.

'Sure.'

'It's just there's been so much going on, I think I need to veg out this evening.'

Phil laughed. '*You*, veg out?'

'I mean it. Let's watch a film or something.'

598

'I'm not entirely sure you'll be impressed with my DVD collection,' he said, opening the TV cabinet where they were all neatly stacked up. Taking her wine, Sasha walked across to flick through them.

'The Hundred Greatest Rugby Tries,' she read, pulling a face. 'The Sylvester Stallone collection . . . *Die Hard* . . . *Crank 2* . . . Well, it's nice to see that you're in touch with your feminine side, Bettany.'

She walked across to a leather sofa and sat down, curling her legs under her. 'OK, forget the DVD,' she said. 'Let's just finish the bottle of wine and you can tell me about Australia. Why did you leave, or is that a stupid question?'

'Actually, I haven't really left,' said Philip, sitting at the other end of the sofa. 'Lily and her mum are still out there, so I couldn't move back to London permanently. This job is just a twelve-month secondment, so I'll be going back to Sydney next April.'

Sasha tried to hide her disappointment. Philip had never been the one who excited her; he had always been her partner, co-conspirator, friend. He'd believed in her when everyone else thought she was an airhead fashionista unable to run anything except a bubble bath. And a decade ago she'd been so certain he wasn't right for her. Too dull. Too steady. But now? What was wrong with someone who treated you with respect, who knew you inside out, good bits and bad, and loved you still? She felt a stinging sense of regret.

'I'm so sorry about the way things ended between us,' she said softly.

Philip shrugged. 'I loved you and you hurt me. But when I eventually heard the whispers about your relationship with Robert I knew there was no point being with you when you just wanted to be with someone else. And for what it's worth, I'm sorry how it ended with Robert. The accident, I mean.'

'Thank you, but you didn't have to say that. Other men would have secretly gloated.'

'Gloated? How could you gloat that someone got killed?'

'What I mean is that not everyone has as much dignity and decency as you.'

Tension crackled between them and, unable to stand it any longer, she reached out to touch him, but Philip pulled away.

'That's not why I invited you here this weekend.'

'I know,' she said, her eyes beginning to glisten.

'Oh Sasha ...' he said, taking her hand and kissing her fingers gently. It felt so good, so right. She gave a nervous little laugh.

'I feel like a teenager snogging on my parents' sofa,' she said.

Philip smiled. 'In which case,' he said, 'why don't we take this upstairs to bed?'

74

He couldn't sleep. How could he? Nobody could rest with such a weight hanging over their head. Miles Ashford turned over and looked at the red digital numbers of his bedside clock: 3.45 a.m. He had taken a Xanax at midnight; it hadn't even made him drowsy. Had it been only six hours since his attorney Michael Marshall had called, telling him that a detective superintendent from the Royal Bahamas Police Force wanted to question him?

Miles sat up and reached for his cigarettes, hoping it would do something to relieve the anxiety – an emotion he was unused to. A man as successful as Miles Ashford had not got where he was today without being able to handle extreme pressure; he just didn't get rattled. Not when his $500 million residential project had to be shelved in Dubai last year. Not when the banks were breathing down his neck after the collapse of Lehman Brothers. Not even when he had run into a Kosovan gangster when he had tried to buy a series of brothels in London's Soho. All those things were just setbacks, concerns or irritations. This . . . well, this was different.

He swung his legs off the bed and reached for his navy silk robe, pulling it tightly around his body before walking through to his study. It was Miles' favourite room in his Fifth Avenue duplex, with a huge bay window that looked out on to Central Park. After dark, it resembled a black hole in the heart of the city. Whoever coined the expression 'the dead of night' was thinking of 3.45 a.m. in NYC. Even in the city that never sleeps, this sliver of time after the party people had gone to bed and the early risers – the market traders, the workaholic Wall Street tycoons – had not yet started their day was a moment that was eerie and still.

Miles didn't turn on the light, content to just gaze out on to the city, letting the darkness and silence soothe him. He closed his eyes and immediately felt himself transported back to the island. For a second, his memory of that night was so clear he could almost smell the sea air, the pineapple bushes, the mangrove. Growing up, Angel Cay had been his Eden, a private pirate island to explore and to run wild in, rich with imagination and adventures. But not any more, not now.

He turned from the window and sat at his desk. His empire spanned a dozen industries and six continents, yet the glass surface of his work station was remarkably uncluttered. In two hours' time it would be set for breakfast by his butler Stevens and the world's most influential newspapers would be in a neat pile ready for him to read. But now it just contained a stack of contracts, a phone, a copy of *Fortune* magazine and a small desk lamp which finally, reluctantly, he turned on. Blinking in the yellow light, he picked up the sleek black phone and dialled his attorney. If he had to go back to Angel Cay to confront this, he wasn't going to do it alone. Sasha Sinclair, Alex Doyle, his sister. They were going to come with him.

75

Sasha lay naked in Philip's bed, enjoying the sensation of crisp Irish linen on her bare skin. Her head was foggy from too much red wine – just a couple of glasses was enough to do that these days – and as she started to feel more awake, she felt torn between relief and happiness that she and Philip had got together again and a flood of discomfort from being here, in her ex-boyfriend's bed, when she should have been in the spare room concentrating on sorting out her career. Hearing a creak at the door, she looked up and pulled the sheet up to cover her bare breasts.

'I think we're past that stage now.' Phil smiled, bringing her a mug of tea.

Sasha giggled, immediately feeling herself relax. *Don't be so uptight*, she thought. *This is what you wanted, isn't it?*

He sat down and stroked her bare shoulder. 'You were dead to the world.'

'What time is it?'

'Midday.'

She sat up. 'You are kidding me!'

He laughed and shook his head. 'How about going out for breakfast at Daylesford?'

She gave him a saucy smile. 'How about breakfast in bed?'

'Or lunch, as the case may be.'

Sasha stretched out, smiling. 'How completely decadent,' she said, feeling happier than she'd felt in ages.

'Well, in the spirit of decadence, I'll see if I can whip up something full of fat and carbohydrates,' said Philip, heading for the kitchen.

Faintly she could hear her mobile ringing. Swinging her legs out of the bed, she scrabbled it out of her bag and pressed accept.

'Sasha Sinclair?' The voice was unfamiliar, the accent foreign.

'Yes.' She hesitated. 'Who is this?'

'Detective Inspector Carlton from the Royal Bahamian Police Force in Nassau.'

Nassau? She felt her skin go cold, her heart fluttering with panic.

'How can I help you?' she asked as evenly as she could.

'It's in connection with a body found on Angel Cay, the Exumas island belonging to the Ashford family.'

'Yes, I know it,' she said. 'A body? Has there been an accident there?'

'No, Miss Sinclair. It's a very old body, discovered buried near one of the beaches. Initial forensics have put time of death around twenty years ago. Mode of death blunt trauma to the head.'

'That sounds awful,' said Sasha. 'But why are you telling me all this?'

'Because you visited the island regularly around this time on account of your relationship with Miles Ashford.'

'That's true. But I don't know anything about an accident. Or a body.'

She willed herself to stay calm, stay vague with what she said, although her pulse was racing.

'We've interviewed several former staff from Angel Cay working there at that time. Apparently twenty years ago a boat boy disappeared from the island. At the time everyone assumed he'd just left as he was about to get dismissed.'

She sipped her tea, but it just made her feel nauseous. Her

604

heart was pounding fiercely. Her skin felt crawly. *Breathe, Sasha, breathe*, she thought, focusing on her yoga training.

'Really? I don't remember hearing about that.'

'The week he went missing, you were one of the dozen or so guests on the island,' pressed Carlton.

'As I said, I don't recall anything about a disappearance of a staff member.'

'Well even so, you will appreciate that we need to interview you.'

Sasha paused, anger beginning to overtake her fear. What if she really didn't know anything about it? Did they expect her to drop everything and go running off halfway around the world to tell them that? And anyway, if she did, wouldn't that be tantamount to an admission of guilt?

'I appreciate you have a job to do, Detective,' she said. 'But I have a job too. I run an international fashion label. I don't have enough time for breakfast, let alone to come to the Bahamas to help you with your inquiries.'

His voice took on a sterner edge. 'Don't make this more difficult for yourself, Miss Sinclair.'

'With respect, Dectective, the difficulty is yours. I have told you everything I know about this. If you wish to speak to me further, please contact my lawyer. I would be more than happy to give you his number.'

She took a cold shower straight after the call, shivering in the tiny cubicle as the icy water pinched her skin. Any thoughts of Randall Kane, Assad or saving her business had evaporated to be replaced by a sense of dread that Angel Cay, the boat boy and that horrible summer were finally coming back to haunt her.

Grabbing a fluffy white towel, she rubbed her face in the luxurious, comforting folds and quickly dressed. She went downstairs and passed through the kitchen where Philip was cooking bacon, eggs and beans on the Aga.

'I'm going out,' she said, reaching for the latch of the farm-house door.

'Hey, what about the food?' he said. 'And anyway, your hair's wet.'

'I don't care,' said Sasha, fumbling with the lock.

He moved the frying pan from the heat. 'Sash? What's going on? Who was that on the phone?'

She pulled open the door and ran outside. It was raining, but she didn't feel it; she just had to get away from the house, to clear her head, try and think.

'Sasha, wait, please.'

Turning, she saw Philip striding to catch up with her.

'Leave it, Philip, you can't help,' she called, but he had already reached her, grabbing her shoulders and holding her firm.

'Sasha. What's wrong? Tell me.'

The rain was soaking his shirt and he was shivering.

'I can't,' she said, the words feeling strangled in her throat. 'I just, I can't . . .'

'Yes you can,' he said, taking her in his arms and leading her back to the house. 'You can tell me everything.'

He towel-dried her hair, wrapped her in a dressing gown and sat her down at the farmhouse table, putting a hot cup of coffee in front of her. She wrapped her fingers around it and began her story.

'It's Miles, Philip,' she said. 'It always is. I can't seem to get away from him. From the second I arrived at my old school, Danehurst, I was drawn to him. He was everything I wanted to be. Rich, successful, glamorous. I thought that just being with him would make my life so special.'

Philip nodded, but stayed silent, letting her talk.

'I loved him even though he didn't make me feel good about myself a lot of the time. Miles liked to play power games even then, liked to keep me in my place. But I didn't care. When you're with Miles Ashford, you feel untouchable.

People would do anything to be my friend and I could see a future for myself beyond my middle-class Surrey background that my mum had brought me up to despise.'

She glanced at him with a sense of deeply buried shame.

'After our A levels we went to Angel Cay, the Ashfords' Caribbean home. I loved it there, it was like Paradise. On the last night we stayed up all night. Drinking, smoking, taking drugs. Just before dawn, four of us, Miles and his sister, myself and Alex Doyle – you know, the musician? – went skinny-dipping in a cove, and on the way back to the house we found a dead body. Or at least we thought it was dead.'

'Who was it? Did you know?'

'A boat boy called Bradley,' she said, feeling more courage as she told her story. 'Miles said we should do nothing about it. That we should leave it for someone else to find. People would point the finger at us, the police would investigate us. So that's what we did. Left it. Miles said he would get his father to sort it out.'

Philip creased his brow. 'So why are you so freaked out about it today?'

'Because that was the Bahamas police on the phone. They've found a dead body buried under the beach at Angel Cay and they want to interview me about it.'

'And you think it's the boat boy?'

'Who else could it be?'

'But I thought you said you weren't sure if he was dead.'

She sighed. 'Robert Ashford told us the body had disappeared and a boat had been stolen. He said the boat boy had taken it and fled the island.'

'And you believed that?'

'I had to believe it,' she said, clenching her fists together. 'I've spent twenty years telling myself that was what happened.'

'Why?'

'Because in my heart of hearts, I've always thought that it

was Miles who attacked him.' She shook her head, knowing she had to tell him everything. 'I'd slept with the boy earlier that night and it was just like Miles to find out and take revenge. I wanted to believe that he was OK and had escaped, because the alternative was suspecting that Miles had murdered him. But if there's a body, well, it looks like he didn't steal a boat and escape, did he?'

There was a long pause as Philip tried to absorb the information.

'You have to tell someone,' he said finally, his face solemn.

'And dig myself into a deeper hole? We found the body, Philip. I'd had sex with the boat boy an hour earlier. I doubt the police know that detail; then again, who knows what they know?'

'Precisely. And the last thing you want to happen is to get done for misprision of felony. Still law in the Bahamas as far as I'm aware.'

Sasha shook her head. 'Misprision of felony?'

'Concealment of a crime.'

Her hands were trembling, but Philip came over and took them in his. She felt a surge of strength and comfort.

'What should I do, Phil?'

'Don't worry, for a start. We'll sort this out together, OK?'

He put his strong arms around her and she felt safe and protected, knowing she had someone who would fight her corner. And Sasha Sinclair had never been one to lie down and take what was being thrown at her.

'Sod this, I'm calling Miles,' she said suddenly, standing up and going to the bedroom. She flicked through her BlackBerry until she found Miles' assistant's number. The number was over ten years old, but she was still connected to a polite British voice.

'Mr Ashford is in New York right now,' said the woman. 'Can I ask what it's regarding?'

'I'm an old friend and this is urgent business.'

608

'I'll pass on the message.'

Sasha was in no mood to be fobbed off. 'I need to speak to him right now,' she said firmly. 'Tell him the Bahamian police have been in touch with me about a matter on Angel Cay.'

'I'll put you straight through to Mr Marshall,' said the woman with clipped efficiency.

'Who's he?' asked Sasha, but she was talking to dead air. There were a few clicks and then a rich-toned American came on the line.

'Miss Sinclair. I'm glad you've called. I wanted to speak to you.'

'Who are you?'

'Miles Ashford's attorney.'

Typical of Miles to put some lackey in between them. Never did like doing his own dirty work.

'So you'll know why I'm calling,' said Sasha.

'About the discovery at Angel Cay?'

She didn't know what he knew, but as a trusted henchman of the great Miles Ashford, it was certain he had more information than Detective Carlton.

'Don't worry, we're going to get this all smoothed out, Sasha.'

'Really? And how precisely do you propose to do that?' she said, irritated by his condescending tone.

'Miles wants you all to meet to discuss your position.'

Sasha swallowed. 'All of us?'

'Yourself, his sister Grace and Alex Doyle,' said Michael. 'He wants you all to come to Angel Cay.'

She felt a cold sweat break out on her forehead. 'Why on earth would I want to go there?' she hissed.

'Would you rather this was first discussed at Nassau's police station?'

'I suppose not.'

'Miles thinks you should all talk about this privately and

make a strategy,' said Michael smoothly. 'And I think that's a wise move. We will send his personal jet for you. You'll land in Nassau and be taken directly to Angel Cay. Can you be ready by first thing tomorrow morning?'

Sasha had the sense of being pushed into something she wasn't comfortable with. *That's a feeling I should be well used to with Miles Ashford*, she thought.

'I need to think about this,' she said, playing for time. Most of all, she wanted to discuss it with Philip. He would know what to do.

'Well, call me as soon as you have thought it through,' said Michael. 'You're all in this together, Sasha. And right now, I think you all need to stick together.'

Part Three

76

Sitting at the back of the six-seater plane, Alex gripped the armrest of his seat and watched Angel Cay get bigger and bigger, the white sands growing brighter and more dazzling as the small craft circled the island then spluttered in to land on the tiny airstrip along the south shore. He simply couldn't believe he was back here. Stepping off the plane, the scented tropical breeze warming his face, squinting at the perfect stripe of sea beyond the dunes, it was as if the summer of 1990 had been yesterday.

He glanced over at Grace and gave her an uncertain smile, knowing she was feeling it too. But Grace had other things on her mind; she had barely spoken on the flight from Heathrow. He experienced a huge wave of emotion for her, feeling the weight of what she had just been through on his own shoulders. After her hysterical phone call three days ago, he'd found her wandering aimlessly along Chelsea Embankment, her face a pink puffy mess, stuttering and shaking. He wasn't entirely sure whether it was Julian's affair with her daughter which had destroyed her, or the brutal words Olivia had spoken when Grace had walked in on them. Whichever it was, she had fallen completely apart, and while his first instincts had been to track Julian down and beat the living shit out of him, he had done the grown-up thing and taken her back to his Highgate home to look after her, protect her.

That was where they had been when Michael Marshall had called. A body had been found, he had said. The police wanted to question them. They had to face this together.

Standing on the dusty runway, the pale pink house looking down on him from the bluff of the hill like an imperious maiden aunt, he wondered how Grace had persuaded him to come. He always knew this day might happen, of course; in fact he had somehow known in his gut that it would, but his time in the clinic had forced him to look at his motivations in life, and he had realised that the desire to be rich, powerful and adored was really a desire to be protected, so that he would be cushioned from things like this, hiding away behind an army of expensive lawyers and legal loopholes. If he'd wanted, he was sure he could have paid enough to make this go away, but as always, Grace had broken down his defences.

'We can't hide for ever,' she had said, and there was a certain simple truth in her words. Alex had made himself unhappy all his life because he wouldn't face things. Maybe now he could find some peace, however painful it was to do. He looked over at his friend with affection.

'You OK?' he said, and she nodded.

'Under the circumstances.'

Alex suspected that from Grace's point of view, Michael Marshall's phone call had been a relief. She was the one who had carried this burden around with her, trying to make amends with her good works, by living a good life, but it hadn't been enough – and now here was a chance to make it right, or at least own up to what she – they – had done. He also suspected she'd much rather be facing a police grilling than dealing with the horrible mess that her personal life had become.

A white Mini Moke appeared through a clearing in the palm-trees, beeping its horn as it approached the runway.

'Here he comes, the lord of the manor,' said Grace as they saw Miles in the driver's seat.

614

'You know, even as a lad I knew that having a friend like Miles was trouble.'

'But he sucked you in anyway?' asked Grace. 'He does that. Even now.'

Miles stepped out of the car in shorts and a white open-necked shirt, looking for all the world like a carefree tourist rather than a cornered felon. He strode over and slapped Alex on the shoulder.

'Good flight?'

'Good enough,' said Alex.

Miles grabbed Grace's bag and pointed to the car. 'Tight squeeze I'm afraid.'

'Is Sasha coming?' asked Grace.

'Of course. Rejected the offer of the jet and she's staying at the White Sands resort on Emerald Cay. You know Sasha. Always has to be different. Awkward. Still, she should be here in a couple of hours.'

They clambered into the Mini Moke and Miles gunned the engine, propelling the car up the hill.

'Benny, the temporary caretaker, is doing a barbecue later for old times' sake,' shouted Miles over the roar. 'No one turned vegetarian as well as teetotal on me in the last few years, did they?'

'Old times' sake?' said Alex. 'This isn't a bloody holiday, Miles.'

'Exactly, but neither does it have to be purgatory.'

They pulled up to the house. Since he had left this place, Alex had been around the world dozens of times and had lived a life of luxury most people only dreamt about, but still, there was something magical about Angel Cay. The view of the island from this elevated position was unmatched for drama and beauty anywhere on the globe. Somehow the sand here seemed whiter, the trees greener, the breeze more fragrant and sweet. It had a more potent tranquillity too, now the hordes of staff had left the island in preparation for the sale.

Benny the caretaker took their bags and they went out on to the terrace where ice-cold drinks and a huge fruit platter, piled high with mango, pineapple, papaya and starfruit, were waiting for them.

'So what now?' asked Grace.

'How about sailing?' said Miles, picking up a slice of mango.

'We're here to talk, Miles,' said Alex with irritation.

Miles wiped the sticky orange juice from his chin with the back of his hand. 'No point till Sash gets here.'

'And when are we seeing Detective Carlton?' asked Grace.

'Tomorrow. One of his forensic goons is over the hill on the beach, though. Probably best to avoid that side of the island.'

'I hope your lawyer's here,' said Alex.

'Michael's in George Town. Just left. Apparently Carlton and his colleagues are talking about doing a reconstruction of "the night in question",' he said, making quotation marks with his fingers. 'You'd think it was bloody *Crimewatch*.'

Typical Miles, thought Alex, *still fiddling while Rome burns*. He had expected a little humility to have crept into his personality after twenty years, but it seemed Miles Ashford still saw himself as Superman – bulletproof and unbendable. Suddenly Alex felt clammy and unclean.

'I think I'll go up to the room to change,' he said.

Grace followed him up and they were only mildly surprised to find they had been assigned the same bedrooms they had slept in on the 1990 holiday. Miles' sense of humour at work, Alex assumed. He changed into a fresh shirt then went down the corridor to Grace's room.

'I can't believe how little this place has changed,' she said as he walked in. She held up a copy of *Valley of the Dolls*, the novel she had been reading that trip, with her bookmark still in the place she had left it. She shook her head. 'This is going to be hard.'

'We did nothing wrong,' said Alex, trying to put a brave face on it, but Grace just gave him a sad smile.

'You know that's not true, Alex.'

He put his arm around her and she looked up at him with big blue eyes. 'You know, all the bad stuff that has ever happened to me in my life – Caro being killed in the car bomb, the collapse of my marriage, the death of my dad, my mum, Julian and Olivia . . . sometimes I think it's karma. You felt it too, didn't you, when you were in the clinic?'

Alex gave her a squeeze. He knew that hot summer night in 1990 had damaged them all.

'I try not to think about it too much. What's done is done.'

'But we can always do our best to make amends, can't we?' asked Grace.

'We can try.'

For a moment they stood like that, both enjoying the moment of closeness. Miles might have called them all back saying they needed to stick together, but Alex seriously doubted that he – or Sasha for that matter – was motivated by that sentiment. He and Grace would just have to back each other up.

'Come on,' he said, pulling away. 'For once, Miles is right. No point moping around here; let's go sailing.'

'Miles is right?' she said with a cynical half-smile.

'About some things . . .' he said, pulling his sunglasses over his eyes and leading Grace outside.

It was time to go. The hotel boat was waiting by the dock and Sasha knew it was now or never. She had to return to the island, or run away, never looking back. At that moment, neither option seemed particularly appealing, but she knew she couldn't keep running. She was too bloody tired.

Phil walked over, standing behind her, where she was looking out of the French windows leading to their private terrace.

'You sure you don't want me to come with you?' he asked, putting his hands on her shoulders.

She shook her head. 'I'm grateful for you coming this far but I don't want you to get more involved than you have to be. I'm just going to go over there and get this done.'

Philip tilted his head to look up at the grey clouds gathering across the horizon. 'Well you'd better be quick. The concierge thinks there might be some bad weather coming in and you don't want to stay on that island overnight.'

'I'll swim away if I have to.' She smiled.

Phil put his arms around her and planted a soft kiss on her lips. She relaxed into his body, and didn't want to pull away. There had been so many places that had just felt *right* over the past twenty years: on Pampelonne beach in St Tropez in the summertime. On a yacht in St Barts on New Year's Eve. At the CEFA designer of the year awards picking up a gong. But right now, Sasha could not think of anywhere she wanted to be more than here in Philip's gentle, protective embrace.

'I should have said yes,' she said quietly.

He turned to look at her. 'What do you mean?'

'That night in your flat. I should have said yes.'

His eyes twinkled with pleasure, but Sasha knew she didn't have time for this right now.

'I won't be long,' she said quickly, grabbing her bag and striding out of the hotel with a purpose she had not felt in a long time. She had to get this finished. Only then could she get back to Philip and the life she had been searching for all these years.

The boat taking her to Angel Cay was fast and powerful, slicing through the green water with such speed that a journey that should have taken forty minutes took only fifteen.

'Shall I wait?' asked the captain as he helped her on to the jetty.

Sasha glanced at her watch. 'No. I don't know how long I'll be, but that journey was so quick I'll give you a ring when I need to be collected.'

He lifted a finger to his cap. 'Sure thing, madam. But don't leave it too long; the weather's turning.'

'I'll be two hours tops.'

She walked along the pier, her heels tapping on the sun-blanched wood to where a man was waiting by a Mini Moke. He was about forty, with weathered skin and a clipped moustache.

'Benny Law,' he said, extending a hand. 'I'm the caretaker.'

'What happened to Nelson?' asked Sasha as she climbed into the little jeep. 'I thought he was part of the furniture around here.'

'He retired,' said Benny vaguely. 'Now let me take you up to the house. Grace Ashford and that musician fella arrived a couple of hours ago.'

'So everyone's here?'

He shook his head. 'Naw, miss, not right now. They've all gone sailing. Should be back in about an hour.'

Sasha tutted and looked anxiously at her watch again. She wanted to get this over and done with as soon as possible, and Phil was right – she really didn't want to spend a night on the island.

Benny took her up to the house, then drove off in a cloud of dust towards the caretaker's cottage. Left all alone, Sasha wandered from room to room, feeling the years slip away, remembering what it was like when she'd had the run of the house.

God, I really thought I was going to marry Miles, didn't I? she remembered with a smile, trailing her hands over the familiar furniture. *I thought all this was going to be mine.*

Upstairs, she stopped with a pang of melancholy at the door of Miles' old bedroom. She wondered idly what would have happened if she had got her wish and become the next

Mrs Ashford. Would she have been satisfied? At eighteen, she had believed it was her destiny to settle down and spend her life being a chattel, a possession, Miles Ashford's wife. Instead she had gone entirely the other way and been completely independent, beholden to no one, making her own way in the world on her wits and her talents. She hadn't needed anyone. Apart from Robert, of course. As much to distract herself as anything else, she went in. Laid out on the bed were Miles' clean clothes, a pressed pink shirt, Ralph Lauren chinos. This was obviously where he was sleeping tonight, she thought, wondering why he hadn't moved into the master bedroom with the best view of the beach. *Same reason I'm not going in there*, she thought. *Too many ghosts.*

Her eyes was drawn to the laptop computer sitting on the walnut desk by the window, a white light on the front blinking at her. Glancing back towards the door, she walked over and sat down. *I wonder . . .* she thought. In all the maelstrom of the past forty-eight hours, she had not entirely forgotten about her business and in particular how Miles was trying to pull it from under her. She knew he was in league with Simon Assad, but how exactly and why? Maybe there would be some clues on his personal computer.

She made a few clicks, but it was immediately clear that he had protected his emails with a password. Dammit, she thought. If there was going to be evidence, it would be there. His desk-top files, however, were not protected in this way. Systematically she began opening them. Most were dull Ash Corp.-related items. Spreadsheets, projections, PowerPoint presentations with pie charts and endless contracts in dense legalese. She was just about to give up, when she found a folder full of dozens of photographs. Miles skiing. Miles on a yacht somewhere hot and sunny. Miles with his arm around a clean-cut handsome ski instructor. Miles in bed with another man, laughing at the camera. She recoiled in surprise and then almost laughed out loud. *Of course!* So many things began to fit into place. Their strange sex life, which had swung between the borderline kinky and the lacklustre. He was either at her like a piston or couldn't get it up. It also explained his remote relationship with Chrissy – perhaps even his bond with Alex Doyle.

She clicked on another folder entitled 'Dubai' – it looked like some sort of Ash Corp. company jolly, or maybe the launch of one of his resorts – there were loads of shots on the beach, various men and women in swimsuits horsing around on the sand and in the water. Lots of shots of Miles with yet another good-looking man in aviator shades and surf shorts. And then she saw something that made her heart beat faster. It was such a small thing, she could easily have missed it, but there it was – and she was sure she had seen it before. The main photo was of Miles smiling as he held up a cocktail in salute to the camera, but what was grabbing Sasha's attention was in the background; the good-looking man was running out of the surf, which had pulled his shorts low. She enlarged the image as far as it would go; it pixelated as it expanded, but it was enough to see the mark on the man's hipbone. It was a tattoo of the sun, its rays curling outwards. A tattoo she'd recognise anywhere. Bradley the boat boy – the *dead* boat boy – had had exactly the same tattoo, in exactly the same spot. Was it simply a coincidence? *Could* it be? Sasha's palms felt clammy; intuitively she knew it was the same tattoo, the same man. But who was he? Why was he with Miles?

'What the bloody hell is going on?' she whispered to herself.

She shut the laptop and glanced around Miles' bedroom. There were few personal possessions here, just the clothes and a small overnight bag, nothing to give her more clues.

Who are you, surf boy? she thought frantically, her mouth feeling dry. *And why are you with Miles?*

Unzipping his leather holdall, she looked inside. Toothpaste, floss, deodorant, nothing out of the ordinary. She pulled out a magazine: *Forbes*, with a picture of Miles on the front cover, a fat cigar between his grinning teeth. *Typical*, she thought. *Miles' idea of porn: a picture of himself.*

Sitting on the bed, she flicked through the magazine until she found the feature about Miles. And then she stopped as she saw a small black and white photograph inserted into a body of text. It was the same man in the surf shorts, but instead of sunglasses he was wearing small wire-framed spectacles. She ran her finger across the page. Was it him? Could it be? His face had slimmed out. His hair was darker, not as blond. The nose was different too – thinner, straighter, with the perfect nostril shape; the work she knew instantly of an expert cosmetic surgeon, because she'd had similar work done herself. But it was him. Her breath was ragged, her hands shaking. *It was him*. She read the caption: 'Miles Ashford and Ash Corp. director of business affairs Michael Marshall.' *Oh shit*, she thought. She had no idea what was going on – was this guy scamming Miles? Was Miles in on it? Was this some sort of sick game he was playing? Whichever way you looked at it, it wasn't good, and instinctively she knew they were in danger. Putting the magazine back, she slipped out of Miles' bedroom and went into her own, pulling her BlackBerry out of her bag.

Who to call? Whether Miles was manipulating them or not, he had to know something. But when she dialled his mobile number, her heart sank as she heard it ringing back in his bedroom.

Shit, shit, shit, she whispered.

She scrolled through to Philip's number and walked towards the window, her eyes searching the sea for a sight of Miles' boat.

'Phil. It's me,' she said, keeping her voice low.

'You're there already?'

'Yes, and I have a horrible feeling that something weird is going on.'

'What's up?'

'You know we found the body of the boat boy?' she whispered. 'Well, he's not dead. He's Michael Marshall.'

'The lawyer who invited you here?' said Philip. 'So whose body have the police got, then?'

'I wish I knew.'

She was shaking her head, trying to process the facts in her mind, trying to work out what made sense.

'Look, the boat boy had a tattoo on his hip; it's one of the few things I remember about him. I've just seen a photograph of Michael Marshall on Miles' computer. Phil, he has the same tattoo. He's changed his appearance, his name, but it's him. I know it.'

'Why on earth would Miles have the boat boy working for him?' asked Philip.

'I don't know. Maybe he doesn't even know it's him. I don't know what to think.' She closed her eyes tightly, trying to blot out her fear.

'Do you want me to come to Angel?' asked Philip.

'Yes.'

'I'll be there as soon as I can, but the weather's changed. I'm guessing that's going to slow me up, but Sasha, I'll get there.'

She felt a wash of relief, but she hated being so vulnerable. She was Sasha Sinclair, the arse-kicking global style icon, but she was just grateful that Phil was on the way.

'Where is Marshall now?'

'I don't know. He told me he was going to be here, but the caretaker didn't mention him.'

'Is Miles with you?'

'No. He's out sailing with Grace and Alex.'

'Well find some company. Stay with them.'

As she clicked off, she heard a noise behind her and whirled around.

A smartly dressed man with cocoa-coloured skin and short hair was standing in the doorway.

'I'm sorry, I didn't mean to startle you,' he said and extended a hand. 'Detective Carlton. You must be Sasha Sinclair. I recognise you from one of my wife's magazines.'

Her shoulders sank with relief and she clasped a hand to her chest. 'A detective,' she said, breathing out. 'You scared the life out of me. Are you with Miles?'

'No. A boat has just brought me from George Town. Perhaps we should go downstairs and wait for him?'

'Good idea. I think he's in danger.'

'Danger?'

Sasha wasn't sure she should tell the police anything until she had spoken to Miles. Then again, what if Michael Marshall was with them? What if he was planning some sort of revenge?

'Yes, I think there's a man on this island who might not be who he claims to be.'

She turned around to retrieve her BlackBerry. She didn't realise that Detective Carlton had come up behind her until she felt an arm around her throat, choking her. She struggled, but he was too strong, his arm pressing into her windpipe. For a split second, the pieces started falling into place. But then it was too late, because a moment later, she had lost consciousness.

77

Miles decided to cut the sailing trip short. Thick grey storm clouds were gathering quickly and both Miles and Grace had spent enough summers in the Exumas to know that when bad weather came, it could be bleak and torrential. As they tied up the boat and walked up to the house, the tall coconut palms had begun swaying from side to side and the once cloudless sky had become dark and brooding.

'I hope Sasha has managed to get here,' said Alex, looking towards the house. Where before it had looked idyllic and welcoming, now the dark windows made the place seem cold and unsettling.

Miles tutted. 'I still can't understand why she refused to come out from London with you two.'

'I should think the prospect of an eight-hour flight sitting next to Grace probably put her off,' said Alex quietly as Grace walked into the house out of earshot. 'After all that business with her and your dad.'

'I see your point,' said Miles as they followed his sister in. It was obvious that no one was in the house; there were no lights or signs of life.

'Where's bloody Benny?' snapped Miles. 'I need a drink.'

'The bar's only over there, Miles,' said Alex, nodding to the corner of the living room. 'I think you can manage to unscrew a bottle by yourself.'

'I'll do it,' said Grace, obviously trying to head off a confrontation. She handed them all glasses, then sat down on a high-backed cream sofa.

'Look, Miles, I know Sasha's not arrived, but she might not even get here tonight. So I think we should start talking about what we came here to discuss.'

Miles glanced out of the windows at the dark, rolling sea. There was no way a boat would bring Sasha over from the White Sands resort unless it had left already. He shrugged.

'Fair enough.'

He was just sitting down when his mobile started ringing, a faint, shrill rasp in the distance.

'Bollocks. Where did I leave my phone?'

'Sounds like upstairs,' said Alex. 'Why don't you leave it? We need to get started.'

'Might be the police,' said Miles, running up to his room and pulling his phone from a pocket of the jacket hanging behind the door.

'Mr Ashford?'

'Yes.'

'DeShaun Riley. I'm doing forensics on the island.'

Miles had met the man earlier. He had taken the Mini Moke out to the west beach that afternoon to see how he was getting on.

'Can you meet me by the boathouse? As soon as you can. There's something I need to show you.'

Miles frowned, feeling a flicker of distress. *The boathouse?* What the fuck was he doing there? Hadn't Detective Carlton said that the only scene-of-crime work was being done around the site where the body had been found? *God, I knew it was a mistake to let Michael go back to George Town.*

He grabbed a windcheater from his wardrobe and ran downstairs, where Alex and Grace were still sitting expectantly on the sofa.

'I have to go out,' he said, heading for the door.

'Miles, we're here to bloody talk!' said Alex.

'I won't be long.'

Outside, the temperature seemed to have fallen by ten degrees and the first drops of rain were beginning to fall, spotting Miles' expensive suede leather deck shoes. The quickest way to the boathouse was to weave through the mangrove at the back of the house. It was darkening as he walked through the forest, the wind beginning to rush through the treetops. *I won't go down for this*, he told himself. *I did nothing wrong.*

As he approached the west beach, the vegetation thinned out and he could see glimpses of sand through the trees. A man was standing in the shelter of the rickety boathouse, but it was not DeShaun Riley.

'Michael?' said Miles with a puzzled expression. 'What are you doing back? Where's Riley?'

Michael waited until Miles had joined him him before he spoke. 'I sent him away. I didn't want anyone to overhear this.'

'Overhear what?'

Michael's expression was serious. 'Miles, you have to tell me what happened that night.'

'Why? What did the police say?' said Miles, pulling his collar up against the cold.

'Forget what the police do or don't know. I am your lawyer, and if we're going to fix this, I need to know the truth.'

Miles nodded; Michael was right, he supposed. So far, he had been selective with the information he'd told the lawyer, but then what really *had* happened? Over the last two decades he had rewritten history in his own mind. He remembered the key events: the spat with the boat boy when he'd caught him and Alex together. Finding out that the body on the beach had disappeared. The stolen Boston Whaler that had never reappeared. But everything in between had faded away, forced into some dark corner by his own reflex to protect himself.

627

'Tell me, Miles,' said Michael.

Miles felt a flicker of irritation at the expression on his lawyer's face: hard and disapproving. That's a bit rich, he thought, considering he paid Michael handsomely for his moral ambiguity. Still, he needed to tell him, even if it was only to cover every angle. He pulled a Camel Light packet from his shorts pocket, cupping his hand around the tip as he lit a cigarette.

'I came to the island after our A levels with a bunch of friends,' he began, breathing out a plume of smoke. 'It was our last night and we got incredibly pissed. I'd been drinking absinthe, taking coke. I was a bit of a mess as I remember. Anyway, Alex and I went to the dunes for a smoke. We kissed. Just schoolboy stuff, messing around, but we'd been seen by this boat boy, who began taunting me. We had a fight. He ran away.'

He glanced at Marshall for a reaction, but the lawyer's face was hidden in shadow. It was overcast now and Miles began to worry they might be caught in the storm.

'After that, I went for a walk around the island. Maybe an hour later, I saw this boat boy again. He was drunk too, which I pointed out was reason enough to get him fired, the cocky little prick. So he starts having a go at me again. Called me a fag over and over. And then he tells me that he's just fucked Sasha back in his quarters, because I wasn't enough of a man to satisfy her.'

His mouth pressed into a sour line. He could still hear the boat boy's whiny American voice now, taunting him. *You fucking faggot.* His words had been like acid and Miles had hated it, because deep down he had known it was true, and it was the one thing about himself that he could not accept.

'So you were angry?' asked Marshall.

'It made me mad,' he snapped. 'Of course it did! Sasha was bugging the shit out of me, but how dare that boat boy have sex with *my* girlfriend?'

'So you killed him?'

'No! At least,' he said, shaking his head, 'I didn't think so. We fought, a bit of a tussle, but he had a beer bottle in his hand. Somehow I got hold of it and swung it ...'

His voice tailed off. He screwed his eyes tightly and he could almost see the boat boy's body crumple to the sand. In his rage, Miles had kicked him, and he remembered the feeling of sinking terror as he watched the body rolling down the dune on to the beach. He had been so scared. *So* scared. His first instinct was to go and tell his father, but Robert Ashford was such an unpredictable man, he couldn't take the chance. It was the first time in his life he had felt absolutely alone, and even today, the thought of it made him shiver.

'So I left him there. Hoped someone else would find the body. It was bad luck that it was my friends.'

'But why didn't they help him or report it?'

'We all agreed it was best to let one of the staff find the body. But ...'

'But what?'

'Alex and Grace went to see Nelson – the old caretaker – and when they came back, the body had gone. My father convinced me the boy had simply been drunk, feared getting the sack, so had stolen one of our Boston Whalers.'

'And did you believe that?'

'Why wouldn't I? There was no body there.'

Michael moved out of the shadows, his face grave. 'But you suspected Robert had made the body disappear?'

'Yes – no! – I don't know,' said Miles, running his fingers through his hair. 'I certainly wanted to believe he had got up and walked away. But if that was the case, whose body is DeShaun Riley inspecting?'

'He isn't inspecting anyone,' said Michael in a low voice. 'There is no body.'

Miles looked up at him sharply. 'What? What do you mean? Have you done a deal with them?'

Michael shrugged. 'In a way, yes. But not in the way you mean.'

Miles found his mouth had gone dry. 'What are you saying?'

'I'm saying he didn't die, Miles. The boat boy . . . it was me.'

Miles shook his head in astonishment. Was this a joke? But he knew from the hard look on Michael's face that he was deadly serious.

'You . . . you're the . . . ? Don't screw me around, Michael!' he shouted in confusion and fear. Michael's face was like stone; hard, unyielding. And there was something in the lawyer's eyes he didn't like, something he'd never seen before. Triumph, or fury? He began to back away, but Michael brought his hand up. He was holding a gun.

'What is this, Michael?' shouted Miles. 'Who are you?'

Before he had finished forming the words, Michael stepped forward and whipped the pistol sideways, catching Miles on the temple and sending him crashing to the floor.

'I am revenge, Miles,' he said, his voice quiet and controlled. 'I am your conscience finally catching up with you. I am the last thing you will ever see.' He raised his hand again, levelling the gun.

'No, please!' said Miles quickly. His head was swimming from the blow, but he had to think. This couldn't be the end, he had to find a way out.

'Tell me,' he pleaded, playing for time. 'I have to know.'

Michael didn't lower the pistol.

'It wasn't your father who got rid of the body. It was Nelson. Except I was alive. He saw you and your friends coming back to the house, scared and jittery, and went out to investigate. He found me just before daybreak, took me back to his house. Nelson knew your father well and knew he would have taken your mistake out on me, possibly had me arrested. "Mr Ashford's a bad man," was what he said

630

to me. "A very bad man." So when you'd left the island and your father's guests had arrived, Nelson got me off the island to a doctor.'

Miles knew the only way out was to try and reason with him. 'So you were OK,' he said. 'It all turned out OK.'

He could see Michael's hand trembling with simmering fury.

'OK?' spat his lawyer. '*OK?* You tried to kill me, Ashford, you put me in hospital, my brains scrambled. You almost ruined my life.'

'Clearly not,' hissed Miles. 'You have a good life now, because of me, not in spite of me.'

Michael's voice was level and hard. '*Two months*. That's how long I was in hospital. I had a broken nose, ribs, jaw. Thanks to my head injuries, I lost my short-term memory. I woke up screaming. It goes without saying, I lost my place at Harvard. Not that I could take it up anyway – far too dangerous.'

'What?' said Miles.

'Even as an eighteen-year-old hick, I knew how powerful the Ashfords were. I knew how you might come looking for me. To check I was really dead, and if I wasn't, to silence me.'

'That's just insane . . .' said Miles, trailing off. He didn't want to provoke a madman.

'What were you going to say, Miles? That's insane? Paranoid? You think I'm crazy? You're talking to the wrong man. I've spent five years doing just that for you, haven't I? Digging up dirt, smearing people, having people "dissuaded" from doing things. Do you really think your father was any less ruthless?'

'If you were so keen on staying hidden, why did you come back to find me?' asked Miles slowly. He had shifted his position to look back down the path behind him, wondering if he could make a run for it. He had to distract Michael, keep him talking.

631

'Because you had to pay for what you did!' said Michael, spittle flying from his mouth. 'So I changed my name, went to state uni, law school, joined Weinstein Fink on Wall Street, a small outfit. Tough, alley-cat lawyers. The truth was, I'd almost forgotten about you, Miles, until one day I heard Ash Corp. was looking for a business affairs manager. Dick Donovan, your father's right-hand man, had put a discreet word out around all the hard-nosed, streetwise firms like Weinstein Fink that Miles Ashford wanted a fixer, and suddenly I couldn't *stop* thinking about you.'

'So you came to meet me,' said Miles, remembering their first meeting in an anonymous hotel room in midtown. What had Donovan, his father's business adviser, told him? 'Come and meet an impressive young lawyer I've found. He's sharp, ruthless. Just what we're looking for . . .'

'I just wanted to see what you had become. It was a risk, of course,' said Michael with a hard, brittle laugh. 'But I knew I looked different, my fixed nose, the long studenty hair had gone. My new glasses. I have to wear these because of you, Miles. You ruptured my right cornea in that "bit of a tussle", as you put it. A man like you, I'm not surprised you've found a way of justifying it to yourself, but it was a vicious, cowardly attack. "Frenzied", that's what the doctors said.'

Miles took a second to study Michael. He had never been able to recall the exact contours and features of the boat boy's face. Even examining Michael's face now, he could barely remember it. But then, he'd only seen him twice, in the dark, twenty years ago. Why would he recognise him?

'But if you hated me so much, why did you take the job?'

Michael snorted. 'As soon as I saw you again, I knew what sort of man you had become. Weak, arrogant, in need of other people to cover up your mistakes, just like you did that night on the island. I wanted to stop you, Miles – and get my just reward for what you did. And because of the power and influence you gave me, I now have five million dollars

632

sitting in a bank account in the Cayman Islands, all slowly siphoned off from Ash Corp.'

Miles creased his brow. 'Take the money and just fuck off then. You've made your point.'

'Oh, this isn't over, Miles,' said Michael. 'I'm not going anywhere.'

Michael's eyes were like dark, angry hollows. Miles forced himself to remain calm.

'Put the gun down, Michael. Do you really think you can just shoot me and get away with it?'

The lawyer smirked. 'I know how to get away with anything, Miles, you know that. I'm the master of the disappearing act; I've done it over and over again for you. But this time it's going to be messy. This time I'm going to leave a bloody trail leading right to your precious friends. Alex, Sasha and Grace will take the blame.'

'They don't deserve that, Michael.'

His brows arched in surprise. 'Don't they? They were happy enough to leave me to die on the beach. Happy enough to put it out of their minds as if it simply didn't matter. Happy to go on with their lives hoping I had just been a bad dream.'

'They thought you were dead,' he said defensively.

Michael leapt forward, grabbing Miles' hair and jamming the cold barrel of the gun into his eye.

'Oh, I am dead, Miles,' he whispered. 'I've been dead for twenty years. And now you're going to join me in hell.'

'Can you go any faster?' shouted Philip, desperately trying to hang on to the side of the boat. The weather was filthy and waves were splashing over the bows so that he was ankle deep in water. At first the captain had refused to bring him across to Angel Cay from the White Sands resort, but he had relented when Philip had given him a thousand dollars in cash.

'Boat only does thirty knots,' said the old sailor.

'This is an emergency,' Philip pleaded, fumbling another note out from his pocket. The captain reached over, took the money, then turned back to his wheel.

Twelve long minutes later, the boat finally thumped up against Angel Cay's jetty and Philip vaulted up and hit the ground running towards the house. His rugby training was a long time behind him, and at forty-seven his legs felt like lead as they pounded through the sand. But adrenalin and fear pushed him on through the rain, the wind whipping his jacket away from his body. Sasha had said she had thought something was wrong on the island, but now Philip *knew* there was. As soon as he'd hung up from Sasha, he'd called Nassau's Central Detective Unit and asked to be put through to Detective Inspector Carlton, only to be told that there was no officer of that name.

'At the station?' asked Philip.

'In any of our divisions, sir,' said the officer on the line. 'The Bahamas is not a big place.'

Confused, Philip had said he understood Carlton was in charge of investigating the discovery of a body on Angel Cay. He was put through to the Great Exumas police station in George Town only to be asked, 'Is this a hoax?' Nobody had heard of a dead body on Angel Cay. There was no police investigation and as far as they knew, no foreign surveyors on the island.

Philip was panting when he reached the house. He pushed through the front door and almost ran into Grace Ashford and Alex Doyle.

'Who the hell are you?' said Alex.

For a moment Philip couldn't speak, he was breathing so hard. He bent over, hands on his knees.

'My name is Phil Bettany,' he gasped. 'I'm . . . Sasha's friend.'

'Is she with you?' asked Grace.

Phil looked at her anxiously. 'What, you mean you haven't see her? She arrived here over an hour ago. I spoke to her – she was in this house.'

Alex shook his head. 'There's no one else in the house. We assumed she hadn't got here yet.'

'Shit,' whispered Phil, a sinking feeling in his stomach. 'Who else is on the island?'

'Just Miles. And that caretaker who met us off the plane,' said Alex. 'But you haven't told us what's going on. Is something wrong?'

'Listen, I know why you're here,' Philip said urgently. 'Sasha told me all about that night on the beach twenty years ago. Finding the body. Leaving the body, all of it.'

He saw Alex and Grace exchange a troubled glance.

'But what's that got to do with us?' said Alex.

Philip pulled a face. 'Sasha was told the police got involved after finding a body dug up by the Fairmont Hotels site surveyors. Alex, I told you, *I know.*'

Grace's cheeks flushed. 'We are going to speak to the police. We're going to tell them everything we know. Two officers are coming here tomorrow.'

'No, they're not. The police don't know about any body dug up on Angel Cay. I just spoke to them.'

Alex frowned. 'That doesn't necessarily mean anything. It wouldn't surprise me if only one or two officers knew about this. Miles has his fixers on it, crisis-managing it. He wants to keep this as quiet as he can.'

'Maybe, but there's something else,' said Phil. 'Sasha said that Michael Marshall, the guy who brought you all here, is the boy you found on the beach.'

'The *dead* boy?' said Alex incredulously.

Phil nodded. 'That night in 1990, Sasha had sex with him. Apparently this afternoon she found a photo of Marshall and she recognised him. Same face, same tattoo on his hip.'

'A coincidence, surely?' said Grace, looking from Philip to Alex. 'I mean, it has to be, doesn't it?'

It was clear from their faces that they all felt it wasn't.

'You know, I never actually saw that boy's face,' said Grace.

'Just his head facing down into the sand when we found him. All those times I've thought of him, it's just a projection, a guess what he might have looked like. And anyway, I've never even met this Michael Marshall.'

'What about you?' asked Phil, turning to Alex.

'I met Michael a couple of times; he helped out when I was in the clinic that time, but he's never looked familiar. That said, when I saw him in 1990, it was dark, I was drunk, high. It was a long time ago.' He threw up his hands. 'I guess it's possible, but it's so crazy, isn't it?'

Philip felt a growing sense of unease. *Something weird is going on*, Sasha had said. From the pale expressions of Grace and Alex, he knew they felt it too.

'Let's go and find Miles,' said Alex. 'He disappeared twenty minutes ago. Maybe he went to meet Sasha.'

'I'll call the police,' said Grace, walking over to the phone.

'Good idea,' said Phil, following Alex, who was already at the door. 'And tell them to hurry.'

Miles was frightened. The sky was dark grey and the rain was getting harder. It was hurricane season this time of year in the Bahamas and a storm was definitely on its way. But it wasn't the weather that was scaring him; it was his chances of living to see it.

'So you intend to just kill me? Is that your masterplan?' he shouted over the wind. 'Why drag yourself up from West Virginia only to have yourself thrown back in jail for my murder?'

'The police aren't going to think I killed you, Miles. They're going to think it was Alex Doyle, Sasha Sinclair and your sister.'

Miles laughed bitterly. 'Why?'

'Because they're the only ones on this island. Carlton, Benny the caretaker, they're my people.' He laughed. 'Carlton's an ex-mercenary I've sometimes used for strong-arm work. I have to say, they've really thrown themelves into their roles. And when you're found dead, Miles, the natural suspects will be your dear friends. All of them have motive. Grace hates you; so does Sasha after that nasty stitch-up with Simon Assad. And there's bad blood between you and Alex too. His rejection of your Vegas residency plan, the mugging – which I was behind, incidentally. Benny will find your body. He'll call the police, who will naturally suspect the island's vengeful house guests. Meanwhile, I've got five guests at the Nassau Ashford prepared to vouch that they saw me in the hotel at the time of your murder.' He glanced at his watch. 'Which is going to be at roughly six thirty p.m.'

He levelled the gun, using his other hand to steady himself. Miles had the crazy notion that he looked like Dirty Harry.

'Why? What the fuck are you doing this for, Michael?' he shouted desperately. 'Do you want money? I can get you millions in cash, jewels, whatever you need!'

'I don't want your money,' spat Michael. 'But I want you to pay.'

At the edge of the mangrove, Alex stopped suddenly. He was walking in front of Philip and had seen Miles and Michael on the beach before him. Crouching down quickly in the bushes, he instructed Philip to do the same. They could see Michael standing over Miles, pointing down at him, his body turned away from them.

'Shit, I think he's got a gun,' Alex whispered.

The two men stayed low in the undergrowth. Between them and the boathouse was a hundred feet of sand and scrub, completely open ground.

Alex felt his palms sweating. He knew instantly they were all in danger, Miles more immediately, but would Marshall stop with him?

'What are we going to do?' he said.

He hoped Grace had called the police but wondered how

long it would take them to arrive – if they could get here at all in this awful weather.

Philip puffed out his cheeks lightly. 'I could tackle him from behind but he could fire at Miles before we got halfway to the boathouse. He could fire at us too, for that matter.'

'Tackle him?' hissed Alex incredulously. 'Who are you? The SAS?'

He watched Philip's eyes scan the ground around him. Then he crawled across and picked up a small rock the size of a squash ball.

Alex looked at him cynically. 'You are kidding me?' he hissed.

'Nope,' said Philip, moving into a crouch.

'Tell me you're a good shot.'

'As well as my rugby, I was in the England Under-Eighteen cricket team,' he said.

'*Under* eighteen?' said Alex. 'I hope you've kept in practice.'

Knowing he had no time to argue, Phil stood up and threw the rock. It sliced through the air in a perfect arc, hitting Michael Marshall on the back of the neck. He slumped forward, the gun going off with a bang.

'Fuck me,' whispered Alex. 'Great shot!' But Philip wasn't listening; he was already sprinting across the open ground. In a flying leap he landed on top of Michael, forcing his arm across the lawyer's throat. Without stopping to think of the danger, Alex followed him, struggling for speed across the cold, wet sand.

'Where's Sasha?' shouted Philip. 'Tell us!'

'Fuck you,' growled Michael.

Alex spotted Michael's gun a few feet away from him on the beach. He scrambled over to it, pausing for a moment before he picked it up, heavy, menacing in his hand.

He pointed it at Michael as Philip repeated his question. Michael hesitated.

The gun felt alien in Alex's grip but he kept his hand steady. 'You've got three seconds to tell us. Be quick, I was almost sectioned once, no telling what I'll do. One, two, thr—'

'At Nelson's old place.' Michael winced.

'Miles, get some rope from the boathouse,' said Alex.

Miles struggled to his feet and obediently followed his instructions. Philip bound Michael's arms and legs together and the three men lifted him into the boathouse, where a third length of rope tied him to a cast-iron table.

'That should keep him quiet,' said Alex. 'Now let's get back to Grace.'

'No, we have to find Sasha,' said Philip urgently. He pulled his phone out and handed it to Alex. 'Call Grace, make sure she's OK.'

Alex nodded with anxiety. If Michael's men had even touched her, he would kill them.

'Are you all right?' he asked when she answered.

'Just wondering where the hell you are. Is everything OK?'

'We've got Miles, he's fine. Have you called the police?'

'It took some persuading, but they're on their way.'

'Have you seen Sasha or the detective?'

'No.'

'Good. Now lock yourself in your bedroom.'

'Alex, what's going on?'

'Please. Just do it,' he pleaded.

The three men ran around the beach path and through a stretch of mangrove towards the caretaker's cottage. Philip asked Alex to give him the gun, which he did willingly. The rain was lashing down on to the island and their hair and clothes were soaked. Seeing the staff buildings, they stopped behind a bike shed.

'What the fuck do we do now?' asked Miles, wiping the rain from his face with his sleeve.

'You knock on the door and wait for Benny to answer,' said Philip calmly.

'I'm not doing that! He might be with Carlton. He might have a gun. He could kill me.'

Philip frowned. 'I've got a gun and I'll fire it at you if you don't bloody knock at that door.'

Seeing he had no choice, Miles puffed out his cheeks and walked up to the cottage's front door. Alex and Philip crept closer around a thick line of trees until they were just ten feet from the cottage. The light was poor, which Alex hoped would keep them hidden from view.

After a minute, the detective answered. 'Mr Ashford,' he said, looking ruffled.

'I was wondering if you'd seen my sister.'

'No,' said Carlton, 'and I have some very important calls to make.'

'I'm worried about her, Detective,' said Miles quickly. 'And I've just found something up at the house I need to show you. I think it might be important.'

Carlton looked dubious, but he nodded. 'OK, but make it quick,' he said, wiping the rain from his forehead.

He stepped outside on to the path and Miles led him to just a few feet from the line of trees. Philip jumped forward, pointing the gun at him, but Carlton was a professional; he ducked and spun around, slipping his hand into his jacket pocket as he turned. Miles, who was standing right next to him, slammed his fist into the man's ear. It was a pathetic punch, but enough to make Carlton stumble. Carlton threw a punch which landed squarely on Miles' jaw, but the scuffle had given Philip enough time to push the muzzle of the gun against Carlton's temple.

'Fucking hell, Phil.' Alex whistled.

Phil grunted. 'I'm glad two years at Sandhurst came to some use.'

They marched the fake detective back into the house.

'Any more of your little friends on the island?' asked Miles, regaining his bluster.

640

Carlton shook his head as Alex removed his gun from his pocket and bound his wrists with a length of washing line he had found in the kitchen.

'Miles, you watch him. Alex, help me look for Sasha.'

At the back of the kitchen was a washroom. Alex flung open the door and saw Sasha, slumped on the floor.

'Phil!' he shouted.

She was unconscious, but she was still breathing, although her skin was cold. Phil ran in and cradled her in his arms.

Alex heard his mobile ring. 'Grace?'

'Tell me what's going on, Alex,' she said. 'The George Town police have just called. The sea's rough but they're on their way and someone should be here in thirty minutes.'

He left the other two and ran for the door. The only place he wanted to be was by her side. 'I'm coming,' he panted as he ran through the rain. 'I'm coming to get you.'

78

Sasha could only vaguely remember what had happened. There was a jumble of images on Angel Cay: Phil's concerned face, some uniformed policemen, an air ambulance on the beach. Then she had woken up here, in a private room at Nassau's Princess Margaret Hospital. Philip had filled in the gaps. Michael Marshall had been arrested by the *real* Royal Bahamian police and thrown into a *real* prison cell, as had his conspirators, although none of them were talking. Sasha shivered at the thought of how close she had come to death. It was actually lucky that Detective Carlton – or whoever he was – was a trained killer: the pressure he'd applied to her neck had been just enough to knock her out, rather than break her neck. Her head and throat were still throbbing and her entire body felt bruised from where she'd been dragged to Nelson's house. *But I'm alive*, she thought, feeling emotion swell. *That's enough for me right now.*

She heard movement in the doorway and looked up, hoping it would be Philip, but flinched as she saw Miles standing there. A memory of the last time they had met flashed before her – another hospital, another time she'd rather forget.

'Hi, Sasha,' he said quietly. He looked pale in the fluorescent light. He came and sat on the wooden chair beside her bed, his eyes cast down. 'How are you feeling?'

'I've felt better. What about you?' she said, pointing at his bruised jaw.

He shrugged. 'Listen, if there's anything you need ... The jet can take you anywhere you want, an extended holiday to recover, whatever.'

'Miles, look at me,' she said.

Reluctantly, his eyes slid up to hers.

'I don't need anything from you. It's enough that it's over.'

She had expected to see the usual arrogant pout, but Miles looked different. Smaller somehow. She couldn't believe the great Miles Ashford had learnt any humility after facing death – facing his past. But there was something she hadn't seen before in his face. Vulnerability, perhaps?

'You do know that we could all have been killed, don't you, Miles?'

Miles shook his head slightly. 'Michael didn't want to see you dead. Only me. He wanted you, Alex and Grace to pay for it. He wanted you to suffer.'

'Well I think we've all been doing enough of that for ourselves,' said Sasha. 'But Miles, you worked with the man for five years. How could you not have known?'

He glanced at the floor. 'I've spent twenty years forgetting that night. I thought he was dead. I thought my father had got rid of the body.'

'Is that why you hated each other?' she asked softly.

His eyes flashed at her briefly, then he looked away again. 'Is that what he told you?'

'No,' said Sasha. 'We never talked about you.'

'Well, it's all in the past now. My father, Michael Marshall, the island, all of it.'

She looked at him. 'Is it? We still left that boy for dead. Yes, it was twenty years ago, but you almost killed him that night.'

He stuck his chin out. 'But I didn't.'

'Everything has a consequence, Miles.'

He blinked, longer than necessary, and when he opened his eyes, she thought she could see the shimmer of a tear.

643

'I'm sorry, Sash.'

She looked at him and realised that she'd hated him for almost half her life. Hated him for his rejection of her on the island. Hated the power he had over the business by being their first backer. Hated his reaction after the death of Robert Ashford. And underpinning everything, she had hated him for the secret he had made Alex, Grace and herself carry for all these years. But of course the truth was they had carried it for themselves, not because Miles had made them. They had thought it would be easier to keep quiet, to let the memories fade, but they had been wrong. Dead wrong. Those memories had stayed with them, festering, spreading into their lives, colouring their decisions, changing the way they were. And now, at the other end of all that misery and heartbreak, Sasha found she drew no comfort from the ordeal Miles had just been through. It had always been her weakness; she wanted to please Miles. After all this time, she still wanted him to be happy. Not that he deserved it.

'Actually, there's one thing you can do for me, Miles.'

'What is it?'

'I know you put Assad up to buying my company. You can call it off.'

Miles bristled. 'Simon is his own man,' he said. 'This is a business investment. It's nothing to do with me.'

'Miles, you're lying.'

He looked thoughtful and then nodded. 'I'll have a word.'

'Thank you. I appreciate it.'

There was a discreet cough behind them. 'God, I can't believe you're actually talking business,' said Philip, walking in with two drinks.

Miles stood up, hearing his cue to leave. 'Remember, you two. If you want time out after all this, pick a hotel. Call me on my cell and I'll sort it for you.'

'Thanks, Miles,' said Sasha. 'I mean it.'

He looked at her quickly, then nodded and walked away.

Philip smiled into his Pepsi. 'I leave you for two minutes and you've got Miles Ashford's balls in a vice.'

'I'm battered and bruised but I'm not brain-dead,' she said, pulling herself slowly up on the pillow. 'He was feeling weak. I used my moment to gain the commercial advantage.'

'You never stop,' he said, perching on the bed and taking her hand.

'My hero.' She grinned.

'Is a mistress of the universe allowed a hero? I thought feminism had killed them off.'

'We're allowed to make an exception for heroes as cute as you.' She held his hand and sighed. 'Is it true I can leave hospital in a couple of hours?'

'I think the doctor wants to take one last look at you and then you can be discharged.'

'Then get me back to reality as soon as possible, wherever that is.'

Philip looked down into his drink. 'Were you being serious about what you said at the hotel?'

'Sorry, I'm a bit fuzzy about stuff at the moment. Which bit?'

'What you said about that night at my flat. How you wished you had said yes.'

'Phil, we're in hospital. This isn't the time to talk about that.'

She felt flustered. It must be the medication. Or the heat. She was Sasha Sinclair. Always in control. An independent woman in charge of her future. Except that when she thought about the future, she wasn't entirely sure about anything any more. Whether she could keep her stake in Rivera. Whether she *wanted* to keep her stake, or whether she should sell up, ship out and take her considerable talent and fortune to a new business, a new challenge. The only thing about her future she felt sure of was that she wanted Phil Bettany in it, and that was what was scaring her the most. Not the crazed killer or the mercenary with his arm around her throat or the terrible consequences of that one dark night. No, what was scaring her was love.

A side door took Miles out on to a back street. He closed his eyes and inhaled the hot, dusty air. He was glad Sasha was all right; it had been important to him somehow. Now he just had to take care of Michael Marshall. Fraud. Attempted murder. Possibly a nice secure mental hospital would be the best place for him. Either way, Miles had wasted years of guilt on that boat boy. But now it was over. He would push the Fairmont deal through as fast as possible and bury the whole episode next to that non-existent body. He certainly knew he would never set foot on Angel Cay again. At the end of the alley, the main street looked bright and he walked towards it, stepping out into the sun feeling light, happy and back to full strength. *Nothing like a gun to your head to pep you right up*, he thought with a smile. No, he felt good. In fact, the last seven days was already beginning to feel like a simple irritation. That was the key to life. Let problems wash over you. And if they wouldn't wash, screw 'em. There was always another deal to be done.

Grace sat on Catseye Beach, running the oyster white sand through her fingers as she stared out to sea. She was glad she had chosen to stay on Angel Cay once the police had left. Miles had volunteered to accompany them back to George Town to fill in the blanks, which everyone said was nice of him. Grace, however, knew her brother well enough to guess that he had an ulterior motive. He certainly wouldn't want Michael Marshall – or whatever his name was – shooting his mouth off, telling his side of the story in open court. People would have to be paid off, ears whispered into, hands shaken. She laughed to herself. She could imagine her brother at the pearly gates, trying to cut a deal with St Peter. No, whatever happened, Miles would never change and there was actually something quite comforting about that. The island, however, would never be the same. The innocent, idyllic paradise of her youth was long gone, but at least they had found some peace again, which Grace wanted to enjoy one last time before it was finally sold.

Ahead of her, the clear waters stretched out towards the horizon and blended seamlessly with the sky, which was so cloudless and blue it was almost impossible to believe that yesterday a storm had circled the island. How fluid life was. How quickly things could change. She thought of the moment she had caught Julian with Olivia. And the phone call from Miles telling them a body had been found on Angel Cay. It had been like stepping on to rotten floorboards and falling into a deep, dark well.

But that was life, wasn't it? Things jolted you from your comfortable groove and put you on to a different track, but it wasn't always a bad thing. She was free of her loveless relationship and she was back on the island she never thought she'd see again. Although the last twenty-four hours had been a surreal nightmare, it had been the most liberating time of her life. There would never be an absolute finality to what had happened on that hot summer night in 1990, because Grace knew she could never forgive herself for leaving the body. But there were plenty of positives in the situation. The boat boy wasn't dead. Miles hadn't killed him. Her father hadn't covered anything up. It was too late to mend that relationship, but life was full of possibilities. There was still time to work on Olivia – even Miles.

And then there was Alex. Squinting in the sun, she could see him waving at her as he came down the dusty track from the house. Giving him a lop-sided grin, she walked up the beach to meet him.

'A plane is coming for us at four to take us to Nassau, which gives us an hour to kill. Where are you going to take me, Ashford?'

'I know a lovely little rock over there. Very exclusive. Very you.' She smiled.

'Sounds good. Let's walk.'

They ambled along the shoreline in the sun, Alex picking up pebbles and throwing them into the surf.

'So are they going to be able to charge Michael and Carlton with anything?'

'Miles will get the hottest lawyers on the planet to make sure they can pin something on them.'

'Either that or make it all go away.'

Grace smiled. 'Exactly what I was thinking.'

'Imagine if Sasha hadn't come and recognised that picture of Michael. Or should I say Bradley.'

'I don't want to imagine it,' said Grace, shivering.

'I hope Sasha is going to be OK.'

'I've already called the hospital in Nassau and spoken to her. Sore, but fine. She's a tough old bird.'

They rounded a headland on to another stretch of beach. The shore was littered with a trail of tiny white shells that crunched as they walked across them.

'So you are coming back to mine when we get back to London?' asked Alex. 'That's an invitation, by the way, not an ultimatum.'

'I'm sorry for being such a pain, but I can't go back to Stockbridge or the Spitalfields house and a hotel room feels too soul-destroying.'

'You're not a pain, Grace. You're very welcome. And we'll get it sorted.'

She puffed out her cheeks. 'I've been trying to think of what I'm going to say to Olivia the next time I see her.'

'So you're going to see her?'

'After everything that's happened in the last twenty-four

hours, it just seems like another thing I've got to do. Nothing feels too difficult.'

Alex looked at her sideways. 'You know this island saw a lot of firsts for me. It was the first time I'd ever been somewhere so beautiful. The first time I'd had a perfect martini and tried oysters, even snorkelling ...' He paused. 'And it was the first time I realised that people will disappoint you. That some people aren't very nice. Some people will never be what you want them to be. Like Miles.'

'Like Olivia?'

He nodded. 'But maybe she's young enough to change.'

'And even if she doesn't, she's still my daughter. I'll love her whatever happens.'

'What about Julian?'

She snorted. 'What about him?'

It was only then that Grace realised she had barely thought about him. It was Olivia's treachery that had torn a hole in her heart, not the loss of Julian.

'I'm not sure I ever really liked him. Let alone loved him.'

'Then why were you with him so long?'

She wanted to remind him of something he had once told her about his own relationship with Melissa: how they were two people brought together by circumstance rather than compatibility. It had been exactly the same with herself and Julian. They had met the night she had found out that Alex was getting married, the day before her father had been killed in a car accident. She had needed him then; love hadn't come into it. But she didn't want to ruin the moment, to remind him of his own mistakes, so instead she just shrugged and said: 'You know how it is.'

Alex smiled. 'I do indeed.'

She looked at him and for the first time she noticed the lines on his forehead. They suited him. Experience and hard knocks had rubbed away his pin-up prettiness, but even so, he was still the most handsome man she had ever seen in her life. She felt a flutter in her stomach and suddenly she was twenty years old again, thinking of that letter he had sent her, signed off 'Just Like Heaven'.

He was glancing at his watch as the sun started sloping down the sky. 'We'd better head back.'

'Just a bit further,' she said, not wanting it to end. A line of dark rocks blocked their way and Alex put out his hand to help her across, but she slipped on some seaweed and he caught her as she stumbled, their faces just inches apart.

'What's so funny?' she said, catching his smile. 'You never seen a lady slip before?'

'It's not that,' he said. 'I was just remembering this spot.'

They were on North Point Beach. The very place they'd been skinny-dipping the night they'd found the body.

'That night, right here,' he said, 'I was about to kiss you.'

And immediately Grace could remember it as if it had just happened. *He had!* He had held her hand to cross the rocks and she remembered feeling as if she never wanted him to let go.

'The whim of a drunk, horny eighteen-year-old,' she said, trying to make light of it.

'Not really,' he said, kicking some seaweed. 'I just had a bit of a crush on you.'

Grace stopped and gaped at him. 'You?' she said with amazement. 'You had a crush? On me?'

'Don't sound so surprised.' He looked more like an awkward teenager than a thirty-something rock star.

'But I am,' said Grace. 'I mean, that letter you sent me in Bristol, boasting about your sexual conquests at Danehurst, then copping off with Freya that night. I thought . . .'

Alex looked affronted. 'I never copped off with Freya.'

She grinned. 'I forgot. She was gagging for it but you beat her off with a stick. You were such a shy, retiring youth.'

'I didn't kiss her, because I wanted to kiss you,' he said seriously, like it was the most important thing in the world.

Oh God, oh God, she thought. Her heart was hammering so loud she felt sure that he could hear it. The thought of what she wanted to do next, *could do next*, made her light-headed. *We never really grow up, do we?* The thought of two decades of wrong turns and missed opportunities ignited something inside her.

Just do it, Grace, she told herself as she stepped towards him, taking his face in her hands. And as their lips touched, his hand slipped behind her neck, pulling her in for a deep, warm, sweet kiss that seemed to stop time. Opening her eyes, she saw him look at her wide-eyed, his cheeks flushed with surprise and pleasure.

'Why didn't you do that twenty years ago?'

She breathed deeply, opening her heart, sharing his air. 'If I'd have known it was going to be that good, I would have done.'

He wrapped her in his arms and spun her around, laughing.

'I love you, Grace,' he said. 'I really do. And you know what? I think I always have.'

'Why didn't you tell me?'

'The timing was never quite right, was it? Here on the island. In Ibiza. You know I really wanted to kiss you in the nut-house but I thought better of it. You'd have called the nurses and told them to top up my meds.'

'Better late than never.' She smiled, kissing him again.

They began to walk back down the beach, hand in hand. He reached up to help her back across the rocks, but she paused, bending down to touch their warm surface.

'What are you thinking?' said Alex.

'Oh, just about those little decisions that we don't think are important at the time but which actually change our lives.'

'You mean how different things might have turned out if I had kissed you right here? If we'd turned around and gone back to the house for a long last night in bed together?'

She nodded, her mind distracted for one split second away from the delicious thought of them in bed.

651

'Well, we wouldn't have found the body.'

'I would have gone to the Royal Academy, maybe never ended up in a band.'

'I wouldn't have gone to Australia, I wouldn't have met Gabriel. I might not have two children.'

'Hey, Sasha might have married Miles.'

Grace puffed out her cheeks. 'Doubt that.' She smiled. 'But we'll never know.'

Above them, they heard a roar as the small aeroplane swooped over the beach and banked, heading towards the landing strip.

'God, I wish I had kissed you that night,' said Alex as they jumped down on to the sand together.

But Grace shook her head, then kissed him on the shoulder.

'You know what? I think we've ended up exactly where we're supposed to be.'

Acknowledgements

A big thank you to everyone at Headline for making me feel so welcome at my new publishing home. Jane Morpeth, Kerr MacRae, James Horobin, Kate Tindal, Jo Liddiard, Rosie Gailer and all the fantastic sales team – I'm so grateful for your support, hard work and passion. Sherise Hobbs – you are a star and working with you this year has been a pleasure.

Continued thanks to Sheila and Wayne (long may our Christmas lunches continue). Also to Sarah and the foreign rights departments at both Curtis Brown and A P Watt.

Wendy Birch and her team came up with a great new cover look. Thanks also to Jane Selley for copyediting the manuscript up against the clock, when a stint in hospital put finishing the novel on the back seat.

Thank you to John Kelly, Alison, Quentin, Tamasin, Nick Stewart, Will Storr, Sam, Riggster and Antoine McGrath for their time, knowledge and generosity. To the team at Kingston hospital for looking after me and for all the incredible work they do. And to all our friends for their help at that time. To my great friend Suzanne Parkinson for the original brainstorm around her kitchen table. One day I'll have to write about Tarbert! To my family, especially Mum for the hours spent looking after Fin when I've got a hot date with the laptop, and to Dad for the dozens of titles he has thought of for my books (not to mention the hours of entertainment when he unveils them!).

To all the retailers and sales teams who have supported my books from the beginning, and to the journalists who have reviewed the novels and helped get the word out there. And to anyone else I've forgotten – forgive me but the book is about to go to press!

As always, much love and thanks to my boys Fin and John, without whom I don't think there would have been one of my books out this year. Pez Gang for ever.

Read on for an exclusive extract
from Tasmina Perry's sensational new novel,

Private Lives...

Prologue

She looked around the flat and smiled to herself. Silk drapes and tall windows looked out on to an iconic view: Tower Bridge and the slick black ribbon of the Thames glistening in the night. Sometimes she wanted to hug herself with excitement; just being here, in her own luxury flat, surrounded by all her nice things. Who'd have thought that someone like her would live in such a smart flat in the centre of one of the most exciting cities in the world?

Walking over to the kitchen, she poured herself another large glass of wine from the open bottle. Would he still come tonight? The thought of their last conversation jumped into her head, but she shook it away. No, of course he would come, he always did. She admired herself in the mirror: the long legs, the high breasts. Even in leggings and a tee-shirt she looked fantastic. No, he'd come. She knew he'd come.

She sank back into the sofa then flicked through her favourite celebrity magazine. In her more honest, introspective moments she knew it was her obsession with magazines like this that had led her to choose this career path. Not that she could imagine Miss Davies, her careers adviser at school, calling what she did a 'career'. But what was wrong with wanting to be rich and famous? She bet Miss Davies didn't have a flat like this one.

Tossing the magazine to one side, she knew she should get ready in case he did drop by. A bottle of nail polish was on the coffee table and she held it up to the light. Scarlet. He

657

always said he loved it when she painted her toenails red. *Slutty, that's what he meant.* Well, she was happy to oblige in that department, especially when they'd be making up tonight.

One toe nail had been painted when the doorbell rang. Flustered, she put down the polish and went to the door. She peered through the spy-hole, expecting to see flowers or some small, tastefully wrapped box clutched in his hand. But instead she saw another face. An unfamiliar man in a suit, his face stretched and bulbous in the fish-eye lens.

'Who is it?'

'It's Jack. Jack Devon. I'm a friend of Peter's.'

She frowned. Who was he? Had Peter sent him? Attaching the chain, she opened the door and looked through the gap. The man was about forty. Smartly, but conservatively dressed, like an accountant. Pale watery eyes blinked behind small, rimless glasses.

'What do you want?' She hadn't meant to sound rude, but it was past nine o'clock and she wasn't used to having strange men turning up at her door, no matter what other people might say about her.

'It's about Peter.' He glanced behind himself. 'Do you think we could talk inside?'

She felt a jolt of panic. Was he hurt? Was something wrong?

'Is he okay?' she asked.

'Under the circumstances,' replied the man.

'What circumstances?'

'I think it's best if we discuss this inside.'

She wavered for a moment, then slid back the chain and opened the door. He walked inside, looking nervous, uncomfortable.

'I'm sorry to have to visit you so late,' he began. 'I don't enjoy this any more than you do.'

'Who are you?' she asked, folding her arms across her chest. 'What do you want?'

The man shrugged as they moved into the open-plan living space. 'It's not what I want. It's what Peter wants.'

She didn't like the direction this conversation was taking. 'And what's that exactly?'

He pushed up his glasses and rubbed his eyes. 'He wants you to start acting reasonably.'

Her heart was beginning to hammer in panic, but she was determined not to show it. 'So who are you? His lawyer?'

'No, not exactly,' he said. 'But that might be next. Blackmail is a criminal offence, after all.'

'Blackmail?' She almost laughed. 'Is that what this is about?'

Okay, so she had applied a bit of pressure, told him she wasn't prepared to wait any longer, maybe said a few things she shouldn't. But that was hardly blackmail, was it?

'Does Peter know you're here?'

'Of course. He simply wants a solution that works for both sides. We really don't want to have to involve the police.'

She snorted nervously. 'You and I both know that Peter is not going to go to the police.'

The man blinked at her, then nodded. 'Indeed. Which is why I'm here.'

He moved over to the table and opened his leather brief-case. He pulled out a cheque book and held it up. 'How much?' he asked.

She glanced at the cheque book, then looked out of the window. 'I don't want his money,' she said.

The man allowed himself a small smile. 'Really. And who paid for all this?' He glanced pointedly around the apartment.

'I don't want *money*,' she snapped, trying her best to sound indignant. 'What I want is Peter.'

'Well, I'm afraid that's not an option any more,' he said flatly.

'We'll see about that.' She strode to the coffee table and snatched up her mobile. 'I'm phoning him.'

He shook his head, that half-smile again. The bastard was enjoying this.

'I don't think so.' He peered at his watch. 'It's two a.m. in Uzbekistan.'

'Uzbekistan? He's supposed to be here.'

'Just us here,' said Devon, gesturing with the cheque book again. This time, her eyes followed the book, unable to look away.

'So give me a figure,' he said, sitting at the table.

She grabbed her glass of wine and took a fortifying sip. 'I've told you, this isn't about money. This is about Peter and me.'

'How much is it going to take?' he asked, taking a fountain pen from his inside pocket.

'And how much would you suggest, Mr Devon? How much would you say a relationship is worth?'

'In this case, nothing, because your relationship is over.'

His words were simple and stinging, their impact cruel because she knew they were true. She had pushed Peter too far, overplayed her hand. And now he had sent a lackey to mop up his mess. A thickness filled her throat and her vision blurred in a cloud of tears.

'I think you'd better leave.'

Devon remained seated. 'Believe it or not, I'm here to help you.'

She hated the note of sympathy, the pity she could hear in his voice.

'Take my advice,' he said slowly. 'Accept the money, move somewhere new, forget what's happened and just get on with your life. It's the smart thing to do.'

'It's never that easy though, is it?' she said, her voice cracking. 'Not when you love someone. Now please, just go.'

Devon hesitated, then put his cheque book back in his briefcase and stood up. 'Very well,' he said. 'Could I just use the bathroom?'

She nodded without looking at him. 'Upstairs.'

Her bedroom was on a mezzanine platform over the living space below. She watched him disappear towards her en-suite, his sensible brown shoes clumping up the glass staircase.

His briefcase was still on the table. How much would he have paid? A decent amount, that was for sure. And Devon was right, it was the smart thing to do. Her own money wouldn't last long in this place. A person could quickly get used to expensive linens, parquet floors and stainless steel kitchens. Nice things. Pretty things. Things which made her feel safe, secure, smart, successful. This was the life she'd always wanted. But still . . . for once, she had been telling the truth. It wasn't about the money this time. All she wanted was him – and she couldn't have him. No amount of lovely sheets would make up for that.

She rubbed her eyes with the palms of her hands to stop the flow of tears. Taking a few deep breaths, she tried to compose herself. Maybe she would call Peter herself, apologise for what she'd said, explain that he'd taken it all the wrong way. Yes, that would do it, she thought, feeling a little better. Maybe this was a test; when Mr Devon reported back that she had turned down the money, he would see that she truly loved him, not his credit cards.

She glanced up the stairs, frowning. He'd been a long time in the bathroom.

'Mr Devon?' she called. 'Is everything alright up there?'

There was no reply. Shrugging, she walked up the stairs towards the mezzanine platform. 'Mr Devon?'

At the top, she tapped on the bathroom door but couldn't hear a sound inside. 'Are you alright? Mr D—'

The door opened and Jack Devon stepped out. 'Yes. I'm fine.'

'Oh, good,' she stuttered, flushing with embarrassment as she turned to walk back downstairs. Her body jerked forward as she felt a hard push from behind. Instinctively she reached for the banister, but she was moving too fast and momentum carried her forward, her head slamming against the wall. Her body twisted as she fell, her shoulder cracking into the glass steps, her torso pin-wheeling over, snapping her neck, her body landing splayed and broken like a puppet with the strings cut. It had been mercifully quick. Aside from one moment of air-sucking terror as her hand missed the rail, she had felt nothing.

She lay there staring up, her body motionless except for the faint flutter of her eyelids, barely aware as Jack Devon walked slowly down, taking a pair of latex gloves from his pocket to finish the job. When he was done, he moved methodically around the flat, making sure everything was in place for whoever found her. Sometimes he had to create a story: the lovelorn jilted lover who had taken their own life, the break-in gone wrong, but here she had done the job for him. The half-empty bottle of wine. A simple case of a tragic accident, slipping on the steps after too much alcohol.

Satisfied with his work, he pulled out his phone and made the call. 'It's done,' he said simply, then hung up. Removing his glasses and putting them in his pocket, he picked up his briefcase and let himself out. Out of her flat, on to the street, as if he'd never been there.

COMING SOON...

Private Lives

**How far would you go to keep someone else's secret
when *you're* the one who stands to lose it all?**

Anna Kennedy loves her career. A young associate
with a top media law firm, she's the lawyer to the stars,
hiding their sins from the hungry media.

When Anna fails to prevent a damaging story
being printed about heart-throb movie star Sam Charles
she finds herself fighting to save not only his reputation,
but also her own.

But Anna is about to uncover a scandal
more explosive than even Sam's infidelities.
A party girl is already dead and those responsible are
prepared to silence *anyone* who stands in their way.
Not least a pretty young lawyer
who knows too much...

**Take a thrilling journey into an intoxicating world
where games are played to mask the truth, where
there is no one you can trust and where being too
good at your job could put your life in danger.**

headline
review

WIN £500 worth of nails inc products

Tasmina Perry and nails inc have joined forces to bring you this amazing prize. Ge everything you need for beautiful hands and feet – just in time for the holiday season! Th exclusive prize includes a year's worth of manicures, professional high quality na polish and luxurious hand care products!

Founded in 1999, nails inc is the UK's leading nail brand with 60 nail bars nationwide and bestselling, highly sought-after product range.
nails inc combines luxurious, professional formulas with a sense of fun and up-to-th -minute fashion sense.

Visit **www.headlinecompetitions.co.uk** to enter

*No purchase necessary. Closing date 31st July 2011. Terms and conditions apply.

15% off at nailsinc.com**

To celebrate the publication of Kiss Heaven Goodbye, nails inc would like to giv readers an irresistible 15% discount on products. Take advantage of this fabulous offe and stock up on the latest trend shades. We recommend the ultra glossy "I can paint rainbow" collection – 6 mini must-have colours and a professional mini nail file. Thi collection is perfect for taking with you on holiday.

To redeem this discount please enter KHG15 at the checkout.

Offer ends 31st July 2011.

**Offer valid at www.nailsinc.com only. Valid from 9th June – 31st July 2011. Excludes sale items, gift vouchers, creat your own gift and postage. Not valid in conjunction with any other promotional code. Not valid in conjunction wit the reward scheme.